I0819785

ShadowWalk

Other Amos Keppler novels published by Midnight Fire Media

Your Own Fate
Night on Earth
Dreams Belong to the Night

The Janus Clan series:

The Defenseless
The Slaves
Birds Flying in the Dark

Poems:

Amos Keppler: Complete Poems 1989 - 2003

(A few of the) novels to be published:

The Afterglow trilogy
Season of the Witch
Alarums of Reality
Thunder Road: Ice and Fire
Falling
Black Dragon

For a «complete» list of current and current future Amos Keppler and Midnight Fire Media projects see the back of the book and the Midnight Fire/Midnight Fire Media web pages.

ShadowWalk

by

Amos Keppler

∞

MIDNIGHT FIRE MEDIA
2011

Midnight Fire Media

http://midnight-fire.net/mfm
For more about ShadowWalk:
http://midnight-fire.net/sw

E-Mail:
amos13@midnight-fire.net
manofhood@yahoo.com

Cover, text, design, art, premedia and photos Amos Keppler

ISBN 978-82-91693-12-5

Previously published as paperback in 2003.
(no longer in print)

We walk
Through fire, through shadow
From the night we are born
An owl howls between
The dark trees
The Hunger of life
From the newborn

Amos Keppler - **Witchsong** (1995)

«And God will wipe away every tear from their eyes;
there shall be no more death, nor sorrow, nor crying.
There shall be no more pain, for the former things have passed away»
Gideons' bible Revelation 21:4

«But there shall be no means enter it anything that defiles, or causes
an abomination or a lie, but only those who are written in
the Lamb's Book of Life».
Gideons' bible Revelation 21:27

Names might be important...

You may have heard about him. He, too, is known by many names. He is Wanderer, Sorcerer, Searcher, Shadow Walker. And many more. He himself has, during his lifetime taken several different aliases. His best known is, coincidentally, that given to him shortly after his birth, *Ted Warren.*

Birth names may have some importance, but taken names carry great weight, especially to those who walk in the shadows... Coincidentally, his best-known name is his given and taken name both. It's one he has had to fight for and thus it carries immeasurable weight.

This is not a story about Ted Warren, though. He is part of the story, like many others are parts of the story, but he isn't the main character. Not this time. Far from it in fact. This is about young girls and boys gaining insight, gaining self-awareness, gaining good and evil. Ted Warren did that many years ago.

But it's the start of his story. Or maybe one start. Or the end of the beginning, the beginning of the end. A start of the ascension. It is perhaps about Elizabeth. Or the Janus Clan. Their start, end and new beginning? Life and Death and the End of Time. They are *present* all of them. Even if they're not seen, even if they're not heard. They might not be physically on the actual spot, all of them... Ethel, Nick, Ruth, Linsey, Stewart, Martin, Lydia and Kyle... but they're *there!* Everybody knows this, now, all these years later. Very few knew it at the time, but Mankind, once countless as ants in the ground, so few now, had started on their way back, their way *home.*

Chapter One: THE WALK OF VISIBLE SHADOWS

It was the Day of the Dead, the day when, according to ancient mythology, people long dead caught up with the present. How appropriate this day, with wreckage and ruins visible as far as the eye could soar.

And Beyond.

They came from faraway. From faraway they came.

One image dominated the view, one single sight of chaos incarnated. This was not your ordinary 2.4 kids' family picture. Oh, no, not at all. It was a beyond staggering departure from that.

The black dome filled the horizon.

Even from several miles away through the clear, bright air, it was clearly visible, seemingly sucking light from the Sun itself. The two passengers in the helicopter, surrounded by their very own, very nervous honor guard saw that it easily covered what was supposed to be a nice, quiet little town. Not many buildings were visible. Only a few, outside all the black inside. There were supposed to be quite a few of them. In fact, this was, had been one of the fastest growing, emerging urban areas in this part of the country.

There were really no visible shapes on the dome except for the shape itself, a ball cut in half. Nothing more than the black surface, some incidental sparks of half visible, ghostly lightning close to the rim were exposed to the people in the chopper, as they descended and landed in relative safety well over five hundred meters away from the damn thing.

The army had made a tight perimeter ring almost twice that distance around the whole diameter of what was already all over the world referred to almost unanimously as the Black Dome. The Army, the American government had tried to put a heavy lid on things, of course, they always did. But this was too big, too gross, too huge to hide. All the shouting reporters, all the starving cameras, every single hungry eye were kept very safe, very far away, but they had a nice unavoidable view and could easily see everything and everybody inside the enormous, closed ring. It was not difficult, not difficult at all, for anyone to recognize Ted and Elizabeth Warren the moment they emerged from the helicopter. The hunger of curiosity grew, and the shouting became a crescendo of frenetic shouts, high-pitched, distorted calls of the wild.

It was a riot, even a laugh riot, the whole thing, a spectacle to warm the hearts of even the most cynical rebel. The male and female Warren couldn't say they didn't enjoy it all.

And they wouldn't...

The secret smile they exchanged spoke volumes.

By their arrival it became even more of a spectacle, a ruckus, an event. But strangely enough, even if you couldn't convince yourself the decibel count actually went down, there seemed to suddenly be more... silence in the air. To anybody who stopped a minute, a second to listen it just might be possible to hear what was being shouted, what was being said and done.

– HEY, Wanderer, what are you doing inside the ring? You aren't cooing with the military, are you?

– Don't listen to that IDIOT, wanderers! Just go an' give them one *hell* of a time... for me, please!

Both Ted and Elizabeth were quite infamous already in their early youth. Their reputation had not improved over the years.

It was indeed easy to read that fact in every expression, every movement of the man waiting for them inside the military tent some hundred meters away from the dome.

An aide led them deep inside to something that was certainly through several security checkpoints and levels. The man in front of the wall of video screens, the head honcho of the operation smoked his cigar a little more anxiously, puffed on it a little harder than he usually did, something that didn't escape them.

– Warren... he nodded. He ignored Elizabeth, he always did. And her reply to his «lack of interest» was of equal measure.

– McKenzie... Ted said in the same officious manner, smiling his famous, sardonic smile.

Floyd McKenzie was not military. He was not FBI or CIA or NSC or Homeland Security.

He was all of the above.
The sound was turned on loud, giving voice to one particular audio image.
A man, dressed in white stood on a platform, speaking to a crowd that was evidently a congregation. They recognized Brian Garrett instantly.
– Sons and Daughters of the Light, he cried.
His opening gambit brought, as always, a rush of hot air through the listeners. Some of them raised their arms to the heavens and some started crying.
– My friends, he said in a loud, intense, officious manner. – We're living through trying and often frightening times. It's more important than ever that we're drawing strength and comfort from each other and from each other's faith. We, the resurrected faith, drawing inspiration from many cultures, many creeds have a unique opportunity to lead mankind through these rough waters and into the promised Golden Age…
He was on several of the screens, but most showed the dome from various viewpoints. The images of the dome closeup flashed and blinked as its currents and electrical fluctuations disturbed the video feed.
McKenzie gave a signal to the operators, the underlings sitting at the back of the room, people staring blindly at all the screens, listening to the screen's sound with all the remaining external noise cut off.
– We have one hell of a situation here.
Liz and Ted stared at him, at the screen, and back at him again. They could practically observe as he pulled himself together and became colder, businesslike, more the way they had learned to know him. Whatever animosity he bore towards them, and there was a *lot* of it, he had resolved it with himself well before he with his teeth gritted had decided to accept their... unique expertise. He had without doubt tried virtually everything else first.
– You can say that again.
The male Warren looked impressed at the towering structure showing up on most screens, dwarfing all the technological equipment, all its spokesmen in the foreground, speaking into their toys, their microphones flushed in spit and saliva. A majority of the world's well-known journalists and public figures had already descended on this place.
Not Garrett, though - the Bishop of California. He remained in his home state, consolidating his position.
It could be a recording, though. Ted thought he had heard something familiar there, and he had, but he couldn't be sure it was an exact match. Garrett wasn't exactly known for variety in his life and speeches.
At least not among the Warrens… and neither in what could be described as McKenzie's inner circle.
– I can have you both briefed thoroughly before dark...
If he had shown them, made sure they saw the screen to rattle them, it didn't, wouldn't work.
– There's nothing you can teach us, Floyd... about the structure or anything connected to it, the female Warren said relaxed and without any animosity in her voice. – Besides, we prefer, as you know, to make our own independent scrutiny.
No doubt he also wanted to use this opportunity to study them more closely. That was quite okay, even if they couldn't learn anything more from him. They knew who and what he was. It was enough.
– The President acquiesced to your rather unreasonable demands and terms. You are to have free reign of the vicinities and are effectively, within reason, in charge of the operation.
– That's good of you to confirm for us, Floyd, Ted said extremely good humored, – but totally unnecessary. The president's aide took us through the same lecture hours ago.
They all knew McKenzie could have the President killed within hours if he really wanted and found it to serve his long-term interest.
The two of them went outside, took the long road away from there and they breathed easier almost immediately.
She stopped a little bit and turned back towards the tent.
– May I borrow your watch, Floyd, she said in a light tone. It wasn't a question or a request.
– Why? McKenzie did not show himself in the tent opening.

But he couldn't hide the fact that he had followed them, chased after them like a hawk.

Fortunately, they didn't need to hear his voice to confirm he was there. They had known, they knew, feeling him like a festering sore in their consciousness, assaulting their senses.

– We're going to take a closer look at everything, she said teasingly. – And want to keep track of time, that's all.

The watch came flying out of the tent, as if thrown by an invisible force. She caught it with an elegant swing of her right hand.

Their sharp senses started taking in the atmosphere, the mood of the area. Every place they had visited or lived had been different from each other, but in most cities and areas they only spotted minor differences. This place... was *different.*

There was, except for the obvious nothing obvious. Not even to them, who always looked for strangeness wherever they traveled, who were able to smell a city, a place. Though it had to sink in slowly. They had felt *something* of course, when they first landed here, but it wasn't until now it started to «surface». Under the ruckus, under the laugh riot, they sensed something... deeper.

A fundamental... Change.

They walked towards what scientists probably already loved to call a «phenomenon». When they looked in its direction it filled their entire view, long before they got close. Now, on the ground, confronted by «it», it became almost impossible to measure the distance to the beginning of the black surface. They proceeded with caution, but not excessively so.

Four eyes caught the sight of them, the bodies, the statues, the soldiers frozen in time. There were four of them, just under, inside the surface. They were obviously aiming to run forward, but hadn't been able to advance very far. One step, perhaps two, it was hard to tell.

The Black Dome was not completely black, at least not on its outskirts. A kind of twilight allowed a view to the first fifteen meters of the main road leading into the dark. The two saw no more humans, but while looking more closely at the details they discovered birds and objects floating perfectly still in the air. As if it wasn't air at all, but glass or some other form of transparent, solid compound that had captured it all.

Elizabeth stretched out one arm. The hand penetrated the surface quite effortlessly, the lower arm, too, and the elbow, all the way to the shoulder.

– It tingles, she reported. – It... hurts and... I cannot move my fingers.

The withdrawal happened slowly and with some effort. When she managed to pull out the hand it was clearly swollen. The change from wonder to pain had happened over a span of seconds.

– Its border is fluid, she said. – It's hard to say where it actually begins. You can't penetrate very far before the effect becomes quite... pronounced, though.

– Come on! He knew she didn't need coddling and they started walking along the dome's edge.

They took their time, circling around it all, walking through urban areas, fields and abrupt wilderness, back to the few remaining houses and streets, stopping by the big dig in the ground they had noticed earlier.

– So, they have tried to dig under it, she said bemused.

The tunnel was more than big enough for a man to walk upright in it, big enough for cars and bigger vehicles. He went down inside it. There wasn't much light, but he had always seen well in the dark. The military had, with their usual thoroughness started the dig at least twenty meters away. It didn't help much. Almost before the tunnel opening disappeared, he could decide decisively that, as usual, the world was the same below as above, above as below. The Dome literally sucked light out of the air. His hand started tingling. It was enough. He withdrew it after a few seconds. The tingling persisted a little, then vanished. He turned and walked out of the dark pit.

– It's a ball, a sphere, he reported quite unnecessary. – No way in through the backdoor.

They went in among the houses and streets, rang bells and made the locals react. People opened their doors reluctantly, but because of the military presence without any tangible resistance.

– We would like you to tell us, in your own words what you've seen happen here. Ted spoke quietly, sweetly and was straight out uncharacteristically charming. Elizabeth shook her head in frustrated admiration. She had always taken care of tasks like these in bygone years.

Slowly, hesitatingly the few remaining inhabitants of the area started to speak, started to tell.

There was no electricity, no artificial generation of heat or light. Torches burned on the porches and seeded the air with soot. If not for the modern look, the architecture of the living quarters, the scene itself, they could just as well be visiting a genuine medieval village. It wasn't so much the look as much as the feeling it gave the two outsiders. It was the people, how they behaved, how they moved. Both Elizabeth and Ted had long ago learned to see beyond appearances, beyond skin and bone, the surface of the living daylights.

Away from the tents and the soldiers, from the workings and trappings of technology, among the few houses that remained on the outskirts of town, it reminded them both of New Orleans. Mixing the old with the new, the future with the ancient...

It reminded them more about New Orleans than New Orleans did.

– Before this, Elizabeth asked, – did you notice anything extraordinary, anything at all? We would like you to tell us everything, even if it seems trivial and unimportant.

– There's always *something*, a young man said, a little less timid than the others. – This is New England, after all. We've lived with the strange and offbeat since they hanged witches in Salem, as part of the local folklore, so to speak. There's a trail up to a hill where nothing will grow. Nothing at all. I've never heard a satisfactory explanation to that one.

– On that hill there's an old castle. It's supposed to be haunted. When I was a kid the adults told us that there were no such things as ghosts, but on the other hand, we were also forbidden to ever set foot there, even in the forest surrounding the old house. I'm not sure it can be called a castle... We went there anyway, and nothing ever happened. It wasn't boring up there, but we felt somewhat cheated, I guess.

– The last two months, though, that's a different story.

He did speak rather hushed. Sometimes his voice was so low that even they had problems hearing what he said. He didn't speak in a hushed whisper like most of the others here did.

– It isn't easy to put into words, he began hesitantly. – Events that didn't seem to matter when they happened, are now gaining, in hindsight, a lot more importance. I didn't see much. I didn't see the floating fireballs, the shimmering lights others told me they had witnessed. What I saw was the slow, inexplicable changes. We've always had witches, of course...

– Hush, a woman whispered in a mixture of fear and rage. – Can't you see that he's one himself, and she is, too?

Ted and Elizabeth exchanged glances, good humored. It was the eyes, naturally. They had stopped using dark glasses many years ago. They did not hide themselves any longer.

– The correct, general name, if there is one, should probably be mutant, ma'am, he said with a huge smile, one definitely overdone, as it showed off his big, juicy fangs.

– You said witches...? Liz prompted the young man.

– Yes, he pulled himself together, recovering from her dazzling smile. – There have always been some. Every town in New England seems to have them, do they not? Even if they, like here, tend to keep a low profile. That changed here, especially during what they called the Festival of Samhain. As I understood it, it is the time leading up to Halloween, what Christians call All Hallows Eve, and they called All Souls Night. They grew in number and importance. Many treated them badly, but it hardly seems to matter anymore, does it? They managed to do their thing anyway and what they did engulfed the whole town... Didn't it?

He stared up on the older, taller man that seemingly towered over him.

– She *flew*, a girl spoke up. – She flew over the city embraced by Fire.

– That's a witch for you, Liz laughed, – as always, a disaster waiting to happen.

– Yeah, isn't it GREAT? Ted exclaimed.

She tried her utmost to stare him down, in vain. It was she who was supposed to have said that. He had changed significantly since his younger days. He had developed humor and self-irony, for one thing.

– Do you think she did it all... alone? She asked burning with need, with curiosity, mirroring his fireeyes with hers.

– No way! He said quite decisively. – No one can manage such a feat alone.

The townspeople imagined that the torches burned brighter and taller when the two walked away.

The frightened and the lost hoped for reassurances. There were none. They hoped for comfort. No one answered their prayers.

The two with dancing fires in their eyes didn't lose an ounce of their good mood on the walk back to the camp. Not even the sight of all the uniforms and subsequent scenes affected them as it had before and should have done now. They entered the bus where more electronic equipment was stashed. It was almost darker here than outside, where ghost lightning often flared and didn't illuminate anything. The machinery was supposed to be shielded from any outside interference, but still it struggled as most people in this place, «faced» with the unknown.

They walked straight to the head honcho, as if they knew by instinct the spot they would find him.

– The people you sent in, they're alive, are they not?

McKenzie, unbelievable enough, looked exasperated. He allowed by a glance one of the scientists to answer the question.

– We can't really be *certain*, but we believe they are... They were sent in with sensors on each body for us to monitor their life signs. First, we were convinced they became... deceased the moment they entered the dome. Later we found that they still have heartbeats, though highly irregular ones. There can come one shortly after the previous or pause for minutes. They're fluctuating, varying wildly.

– They're moving, another said and pushed a button. – This is a video constantly monitoring them all. It's speeded up ten times. The movement is still painstakingly slow, but it's *there*.

The two noticed and it helped confirm what they had already surmised.

– So? McKenzie blew against Elizabeth. – Any theories?

– Look at this watch you so graciously contributed earlier today. She held it up, then handed it to him, smiling a bit. Ted brought another wristwatch out of his pocket and held that up. – Both these mechanical devices show the same time, which is coincidentally half an hour late compared to your watches.

They stared at her, as uncomprehending as ever.

– It's a Time Distortion field, she shrugged. – Time moves much more slowly by the rim of the dome than hundred meters away from it. Not as slowly as it probably does inside, but *noticeable.* You must have gathered as much yourself. You have the world's biggest brains at your fingertips. Beyond that... We don't have a clue.

– WHAT! His patience already running thin, his cautious calm gave in as the thinnest ice.

– The only way to really find out more is to confront the beast head on, face the music, pay the piper...

– Going in, the male Warren confirmed, not without some modicum of satisfaction.

– But... who's behind it? McKenzie said with a despair impossible to hide. – Who can do such a thing?

– Who says it's *done?* Ted challenged him. – Can't it just be a random, rare *phenomenon?* Who are you who claim to know everything there is to know about the Universe?

He didn't get an answer, had not expected, and did not expect any.

The early morning dawned for the third time over the Dome. He saw it before his inner eye. Suddenly, slowly, he seemed to look at McKenzie and everyone and everything from outside himself. This wasn't unusual for him, but he had hardly experienced it this pronounced before. Also the world outside the dome seemed to slow down to a crawl. There was no wind, but the curtains still did flap in the wind. The air blew under the door. He remembered another bus, long time past, not the past. He didn't want to, but he did.

Dawn, the color of blood and rust. They stood there, alone, facing the dome.

He heard a rusty voice, one from the past, clear as day, his brother's voice:

I saw everything. I saw the Phoenix rising.

– I keep seeing rows of open windows, he said.

– I do, too, she said. – In a long hall. There's no one else inside, I see nothing outside. There are white curtains floating in the wind, straight out from the wall. I know there's sound, but I can't recognize it. A therapist would have a field day here.

– Good thing we don't believe in them, then, he said.

Again, she looked at him with a half-humored sting in her eyes.

– We don't need a crystal ball to realize the obvious. She cocked her head in contempt.

They started walking. Behind them McKenzie and his men stood, close by the best technology money and power could buy, everything totally useless. Ted enjoyed that, they both did, and they embraced that enjoyment with everything they had, everything they were.

– This is... monumental, something I never would dare expect.

– And it's just the beginning.

Behind his eyelids he once more saw the bird, the bird of Shadow rise in the twilight.

He embraced yet again the feeling of the moment. This time she didn't give him any look, but shared the joy with him.

– We're at the top of our Power, she said with for her an unusually quiet confidence, confidence edged with just a little lace of bravery. – Whatever is residing in there should have some problems gobbling us up for breakfast.

McKenzie and his crew heard everything through the microphones.

– They're joking, an assistant gasped. – How can they...

McKenzie silenced her with a sharp move with his hand, a hand, a movement that killed and mutilated.

Ted and Liz started tearing off all the microphones and the ridiculous army clothes they had been fitted with. One microphone had been hidden under the skin by the right shoulder. Liz tore it off and a lot of skin and blood went with it.

– A good thing we refused all those idiotic and beyond silly inoculations, she murmured. – Otherwise, we would have had work until Christmas.

– HEY! The Man screamed well behind them, unusually and uncharacteristically *excited.*

That, too, pleased them more than they could ever express.

Thoughts dwindled as they the last few seconds prepared, braced themselves. They felt it, how outside influence slowly was cleansed from their bodies and minds, their soul and their fire. There was only the boiling of the blood and what was ahead.

They ran the last ten steps as fast as they could, they held nothing back, and just before they could feel the first stiffening of limbs and muscles they jumped. Onlookers might even be tempted to think they were flying, levitating as easily as a bird flapping its wings. The blood flowing from her shoulder seemed to jump straight up and the drops, shining like sapphires, seemed to be freezing in the air.

And just as with the soldiers and the birds their two bodies... *stopped* the moment they dived under the transparent surface of the darkness, a darkness strong enough to keep the day at bay. Facial features already hardened by intense concentration and wild passion were captured as if on a giant painting. All their power, all the power of will they could muster, was for nothing. They, too, had become prisoners...

Of the Black Dome.

2

What is reality and what's fantasy? Who can say for sure?

From far away they came. All of them. They came from far away.

The bus moved slowly through the landscape, through the pockets of heat and air.

Jill Stafford ate rolls of chocolate. She knew she wasn't supposed to, but she couldn't help herself. Besides, she had to eat the chocolate fast. She had bought it at the gas station just a few minutes ago, and it was already melting.

She licked chocolate from her fingers and dried the remains off her skin on the seat beneath her. It left a visible brown line. Nervousness mixed with excitement whether or not anyone noticed or would notice.

It was hot outside, she supposed, but the heat inside the bus reached monumental levels. Her body and her clothes stank of sweat. Everybody on the crowded bus stank of sweat. All the deodorant, anti-perspiring stuff in the world couldn't stop that from happening. The bus was a charter, just like the driver, hired in to do a specific job. The thought was condescending and cruel. She knew that, but couldn't help herself. Most of the girls and boys had been sitting on the same spot all the way from

Boston, without being able to move much around. It was an uncomfortable, unpleasant and worst of all, boring ride. Some of the passengers had the nerve to move around a bit and amuse themselves. She didn't want… to do that.

The year had reached the first days of September. Jill knew the summer lasted longer here than in Wales, where she had lived for most of her life. But shouldn't it at least be waning a little at this time? Just a little bit compared to... August, for instance? It did not wane, that's for sure.

It was waxing.

During the days since she had arrived in the United States the temperature had risen from hot to red-hot.

– This is the hottest summer in New England *ever*, she heard someone speak out. – I grew up here. My father and grandfather, too, and they say the same. This isn't «Indian Summer», but Hell.

She had tried reading a book. It was hopeless. Sweat got in her eyes and almost blinded her. Besides, she was fucking tired of books. She couldn't even remember the title or what it was supposed to be about.

She looked up, suddenly startled. Tried to remember what, if anything, had caused her to react the way she did.

The bus had passed a turn, a hill covered by trees. She could see it with something akin to sudden, photographic memory. There was a house up there somewhere, a huge building, or rather a structure, hardly visible, hidden in the land as it was. But she had seen it and the sight of it made her turn strangely cold.

It was like she could imagine long, dank corridors filled with screams.

She had stopped looking through the windows hours ago. It was too hot, too boring to bother with exploring anything or satisfying her curiosity.

But still she had. She awoke with a start, a start from her slumber.

– Did you say something?

– Eh? She looked up, startled, with big, weary eyes.

– You said something, the boy in the seat next to her said. – I couldn't hear exactly what. I realize now that you dozed off and were dreaming.

– I thought I heard a scream, she said. – Someone was screaming, I'm certain of it.

– In this terrific place, he joked. – Pretty improbable, don't you think?

She smiled, in spite of the awkwardness she always felt in the close presence of boys.

– You see, that's exactly what I was talking about. He leaned a little closer to her side of the seat. – Do you remember what I told you?

– Yes, she replied. It was not necessary for her to concentrate. – You quoted a man called Havelock Ellis. You didn't know anything about him, who he was, but you liked the quote. It goes like this: «Dreams are real as long as they last. Can we say anything else about life»?

She looked him straight into the eyes. He was not put off, as she had thought he would be.

– I *knew* you heard me, he said excitedly. – A little shy, are we not?

And on that note, her shyness returned vengeful and with the usual foulness. She nodded and felt very small. He was... experienced. She saw it in each and every one of his movements, his very being, fuck him.

– I still want to know you better, he told her compellingly. – Not because of the shyness, but because you're special. That's why I told you I wanted to appeal to your intellect.

He touched her generous chin and wiped off some chocolate. She was blushing, she knew she did. She always did!

The bus stopped quite suddenly. She was ill prepared for it and would have been thrown forward if he hadn't grabbed her.

– This is my stop, he explained to her, as he would to a small child. – I live here, you know, I have just stayed in Boston the last week. See you around!

He went off the bus, with several of the others. He said something to a tall, beautiful blonde and she threw her head back and laughed. She kissed him on the chin. So casual, so easy.

The brief stop made Jill even hotter. That didn't seem possible, but as Havelock Ellis probably or possibly would have said: «Things can seem very unlikely sometimes, but who are we to argue with facts»?

She moved hesitantly on the seat until she sat where the boy had been sitting. The reward came in the form of the wind from one of the open hatches in the ceiling blowing straight at her. Her long, black hair that ordinarily fell down on the brow was pushed backwards and she felt she could breathe for the first time since the trip started. It felt great. A fleeting feeling quickly fading.

The bus drove into Northfield, Massachusetts. The town was far enough away from Boston that its location was on the outskirts of the enormous Metropolitan Area stretching all the way down to Washington DC.

Northfield was a field. A field part of a bigger, flat land. It lived up to its name where there were houses and streets, and the farmland to the north. There were no houses where the land started to curve to the west. Jill could see the path leading up the forest-clad hill, because of the lack of vegetation. After they had passed the hill, she saw that the land leveled out behind it and the plain continued westward. Jill could glimpse more woods and single trees and far beyond that, haze-covered smaller hills.

Now, that she was almost at the end of the tiresome trip, her mood improved decisively, and she even felt a surge of low-level excitement. After all, this was the place she had chosen to live the next few years. She realized this suddenly, with a start. This had been a distant place, until now, now when she was here.

The main road reached a sharp curve in the otherwise flat landscape towards what she suspected was their destination. The school, with its adjacent boarding area, was situated to the east, at the opposite side of the hill, with the old part of Northfield between. The bus drove on to a surprisingly big parking lot. Jill was not used to the typical huge American education facilities.

There were three tall, interconnecting buildings on the campus. The driver stopped the bus and killed the engine in front of what was supposedly the school itself, with the living areas on each side.

Sleep and work, Jill thought for no specific reason.

The heat hit them all almost immediately. No more cooling air through open hatches. She grabbed her black, flat-brimmed hat from her lap, the one she had carried with her since leaving the house in England, and hurried off the bus with the others.

The students collected their luggage from the cargo bay under the bus.

In spite of the impractical color in the heat, she put the hat on her head. The long, flat brim hid her eyes, and she could look at the world without the world looking back.

They were, after a remarkably short wait led the modest stretch to their destination by a girl and a boy dressed in a school uniform. Jill recognized the blonde bombshell from the bus.

– Boys with me, the boy called.

He brought the boys in one direction. The blonde bombshell signed for the girls to follow her in another and led them even closer to white paint, to walls of heat. There was no defense against the searing sun anywhere. They stood there sweating and suffering, while the girl talked with what was probably one of the supervisors.

– Thank God for the wind, a girl close to Jill moaned.

– I've been told that it's always windy here, another whispered.

Only a short walk now, to the shadow, but it felt like miles and miles.

The air in the hall inside was surprisingly cool. In the big house, that almost certainly had hundreds and hundreds of rooms, it seemed like stairs and hallways went on forever.

The blonde turned towards her wards for the first time and held up her hands. It became quiet except for the murmur created by the echo in the halls and the passages between halls. It was the first time she talked to them using her voice. Outside she had used hands and eyes, with an obvious patronizing flair.

And they had followed, like good sheep.

– Hello, she greeted them (sort of), – my name is Victoria. I wish to welcome you all to Northfield College Campus. I will guide you to your rooms and also help you to get settled. I know it might be difficult for some of you to come here to a totally different environment from what you may be used to, but I and the other student contacts are here to make the transition as smooth as possible. We pride ourselves on our friendliness here at Northfield...

Jill listened only halfheartedly, without really registering what the well dressed, well-done-hair girl said.

– Then there's the matter of your rooms. We've already assigned them to you, though, so individual wishes to move or trade places may be difficult to fulfill. This is made twice as hard by the fact that the lot of you is the last to arrive...

Stafford was one of the last names to be called. Jill didn't need to call out or otherwise identify herself. Victoria, apparently and obviously had already made her.

– Your room is on the top floor. Victoria enlightened her. – You're lucky!

Jill didn't feel lucky, but inside her sparked the small ember of rebellion, the same that had led her across the vast sea.

– That's GREAT! She exclaimed. – I can slide down here on the banister.

The joke was not appreciated.

– We've got quite extensive rules of conduct here. Especially for fresh meat like you, young lady. Some things are allowed, but we practice freedom with responsibility here. If you cross the line...

She obviously had a desire to repeat points more than once. Jill did not say anything.

– Your roommate is expecting you upstairs. We couldn't let all of you meet down here and she is also quite *busy,* if you must know.

Welcome to Northfield College, Jill thought sourly. She was on her way up the stairs before the other girl had finished speaking.

Halfway up she stopped, suddenly curious, wondering. The diminished rays from the sun spiraled through the dust (there was dust here), and seemingly made shapes, shadows out of nothing.

Whisper, *whisper,* Shadow cried silently.

She reached out for one of them, but it disappeared when she held out her hand. The dust blew away. She looked around. There was, in fact, possible to slide down the banister almost all the way from the top. The staircase went from top to bottom in a broad spiral along the wall. It was at least as old as the house itself. She smiled then, without quite knowing why.

Jill Stafford was tall, a fact she was quite aware of. She had been both lightheartedly and heavy handedly teased about it her entire life. The girl waiting for her at the top of the stairs was even taller, though. Jill doubted that she had met boys or men who were taller.

– You are Jill? A smile and an outstretched hand. – They call me Tamara Farley. Nice to meet you.

– I'm not so much into shaking hands. It came out as a mumbling, hesitantly, slightly out of breath. She had always hated stairs.

– Traditional bullshit, I know, but let us make an exception this one time, what do you say?

Jill did shake her hand and the girl's smile widened.

Jill felt her skin pressed against hers, the feeling lingered long afterwards, of skin, of more. Words pressed ahead from behind tight woven lips, but she held her tongue.

– It means so much more when it's done only occasionally, Tamara said.

They walked the vast sea to their room, at the end of another long corridor, by the dark stairs to the attic.

– «Your room is on the top floor». Jill mumbled. – «You're lucky»!

– That's Correct Victoria for you, Tamara laughed. And then more somber. – You know, you're really good. That really did sound like her. You might wanna consider a future as a mimic.

– Why did you meet me by the stairs? Jill asked curious.

– I arrived yesterday, and nobody was there to meet *me.* I searched very far and very long before I finally found my room. It's an experience I wouldn't want anybody to repeat.

They grinned at each other.

Tamara unlocked the door and opened it and allowed Jill to enter first. Jill entered cautiously, sought and took in the sight with her gray eyes and her senses opened wide. The room opened up to them. It… welcomed her. A shiver passed through the tall and big body. She straightened.

– It's big and... bright. I like it.

– Our home for a looong time to come, it came merrily from behind from the other girl.

The room turned westward, where there were two big windows. Everything was huge here although she suspected there were other rooms, where more «important» students resided, which were substantially bigger. Under the windows someone had placed the beds, far from the cool shadows in the corners and straight in the path of the white heat rays.

– Don't look at me, I didn't put them there.

– Good. Jill moved in one sweep her bed into her corner, into the shadows.

Tamara, after a brief hesitation, did the same.

– It isn't so bad in the afternoon, she said. – The Sun sets fairly early behind the big hill.

– Yes, Jill mused, – and a shadow is cast all over the place.

She shook her head wondering if she herself knew what she meant by those words.

– They have named it Frazer Hill, but the way I understand it, everybody calls it quite simply the Hill, the other girl told her. – Funny, isn't it? As big as it is, they could just as well call it the Mountain or something...

– Yes, it is strange, isn't it? Jill still thought she herself sounded a bit far away. – That it seems so much bigger than it really is, how it seems to draw light from its surroundings. Look, it's dark even now, in the middle of the day.

– If you say so. It was uttered with obvious embarrassment. Jill didn't notice. – Uh, do you have any more luggage? We should perhaps carry it up.

– This is it. She pointed at the small suitcase on the bed. – I do plan to buy myself more clothes...

She knew her insecurity was exposed in her voice and her pose and hated herself for it.

– Don't worry, Tamara grinned. – Not that it matters, but as you can see, even if my suitcase is a little bigger than yours, it's not much to brag about.

Jill felt strange, skittish, but not skittish at the same time. Strange!

– Even if you probably have traveled wide and far just to get here, the bigger girl continued hesitantly. – Your accent is pretty strange, far from anything I've ever heard before.

– I guess it's my Gaelic upbringing, Jill replied with a calm voice. – I grew up in Wales. Everything is... strange there, even the language. It's pretty boring actually. I know I would've been disappointed if I was a traveler coming there seeking something... special.

Someone played some kind of string instrument somewhere in the building. It sounded like a harp, but could just as well be a guitar. A cloud passed the Sun. There was no cloud. A fog not chilly, not visible, gave her gooseflesh all over.

– Funny, isn't it? Tamara laughed nervously. – And at a *school.* Too bad it isn't prolonged aid against the heat.

Jill looked out the open window and did nothing else than breathe in and out, in and out, a couple of minutes. She regained her calm, but maybe not her center. She wasn't certain she had one, feeling the same restlessness she had felt her entire life.

Breathing was the very reason she had come to this place, so far away from what had passed as her home. That had seemed distant, or sickeningly close, not like this. She had traveled far, to think through her life.

No one would claim that their new home of a room was filled with personal stuff or even stuff. A brig or a prison cell could be more accommodating. Tamara had put a few posters on the wall. And she owned a Walkman. That was all and everything. Jill had nothing to contribute, except the hat she hung over the bed.

The heat, never truly gone, returned with a vengeance. The temperature rose even a few notches more during the seemingly endless hours remaining of the day and the sun shone mercilessly on the rooms on the west side. It became nearly intolerable. Doors and windows were opened wide, but the wind racing through them was so hot that it didn't help much. Not much at all. Rather it served to dehydrate poor bodies even more.

– I apologize about my claim concerning the livable temperature here earlier, Tamara moaned.

– Don't… sweat it. Jill made a poor attempt at humor. – I presume the heat has turned even worse since yesterday afternoon?

Tamara nodded glumly.

They thought about leaving, decided against it, thinking it couldn't be worse. Regretting it one hour later when every part of their clothes was soaked in sweat. Shy eyes looked in the mirror and at each other. Everything was visible, or so it seemed. They couldn't go anywhere like this, just couldn't.

– I must take a shower, Jill mumbled. And then, with something like renewed energy she pulled and pushed off every piece of cloth on her body.

Tamara was not used to such immediate, impulsive behavior. Eyes widened. Hers - and Jill's own.

– Your body is golden all over! she said most of all to say something.

– The family is supposed to be descendants of Vikings. A shrug. – I guess it must be correct. Both my parents have fair skin and hair. But I would gather it isn't the whole truth...

– It wasn't meant as an insult, Tamara apologized. – As you can see, I'm pretty ethnic myself.

A pause, if not hesitation.

– I'm Jewish, she added explanatory.

Her hair was as black as that of the other girl, but while Jill's hair was smooth and shiny, hers was curly and disheveled.

Jill used only cold water in the shower. She stood under the endless waterfall long after she was reasonably clean of sweat and dirt and allowed herself to be cooled down as much as possible. The water was warmer than it was supposed to be, but it did help. She was still somewhat chilled after carefully drying herself with a towel and dressed up in her last change of clean clothes.

Tamara took the plunge, too, and afterwards showed her roommate around the campus, the few places she knew. She had only been here a little more than twenty-four hours herself.

Outside in the hall, it was merely moderately less hot. No respite from anything there. Doors had been opened to every room and the sun easily reached those who sought refuge from it in the bleak shadows.

– That door is closed, Jill noted.

They had reached the big hall by the stairs. The door to the opposite wing was closed.

Strange, not so strange at all, she suspected.

– They have air-conditioning in there, Tamara sighed. – The door is probably locked, in order to keep us ordinary mortals from entering or benefiting from it.

Jill turned and went back to the door and touched the handle, pushed it down, pulled it to her. It didn't budge. For a moment she pushed her entire body against the door. She had sensed the cold in there and now she felt it. It felt good.

She shrugged and they went on their way. Half expecting to see the same dust shapes, she felt something almost identifiable as disappointment when they didn't appear.

– The boys live over *there,* as I suppose you can guess, Tamara giggled and pointed through the window. – As you can see, they live *bigger* and probably better. There are more of them and they're not gonna be housewives and give birth to a bunch of kids.

They set down in the mess hall, the school's dining room. There were blessed few people present and the air conditioning was on, had to be, with all the food close by.

And even the rich brats have to eat here, Jill added cynically in her mind.

– ... so I'm a real happy camper because of the scholarship, Tamara said in a somber way a while later. – I wouldn't have been able to keep it going at home much longer. I had already distanced myself in a major way from the religion and everything connected to it. I couldn't bear all the hypocrisy, for instance my father's defense of the murders the Israeli nation and soldiers did in Jenin and on the West Bank and in Gaza in general and the government sabotage of the peace process. I expressed my fervent desire to hunt down Ariel Sharon and his entire terror cabinet.

There was Passion, wide open and boiling. Jill froze in joy.

The TV was on. They sent even more reports from New Orleans and Louisiana about the devastating effects of the Hurricane Katrina. For some reason it made the strange chill and heat burn even stronger somewhere inside Jill.

– Reporting such events is very important, Tamara said. – Usually they don't, you know, but this is quite simply too big to ignore.

– You're an avid political beast, aren't you? Jill said with a grin.

– I am! Tamara said, clearly agitated. – Established media won't report on important issues, because they want to lull people to sleep, so I rely on the Internet and alternative venues in an ongoing effort to find out what's happening, what's truly happening in the world.

She looked a little hurt and clearly vulnerable just then.

– I think it's great, Jill assured her.
The big girl visibly brightened.
– You do? Really?
– Most certainly, the Welsh stated firmly, - I have despaired in my ongoing effort to find astute friends, people able to see beyond the veil of deceit and lies so prevalent in the world today.
Hearing herself speak like that felt strange, too, felt so good. When the two grabbed hands she did so without thinking, without anxiety, forgetting herself. She gasped and blinked.
Tamara didn't notice. She had her attention on the TV. The news broadcast ended.
- Did you *see* that?
Jill grinned and shook her head, and waited for the other to explain, and Tamara understood, too, and she was also grinning.
– There have been major protests against the construction of the Israeli «security wall» every day since January, largely unreported by US established media, and just a few days ago I heard about major clashes between protesters and the Israeli army in Bil'in, the *correct* version of events. US media is so Israel-friendly that it makes me want to hurl.
– Western media in general is, Jill said, – even though an increasing number of Europeans have grown aware of what's going on.
They had a lot to talk about, both equally agitated and passionate, and Jill almost forgot again, forgot about the tingling in the hand from Tamara's touch and the vivid impressions it created.
It happened as they were about to leave, as the eager exchange of thoughts halted a bit, turned sober.
– Sweet Daddy expressed his desire to beat me up the day I left. «To teach me to respect authorities and tradition». I threatened to go to the police. Then he threatened to throw me out, but I was already standing on the stairs outside...
– It was a bit different with me, Jill said with burning eyes. – They stated that they wouldn't give me permission to leave. They wouldn't even discuss it. If I hadn't been eighteen already, I would've had great trouble getting away...
– ...escaping, her new friend completing for her.
– *Yes!* She agreed.
Jill noticed something then, in her moment of vulnerability, a sore, raw spot of feeling spreading all over her. She looked around her, at the other people in the room. It wasn't just her, feeling the way she did about the past. Everybody looked, glanced uncomfortable... at the Hill. And so she joined them in their venture. And she saw the Sun hanging there, a moment, not over the horizon, but over Frazer Hill.
And then disappear.
It happened so sudden, from one moment to the next, so abruptly that it seemed like the whole shining disk had been swallowed whole. It wasn't any transition like with daily sunset, hardly any shifting to red. One moment the entire disk was visible, the next it was gone. Someone screamed. Jill hardly noticed in her excitement, didn't even notice the tingling of fear running down her own spine.
They all felt it, it was tangible and real, how the shadow and the cold reached them at the same time, immediately and without the slightest delay.
– Isn't that something? One of the teachers said proudly. – Scientists from all over the world have visited us, but even through extensive studies they haven't yet been able to solve this particularly fascinating riddle. They assured us that there is nothing to fear, though, a conclusion I wholeheartedly agree with. For no matter people's unhealthy reactions to optical and sensory input *illusions,* the Hill is still *there,* is it not?
Jill wondered if the man understood the implications of his own words, or was merely grandstanding. She decided it didn't matter. Not now, when the mystery was still fresh in her mind.
The two girls stopped at the top of the stairs outside. It wasn't cold in any way. A typical New England summer afternoon, Jill guessed. They would still sweat easily, if they moved, walked faster than a slow stroll in the afternoon heat. But...
The Sun hadn't really set between the trees on Frazer Hill. There was no residue of sunlight there whatsoever. In fact, there were no trees, no details visible up there at all, except the smooth edge of the huge Shape.

– The rays from the sun are visible not far from here, a boy enlightened them. – Everywhere else, in fact, except on that damn heap and in its shade.

It was true. When they looked, they saw the effects of sunlight both north and south of the «phenomenon». But the entire older part of the city of Northfield was cast in Shadow.

Tamara fell. It happened so fast that she almost tore into Jill and took her with her all the way down. Jill swayed, but stood her ground. Tamara was lying by the base of the stairs, whimpering slightly. Jill hurried down to her.

The other girl already rose and straightened herself.

– I'm fine, she said. – I don't know what the fuck happened. The lovely sight took me in, I guess, and I lost my footing. It is a lovely sight, isn't it?

– Yes... Jill hadn't thought about it that way before, but now, when the thought had been spoken aloud, she did. She took it all in. The Shadow tempering the full daylight, the sunlight, rays on the edge of it, like waves of fire, the sea of humming voices surrounding her...

She «awoke» with a start, from what resembled a dreamlike state.

Many of those around them did stare bemused at the two. One girl walked over.

– Is everything okay? She asked and seemed worried, surprisingly enough.

– Everything is okay, Jill reported with a skewed smile. – We were just a bit too eager admiring the view...

– It is a nice view, isn't it?

– Yes! Jill said.

She stared into eyes as gray as hers and so alike her own. She felt dizzy. The strange feeling of familiarity overwhelmed her momentarily, before it subsided.

– But you didn't fall?

– No, I didn't.

– We'll meet again, Stacy said.

– Yes! Jill acknowledged.

Stacy? Was Stacy her name? Had she said what her name was? She was gone before Jill managed to ask her.

– Did she say what her name was?

– Who? Tamara asked good-natured.

– The girl who was here.

– Which one?

Frustrated Jill held back, well aware of the fact that this wasn't the first time something like this had happened to her. Had Stacy been here at all, or had she been a part of Jill's usual overactive imagination? She knew she had one. Her teachers had always told her so. Her parents and friends had, too. And the therapist they had sent her to, when she was twelve. She feared now, more than ever, that they had all been right in their assumption. Stacy had, when she thought it through, seemed more like a mirror image, than a real person.

She knew she wasn't crazy. She knew there were other explanations. Better explanations. If a person... dared to believe, trust in oneself. But a bit of fear always remained.

She walked away, half hoping that Tamara would follow her, half hoping she wouldn't.

Tamara did, and the hope inside her dwindled and died, died and was reborn a thousand times. The afternoon daystar crept forth from the Hill this day, too, like she had been assured it would do. And she wasn't certain at all whether she preferred it that way or not. The cool shadows had always been a source of both joy and fear to her.

– I've always seen... things other people don't, she said quietly to Tamara. – Here everybody is seeing something, and they still don't see.

Tamara did not reply at first. They had walked more steps in silence than any one of them dared to count, when the bigger girl grabbed her arm and stopped them both in their tracks.

– Your scholarship, where did you get it?

– Prometheus Corporation, Jill said. – They tested the whole class, both physically and mentally. As far as I know I was the only one they offered anything. They didn't do anything really weird with us or asked us strange questions, not weirder or stranger than many other tests I've seen. They do all kinds of tests on everybody these days, don't they?

– In my class they called themselves the Phoenix Foundation, but otherwise everything seemed remarkably similar to your description.

Disappointment and hope warred for dominance in both their faces. They exchanged slight smiles.

– Prometheus, according to mythology, was the ancient Greek god who gave humanity the gift of fire, Jill said. – Fire to survive the gathering storm. And Phoenix is the bird of Fire, the ancient symbol of Life, reborn through life, throughout Eternity, from the ashes of its own fire.

The slight smiles broadened insanely so.

The matriculation started in full the next day. Jill hardly remembered the night before. She was kept so busy that she wasn't certain she remembered anything or even her own name. Even if she had to repeat it numerous times during the day and the days that followed. Her first conscious memory of that day was the precise moment

She saw Stacy pull out a chair from a desk not far from hers. Stacy didn't seem to notice her, to acknowledge her presence. And why should she? How would she react to a stranger staring at her like that? Jill disliked the sting of shame coursing through her, cursing her, but the feeling persisted, until she felt the overpowering need to look away in embarrassment. The strange feeling, so seldom felt earlier in her life, returned to her several times this day, though, like a shadow, a whisper, also this time hardly noticeable. Not so strong as the first time, not only Stacy but others, too, brought it on. Brought exhilaration, brought fear and numerous other layers of emotion.

She and Tamara took a stroll in the school park in the afternoon. The Hill started to tower over them as Jill imagined it did every day. But the wind blowing through the town and the surrounding farmland was just the same soft breeze. Jill looked for Stacy, but didn't see her. She remembered herself as a girl, a sharp pain memory, both unwanted and welcomed. She had loved to stay on high ground and feel the wind blow. Her parents always asked her why, no matter what she did. Both with the wind on the high ground and most of her other activities. The worst part of it all was that she could never really explain it to them, no matter how much she tried.

She looked at the trees and growth around her, how it all needed water, in order to grow and thrive. How much they lacked even the most elementary manure nourishment. Year by year now, she had felt the winds grow hotter and fiercer. The summer in Wales had been uncanny hot this year, as was the case with all of Britain and the rest of the world. The weather, the mood. As the wind had blown more and harder and the rainfall had beaten all former records in the colder half of the year. The wind blew ever harder. Everything seemed ready, more than ready, to... to blow.

The increasing heat wasn't so bad. She had really adapted to it a long time ago. It had never represented much trouble to her to adapt to a changing environment. It was those that didn't change she couldn't stand. The excitement connected to the Journey and what she traveled to, had for a while put her inner balance in turmoil, one now clearly abating.

– Why did you leave?

– What? Jill raised her head. Her thoughts had wandered off there, for a while, wandering off yet again.

– Why did you leave? Really. It wasn't merely your parents doing, was it? Why did you seek out a place like... this? You did, didn't you?

Tamara spoke mostly to keep the conversation going, but the question had a certain quality that clearly revealed that there was more to it, somewhere in her soft voice. Something was nagging the big girl.

Jill decided to reply to her. Tamara was nice and they had spoken so much that they had taken the first steps towards what could be friendship.

– Truth to tell I don't know. Not fully, at least. It was, is more like a series of hunches showing up simultaneously. I wanted to experience more of the world, of course, but it's more than that. I was lonely, in a way I couldn't define. I've heard it be said that loneliness isn't a need for company, but a longing for kindred souls. I believe that to be true. There were friends, even close ones, but there was a part of me they couldn't reach. The whole of Wales is so mundane, you know, like a painting, unmoving. It was almost funny the way the tourists talked about it and so much of it that seemed to me like ridiculous myth. I did some sabbaths, witch sabbaths, with a bunch of sun worshippers, but nothing much ever happened. Their heart was clearly not in it. It was more of an excuse to drink herbal tea. And such. I wanted to do... more.

– So you never found out... if you can do Magick… do Witchcraft? In spite of the cheerfulness in the big girl's voice, there was, to the other girl, an easily detectable edge there.

– No, Jill replied embarrassed. She gave away a short snort that might be called laughter, filled with nervousness and no small part of repressed animosity. Many promising friendships had ended this way. She decided to answer as truthful as she possible could, in an attempt to explain. Explain what couldn't possibly be explained. – There were flashes of... something, there always have been. Nothing convincing or conclusive.

Tamara did not seem to have heard a word of what she had said, merely what she maybe wanted to hear. Or maybe not.

– Are you psychic? What can you tell about me?

They had stopped now. Tamara held her in a firm, painful grip.

– I shook hands with you, Jill said carefully measured. – I touched you.

Inside her something happened that led her to forget the pain. A flow, a release.

– I don't mind, Tamara Farley assured with eagerness imminent in her voice. – Don't worry, I'm interested in this.

Jill had attempted to shove her away. Tamara released her grip. They both smiled apologetically. It was refreshing in a way, to experience interest, as it was, instead of the usual distant treatment.

– All humans are sensitive, I guess, Jill spoke in a low voice, akin to a whisper. – Curious, too. At least they have been once. At least in the cradle. This vital part is shredded off during childhood and adolescence. We're taught to fear the strange and the different. A certain degree of respect for the unknown is healthy, but in our present age hatred toward strangers has become a way of life. You yourself, have managed to fight off the brainwashing pretty well. You're just *a bit* afraid of me. Much more anxious really, about the possible consequences of your last adventure before traveling here. Don't worry, there aren't any. Therefore, you don't need any shoulder to cry on.

They both stared shocked at the other.

– How DID you know that? Gasping in horror, Tamara practically slapped her own cheeks, as she hid her face in her palms. – You couldn't know! There is no way you could know!

Totally out of it, she ran away from there.

Jill remained, frozen on the spot, almost as out of it herself. She felt shock, mixed with a number of other nuances of impression. She hadn't known what she was about to say before it left her mouth. Her aim had been to expose something superficial, harmless, anything non-conclusive they could laugh about and forget. But she had slid into some kind of *trance*. And her dormant abilities had shown themselves with a vengeance, beyond reproach.

In a second, between one heartbeat and the next, everything had changed. Eternity revealed itself to her. The very air. Even to her plain eyes the very air seemed changed. And the trees...

There was one tree in particular, to the left of her. She turned and faced it. To her it seemed alive and of course it was. Seething with Life's energy, as it did. She started to laugh, giddy with sudden happiness. It threatened to grow to euphoria, when she noticed the stares and the attention she attracted from the nearby people. Better not gather too much attention to herself. Virtually crestfallen, she forced herself to calm down. She became calm in her outward manner, but inside she was seething and boiling. Something akin to labored breathing became close to normal.

But the tree still seemed to glow to her inner eye. And the need to embrace it grew close to a compulsion.

And then, the flow in her mind transformed itself into a flood.

So strange... People around her, not close really, in a wide circle... felt as if they were closing in on her. They were steps and steps away, most of them. They didn't come to her. She came to them. Their *thoughts*... she could feel them. Their loud thoughts closed in on her and she was unable to resist them. She started to walk, hardly knew where she was headed, knew only she had to get away. The walk broke into a run, she broke into a sweat, and feared she would soon lose control over herself completely. One thousand feet drummed against the tarmac, a narrow path between bushes and low trees, the school park. Everything filled up her brain and it threatened to burst. She moaned, in fear, in terror.

Slowly, slowly, it dawned on her that the flood of voices in her mind had vanished. If it had happened just now or some time ago, she couldn't say. But they were gone. Once again, she heard only the sounds the ears could hear. A few more hesitant steps and the rampant run halted.

Slowly, slowly, she calmed down, calming herself. With labored breathing and leaden legs and thighs, she felt as if she coughed her guts out there on the ground. The taste in her mouth was sour and bitter.

For a long time afterwards, she stood absolutely rigid, while she listened and waited and tried to compose herself.

She turned around and slowly, hesitantly started to walk, walk back. Each step, every moment, she feared she again would hear the terrifying chaotic sounds in her brain. She didn't. Not in the park and not in the schoolyard in the middle of the crowd. But she felt a splitting headache coming on. It was the worst she had ever felt. During the next couple of minutes, it grew to such proportions she feared she had popped a blood vessel or something. She wanted desperately to run to the school's nurse. She didn't, but steered her steps towards the girls' dormitory, up the massive staircase. Climbing a mountain, almost blacking out.

Bed, head on the pillow, wishing she could actually black out. The pain kept just below unbearable and kept her from slipping into unconsciousness. Every time she moved only the slightest, knives of pain cut through body and mind.

Tamara entered the room. Her hardened expression softened when she saw the state of the other girl.

– Jeez, you're pale as a ghost, she burst out.

– Killer headache. Do you have any... painkillers, aspirin, anything?

– I'll get something. Just a minute.

She left the room and Jill imagined less than a minute passed, before her return.

– Can you sit up? She held out pills and a glass of water.

– Yes, I... The pain tore into her. Thoroughly frustrated she couldn't keep tears from flowing from her eyes.

Tamara helped her sit up and held her head, stroking her forehead carefully. She put the pills between quivering lips. Jill swallowed hard.

– How many... how many did you give me?

– Two. Hesitantly, worried.

– Give me one more!

She swallowed the rest of the water in the huge glass in one swap. Whimpering like a child as her head hit the pillow.

Someone had said something she had overheard during childhood. Something about joy being fleeting, lasting only through moments and flashes in time, but pain... pain was forever.

It subsided painfully slow in her head, turning from unbearable to a soft stab somewhere and sweat began pouring from her skin, while the poison she had taken to dull her senses spread through the body.

– That seemed to be *terribly* painful, Tamara finally said. – Have you ever gone through something like this before? I mean, I searched your bag, but found nothing there to...

– I don't believe in painkillers. Jill still had to mumble, but she could talk somewhat. – The few times before was not pleasant, but now it was…

– Yes, I know. Tamara smiled a wicked, sympathetic smile. – There comes a time in life when you may find it absolutely mandatory to kiss high and mighty principles goodbye.

Jill smiled, too. It did hurt, but was well worth it. She fell asleep a few minutes later with that slight smile around her mouth.

She slept.

And dreamed nothing in the dreamless sleep. Nothing at all. As if all her energy was conserved to... to sleep.

She awoke with a start, some time later.

And Jill Stafford started dreaming, started imagining.

She stood by the open window, watching the gathering Night, with a feeling, both good and bad, of water in her eyes, her eyes resting on Frazer Hill. She had to look a bit to the left. The sun had, seemingly ages ago, set behind the Hill. In midsummer or winter, it might (probably) set left or right of it. Now at least, if not also in spring, it seemed to have swallowed the gigantic fireball whole. The forest at the top still seemed completely... gone. Something up there both attracted and repulsed her. What could there be with the giant Shadow and this entire city that affected her so? She knew some of the history of both this and the entire New England area. That had to be something any promising young witch had some rudimentary knowledge of. She smiled slightly.

Even that was enough to remind her of the pain behind her forehead. It had faded now, merely a weak reminder of what had been, but remained more than potent enough.

To her it was unnecessary to do as most others, take a look at the map. Many of the places and names were like pulled from legends. Boston was, for instance built by the mouth of *Mystic* River in Massachusetts Bay.

– How is the ol' head? Tamara asked from behind.

– Let's say it's a definite improvement.

Tamara laughed a bit, before continuing haltingly.

– I saw the book in your bag, looking for painkillers.

– Oh, that book, Jill shrugged.

– Such books are a particular interest of mine, Tamara said with something akin to enthusiasm. – And I haven't seen its equal since mom burned mine. It's *old,* isn't it?

– I found it on a market in London when I was eleven, Jill's voice become even more distant. – In a stretch called Camden Street. It was the one and only time my parents brought me anywhere.

– You remember the name of the street? That's really impressive, I can hardly remember anything from I was eleven.

She took the book out of the bag, hesitantly at first, more confidently when her new friend didn't object.

– It certainly looks old.

She brushed a hand over the front cover, as if to remove dust. And the entire cover really seemed to be covered in dust. The original color had almost faded entirely, the edges worn down. The once white paper faded to yellow. It was a well-kept book, but it was... old.

Tamara opened it and started reading.

– «Folk sayeth that a girlie is not fit to writ, but ah know ah am Wise and am fit and wilt do as I pretty please».

She looked up.

– Handwritten and in some kind of old English. What's this?

– It's a diary. Jill still stared with a fixed look at the Hill. – Basically, in two parts. The first contains the partly personal account of a young girl burned as a witch in these parts 300 years ago.

– My book was about that, too, in a more generalized way, I guess, but no less frightening and *interesting*. Most of it emitted from history books. Definitely emitted! It was about witches and their craft, the execution of witchcraft, Sorcery. Some of the tales were from this area, New England. The first immigrants, *refugees*, from Europe came here. In history books there are a lot about the pilgrims, the orthodox Christians and the learning places founded here. I guess that the victorious write the history books. It doesn't say much of the most important facets of it, does it? About the fact that all kinds of persecuted people sought this land, among them witches and «followers» of the ancient «heathen» ways. One of the few accounts is about the Salem witch-trials, as if they should be one of the rare and proud. Do you know what? I'm pretty much convinced by now that there were far more. The victorious wanted their triumph to be well known, but didn't want to draw too much attention to the extent of «paganism». Their belief, the only right belief, should be the only belief in the new world. But they failed. Belief in witchcraft survived, even some witches, despite the fervent persecution. Later more arrived. And Africans... in addition to the natives already present. Do you know that the coast Indians are supposed to have been exterminated by *measles?* That lie is up there with the Nazi's claim that 6 million Jews died of exposure to water...

– There is a witch coven here still, Jill said, seemingly unfazed by Tamara's sudden exaltation. – In

Boston.

– I've heard they don't do much. Mostly social work and such and keeping mostly to themselves.

– Maybe they're waiting, Jill said slowly.

Just as slowly, seemingly, she felt the dampness in her eyes evaporate. She opened them wide and their look turned firm, focused. She noticed the change in herself, as she noticed Tamara noticing the change.

Still hesitant, she leaned a bit out of the open window, the wide-open window... and stretched out her senses, herself. Backwards, forwards, right, left, down, up and none of the above.

Northfield wasn't really one city, but two, two cities distinctly and radically different from each other. This one, the Old City, with low buildings centuries old. That one, the New City, the modernistic, post modernistic town to the east. She flew then, floated, following Mystic River all the way to Boston.

The Old City, the New City, and the hidden, ancient, hidden one, so old that it didn't have any name. Other stuff not seen with eyes, without eyes.

In this area, so shockingly full of contradictions, the girl felt she would do her Journey, her non-moving traveling. It started here, the Journey. The crossing of the sea from Great Britain was merely foreplay. She more than imagined she was destined to come here. She didn't understand it, as little as she understood herself. *But she would!* She realized that much, as the joy of expectation coursed through her.

She was «back» in the room. The headache was back, too. She bit her lower lip in frustration, bit deep into a tightly clenched fist. Her eyes stayed focused, her vision clear.

Something... *happened.* A pressure shift in the air, behind her eyes. The hill was no longer dark, but glowing. Glowing, she suspected, just outside the normal spectrum of light... or dark.

Somebody stood behind her. The certainty made her flinch and turn around fast as a whirlwind.

Tamara sat quietly on her bed. Her eyes grew large.

– You had a really lethal look, just there, do you know that?

Somebody had stood behind her. In this room. Not Tamara. Another. In front of the closed door, but there was no one here now. Jill didn't take her eyes off the door.

Jill stumbled a bit, catching her footing, catching her breath.

– I saw… It was as if I saw… saw a misty black hole sucking me in, sucking me in, forming words like lips, a hungry, giant mouth devouring me *whole.*

Still visible in her mind, in her black, black vision, her eyes staring at it, seeing nothing besides. She shivered visibly.

Seconds, minutes passed by as she pulled herself together.

She stopped, smiling embarrassed, still shaken at the other girl.

– Sorry if I scared you...

– Not scared exactly... but... with that look... The girl paused, and struggled a bit, before she managed to continue. – It's easy to be afraid of you. I think you somehow communicate *something* even to the most insensitive.

She crouched a bit, rubbing her upper arms, the big, strong girl, nervously awaiting the ax to fall.

– I felt it, too, you know, the pressure shift. But not with your extravagant intensity.

The apologetic smile did nothing to improve the pale color of her face.

Jill had already turned back towards the window. It was even more difficult than usual to interpret her feelings.

– It's okay, Tam, I'm a bit... scared myself.

Chapter Two: GATHERING

Many voices. Many new voices, mixing, blurring by the edges.

A condensed cloud of dust and gases formed the planet Earth approximately 5 billion years ago. At the center of the solar system gravity collected the majority of this dense matter and transformed it into a glowing star. Whatever was left formed the planets and other minor fragments. Nigh suns like Jupiter, Saturn, Uranus and Neptune... and tiny planets like Earth. From the remains of their dense matter, were formed more smaller satellites.

The third planet counted from the Sun, Earth, is remarkable in several ways. Its moon is so big that scientists are talking more about a double planet system than the moon as a moon. And this double planet system is placed in the so-called Life Belt, a certain distance from the life-giving Sun, and Earth had the right size.

A billion years later, in an atmosphere of lightning and heat and methane and ammonia, Life formed itself in a microscopic drop of water. Something akin to a cell reproduced itself for the first time. A timeless time later the exchange of genetic material started between two independent creatures, with the result of this union being different from them both. Countless millions of years later, merely a moment in geological terms, Life's diversity began to reveal itself in earnest. While the land was still lifeless and desolate, the sea swarmed with Life.

260 million years before present time, this diversity had long since spread across the globe. The 200 million ensuing years were the age of the dinosaurs, the biggest creatures ever seen on land. Hundred times longer than Humanity and its close ancestors have existed, they were masters of the Earth. These giants were perhaps not even aware of the tiny, rat-like creature crawling by their feet, hardly the size of one Tyrannosaurus Rex' claw.

Approximately ten million years ago a bunch of strange and dissimilar creatures left their ancestors' home in the trees and set out on the open plains. Why they did it, nobody knows. Perhaps they couldn't have told us themselves, if we could've asked them. Perhaps it was curiosity or hardened competition resulting from lesser access to food or a fight about territories... or a combination of many things and events. They were a small group. Smaller groups have ever led on down the road of the Long Walk.

Scenery kept shifting. Voices mingled and were singled out and mingled once again, blurring around the edges.

They followed a mixed special anthropology and biology course, led by Laurie Isherwood. They sat in a dark planetarium and watched an illustrated account of the Universe from the Beginning to Now. They heard the teacher speak. Even behind the recorded male voice. They kept seeing the images in the classroom, long after they had faded from view.

– There is no clear division between Man and apes, Laurie Isherwood said from behind her master desk, sometimes sitting in her chair. – No one has ever really proven that any exists. A friend of mine, a kind of a brave bastard, says it is because there isn't any. We are still apes. The similarities, quite simply far outweigh the differences. In his eyes the question of when and why the separation happened is therefore irrelevant...

Jill sat by her desk and listened as silent and transfixed as the other students. Was this modern science? The images (from the planetarium?) still seemed vivid in their minds and haunted them in the hot sunlight. And even if Laurie used no visible aid in her lecture, they still felt in a strange way, as part of her story, and they saw it unfold. At least they imagined they saw it. It was something quite different from the lifeless images they had seen in books.

They heard music. At least Jill was certain she heard it. Considerable time went by before she realized it had nothing to do with Laurie. It was Ragnarok Metal, the newest, heaviest part of rock music. It felt wrong in connection with Laurie. Jill looked around to see if any of the students present had a Walkman or MiniDisc player or something, but she couldn't discover any. She realized it came through the air, from far away. Not from the room, not from the schoolyard, but from outside the school's area... but they could still hear it.

– The air carries sound far in these parts, Laurie said, slightly irritated, acknowledging the disturbance. – Don't worry about it.

– Anyway, she continued, – the most decisive differences between apes and mankind, developed in the Pliocene age through what is mistakenly called «the Missing Link» period, the Dark Age without any preserved skeletons. But as you can see and will later recognize quite easily, it's easy to spot the similarities between Namapithecus fourteen million years before the present and Australopithecus two million years ago. The first tools were in use by then, tools difficult to distinguish from rocks and bones, but tools, nevertheless. The oldest manmade tools were found in the Olduvai canyon in Tanzania in levels a hundred yards below ground level.

They walked in the streets, Jill, and some of the other girls, on the cusp between New Town and Old Town. They heard the music now, and were led to it, by the rage, the beauty, the siren song.

Somewhere between the building aptly named the Pyramid and the factory spewing out smoke and poison, a group of girls and boys played the loud and aggressive, but also melodious music, incantations of another reality.

The lead singer/performer was a tall, slender girl, noticeable younger than the others, but seemingly far older.

– That's Gabrielle Asteroth, one of Jill's classmates snickered. – She's more than a little weird little cookie.

The music died down, rising to a roar of silence. The younger people on the marketplace applauded vigorously and the older ones applauded, too, beside themselves with conflicting impressions and emotions.

– Thank you, THANK YOU! Gabrielle had said some time ago. Now she was talking in a long, eager monologue. – I am *Asteroth.* These are my demons, the *Thornbirds.*

– Humans are so self-conscious, she said smiling, a smile very much in contrast with her makeup, – so assured of our position as masters of the Earth...

She had spoken for a while now, like Laurie, about Life on Earth and its implications.

– Compared to the span of time dinosaurs «ruled» the Earth and the span of the planet's existence, Humanity has existed for a very short while.

The band accompanied her voice with low keyed, yet haunting, background music.

– Homo Erectus, the Erected Man, the first human animal with a body adapted to a life fully erect supposedly developed, depending on interpretation, approximately 500 000 years before the present. A bit less than that and we, Human Sapiens, Thinking Man, have, through evolution achieved all abilities necessary to be the globe's new masters. It took 65 million years after the fall of the dinosaurs.

– This is Earth's entire history. She held up a rope, a meter in length. – I call your attention to the black ink, the small mark, on one of its ends... This is how long Humanity has existed.

The black ink was strangely visible, even to those at the other end of the big, dusty marketplace.

They did not speak in tandem, or simultaneously, she and the teacher, but Jill heard them that way... except for the blurring around the edges.

– I've heard she's a genius, a Wonder Kid, another one whispered. – That's why she gets away with everything.

She is a genius. Too bad, she's wasting it.

– Laurie? Jill said aloud with doubt in her voice. Had Laurie said that, or was it just something she had imagined?

Gabrielle didn't use the microphone when she made her speech. There was nothing strange when she told her story. At least her strangeness was on another, more subtle level.

– Still, before mankind's arrival, there was in many ways nothing here. No gods, spirits, nor soul... Oh, I believe what we call animals are like us, in many ways, but also different, as we are different from them, as we are the same. We are the first species that decidedly, in good ways and bad, have the ability to look beyond ourselves. We have created a world of mind in addition to the world where our bodies are residing. The Earth was not really born, before a certain point of human development. It was most assuredly alive, but we consecrated it, gave it a soul. Memory is something we share with all life on the planet, perhaps with the planet itself, if we do an in-depth philosophical study... all the way back to the first amoebae-like creature, in its atmosphere of lightning, methane and ammonia and water. But extensive fantasy, imagination and creativity, at least its outer manifestation, is something

unique to us.
– So, she doesn't really believe animals have a Soul? Someone unknown whispered.
Jill wanted to ask the annoyingly close girl creature if she had never heard about the fine art of irony, tell her that she'd missed the point entirely.
Laurie drew a line on the blackboard, another line, to complete the one above.
Jill looked at Stacy again, Stacy Larkin, the girl she *probably* had first met two days ago, or the very least, the day before, when all the new classmates had stood by their desk and introduced themselves to their fellow students. Stacy sat just two rows away. Jill looked away before the other girl could turn and meet her eyes. Stacy felt very familiar to her, even more so than several others in this room, this parking lot.
– Now, imagine this rope as recent human history. This particular story was about to conclude.
– Let it be the last ten thousand years, with one end being the start of human progress leading inevitably to the present-day civilization, with all its advantages.
– Let it represent, if you please, from present time to 35 000 years hence, to the «birth» or Cro-Magnon Man. Over half of its length, nothing much happens. The first major, decisive changes didn't occur until the first major settlements were «founded» ten thousand years ago.
– ... but the truly vast improvements, Laurie, said – may be represented by this tiny dot by the end of the line.
– But most of the major disasters didn't begin to show their ugly faces until 200 years before the present. Gabrielle smiled wickedly. – All the things we lazy slaves take for granted today, the factory, chemical pollutants, poisonous levels of radiation, TV, the car... have their roots at the start of what most people call the beginning of the industrial age. This small drop of ink is the equivalent of the short time span, in which we've made a tremendous effort to seriously screw with the Earth and everything resembling Life here... In short, we're shitting in our own nest. This is happening because we've removed ourselves dangerously far from living Nature.
– There are problems, sure, Laurie said, – but we're solving them, bit by bit, little by little. There's a growing awareness today that we must take the environment into consideration in our decision making, when creating the future world. We're about to grow up as a species, heading towards a society where people and possible antagonists are cooperating towards common goals and are not wasting their effort on fruitless struggle.
– Virtually every move we make today, Gabrielle cried out, – everything we take for granted, except a clean environment, is removing us from our origin. Mind and body are no longer one and as a result, we're suffering, without really understanding why. Most people walk around dissatisfied, a dissatisfaction present wherever we go, whatever we do, a nagging feeling that everything is not right in the world. All the things we experience, what is making us happy are the things reminding us about the world, *and us,* as we once were.
– You may ask, what the hell you, yourself may do concerning this. She spoke into the microphone now, once more. The band continued playing low-keyed, minimalist music, accompanying her. – As I've suggested earlier *Memory* is an important part of it. Memory far more than ordinary recall, what we usually experience on a daily basis. The «solution» is, simply put, in each and every one of us. There is hope if humanity as a species and as individuals can remember our stolen, or rather misplaced past and use that to recover what is lost. We are lost. We need merely to find ourselves.
The music rose slowly to an exuberant wall of poetic sound.
– That's all there is to it.
The bell rang. They hurried outside, easily forgetting the teacher's parting words:
– We can do a lot to make this world a better place to live.
Seeking eagerly the siren sound of the airwaves.

2

From far away they met, the emerging Strangers, strangers not just in this town, but the entire world, to each other and to the society of their birth.
Sound, like a wall, a velvet wall, a silence of wilderness and mystery roared at the parking lot. The

concert ended as it perhaps began, with an intensity that literally made the «audience» gasp for breath.
The scene, the setting, should be all wrong. The white, hot day, a gray, dusty parking lot, a family gathering.
Jill felt something, a pull, not merely towards Asteroth, but towards... everything. There was something here, someone...
She looked at Stacy Larkin then, met her eyes. Stacy nodded.
The crowd left the «arena», giddily, but not particularly contemplative. Concentration broken, contact lost, Jill drifted away the same as everybody else.
Old Town... it was old, but it was more than that. It couldn't be that old, a few centuries tops, probably not more than sixty or seventy years. The «feeling» she got from it, though, was as if from something far older.
She looked up.
The band had packed their gear. It was later in the afternoon. Jill realized she felt warm all over. Not hot, but warm, like she was bathing in sunrays, without the heat.
– What did you think about the performance? Gabrielle asked her with her open, eager smile.
– It was... great.
– Yeah! But what did you really think? Gabrielle asked.
– It was indescribable! Jill laughed wildly.
The girl's father, who had obviously wanted to drag her away immediately after the concert, came charging with his bad mood and grim demeanor.
– I hope she didn't bother you, the father said with a stiffened smile a while later, when the girl had bothered half the audience still gathered on Main Street.
– On the contrary, sir, Jill replied politely, but with unmistakable intensity. – Both her performance and stories were both unusually interesting and inspiring.
She held back. Asteroth had not really been performing, but rather shown a piece of her (inner) self, an invaluable piece of the world, of reality.
Not long after that, the father led the daughter away.
Jill heard her repeat her question to her father, just as they walked beyond hearing range:
– I know what you said. A haughty, almost nasty sounding, humorous tone. – But what do you really think? «Who are you, what do you want»? «Why are you here? Do you have anything worth living for»...?
Jill wasn't one hundred percent sure, of course, but she strongly suspected that the father wouldn't exactly appreciate the daughter's wit.
Jill did. And others. It was a bit strange to feel that way towards a kid considerable younger than herself, but only, she realized, because youth usually was seen as synonymous with «inexperienced» and «unwise». In spite of the fact that everybody realized that Gabrielle wasn't an ordinary thirteen-year-old girl. Not by far.
But it was strange still. Heading back to the dorm they walked down Main Street of Old Town or Oldtown. And the feeling of perpetual strangeness prevailed. Jill laughed, laughed out loud, without a single, discernible motivation. And it felt good. She couldn't remember feeling exactly like this before. It dawned on her then, that in that moment she hadn't considered the consequences of her actions, in any way. She had just done what felt... good.
Main Street was really the main part of Oldtown, going through the entire length of the old part of Northfield, except for the church and its backyard. The buildings were made almost entirely of mortar and bricks. Some had gone through some modifications, with roofs made of wood, but all in all they looked remarkably the same as they probably did just after they were constructed. And any one of them could be interpreted as one geometric figure or another. A triangular, a square, a circle, even an obvious octagon. From the air they would probably be able to see even more variations. So strange.
And that word again.
Jill stopped. She realized that they, most of the «freshmen» were on their way back to the dormitory.
– Now, that is weird, she said out loud.
– What is? One of the boys, she believed his name was Jason said.
– We're on her first «leave» from the barracks, she said grinning, – and we're already on our way back,

after just one great experience.
– We are expected, Stacy shrugged. – We have only been here a few days, and they wanna know where we are.
– I want... more. Jill turned to her. – There's so much more!
– Of course, Stacy said hesitatingly, almost tenderly.
Jill didn't notice, too busy with looking around, with surveying the terrain.
– Where? Jason looked around, too, with a conspiring look in his eyes.
They heard it all at the same time, or so it seemed, the music from the open windows in one of the bigger circular buildings. Nostrils vibrated by the scent of food and spices from the many hot dishes.
They hesitated a bit before the open door, before tumbling inside. A draft greeted them and gave them a momentary relief from the searing heat.
It was a pub, a real life honest to Goddess English pub, mixed with a medieval tavern setting and mood.
Something designed to serve the students the whole year around, Jill thought cynically.
On light feet they danced around, exploring the place. It was big. The pub itself covered approximately one tenth of the big-circled building, but the entire backyard inside was used as extra space, with chairs and tables. There was a performer stage in the bar. No one was performing live here now, but there was quite a number of guests, both inside and outside, both shadow and sun. The sun hadn't even set behind the Hill and the place was already crowded, filled with many thirsty people in the wild Indian Summer.
Jill stopped a bit, just before they were about to sit down by a wide table. She had been to pubs before. Almost any British child had been, at some time or another, with parents or relatives. But not alone like this. She couldn't help but feeling disconcerted. The fact that her bravery had been so short-lived made it all worse. But she wouldn't leave. She wouldn't!
There was... *energy* here. Here, too. People sat (down) by their tables and talked. And more. They talked with an intensity foreign to the newly arrived students.
– I am Sharon Haldoway, your *host.* A younger woman, perhaps no more than ten years older than themselves, greeted them. – I wish you welcome to *Haldoway's Inn,* my young friends. Is there anything you desire?
She was wearing a dress, more akin to a medieval costume than not. It was her place. They had seen how she had greeted every group personally. She was not the only staff member, but she greeted every group before she sometimes left the ordering to her employees.
– We want Guinness beer, each and every one of us, Jason exclaimed cheerfully. – Not watered down, no substitutes, the real thing.
He was from the United Kingdom, too. Jill easily recognized a London dialect.
– You are, I trust familiar with the strict laws concerning serving of alcohol in the state of Massachusetts? Sharon said good humored.
– Eh, no. Jason reddened all over.
– Fortunately for you, none of them apply in this case. Just a minute or two, young ladies and squires...
Jason laughed, too. Laughter seemed suddenly easy and took a long time before fading.
– Strict, my ass, one of the men on the neighboring table exclaimed quite pronounced. – *Strange,* preposterously strange is more like it.
The «minute or two» felt like just a moment, a flash in time. One of the serving maids put the big pint glasses on the table with practiced ease.
Jill tasted the beer carefully before taking a bigger sip, and then she took a big dip. It was... it tasted great. Even if she, unbelievably enough, for a short while smelled something akin to bile.
On light... asses (Jill giggled) they rocked on their chairs, almost dancing where they sat. Freedom cursed through them, in their first, prolonged time away from parents, from responsibility put on them by guardians or society as a whole. They were no different from other kids in this respect. But they felt it stronger, more pronounced. Jill was certain of it. Most eighteen-year-olds couldn't feel this euphoria, feel this good, and ever expecting, *accepting* it to end?
But they did! She knew that. And so, they would.

– Hey, do you guys see the TV over there? The brown skinned blond South American Native girl, Rae Morgan said.

– Yes, said Kieron. – That does indeed look like a television set.

Everybody laughed, more than a little wickedly at Rae.

– Oh, what a cruel, cruel bunch you all are, she said sheepishly, unexpectedly. – Perhaps I should find myself a room for myself, fitted with a «television set» and leave you hens to hang.

– You know something we do not, Stacy said abruptly. – What is it?

Her expression changed almost immediately into something akin to awe.

– Yes, TELL US! They didn't notice anything out of the ordinary, but deluged poor Rae in a flood of persuasive argument.

– Well? Loeh said with a threatening gesture.

– Do you know who are the guests of «honor» in Mystery Hour tonight...? *Ted and Liz Warren.*

She virtually cried it out. Everybody in the room seemed to have heard it, above the music and buzz and everything. She reddened.

Incredulous comments echoed throughout the place.

– How did they convince them to partake?

– How on Earth did the executives approve their appearance?

– How could they let those two get any airtime?

– Oh, he's so cute and desirable! a girl moaned.

– I, for one, would claim that she is far more desirable, her date said sourly.

So many opinions, so many conflicting emotions. Jill had heard it was ever thus, when Ted Warren was concerned. He walked his own path and the world responded in confused ways.

– So, how about it, Sharon? Kieron queried fully confident.

Everything, the room, the tavern, the guests turned quiet pretty fast.

– I guess there can be no harm...

The owner of the establishment turned on the TV.

There was yet some time left before Mystery Hour started. People began to talk again, in considerably lower voices, though.

Sharon's reaction confused Jill. There had been something, in her voice, in her body language, not formerly present.

She knows him! Incredulity warred with amazement in the girl's mind.

– I don't know what's so great with either him or her, Jason said. – People seem to give them far more consideration, both hostile and otherwise, than what is really warranted.

Jason's reaction confused her even more. And here there was no explanation forthcoming, no big, blue bolt of understanding from the sky.

Mystery Hour started. There was always an entry, introduction. Music from the Sixties floated from the speakers from all corners of the room. Ted, and especially Liz had been too young to actually participate much during that legendary time period, but they were seen as a part of it anyway. They had both been very young when they started to make their mark on the world. When rising from obscurity

To infamy.

And they didn't look much older now, at least not in a purely physical way, not that much older than Jill and her new friends. There were the eyes of course, or rather the expression, the totality of their facial expression. A certainty, a confidence, probably not present in their younger days.

And those eyes, the color of fire and dawn. Not really a color at all, but dancing flames in a dark night.

Jill didn't remember much of the interview itself. Bits and pieces, that was all that would surface in her mind occasionally. She remembered the sound of wind and flying sand in her ears, the wind of change running wild.

The female interviewer asked Ted something. The question didn't register in her brain, in her conscious thought. She heard his reply, though, clear as rain.

– Many people voicing an opinion, do not really give their own view on any given matter, but are merely repeating what they've heard, what's often the lies of others.

– Why is that, in your opinion?
– My position on this is crystal clear, Gayle. Warren smiled self-consciously and with no small bit of irony. – They are brainwashed, they even aid in the brainwashing themselves, since they early in Life have forgotten how to Live. Present day society places bars around our emotions, our Passion, to keep us from being Human Beings. But then it isn't really working, you know, since we, among many things, *are* creatures of passion, wild, savage animals roaming the forest.

Jill drank more beer. She drank a lot more beer. She drank a lot of water and orange juice. In vain. She remained thirsty.

Stacy paid for it, she paid for it all, with her handy plastic card. The TV program had ended a long time ago. They sat by the same table talking in exciting tones and hushed whispers.

– People surely are different here these days, Kieron said. – Different, I suspect, from how they usually are.

– It's the rush week, Stacy said somewhat brusque, seemingly «biting» every word. – The old club system existing inside and alongside the American university system. Except it's not really clubs, but a fraternity pattern. Included you're set for life, excluded and your chances of succeeding in society are far less. You have to arrive on campus a week before the official tutoring starts to be considered. My parents wanted me to apply. The family has a long-standing tradition in the «Greek» system. But I refused.

– Have we, any of us here been included? Jason said, speaking up, mischief in eyes.

– I did apply, a boy said. – None of the Chapters accepted me... They don't accept more than approximately twenty-five percent of the applications. I got a few peeks inside, though, before they rejected me.

He didn't sound too excited or too crushed about being rejected, not even if they searched for sincerity behind the words.

– I got accepted, Rae said. Everybody turned and scrutinized her.

– You did? Stacy said.

– Yes, indeed, you're looking at a proud member of Tau Beta Delta, «one of the most prestigious Chapters in the history of mankind». She smiled and somewhere during the sentence her voice turned to a qualified irony. – I got wind of it, learned about it, by coincidence, I guess, and I got curious and decided to waste a week. It is truly a waste. Boys and girls in different Chapters, a lot of singing and an implied understanding that we're all supposed to bond for life, that's all.

– Ah, Jason said quite smug. – You're all aware, I trust, of what we're looking at here, people?

They looked at him, not quite realizing what he was playing at.

– Freemasons Junior. And he rewarded them with a big smile when his words and its implications dawned on them.

– Secret handshakes, passwords, that sort of thing, a miniature society mirroring the bigger one...

– It's true, Loeh said, quite heated. – Very few are really thinking about the implications of it all.

– And Magick, of course, Stacy smiled, too. – Or at least the pretense of it.

They all looked at each other and they did not forget.

More Time flew. Even more. It was dark outside, and they knew they should return to school, to duty and all that, but they were clearly reluctant to do so.

They were drunk, all of them. Bodies were getting numb, but they didn't forget. Their minds soared along infinite treks.

Jill couldn't later really recall what the present conversation had been about, if it had been anything, anything remotely interesting. But suddenly... Suddenly she and most of the others got the distinct impression that this wasn't a party, at least not in a traditional sense. It was a party, but not one where inexperienced youths visited the nearest bar for the first time in their life and got thoroughly blitzed.

– I've heard there's supposed to be an old house somewhere on the Hill, Stacy said casually with big, shiny eyes, seemingly out of the blue, – is that true?

They all focused on her, focused on each and every one's illuminated eyes.

– I've heard that, too, Kieron said, clearly slurring.

They all did. The alcohol had without doubt partly paralyzed their tongues and lips, and perhaps even their vocal chords.

Even their voices didn't seem normal. Oh, no, not at *all!*

– Magick lies scattered, Loeh said. – After years without number of non-use it has dwindled and retracted from sight, but it's still *there.* There are houses and hills, and places where it may be picked up. Places of imagination and Power, where mighty witches once lived and thrived.

– Why don't we... go there? Jill leaned forward and looked at the others with a daring smile, full of mischief. – Go there... and pick up some Magick?

– Why don't we form a club, our own unofficial Chapter, Stacy said, – a *coven*, and let this be our initiation?

– A witches' coven? Rae burst out, visibly shocked. – I don't know...

– Why not? Jason shrugged. – It might be fun.

– «When in Rome»... Loeh laughed subdued, full of expectation, – «dress like a Roman». Right? And then we wait and see if we're truly Romans...

And thus, it began, slowly, hesitantly, like a coincidence.

Hands sought hands, eyes sought eyes, and they all smiled conspiratorially to one another. Hands sought hands at the middle of the table, weaving into each other. Eyes found eyes, shimmering and dancing of clouds and twilight.

And it felt so right, so natural. And there was nothing strange about it at all. And that was okay, too.

INTERLUDE: The city that was not New Orleans (I)

It was not Sunday.

Joseph Parnell, the Father of this particular christian parish, in the old town of Northfield, was lurking behind the heavy door, looking through the thick glass, at the people walking by outside.

People walked by, quite the lot of them. The church was open. It was always open (well, almost always). But very few but the regular flock entered. It was not Sunday.

The Father looked around him with scowling eyes, as he walked the floor close to the exit, as he wore down the carpet, the worn-down carpet.

– This is an evil time, he mumbled. – You are worshipping false gods, all of you, and do not think twice about it. You're all evil. You will all be cast into the Lake of Fire.

It wasn't Sunday and people stayed away from the church.

He closed the door and returned to the Great Hall, the room where he spoke to the congregation in times of need and ritual. Empty. Most people would find it empty. But as always, he sensed the presence here. He had done so since he had been a little boy.

He fell down on his knees before the altar, in a dramatic gesture.

– God, he cried, – hear thy humble servant. Maketh me do thy work well, so you may strike all the heathens with impunity and cast them into the pit.

And he knew that God heard his prayers and that his wishes would come true. It would all happen.

Chapter Three: TEMPLE OF FIRE

Stepping outside was like being hit by a wave of hot air. You looked around for the walls of the oven, for the leering face of the person outside ready to turn the switch. She had heard this was how it was in the desert, in Las Vegas and other places where humans lived in the midst of the sand and dust.

But this was New England in September, supposed to be a green and pleasant land.

She bathed in sunlight, in the searing heat, as she started on her Journey from the campus towards Frazer Hill. The sun was traveling the open sky, a sky seemingly more *open* than Jill ever could remember, baking the earth, at least as heavy as it had done for months now. The trees marking the avenue had dry, yellow leaves, suffering from the lack of water, the most inconsequential moisture. There had still not been issued a water-rationing edict for the area, but gardens and plants were, as a rule, not given water. The powerful winds whispered, shook the treetops, and dried the land further, violently moving the girl's hair. She had to tie it up and make a ponytail, or she wouldn't have seen where she was walking.

She walked hesitantly at first, as if people could see where she was headed, the dirty deed she had in mind. So silly! What if they did?

The smaller road turned into Main Street. A street covering the entire length of the older part of the city, almost all the way from the campus area to the Hill. Jill enjoyed herself in the sunshine. She could do no less. It was such a beautiful day. Like yesterday many people traversed the broad main street, broader than every other in the entire city. And it was teeming with activities and assorted modes of being, like fish in a river dance of spawning. There weren't that many cars, even though they were not banned. People preferred to use them in the modern parts of the city.

Jill looked briefly inside Square, as she walked by. She felt a pull towards it, as she had done the day before. Then as now, another pull was stronger. Yesterday it had been the tavern. Today it was... Twinkling gray eyes looked up, couldn't see the house up there, but she could picture it in her inner eye. She hardly had to picture it. She passed «Circle», too, seven portals leading into the big, open space. It had been used for public offices, but had been empty and virtually derelict a while before the opening of the tavern. Jill crossed Cross Avenue. As she had noted several times since her arrival, it was really peculiar how many names in Old Town weren't really names, but more descriptive.

And she noticed something else, as she cast a brief look towards the church and the reverend half hiding in its entrance.

It was impossible not to notice, how easy she was on her feet, how light she moved. Her body was about to awaken, along with the mind. She thought dumbfounded:

I'm so awake!

She didn't merely feel awake. She was!

Her mind reaching out, almost by itself, as she managed to achieve a modicum of control, felt the throb and the pulse around her, the excitement and the fear, mirroring that of her own.

She wondered what the good people around her would do if they saw her as she really was. She was examining her own feelings, how she felt, seeing her own potential in not more than glimpses, knowing fully well how overwhelming that was.

There were two teenagers by the bus stop, a boy and a girl. She could imagine that she stood there, close to them, and then she was, their emotions raw, unbound, open to her, stronger than she had ever known. Like lightning, like thunder, she couldn't stifle a gasp. No one noticed, but she blushed all over her body and she had to stop, and she couldn't move. And the headache was just a faint reflection of what it had been, as it had decreased to virtually nothingness the last few days. Her clothes got attached to her moist skin from one second to the next. She almost fell and almost in self-defense she managed to take one step forward, then another, until her walk had regained a semblance of normality. Her labored breathing continued for several minutes.

She consciously distracted herself from her woes. And it worked. Slowly, painfully she managed to continue in a somewhat composed manner.

The Hill still pulled at her, harder than ever.

Her eyes, her senses, opened even further, took in impressions, pulling them inside, pushing outside what was inside.

This city, this place, was so *old!* So much was hidden here. Many times older than even the oldest building. But it was so vague, like an echo from ancient times. The wind... was blowing, the wind was increasing. Not far into the future it would grow to a *Storm.*

She overheard people talk about the weather. People have always talked about the weather, as an excuse for having a conversation, but it was different now. They spoke with fear in their voice. They could no longer deny what was about to happen.

The Earth's climate was changing. The news was full of evidence to that effect, each and every day. A human created change, going full throttle, far beyond human control. Poetic justice at its best.

And even «better» were the diseases caused by the smoking and leaking factory close by. She swallowed hard, in anger, in despair.

She had been a part of an environmental group in Wales, but it, they, had really never amounted to anything.

Her thoughts, after the arrival here, had been focused in more than one way.

Main Street narrowed into smaller streets and the smaller streets turned to paths, fine gravel to hard ground. She sensed it as she saw it with her eyes, as she started walking the trail leading to Frazer Hill.

The dark forest beckoned and awaited her. She sensed it had awaited someone... like her a very long time. Like her! She walked on the ancient Trail on her way up. It spoke to her, about times past. She noticed it immediately. Nothing grew on it. People rarely walked here, but nothing in the dark soil sprouted and grew. In the grass on both sides, however, growth and Life was abundant. But the girl suspected that no animals, no other animals crossed the emptiness.

The forest began where the terrain started to flatten at the end of the slope. A few trees became a forest. Shadows swooned in tandem with the treetops and surrounded her. She stopped her walk for a while, between light and shadow, turned a bit and could see the entire city below.

She was out of breath and painfully aware of what a bad shape she was in. Cold and hot sweat fought over her body as the light and shadow did over her mind.

The city unfolded for her eyes and revealed itself to her.

To the north were the agricultural areas where there was still only limited population growth. The «Trail» disappeared there and appeared again on the east side, close to the school. Somewhere in No Man's Land there, it disappeared. She saw how Main Street and Cross Avenue formed a big cross. At first sight it seemed to be two, ordinary crossing streets. Other streets, after all, were mixing with, crossing them. But something was different. The special form stood out from the rest of the city. It seemed as eternal as Trail... as this forest. Cross Avenue formed another, minor cross with Cross Street to the east. But this one a person noticed just because of the church at the end of the avenue, bordering on the modern part of the city. It was so obvious. Further east the new city, buildings of metal, glass, plastic and concrete stretched its wings. It widened to a kind of T-shape. How small the size of Oldtown was in comparison. It seemed so insignificant. Buildings of offices and condos and homes grew like trees, stretched out towards the yet distant Metropolitan Area and would probably be swallowed by it one day. Newtown was the pride and joy of the people at the top of the pyramid.

Jill Stafford continued her venture deeper into the dark forest. It... called to her and she wanted to reply, but couldn't. Something blocked her, the veil-like wall she had sensed, imagined a few times earlier in her Life. She ventured deeper into the forest, the forest truly mobile, noticeably Alive. Smoke rose behind a tree, surrounding it in a bluish radiance reminding her of silver moonlight. She saw no fire, but there was smoke and not mist. Everything moved around her. She would have moved, even if standing still, moving herself without moving. It didn't frighten her. From her first, earliest memories, she had always seen the Earth as being Alive. That and other forgotten memories surfaced, flowing first like a river, then a waterfall.

The forest surrounded her completely now, on all sides. She couldn't look out of it, without looking up at the few, distant flashes of blue sky, flashes as far away from each other as the few spots of sunlight reaching the forest floor. And all light seemed dimmed, subdued, gray, in a way. This forest was probably not something akin to other forests she had ever walked through.

It wasn't a problem to her. She had sensed so much, so much new to her, fresh in her memory, and yet it was merely an appetizer. She realized that the world truly was much bigger than she could remember imaging and alien emotions of happiness cursed through her. Her mind had opened like a flower. A stray thought making her sad. As a flower knowing that it must soon wither. She had already learned well, early in her life, the necessity of narrowing an opened mind.

A stray thought now, as she was pulled, as she pulled herself further. Her vision was locked forward. Whatever pulled her further on dominated more and more of her attention, dominated her like a storm. Besides she didn't need her eyes to see the wonders around her. Yes, she walked on a trail not a trail. There was no trail that her eyes could see. And yet there it was. And more. By her feet, as she imagined them, and the surroundings kept shifting and pulsating and changing. And she could smell the almost painfully strong scent of the forest. There was a slight irritation in her throat, probably because of the excitement and perhaps the multicolored mood. *Variety.* What a wonderful word. She hadn't experienced enough of that in her young life, even if she had experienced more than most.

She walked without a conscious sense of direction. Everything looked the same, hundred meters ahead like hundred meters behind. Sense of time and space was... seemed to be gone, and time/space led her on, eventually, to a clearing in the forest, a huge one, where there was still a forest on all sides. The long walk had made her even more short of breath, but she hardly noticed. It wasn't the reason she had stopped. She saw water, and she saw waves of fire, until her vision cleared.

The close to circular clearing was surprisingly big, but then it had to be. The water covering virtually the entirety of the open space gave her the impression of being a small sea. Surely a kind of optical illusion, because it couldn't be that big, could it? Somewhat at the center of the wide, vast water there was a house, an old house, made in an old style. There was only a small amount of land on the lot around it and no road, no path to it, except the water rippling in the wind. What Jill saw was a house, but what it reminded (her) of, was a medieval castle. A house of considerable size, true, but that wasn't unusual, was it? Her eyes told her one thing. Her newly awakened senses something different, something else... about the house, the castle at the center of Fire Lake.

Sorceress, she told herself, full of spite. *Witch!*

After just a slight hesitation, so slight that she surprised herself, delaying a moment longer than she would have wanted, she kicked her shoes off and left her t-shirt and shorts on. She walked out in the water until it reached her navel, and started swimming in a somewhat calm manner.

She let water into her mouth, so cool, so refreshing. Why did so few come to this place? Did anyone? There couldn't be any other places for miles and miles comparable to this. Was there any, even remotely close these days? And still people stayed away.

An attempted dive wasn't very successful. She had never been any good at swimming. But she got her head under and got a glimpse of a deep, deep, clear, clear well. The water had to come from far below and be pushed upwards from an infinite source. So clean and so fresh. Floating on her back, with the ears under the surface, she could hear the low roar flowing towards her from all sides.

Who would do such a crazy thing and build a house on a spot like this? How had they managed to raise it at all? There was no road up here. No communication and electricity. But the house had been raised and people had lived in it, at one time or another. Surely, they had used a boat, in order to reach their home from the shore. There was none to be seen anywhere, now. She walked up on dry land. There were stairs she could walk on, and a natural pier overgrown by growth. She crossed what must once have been the lawn of a well-tended garden. Her hand pressed against the wall. It felt just like... a wall. Of course, what had she expected...

The sun, the heat, dried her clothes, dried her, before long. In these days all moisture evaporated faster than fast. Even her groin dried quickly. A thought bringing excitement to her already addled thoughts. The grass warmed the skin of her soles. The big flagstones, not yet completely overgrown burned hot. The walls were dirty, but she didn't see any signs of decay. The entrance had no door. The path inside was free of obstacles of any kind, through a tall, broad and open portal.

There was hardly any sound as she moved with her naked feet over the wooden floor. There was dust everywhere, whirling like desert sand, with every movement, every breath. Was she the first? Or would everybody see the house as she saw it, untouched, with no sign of anybody ever entering?

Light paled shining through the dirty windows. Old, everything here was old, the building itself, a huge, sumptuous manor. Somebody had planned to live here for a long time. And perhaps they had done so - forever. She felt death here - the novice, but Life, too, and Fire. The Fire was first, the fire as it existed in the Universe from the first small, infinite moments. And Life had Become in a scourge of Fire and Heat. The young, aspiring sorceress felt cold flow down her spine.

So many old things. But what she saw, and the furniture here, didn't have any age to speak of, compared to the mood, the atmosphere, of the place itself. She got gooseflesh all over, both because of expectation and apprehension.

The outer rooms in the manor had no doors. All passages from room to room were merely just that, passages with a highly artistic and deliberate design. None led to the castle's... the manor's inner sanctums, though. Every room had a window, to the garden, to the sun. She walked into a room, a living room, but one of the smaller ones. There was another portal there, for her to continue the circle walk. She stopped. Before her, on her left, was a door. It had no lock that she could see. She was fairly certain that she could just turn the handle and open the door, and walk inside. Just a door. Why then, did it feel like… like a mouth?

The small living room had a fireplace. On a shelf above it, there were candlesticks and candles. More candles in boxes. The fireplace, obviously, couldn't have been in use since the candles had been placed there, or they would have melted.

There were no windows beyond that door, she realized, nothing but Complete Darkness. She needed the candles. Eager, apprehensive, inpatient, without conscious thought, she reached out a hand for them, before she was really close enough... and stopped, frozen in her tracks. She saw, as if in a dream, how one candle floated out of a box, up in the air and into her outstretched hand. The candle dropped from her numb hand, from a grip weak as air. She turned abruptly and with horror painted in her expression, in her very body language, she attempted to look in every direction at once, as she had done when she was a child and walked a dark road in the night. There was no one to see, and... she had no sense of anybody being here either. She stared at the broken candle on the floor, then at her hand. Did she do it, or was there someone, *something* else... She held out her hand again. Nothing happened.

– Sorceress, she told herself, full of spite. – Witch!

The candle flew out of the box and into her hand so fast that she almost dropped this one, too. She made a fist around it.

– Sorceress, she said triumphantly, as a broad smile centered on her tightly woven lips. – Witch!

She held the other hand close to the top of the candle and concentrated. First there was a spark and some smoke from the old material, then the flame rose, tall and brilliantly. And then the headache returned, faint but unmistakable. Comforting. She focused on the door. The handle was pushed down as if by itself, but she could feel the movement as if she did it, and she did. The door opened. She looked around her one last time, at the day world she left behind, before walking the last, deliberate steps into the dark. The door shut with a bang behind her.

She stood still a long time, perhaps for minutes, while waves of frost washed over her. Everything was dark. The tiny flame was all she could see. Her glance sought first, naturally, towards her own body. The hand, the other hand, further down, to the feet. And the floor. The flagstones. There was a floor. She didn't levitate high above in the air. Of course not. What a stupid thought. The floor seemed to stretch ever further away, as her night vision adapted to the changed environment. But not far enough for her to glimpse any wall on the other side. But something huge in what had to be the middle of the room caught her attention. She floated, slid, walked over there with her nude feet on the naked floor, the stone floor in here, what would be found in an old castle. When she stopped, she stood before a wide staircase, leading upstairs. There were no turns in it, but it continued far, far up, to what could be interpreted as a ray of light. She sensed a gust of wind, a draft, from there, from below. She turned and discovered a smaller, more modest stairway, stairs winding downwards. She held the light above it, and she could see impossibly far below, as it turned and turned ad infinitum. The small flame burned in the wind, and didn't go out. She kept it burning. She considered going down... down there, but decided to go for the attic instead.

It felt as if she floated up the stone stairs. She would sense the stone under her feet, under the ancient, dusty carpet, attached long ago to the solid rock. She knew that if she had remained down there, she would now have seen herself, as a silhouette against the dim light up there. And in a way, she did. And the weird thought persisted, even if she was most certainly on her way up. Even if what she experienced did have certain dreamlike qualities, it was most certainly real.

The light shone through a window somewhere in the distance, by a half-closed door. She still needed the candlelight most of the time, though. Even where there was daylight, there was a distinct... quality of darkness. And walking through the lucid darkness took minutes, hours, years. She arrived in a great hall, in one of the wings of the... the castle. And there were windows, more than enough of them. At least there had been once. Big doors of glass, leading to balconies. Now, they were all nailed shut, with huge shutters. At least they seemed quite solid. She didn't bother to check on them now, but kept walking further on her non-designated path. Flashes of images visited her then, as she imagined how it might have been to walk by the open windows, with shining white curtains blowing in the wind, a hot summer day a hundred years ago.

Certainly, no attic this.

And if there was one, it would not be much smaller than a floor in an average house.

A mirror grew out of the dark, just appearing in front of her, like a specter, a ghost of the mind. Her height, her features. Out on a floor some distance away from furniture covered by sheet, probably once white. Christ, this had to be quite valuable, and no one had ever arrived and collected it. Not thieves. Not even thieves. She saw small signs now, had seen them for a while, that there had been humans here recently. But nothing had been removed. Nothing had been moved. The house as she saw it now, was exactly as it had been on moving day a hundred years ago.

«Mirror, mirror on the wall, who is the most beautiful of all»?

She smiled protracted to herself, quite different from how she remembered herself. The mirror image returned the smile. Wasn't it amazing, how Life began with a slow, windy dream, how the strength of the wind picked up as the years went by? Most people didn't realize this. Only those who were either warm or cold did that.

«Who is it that you ask, girl, ask a thousand people and you get thousand different replies. Whether asking about skin or skin deep, skin or bone».

She made a slow pirouette in front of the smooth surface, as she discovered the contemptuous smile of the mirror image.

«Mirror, mirror on the floor. I came here to query, to search the winding ways, I want to *know*»!

«You don't need to come here for *that*, you daughter of witches. Every secret there is in this world is yours for the taking. You can become a goddess and humans will bow down in the dust for you».

A Goddess, Jill thought proudly.

She frowned. She knew she did. The mirror image did not. Jill shuddered. The girl in the mirror continued to smile her teasing, mocking smile. Jill looked around, turning abruptly. There was no one there, no one here but her, but Her. It was so strange, so horrible. Mirror images weren't supposed to behave this way, not behave differently from the person they... mirrored? An echo didn't return more than what was said.

Time stretched out. It was bending behind and in front of her, and to her sides. As Time so Space. Reality itself shifted. Light reached her from all directions. She - was - not - here - and - now - anymore (whatever that meant), but Somewhere Else, in another big house. She heard the faint noise of drums, but there were no drums to be seen. Faint singing, chanting, mysterious, enticing, but she saw no one actually singing. A big modern manor appeared to her. The sun shone through the many windows. She laughed out loud in the hot sunshine, passing all the open windows. The ceiling seemed to be so much higher above her, so far away. And so it was, she realized with a start. She was much shorter. A little girl. The little girl looked angry down on her high-heeled shoes, making her walk considerably less than elegant. Clothes were not so bad. The tiny, white dress felt light and airy in the summer heat. She was held in her short, brown-skinned arm by a maid in uniform, led into a smaller eloquent living room. Little Jill sat on the couch between her parents. The maid curtsied and withdrew respectfully. Jill saw herself in a mirror, but the girl in the mirror behaved strangely. She might do exactly like Jill did. When one girl lifted an arm, the other did the same. They were so alike. But quite surprisingly the other girl could suddenly move completely different from the other, but they were still the same. But then, one moment, when Jill turned around, there was no one there. No girl, no mirror. She missed it so. And the sun turned to black. The wind was blowing so terribly. She was dragged into a huge car, taken away. Thick smoke stuck in the air and the throat. Ugly flames rose and Little Jill watched them as she sat in the back of the car and cried.

She was once more on her way down the stairs. Small, single tears rolled down her cheeks. She used her arm to dry them with quick, frantic movements. The dark below seemed at first to be as impenetrable as ever. But step-by-step this changed. She sensed images, impressions. For every step and every level down, more was revealed. There was so much here. This place, this place had existed through the ages, not only here, but many places.

As one girl walked up, another girl spiraled down, down, down. Time shifted. Reality shifted.

She was walking through the forest, her body nude and sweaty. She collected red soil and she made a wound in her skin, making the blood drip, drip into the red, red soil. A piece of her soul pushed itself into the soil, into the amulet she made, the necklace she made and hung around her neck. And it was a focus, a way to connect with the dark wings moving inside her. Dark fluttery wings gaining substance merely by her dreaming about them. Something turned inside her, merely by dreaming about this… about the dream quest of a witch.

As she blinked, as she gasped something turned, something shifted, like a switch somewhat turned off, was turned on. Merely by thinking about it she focused on it, and she stepped Through, stepped through something in front of her, in front of her so long, invisible so long, tangible now. Real. She started her Walk and the ground below her trembled.

The fires burned high. Drums, flutes, ancient strings and voices resonated in the Night on a darkened Earth. A door somewhere opened. A procession carrying torches was walking slowly. In the second row two priestesses led a girl between them. Murmurs of expectation rose from the crowd. Jill stood in the shadows, hidden, unseen. She observed the offering stone and the offering. The young girl was dressed in heavy, deliberate clothing, a beautifully woven skirt showing her thighs and a jacket without arms, exposing her breasts. She walked with slow, woozy movements, with a distant look in her eyes. It seemed like she was somewhere else entirely. White flower petals fell on the floor. People threw them from their positions close to the ceiling-arch far above. The girl's body was continuously shaking, her entire attention directed towards the man awaiting her by the altar. The air was dense with desire and sensuality. Only deep within the girl did Jill observe the limitless fear. It wasn't her body he was after. He wanted her soul, wanted to steal it from her, and keep it as his. He, the Witchmaster. Jill discovered that she now did wear the same clothes as the girl, but she sat on a throne above the altar, aloof, above it all. Light came from everywhere, but it was still dark. The tall Witchmaster, he was heavily built, so impressive and foreboding, took the knife from the altar and started chanting magical words and increased the enchanted mood, while the light and darkness shifted and shifted. He was the Magician, the Big Illusionist. The Queen, on her throne felt nothing particular about what was transpiring, except an unruly curiosity. She had witnessed a lot of sacrifices in her young life. Every time the blood bled off another young virgin, she had kept her ambiguous emotions to herself. But the Witchmaster had drawn her, too, ever closer to himself. She had wondered... how did it really feel to stab another person, another human being? She would perhaps never know... unless she killed them herself.

The two priestesses released the chosen one. She started walking, still with the same, sleepy movements. The two priests in front let her through. The entire procession stopped and the singing of a thousand throats rose in the night. By a powerful wave the Witchmaster called the girl to him. She swooned and knelt down in front of him. He made a dramatic move with his hand, and she started to levitate off the ground. She was stretched to her full length, horizontally above the altar. The crowd gasped in admiration and awe.

A cheap trick, the Queen thought unimpressed.

The girl was lowered down on the altar, on her back. She stayed that way and squirmed sensually and her throat released loud moaning and calls. Her eyes conveyed trust, longing, humility. Nothing suggested that she saw the golden knife in the hand of the man towering above her. He lifted his other hand. The crowd, the entire assembly turned quiet. Then, the choir of his servants started chanting and nothing else was heard between heartbeats. Now was the time for him to stab the knife into the fragile, helpless sacrifice.

Instead, he turned to the Queen. He held the knife out to her. Startled Jill attempted to compose herself. His facial features betrayed no emotion, no secrets. As so many others here, he hid his inner being. There were many here... in *Northfield*... who weren't what they seemed.

She rose from the throne and walked to the altar. She couldn't hold herself back. He welcomed her with a genuine smile. An expectant murmur from the assembly rose to a roar. Something fundamental happened before their eyes. The Virgin Queen had at least passively opposed the sacrifices, until now. The Witchmaster put the knife, the shaft in her hand and closed her fingers around it. His dark look challenged her to push the knife into his abdomen instead. Why not? It would save more lives than it took, wouldn't it? He dared her to do it. But she had already given in to him. She didn't bow her head and kneel in deference to him, but she could just as well have done so. It would be just a formal acknowledgment of what had actually taken place. She displayed herself by the altar with the knife raised above her head. She had given in.

She looked down at the skinny figure on the flat rock. The girl had only experienced one single bleeding and had just begun developing female attributes. A perfect sacrifice. Thunder rolled and the wind became a storm. The chanting choir increased to a peak. The flower petals turned black. The knife flashed through the air, lighting the darkness.

«Mirror, mirror on the wall, who is the most powerful witch of all»?

You are!

Chapter Four: FUN IN THE STONE DESERT SHADOW(S)

Indian Summer burned in Boston, Massachusetts. Fall should have shown its cold ass long ago. There wasn't any sign of it, none what-so-ever. It was a glorious day. Everybody would agree on that, in spite of the heavy stench of pollution everywhere. Even the strong wind from the ocean couldn't take care of it all. This Sunday people took to the parks, to the streets and did their best to amuse themselves, to do so with a more than distinct frown marring their smile. There had been too many glorious days lately, so unexpected, so alarming.

The three girls, not from this town, didn't really care. They wanted to enjoy themselves, no matter what they might feel in others. In this respect, they were no different from most people. Stacy, Jill and Tamara roamed willfully the city's enormous wharf area. They were all dressed light, in shorts and sleeveless blouses. Jill carried her black hat on her back, hanging in a string from the neck. She didn't let herself be taken by the bothersome heat, distracted as she was by all there was to see around her. So much to see, and not the least *feel*. Even if Boston was just a few hundred years old, it represented history and events far older. A mix of old and new, science and Magick. Truly fascinating.

Most Bostonians, not talking about the weather still conversed about «the Big Dig», a hole in the ground throughout the city, supposed to be a new central road, supposed to take care of the city's long standing traffic problems. A mire of federal and local funding and lack of such. Charges of embezzlement and worse. The work had stopped several times, to be restarted, to be stopped again. The girls had seen it and passed it several times already. And «the Big Dig» had so far plagued Bostonians for over ten years, and no immediate solution was forthcoming. When they listened to all the wild stories, it was hard to tell if they were in fact facts, or plain and simple urban legends.

Life in the city... Jill shuddered and smiled simultaneously.

– I need an ice-cold ice-cream, Stacy announced cheerfully. – I need to cool down before I go insane.

It was a bit odd to hear that from her, since she seemingly endured the heat better than her two companions. Jill and Tamara didn't object, though. They had wanted to make similar suggestions for a long time now, but had been unable to move their lips...

They were grateful to how fortuitous it was to locate an ice cream café. They hardly needed to «locate» anything, as there were found such places on almost any corner. Sales were gratifying indeed, at the very least double the usual. Even places opened merely a month ago had probably already made a fortune. The three girls didn't find a place in the shade, but by being patient and taking their time, they found their reward in the guise of a table located under a HUGE parasol. Stacy gave her American Express Gold card to the waitress and not much longer after that, they sat by the table and ingested their very own foot high ice-cream and can of ice-cold coke. It was too hot to be concerned about health and they enjoyed their «meal» in full measure.

– Isn't life grand? Tamara leaned back in the chair with a huge grin on her face.

– It sure can be, Stacy said, and for once, there was no hint of pretense in her voice or posture.

Tamara did her best to act naturally in Jill's presence, but Jill could easily see through her veneer of self-assurance by her deeper senses. Jill's deeper senses, that she now was almost certain she possessed.

They had to eat the delicious vanilla ice cream fast and furious, before it melted in their hands. They sat in the shade under the parasol, and were not hit by rays of sun, but the very air seemed like it was burning. And moisture evaporated inside their mouth.

– I read about traveling in the desert, she said, almost in a hushed, soundless voice. – How you have to drink all the time to not get dehydrated and «stones» will develop in your kidneys. This is like that, except the desert is not of sand, but of stone.

– Stone Desert... Stacy mused. – I like that, little sister.

They drank up all their soda and ordered more. They had to, anyway, or they would be asked to vacate their seats. There was an ever-growing queue on the sidewalk, outside the fence.

The waitress didn't seem pleased by their new order, though. They noticed that she didn't bring them more glasses filled with refreshing fluid, but instead a rather sour disposition.

– We've been told your card is invalid, she said to Stacy in quite a cold manner.

– That *got* to be some sort of misunderstanding, Stacy protested in a not too worried posture. – It

worked just fine this morning and there is no reason for it to have been blocked.
– I'm sorry, the waitress said, certainly not very sorry. – The card is definitely invalid, and we've been asked to keep it in our possession, until it can be picked up by the right party. I must ask you to pay in cash, please.

They did, with the small allowances they kept in their wallets. Then they were practically butted out of the cafeteria. A big bruiser of a man studied it all from a distance, in case there was any need for muscle. There wasn't. The girls played it nice. Besides, at least Jill and Tamara were too stunned to raise much of a stink. Stacy, as usual, seemed curiously unfazed. Though there was no calm in her voice as she uttered her next words.

– *Damn them!*

– Who? Tamara asked in a mystified tone.

– My parents, Stacy raged silently. – They've sealed all my accounts. I suspected as much, as I received a minor check through the mail yesterday morning.

– But your parents are rich, aren't they?

– They wanted me to go to Harvard. It has always been like that. If I don't do exactly as they wish, I'm punished for it.

– But if you knew...? Jill looked disheartened through her wallet. – What do you suppose we should do for the rest of the day? Our scholarships, mine and Tamara's, don't exactly warrant wild parties and such...

She knew she sounded like a spoiled child, but she couldn't help it. The thought of wandering around in a big city all day, doing nothing, and just about have money left for the trip back, didn't exactly fill her with joy.

– Yes, I knew, Stacy said firmly. – From before we left this morning. That's why I didn't attempt to use my remaining cards, since they, too, would probably have been confiscated. I didn't know when, though, because most people don't check an American Express Gold card... The fact that they did, is telling me something... that they perhaps in fact didn't... I think my parents have me followed and that he or she or they... enlightened the manager of the cafeteria.

– But why didn't that happen earlier today, when we bought the bus tickets...

Tamara's voice trailed off. She understood. As did Jill. Easily. And she understood to what length Stacy's mother and father were willing to go, to punish their wayward daughter.

– I knew, Stacy continued, very deliberate and very direct, in both stare and tone, – and I didn't tell, since I wasn't really considering the matter as being of any major importance... since we're not, in any way, ordinary maidens in distress or jeopardy...

She knows. The thought crossed Jill's mind immediately, even if she didn't realize immediately the further implication of her own thought. She felt a tingle inside and blood that slowly, slowly began to boil. And not because of the external heat around them. She also felt an almost irresistible urge, just then, to behave with a bit of decency. But she couldn't resist, didn't want to either. Stacy's suggestion was too tempting. Suddenly she longed to prove herself, like a child learning to walk.

– You mean... Smiles dawned in both their faces. They understood each other so well, Jill thought.

– You both mean... Tamara made an attempt, destined to fail, to look shocked. She, too, started to smile.

But then, incredulously:

– But will it work?

– I don't know, Jill giggled nervously.

– Just do it, Stacy said.

– We can do it together. Jill stretched out her hands to hers. She pulled hers away.

– You first.

They walked into Boston Common, the enormous green area at the center of the city, under the torn shadow of big trees without the full cover of green leaves. Jill began to stretch her senses, carefully, apprehensively, trying not to open her mind too much. The tarmac paths in the Common were crowded to a point where people sometimes couldn't see their own feet. Experience had taught the aspiring sorceress how dangerous that could be to a young, unskilled witch.

A young couple, occupying an entire bench of their own, was making out, kissing and snuggling to the point of oblivion. The impressions she got from them made her even more hot and sweaty. She turned her attention away in total and humiliating embarrassment.

– Oh-kay, let's see now, who can afford to lose a load of money...

She said in a hoarse voice, close to a whisper. What she had meant to sound confident and cheerful. But no such luck was bestowed upon her. Tamara didn't notice anything, but she was convinced Stacy did, carrying her usual, enigmatic smile. Jill managed a smile, too, a bit self-consciously and ironic.

There was joy around her, even if it was, as ever, fleeting. She wouldn't want to take that away from anyone, no matter how much and how hard Stacy was pushing her. The day was such a fine one. In spite of the day being *too fine*, in spite of its causes being pollution and pollution's vast inherent dangers. Life could be light and joyful, she thought dreamily. Why not? Or... was the question rather how long the bad times could be kept at bay?

Children did play in the streets. They did have fun, running and chasing the dust devils on the coal-like tarmac, coal glowing as if on fire. And they didn't burn their naked feet.

Not many people here were carrying much cash, and those doing so didn't serve the purpose Jill wanted them to serve. They didn't carry enough of it to make it worth the effort. Most had a lot of plastic in their wallets, useless to Jill's purpose. It wasn't easy... picking a mark. She had heard that word used in connection with pocket pickers once or twice. It did fit. She supposed most people in that profession did it very much as she did now, zoning in on people, assessing them, throwing them back into the water.

Stacy looked at her, humorously, questionably, Tamara apprehensively, nervously. Jill shook her head.

Then, as she was about to lose patience, with the search, with herself, her attention was drawn, in quite a normal sort of way, to a large group entering the Common. One man, crowded with bodyguards. Fear, anticipation, the thrill of the challenge washed over her, all at once... just as Stacy had expected... and wanted.

She sat down and her two companions did as she did, on a grass knoll in a fractured shade under a tree. And she focused; they focused on the group of people walking on the tarmac towards them. The group of men didn't wear black suits and dark glasses, but were dressed rather casually. Still, their demeanor, their body language suggested they were indeed such classic stereotype characters.

Jill concentrated on the leader. Eyes were half closed, almost unfocused. She could see the thick wallet in the breast pocket of his jacket, see it bulging, imagining she could actually feel it in her hand.

– Lift, she mumbled. – Come to me.

Nothing happened. She did another attempt. And another. The crowded group walked by, and continued on their way. She stood up and signaled for the others to follow her, chasing their target.

– What happened? Stacy asked inquiringly.

– I couldn't do it, Jill replied, subdued, irritated, angry. – I don't know why.

It had been so easy with the candles. It hadn't been necessary to think, only do, and a material object had levitated into her hand.

She stopped a moment, before continuing, walking faster, with eager, quick steps. What if...

What if that was the answer?

What if concentration, in this particular case, didn't aid her, but rather the opposite, that it instead of making... the rope soft and malleable, tied it in knots, making it useless?

The use had to be natural, instinctive, a flow, not a rock.

Like walking. If a person concentrated on how to walk «right», it tended to be anything but.

Yes! That was it. That must be it.

Eyes were half closed, with a dreaming quality. The girls closed in on their quarry, their dangerous prey, in one of the crossroads.

They were ten, fifteen steps behind when the mark virtually disappeared among people crossing each other's path ahead. For some reason, unfathomable to most, a woman stumbled into the big man. What she might have stumbled on nobody could tell. But before his obvious bodyguards could react, the completely unknown woman flew forward and knocked him down on the ground.

The wallet flew so easy and so unnoticed out of his pocket that Jill couldn't really be certain that she had anything to do with it. Distance, she thought, *keep the distance*. And then she was certain, as the wallet failed to hit the ground and floated right above it, floated by people's whirling feet. She felt it, a nip in her mind, a rush, a flow. And now she had to concentrate, not to concentrate. Sweat began flowing, dripping from her nose and jaw, making her eyebrows thick with salty fluid, filling her eyes. With a low thud the wallet made it into her hand. A quick move and the object of her most present desire was released into the bottom of the bag. She touched her head and felt the thud thud thud in her fingertips. Something broke someplace, in her nose, she felt fluid float out of it. She touched the skin above her mouth with her right hand and it turned blood red.

– Watch where you're going, you FAT COW, the man shouted.

Jill shook, as if struck, even if she realized he wasn't talking to her.

She relaxed. Slowly normal respiration and heartbeat was restored. And then she heard the buzz, or the beginning of a buzz in her mind, she just knew too well. She concentrated, she concentrated about relaxing, and she didn't relax, and the buzz buzzed out, before it had a chance to seriously stagger her. There. She could finally calm down. Neither the former owner of the wallet, nor his compatriots had noticed anything was amiss. They were walking one path from the crossroads, the girls another.

Stacy dried her forehead and brow, and then using a pocket-handkerchief, her nose and lips. The burst of blood had been pretty fresh at first, but had soon stopped. There was visible pride in Stacy's eyes. Visible to Jill that is. Behind the expressionless mask.

– I've never been able to do that, Stacy said. – I do think I can, and I shall, but I've never been able to find out how. How did you do it?

– I think you're always concentrating a bit too much, Jill said, replying without really replying to the question.

Her visit to the castle, the manor, the temple of fire had released something in her, thrown aside the wall, the veil masking her inner being. Her talent, her power was like steppingstones, revealing themselves one at a time, ever bigger, ever more powerful.

They walked further away, back into the city. They threw a glance, all three of them, from time to time, on the bag Jill carried, so much heavier now than it had been.

– We can afford another round of ice-cream now I take it? Stacy said roguishly, waggishly, unfathomable.

– Perhaps we should postpone that one a bit? Jill said roguishly, waggishly, unfathomable.

– Why is that? Tamara wondered.

– We can afford something better now...

They didn't make haste, as they walked further away. There had been a lot of walking today and their clothes felt tight, uncomfortable from the sweat and dust clinging to them, making the clothes cling to their bodies. Jill felt curiously fresh, not just in mind, but in body as well. She had walked further this day than she had any day earlier in her life, and there was no substantial stiffness in her limbs and muscles.

Stacy looked behind her ever so often, visibly irritated.

– Are you looking for your parents' stooge? Jill asked, not without compassion.

– If there is one, I can't detect anything, Stacy said. – He or she must be very clever.

Jill knew what she meant. In the last few days, she, too, had been able to sense hostility, as in one of the teachers, or even occasionally casual interest. She realized now that she always had been able to do that, to sense projections and emotions in others. But she hadn't been able to identify it as such, and therefore it had been a bother, more than a gift.

If there were people tailing them, they were not projecting. She had read about such people, how good they were at blending in, almost as if they were chameleons.

That was the worst part of being under surveillance, or believing you were. Without tangible evidence you could never be certain there was anyone *there*.

And they couldn't stop looking for the former owner of what she carried in her bag.

Their walk had been quite casual for what felt like hours, now, but suddenly that changed. In a rush of fear, hysterical giggling and excitement, they hurried into the closest public restroom. All three of them pushed themselves inside the same booth and slammed the door behind them. The shockingly loud noise made them even more jumpy. They eyed each other, listening for suspicious sounds, for other guests in close proximity. There were none. Three eager hands dived into the bag and returned with an equal grip around the wallet. Three pair of eyes widened as they opened it.

– There gotta be several thousand dollars here. Tamara glanced around her, on the booth walls, suddenly very, very nervous.

– Probably, Stacy said laconic.

They split it three-ways. There was one coin left. It was given to Tamara. She held it up, grinned, and dropped it in the toilet, flushed it down the sewage pipe without hesitation. They looked at the ID cards. They didn't tell them anything, except that both the face and the name sounded ominous. They resisted the urge to keep the credit cards...

After sneaking out of the public bathroom area, after Stacy had used the opportunity to brush and paint and «fix» her face, and thrown the wallet, completely devoid of cash, into the closest garbage bin, they set course towards a restaurant. Even if they didn't pick the first and closest, they didn't bother to look very far. The one they chose, eventually was a surprisingly quiet and plain, informal, solitary place. But the food was great and tasted even better because of the triumphant boiling of their blood, the beating of their wild hearts. They ate even more than they wanted, since the food was supposed to last well through the evening and the long night.

Lazily, with well-filled stomachs, they left the place. Jill didn't really pay attention to where she was going, and would have been run down by a car, if Stacy hadn't grabbed her arm and saved her.

– Shame on you, girl. Distracted and killed on your first evening as a wealthy Lady? That won't do, that won't do at all...

Jill, with her increasingly sharpened senses had easily felt the interest from the boys by one of the other tables. It made her giddy and her body felt... heavy? Was this how it would always be, how she would always experience emotion, *passion?* As perpetual, heightened desire? So strong, intense?

Sunshine met them outside. Vanishing day greeted nightly fire. Jill stretched out her arms, enjoying herself even more.

– Shall we procure new attire, then? Stacy said casually. – It's long overdue, if you ask me.

Three strange birds on their way into the night, and to increased knowledge, started their search for more representative rags, rags that would, with a little luck, better suit their personalities.

The street was a curious one, or at least it looked the part, with what could be interpreted as early, very early Halloween decorations. And to them even more so. Even Tamara felt it. Or she might have «caught it» from the other two. Stacy and Jill saw the light and shadow shift in a special way, from the other's perspective. Then it shifted back, and back again. Back and forth, back and forth. They couldn't tell if it was anything caused by the place, or by them, or a combination.

– *Wow!* Stacy whispered and for once she was close to speechless.

There were a lot of shops here, both selling... *special* clothes and other stuff, equally far away from the norm, from any average viewpoint. Big eyes bulging, they took a thorough look at *everything.* They found a hidden, intimate shop with a personality, a rare one, too, at that. The localities were big, if not amazingly so, and stuffed with... stuff, with content instead of form. Not your usual fashion show, the prototype of This Month's Flavor Shop. They loved it and lived it.

– How did we *find* this place? Tamara wondered nervously. – *Well* done!

– Smelled it from afar, I guess, Jill grinned. – A small miracle, in an oasis of mediocrity.

– I too, felt like a poet, once, Stacy remarked. – I grew out of it.

Hurt, Jill couldn't find a proper, witty response.

She looked around her, still with wonder in her eyes. There was much to see, to take in. All the clothes, all the costumes and paraphernalia, lots of *witchy* stuff imposed itself on her. There weren't many customers and only one person behind the desk, possibly, probably the owner. They didn't really know what to make of him. They couldn't decide whether he looked like a witch or a gypsy or something different altogether. He had long, curly hair under the bandanna he had tied around his head, and a ring in the left ear and wore something that looked like woven, dark colored, not black, clothes. None of it was really outrageous or unusual these days, but the combination and his presence and the impression they got from him, was still *something else.*

– Good afternoon, good Sire, Stacy said, cheerfully, challenging. – We're three good maidens who want to rid ourselves of our old rags, and procure some new ones.

– Have a look around, he said calmly. – Take your time. If I can help you with anything, don't hesitate to ask.

– Well, there's one thing. We couldn't help but noticing your abundance of costumes here today. We know this is a business where *costumes* are sold, but we don't believe you're always stocking like this, are you?

– It's the rock concert tonight, he said. – It's a costume party, too.

– We knew about the concert, that's one of the reasons we decided to visit this fine city this weekend. We didn't hear about any party, though. How *exciting!*

Jill thought Stacy was overdoing it and wanted to tell her so, but decided not to bother.

– It's one of the best kept, public secrets I've seen for quite some time, the man behind the counter said. – It might be great stuff, you can never know about such things in advance. If it's the right crowd it may take off completely, go through the roof, or it might turn out to be a complete dud.

Jill understood more of what he was about, now. He was probably a *Goth*, a part of the gothic scenery that had been part of the underground scene for a number of years. They dressed outlandish and usually played at being wicked, being evil, but it was mostly an act. Most of them had quite ordinary day jobs and didn't, though they were occasionally, somewhat persecuted by present day society, harbor much in the way of radical thoughts and actions.

It still didn't feel right concerning him, though.

She was still distracted while she allowed her fingers to stroke the black velvet of the combined hood and cloak on the wall, and the edge of the so very fitting dress. And her distraction disappeared more and more, and grew little by little, by each stroke.

– That stuff is quite expensive, he said, seemingly from far away.

– We want the very best! She said, without really emphasizing her words. – We want the real thing!

– They're not that expensive, he said, – but most people would still do more non-expensive pickings. I'm wondering where you gals got your money from, you know...

He had to be teasing them, at least in part. Surely, he, an aficionado had to know, just by a casual look, that Stacy was already wearing very expensive clothes?

– We've stolen every single dime, Jill said coquettishly, suddenly very close, feeling very bold.

The three girls arrived at the inner room or *sanctum*. There was no one else there. And that's where the really interesting stuff was. They stood still, for what was seemingly a long time, gazing around. In their excitement they were certain they forgot to breathe in between. And breathing was important. It just didn't seem like it right now. Or perhaps, *right now,* it felt more important than ever.

Jill stood before the mirror and tried on clothes, big, comfortable sizes, many different types. She spun on her toes. John, his name was John, as he had promised, gave them all the time in the world. He had pulled a curtain before the opening, between the outer and inner part of the shop, and left them in peace (and not in pieces).

Jill started hesitatingly by lifting clothes off the hangers, four or five steps away and made them float to her. Stacy tried a while before she, too, could do it. Impatient and reckless, she soon got the hang of it. Remarkably fast she could do it almost as good as Jill. Clothes floated off and on them both. It was good exercise to arrange the fabric in such a way that it was easy to just make it slide up feet or arms. They didn't manage to do it with more than one item at the time, but to Tamara, who was watching stunned, it was pure revelation.

Jill lost sense of time and place. She tried on another set of clothes. And another. And it wasn't merely clothes she tried on, but different parts of her being. She rotated one more time before the mirror, feeling almost completely relaxed, so peaceful, so... harmonic.

When suddenly... she felt a draft… from *somewhere!* There was no wind, no visible origin of the draft, but it was there. Here. And there was an overwhelming suspicion... of being watched.

There was no one behind her. The mirror showed her that (to the degree she trusted mirrors). Her two friends were in the other room. She could see them admiring a black shining dress, see it through a sliver in the curtain. They weren't spying on her. She spun around. Still no one. She spun back to the mirror, facing it. *The mirror.* Didn't the mirror image stop spinning, stop moving a fraction of time later than she did? She stared into it. Hard. And had to blink. Stunned. The mirror image, her other I, was fading away before her eyes. What was going on here? This was... this was too much! If something like this happened in a dusty, old, spooky house, far away in the wilderness, that was one thing. But here, in the center of the great city of Boston, in a well-lit store?

Eyes had been closed. She opened them yet again. The mirror image was still gone. But then, as she turned, she glimpsed it by the exit. And then, as she completed her turn, she was looking straight at it, seeing it fully, seeing herself from the outside. It moved a bit more towards the curtain, waving, calling Jill to it. Jill couldn't move, but stared as transfixed at the ghoul in front of her. She wanted to scream, but couldn't. She wanted to move, but couldn't move a finger.

– Stacy? Tamara? Come here.

Finally, there were sounds, but whispers more than talk, far from the shout she wanted it to be.

– Stacy? Tamara? COME HERE! She cried out.

The creature by the curtain faded away, returning to the mirror.

– Is something wrong, honey? Stacy entered the room with a both mellow and worried look in her eyes.

– No, nothing is wrong. Jill assured her. – I just figured we should think about getting out of here. It's getting dark and we should arrive early at the festivities.

– Good idea. Tamara stuck her head out from the curtain. – Let's rock'n roll.

Jill started dancing softly to the music in the store. She returned to one of the first costumes she had tried on. The black dress, the combined cloak and hood. The golden mask, covering half the face. The forehead, the eyes, the nose and most of the cheeks were covered in golden, hardened cloth. She looked at her eyes, through the holes of the mask. She put on the cloak, drew the hood over the head.... and the transformation was complete.

Tamara whistled and stared, stared at herself in the mirror, at her two companions. Stacy and Jill stared at each other.

They went back to the counter and to John, in the outer room. Jill also bought a set of jeans, a jacket and pants in deep blue. The others similar stuff. All three bought silver colored pentacle necklaces and an assortment of other things well known as magical ornaments. It didn't feel unnatural in any way. Not anymore. Jill kept the hat. It did fit her, no matter what else she might be wearing. For some reason or another, the thought made her smile.

She looked excitedly around her as if to memorize the place. Her life had become so challenging and interesting. Everything was behind her and so much ahead.

They removed the mask and the hood/cloak and decided to walk to the concert in the dress.

– So how is business? Jill asked.

– People I do not want as customers never return, but people I do want, are returning many times. Business is, in fact, excellent.

– No wonder, this is a great place you've got here, Stacy smiled angel white. – We're studying in Northfield by the way. You must come and visit us there sometime. It's not much right now, but it's gonna be a blast...

– I will probably take you up on that, John nodded.

The evening was, in comparison as hot and humid as the day had been. Compared to what had, once upon a time, passed for ordinary evenings. Hot, but so much colder than the day that they didn't sweat in their clothes at a normal pace.

– You've painted your face again, Jill said to Stacy. – As you did this morning and in the public restroom. Why do you do it so often?

– I like it, Stacy replied. – The boys like it, too.

Jill didn't reply to that, not in words. The chuckle of the other girl echoed inside her.

They shared a sense of the streets awakening, coming alive after dark. People had moved in the heat and the day, too, but measured, more controlled, not so spontaneous and merry. All the artificial lights threw more shadow than light. At least tonight they did. This was how Jill saw it, anyway. And the wild and merry passions were enhanced as they walked closer to Boston Common and Public Garden. From inside the huge park area, they heard the collected sound of the expectant crowd and instruments adapted to the specifics of the area, before the concert began.

A group of youths waited for them at the gate (or so it seemed). Their outward, and also inward characteristics were not very muddled to any of the girls.

– Christ, Tamara exclaimed (with a certain grim satisfaction). – They're Children of Light.

– Fuck, we've heard of them in Wales, too.

They all shared a sense of disgust crawling in their innards, as they forced themselves to push forward, towards the unpleasant task ahead of them.

– Hello, a tall and handsome boy in front of the group said. – Are you by any chance going to the… what is going on inside the park?

– Hallelujah, Stacy cried. – Hail to all you clean boys and girls.

– You are aware, I trust, of the negative effect rock music has on the human psyche and health in general?

– You're such a sweet boy, Stacy flirted shamelessly.

She touched his chin.

Jill cast her an admiring look and expected her to keep it up, to move in for the kill, so to speak, but it didn't happen. She… stopped.

– I trust you're aware that you're all brainwashed? Jill stepped forward, smiling sweetly.

Stacy walked into the park and the two other girls followed, slightly puzzled.

– There was something…

Jill wanted to ask, but she recognized… recognized fear in the other girl, and didn't want to pursue it further.

She looked down at her right hand. There was a leaflet there. She took a look at it.

THE CHILDREN OF LIGHT AND LOVE
Together for a better world

Are you a Christian, Muslim, Buddhist or of an another denomination
Questioning your faith?
Or one without any, looking for one?
We're combining all the world's belief systems
With the very best our modern world has to offer.
We offer ourselves to the World
Perhaps we have something for you, too?

Jill crumbled the piece of paper in her hand and threw it in the nearest wastebasket, shaking uncontrollably.

– The Moonies, the Scientology Church and bunch… Stacy's voice was hoarse and ragged, and thick with emotion. – They're all alike. Pretending to offer seekers and rebels something different, but what they're really doing is to give them more of the same. They have… refined the oppressive methods of the establishment and perhaps even raised themselves to another level when it comes to deceit and fucking with people.

Jill and Tamara looked shocked at each other. The raw, vulnerable Stacy was something new and ultimately frightening. The fact that she was scared was frightening.

They would, all three of them look back on this as a thoroughly negative experience, without really knowing why, and that was the truly scary part.

It took time, but they did manage to calm themselves, as the valve of the park, of the trees and the would-be forest shielded them from the noise, the traffic outside.

People came from all over the area, to experience something different, something beyond the everyday experience (or lack of it). Jill sensed their expectation, experienced it as she did herself. She spit out the sour taste in her mouth. She did it several times.

Layer upon layer of city smoke blocked significantly the rays from the moon. The garbage of the modern world was found in the air, soil and water, here, as it was everywhere, especially in urban areas. Still, Jill felt the undeniable happiness and fullness of Life tonight. She couldn't help it and it was right, she realized. The day all joy was destroyed, it was truly over.

– «Girls just wanna have fun», Stacy hummed.

They stopped, looked at each other.

– It's Time, she declared, grinning her radiant grin.

They started dressing in full. Cloak and hood and mask in place, they took the plunge into the park, walking up the slight slope on the path with the old looking lamps on their left. The special mood didn't leave Jill. If anything, it was growing, in leap and bounds, in rushes of hot night air. Unpleasant thoughts faded to at least momentary insignificance.

The space opened up to her. The people opened up to her. She threw herself out in the wild, wild water.

People crowded the park, but it felt both filled up and empty simultaneously. The night was both dead and intensely alive. Dizzied and giddy she looked up and then she stretched her arms out wide. Slowly she started to rotate round and round and round... observing the treetops high above and the giant clouds in the night sky move in the wind. There were trees and there were no trees, and everything did spin for her eyes. When she stopped spinning, she was so dizzy that her two companions had to grab her to keep her from falling.

– I s-saw something, she said, and shook her head in confusion.

Whatever she had seen, whatever it might have been, it was gone nooowww.

Time stretched and her thoughts with it, to the point of becoming elusive, so out there, in the vast ether surrounding her.

They walked further into the park, really far inside, three strange birds in the night. Somewhere ahead, between the trees, they glimpsed a huge outdoor scene, raised for this night only. A carnival and a fun fair traveled with the band. The wheel of fortune placed by the entrance was spinning round and round and round. Not everybody inside wore a costume, but everyone wore masks, hiding their face, revealing their face. Masks were like that. Jill felt a rush, a thrill, as she passed a mirror and glimpsed herself in it, glimpsed with eyes, without eyes, as she walked a Night far deeper than the one surrounding them.

Batman approached them. Kind of. The mask was Batman, but the costume wasn't really, but more a free interpretation based on a Batman suit. «Red Rain», Jill thought. He has read Red Rain, the comic book. He was dressed in a combination of Batman and Dracula costumes.

– May I wish you three bewitched women welcome to this fine gala?

– You already did! Stacy said curtly. – How utterly gentlemanly of you, sir...

– How sweet, Jill said, sweet and ingenious.

– You will all enjoy yourself here, I guarantee it...

As they made their way further into the festivities, they were certain he was correct, no matter, what he, himself, may have meant with his words.

The place was not filled with people, but this, strangely enough, gave the whole thing a more intimate feel. People did not stand close. They didn't need to, as it was more than enough space. And that was the reason it felt intimate. Most discos and «dance halls» in their experience were quite impersonal, precisely because of everyone's close proximity to each other. When people got close here, it was because they wanted to.

The music started with the cracking of thunder, not that much of a departure from standard rock music, not so... *progressive* compared to what Gabrielle and group had done, but different enough. Heavy, inciting rhythms, raw, pulsing, passionate Rock shook them apart, and they allowed it to happen, embraced the feeling. The Wild Dance began. And their sensitivity grew to the point where they could sense the Earth move. Birds took off from the treetops, flapping their wings over the night sky. Jill cried out while clapping the beat over her head, beating her palms together in excitement. From far away they had all come, to fly higher and further than the eagle. Batman danced with her. She knew it was the same Batman, could «read» it in his mind. She also perceived other emotions from there, which, even if they didn't bring forth the blushing, brought to life even stronger reactions in her.

The dress was a bit too small. She had been painfully aware of that fact when purchasing it, but had stubbornly done so anyway. She had lain off the chocolate all week and had begun exercising. To her great joy it had already shown tangible results. But the dress was too tight and made her pant and breathe harder.

All this, just a fleeting thought, forgotten in the moment.

She felt the intensity on all levels, the influence enhanced by the music and mood around her. The guitar solo was floating through the air, and she floated along. She... *danced.* The realization hit her suddenly, like a jolt. She danced wildly and recklessly. The dominating drumbeats immediately afterwards set her feet on fire. She let herself go for the first time in her life. She had attempted to do that earlier, too, she had wanted to, but had always felt watchful eyes on her. They were still felt, still there, but just now, they were as nothing, they meant nothing. She had set sail on the vast sea, and intended to live her dream, whatever it might be, wherever it might lead.

Something…

The lead guitarist, the singer, suddenly she was focusing on him, breathing with him, feeling the pulse of his beat, his inner, erupting darkness, his rainbow. And the girl, the bass player, the other lead singer. Something... happened. Stacy... Jill and Stacy danced close, encircling each other, to the point of being one. And the lead guitarist, Jared, started *playing,* and his singing turned hoarse and raspy and wonderful, and the band, Stone Walking, started to follow his lead, and then their own. The bass player, Holly, closed the distance between them, and they started a guitar orgasm out of all proportions. The drummer changed his tune, and so did the two keyboard players. The other guitarist started jumping up and down in a completely irrational pattern. Tamara, too, started *dancing* then. The big, full-bodied girl and the two slightly smaller ones soon attracted an audience. And the band played even wilder. And the rays from the moon started dominating on the stage and below. They were rocking between its silver rays and the skin on their faces was glowing hot and cold. Electric lights dimmed to insignificance. Even the electrical sound seemed to be fading, supplanted with something else. Jared and Holly, they were dancing tight, and even though one would believe the guitars were a hindrance to that, it obviously wasn't. Suddenly they had disappeared behind the stage and the keyboard players started their thing, their solo, a duo looking incredulous at each other, but still playing, and feeling. An image, a *Vision,* came to Jill then, incredibly funny, of Jared and Holly making out behind the stage, and she started laughing, and Life, with its hard edge, was evident in the sound. The laughter itself seemed mysterious and challenging, something Stacy might have done, but Jill knew it was her own. The song «Dancing on the edge of Night», forever Changed this very evening ended, but yet echoing throughout eternity. Holly and Jared stood on the precipice of the stage, nearly falling off, bathing in the applause, the wild cries from the participants below, the hundreds of people, completely ecstatic by the performance, by the undeniable feeling of Life present.

– HOLY SHIT! Jared exclaimed. – Did you people *feel* that, or what... Un - BE - liev - able. What a NIGHT!

And as Jill saw the surprising flash of fear, quickly drowned in elation, in Stacy's eyes, she felt it as if every single bit of skin covering her body was alive. In flashes she even imagined it, the two young girls glowing.

And it turned out to be that great night, that great time. Stone Walking started playing again, and played on for four hours straight after that, four and a half altogether.

– Are we recording, people? the rhythm guitarist mumbled with a glassy look. – We must record this. Straight into the microphone.

And there were tape-recorders humming and tapes turning somewhere. Wild rumors would circulate within and without the business the coming months, about the manager, who had grabbed a handful of roadies and forced them at gunpoint to join him on a breaking and entering spree in music and video stores nearby...

There might be *some* truth to it, but the fact was that recording equipment had been... well, routinely recording since the start of the concert. Their manager had always been a man of foresight. He just hadn't realized how much a man of foresight he had been... before this very evening.

The music from the stage faded, the band left, but those who had truly listened remained, and kept listening, not only to the music, but also to the Night. It was quiet now. The talk among the youths, in smaller and larger groups, didn't change that. Silence ruled. The exalted bird chirping from the trees served only to confirm this. The sense of peace brought forth by the relative isolation from the city outside the green area confirmed it further. Stacy, Jill and Tamara sat with a group changing from fifteen to twenty people and back again, as some left and some joined. They sat in a perceived grove a stone throw from the monument.

Jill had felt weird during the entire concert. Still did. The girls enjoyed themselves immensely behind the masks, but the joy didn't explain the major and distinct... quivering, the Burning in skin and body and on the edge of consciousness. She and Stacy, at least, caught moods, catalyzed them, returned them. There was an intense pricking in their skin. They felt like they were… *bloated* with energy. It had been a subconscious function, but self-perpetuating. She couldn't avoid becoming conscious of it.

You feel it, too! That's good!

How could I not?

She raised her head with wide-open eyes, read confirmation in Stacy's green, deep eyes, in the turmoil that was her thoughts.

Telepathy? Jill glowed, not really questioning it anymore, even though it still felt amazing to her.

I didn't think you were ready, but you are. You taught me something, as I had hoped, Stacy sent. *Now, I've taught you in return. Now, we've given each other a gift, the gift of discovery, of Life.*

Suspicion rattled Jill for a moment, about Stacy's motives and the validity of the experience.

But suspicion and skepticism faded. There was clarity this time, not the confusion of old. The experience of power boiling, of power rising inside her was too real, too overwhelming to be denied, too exciting for suspicion to prevail.

There was drumbeat up close, far away, one drum different from others, *a different drum* heralding new, ascending times. It was that close. They were bathing in it. It seemed to come from everywhere. People continued to talk, while Stacy and Jill continued to talk between themselves. Stacy had held Tamara outside the loop the entire day. Now, she did it more than ever.

It's so fabulous, so distinct. Your «voice» is as clear as if I actually hear you speak.

Clearer. Haven't you figured it out yet? Speech is a barrier. This is so much more.

YES! Like speaking in the dark of the night. Everything is crystal clear.

The Night is mirroring our dreams, Stacy smiled.

Jill repeated it, aloud.

– Yes, isn't it NICE here, Tamara cried out, excited. – And I can't seem to get the concert out of my head, and I don't want to. It's so *outside* any previous experience, if you know what I mean. The band turned out to be such a great departure from the norm.

– I don't know about you guys, a girl spoke jokingly, shuddering in a near whisper, – but I certainly enjoyed myself.

– Some left, another exclaimed. – I can't understand that.

– It was too much for them.

– I can understand that. I'm exhausted.

– ... was worth every moment...

Everybody there agreed. It *was* a special night. The comments went on and on, confirming the lights in everyone's eyes. Jill noticed the casual interaction between everyone, including between boys and girls, men and women. She also noticed that Tamara was holding back a bit. Nobody else did, so busy enjoying themselves. Stacy noticed, though. She noticed everything.

The thought didn't bring much peace to Jill's already distracted mind. Her interest, both casual and intense, for the boys present flared constantly off and on, making her feel bad one moment, good the other. She wanted to get to know better more than one of the boys approaching her, but shyness kept her from revealing her interest.

A virgin, eh? The All Seeing enjoyed herself.

Yes. Giggling. *It's almost weird. I've wanted to, many times, but something has always prevented it...*

But you probably know this, she added.

I can't read your thoughts more than you can mine, Stacy explained calmly, patiently.

It was true. A (natural) «barricade» seemed to close off both their minds for more than a casual visit.

It's one of many advantages of our strong Power. Others can't get past our defenses without our consent.

Jill felt an undeniable relief and made an effort to keep herself from revealing it. Stacy's smile didn't falter.

Another useless distraction, a distraction no more. Darkness placed a crimson flow over her eyes, making her see better, so much better. She was rising from the treetops with the birds, flying with them into the Night. Suddenly she was lost in thought. It was like she had finally reached beyond a border, a limit, where she had been under way a hundred years. She had awaited this moment for so long, and still frustration held her in its vice, as she still couldn't look beyond the gate ahead, the Gate of Fire. Flight ended, she opened her eyes, opened her narrow chinks of her cavern. In the grip of her own instinctive mind/self she sought among the people in her immediate physical surroundings. Her burning, hungry glance stopped and rested by Batman… or Dracula.

You want him, don't you?

She pulled her eyes away, until they rested on Stacy, glaring at her.

You don't need to say a word. Your eyes are very revealing, do you know that? I fear that, if you're not careful, the dullest of fools can read you or your intentions, read your mind, so to speak...

Yes. I want him! Jill admitted.

You magnificent little horny bitch! You're burning to know, to experience the Unknown, are you not? As much as is your cunt, as you're itching to be a woman.

Yes!

Pretty interesting fellow. The witch nodded in acknowledgement.

Jill nodded, too, without really registering it, registering anything of whatever she happened to be doing. She attempted to wet her lips, but they never felt wet enough.

He has most certainly conquered many young mares, don't you think?

Yes! At this point she could virtually register the hoarseness of her thoughts. But she wasn't blushing.

Too bad with a popular guy like that. He has probably caught AIDS or something on his many exploits...

All heat and need left Jill, like a drop of water in the desert.

Hey: So cheerful. *Don't look so glum, your head is literally hanging between your knees... I was just kidding, can't you take a joke? He's most certainly a very healthy young stud. Take him as yours, as is the right of a young queen.*

But the expectation was gone for Jill. Without the strong emotions and driving need, she didn't dare to even look in the right direction.

You must overcome that boring shyness of yours, sister, Stacy reproached her gently.

Your eyes are not revealing you, Jill thought unprompted, without sending.

Sending, not sending, it was easy to discern the difference, as if she had done so all her life.

We are... late bloomers?

Stacy continued to look at her with seemingly infinite patience.

I mean, our... powers, our talents, we don't have them from birth, do we? Surely, we can't have, as we didn't realize them until our late teens...

Oh, we're born with them all right, but without encouragement, without nurturing, without belief, nothing can really grow, can it? But it can't be held down, be kept enclosed forever. It's a fire, a rage, one as old as mankind itself.

That felt so right, so very, very true. How could the snotty bitch be so right about one thing, one such fundamental subject... and be so damn wrong about others?

Why do we keep Tamara out?

Why should we include her?

She's our friend. That should be reason enough!

Friend...? What an overly sentimental statement. You've got a lot to learn, little sister. She may be of some limited use for us on some future occasions, but she's hardly worthy of any deep-felt camaraderie.

You cold, arrogant...

The only reply was the usual, mocking echo of laughter. Jill was so stunned that she didn't manage to say more, to even think more. She didn't know how to reply to such a statement, she really didn't.

They moved a bit around, between various groups. Jill heard Tamara talking, she even heard herself reply to her, but the conversation didn't really register in her conscious mind. And she felt ashamed.

She grabbed Stacy, not by her hands.

By her mind, for the first time using her power, the Power consciously in anger.

D-don't you feel the kinship with her, the possibility that she could be...

That she, too, may be a witch? Of course, I did. I can recognize it anywhere. But her «gift», whatever it may be, is a very weak one. As I said, she may be of some limited use, but not much beyond that.

They sat down again, without really knowing why. Maybe there was no reason, wasn't any to speak of. Jill crouched there on the grass knoll. Without really being aware of it she attempted to embrace herself, with her all too short arms.

– ... the world is about to go to hell. The voice of one of the boys finally penetrated her erected screen.

– Everything is dissolving and recreated, Stacy said. – There are some honest people claiming that re-creation isn't a painless process...
– The time is five minutes past twelve. Jill rocked back and forth, as she sang her words, as the ground was shaking. – And the carnival is done. Masks will fall. The present-day world is reaching the end of its final hour. If there has been strife and suffering before (and there has), it is nothing compared to what is coming.
She gasped then, as the air seemed to be stuck in her throat and she stared at nothing.
Was there really any use in fighting against it? Against an ever-bigger snowball rolling downhill, escalating in size and momentum every second? Against hatred, intolerance, poisoning and oppression? Was there really any use dancing to a different drum?
Stacy reached out her hand. Jill took it reluctantly and allowed herself to be led astray.
Impulsive as they were, the many people present continued the playing and the dancing long after the band had ended its performance, towards dawn, where it ended. One guitar, soon to be joined by a drum, was enough. Movement and a cascade of rhythms began anew, even less limited than before. Compared to eternity it didn't last long, but it was enough to bring Jill out of her misery.
The three girls did, occasionally, withdraw from the party and wander off to further explore what was the park, the park at present, explore themselves. And the party did seem to be dying off. There were even people falling asleep where they sat. And the girls moved on. Usually, neon and glittering lights didn't attract Jill, but tonight it did. Stacy was flirting with Batman, but Jill didn't allow herself to be bothered by it. Furthermore, she had admirers enough to be embarrassed for an entire lifespan. Though she didn't blush, and she wondered why not. Didn't she know shame?
Or perhaps she knew too much of it. Her parents had always instilled in her virtue and «responsibility» and the proper behavior where a young girl was concerned. She had fought long and hard to liberate herself from that.
It was way past midnight, and the fun fair didn't slow down. People showed no signs of wanting to go home.
Jill did enjoy this particular fun fair. She didn't know why. Usually, she didn't enjoy any sort of «amusement» park, but this was different. Or perhaps only the situation was or she was. She and her companions danced on, light, flowing steps on the hard and soft ground. All the spinning wheels went round and round. She did recall some fondness, interest for traveling fairs in her childhood. And a burning interest for traveling, the very thought of sailing away, to distant shores. There was a special enchantment in the air tonight, a vague spell of recklessness, of joy. Wheels within wheels. Flying saucers spinning at staggering speed... and wheels of fortune.
The Wheel of Fortune spinning round and round. The Wheel of Life burning.
– Look at the top shelf, Tamara eagerly whispered. – The big teddy bear...
– Let me guess, Jill said sternly. – You want it, don't you?
– It's no problem, Stacy said. – We can have everything we want from the top shelf.
The three of them stopped in front of the booth with their new companions. Lights blinked many-colored as the wheel turned. Jill focused on the task. She stretched her mind and in expectant eagerness she felt its Power. To control the turning of the wheel turned out to be much easier than she had anticipated. She had planned to experiment a bit, prepare herself, before she helped Tamara win, but she did it on her first attempt, without anyone being the wiser. The wheel simply slowed down in a seemingly normal way. But it stopped where she wanted it to stop.
And there was awe and fear in Tamara's eyes. The big girl thanked her in a show of excessive enthusiasm. She made a note to talk to her about that. To not be overly careless
They left the fair, left the park. Jill looked back ever so slightly. Wind moved the trees. Many-colored clouds flowed ever faster across the sky. Life was a game. One played with the heart and with the cards dealt. Eventual pros and cons one didn't count until the game was done. One drew each card, threw each dice, spun every wheel, as if life itself was at stake. And perhaps, when one considered it carefully, that was indeed the case.

INTERLUDE: The city that was not New Orleans (II)

– The laboratory is a safe, solemn, controlled place, chemical and biological reactions easily discerned and controlled.

Felix West spoke with an even, controlled voice, carefully modulated sentences and in a straight, unexciting manner. In short: He was boring as hell. The students took notes, as they were required to do, but they had to fight against the all too human urge to fall asleep.

Before him were second year students, more confident, more difficult to teach.

– Oh, I don't know, a girl spoke up jokingly. – We can always hope for more uncontrollable circumstances.

It took some time before the laughter died down, and he could continue. He continued in the same even voice.

The class ended eventually, as all classes do. The students rallied out in the hall.

West took another route, through the adjacent room.

Anton Berkowitz joined him in the small lounge, the minor wing, a bit away from the classrooms.

– I heard young Joan Davis was at it again.

– She has a way of drawing attention to herself. She is distracting, but I can handle it.

– I'm sure you can. How are the test results concerning her?

– I don't know, West admitted. – There seem to be some anomalous results, but so is usually the case, without it leading to anything more.

– We must get results soon, Berkowitz stated. – You know how touch and go it was just to get the program started. Finally, after three years of preparation we received the necessary funding and approval. We need to isolate the subjects in a controlled environment, you know that. We all do!

– You know I agree with you on the program's importance, West said solemnly. – But if we take them out of school for a longer period of time, we risk raising suspicion. We can attempt to get them enlisted during their holidays on a voluntary basis, using premiums. It's been done before, with qualified success, as we both know. Besides, we shouldn't underestimate the value of random qualities.

– If the class had heard you speak like that, they would've fainted *en masse*, Berkowitz joked.

They walked out in the corridor and the conversation turned more trivial.

West closed the heavy door to the laboratory. Nobody could get in there but him and Anton. They had the only key cards.

– Our minor nemesis has been at it again, I hear?

– Yes, West shook his head. – About the usual, about «wasting time and money on unspecified trial runs».

– Barryman is an idiot, Berkowitz said, smiling, once more showing his unusually good mood, – but a useful one...

West moved to the window, standing there for several minutes after Berkowitz had left the room. He spent some time attempting to admire the beautiful sunset, to no avail.

It always worried him when Anton joked.

Chapter Five: WICCA

Lights hidden in fog. Stars in the sky.

What was the wolf's reply to Little Red Riding Hood when she told him: «What a big tail you have, grandma».

Did he realize, in his arrogance, that he was being tricked? Or did he continue to look forward to an endless row of new, juicy meals?

One could wander through the fog forever without spotting lights. If one wandered too far the gray would swallow you.

Through the dark of the Night there were far more lights and they burned stronger.

The sun burned Main Street and the people on it. Jill stretched limbs and body opposite the bus stop. She didn't wear Walkman gear or its more modern equivalent like most of the people or joggers present, but she could hear the music. Hear it in their minds. She followed the beat with her right foot, moving it up and down in the dust. One girl, in full (expensive) training gear listened to «Nebraska» by Bruce Springsteen. Jill hadn't been born when that song was first released, but there was something eternal about it, something for the ages, speaking of suffering, alienation and desolation, the modern human condition.

She didn't really obtain the same level of clarity as she had done «communicating» with Stacy in Boston. It couldn't be called «mind reading». What she sensed was mostly emotions, an enhanced form of emotional expression. She and Stacy shared the same telepathic talent and they had been concentrating on sending, and at least Jill herself was unskilled. That could explain why she had some difficulty at this time. She knew she wouldn't stay that way, though, and that both exhilarated and frightened her. She wished there was someone she could talk to about this, someone with experience. An older witch would have been great, but she supposed, to her sorrow and rage, that there weren't that many around anymore.

An understatement if she had ever heard one.

Some feelings, though, were easy to interpret, like greed, like the man clutching the handle of his briefcase. To her it seemed like he couldn't take his eyes away from it. She could practically see the knuckles whitening.

Desire was even easier, especially by the way it made her feel. She saw the two teenagers, the boy and the girl she had seen the other day. They sat on the bench inside the shack, hidden from the sunlight, their emotions at least as raw as she remembered them. The two of them didn't have eyes for anybody except each other, but still, they were incessantly moving their eyes, keeping them on anyone that might happen to come close enough to approach them. They didn't kiss and snuggle like that other day. Nervousness had entered their lives now. They... did they love each other? Most certainly, this whirlpool of attraction, she sensed, couldn't be anything else. It dawned on Jill that they weren't considering taking the bus home, at least not their present ones. They did behave like they were on the run, or were considering running. The girl carried quite the heavy bag. Doubt and need alternated in their eyes and body language. Hey, perhaps mind reading wasn't more than being a good observer...

Go for it, kids!

Without even thinking about it, she had wished them good luck. She saw how they froze and stared. Not at her, but straight ahead, not knowing where the eerie voice originated from, not really understanding what it was.

Jill left them, focusing on other things. She started walking, and before she knew it, she was running. Her headband was already wet. During the next minute or so, it stopped being of any use whatsoever. Sweat was pouring into her eyes and the fact that the thin piece of cloth helped keeping her hair in place, seemed like a small, useless detail indeed.

But still, during breaks, she observed others attempting to run up and down the hills west of Northfield. (The school's gym classes, too, kept way off Frazer Hill). At first, she had felt... *distressed* by it, and not because they kept away from the Hill or their fear of the unknown, but because she had never really run much in her life. Not with her feet, anyway.

And she feared she would make a fool of herself.

That they would laugh at her.
She could admit to that not so flattering flair in herself. She could now.
It had been *hard*. But not as hard as she had imagined it would be. She had been highly motivated this time, compared to the few, feeble attempts she had done to get in shape earlier in her life. But she was still surprised. A year ago, two years ago, three and a half years ago, she had stopped almost immediately, the moment it started to hurt. This time she had pressed on, and after a while started to experience some strange elation. She knew about the body hormones, the endorphins released by physical hardship, she had read all about it. She had also read, though, that for it to work properly, a person had to reach a certain level of accomplishment in his and her endurance. And she was far from there, wasn't she?
She hadn't been able to keep pace with most of the girls, and she had pushed herself beyond endurance the first time. And her legs and thighs had been stiff like trees the day after, but it hadn't lingered, and it didn't linger anymore. There were still a lot of girls running faster and farther than her, but she was gaining on them.
Two minutes in the shower, and it seemed like two seconds. Rinsing, soap, rinsing, end. She didn't care. In the heat of the sun outside, she felt great. This had been the last school-related activity for the day. She was free to do whatever she wanted, to some extent and to the next morning.
She couldn't see any of her fellow conspirators around. Perhaps they had already gone to Sharon's pub? Before she knew it, she was on her way, so eager that she almost broke into a run. But no, she walked, and she soon realized that her will was no longer her own. There had been no forewarning. One moment she was her own woman, the next she wasn't. She should be afraid, she knew she should, but it was as if all her senses were dulled, to a point resembling sedation. Walk wasn't hurried, but slow and still deliberate, a puppet dancing to a tune. She knew there were people around her, she could hear them talk, but couldn't tell if they were talking to her. Distant eyes saw nothing but the path in her way. It wasn't exactly a compulsion at first, just a pull she was unable to resist, but it became one as she entered Main Street. Perhaps, at some point, she could have resisted. Not anymore. She saw them now, seven others. Everybody was known to her. She knew that much. But no matter how much she wanted to, she couldn't remember their names. Eight boys and girls walked their puppet dance with the same destination in mind. It wasn't Sharon's Inn, but Square. Square, where they were expected, and they were late, late, late
A little song was singing in their head, a lullaby calming them down, making all resistance melt away.
The gate to Square was hardly visible even to their dazed, extremely focused eyesight. They walked through it. The gate seemed to close behind them. The brick walls around the three-floor house were so tall that very little sunlight seemed to reach the yard, even if the sun should happen to be high in the sky, as it was now. The gate seemed to close behind them. Jill didn't see it happen, but she did sense it, and froze in her complete helplessness.
The door opened by the end of the long staircase. The eight walked inside in line like good boys and girls, into what they perceived more as the cave than a living room. She saw no windows, only a transcendent light, coming from nowhere, candles on the floor, illuminating nothing. It was as if everything beyond a certain point didn't exist to her.
Laurie Isherwood sat there, with one girl to her left and one boy to her right, inside a circle drawn with white chalk.
– Greetings, novices, welcome to my place, my sanctum. I trusted you to heed my call, to find your way here on your own, but you didn't, and that's why I sent out a stronger call.
She rose, towering above them. The chalk dissolved on the floor, candles were unlit, and the room was a room again.
She seemed angry somehow, about something, hiding it behind a stern mask. Jill sensed this, as her reason and self-determination slowly resurfaced. Slowly. When she looked at the others, she saw the same look of bewilderment and fear in their eyes, as she felt herself. They had all felt good about the Change, the Growth they'd gone through and had made, since their arrival in Northfield. But Laurie had taken control over them so very, very easily. Her demonstration had been quite effective, and they looked at her, and felt indeed like novices in her presence.
And then there were windows again. Then the room had details again. And it once more felt like they

were allowed to breathe. The hold she had on them lessened. They kept paying attention to her, kept straining their senses in order to accommodate the demands she placed on them.

– These are my first student witches, Udo Beyer and Andrea Natchios, she introduced her two aides. – They've been my confidantes and assistants for some time now. They've gone to school here and been in my service for one year and can tell you a lot of the pitfalls that may befall a young witch.

She walked to the table at the center of the room. All the new arrivals looked closer at her. They saw her far more clearly than they had when she was merely their appointed teacher. She wasn't old, at least not as old as the gray stripes in her hair or the premature lines in her face were suggesting. She had a slight limp they hardly noticed. There was nothing wrong with the strength of her body. On the contrary, there was something extremely… dynamic about her. And they had felt her natural authority and still did, something akin to a presence, so much stronger than in the classroom at school. She didn't hold it back now.

– This is still class and I'm your Teacher, Laurie said. – On these premises and on my farm in the outskirts of town, we'll cover knowledge not included in official textbooks.

The inside of the house was temperate and fresh-aired, compared to the searing heat outside. But there was more, and they had all sensed it the moment they had passed through the portal, a chill, thoughts like ice in the back of the mind, indescribable and such a departure from anything they had sensed so far in their young lives.

– Yes, the Teacher said, – this is something you must master, like everything else in your life. This is my aerie, my Place of Power, where I am at my strongest, a place consecrated, attuned to me as a witch. And because this is a place of Magic, you're also feeling stronger than usual, the inherent dangers and threats.

– What's happening to me? Jill asked fervently. – To us all?

The woman looked at them again, with a penetrating stare including them all.

– You know! You all do! Below ephemeral layers you know everything you need to know. You've felt an undefined *unrest* your entire life. You've come here in search of guidance, and to learn the secrets, pay the price. You've come here, to me, and I will guide you, steering you outside approaching pitfalls.

She waved, calling them to her, to the table and its... *varied* content.

– Please, have some fruit. Eagerly, Andrea made them aware of the huge basket of apples and oranges and a variety of both well-known and more exotic fruits. – We grow everything on the farm, using ecological methods.

The table was big and circular and had three legs. It had eight chairs. On it, in addition to the basket of fruit, there was certainly a lot of other stuff, not fit to digest.

– What is that? Jill asked, pointing to a powder in a mug formed as a nasty looking face.

– For curing stomach cramps, Udo offered in a teasing tone.

– Permanently then, I gather, Jill snorted.

Provoking a spontaneous laughter around the table. She laughed, too. It felt good to laugh.

Laurie, after drying her tears, covered all the windows with several layers of black curtains; making the huge and cozy living room turn dark and moody. She did it with her power, without physically touching the fabric, making her young charges gasp in awe.

And had, just like that reinstated her authority.

Jill grabbed a big, juicy apple and took a bite. She could just barely make out a taste of industrial pollutants. The factory was on the other side of town from the farm, without that being of much «help». Ecological farming did use lesser poisons then the usual agriculture venture, but it couldn't protect life from general pollution.

– You have chosen to walk the Shadows, Laurie said. – None of you will ever leave that path. Once one enters it, one can never leave. Looking back, the road you walked to that point isn't there anymore. Looking forward, a new path, not previously there is reveals itself.

The newcomers were using the chairs. The hostess and her brood faced them from the other side of the table.

– Yes, she said, I did find you; I brought you here, from various ends of the Earth. As you may have gathered, I have considerable resources at my disposal. I've made preparations for such a venture for some time now. I took Udo and Andrea and others under my wings last year, as another stepping-stone to what I've planned.

Jill wanted to ask her what she had planned, but she couldn't get the words out through a seemingly constricted throat.

– As I soon will demonstrate for you, we live in dangerous times. The way of *Wicca,* the modern pagan beliefs, is to live a non-confrontational life. We do call ourselves witches, but don't stress it at every point, making it more difficult for the ignorant to point at us.

– Wicca? Stacy said, very deliberate, – isn't that a religion? You won't force us to conform to that, will you?

– I would ask you to humor me on this. Hear me out and then you may decide for yourself what you want. You won't deny me that, will you?

She turned her entire attention to Stacy and the girl shook slightly, being diminished under the wrathful stare of the experienced witch.

– N-no.

– Leave her alone! Jason spoke up and rose from his chair. – We're not your subjects and won't be treated thus.

Jill blinked. Was it a trick of the light or her imagination, or had his eyes... glowed slightly just then? Slightly, for just one, tiny moment?

– ... Forgive me, Laurel apologized. – It's just that there's so much I have to teach you, so much you need to learn, so fast. You're of course under no obligation to stay, but I'll ask that you do, that you will follow my teachings, my ways, for a while, before you decide if it's right for you.

There was something in her voice, in her wording, that Jill didn't quite care for, even if she couldn't pinpoint exactly what. And she did feel excitement. In fact, merely the sight of the regal Witch made her occasionally all tingly with anticipation.

– You'd want to proceed with... caution? Making the general population used to witches, as an integrated part of the community?

– That is *exactly* what I'm «up to», Kieron. The very context of non-violent beliefs is to act non-aggressively confronted with intolerance and ignorance. Education and a careful approach are essential here.

– Everyone, please let me introduce you to this fine young gentleman, she continued, sarcastically, deliberately using comic relief. – This is Kieron Dane, coming to us directly from the Outback, Australia.

– Hello, people, nice to meet you all, I want you all to know I feel great being here in your company.

It felt like meeting him for the first time.

And he bowed before the audience. There were cheers and applause from first to last row.

His accent was not particularly Australian. They were told that he hadn't lived much in Australia, except for the last few years. His facial features clearly illustrated that he at least was from three different «worlds». He was dark skinned, as were all of the eight newcomers, and a synthesis of Negroid, Caucasian and Mongoloid races, and absolutely fascinating… like everybody here, Jill thought, quite proud.

– Say: «I am a Witch», Laurel bade him.

– Gee, I don't know... he said a bit flippant. – Do I look like one?

They were all grinning a bit. It was a good joke.

– Go far enough back in time and «witch» is a word used for all practitioners of Witchcraft, the woman said icily. – Man, Woman, Bearers of Knowledge... and Power.

Suddenly, without any preceding warning, Kieron and the chair he sat on were thrust backwards. He hadn't done anything. They knew that. Nothing visible had done the pushing. Nothing even close could have done it. The chair stopped, as suddenly as it started moving, and Kieron flew up from it and up in the air. He was stretched out in all his considerable length, from a visible distance above the floor, to the high ceiling. His expression made it clear to the others that he had nothing to do with it, if they should ever entertain such notions. He was levitating and it seemed like gravity didn't have any influence on him, any at all.

And just like that, their world had changed forever. If they had entertained the thought, in moments of doubt that the last few days and nights had been a dream, they did so no longer. It had a tremendous impact on them all.

– You win, he said in a hoarse whisper. – I'm a Witch.

Nobody laughed this time. They were simply too stunned.

Laurie circled the levitating boy with a slight, sarcastic smile on her lips. Her forehead was slightly lined in concentration.

– You're being watched, studied, assessed. Get used to it! It's the way of the world.

She turned her hand around. His body started spinning slowly, the right leg of his pants sliding up to the knee. There, on the leg, they saw a big mole - a birthmark. Jill felt a cold tingle down her spine.

– Yes, this is your witchmark, the sign of your stature as an elevated being. You all have it, share it. I don't know why, but the reason is no doubt hidden far back in ancient times, and has no doubt, significance to your present and future.

Kieron (was) dumped back into the chair. A girl was lifted up in the air.

– This witch was an aspiring voodoo priestess in New Orleans and has quite a bit more advance experience than the rest of you. Say hello to Henriette Gallier.

They did so, even if they had known her for days already.

– I am *Loeb,* the girl said forcefully, – and that's also my given name. The other one was given me for the sake of family «harmony». They attempted to hide my roots.

Stacy Larkin was lifted up from the chair, from the floor. Her long brown hair fell like a waterfall down her back, seemingly combed back from her forehead.

– Yes, I'm a witch, and I'm gonna fly through the Night by my own Power.

The next was Rae Morgan. She was from South America somewhere. Laurie didn't specify it. She was the only one of them that had light, blond hair. Her Native inheritance, though mixed with others was clearly visible in her features. And in spite of the color... her hair had a strange, undefined quality.

Jill was drawing in everything she felt, and everything being said and done inside the room. She was reintroduced to Travis Nichols and Ivan Silvestri and didn't mind. And then she felt the pull in her body and she experienced levitation under the ceiling. Telekinesis, she thought, mind over matter, remote control of energy. She and Stacy had both accomplished it, but that, in retrospect, felt like parlor tricks compared to this.

– It tickles, she giggled, clearly excited, her wild heart beating.

She felt... at home here.

– As you probably have gathered, you're all showing major traits of mixed blood, as people are fond of saying, Laurie said. – I sought that. You have Magic from many tribes in that blood, variety and diversity. And strength.

– Jason here, Jason Gallagher, can, for instance trace his ancestral path back to they who were the People of Legend in Europe and North Africa, not those called it centuries later. But this is just some centuries anyway. If we measure in millennia, you may all stem from the same source or similar sources. Anyway, you have a bond, a similar aura I noticed immediately. You, too, will sense it, stronger by each passing day.

We already do, Jill thought. Did she imagine it, or was there a flash of anger on the edge of the teacher's vision?

Jason was the last one lifted up in the air and displayed. Jill noticed absentmindedly that his mole looked different, that it wasn't really a mole at all, but merely a pale discoloration.

The initial demonstration was done. The newcomers held their breath.

Jill cocked her left eyebrow. Was Laurie tired? She seemed unfettered enough, even unfazed, but something... there it was... Jill concentrated. For a while she did nothing but look, and she noticed the change in the aura before her.

She had always been able to see «auras». Not all the time, but often enough, to take it for granted. Never anything as clearly and easily made out as this, though. Her Talent had improved, and not just because she had realized its potential and how it was part of something much, much more.

Laurie left the room. They weren't certain they should follow her, so they remained. Udo and Andrea did, too, even if they placed themselves on the opposite side from where the newcomers sat.

The time outlasted an odd while, and one by one (Stacy was first), they left their chairs and started exploring. If there was one thing they had in common, besides the Talent, it was curiosity. And this room alone and the entire place contained so much interesting stuff. They felt clearly that this one room in this small house was merely the beginning. Still, it contained more impressions than they had experienced in entire cities. One second gave them more than hours had done in their existence before this one.

They studied, sensed the room, seeking out, savoring its treasures. It wasn't their arrival here in itself that had heightened their awareness, their sensitivity. The entire town had a history filled to the brim with impressions. Most of all it was caused by their newfound confidence, in themselves, in their ability to confront adversity. Their inner self, what was hidden in their innermost being, had not been a certainty before, as it was now. Now, the Shadow World, to this point merely existing in their half-awakened dreams, slowly turned into a tangible reality, to enthusiasm and creepy fear.

Jill's eyes singled out a statue, lonely in a room full of similar statues, of artifacts and ancient dust. It was placed on a shelf, admittedly a bit removed from others, but why had she singled it out? Lonely... what a strange word to use in connection with a statue.

It reminded her of something, she didn't know what. It was supposed to be of one human, she convinced herself of that fairly easy, but it was a representation of two melded bodies, two heads, turned away from each other. Two faces, identical as not even two snowflakes out of millions could ever be.

– *I'm a Witch,* the girl muttered to herself, being able to say it for the first time, without picturing a dried out old hag with an evil eye and fangs, in her mind.

She stroked her fingertips over the surface of the statue, attempting to hypnotize herself to more sensitive skin, to increase her sensitivity. She didn't receive more than general impressions of age and distance. Then a hand reached out for the statue from her opposite side, stroked it as she did, and the impressions were enhanced tenfold. There were images now, suddenly, lives to be experienced, to be lived. And the statue wasn't two, wasn't merely duality, but manifold, many, countless sides. Another body stood by the side of hers. She was only vaguely aware of it, as if this world was the dream, not the impressions from the statue. She turned her head and she and Stacy Larkin stared into each other's eyes.

– Cool, isn't it?

– Yes, great, Jill smiled.

Both comments encompassed a broad specter of emotions and subtle meanings.

– So, what are you doing here among this bunch of losers, Stacy inquired merrily. – For some *weird* reason I don't think I've actually asked you that pertinent question before.

Here, this town, not only this room, this smaller gathering. The question, aided by Stacy's mind contained so much more than mere words.

– I've always been a... stranger. Jill, her mind filled with images, sensations thought about it a bit more. – I've always longed to live among strangers.

– I see, Stacy said.

Skin touched, touched cold metal frame. Together they were capable of hearing distant thunder, ancient thunder, thunder from the gathering, approaching Storm, a glimpse of understanding. No more, of things unclear.

A burst of smoke suddenly appeared in the middle of the room. When the cloud dispersed Laurie once more stood before them.

– Parlor tricks! Stacy cried out in contempt.

Laurie was dressed in darker clothes now, a suggestion, a hint of Mystery.

Very clever, Jill thought impulsively.

– We Witches stand between the visible and invisible world, Laurie began. Voice seemed different, more penetrating, and impossible to close off, as she closed off Stacy's remark. – Many See, but don't know they do, or they refuse to. Many know, but refuse to see the obvious.

She didn't look at Stacy. It wasn't necessary to do that, to convey her displeasure.

– One crucial fact is that Witches are not created, they're *born.* But many possessing the talent are squandering it, by not using it, or merely dabbling. Like any other talent, for music, art or carpentry, it must be stimulated and directed to work. Or to not work wrong.

– I'll train you, teach you to not take wrong steps. What being pagan, what being Wicca, is about, is to live in peaceful coexistence with the rest of the world, to share magic, to share the world and to live by the word of the Goddess and God.

Jill recognized something in these words. She couldn't quite identify it, but wasn't certain it was anything positive. It made her shudder. She sensed that Stacy wanted to say something, but didn't dare.

But weren't the lot of them really brainwashed to react with contempt and enmity towards Wicca or any alternative belief? She should give Laurie and her teaching the benefit of the doubt, shouldn't she?

– The Goddess is the center of our existence and our only comfort in difficult times. I've felt her several times, like a warm blanket surrounding me, strengthening me, through fear and hardship and adversity.

A panel in the wall slid aside without any «traditional» act leading to it. No one was close to any buttons, no one moved anything. It could, of course have been a trick, if they hadn't already seen what they had seen. The boys and girls were more surprised to see a TV and a video player revealed in this «old» room.

– There are lots of interesting things hidden in this area, much of interest. Not all of it free of danger. The world is a dangerous place, both because of sorcery and other, mundane aspects of it. I won't deny that. Instead, I feel I must stress it to you. You must learn. We live in a hostile world and it's paramount that we know how to counter this. Both the incredible and the mundane may break you. There *is* a price to pay, seeking forbidden knowledge, but I do know about the pitfalls and I will teach you how to avoid them.

Her words and seriousness made them uneasy.

– I do not wish to frighten you, children, but you've got a lot to learn, and this is a good place to start. Let it be a lesson in human behavior.

An outsider here, something they were not any longer, would have wondered and believed the electronic devices turned themselves on by themselves or they (the outsiders) would have believed they were being conned. The youths knew Laurie pushed the buttons and turned everything on without physically touching anything.

The video player started humming and images filled the screen. Flickering, flowing, flickering, flowing. Anyone could see this wasn't anything even approaching a professional recording, and that the same could be said about the equipment being used, that had been used. The objects were often unfocused, especially the telephoto recordings and the camera - or the person holding it - had been shaking quite badly. Shaking in body and, as they could hear, without trying, in voice. Both his «live» comments and also everything recorded afterwards. He couldn't forget and neither could they, as if it was already burned into their mind. They felt the horror before they saw it.

– There was nothing I could do, nothing I could've done. I realize this, even as I'm torn apart by guilt. They would've just torn me physically apart, before proceeding with their unholy mission. They... the people down there... just a few days ago, they were my friends, my brothers and sisters in the congregation. These human beings with the most hideous, demonic appearances...

The fleeting overall pictures showed a typical American small town. There were farms around forest-clad hills, cows and sheep grassing on the field, small shops without built-in, pulled-down fences on the windows. Picturesque to the max.

Suddenly the scene shifted, in focus, in mood, to a narrow backstreet. Twilight had set in. The modern houses could just as well have been other buildings, built three centuries earlier. The movie was recorded from a viewpoint above the street, through a window on the first floor. There was movement, swift and deadly, one girl backing away from a huge, threatening crowd. They walked one step forward every time she took one step back.

– Keep away from me, she screamed hysterically. – Don't touch me, don't come near me. I don't know what's happening. PLEASE! I don't know who's doing it, I can't control it.

A man took one step more than the others.

– Don't come any closer, she screamed wailing.

The man rushed forward. She desperately struck a hand in empty air. The man, huge and powerful halted abruptly, howled and fell on the ground, silent, still.

– *NO! NO!* She pressed a hand to her mouth, turned abruptly and started to run.

The mob had stopped a moment, frozen in their tracks, but now they resumed their forward movement, chasing her like a single, undulating mass. They caught up with her and grabbed hold of the shivering body, hooked her paralyzed mind. Without further ado they started beating her up. Strangely enough it got orderly quite fast. The senseless attacks ceased. Two held her arms, while the others took turns of hitting or kicking or punishing her.

– *STOP!* A man shouted in a commanding voice. He stepped forward. A priest. A small hope was lit in the girl, in the onlookers. Why the onlookers couldn't say. – *We must do this right. She's a witch, a servant of Satan. She must be punished!*

The agitated crowd calmed down, overpowered by one of their foremost authoritative figures.

– *She must Die!* The horrible voice continued. – *But not before she's correctly punished, according to the law of God. She must suffer the death all witches have made themselves deserving of.*

– *I couldn't do anything,* they heard the desolate, despairing voice of the man recording it all. – *Except the smallest, most cowardly thing, to make sure this atrocity is revealed to the world. Perhaps it will do other potential future victims some good.*

The scene shifted again, into clusters of trees, a country road and hill, a sea of burning torches. The good, righteous people of the town had tied the girl's wrists together on her back. Several loops of rope tightened around her neck. She was pulled and sometimes pushed forward, but they didn't dare get too close to her too often. They pulled her with the ropes over the field, towards the hill, the slight rise in the terrain. The yet unlit pyre awaited in silhouette to the horizon just after sunset.

The very young girl, she couldn't be a day over fifteen, stumbled forward with a completely unintelligible expression in her white, bloodied face. Clothes were torn and she was dirty after having fallen countless times. Every time they used the ropes and whips to force her back on her feet.

– *You can't do this,* she droned on in deep apathy, – *I have done no wrong. I have done no wrong.*

– How can they DO something like that? Rae cried out in disbelief.

The girl wavered and stumbled the last stretch to the awaiting pyre, to a crown of branches and sticks, with the thick stake raised in the middle. One pushed deep into the ground. Very elaborately done. The mob had never done this before in their entire life, but they seemed to be very good at it.

They removed the nooses around her neck, not wanting her to strangle herself. She was pulled to the stake and placed there with her back to it. A man signaled for rope, and some was thrown to him. Suddenly he grabbed his own throat. Eyes bulged in his skull, and he fell, rolled off the witch's crown. Tears jumped from the girl's eyes. She shook her head in shock and denial. They hesitated a bit, before charging her from all sides with fear and hatred in their eyes, tying her hard and brutally to the post.

– *I can see the police chief down there,* the observer's strangled, hardly noticeable voice was heard. – *The mayor, Robertson, Webster, Bennett and a slew of our town's prominent members.*

– *«Thou shall not suffer a witch to live»!* The priest cried out in a dramatic gesture.

– *Burn the witch!* A woman shouted her hatred.

– *I know her, too. God help me. In this eternal night I don't know if I can beg His forgiveness for any of them. Their manifested hatred seems, after all, so pale compared to my own.*

– *Light thy own fire, witch,* the priest roared. Saliva flowed from his mouth. Nobody seemed to notice.

The girl's eyes cleared a moment. Her mouth formed a single word.

Burn! Jill thought, cold deep in her soul.

The jacket sleeve of the arm the old, strict man pointed at her caught fire. He screamed and started to *howl* when he couldn't put it out. Many threw away their torches and started to walk away, a walk soon to break into a run. But most stayed and threw their torches on the dry wood and hay. Fire rose immediately around the young and untrained witch.

– *I know who I am now,* she cried into the night. – *What you've made me. May you all burn in hell for doing this to me, who has never done you any harm.*

The priest struggled to free himself of his cloak. He finally made it and threw it on the ground. It burned so fast that one was tempted to believe someone had soaked it in gasoline.

His face ashen, but ever contracted in wrath.

The girl's face and eyes were to the last filled with an infinite incredulity, even when the thin wails reverberated through the night air, and tore into those who heard them.

– NONONO, why didn't she DO anything? Loeh pressed her hands to her ears, of course in vain. Long nails ripped the skin of her cheeks. There was no warning beyond this. The television screen cracked from one side to the other, with a laud, sharp sound. There were more cracks. Everybody twitched. Loeh's eyes widened. She was paralyzed to the point where she turned calm immediately. Arms fell from the face and down. She looked incredulous at the smoking, totaled heap of a television set.

– Sorry, she mumbled, without really realizing why.

– She didn't have any control over what she could do, Rae said. – She didn't discover it until it was too late.

At first it, being a witch, had been a source of embarrassment to them. Now, seeing the movie, they got a taste of what it could mean. They had always known that people feared what was different, but had not realized, not consciously, to what extent.

Frightened, on the verge of tears, they gathered around Laurie.

– This recording was shown on a few local TV-stations, Laurie said, as she comforted Loeh, pleased because her students had realized what the lesson was about, – before it was stopped. Very few really wanted to see it, you see, wanted to have their cozy little fantasy about life screwed up. No steps were taken to punish the perpetuators, not even to find out who they were or what town they came from. The united states' parliament, the congress, you see, has long since passed laws minimizing the possibility of Wicca practitioners to practice their religion. They're not allowed to have tax returns on income stemming from practicing the Craft, an «arrangement» all other «clean» religions have. And there are a thousand large and small obstructions to make it all the more difficult for us. Representatives do not wish to go on record supporting Witchcraft, a belief that for centuries now has been seen as the Devil's work.

– But people practicing Wicca do not believe Satan exists? Jason said.

– No, they don't! Laurie said.

Laurie had released Loeh. The girl leaned against the wall. Tears still flowed freely down her cheeks and made the wounds sting even more. Jill moved to her side without really knowing why. She suddenly had this strange feeling, compulsion inside. This moment, now, it was all that mattered. She wanted to comfort the girl, lessen her suffering. She put her hands on the wet and bloodstained cheeks, these hands, suddenly so warm. She felt energy passing through them. Both she and Loeh whimpered, but stayed put.

Jill let her hands sink down in her lap. She felt the headache this time, too, but far from the paralyzing, crippling pain she had endured just a few days ago.

Everybody, including herself, stared astonished at the brown and fair-skinned face, so torn just a few seconds ago, a face where the scratches were hardly visible now.

Loeh ran to the closest mirror, on the wall, on the other side of the room.

– It isn't just the... scratches, she said devout. – I feel so much better, too... in spite of it all. Better mood, better everything. It feels fantastic, Jill, how did you do it?

– I... don't know, Jill replied, hesitating, still staring at her hands.

– Light one of the candles on the commode, Laurie told Loeh lightly, – you'll see better.

– But I don't need... I don't have...

– You'll want to see better, won't you? I said: Light it!

Loeh Gallier seemed to jolt or something. There was a loud crack and fire rose from the candle. The girl almost jumped in shock.

– It made the headache return.

– Look at it as a muscle needing exercise, Laurie explained. – After a while with regular use, the soreness wears off.

What they had seen and heard and felt sank deep in. Contradictory reactions were revealed in their faces and eyes, sinking deep, like hooks and fangs buried in their throat.

– I've always seen myself as a rebel, a Stranger, Travis began hesitatingly. – What I mean is... Hell, I've always wanted to be a part of something like this. Perhaps *she* never thought like that. And that's why the shock was so big for her, too big for her, paralyzing her to the point where she couldn't defend herself as she could have done, if she had accepted her talent, accepted herself.

– What happened to her can happen to anyone, and anyone of us, Kieron stressed.

– I know! Travis said a bit agitated. – My point is that we have a better chance, just by coming here.

Stacy didn't seem to listen to the discussion. Smiling and in control she sat down in the sofa beside Loeh.

– There will be no scars, she told her.

– Are you sure? Loeh said, still with tears in her eyes. – How...

Stacy touched the other girl's cheeks with only one hand. It glowed just a bit in the dark room. The last, remaining scratches disappeared.

– Yes! Stacy said.

She's really confident, Jill thought.

– Wow, two of them, Kieron said. – We could have taken quite a bit of pain if all of us could've done that.

– That's not very likely, Laurie interjected. – Two healers are a lot in a group of eight, eighteen or even hundred witches. Like Loeh, you have other talents. We'll find them soon enough, find them together.

– But we, Stacy and I have more than one, Jill burst out, ignoring Stacy's cautious look, it was too late anyway. – Like y-you.

– Yes, Laurie said.

– No matter, with two such sweet nurses we're off to a good start. Ivan stressed that he was teasing with an admiring smile.

It didn't fully work, though. Jill flushed like the biggest of toilets and hated herself.

They laughed together, couldn't help it, couldn't resist it. Slowly the numbing scare released its hold on them. It dawned on them that they really did belong together, in ways they never could have imagined before *exactly this moment.* And it had happened so quickly. They hardly knew each other. They didn't know each other. But they did. Everybody recognized this feeling of... companionship as real. All of this was real.

They looked at Laurie with anticipation and gratitude.

All of their thoughts were focused inside this room. Laurie smiled, a thin smile. The first step had been successfully implemented.

– I can read your minds, you know, she said, rewarding them. – I am a telepath. But my major Power in that regard, as you may have noticed, is in terms of projection, in my ability to transfer my thought patterns to others.

– Yes! Jill nodded excited. – To hear you tell stories is almost like being there, so lifelike.

You're a treasure, dear, so young and full of life, so eager to learn.

And Jill blushed some more.

– You have, all of you, looked your entire life for a teacher, someone to guide you in a dangerous and uncertain world, to teach you about the world, give you your devoirs, your totems, the proof of your existence. You're lucky. Many people do look their entire life, without finding more than scraps and pieces of the necessary information. I'll teach you, as you'll support me, and support the decisions I make on your behalf. What I've given you so far is indeed only the first bits of knowledge, insight. It's nothing compared to what I *will* give you. You are bright students, but you need dedication and must want to learn, too.

She gave them a token, a nudge of joy in their mind, and they were grateful.

– Go now, digest what you've learned. It will not be long before you're ready for more.

2

The white inside Square bathed in sunlight. The day after, after school, eight eager witches and one, showed up like clockwork outside Laurie Isherwood's Sanctum, standing in line like good girls and boys.

Laurie appeared in the door, and somewhat easily made her way down to them. Jill held Tamara's arm in a comforting grip, pushing her slightly forward.

– Ah, you've brought us another recruit, Laurie beamed, – what an inventive mind. So, little one, do you have anything to tell me?

Tamara towered over her, as she did with most people.

– I am a w-witch, the girl said.
– So, tell me, what can you do... as a witch?
– I don't... know.
– That's fair enough. The teacher waved off her regrets. – That's a difficulty you share with several of those present. Whatever you can do, making you Special, we'll eventually discover together.
Gratitude and admiration immediately lit the big girl's face. A slight nudge and a few kind words, and she was won over.
Laurie started circling the nine, steady and confident.
– You've returned to me, of your own free will, she began. – It's time to begin. Your personal Hell Week starts this minute, and if you think the mundane boys and girls got it rough during their Week, you should really reconsider. Theirs are just a pale reflection of your perils. Yours are a true Initiation, as it was done in ancient times.
Jill felt a start in her own body; so slight she didn't think anybody else could notice it. She saw the flames, the fires, already. The many fires and torches, making the witches sweat. Tongues of the yellow and red light from the fire illuminated the ground. The Night remained dark. She heard drums and voices, and she felt the pull tug at her. The trees, the trees cast their Shadow, and so did the witches. She saw Stacy, in the night, in the present day, and knew that she saw, too. Just an eternity of a second, then the images, no, the visions were gone.
– Fortunately, the school board didn't give me any significant trouble when I wanted to remove you from the traditional curriculum for a week. They shouldn't either, of course. I've prepared them for you, for the fact that your personal curriculum would require my personal touch. Special… *gifted* people need special teaching. Anyway, you'll be required to catch up fast with the rest of your classes, so there's really no problem.
– But we do not aspire to belong to a fraternity? Rae said.
– You most certainly do, one of the oldest on Earth, to the Coven, the Circle of Witches.
– All the modern ones are just pale reflections of that, Stacy said with a proud stance.
– That's right, Maiden, that's right, Laurie said pleased.
She got to her, Jill thought impulsively, *by appealing to her vanity.*
Like she got to me...
– Follow me, witches, Laurie said.
And so, they did.
There was a shed in the backyard, a pretty worn-down attachment to the house. It was still standing. Aside from that, how long it would remain so was an open question.
– There are workbenches inside, they were told, – and tools and stuff. You will clean up the place and fix it up. When that is done to my satisfaction, I may tell you some secrets...
She left them then. But they felt her presence in their mind, they always did.
The shed was hot, even hotter than the inferno outside, and they were soon soaking wet. Skin and clothes and hair were covered by dust and dirt and hardened sweat.
S-spiders, there are spiders here.
Nothing is really wrong with spiders, she corrected herself forcefully.
Phobias were stupid, and fear of (most) spiders was high on the list of the silliest around.
But it didn't exactly improve her spirit.
None of the nine were used to any kind of labor, far less this hard, unrelenting version of it. And it didn't stop, but continued, continued, continued... And suddenly they were working in the field, picking potatoes, digging in the dirt. Digging, digging, digging... There had been some sense of accomplishment in the shed there at the end... or had it? Was it merely a Mirage the clean, spider free room they had seen? In their fever, in their fever dreams, constantly digging into their skull, their self. They were really working in the field, picking potatoes, picking fruit, were they not? Jill wasn't certain, she couldn't feel any fresh air in her lungs, any at all. And each breath she drew caused untold suffering of fire and brimstone. It was like working in a mine, a lava pit, the way she had always imagined it.
You are cruel, cruel, cruel, she wanted to shout at Laurie.
But no sound vibrated through her larynx, no words were formed on her lips. She wasn't even

allowed that.

And worse. She feared she couldn't sense anything but the heat and the suffering.

But... that was okay, wasn't it? This was an initiation after all, and initiations were supposed to be tough... right? Who was she who could say how it should've been done?

They sat crouched in a shade, in the grass, hidden from the relentless sun by bushes. Andrea administered fruit juice to them all, effectively, remote, silent. They could see again, feel again, sense again, see, feel and sense each other, the surroundings. They noticed two things: Laurie wasn't here. And Andrea bled from her nose. As did Jill, Stacy and Jason.

– I heard a scream... of Rage, Loeh said uncertain.

– You were just imagining it, don't you think so? Andrea corrected her.

They wondered. Was this the first words they had heard her speak?

Birds were still ascending from trees.

– My throat is sore, Jill half whispered.

– The heat can be a killer out in the fields these days, Andrea said sweetly. – Here, have some more.

Jill drank greedily from the big glass. Andrea filled it up to the rim and she emptied it thoroughly. She could feel the cold, refreshing fruit juice flow down her still dry throat, all the way to the stomach.

The surroundings were quiet, peaceful and the air had a fresh quality not present in city streets. The wind cooled their bodies and minds, even if they didn't, in any way feel chilled in their dripping wet clothes.

– Come, Andrea said, – Laurie is waiting for you.

The nine novices followed her between rows of apple trees and through tiny valleys between tiny mounds, but most of all across one enormous field. And even when most of the land was behind them, there was a considerable stretch through what was essentially a garden.

– How big is it? Rae asked big eyed.

– The farm is one of the major ones in the state, Andrea explained willingly enough. – Laurie's influence is also stretching way beyond this small piece of land.

She sounded almost... proud when she said that.

There were other people on the farm. The nine could see them now and then, working in the garden. But there weren't many compared to the size of it all. Jill guessed it was a seasonal thing. People were called in when it was time for the harvest.

If there would be any this year. This place wasn't much better off than the rest of draught-ridden New England.

Laurie sat on the porch. It was a big porch, a big house, and she sat in a throne-like chair, high above the floor. Flanking her were seven people, including Udo, dressed in what could be described as formal «witch wear», cloak and hood. The neophytes stopped. Andrea joined the others on the porch. She was handed the cloth and immediately let it slip over her head. Then, she was suddenly indistinguishable from the others.

It can also be described as a costume, Jill thought, good humored and she strove to guard her thoughts, probably in vain. For some odd reason this added thought made her feel even more... good humored.

– You've all visited the Hill, I presume Laurie stated.

– Oh, yes, I did it yesterday, Tamara exclaimed, still eager. – Some... place!

– This will no doubt aid you somewhat in your Initiation, Laurie continued unfazed. – From now on, however, I'll determine your further course.

And I'll show you wonders you've hardly imagined.

Everybody «heard» her, clear and distinct in their head, words, but also a texture so much richer than ordinary speech, not just the words, but their deeper modulation.

This is all so absolutely fantastic, isn't it? A silent cry of pure joy came from Jill.

Everybody turned to look at her and stare. Her transmission had been almost as extensive and all-inclusive as that of Laurie. They wouldn't have believed that anybody but the teacher could speak to them all simultaneously and not with that kind of strength. And Jill was a novice, a newbie, just at the start of her Path. What that very fact entailed hit them, suddenly, not to be ignored.

The girl could sense it in them all, transparent as glass.

– A... voice, not ours, not yours, Udo, Udo the aide, Udo the blockhead said to Laurie. – Who...
– Oh, it's just young Jill here, strutting her stuff. Don't worry about it. It's perfectly natural. Inexperience will lead to subconscious use of power.
The laughter, however, did not seem natural. Jill did laugh with the others. She couldn't help it. She felt joy, after all. But what she did most of all was waiting. And then, just after a short break she felt it, Laurie's intrusive and probing mind inside her own. She was helpless to deny the more experienced witch access. An imagined shield didn't do much good. She felt so light, everything was floating... while the other accessed and assessed her.
Don't worry about it. Be calm. I could've enslaved you at any time, if that's what I truly wanted. Trust me!
She didn't, but that was beside the point. She felt anger... and more. With a force of will she had no previous conscious knowledge of, she tore herself out of the other's «grip», the velvet spell she had been under. The ceiling lamp exploded in an infinite number of pieces, and they rained down on the amazed onlookers. Jill felt the terrible headache from the first day return with a vengeance and was very relieved when she saw that Laurie couldn't do anything to keep her own hand from her head.
– As I was saying... Laurie joked, but her smile was strained. – These things happen from time to time. You'll get used to it.
Just a moment there, while Jill had been counterattacking, she had felt Laurie's thoughts. Felt more of her being. Jill began to fear that the teacher's authority was a bit too strong. She had an agenda, one possibly blinding her to the means she used.
Jill had made some attempts as an actor, at the local theater in the city where she had grown up. She wasn't very good. What she was most lacking was the ability to spin illusions. She didn't feel quite okay when doing that. In spite of what she knew, that illusions were no more right or wrong than other tools or methods. Still, it made her feel uncomfortable. But she recognized a Stage when she saw one.
And this was one.
– We'll eat now, Laurie said and motioned them to follow her inside.
They sat by the long table in the huge living room. Servants put food on the table. Laurie dismissed them with a wave of her hand.
– Praise the Goddess, Andrea intoned, – for the food we're about to eat.
– *Praise the Goddess,* all the witches repeated. The novices automatically following the lead of the older and more experienced.
The food was basically vegetarian. Jill had tried it out before, and discarded it as a way of life, but never food as good, as delicious as this. Paprika, fruit, oyster (which, by the way was an animal) and all sort of grown stuff. There were animals on the farm, though, and animal food on the table. Milk, meat and butter. Jill tried it all and everything tasted great. Only with the greatest regret did she manage to hold herself back.
And she felt great otherwise, too.
The headache was obviously waning already, much faster this time. She could feel it... fade by the minute, and even faster when she concentrated on it. She realized she could make it disappear, that she could heal herself. And amazingly, the pain in her limbs subsided, too.
After a time, she reached out with her power anew, and didn't experience any pain or difficulty.
She did feel, with her heightened sensitivity, a change around the table.
Dinner was about to end.
They all sat back, filled up, still filled with Hunger.
– I'm going to tell you about the Goddess now, Laurie said, standing.
The chatter died and they listened.
– I met the Goddess in a time of great despair, at my lowest ebb. I took a walk through the forest, an act that had always sustained me before. This time, however, it made everything worse. All my sense of failure was accumulating inside. Then I came to a glade. And I «saw» her. She gave me the feeling that it was all worth it, and showed me what I should do, to turn my life around. Everything in my life had been building to this moment. I found my Destiny. Everything opened up for me, by the end of the forest. I did her bidding and felt how right it was. In my former life I had disliked society to the point that I didn't want to involve myself in it, instead of attempting to instigate positive change.
– Ted Warren says that we shouldn't participate in society, Jill said. – Or participate as little as

possible. That it's a hopeless task to build on a rotten foundation.

– Warren? Laurie snorted. – An anarchist, a nihilist, and completely without social skills to boot.

Once again something in her voice alerted Jill to a deeper, possibly concealed context.

– No, that can't be right, Rae said dreamily. – The way I've heard it he's not lacking any in social skill...

Laurie pulled herself together, calming herself with a force of will.

– We must show him and all like him that it is possible to work within the system.

She showed them her image of the Goddess then, and many of them gasped, and forgot almost everything else. They couldn't recreate it later in their mind, but it filled them to the brim, leaving room for nothing else.

– It's time! The Teacher stated. – Do you nine want to be initiated into our circle, our coven? Are you *ready?*

– Yes! They replied in unison.

– *Yes!* Jill, Jason, Stacy and all the others said, with stars in their eyes.

– Then follow me!

She has been preparing this for a long time, Jill thought, woven her spells, her web, made her keys to her Kingdom.

The Teacher walked up the stairs, to the attic. They followed her, walking in line, as well behaved and attentive students.

They emerged into the attic, a huge single room, covering the entirety of the upper floor. Laurie's other witches, all eight of them, welcomed the newbies with silence and cold stares. They stood upright in their hoods and cloaks, forming a perfect, almost complete circle.

The sun burned them through the open windows in the ceiling. There was a lot of light, surrounding them all. And all the open windows made them imagine they were standing completely outside. They felt like they were standing on air. But there were walls, and the air was thick and difficult to breathe. Laurie stood in the center of the circle, with one young witch on each side.

– We have nine novice witches who want to join our Coven today, she said. – They're nine, as we are nine. Welcome them.

And (as if) on cue.

– Welcome witches, the choir of voices and minds greeted them.

So friendly, so friendly, friendly. Through Laurie they could sense their presence in their own minds.

Laurie gestured for them to join her, join them in the Circle, and they did, one by one.

– Leave your clothes behind, as you leave yourself behind.

Jason was the first. He undressed and stepped into the circle. Jill saw him fully. She couldn't avoid it, as he turned towards them. There was no shame. Even she didn't feel any. She wasn't sure it was a good thing.

Laurie touched Jason's forehead.

– Be embraced by the Goddess, accept her blessing. Blessed Be.

– *Blessed Be,* everybody repeated.

He was given his cloak and hood, dressed by the two aides, and then he took his place in the circle.

Stacy was next. She had the same dreamlike look as Jason, so distant from their usual cocky demeanor that the wrongness of it made Jill want to cry out. But she couldn't move. Not her body, not her lips. She was the third entering the circle. Clothes just fell off her. Everything felt dreamlike, but it was real, real, real. She stood outside herself, and saw Laurie touch her forehead, saw herself be dressed in the ceremonial garb. And at the same time, she sensed the fabric of the cloth touch her skin, she registered when she joined the circle, and felt its Power.

Felt its power increasing, as the number of witches increased, the jolt, as they were all holding hands. Saw Laurie smile. Saw everybody else smile in Joy.

– Witches, Laurie said to them, – feel the Gift of the Goddess.

And this time it wasn't a jolt, but something far more powerful.

– Praise the Goddess, Rae suddenly gasped. She was immediately joined by the others, in a burst of indistinguishable outbursts.

Jill joined them, without thought, without will.

But there were flashes, images unique to her, she suspected, she fervently hoped, because of their unique quality, bursting with thought, with will, free of Laurie's manipulations.

Had she slept, or just missed something? Hours had passed, if not necessarily being lost. She could sense them. Andrea drilling them in the field. Udo enlightening them, in something resembling a classroom. This, she recalled, was merely the first day of their personal Hell Week.

Flashes came and went. And she had no control of either.

Sunset in Northfield. She sensed the coming of the darkness.

Jason came up behind Jill, gently, teasingly grabbing her shoulders. She turned and looked at him, looked around. She had been in the... kitchen, hadn't she, preparing evening supper? They were standing by the apple trees. The sun was about to set in the west, in the boiling sea, far beyond the hazy hills.

– There were at least two distinct screams, he said. – First one of pain, then the one of Rage.

She looked blank at him.

– Earlier today, he insisted, – before dinner?

She sensed he wasn't certain himself, but she sensed the Will in him, the anger.

– Laurie was in pain, you were the Rage. You smashed her thoroughly. She's playing smoke and mirror games with us, pretending to be much more powerful than she really is.

– Yes, she's... weak, isn't she? Without her lead in experience, we would be far... superior to her.

– Precisely my point, he said, suddenly very close to her. – I like the way you said that, more than suggesting what attitude is reasonable towards inferiors...

Before she could protest, tell him it wasn't like that, that she hadn't meant it like that, like it sounded, he bent forward and put his arms around her, kissed her fiercely, his hands roaming her body at will.

She pushed him away, just as she felt the first sting of arousal, pushed him away with arms and mind both. He staggered backwards, but didn't fall, and kept smiling his teasing, irritating smile.

– Manhandle me again, and see where it gets you, she said enraged.

– I just love that Rage. He just kept smiling as he waved and left her.

– You're just like Laurie, she cried after him, a bit calmer, but even angrier. At him, at herself.

– Isn't everyone? He said, before disappearing in the twilight.

And she couldn't be certain that he had been there at all. And she got even more angry, angry and uncertain, uncertain and insecure.

There was a black cat, a kitten on the farm, one of five siblings. She saw him play with them, rough, «affectionate». Sitting on her heels, she called out to him. He ran to her immediately, jumping into her lap.

– Malvin, she said. – Your name is Malvin.

And the small furry beast started purring. She let go of him and he ran back to his siblings and took up the game of rough pawing and kicking with renewed strength and eagerness...

It had been so easy. They had learned a bit about mental discipline since their arrival. It didn't seem difficult, not really. Not much different from moving arms and legs. This was however something they had done extensively since birth. And since then, their thought-processes had been steered towards more mundane knowledge and pursuits. Almost all knowledge during a human lifetime, language, foundation of physical and mental development, emotions, much of what becomes natural, instinctive later in life is learned during the first months after birth. It was quite another matter to start on something new and strange in the late teens.

Or perhaps it wasn't completely new and strange? There had been moments earlier in her life, where she had felt unique, extraordinary, had felt fear, elation. It dawned on her slowly, almost painfully. Just tiny flashes, not enough to carry any weight, not enough to conquer the maniacal skepticism dominating among the grown-ups, taught their children from an early age. One is picking up the phone the very moment connection is made, before it even starts ringing. Two old friends are starting on the same sentence simultaneously. She remembered once... yes, she remembered now. A ball she was playing with had rolled under the hedge. She couldn't reach it without lying down on the grass and become dirty and wet. Then suddenly she had reached it, seemingly so. She had it in her hand without being dirty or wet, and there was a long stretch under the hedge, to the ball. And there had been other incidents. Another of her cats had been hit by a car. It had been bloody and crushed when she took it in her arms. Her harsh crying had alarmed her parents, but when they came running, the cat had been virtually kicking again. Such things happened, but when one waited for days for it to happen again, in some manner, and it didn't, one rejected it as flukes or impressions of an (over)active imagination.

But now she was awake, and no one told her anymore that she was imagining stuff, and it didn't feel wholly bad.

She sat on the ground, in the grass, with her fellow novice witches. Laurie sat on the porch, in her High Chair, flanked by her Coven.

– Tonight, you'll walk out in the world, she said. – You'll be walking alone, cast out from the Circle. You'll be facing the world as a Witch, for the first time, facing the intolerance and ignorance of the outside world. There will be dangers and you will be hounded and bullied. Your Spirit Quest has begun, and I assure you it will be a long and hard trek, before it's ended, before it will either break you or empower you.

They brought their pouch, hidden under the cloak, given them by Udo, during his lecture in the kitchen.

Other than that, there was nothing. They were completely naked under the hood and cloak, and that was precisely how they felt. Naked.

– Go now, Laurie bade them. – Reveal yourselves to those with limited awareness...

Jill walked with measured steps through the city streets. Images, sensations had assaulted her from all angles, almost immediately. She had few problems with sensing the variety of impressions she «created» merely by her presence. People stood under the streetlights, propagating the rumors already flying. Or they were silent, watching. But not mute. Not to her. Not anymore.

The late evening air was hot and dry, as it had been since her arrival here, in northeastern United States. The cloak blew around her in the eternal wind, the wind touching her naked legs. The sandals felt wonderful on her feet, like a part of them, of her. She had all the advantages of walking barefoot and none of the disadvantages. Just that tiny bit felt almost intoxicating in its simple freedom. That and everything about this, the fear, the elation. Was this how it felt to be blind your entire life, and then suddenly be able to see?

And Laurie claimed that this was merely the beginning.

She had spoken continuously while they had made their preparations for their first, minor Journey. Told them what to bring and what not to bring, which, as it turned out, was almost everything. Advised and admonished them. Which they could decide to follow... or not, Jill thought clearly skeptical. But she and the others had listened, because they couldn't escape the fact that she had a lot to teach them, necessary things, downright essential stuff. They recalled clearly the image of the young girl, the untrained witch, embraced by fire, her shrieks of pain and boundless terror. They couldn't get it out of their heads.

Jill passed the church and pushed into the modern part of the town. She had walked along Cross Avenue and crossed Cross Street, the intersection of the small cross. It was illuminated to such a degree that it was clearly visible from the air. It had to be. She could almost, almost see it in her inner eye, as if she was a bird flying over the city. The entire arrangement must have cost a fortune. She had heard that one of the town's favorite (and rich) sons had made a considerable contribution to it all. What a waste.

The lights were still on inside the church. She had almost missed that fact because of the illumination outside. There was no congregation gathered tonight, no singing, no sound, but silence. Was it the priest? Did he spend the entire day there?

She dived, stubbornly, into Newtown. Then she felt it, suddenly, inexplicable. It was a feeling she had sensed a few minutes ago, too, faint then, strong now... of being watched. She turned her head, couldn't help it, and thought she heard laughter. It didn't originate from any of the people around her, or someone she could see with her naked eyes. She had gotten used to the staring quite fast, sort of. No, this was something different. As if she was being weighed and judged. Someone did watch her, followed her every movement, followed her. She turned her head several times, but didn't see anybody. Claws and fangs of darkness were reaching for her. There was so much to see and sense, but nothing overtly suspicious. Sending out her thoughts, searching, probing didn't change that.

It frustrated her. She had to admit that to herself. Whoever or... whatever it was thought it was possible to play with her. And whoever, whatever was correct. She was inexperienced yet, so damn inexperienced. But that wouldn't last. That...

She relented, attempting to calm herself. She had so much anger in her. Tonight, it felt like something recent, but thinking about it, thinking it through, she realized it had always been there. And not just anger either.

Fury!

Was it Laurie? Was it she who was watching her, using her Power, letting her know that she was there, showing her how powerless she was? Laurie had been playing with them constantly, from the very start, using her telepathy to control them, making them do whatever she wanted. *Using* them!

Jill had thought about leaving. She didn't think Laurie would actually keep her from doing so. Jill wanted to leave... But she wanted to learn more. And Laurie knew that. Of course, she did!

The Pyramid rose before her. This was a well-known landmark in New England, Big Man Thompson's gift to himself, his personal symbol of power, a building dwarfing all others in the city, both in height and width. The lights were lit all over the place. Work went on there in shifts twenty-four hours a day, like it did in his factory not far away. There was smoke, and glass and steel, and tarmac and concrete everywhere. More waste, so much waste.

She could «see» so much better now. The anger had seen, saw to that, breaking up chinks of narrow cavern eyes, pawing the way to the Deep Below. She smiled then. *This* was what Laurie couldn't control, what no one could ever control.

The people around her were, if not open, uncomplicated to her senses then. She was searching with her eyes, without being conscious of what she was seeking. Her eyes stopped by a little boy. He stood alone in a dark alley. Thin, so sad, so down, with lowered eyes. It felt to her as if he had been looking for her. She knew he hadn't. He was just looking for help, any help.

– Are you here on your own? She asked carefully, to not frighten him.

– My sister is ill, he squealed. – Mom and dad are just... sleeping.

Why don't you guys go to a physician? She had asked.

They couldn't afford any.

– Well, I can come home with you, if you want me to, she said lightly.

– I don't know... She could see how the muscles worked in the small, adult-like, too serious face. – You don't seem to be much of a witch. You're not even ap-approaching the necessary level of ugliness.

Well educated or well read, too.

– That comes with Age. The young witch was striving to keep a serious-minded appearance. – But I'll make a deal with ya. Allow me to take a look at your sister, and if I can't do anything to help her, we'll send for the master witch, okay?

– Oh, he said impressed, – she's ugly, right?

– Ugly as sin, Jill assured him. – She'll scare you shitless.

He led her through narrow alleys. Kids were playing there, dressed in rags and sad eyes, attempting to live. The sight and the impression she got from them made her even sadder, even more furious. She welcomed the Fury. Through dark alleys and cellars it helped her see.

Candles were blowing in the wind, just a few candles. In winter it just had to be ice cold down here. Now, it was as hot as any imagined and true to life hell. In spite of the open windows (there was no glass) the air reeked of closed in smells, and it seemed far hotter than outside.

The sick girl was sweating between a mattress and some dirty blankets. The man who had to be her father was standing by the wall, his shoulders sagging. The look in his eyes was empty and subdued. There was not even the slightest anger left in them.

– Her cold won't disappear, he said with a rusty voice. – Pneumonia, I guess. Bacteria are spreading like wildfire in this heat and moisture.

She nodded slowly as she sat down on her heels and let her hands move over the meager body. It was evident, even as untrained as she was that malnutrition had given the disease easy access and roaming capabilities. Jill knew what had to be done, but she did hesitate, even if it didn't show. It was so new to her, all this, so old, so much a part of her. She concentrated, sensing the sensitivity in the fingers increasing, searching her way to the center of the disease, to the lungs.

The girl mumbled in her pitiful and painful sleep, more unconscious and slumbering half-awake than actually sleeping. Death, Death was not far away. It might have lingered a few more days, but it was Present. Jill was freezing, not because of the cold, but because she was cold. She concentrated and started meditating, attempting to put herself in a meditative trance. She sensed the Calm then, the Rage, the Despair. She could almost touch it all, as she sent the first jolts of heat and calming thoughts, what she prayed was healing energy inside the fever hot body. *The girl, her name was Toni, and she was seven.*

– It hurts. The small mouth moved slowly, but it moved.

The Witch moved a hand over the too hot a chin and pulled forth a bottle from the small pouch under the cloak. The fluid inside was still hot. It was a potion made from willow juice reducing pain and fever without damaging side effects. It didn't, couldn't cure the disease, but they didn't have to know that. She held the girl's head while making her swallow the fluid. It evidently hurt each time she did manage to swallow, but the girl smiled bravely up on the sinister, kind stranger. The gray eyes burned in all the colors of the rainbow and Toni strove to breathe without coughing, while still conveying her trust.

Jill crawled and crouched over the skin and bone girl and in a swift, decisive movement spread her cloak over them both, also over her own head, entombing them in darkness. She pressed her palms against the practically exposed ribs and pushed the healing energy into the ailing small form. There was careful probing, insecure at first, then ever stronger bursts, doing so in wonder and growing joy. A flow of energy not only healing, she sensed, but also strengthening the other. It did hurt, for both of them. Toni moaned. Jill bit her lower lip. She realized that the healing couldn't be complete. She lacked both the control and the power - yet, to finish the job.

You will be healed, do you hear me, Toni. Life is Great and there is so much awaiting you, an entire world of emotion and experience, leading to joy and growth.

The Witch calmed down, calmed herself. And she... felt something. A tingle down the spine unlike anything she had felt before, or could remember feeling before.

Something *happened* then, as she entered (close to) the desired meditative state (of consciousness).

Suddenly she was somewhere else. There were flashes. Each lasted only a microsecond (which were hardly any time at all), but in each of these flashes there were thousands of years. There was a forest. Just outside that forest there was just a small cornfield. But there was... a corruption, almost unseen at first. There was movement in the glen, of tiny specks swinging axes. The Earth glowed red and sickly yellow. Trees... vanished, the forest vanished and then the field covered the entire area of what had been a forest. And the corruption continued. Houses arose in the outskirts of the field, then many houses together, and then buildings, a sickly tone of gray, the Gray Fog spreading across the land, destroying it, destroying Life.

Jill straightened. The upper body rose. The cloak floated down her back. The eyes of the witch were closed slightly, before opening, her head sliding back and forth. Blood flowed from her lip a moment before it stopped. She rose, refitting the cloak and hood, eyes already fixed on the husband and wife. They stared at her with a stiff look.

– You will never speak about this, she told them.

Toni blinked, her foggy eyes already clearer than just a few seconds ago. Jill bowed down again a bit and touched her forehead. She was still hot, but already cooling. Respiration was normal, or so normal that it was virtually impossible to detect irregularities. Jill could, but she had, as she now knew, in her possession one of the better instruments around, her sharpened, enhanced senses.

– She isn't yet out of it. It will take a few days. If she hasn't recovered by then or is showing signs of getting worse again, you call for me.

All four of them, nodded in tandem. Jill had to smile. In exactly that moment, in spite of the unnerving visions, she felt as if all doubts she had ever entertained were gone or just didn't matter. The father, Luke, took an uncertain step forward.

– I saw an angel once, he began, moved. – On an airplane, an angel with huge wings. It talked to me. I've never been able to forget it. Since then, I've always sought the mysterious, the unknown.

– I can tell you one thing about that, Luke, Jill said with deliberately careful humor. – It wasn't me. What did she look like?

– Transparent, really... She... I'm not positive it was a female, it seemed more like… a mix, I think. Or neither. But it spoke to us, and it went through the plane and solid objects like it wasn't there.

– Others on the plane claimed to have seen her... or him, too, his wife added. *I believe him,* her entire posture said. – I've read several news-clips about it. It happened between Christmas and New Year's Eve 1974, the day a hurricane demolished the city of Darwin, Australia.

Jill had read about it, about the strange things happening at the time, long before she was born. Several inhabitants of London had claimed to see incidents from Darwin. And both in London and Darwin the «angel» or «ghost», as it had been called had been observed.

– The angel patted me on the head, Luke said a bit preoccupied.

Jill Stafford, the Witch was curious about this family in more ways than one. It was their story, Luke's story, of course, but also more. In spite of their obvious poverty, they were quite articulate and well «educated», a sign of they having taken a fall not so long ago. Jill could have asked about that, but didn't need to. During her close contact with the girl, she had learned everything necessary about the entire family. She had been closer to the girl than she had been to anyone she could remember.

Strange, wasn't it, a complete unknown?

Unknown no longer.

– We may need help on the farm, she said tightly. – There may be work there, for all of you. I'll check out the possibilities. Think about it. You should come to our market anyway. We'll probably do it quite soon. There you will get nutritious, inexpensive food.

But Laurie hasn't said anything about a market, she told herself.

So, what! she replied.

She turned to leave. Fully aware that they wanted to inquire about payment, but couldn't afford to pay, she ignored it.

– You're so young, the mother said. – How can you be so cold and unmoved?

– Perhaps because I must, she replied.

The streets outside felt cool and comfortable compared to the damp air and decay in the cellar. Seen from the outside the entire building was clearly about to collapse, and it wasn't any walk in the park living upstairs either. But again, compared to the moist cellar...

She drifted a while, aimlessly, to the big, dusty parking lot, glittering dust one moment, and then just dust once more. The factory. A big, pestilent hole. And the feeling of the big, pestilent, festering hole didn't disappear. The nice suburban neighborhood, with straight streets and nice gardens, with dry lawns, no longer nicely cut green grass. She was drifting, until realizing she really wasn't, that she was on her way... on her way... home. She was circling back, back to the farm. Not to the school. To whatever was awaiting her there. She took the scenic route, not the shortest along the short part of the highway, touching the town. She had had enough of cars, heavy traffic and concrete.

It was strange. The moment she reached the limits of Oldtown, she could hear the grasshoppers by the road. Well, perhaps not so strange. A city was an unnatural environment. Here, after all, wilderness, the green wilderness was a lot closer.

People kept staring at her with obvious curiosity, disbelief and hatred, one of the three, or a variant mix of it all. «You're being watched, studied, assessed. Get used to it! It's the way of the world». Laurie's words came back to her. She felt alone, lonely, cut out of her world. She stood out here, exactly like a sore thumb. And that was how she felt, too.

A crowd she had known about for a while now, followed with her eyes, from the edge of her vision was speeding up, closing in on her. They seemed to be very eager, quite insistent. She stopped and turned, waiting for them to catch up.

She recognized a few of them. Some of the older boys and girls from the school, and the boy she had «met» on the bus on her first day here. There it was, immediately, the idiotic urge to blush.

– HI, GIRL, we want to jive a bit with you, girl.

They looked into eyes colder than the moon, stopping a considerable distance further away than intended.

A tall, powerful built boy stood closest to her, half a step closer than the others.

– We heard there were witches on the prowl tonight, he said, – and we decided to go looking for them. But we're a bit disappointed, see. You're the first we've found who's looking even remotely the

part. So... are ya a witch?
– Yes! She replied, drawing breath. – I'm a Witch!
Her words, her «admission» changed her in their eyes. She imagined they looked at her with cruel stares.
– Now, that's good to hear. We heard you were visiting the derelict buildings by the river, their cellars. Good old Luke's cellar, to be specific, Luke and his sinking rats. Do you know he has spoken up against the factory, that he has in fact been fired from that very factory? What did you do there? Did ya heal any of the people there for their sick, subversive ideas?
– From your point of view, I undoubtedly made them even sicker, she said pleasantly.
The conversation had, to this moment, seemed pleasant enough.
– Have you ever asked yourself why he was fired? She asked them quietly.
– Did ya heal anybody? The boy said angrily.
– Hey, do a trick for us. One of the girls spoke up.
– I'm not a performing animal, she said softly. – Listen, you're all welcome to visit us anytime. That's a standing offer from us all.
– Why haven't we heard anything about that before? One of them asked suspiciously.
– Perhaps you haven't been listening?
Her voice was calm, but there were drums in her head. Distant thunder that would, in time, grow to a crescendo.
– You're one of the new ones, a boy said thoughtfully. – I saw you entering the forest. The older... witches have never done that. Perhaps you're more open, more attuned to new ideas?
– Everett has studied the problem, one of the girls laughed.
The boy reddened.
– Studied it carefully... another said, and everybody laughed.
Everett... Everett Moran. Jill's eyes started to glitter. His voice, its tone... It was as if she had heard it before, heard it many times. Something made her seek his eyes, but he had turned away after the others' sarcastic comments.
– Everett is a sharp one, another boy, the one from the bus speculated. – You are one of the new. Listen girl, Jill, isn't it? We're gonna have something of a late initiation party tonight. You are, as a sign of good will, cordially invited. Why don't you accept, as a token return of good will? My guess is that you've got... *sensitive* hands, right? You'll be a great asset on the party, trust me...
– Thank you, that's very kind of you, she replied in a quiet, polite manner, both hot and raging hot inside, – but I've already been asked to participate in another party.
– But you're not a member of any fraternity, are you?
– Sort of, she mumbled.
– Ah, you're having your own party tonight, ain't ya?
– Yes, she nodded, – we're starting our hell week.
She reached out, instinctively, with her mind, attempting to calm them, to brunt their anger, not knowing how, not convinced if it was the right thing to do.
– I'm certain we can convince you. The big boy spoke again, while taking another step closer to her.
– *Another time.*
She... felt something then, a black, swelling nudge inside. Her icy tone and the coldness she projected was more than enough to keep them at bay. They had meant to just grab her and drag her off, some jokingly, innocently, some not so jokingly, innocently. They didn't just stop, they froze. And she knew she could have done more, if necessary. *Pick the leader,* Laurie had said. *The train stops when the locomotive stands still.* But she wasn't certain she had really done that.
– Of course. Insecure, barking, like a good dog. – Another time, right? Okay for me.
The pack turned like one single entity and walked away, left her alone. She had scared them and now they feared her. She felt something, and what she felt was Power.
Applause from a single pair of hands made her turn around. She discovered Jason. He had stayed hidden, observing from a distance. Now, he walked towards her with a grin on his face.
– My compliments, he praised her. – They didn't see me, and I did nothing, but you got rid of them easily enough.

She eyed him with suspicion and skepticism, and made no attempt at hiding it. His grin widened. Fully aware of the implication in his statement, he continued:

– But I must say I wasn't overly impressed. There are far more effective methods you could've used to get rid of them. You could've really scared the living bear-shit out of them, showed them that beautiful Wrath you're hiding. Or you could've indeed *punished* them all, making them regret they ever dared insult you.

– The one wasn't necessary, the other not desirable, she rejected his words.

– I *know* you, you see, he continued unfazed, as if she hadn't spoken at all, – you long to strike them down, strike down those impudent enough to behave in a disrespectful manner towards a *Homo Magi,* or shall we say *Homo Superior?* You wanted to know how insignificant they are. You longed to see them crawl on the ground in your elevated presence...

– Stop! She held her closed fists in front of her face. – You will STOP!

And then the anger took her. Forces grew like Fire between them. Nothing happened. Their power level was the same.

– I knew there was fire in you, he said triumphantly.

He pulled her to him and kissed her violently. She froze. There wasn't much she could do in his grip. His physical strength was far beyond hers. And she wasn't certain she wanted to do anything. She felt the heat rise in her, the burning heat. And he didn't use any «tricks», she knew that. If he had, she would have burned him on the spot. She stopped struggling, and started pushing her body tight to his. He released her grip. She put her arms around him, couldn't believe her own daring behavior. She moved one hand over his back, buried the other in his long hair, and pulled it so hard that it should have made him cry out in pain. He didn't seem to notice. She realized he had to be as... out of it, as she was, filled with raging emotions.

It took a while, until they released each other. She smiled, while putting one hand around his crotch and tightening the grip slightly. He gasped. Her smile widened and she felt the Power again. Without actually using it, she felt it. He had the fabric of her cloak in his closed fists. They very nearly forgot they were standing in the middle of a busy street.

Let us send them all away, she sent frenetically, *send all the servants away.*

Reason, or rather fear won. They let go of each other.

We could have done it, or we could've found a place, he sent, and she «heard» him clearly, much more clearly than if he had used his mouth to speak. *We can do anything. But Laurie is waiting. From her we must learn everything she has to teach.*

– You, hot virgin, have something special coming for you, he said.

– And such an experienced stud like yourself will know how to treat me sweet, won't you...

She fingered his hood, stroked the tip of her fingers teasingly, deliberately teasingly along his jaw.

– You are experienced are you not?

All her shame, all her embarrassment, all the shock over her own behavior buried deep, she smiled and showed him herself, through posture and a sensuality she could taste. She felt dizzy. For just a moment, it was as if she had been a different person. She attacked him, with her wiles and her womanhood, and he withdrew like an ice-cube before the Fire.

– I have some experience, he said almost apologetic. – I thought it was my irresistible charm, and in a way, I was right, of course... in a way I never could have imagined.

– Poor boy, she said softly. – The other boys must have been quite pissed off.

– It did lead to some bloody noses occasionally, and some of them were mine.

She straightened herself self-consciously, extensively masking her face and her thoughts, to hide the chaos of conflicting emotions raging through her. It was obvious she was inexperienced... in a lot of areas, and therefore vulnerable. She had to correct that.

Because it wasn't true what he had said about her... was it?

She wasn't like that, was she?

– An innocent little thing like you shouldn't behave like that, he said, laughing, only partially pretending to be shocked. – I've seen whores acting more prudent.

He was right. There had been a moment, where she suddenly had known all the right moves, what it would take to turn the tables on him, for her to *be* an aggressive, experienced woman, accompanied by the insecure, young boy.

– If you weren't such an asshole, I could've actually liked you...

– Come on, you like me because I'm an asshole. Be honest.

– Oh, you're such a sweet boy...

She leaned over his shoulder, pouting, inviting lips pointing at his. He pulled back, clearly embarrassed. She laughed throatily, triumphantly. She had done it again, and this time it had been a premeditated, conscious decision on her part.

– Time to go back, he said curtly.

She nodded and took his hand. She decided to be on speaking terms with him. He wasn't so bad. She had met people who were far worse. She had won anyway.

Won!

They kept to the heavily illuminated roads on their way back, perhaps because they didn't want to hide themselves, perhaps because they wanted to hide in plain sight. They didn't know, and then they forgot their pondering.

Just as they turned into Main Street the grasshoppers stopped singing. Just like that, from one moment to the next all the animals, all the sounds of the night grew silent. Jill froze. She stopped and looked behind her, prone to the identical feeling from earlier in the evening, the certainty that she was being Watched. She turned and this time she did see something.

He, too turned, looking at her, sensing her unease.

– Do you see it? She asked.

– Yes, peculiar for sure. He whistled, not without a certain anxiety.

He saw, as she did, a creature covered in cloak and hood walking under the streetlight, becoming visible under the streetlights, disappearing in the darkness between. It was walking in their path, walking towards them.

– I can't sense anything from it, she said. – Anything at all.

– Neither can I, he concurred, – and I always get something from everybody. I got it, even long before I arrived here.

As they spoke «it» was walking under the light, the last light before reaching them. And it disappeared in the darkness. They took a few steps backwards, until they were standing in the center of the light. They waited, holding each other's hands, tense in muscles, limbs and mind.

There was no sound of steps, no footprints in the sand, nothing.

Nothing happened. They stood still, frozen, but no hooded ghoul assaulted them. After a while they even started to look around them and up in the air, on their feet, and every other place a scared kid may look, while walking a dark road at night.

They stood there for minutes, before moving on, walking down Main Street. There were more lights here, also from apartments, shops, restaurants and pubs. They looked back often, but saw nothing. Not at first.

– Jason, Jill said worried.

And there it was again, three lights behind them, as it had been when they first discovered it, appearing in spots of light, turning invisible (or disappearing) in the shadows. They kept walking. It seemed attuned to their speed, because it kept that distance, that exact distance. When they slowed down, it did the same. When they speeded up, it did the same. And this time, when they stopped, it did the same.

– HEY! Jason shouted. – WHAT'S YOUR PROBLEM?

There was no reply. She could sense his anger, his fear, as a mirror reflection of her own.

There was no face that they could see. In an attempt to see a face under the hood, they spotted only darkness. There were no legs, no discernible arms, just a cloak and a hood, levitating in the air.

They attempted to contact it with telepathy, control it with their minds, in vain.

Reply! I/We command you to appear.

They saw it with their eyes, but other than that, there was nothing there, as if what they could see had neither form nor substance nor thought.

They looked at each other, then, in sudden inspiration.

– Someone is putting us on, she mumbled.

She bent down and picked up a stone, throwing it at the cloak, where the chest was supposed to be. And the stone went straight through. There was no cloth either. And like a mirage the apparition dissolved into the air. The two exchanged glances. And the cold trickle down their spine intensified.
Nothing there.

3

The farm. Quiet, sort of. At least peaceful. There were drums. And there was rhythm. The youths danced and swayed to the rhythm of the Night. Fires were lit, fires stretching into darkness. Jill felt the heat, without forgetting the cold.

It moved, she thought stricken, moved with thought, with purpose. It was there!

There was no sleep, there were no days, and no food anymore. Her senses were sharpening. Her astuteness, seemingly so dulled the first day or two without sleep, grew to staggering, frightening proportions. The farm... she could feel it. And she could feel the forest, the wilderness beyond it, beyond it all. She could feel the growth. There were no artificial fertilizers in use here, causing the growth pain and misery, and pain and misery to their consumers. No heavy machinery compressing the soil, destroying its breathing, pushing out of it the life-breathing oxygen.

Around her were her new friends, her eternal siblings. Around her in the Night, not necessarily visible, but they were There.

– Yesssss. A serpent's hiss, the distant/close voice of Laurie, their teacher, their guardian, their keeper. – Stretch out your senses, feel your surroundings, feel the Night.

And they did, swaying and dancing in the darkness, the moth attracted to the flame. So hot, the Fire so hot, and it burned them, burned them terribly.

And they were screaming, screaming terribly, alone there, in the infinite Void. And in that Void, in their boundless Hunger, they were screaming for food and for thought, and there was None to be had.

She was kneeling in a circle, her circle of Nine. A hand, a wet cloth was moving over her forehead. Clothes were... clinging to the body, to the skin, wet, soaked in stinking sweat. Uncomfortable, disgusted with herself, she threw up the remains of the garbage she had digested so long ago.

There was wind against the face then. There was water. And when she had drunk for ages, when the water was withheld, she still wanted more.

Gaps... in their memory, extensive enough to fill lives. Filled in flashes, remembered, forgotten, remembered, forgotten, everything she would never forget.

She saw a boy, sitting on a hill alone. *The* Hill? She couldn't tell. He drank, but didn't digest any food, feeding his hunger, his Hunger beyond words, beyond thought. Through his eyes she saw the witches in their circle, saw them dance, saw them sway.

I remember you... *I remember!*

There was Kieron. Wherever he walked, plants danced in his wake. They seemed to perform for him. She remembered laughing, in joy, in a reckless, devil-may-care attitude. When Rae walked the very ground seemed to shift beneath her. Sound «behaved» around Ivan, bending, bouncing and expanding. And Loeh, playing with Fire. There was Stacy, picking up the Fire, making it bigger, expanding it, not like sound, but like Night. She saw her own hands stretched before her, burning. And there was no pain, but illumination. She and Stacy and Jason stood by each other's side, distant from the others. There was one vacant spot.

Blind, blind is the Human Being of today, blind for the Destruction. Destruction of Nature, of Life, of the Human Being itself. Exploiting two-legged beasts. Predators confined. Parasites.

Random thoughts, pieces of a jigsaw puzzle making sense. Jill gasped in wonder and horror.

It was not Laurie's voice. She did recognize it.

Gabrielle.

– To understand Nature, one must become (be) a part of it, Jill Exclaimed, a huge smile on her lips (and there were echoes). – It's that simple. And the other way around...

(or the same)

to become one with Nature, one must understand it.

She saw herself turn around and around, whirl round and round with her arms stretched to the side.

Faster, ever faster. Until her hands were but a line and the only visible part of her. She turned into a wheel, turning into herself. And the beginning and the end were just words, without any quantifiable reality.

Freedom kept swelling inside, outside, from a previous general feeling of wellbeing to this powerful experience, a divide that could never be measured. She was looking out, looking in, so much in tune with her surroundings. She felt closer to the borders, out there, where sea and sky were one.

– It's a pity that not everybody is sharing our expanded awareness, Laurie said, – our expanded potential, but we're going to show them, all of them.

– We're gonna show them! Jill cried.

– What's that saying again... Jason leaned forward, with pointed, burning eyes.

They burned, like the fire in the night.

– That saying, yes. Jill's eyes were half closed, half open. – «One who can't see what's happening in one's surroundings is an idiot... but one who does see and does nothing, is a criminal»: Something like that. I never seem to get it right.

– Astute girl, Udo acknowledged.

There were many colors here, many creeds. That was good... if everybody was allowed to freely express themselves.

And in her soul's mirror, the young witch could read every question, every reply.

What is your game? Jill wondered and didn't look at Laurie, didn't really bother to hide the caustic thought either.

– My dark nature. Suddenly she was alone with Jason. – I can feel it in the soul... a darkness.

– Don't run from it, he insisted. – It will always be a part of you. Embrace it!

Like moths they were, indeed, the youths, pulled towards the flames of purification. The fire rose in what had, since ancient times been called a Witch Circle, a ring of mushrooms big enough to give the witches plenty of room within it. They felt a good awe, as they sat down. All of them crossed their legs in front of themselves. They had waited so long, they thought, here, on the borderline between realities. It seemed like a hundred years.

Laurie removed her hood. The others followed her lead.

Tamara shifted and changed position uncomfortably. Jill realized that she had done so for a while and that there had been pain in her eyes when she had touched her head.

– I'm fine! She said reassuringly. She had noticed Jill's look. – Suit is just a bit tight, that's all.

– Comforting in a way, isn't it? Jill commented with an interested glow in the eyes. – Laurie actually gave you the wrong size. She's human, after all.

All the other newcomers had been given a perfect fit. Some time after returning from the «Dare Journey», they had been given approval, and the remaining part of their suits, their robe. It was dirty now, and soaked in sweat and body fluids, but it wasn't tight.

– ... and I've got hurting ears.

– Hurting ears? Jill chuckled softly. – Then it doesn't hurt inside your ears?

– No, they sting and itch on the outside, but it's no picnic, I assure you, Tamara said almost apologetic. She scratched carefully the ears sticking out from the thick, curly hair. She shrugged then and relaxed. – It's no big deal. I look forward so much to what we're about to do, that a bit of nerves isn't really strange.

Laurie rose, easily, in a single, flowing movement. Her handicap was still there, but hardly noticeable, and they thought about it less and less.

– Witches... she said with an obvious dramatic flair. Like an actress, a politician. – It is time!

Everybody there looked attentive at her, at the revered teacher.

– This is your foray, your initiation into magic. It's a test of your will, of your courage, of your ability to see the world beyond. You will walk there afraid, and you will be reborn into the service of the Goddess. I, her servant will aid you, keeping you from going astray.

Jill felt her heartbeat. She heard the Heartbeat, slow thunder rippling through the ether. She'd had her doubts, if she wanted to continue on this path. Not so strange that. But she heard the sound of her own heart, and she heard it match that of the big drum of the Earth. Sketches, she had done sketches and poems as a child. Her parents had not approved, and she had stopped. But never in her heart! Everything repressed, every emotion, every notion not expressed was about to break out, break out here, now, and she welcomed it!

– There is a special place for us all in the future world order, Laurie said. – We don't need to be outcasts.

And she enticed them with the temptation to fit in, to adapt.

– Your stomachs, your minds are empty now. Forget it. *You* are empty now. *You* will be filled to the brim.

We're vulnerable.

Jill thought.

Thought one moment, gone the next.

There was misery, and she didn't forget that. But she wanted this. She needed this!

I want this!

Did Laurie smile to her?

A jar stood in the middle of the mushroom ring, suddenly rising from the ground, floating into Laurie's hands. She sent it around. In it there were many spongy pieces of something that might be fruit, they couldn't tell. They couldn't tell who ate the first fruit, as they took one piece each and put it in their mouth. There was no taste, or no taste they could discern. She wondered if their taste wasn't paralyzed instantly by the juicy, tasty stuff. Mouth and tongue turned numb and muscles in the body slackened. The mood in the circle changed irrevocably.

They were chewing. Mouth was filled with fluid, the taste so sweet. More sweat flowed from skin all over the body. Saliva dropped from their mouth. Head was rolling on the shoulder, rolling off, rolling off the cliff.

You'll find what is missing, trust me.

This is a shared experience that will strengthen you, strengthen us, strengthen the group, the coven. You'll go looking for your totem and return it to us, return to us a possession, a prize of the highest value.

Then there was the projection of the Goddess again, and all of them kneeling and singing her praise. A sound rose from her, from them all. They sat still, they didn't move. Chanting? It was impossible to tell whether their song rose from their larynx or not. And the last words they heard were not coming from Laurie. Speak to me, Shadow. Speak from the Wheel. Nothing at all.

Then, for just a moment, Jill could focus her eyes. She saw the dancing Ghoul, saw it in the Fire. Its clothes didn't catch fire, but it burned. *She* burned! Jill could see its face, it had her own face, and she screamed.

The fire seemed to grow, grow until it filled the entire circle. But in spite of the flame licking them, there was no heat, no pain. Silence grew, until Total, slowly releasing them from their burden. They weren't weightless, there just wasn't any weight, and they floated in the air. All measures turned meaningless. They floated in silence, rising from their bodies, screaming in pain, in rage, in fear. Their skin and bone and blood were gone. Only their astral body remained. They stepped out of their physical bodies… into the lap of the gods. They took the first, major steps towards their fate.

Chapter Six: (INTO) THE UNKNOWN

The gray road stretched out before her, able to glow in all the colors of the rainbow. She was walking through the streets, crossing the fields, and it was another world. She stood straightened out in the attic at the school, with her arms outstretched. In a dream one could easily set aside the current rules. Why was it so difficult otherwise? The attic, empty except for light and dust, felt so different from how she had imagined it. Dust whirling round and round in the light and the emptiness surrounded her, invaded her.

She's playing us against each other.

Laurie does. Why is she? How dares she? It doesn't fit with her words of coexistence and her stated wish to «do good». What does she hope to gain? *It's more! We're more powerful than her, some of us, if not all, she wants control.*

Jill's thoughts drifted, as she didn't seem to be able to hold on to one thought. It was like a bombardment, overwhelming and Total, something beyond her present experience. She thought about Luke. Life hadn't been kind to him. He hadn't achieved much with it, and he had expected so much, perhaps too much.

Flashes again, millions on a pinprick of a second assaulted her. Voices whispered to her, a constant noise in the background, a presence wherever she sat course. She couldn't make out the words, but they were warnings, fawning, threats, trusting and so much more. She had heard it was Death to acknowledge them, so she strove to not do that. She felt both fear and eagerness gnawing at her under the surface.

A small dip under the surface, and awareness kept increasing. They had been sitting around the fire, being consumed by it, stepping out of their physical bodies. And then? What had happened afterwards? Everything had turned blinding white and suddenly there she was, walking through the city streets in the light of day. And then she found herself on the fields, in the forest, before the temple on Fire Lake. There was smoke on the water, and the lake, with its calm, dark surface was burning, burning with slow flames. They spoke to her in kind and challenging and cruel voices. She found herself in Square, in Circle, by the pyramid in Newtown. No, she was about to lose control. Concentrate, Laurie had said. Focus.

She looked up at the sky. She could see the sun. But the stars were equally visible. It was as if she could see everything. She could see a lot. There was the pyramid again, gray and black and dirty and a construction crawling with worms. She fled from there, couldn't stand the sight of it. It wasn't in any way like she remembered it and she couldn't tell why. There was something she couldn't quite grasp, something hidden just beyond her understanding. The confusion and horror were almost tangible.

She felt it, similar to a physical force, strangling her, depriving her of strength.

Stacy's face materialized in a shopping window. Jill turned around and saw no one. Stacy wasn't here. And then her face faded from the window, too, and only her voice remained.

– You'll understand. One day you will understand!

She descended some unknown stairway, where oozing torches placed in rings fastened on stonewalls burned, but where she emerged was the roof of Laurie's house. Laurie lay on her back on a table, dead and still, embraced by flowers on all sides. Andrea sat by her side, alone.

– I can take over now, Jill said.

– Yes, you can take over, Andrea said.

And she took the cup handed to her, the golden cup, a powerful symbol in many belief systems. And the cup was transformed into a torch, and Jill put the torch under Laurie's bed, and the bed turned into a burning canoe, drifting down a misty river a bright morning. The fire consumed Laurie and her ashes floated further down the river, until the water and the ashes had mixed and become interchangeable.

Jill turned an unknown corner into an unknown street. It was an empty stretch, filled with nothing. Andrea and the others joined her, carrying tables and chairs. They put fruits on the tables and sat down in the low chairs. Suddenly the street was filled with people, and it had turned into a busy marketplace.

It was late in the day. The others had left, and she remained there a few minutes, to take it all in. To sit there alone felt strangely peaceful. She recalled the day in tiny, prolonged flashes, in flashes within flashes. People visited her where she sat. They were talking, asking questions, trading. She had to take some pointed looks and nasty remarks, but they seemed to have lost their potency, their sting, at least to her. She heard the same melody she had heard when she was nine and had walked through the hall of her parents' house, walked on a floor covered by white petal flowers and dreamed she had been dreaming. The song was the 1978 live version of Mighty Quinn by Bob Dylan, played by Manfred Mann's Earth Band. She hadn't been born when this melody was performed the first time either. But she remembered it well. The words sang in her, and the melody resonated with words. She knew their meaning even then.

She saw him as if from far away. The face of Everett Moran seemed calm like a mask, but she knew he was staring at her. He approached her.

– What day is this, she said faint. – Are you real?

– I have no idea. He was shaking his head. – They say you're a Witch. Are you?

– Sure, certified and loony. She straightened herself proudly in her low chair. – You know what? Witches are rare, but exist in higher numbers than most people believe. You may be one yourself.

– I've always thought so, he said. – I'm born and bred in these parts, you know, but it's the first time I've felt at home here.

She hid her face behind hands, peeking out between fingers.

– Sorry. She laughed nervously, hysterically. – I can't seem to get a grip on anything. Everything is slipping away the moment I focus on it. Solid, tangible one moment, puff of smoke the next. Life is both physical and spiritual. There's no inherent contradiction here.

There are no contradictions.

... (felt homesickness, but this was a feeling she had carried with her, her entire life. She was far away from home. Not necessarily in space, but in Time)

Out of the smoke Stacy walked. Everett was gone.

– *Onward, brave sorceress. The time is here.*

Teasingly:

– Or do I have to put a collar around your neck and pull you on your way?

No, no. An energetic shaking of the head. Never a collar, never!

A laughter, cruel and with hard edges.

Jill left everything to follow Stacy. She stopped only a moment, to look back, and Everett was still there. He followed the two sisters from a distance.

They reached the gathering, on the big, open marketplace. Not really like she remembered it. The big parking lot emptied of cars, like it was during markets. But there were no stalls, no market, no people... except the seven witches awaiting them. But they were not exactly as she remembered them either. They were different, even their indifferent, burning smiles and the light and shadows reflected from their bodies were different. And attempt to look directly at them, or any given point, and it was like looking at... nothing. And then, suddenly, it was like she could see them; see everything, from all viewpoints, from every single point in the air. She felt everything, more than she saw it with her eyes, felt like a hit in the belly thousands of eyes shining and burning in the Night.

– *This is the crossroads.* The voice was not a voice, but several growling, indecipherable, distorted, unrecognizable sounds. For all she knew, the voice was her talking to herself. – *All paths, all time, lead here. All paths are wrong, and all are right.*

Covered with dangers, as well as opportunities, Jill thought.

– Humans desire or may desire willing tools for their ambition, Laurie said sternly. – You must guard yourself against others, as well as yourself.

Had she said that before? Had Jill heard her say it just now, just then?

Or was that Laurie at all? Really her? She seemed to be present all the time, but there were others as well. Impulses were sent towards the clusters of nerves and cells. It bombarded those very clusters, and what was Beyond. So much information, impossible to process. Move Beyond, beyond the process, and look towards what isn't, what is. Now, well, a good advice could hardly be repeated too often, could it? If it was just good, that is. A careful approach and a certain critical view of new things were okay. Full blown paranoia wasn't.

The trek revealed itself to her. The gray road turned into a brown path, through the forest of eternity. She jumped and bounced in joy on it, until she reached the Fire Lake. It was a sea of fire, but it wasn't burning. She pulled herself up in the air and floated in a flowing motion above the flames, to the temple in the middle of the Lake, the Temple of Shadows. A place, a point filled with untapped Power, power that anybody might use as they saw fit.

She paced devoutly over the threshold. A few flashes of impressions inside, and then, in a flash, she was outside again, in Nature. Another forest now. She knew that, even if this one was the same as the previous, in all the ways her eyes could see. Her Eyes. She saw not only with her eyes now, but with her Everything. So much that she could hardly endure.

Rays from the close sun shone through the treetops, the moonlight illuminating the shadows. She felt strong and confident as she was crossing the forest. There was something here she expected to find. She didn't know what, but the realization sent a veritable tingle through her, through her very being.

She arrived at a small clearing. There was a tree in its center. A small tree for sure, but with thick branches. On a withered branch close to the ground sat an old woman. No, an *older* woman. In more ways than one, she didn't seem old. Her hair was long and white, her face wrinkled, but her clear eyes had no trouble looking at the world, and she didn't look tired in any way. She contained more fire than many of Jill's age. The young girl admired her already.

– Greetings, young sorceress. I have a short message for you, before I must be on my way. Short, but important.

– What... A sense of familiarity that couldn't be denied flooded Jill's being, but she couldn't recognize it.

– The tail of the two-legged wolf, maiden isn't always visible. Very few things are what they appear to be these sorrowful days. Illusions are the true danger. Illusions must fall! If they fall the enemy can be faced and dealt with. The Book of Shadows is written unseen.

– Who are you? Jill exclaimed in irritation, anger and fear. And then quieter, almost subdued: – Who am I?

Then, so sudden that she wasn't really able to register the change, the blue sky turned gray and cloudy and dark gray. Lightning and thunder flashed violently through the air, but no rain fell.

– My cue to get the hell out of here, the older woman winked cheerily, waving merrily. – Live well and grow, girl. We'll never meet again.

– Wait...

But the woman had already risen up in the air with a skill signifying long-term experience. And then she just faded away. But before she vanished completely, Jill saw something that stunned her even more.

The tight skin on the right leg had been clearly visible and Jill had spotted the characteristic mole. She couldn't have imagined it or been so wrong, could she...

What happened around her turned even more distracting then. So extensive that all thought, all mind had to focus on it. The wind started blowing. At least she felt it blow her hair back. There were a thousand fires and darkness, and everything changed. Tall buildings seemed to grow up everywhere and the green grass under her feet turned to tarmac. The few trees remaining withered to leafless husks.

She shivered suddenly, in the humid, ash-filled cold. It started raining. She stood hidden in a dark alley and watched things unfold. Crystal clear sensations, so real assaulted her. Everything looked completely real, as if it was really happening. Sound was deafening, the images blinding, paralyzing. This could be any city, any city at all, but it was Boston. The huge public library was around here somewhere, wasn't it? Water flowed down her forehead. She blinked in an effort to keep her vision clear.

An enormous crowd gathered around the old building, surrounding it. It took time. The woman standing in the dark alley couldn't be sure of how long. It felt like hours, in flashes, years. She saw them. Faces distorted. She heard them. They shouted and cried. She knew how fanaticism looked like, how it sounded. Seen and heard it, as she had, many times. The smell of the sick burning resonated in the air. She would never have thought that the sight, the smell of fire would sicken her.

They burned books, videos, films, comics, furniture... everything being carried out of the building. Tore and smashed everything and threw it on one of the countless fires. The fires stretched high and low in the moist, dirty atmosphere that perhaps could be mistaken for air, if one pretended *very* hard.

Everything Jill saw made her breathing hard and painful. All she heard and sensed and smelled and tasted, took in. She didn't know what was going on, but it made her sick, sick to the bone. She recognized the library, but the tall buildings around it...? The neighborhood blocks seemed completely transformed from how she had experienced it all... was it just a few days ago? It had been transformed into a place consisting solely of glass and steel and plastic and concrete. *So hideous!* And the sirens, heard everywhere, turned louder, drew closer. The crowd murmured in anticipation. Blinking blue lights turned the nearest corner and there were shouts of joy and exaltation. The police cars didn't look much different, but they most certainly were. They didn't have any wheels, but floated a short distance above the ground. Jill froze in sudden realization, understanding. This was the future. The Earth as it would, *or could* become.

The levitating vehicles stopped in front of the worn stone stairs. Females and males dressed in full protective uniform stormed out in tight formation. The backdoors were kicked open. The police officers pulled their guns, big, destructive handguns from their holsters. More uniformed officers stormed out. They lined up with their rifles pointing straight up. Their uniforms differed slightly from the others, another department evidently. But they wore the same white helmets, with their characteristic engraving. They could easily distinguish between each other and other people during crowd control.

The vehicles weren't yet empty. Jill strained her eyes to see better. Then bowed, broken figures appeared. They were pulled and pushed. Several fell where they landed. They were immediately forced back on their feet by hammering clubs and whining whips. Everybody was made to stand straight, in line, men, women and children nude, with shaved heads displayed to the wrath and scorn of the assembled crowd. They were heavily chained and had great trouble remaining on their feet. Around their neck they had been fitted with a shining ring with an engraved number.

A new floater appeared, one of yet different markings. A bigger model, one evidently not constructed for speed and maneuverability, but for comfort and space. It halted before the library. The driver jumped out and opened the door for the distinguished passenger. A woman stepped out, walked down broad stairs with measured, deliberate steps, impeccably attired in suit, tie, hat and high heeled boots. She raised her arms above her head and the mob suddenly turned very, very quiet.

– THE END OF THE WORLD IS NO LONGER NEAR, she shouted very loud. – IT'S HERE, NOW! THE HIGH COUNCIL'S ADVISER, THE PROPHET HAS CONFIRMED THIS. Our Lord's High Spokesman the Bishop received the message last night.

The mob cried out in joy, with shining faces.

– THE TIME IS RIGHT, she howled and whined. – PUNISHMENT IS AWAITING THE UNJUST AND UNGODLY. THE HEATHENS WILL BE DENIED ACCESS TO PARADISE AND THOSE CARRYING THE MARK OF THE WITCH, THOSE RESPONSIBLE FOR ALL SUFFERING AND FOR POISONING THE MINDS OF OUR CHILDREN WILL BE PUNISHED IN ALL ETERNITY. THE TIME FOR GOD'S RETURN IS CLOSE.

– closecloseclose, the mob chanted again and again.

– THOSE CARRYING THE MARK OF CAIN SHALL BE MADE TO SERVE US ALL THE DAYS OF THEIR LIVES. SOON THEY, LIKE ALL OTHER *CORRECTED* WILL BE OUR SLAVES AND SING OUR PRAISE, HAPPY TO BE LOWER THAN WORMS IN THE GROUND.

The middle aged, far too experienced woman pulled back into the shadows once more. She got a last flash of the prisoners being pushed brutally into the derelict building. The woman turned back into the young girl once more. Jill increased her pace, her heart hammering wild and desperate in her chest. The sense of relation was so obvious and made the lump in her throat so big that she could hardly draw breath. Why had they not used their powers to protect themselves? What she had seen didn't necessarily have any significance, but she believed it did. The chains and collar could have neutralized their talents. According to the legends witches were supposedly weakened by iron. Or it could be an administered compound or a nerve toxin or all of it in combination or whatever other reasons, prolonged torture, brainwashing, various sedatives. She clenched her fists so tight that her palms started bleeding. She was so furious and so frightened and her disheartening so deep, that she thought she couldn't bear to take another step. A proud voice of rage inside, comforting her, whispered: «That's right, use your rage. Show no mercy towards the objects of your hatred. Then you will grow so powerful that no one can touch you».

She approached a clearing ahead. A man, a nice young man sat on a garbage can. Or... was that a treestump, a stump of a tree?

– Will you jump through my hoop? He asked.

She shook her head. She retreated into the shadows and hurried on. A man with hair and beard long and white levitated above the trees in front of her, towering above her.

– Lean on me, he bade her. – I can protect you!

– NO! She raised her fist to him.

The image of a city flashed for her inner eye. Suddenly there she was, Bourbon Street in New Orleans. A big man with hair of gold and red led a group of people down the streets. Rage drove him on and they were his to command. The others didn't see it, but she did, the sparks and dancing embers around his body. His rage, his Fury manifested.

Another big city, with much Light and Life appeared to her sore eyes. She wasn't certain which this time, but it reminded her of... no, it was Times Square in New York. And suddenly she realized something, something that had been at the tip of her hair all the time.

I'm so silly, she thought. *This is all a dream. Of course, it is.*

But she had learned that dreams were just other aspects or reality.

And this felt real, as everything she had experienced had felt real.

It was New Year's Eve, wasn't it? A new year was about to begin. And everyone was happy.

The young girl was new in town. Big eyed and filled with expectations she looked at the tight crowd celebrating, walked among them, as one of them. She felt vigorous and alive, an emotion enhanced by the sight of a group of dancers starting a spontaneous performance under the Coca Cola sign.

She stared with the lump in her throat. Such Life, such Fire, in their movements. Their bodies were whirling and moving, and it was all so real, so authentic.

More started dancing, smiling in happiness. The dancers danced even better; inspired by the response they were getting from the people. One of them was truly great. He was so agile that he seemed almost supernatural. The young girl's blood was boiling, and she danced through the Storm with them.

When looking closer at the lot of them, they seemed, all of them, in all the ways her eyes couldn't see, more than human. One was so big that he towered over everybody present, and his body was enclosed in glittering silver-like covering. A redhaired woman and a black woman with white hair stood on his shoulders and they were throwing off embers and sparks. A man sang so loud that she could swear she heard him above all the ruckus and noise. By his side stood a woman glowing strong enough to be an entire lightshow by herself. There were two more men. One of them was almost as small as a dwarf, but still he instigated a feeling in people of really being a roaring bear... or something. The other had eyes that seemed to cast rays of red, luminescent light. Jill cried out in joy and ecstasy in a wild, hopeful attempt of subduing the Storm.

People started pointing then. They discovered what had been evident to Jill. And they didn't like it one bit. Jill could more than sense their discomfort and disapproval. They became almost like a single, collective mind.

– They're MUTANTS! a man cried out. – Look what they're *doing!*

– May Satan take them, another cried in horror. – They're ever attempting to lure us into sinning. *Demons!*

The mob's motion started, like a mass of lemmings crossing a deep river. Everything turned bleak and threatening, as if the lights in the streets just got turned off. The very walls seemed to bulge in on her. Human characteristics turned diffuse, and in their faces, Jill saw quite different traits. Their inner being appeared, and it was ugly! The girl gasped and gasped while the dancers were pulled into the mass mob and literally torn apart. She pulled herself back while striving desperately, convulsively to keep her outward calm. Away! She had to get away, before she, too, was exposed.

She pulled back into the shadows. Everything had been like transformed out there. People seemed to be completely transformed from what they had been just a moment earlier. She saw them hit the already wounded, how they made blood flow from open wounds. Somebody should *do* something. Somebody did finally cast a glance in her direction. She had waited too long. They couldn't avoid seeing her frightened expression. She was the only one here not participating in the slaughter, the only one. Gasps of terror rose from her open mouth. She turned away and started running, running, until she crouched somewhere in the darkness with heaving breath and stiff, exhausted muscles, a completely blown mind. She was nothing. There was nothing left. And she cried out in her misery, until her voice turned hoarse and useless. She was useless, she cried, and tears flowed down sore cheeks. After hours, after years, there were no more tears, only silence and shame and fear.

Images assaulted her, chaotic, insubstantial, incomplete. They kept stabbing the battered bodies on the ground with their long, bloodied swords. They chained them in heavy metal and carried them off to a place they could make use of them. They dragged them to the pyre and burned them.

AND BURNED THEM

– There she is, the damn mutant. Let's take care of her, take care of her good.

She stood on her feet, but crouched, exhausted. A massive pack of two-legged dogs pursued her. They had done so for days, for nights without number. She had killed so many of them already, she couldn't recall how many. There were so many of them, too many to ever be counted. Hydra raced towards her, and her head drummed and drummed. They had drawn the power out of her, made her use it up. Everything was gone. She stumbled and fell on hard ground, where she remained. She lay on her back when they caught up with her.

They mocked her with words, looks and thoughts, as they chained her and carried her off in triumph, as they refitted the collar she had torn off.

The young witch ran and ran and ran. But while running from one pack she would suddenly encounter another. She froze then, bewildered, paralyzed. Brain and body stopped functioning. They got the shaking, frightened creature in their sight and intensified their pursuit, like a pack of dogs, smelling the prey. The mutant didn't have any more resistance left in her, and they overcame her. Dragged her to the bonfire in triumph and brimming with their just wrath.

She was back in Northfield. She was. There wasn't any doubt. She could smell the smoke from the factory; see the streets, the pyramid, the bridge over the river… and feel the rope around her body and wrists They had tied her to the pole, on top of a heap of dry, dry branches, lit by a long line of faceless masks. That the endless scream was her own never occurred to her. She fought, fought so hard, against her own aching body and mind, in an attempt to put out the consuming flames. In vain. She held her breath to not inhale the poisonous smoke. In vain. She was capable of seeing the fire and herself, outside herself, on one of the fields north of the city. The crown, her crown of dry branches and wood was elevated to a small hill, and it seemed to her that the entire population was present in the circle around her. Eyes burned in hatred and ignorance, in darkened, indistinguishable faces. The fire reached her. The scream of fear became one of violent, unrelenting pain. Broken in body and soul everything she was, was consumed by the flames. And she was awake to feel it, feel it all. She could feel every tiny bit of skin peeling off. She was conscious while her entire being turned to ASHES.

2

It was as if the hard strung body was pulled up, from outstretched to sitting position, in one single, terrible movement. Completely beside herself, she screamed herself hoarse during that short time. Soft, calming hands touched her, there were comforting words and speech. Eyes were pressed so hard open that she was incapable of closing them, even of blinking. Slowly, only slowly, she became aware of her surroundings.

She was in a bed, in a room. A woman sat by her side. She knew her, didn't she?

– Where am I? She cried out, utterly distraught, breathing hard, gasping for breath. – What HAPPENED?

And then, as a stray thought.

– Who am I?

– I brought you here, the woman said. – You needed shelter, needed rest.

– I know you, the girl gasped. – I knew you, an eternity ago. It's been so long.

She sat in a bed, in a room, in Laurie's house. Laurie held onto her, both in body and mind. Every time she feared she would lose it completely to the panic ravaging her, Laurie was there and kept it from happening. The girl slowly gained consciousness, awareness of self, thoughts and body.

– I'm sweating like a pig. The embarrassment was evident in her voice in spite of the hoarseness.

– That isn't unusual, the older witch pointed out. – This is your Spirit Quest. Most people are completely exhausted when they're done.

– It was HORRIBLE! The girl cried out in her distress, and started sniffing, whimpering. – I was nothing, less than nothing, I'm so useless... *useless*

She whispered. She whimpered.

Her eyes focused once more. She clawed at Laurie, dug into her body and mind.

– But what was it that I experienced? You're familiar with it. *Talk to me!*

– It's a test, a trial. It has to be like that. You're reaching in and out, to the world of dream and not-dream, where life and death are One.

– No, no. Eyes turned pointed, capricious, insidious. – What I saw, what I experienced, was not a dream. I met people there I didn't like. Are they real? Do they exist?

– There are others...

What others? Other things? Other humans? What are you talking about?

The girl didn't move her lips. The voice of her mind echoed in the room.

– Both... Laurie paused, hesitated even more. – There are immortals in this world, and also other, powerful witches... And some who are not even satisfied with that.

– Is that it? You're building an army? Is that why you want warrior witches and not nice little flower worshippers?

A light slap on the cheek, incredibly painful and humiliating. Jill felt the pain, throughout her entire body and mind.

– Impertinent, insolent girl, Teacher scolded. – You must be both to survive, sorceress. Be all things to all people. Since you're born different people will fear you. And their fear and ignorance will make them hate and hurt you, if you do not learn to fit in, to acquiesce to their needs. You know this, don't you? You've always known it.

– I discovered a long time ago, the girl said in a low, subdued tone and posture, – how it feels to be different. People's judgment, their p-power is great and horrible. They made me... they all made me... hate m-myself!

Jill burst into tears. She felt like a little child again, afraid of the dark.

Laurie put a hand on her shoulder and spoke in a soothing, hypnotizing voice.

– For that and many other reasons, you need all the strength you can get, all the strength you little upstarts can contribute to our Coven. You'll sleep again now, you'll find Power, and you'll bring it back to me.

An uncomprehending look dawned in the tearful face. Laurie continued speaking in the same, demanding mode.

– Yes, it's a Hunt, and it isn't done yet. One part is missing, the essential part, the price you'll gain and return with. Your gain is our gain.

– My gain is our gain. Jill echoed. – My gain is our gain.

She blinked, and couldn't understand it. She had been wide-awake just a moment ago, had she not? Then understanding dawned on her, and her face mirrored her paralyzing fear.

– NO! I don't want to. She felt her neck meet the infinitely soft pillow. – I don't like it... there. It's... ugly. Please, Laurie, pretty please.

Laurie's presence in her mind intensified. Her will, her resistance melted away. But her fear remained. Laurie wanted it that way, she realized. A moan rose from her throat, a small, useless sign of defiance.

– You must, you shall, Mistress commanded. – And I'll be with you, shelter you and protect you every step of the way.

– NO! She shouted. – NO! A Spirit Quest/Vision Quest is traveled alone. Everyone knows that! You, too! What are you trying to do to me? What is your... agenda? Are we here? You created this place didn't you, drawing me to it. Why, why?

Was this really a room, something tangible, or was it just ghosts and shadows like the rest? Focusing on the walls was no good. They just seemed to slip away, become immaterial. And that was good, wasn't it? That was good.

– It's for your own good, girl, Laurie said sternly, softly, calming, relieving. – I know you'll see it eventually, see it my way. *Sleep now.*

Sleep!

Jill lifted her arms, threw them at the giant towering far above. Her body, if that was indeed what it was turned soft, weak and malleable. Her entire being sank into the softness of the bed, and she could see nothing more than the patronizing smile above. Eyes closed. Fear made her voice her protest, far into the nascent sleep. But the Night called her. And the Rage returned. And when the Night repeated its call, it was she herself her who responded. This was Right, no matter what Laurie wanted, or didn't want with her. She had never before wanted something this hard. And it was herself, *Me, Myself, I,* who sent her soul, her psyche, her Core, further on her Journey.

3

And the world changed and twisted into something new and unrecognizable and wonderful.

The sound she heard was the sound of riders, but here, now, it was only a tiny, tiny part of the multitude.

I sit in a chair. The room is dark. I'm dark. There are colors, but not the right colors; they're all so right, so different from what I see in a mundane light. There are patterns of complexity and I'm everywhere. I sit here talking to myself, and I'm present in every single point of Existence, in this room, and outside. I can see everything from all angles. I start dissolving then, breaking up into my separate points, and I'm as whole as ever, as Whole as I've ever been. And I can't think as my mind is spread throughout Eternity, Infinity.

What the fuck did you give us?

And I sit in my chair, and I move Beyond. Beyond duality, beyond everything limiting Life.

Beyond fear, even if fear remained. Beyond bravery, even if bravery remained.

why? She heard the thin wail of a cry, inside her head. *why? is there no one else suffering like me? am I the only one?*

And she wasn't certain it was a voice at all, but nothing but the eternal whispering of the wind.

She was tossing and turning in her sleep, moaning in fear and rage, an empty, desolate landscape, not a wilderness at all, filling her vision.

Sometimes there were riders, in the early morning light, in the twilight of early evening.

– WHY? Why are you doing this to me? I've done nothing.

A boy that sometimes was a girl was chained to a post in the wilderness.

– WHY? ARE YOU REALLY THAT STUPID, ASKING THAT QUESTION? said the voice of the city people, the voice with no form, no substance behind it. – WHY NOT?

Sometimes there were riders, tossing the chained human being some bone from the table of riches. There were times when they didn't stop to whip the bony body senseless, but most times they did.

– ARE YOU THROUGH DREAMING THE DREAM OF FOOLISHNESS NOW?

– yes, yes, I am, please, please, please, the brokenhearted child cried out in heartbroken sobs.

– NO, YOU'RE NOT, BUT YOU WILL BE. YOU WILL BE SOON!

She stood before the Mirror. She saw herself with a funny headband, one of metal, glowing occasionally from an electronic source. It was a young girl like any young girl, wearing a pretty dress, well behaved and polite. The image shifted slightly. Another well-behaved and dressed up doll, a puppet of unseen persons. She shivered, Jill shivered where she stood, straight to the bone. The images continued. A dancing doll, nude, performing on a stage, before a crowd of hungry merciless eyes. No mind, no will of her own.

Then in the end, there was the Ghoul.

«Is this what you want»? It taunted her. – «Is this the Life you see for yourself»?

She awakened on a plain, in the same position she had «fallen asleep». To say it was enormous didn't do it justice. Sunshine traced it in all directions, in every possible direction, to where it possibly ended.

Stacy stood in a relaxed, self-confident pose just a few steps away, with her arms folded across the chest.

– I've waited a while for you, she said cheerfully. – You took your sweet time.

– What the hell are you doing here? Jill burst out confused and angry. – Do you want company or what?

– I've been where you're going, Stacy said with some regret. – And no matter how close one otherwise may be, one goes there alone.

– Wish me luck then?

– Good luck! The other one laughed. – Not that you'll need it. What I did with ease, you'll do without major difficulties. Just remember this: You'll not lose control with greater power, but gain it.

– It depends. Jill waved and was gone. She got a last glimpse of Stacy's knowing smile.

She jumped and danced during her crossing of the endless plain, of joy, but also of Hunger, persistent, undeniable. And of conviction. The conviction, ever stronger, that this was right, no matter what Laurie... or Stacy might desire of her.

A rush of wind, a rain of colors not seen blasted her. Where she was on her way, she was pulled. And she allowed it to happen. She pushed forward in expectation rather than prediction, even if what was about to happen was as familiar as a forgotten dream. A part of her, deeper than any civilization had always known this truth.

The plain ended in a huge forest, more massive than she could remember. This forest had not shrunk through the ages, but grown to enormous proportions, so much bigger now than even the last time she had passed through here.

The... previous time?

She halted suddenly in her Journey. There was... something. As a matter of habit, she tilted her head a little to listen. She stretched her arms above her head and levitated into this world's clear, fresh air, until she floated high above the forest. It didn't shrink any from her new perspective, though, rather on the contrary. She was further away, and it had grown in her eyes. As she studied it closely it seemed to close in on her. She was shaking. Never before had anything made her shiver this way. The fear lessened. The anticipation grew further. In there, down there awaited her the hidden, the secret, the forbidden.

Witches do face danger.

A voice from long ago spoke to her.

Especially if it can lead to growth, to further awareness.

It whispered excited in both her ears.

Whatever hid down there pulled and tore her violently. Only iron hard willpower and control kept her from her further Journey.

The forest was round as a circle. It was a circle, a geometric symbol. It was the same no matter the size, the same, but different.

But we and the world are constantly changing, she realized in a moment's clarity of vision. We may allow it to break us, or attempt to grow with the changes, the changes inside ourselves.

Another thought struck her.

– It's better to try, to dare, and fail (a thousand times) than to never risk anything.

It took a few seconds, a few heartbeats before she realized she had spoken aloud.

Her voice echoed from everywhere, returned to her with a vengeance, and then she realized she was laughing. The dark laughter shook the land and air, and forest and distant sea.

The land rose beyond the growth, from uneven ground, to hills and mountains so tall that they tore the heavens, so tall that she could never fly above and beyond them. She had to stay on the path, follow the path, follow herself to her very end, to her beginning. In the forest there would be dangers, but also answers. To learn, to learn more, she had to let go, let go of Control, let go of her self, of Self. She had to gamble it all to gain it all. It was ever thus.

She relaxed, she let go, and thoughts and world turned unclear and foggy.

Around her veiled winds and growth swarmed. Winds quieted slowly and she was aware of her surroundings. a thousand, a million years since last time. A forest, one of infinite size and age embraced her, a world different from the one she had always known. Yet, a part of her had always known this world. A memory of what we all once were touched her somewhere she couldn't identify.

The surroundings seemed swamp-like, but the ground she walked on with her bare feet was dry, sound, tangible. Where was this place? She twitched her brow in confusion. What was it? Perhaps it wasn't so strange that she didn't know. She couldn't recall what she was doing here, even who she was... Could she? She was able to think, to move, to use body and mind... effectively. But everything else wasn't just far away... It was Gone!

She had apparently run far, a long time. Chest was heaving and sinking, even as she sensed she was still a while away from complete exhaustion. Throat was dry. Mouth was dry. Water, she needed water. Smelling it not far away, she increased her speed. And in a flash, she was there. She knelt by a pond to drink. Water was cool and fresh and tasted wonderful. She felt the more than pleasant sensation as it flowed down her throat. After the first life-giving slurps, she paused a bit. The water mirror calmed, and she could observe her own mirror image. She saw a wild young girl. The lively black hair covered her back and reached her hips. Face was familiar, but the body seemed stronger, more agile, functional. Not like that of a... bodybuilder. Was that the word? Yes! No, like one who had grown up in the wilderness, with movements as something natural and right throughout the day, with fair access to nourishment. Skin was the same golden color. As was easy to see. She didn't wear any clothes, except for a modest (was that the wrong word) cloth covering her hips. It didn't feel awkward, merely practical. But these stray thoughts were quickly completely overturned, overwhelmed by others, more important ones. They centered on the undeniable realization that someone, something, somewhere was hunting her.

Would she know who it was, who was hunting her, when it was time? She didn't know who she was. Only that she was being hunted, was haunted. She stopped and listened, tried to hear noises from her pursuers she knew were out there, behind her, somewhere. Nothing yet. But they would come. She ran.

Dirty and bruised and disheartened she moved ever deeper into the woods. At one point on the road, she had lost herself, and she felt down, down, down. She wanted to stop, to give up, to allow them to capture her. In spite of this she drove herself onward. Something... fundamental (that was the right word) inside kept her from surrendering.

Wind increased once more. There was movement ahead of her. Strangely enough, there was little fear. Flashes once more. Painful, but not frightening. Suddenly she remembered. She remembered when she was a little girl. The animals... the animals used to call her name. And she recalled even more. Her parents had used to call her by another name... Aline. Aline had been her name then. They hadn't used that name for a long, long time. But it wasn't the name the animals had cried to her. The name they cried now. They were everywhere around her, even if she couldn't actually see them with her eyes. She couldn't understand their language. Why couldn't she? She increased her speed even more, eager now. Wind calmed and she ran long and hard, all the way to an opening in the middle of the thickest forest. It felt right to take a break there, she thought, so very, very right. And she was less fearful than filled with expectation, in spite of all the shadows standing between the trees. These were not any of the entities chasing her. These were those she had sought.

– *Who are you?* They whispered to her, and she realized that she now could understand their language. – *Say aloud who you are!*

– Jill, she replied. – Jill Stafford.

A creature stepped out of the trees' shadows. He had a human body, but a wolf-like head. A jackal? The ancient Egyptians had called him Anubis, but he was known by many names throughout human history.

– No! He insisted. – Your Name! Not the one others have given you, but the one you've given yourself.

– I don't understand, she said in despair. But she did understand. She knew what a Soulname was, what it entailed. The wildness, the spirit animal, the core of every human being, a Totem it was born with and could draw strength from.

– You're One with all living things, Anubis said.

– In one way or another, we're all in contact, she, Jill Stafford, said.

– No! He corrected her. – *You* are one with all living beings, if you choose it.

She called a name then, her name, the one she had given herself. She didn't hear a sound, but knew she had uttered it in a challenging and brave manner.

A huge cat jumped roaring from the shadows of the trees. A black leopard, a Panther. One of the sacred animals. A female continuing her snarls after she landed *close* to Jill, pacing with threatening snarls. Jill felt an unmistakable need to laugh. The big cat sprang at her and pushed her back, down on her back. Playfully it slapped an enormous paw on her cheek. The girl laughed playfully and tickled the animal on her side, under the left shoulder. She jumped up and threw herself on the black, muscled back. The panther roared and ran into the thick, dense underbrush. The female clawed her fingers into the pelt and laughed loud and throatily. She felt so happy, hell, no, she was *ecstatic.* No use in being modest... Was there? She/Pantha raced forward, hunting the game she/they had caught the scent of. She was still aware of the people hunting her. But they didn't worry her anymore. Let them come. Let them try. She was ready for them, ready to receive them in her loving embrace. Muscles tight as ropes increased speed further. The game was close. A big fat buck. The human knew that, even if she couldn't see it with her eyes. But with her nose, the taste she could already feel in her mouth. And saliva ran from her muzzle. She remembered now, who she was, remembered everything, saw a little girl, Aline inside a burning house. Game appeared within her vision, three jumps ahead. And she was no longer riding the animal, she was the animal, felt, sensed as it did. And something inside her, sleeping for so long, abruptly awoke. Something valuable giving her animal strength in limbs and heart, animal cunning in the mind. Heat rose as steam from the beast's mouth, as from a white-hot forge. A roar of triumph rose from its throat, in the certainty, the conformation of the coming kill. As it made the last, decisive jump human and beast were *One.*

4

She heard the beating of the heart. She sensed the beating of her own heart, re-experiencing the tightening, the explosion of powerful muscles, of being the panther, the tearing of the flesh, the salt blood in her mouth and a thousand sensations more. Moves so easy, so casual replayed themselves in her burning memory. Eyes opened wide. She was standing upright in the field with her arms stretched out to her side. Reborn. A cliché these jaded times, but oh so true, so true. Vision was fixed straight forward. A fire burned on the low rise. The low sun sizzled behind it. She wasn't certain if it was sunrise or sunset, dawn or dusk, and didn't care, didn't bother to find out, or even ponder the issue. She stood upright, wherever she was in the heat of the moment, nude, only covered by the cloth on her hips. Body was wet of the dew in which she had rolled herself. She had no idea what day it was. Neither Time nor Space was important. She knew the other witches were roaming the terrain around her, because she could sense them. They were busy performing their own, private ritual, in their own, private world. She sensed the Power. But not as something separate anymore. It was she. She was it. Stretching her senses further was like child's play. Just a thought, a will. A trifle. By solely using one's eyes one could get the impression that there were few wild animals in the area. Abruptly the image, the impression in Jill's mind changed, and she discovered many, even countless mammals. They were not very distinct all of them, but by concentrating on a single individual she could see so much clearer. A buck, on a cliff. And this wasn't just her own heart beating, but his too, and as she could hear his beating, her own beat that much faster. His blood ran faster as he started running and hers, too. She moved her arms, in hard, intense strokes, playing with the flames in front of the Sun, made them rise high and sink low, as her mood shifted through all possible changes. Dried, dead straws torn from the Earth danced in the air. They were burning and smoking, and forming patterns. As she for a moment, in a flash saw herself from the outside, she was able to glimpse a shape, a shape of a bird, and its mighty, mighty wings. Just a glimpse, before it faded. She didn't really understand the patterns. So much was on a subconscious level, she gathered. Too bad nobody took pictures. Perhaps Laurie did, but certainly not to share with anybody. Just then, Jill didn't care. She had *fun!* Is it real what I feel? Am I playing with the fabric of Existence? She couldn't tell, but knew that this was just the start, that she had hardly been wet on her toes, in her wading into the Sea of Eternity. That was what she was certain of. For now, it was sufficient. «May you live in interesting times». She recalled the ancient Chinese proverb. Or was that a curse? She couldn't tell, but knew it to be true. And dependent on each individual, she thought, as everything calmed, within and without. The fire died. The witch' arms fell down by her sides. The sun rose, backwards or forwards. It was complete daylight now, and the sunshine dried her skin. She wasn't cold. Just then she was only warm. Everything was so much clearer now. Not so crystal clear and well defined as the moment she had faced the mythical Anubis, but still bright and shiny and Shadow. It was a wonderful morning, following the deep Night.

I'm Lillith, she thought, the black leopard.

What she really had found wasn't just a part of herself, a slice of her own being.

She had found herself.

INTERLUDE: The city that was not New Orleans (III)

The female and male Warren landed on the dusty ground just inside the perimeter of the Black Dome. The four soldiers disappeared in a flash, as everything around them seemed to dissolve itself into nothing, to be rebuilt into new and unknown patterns. They checked their immediate surroundings, alert and ready. There were no people around them, no visible signs of activity. Liz looked back the way they had arrived. It was night there, too, now, just as much as it was here. They could observe road-lights, fully operational. Normal looking houses. Everything looked normal. There were no army trucks, no tents or crowd of people, the way it had been merely seconds ago, from their perspective.

She released an involuntary cry of pain and hated herself for it.

– Are you okay? He asked, not really worried.

– It hurt just a bit a moment there, she said calmly. – It's gone now.

Years ago, she would've bitten him off with a display of bravado, enjoying showing off her immaturity. She smiled to him, a burning look, full of desire and Hunger. Almost like an afterthought she checked her shoulder. It had already healed and healed completely. There was no scar remaining, no sign of the wound.

He walked back towards the perceived boundary of the Dome. She stiffened, ready to pull him away on a moment's notice. He walked slowly, very slowly. One step, two steps… Nothing happened.

– Something is happening, he reported. – There is a stiffening of limbs, but not very pronounced compared to what we've experienced earlier.

– Your voice is turning higher pitched, speeding up like hell, she said alarmed. – Get back here.

She yanked him back, with her mind, almost into her arms.

– I think the dome is new here, yet, he pondered, – not fully established. On the outside, on the other hand…

– Days might already have passed since we went in…

He nodded.

– But everything here is new, newly formed.

– Fresh. He nodded.

They started advancing into the city. They reached the city.

There were Samhain-decorations everywhere, pumpkins, skeletons, startling drawings of pretty witches and more, a plethora of variety, ingenuity and creativity taking on a new, sinister meaning to them both.

– I'm getting the shakes, she laughed. – Not because I'm scared. Well, perhaps I am a bit scared, sort of. This is unbelievable. We've awaited something like this our entire lives. McKenzie should have seen us now.

She stopped just a second, shaking her fist in the air.

– Can you HEAR me, old man? I KNOW you can.

He did, in the tent, to him several days removed, on a level he refused to acknowledge. And something else heard her, something both unknown and strangely familiar, something giving her the shakes.

– The power here, Ted mumbled. – In the ground, in the very air.

They heard the sound of chaos everywhere, of people smashing windows, tearing at their own fabric of reality.

– I can smell it, Liz whispered cold. – The winds carry the scent… of burned flesh.

Fireeyes met, burning in anger and despair.

They met the first people. Time rushed ahead. A melody just started, played from a store completely without glass in the window frame (completely without the window frame) ended (after being played several minutes to the end) in a cacophony of noise and silence. Earlier in their lives they might have told themselves that it was their perception of Time that was slightly off, and not Time itself, but these days they were no longer sure. And they no longer cared.

They did care, and they cheered.

– The Winds of Change… running Wild.

She laughed and danced before him, and he danced with her.

As they advanced further into this cauldron of human passions and fears, the warm, warm trickle down their spine felt both cautionary and welcomed. The streets, the walls, the very city itself pulled them in… as they, too…

Became a part of the Black Dome.

Chapter Seven: WITCH

It started with a faint idea, but grew to something resembling a compulsion.

Their Hell Week had ended. It had made what ordinary students lived through seem like a picnic, a walk in the park, but now it was over. Jill supposed she was exhausted, mentally, physically, in more ways than one. But most of all what she felt was refreshed and renewed. Energy coursed through her body and mind.

Before breakfast she took a long run twice through the route she usually did. She was exhausted afterwards, but not tired.

Breakfast was like a smorgasbord, an orgy of taste and smell. She felt aware and alive beyond description. They were all like that, the nebulous witches having just completed their Vision Quest. But she felt she was a notch more so than the rest of them. More eager, more... more!

She approached Laurie in a very excited manner, in front of everybody.

– Why don't we have a... a *market* today, one in the middle of the new city, just a stone throw from the pyramid?

Her excitement, her enthusiasm, her innocence was so enormous that it washed over all of them like a wave. They felt it all, and any objection they might have had, melted like snow in the desert.

– You know which street, too, I gather? Laurie was joking, or seemingly joking, not really committing herself.

– Yes, as a matter-of-fact I...

She stopped, a bit taken back.

– That *is* strange, isn't it?

she said, shrugging it off with a Big Smile.

– You'll organize everything then, Laurie told her. – A lot of hard work is ahead of you, young lady. But do take as many you need as helpers, as long as it isn't interfering with their daily duties.

– It won't! I promise, I promise.

And she was off, in a whirlwind of motion, of action.

It was Sunday. The various christian parishes in the area gathered for their weekly duty. Laurie led her young charges in the daily migration back and forth between the farm and her house in Square. It was almost a ritual in itself.

Jill was among them. She had made some preparations for her afternoon quest, but didn't feel quite ready yet, enthusiasm and regret warring inside her.

Joseph Parnell received his Sunday People on the stairs of his church.

Not far away Gabrielle Asteroth and friends had made their stand. They covered most of the street, giving away their proclamation to people passing by, churchgoers and others. They wore dresses and tuxedos and dressed as well-behaved boys and girls. People had to make big circles around them, to avoid being handed a leaflet.

– Thank you, sir, for accepting this political expression (she was smiling broadly, and so innocently).

– SHAME ON YOU ALL! A big man roared in their faces. He grabbed a paper while passing and threw it in the nearest garbage bin.

Expressions of displeasure rained down on the youths.

– Now, now, Parnell said aloud from his elevated position. – We shouldn't judge these fine young girls and boys. They have every right to do what they're doing. We have a reputation for tolerance in our excellent city.

So calm on the surface, but inside he was foaming. His self-righteous anger flared like a lighthouse to Jill's enhanced senses. She hadn't read the leaflet, but had no doubt about its general content...

She wanted to go and get one, but was held back by Laurie's cautionary mental grip.

– But they... she is so great, Jill protested. – We should give them some moral support, at least... shouldn't we?

– Yeah, Loeh laughed. – She's totally Hot...

Mumbles of agreement from the entire group, even from the older witches.

– She's a fucking time bomb, that's what she is, Laurie said coldly, – a manifested aggression, destined to provoke rage and discord.

The image of the young witch tied to the stake surfaced in their mind. And they shivered and initiative was lost to them.

– But shouldn't we help her, then, exactly for that reason?

– Let's discuss that later, shall we? I have indeed given this dilemma much thought, and I'll be presenting a solution shortly.

And they were content, content in their fear, to leave the matter in Laurie's hands.

2

He had seen her a few times before, he had even been close to her, but he *saw* her for the first time then. Everett Moran took a stroll close to the Pyramid, heading north. He didn't realize that he had taken the least used road, until he saw the witches sitting by their booth, behind their tables. This was something new, a recent development and it intrigued him. To this point they had stayed almost hidden, never sticking their neck out, not really being a part of the cityscape at all. There were four of them, sitting and standing behind the «tile», in their dark clothes. He didn't recognize the three others at first, but he did recognize Jill.

She was having a conversation with a «customer». Most people did buy something, he discovered. Even if they hurried off, casting embarrassed glances to the side.

– It's like any given talent, he heard her say. – Any potential we're born with, like writing or playing music. Ours is just a tad rarer, that's all. We were few even before the Burning Times, the Burning Court, put there by the christian church, and afterwards there were merely scattered scared exceptions left. Today we are not many, but more than most people think. And the number is growing with each generation, slowly regaining what was lost.

– So, you're preaching the same crazy shit as that nutso genius girl, then?

– You *are* aware of the crimes Christians and others committed against people of the old faith, are you not? She asked him quietly.

The man left, without another word.

A small group of brave and nervous, and curious people remained, at least a little while. Everett joined them, a bit nervous himself. The witches conversed and entertained them and others standing at various points in the street, half ashamed, half by half interested.

– During the time of the Burning Court massive amounts of knowledge was lost, the dark-skinned girl with blonde hair cried out. – The last remaining bits from what today is called prehistoric times faded away. It's the burden of our times to rediscover what was lost, before it's too late.

Jill moved a hand through the air, and smoke rose from nothing. Their eyes met. She blinked. So did he. Someone was playing a guitar somewhere, with strange, ghostlike chords. It was one of the boys. And Everett hadn't even seen the guitar in his hand. Suddenly he was back to last night, and so, he knew, was she. She did stage magic, completely «harmless» (or so it seemed), while the audience stared and applauded, and he knew she was both irritated and was enjoying herself.

People left eventually, but he remained. Dust drifted in the air, dust like fire. Nervous, but driven forth by a feeling he couldn't name, he walked to her. He stared into her gray eyes.

– I'm pretty sure today is Sunday, she stated, looking at him, seemingly from far away, – but I'm far from certain. And you... are you… real?

She was leaning back, over the table. Was she posing for him?

– I'm confident that I am, he smiled to her. – About both me being really real, and about it being Sunday, I mean.

Suddenly he was no longer sure, about either. Something about the whole *set* seemed completely unreal to him.

– Your Rush Week is officially over, he added. – Congratulations!

– I thought that might be so, she said, slightly mumbling. – But you see, I've «awoken» several times today, and felt as if everything is a dream.

– Isn't it? He dared a joke.

– That is what they say, isn't it? She rewarded him with a smile and a hot stare.

He diverted his eyes, by looking at the others. They teased him with their smiles. He was elevated to a new level of sweating.

The Greek girl, Andrea, he knew her a bit from school, was the oldest, but if she was supposed to act as a chaperone, she didn't do a very good job of it.

– Excuse me a bit, Everett. Jill put a hand on his shoulder, and walked a few steps, to a man standing on the corner.

Everett recognized him, too, even without looking at his bony frame.

– Good to see you, Luke. Jill took his hands. – Welcome!

– Rumor's flying all over town, he said, with unmistakable traces of his old charm. – I had to come and see the circus.

– You've seen nothing yet...

She found a big cardboard box under the table and gave it to him. He hesitated.

– Take it, she insisted, with an edge of anger in her voice. – It's a gift.

– Thank you. He swallowed with a soreness in his throat.

– There is work, hard work, for you and many of your people on the farm, she said rigidly, – if you're interested. We're constantly understaffed.

It was stated clearly arrogantly, but not unfriendly.

He tried to say something. His lips moved, but there was no sound. He left, and the quiet street turned even quieter. There were no cars, no loud noises, nothing, except the humming form of the Pyramid, also somewhat muffled. Usually noticeable over major parts of the city, they only heard the slight humming, as if it was miles away.

Jill turned to Everett once more, giving him her complete attention.

– You know... I'm still not convinced that I'm not dreaming. She seemed to give it some thought before giving him a wink. – Aside from that I'm pretty much convinced it has to be next Saturday or something. I feel like I've slept a week.

– It's said you are witches, Everett queried. – Are you?

With an unmistakably worry sneaking into his voice, fucking up royally.

– You better believe it, mate!

She stood straight and proud before him, her Welsh accent ascendant.

– Great! He released a breath of relief. – When you're free...

– I'm Free now. She took his hands, abruptly and intense. – I'm always Free.

– Greeeat...

– We're just about done here anyway, and these *witches* can pack up and go home without me, can't you guys?

– Sure, honey, Andrea said lightly. – You just go and have a really good time...

She moved to his side with a... catlike, supple quality. With a conspiratorial smile she stuck her arm around his. She made a small wave with her fingers to the others, and they were on their way. To him it was a moment of mixed emotions, of worry and wild expectations. He had certain problems with his sense of reality.

And he didn't mind. He didn't mind at all.

– Hot, isn't it? She smiled blue eyed with her gray eyes.

– Hot, he confirmed, unsteady on his feet, wondering if she could smell his sweat.

– A lovely day, she said hotly. – What shall we do to give it justice?

– You decide, he said. He started to relax more, and could be more himself.

– Great! Then I would like you to introduce me to the people you know.

He noticed that she didn't use the word «friends». She was very astute.

He didn't have many *friends!*

– Okay. An involuntary shrug. – If that's what you want.

– Thank you! She kissed him on the cheek. – I'm looking forward to it.

– A friend of mine, you've met him, Henry Gyrich, is having one of his «get-togethers» tonight. We can go there. The Nice Young People of this town usually go to «Dynasty», during the hours before one of their parties.

– Sounds like fun, let's join them there.

He couldn't read her at all. Even if he suspected she was up to some mischief, he couldn't be certain. She could just as well use him to get access to the future powers of the city.

– You don't think so? She grinned. – Wait and see...

And they started laughing, laughing so hard that they had to sit down on a bench, supporting each other's bodies to keep them from tumbling.

He still didn't feel sure about her.

She kissed him on the lips, sultry and hungry, pulling back before he could respond «properly».

They entered the building called the Pyramid, side by side. The upper floors were offices and a huge hall, the lower a big shopping mall and entertainment center. He wasn't really keen on this. He had been leaving this place. Now he was returning. It helped that he had her by his side. He just wasn't sure how much. In spite of her excitement, her fresh young sensuality.

Was he afraid for her or of her?

«Dynasty» was a kind of mix of a cafe and a disco, one of the «finer» places in town. It didn't have any dress code, since its visitors were usually well dressed anyway. Everett and Jill weren't. Because of this, but not exclusively so, they were noticed by everybody the moment they walked through the inner door. He felt it, like a wind, a draft, and he was positive she did, too. Not everybody was looking directly at them, but they were aware of the new visitors in ways that bordered on the paranormal.

– What a delightful bunch. Jill shook her head, confirming his kind of ephemeral notions. – They're already aware of us in every recess and corner in the room.

Music was low just then. Neither Jill nor Everett had anything against roaring music, rather on the contrary, but this thud-thud-thud massive bass drum shit they disliked quite thoroughly. It was just excellent that it was being played on such a low, virtuous volume.

Henry Gyrich sat in a corner, in his corner, surveying it all. Jill recalled meeting him on the bus. She had been another person then. Even their meeting in the street, on the night of her Initiation she experienced as a thousand years ago. But the old insecurities and sense of shame persisted in her. Even if she knew what kind of person he was. Even if it had been so that she had never met him before, she would have known of him, known the real him, hidden behind the exterior shell. She suspected that the beginning of Everett's friendship with him stretched far back in time, when they were both innocents.

– Ah, hi, Henry let out, chiding her, – what difference a few days can make in a person's make up.

He recognized that she was a threat to his position here, to his position anywhere. She had really changed, not just in obvious outward ways. She recognized that, too, but still got hot and sticky by his interest.

– Thank you, good sir, she chided back.

– Allow me to give you a warm welcome, he said, rising to «properly» greet her. – What do you think of the place?

She returned his kiss on the lips, reflexively.

The churning chaos inside intensified, the confusion, the fear, the undirected desire, chaotic images, forever unfinished puzzles of the Shadow vortex sucking her in. She had expected it, anticipated it, and planned to use it. The smile touching her face made him pause.

– Not... *bad*... She looked around with a pointed, measured stare. – But the music is really lousy, it stinks. I'll fix that. Just a minute…

Quick on her feet she disappeared into the control room, the usual domain of the DJ. But there was no DJ there now. She was there. She switched the resident minidisk with the one she had brought with her.

Images from a television set, the one in Sharon's Inn, rose in her inner vision. Elizabeth Warren's dominant performance, her spot-on revelation of Life.

– Muslim girls in France have once again started to prefer the scout. They say it's «protecting them from the boy's stares». This attitude, in variations isn't exclusive for Muslim girls. It's the behavior of all timid girls of civilization.

– But what you describe as an ideal here is truly promiscuous behavior, is it not? Gayle Tadero, the interviewer pointed out.

– I did expect you to use that word. Liz laughed. – Such words and ways to look at the world are, of course, taught and «beaten» into us from an early age. We're taught to forget Nature, to forget ourselves. Guilt and shame are bred into us, into us all. Don't believe it's any easier for the poor boys. Very few of them dare to use their eyes in open appreciation of the female, and they, too, are looking away, when females send them looks of interest.

– We «poor» boys are even running the risk of a flat hand on the cheek, or worse from a jealous boyfriend or protective father, if we show our interest too openly, Ted said.

– You poor things, Liz mewed. – I do feel sorry for you.

Laughter erupted in among the audience and also more. It was the start of one of the most memorable nights in television history.

Jill was still pissed at herself, because they had turned off the television set, when believing the program to have ended.

Unannounced it had continued after the commercials, continued into the late hours of Night.

Jill stormed out of the booth and pulled Everett with her, out on the dance floor. «The End» by the Doors started flowing from the speakers, from the floor, from the Earth itself, music made many years before anyone present in the room had been born… immortal, everlasting. The rhythm… slow at first, but making the blood boil, anyhow. Slowly, slowly the dance turned wild. Jill led at first, but soon enough she didn't have to.

– I'll turn it off, Victoria mumbled. She went straight to the booth. When she attempted to open the door, however, she couldn't even budge it. Tim «the Bully» Drake, wanting to impress the assembly and the maiden in distress used all his considerable muscles, to no avail.

Jill was smiling. She allowed herself to be sucked in, and sucked everybody else in with her. The cloak whirled and whirled around her and her partner. Sometimes it surrounded them, hiding them completely. Or it could be as if it was blowing in the wind, standing straight out behind her back. *Some cloaks may reveal more than hide.* In spite of this she removed the hood on her head, shaking her head, making the hair flow. She waved to them all, waving them to her.

– Come, she shouted.

– *Come!* She cried.

Many came, and those who didn't immediately did so after a while, to not risk losing face. She smiled more, embracing them with her mind, striving to hold back, not to be found out, making them share her Joy.

After the End... ended, two more conventional melodies followed. In form at least, if not in content. «Break Every Rule» and «Steamy Windows», performed by Tina Turner. The Witch made them listen to the words, feel the rhythm.

Then «Chameleon» by Mystic. With that it truly ended. It was one of the more infamous and famous underground classics in recent years, dark rhythms and harmonies, both calm and wild. Everything ended and began. Faces among the dancing crowd changed constantly between disbelief, wonder, and disgust. And Joy, definitely joy. She didn't imagine it. It wasn't wishful thinking on her part, and she rejoiced.

If a parent had accidentally wandered in during all this, they would have been considerably more than Shocked. The place had changed, from one minute to the next, to a sweaty, scandalous dump.

Lights blinked and blinked. Blinked out, blinked on. Someone had turned off most of them. Only the soft lights were still occasionally on. Someone had turned on the fog machine. Gray, dark and colored fog spread through the room, among the human beings dancing in the night.

Everett and Henry sat by a table, studying her. Henry studied her excessively.

– She isn't the right one for you, he said critically.

– Are you kidding? Everett smiled, shaking his head. – She's exactly right for me.

– What about Victoria?

– Give it a rest, will ya. My parents picked her while we were both in the cradle. We've hardly been able to speak about the weather in our deep conversations. That's the only thing we've ever had in common.

Everett Moran followed her, Jill Stafford, with his eyes. The movements, the changing looks on her face, the shadows dancing on her skin while she sat between them, the center of the attention, though not in any ordinary sense of the expression. One could drown in the very sight of her, in the Pyramid, during the walk through the city, on the Gyrich Estate outside town.

The party transported itself there, during twilight. Not the main building, of course, but a minor one, closer to the main gate. This one was ten times the size of an ordinary house. The main building was twice that size again. Not that much of a difference really. Henry had this smaller version of a palace at his full disposal tonight. The blanket of darkness descended on the land and the remaining guests arrived in smaller or bigger groups.

Jill could see them, as moths helplessly attracted to the light. Any light. The witch had walked out on one of the many balconies. She let her underarms rest on the old masonry, taking in the mood of the landscape unfolding below her. The Moon had risen just slightly above the low horizon, big and deep yellow, soon to cover the trees and fields and buildings in blue silver light. She felt stirrings inside tonight, not comparable to any she had known before. Strange notions continued to excite her, in spite of her present location, one that wasn't exactly the paragon of inspiration. She wouldn't exactly call this a «party». What went on had little to do with actual celebration and much more to do with rivaling and pointers and stickers, finding perceived faults in others, to gain a possible advantage over them. So little emotion, or so much cold emotion. Not the least that.

Her seduction earlier hadn't been that of a Witch using her Power, but that of Joy. She was quite proud of that. But also knew that it couldn't last. More was required to make a lasting impression. Much more!

Everett was looking at her, approaching her from behind. She could easily pick up his thoughts, discern them from those of others. She turned around, meeting his stare as he walked through the double portal. In an aura of fluorescent mist, she saw him. She could be tempted to drown herself in him. She knew his name. The One he had given himself... and it sang in her, was singing in her, in waves and waves of longing.

– What a beauty, he breathed.

– Yes, the moon makes the landscape even more of a sight to behold, doesn't it? She talked the way he did, a bit formally, but her voice had a teasing, underlying quality.

– I hope you won't take this in a bad way, he said, with slightly parted teeth, – but my praise was meant for you and you alone.

– Touché.

They didn't laugh aloud this time, but they heard each other laugh anyway. And the wild cheerfulness hid behind the smiles they sent each other.

– It feels like I've been waiting for you all my life, he said.

And maybe even longer.

– At least since last week, she said grinning, not unfriendly.

– Have you ever been... close to something? He asked. – Very close, for so very long, and never been able to take that last, crucial step forward?

– All my Life. Her eyes glossed over.

She looked at him.

– For instance: I feel «close» to this house, as if I have been here, or somewhere similar before, when I clearly haven't. And when I look at Henry, I see him as not so tall and a lot fatter, instead of seeing his clearly handsome frame and face. It is as if I … know him, too, not just the house, and I *don't* know the house. Therapists would have a field day with me, wouldn't they?

He frowned.

– Some of them did.

– You see, glimpse something akin to an alternative reality, he insisted. – I wouldn't worry about it.

They both faced each other in silence.

– I am, as they say, born and bred in these parts, he said, even more intense. – This is a very conservative area, in spite of the impression they're attempting to create. I've never quite managed to fit in. And I have tried. My innate interest for everything «dark»... ghosts, shadows, haunted houses, witches... werewolves, vampires and everything, has fortunately kept me from succeeding. My parents, in their despair keep saying I'll grow up and out of it eventually.

– I've had it the same way, she stated. – I can't even recall when it started to interest me. It seems that it always has. The Unknown, at the very least has always intrigued me. I know for certain now that there are opportunities in life, to find knowledge and secrets, and I intend to use as many of them as possible.

– Sometimes I feel removed from daily life, he said, kind of testing the waters.

She smiled, brushing a hand against his cheek.

– My take on that is that most people are not sufficiently removed from what passes as daily life these days. And they claim that the world is either spiritual or physical. Me? I think it's both. I see no contradictions in this.

He nodded, understanding her implication. Everything was relative, depending on point of view. There were no contradictions.

They felt homesickness then. But this was something they had been carrying with them their entire life. They were far away from home. Not necessarily in Space, but in Time.

She took his hands and intoned dreamily:

– As if in a dream *(within a dream)*, I can see where we're coming from, and what we may become...

Flashes of Joy, of worry, of wonder, of fear. She kept her Mask on, revealing nothing behind. Even though she wanted to reveal to him, share with him, everything.

The air inside was a myriad of scents. Most of the guests arrived within the next half hour or so. She was there to greet them all. And even though Henry fought hard to stay the dominating presence, he failed gloriously. Everything ended up in a different light, as if transformed. Jill wouldn't exactly call the result a positive mood, but thanks to her own present, cheerful strain, she turned *inspired.*

She proceeded in stride, with an expectant smile on her lips, hardly recognizing the dangerous witch she glimpsed in the mirror. She knew she would enjoy herself in malicious pleasure and enjoy herself simultaneously. Every Human Being carried in them such seemingly contradicting traits. It worried her a bit, but she paid the tiny voice of worry within no heed. Gray eyes sparkled in the lights from the countless lamps. And admiration and envy were hers to enjoy.

– Look at her, Victoria snarled. – She has the nerve to believe she's actually worth anything.

A pair of girls usually following the class president blindly found themselves in the position of wanting to contradict her. They didn't allow themselves to be swayed by the temptation.

Challenge was clearly visible in the eyes, in the pose of the witch, and if there was fear as well, it was well hidden behind the pointed stare. Her entire demeanor spoke of Mystery and Secrets, provoking society's fear of the unknown and what was different. She was full of contradictions as well. At least they perceived her that way. One moment she could sit there, discussing Magic, the next completely mundane tasks and issues. Then she gave them the distinct impression of being a completely *normal* teenager and they almost forgot how she was dressed. To Everett this bespoke a person rich in emotion and content.

Others didn't look at it in quite such a positive light. They turned even more confused, insecure and angry.

«Successful» people were ever striving to ignore those, in their eyes less successful. The Witch in their midst was a chasm in their perfect and ordered world. They found it hard to label her, and were thus lost.

She mingled, walking among them as the most natural thing in the world, both alone and with Everett, feeling exhilaration. Over their reactions, but most of all because of her own bravery. There was a slight drawback in the form of a headache. She still had some problems with shielding herself from all the fevered thoughts, all the close minds. But she persevered. She could handle it. Their energies strengthened her, not the opposite. The relentless disco music, from the many speakers everywhere in the house distracted her however, in its horrible monotony.

There were drugs everywhere. Wherever they went, there was an abundance of it, but most of all cocaine. She had heard that the Americans used more money/funds procuring this than they did on gasoline. After spending the evening here, she could believe it.

She danced when feeling like it, both with and without Everett, casting them all beguiling glances, rotating in her own, self-made circle, and rousing the assembly to thought and Life.

But she couldn't let go completely, and it frustrated her.

More dancing, more accentuated movement, more glances, pointed stares, to the point of her shocking herself. It was as if she kept drawing on experience she didn't have, from places she had never been. A Gypsy in a circle of wagons somewhere, around the turn of the nineteenth century, an Indian girl somewhere in the Old West. *Hide in plain sight. That was the only answer.* She blinked, but didn't allow the sudden thought to distract her. *Closer to present time. A young girl, dressed in revealing clothes, at a party, in a house much like this. And she saw the burning fire-eyes close by.* And the confusion strengthened her. She started to smile, even broader than before.

The Witch started swinging the cloak around her, as she lifted a hand, signaling for them to pay attention. And they all did, as she started ascending the stairs to the floor above. It was in a room clearly secluded from the living room, but there was no wall in between. They could see the stairs all the way up. They saw her. Everett had the crazy notion that he would have seen her, even if there had been a wall there.

She stretched out her arms to the side, turning the hands around, back and forth, back and forth. And the hands caught fire. Somebody screamed. She seemed totally unaffected. No one else reacted.

Cheap trick, she scolded herself, she didn't care.

– Stage magic, a boy said aloud. – It's nothing new. They use an ointment. I could have done it myself.

Ointment, an excellent idea.

The fire hurt. It was the hairs and the outer shell of dead cells that burned. Sweat stung her eyes. She concentrated about supplanting the inner layer of skin as it burned off. She concentrated more, and slowly, painfully the flames changed from being flames to just look that way. The fire became more luminosity than heat. She didn't feel the compulsion to clench her teeth anymore. And it had been easy. She knew then that she was capable of showing them so much more. And that she was only starting to explore her capabilities.

It's like a dancing on a high wire, she thought. *To show them that we exist, but not convincing them of it.*

Everett couldn't be certain of what he saw, and what was imagination. More than the others, at least, he was convinced of that. Whatever she reminded him of, as she danced catlike up the stairs, was buried deep within him, in his Total Recall. The flames, the sight of them embracing her entire body cut into him like a blade only recently emerged from a blacksmith's forge.

She paused in the middle of the stairs. Before she continued to the top, she cast a glance behind her, including them all. They started following her on her ascension. She swept the cloak around her, while floating on hidden feet away from the staircase. She knew they would come, friends, as well as enemies. Good. It would have been too bad if she had put this in motion for nothing.

The evening moved on and no one could say for sure when it turned to night. Who could ever? At the very center of the house there was a room with no windows. All electrical lights dimmed to nothing on the path to that room. Enlightening the path was candles and oils burning in boxes. In the room there was a single table. On it, with her legs pulled in under her, sat the Witch.

A young girl, penetrating them all with her pointed stare. It didn't matter if she sat with her back to some of them. They all felt her stare. She had their complete attention.

So easy. Half in trance, half-awake, half-asleep Jill spoke. Somewhere there was a raven flapping her wings. Jill saw a girl sleeping in a bed, mumbling, tossing and turning. Gabrielle Asteroth slept with open eyes and nightmares haunted her.

– ... remember that witches are born, not created. The rough, silken voice floated in the room, outside the room. They couldn't resist the temptation to listen. – That makes them rare, but there are more than people may think. Anybody might be one. Even if the Power is hereditary, it may stay dormant for generations. In our age, the Machine Age, we live so far away from it, from Life that we may never discover what, who we are.

– Many wish that the world is something... solid, like a brick wall. Just the opposite of what it *is*, namely ghosts and shadows. Modern humanity is fooled into believing in an illusion, taught its validity from birth. The real world is further and further removed each time the child draws breath.

– So... what is the illusion?

– Blind faith, Jill replied calmly. – Authorities, hierarchies, God...

– Blasphemy, Victoria shouted. – I knew it. She's just a lousy Heathen.

Some were hushing her up, but many just «realized» something, falling back on their preprogrammed patterns.

– Yes, call me a heathen, Jill said unmoved, – make me proud. What's next? Are you afraid I'll pull a lovely green apple from my pouch?

– What *are* you talking about? Victoria strove in her lack of comprehension. – What...

Shouts of terror and dismay interrupted her. The Witch sat there, smiling sweetly, with one huge, green apple in each hand.

Several people fled. Those who remained were either frozen... or interested in spite of themselves.

Two blond girls, identical twins, came forward and took the apples, to offer them around. They took one bite each, before giving them away. Everett was the first to take a bite after that, a huge one. Then there were others.

– Thank you, now where were we, oh, yes...

– The Illusion, the Raven, trying her wings, said, – is the belief, the conviction that we may distance ourselves from Nature, from the consequences of our actions, from ourselves. *All* our problems, directly or indirectly, arise because of physical and mental imbalance.

– And you'll sit there on your ass and do your magic? Henry said mockingly. – It's a superb ass you've got there, girl, but surely it won't be sufficient in this case.

There was laughter, but far from everybody participated in it. Jill, however, did.

– What if the motivation behind the Burning Times was not intolerance and that particular version of ignorance, but was just used by the forces behind the motivation, have you ever thought about that? The ancient beliefs of Freedom from state, from church, from constraints were a threat to the emerging christian hierarchy and the new, paradoxical «rational» times both. While these two «new», seemingly opposite directions melded together into one, all true opposition was hunted down and eradicated. But scattered records prevailed, Memory prevailed... Life may be beaten to the ground, but will ever rise again. Life is the dominating force in the universe.

– What is Magick, if not an «invention» of ignorant people to explain what they cannot understand? The natural abilities we're all born with, but have forgotten, things hidden in the shadows for so long that they have become a distant memory, explained by religious fanatics and superstitious fools as «magic». Suspicion is a well-established tradition, centuries old, and has been used for many purposes, not the least removing opposition to tyranny, to cloud people's minds, and condemning the practitioners of the old ways as *heretics.*

– But the ancient ones knew a truth that just now is about to resurface, *that the Earth and the Human Beings are one.*

Moran spoke up, both conscious and not, pondering the validity of his words as he spoke, puzzled and amazed by the sense of wonder they created within.

– Call it Gaia, Maya or a common consciousness, but the planet is *alive.* Not necessarily sentient, as the word is usually understood, but an interdependent «unit». By destroying a part of it, we're destroying a part of ourselves, and are poorer for it.

– You can't be serious, Henry exploded. – Don't tell me that you, too, have embraced the nature freaks and turned anti-technological on me?

– You don't think I stand by my words? Everett felt sort of removed from himself... or perhaps removed from who he had always believed he was? – I do think that «lower» levels of technology and nature may coexist, but that the sanctity of nature must come first in all things.

– BRAVO! Non-aligned shouts sounded from more than one direction. Henry turned deep red.

– You can say that again. The smile Jill sent Everett made him turn quite red himself.

– But I don't quite understand, your Highness... It was Leonard, he who had spoken up, been curious earlier, too, emphasizing his teasing by a huge grin. – You spoke about everybody's inborn, natural abilities. What then is distinguishing the witches from the rest of us poor slobs?

– I'm not sure I spoke about everybody's inborn «paranormal» abilities, Lenny, Jill replied, with a voice, just a bit more «normal». – But it might be that way, I don't know. And if that is indeed so, we who may be called «witches» or «mutants» may be more of a «natural» than most people. I've heard that word be used, signifying that we must work off less of our butt than the majority to gain insight, to develop Talents. Perhaps we are not two emerging, diverging species at all, but rather individuals on a ladder, a flat ladder, branching out everywhere? We're all born *of* Nature. That I do believe is a fact. Close to Life, and all other living «things». That is an understanding we all once shared, and anyone may «achieve». But the awareness of the Witch goes further, deeper, the potential, I suspect, is greater. We're the connection between the old and the new, the Agents of Change, forever upsetting the old order, forever a part of it.

She was shrugging, revealing her uncertainty, her doubt.

– Once in a distant past, I suspect, we humans created an invisible world beside the physical. We did it. No god or alien being. I don't know, perhaps it was then we became Human Beings? We human beings are three parts. We're body and mind, seemingly in conflict. Then there is «soul», perhaps an «evolutionary» attempt to combine the other two. Or perhaps we're even more, more than all three, more than the sum of the parts. Call it a Core, something that is really everything we are, physically, psychologically, spiritually... Perhaps the «seed» has always been there, been present, in the primordial soup, before consciousness, but not before memory. Perhaps memory can precede consciousness? Perhaps it was present in the two amoebas first exchanging «genetic material», in the first lifeforms on land, in the primates first leaving the safety of the trees for the endless plains. The seed has flourished on the fruitful, living planet and now, now, that seed is about to emerge in full...

It had been building, rising as slow steam from the Earth on a hot afternoon. With the last word, something *happened,* something unspeakable.

... *Smoke* seemed to rise from her, spreading among them, spreading among them all.

She shook then, so little that even those sitting closest to her couldn't discern anything or be certain.

– Are you okay? Leonard asked worried, sensing her worry, her sudden fear.

– Yes, she managed.

Something was turning itself on inside her then, turning itself inside out, something more than she had experienced earlier, something new, and with it came knowledge, awareness and chilling understanding.

She «saw» Joe Parnell on his pedestal, in his church. But that wasn't all, not all at all. His image was supplanted by... by Laurie... Laurie on her porch. Was there... Jill realized, for the first time, clearly, that there was no substantial difference between him praising his God and Laurie preeaaaaching about the Excellency of her Goddess.

The girl let go of a tiny cry of revulsion, of pain.

– Hey, *are* you all right? Meta, one of the twins, asked.

– It's okay, really.

– You've fallen into a spontaneous trance and had a vision, Meta said brightly, – glimpsed secrets, gained knowledge. I've read about it. Poor girl...

Her twin arrived with a glass of water. They pressed it against the girl's lips. She discovered how parched her throat had become and drank greedily.

– How come you have read about it? A voice, hoarse as paper.

– Hey, all identical twins are weirdoes. It comes with the territory.

It was Meta again, wasn't it? Melanie, the quiet one, hardly spoke, did she? Jill had read extensively about twins, because Meta had been right, and Jill read everything about everything perceived as weird. The way she had heard it was that identical twins could be as different, often even more so, than most siblings. Even though they had completely identical genetic patterns. Twins growing up apart, perhaps even having never met often discovered that they were remarkably similar, and had lived remarkably similar lives. Perhaps twins were different because they had grown up together, alike because they had grown up apart?

The séance, or whatever it had been, was over. Jill rose from the table, started, suddenly self - consciously to brush her robe. Conversation turned (almost) normal. Jill changed back again, slowly growing more relaxed, once more one of the herd. The interrupted party moved on.

Everett finally managed to be alone with her. Some of the girls sent them both snickering remarks before departing.

– That was amazing, he said, holding back the most of his admiration, knowing fully well that he could hide nothing from her. – I don't want to go off the rocker here, but that was poetry in motion.

– That was crude, she retorted, – an exercise in trial and error. A lot came instinctively, like things I knew, but had forgotten. The rest stemmed from my boundless ingenuity and wisdom...

She rotated a full circle in front of him and made an elegant curtsey, as if on a stage.

– Anger... anger and ... passion. She was blushing. – Erupting from a forge hotter than the Sun.
And in passing:
– It was absolutely, positively weird!
Something looking very much like smoke drifted just under the high ceiling. Some of those present glanced at it with worry in their eyes.
– Is it smoke? A girl wondered. – It might be dust, you know.
– You must be kidding me, her friend said. – There isn't a mote of dust in this house that hasn't been caught and taken to jail long ago.
The very word dust made it tingle so pleasant in Jill and she pondered why, and the thought itself brought further contemplation.
– I'm opening like a flower, she whispered coquettishly in Everett's ear.
Sweaty bodies moved through both the living room and the rest of the house. All windows had been opened wide. It didn't have any measurable effect. This September night was the warmest in recorded Northfield history.
– Damn heat! Henry mumbled. – I'll take a bet from anybody that it's at least 80 outside. This happens night after night. What's happening?
– The Climate Change, Henry, one helpful, sympathetic voice told him.
– Oh, shut up!
Jill danced all over the ground floor in slow, lazy movements, danced relaxed, with half closed eyes. She wasn't limiting herself to one tiny part of the floor. Even so, it was difficult to those who had seen her upstairs to reconcile this experience of her with the previous one. She seemed so completely normal, even ordinary, now.
Everett had a pretty good idea about what went through their minds.
They don't know her, he thought.
She danced with Henry. An act of consideration on her part, she told herself, attempting to bridge the cleft, no, the abyss, between the two of them, for the sake of Everett's friendship with him.
She had never really enjoyed dancing. Lack of exercise had made her legs badly suited to it. That and her fear of letting go. The last few weeks had taken care of both the exercise and letting go problem. Now, she feared she would take the letting go part... too far. The dancing wasn't really with someone most of the time on modern dance floors. Everybody danced solo, closing in on each other at each other leisure. Henry was surely closing in on her, like an arrow… or a bowman, a hunter pointing the arrow at the mark… She found that she didn't mind actually. He reminded her of Jason, except he was far worse, and that was what made him okay.
It took some time until she realized how parched her throat had once more become. She hurried (in a non-suspicious manner) to the kitchen. Throat felt dry as desert sand. She wanted some clean water (no more punch) and some privacy. One big glass first, then two more. She didn't remember to add salt until the third refill. Of course, it didn't really help any. Lack of water in the body (or not) had no direct bearing on her state of being.
Feeling burning hot, she leaned against one of the cupboard doors. What was wrong with her?
Henry entered the kitchen. He sat course straight for her.
– We didn't get to finish our dance, he said.
– It wasn't «our» dance, she replied softly, – and I was thirsty.
– You're some fireworks, do you know that, he said appraisingly. – You're certainly not the right one for Ev. He likes them a bit less eager.
– I don't believe that for a moment, she said with a distinct chill in her voice. – He would have to be quite stupid then, and he certainly isn't that.
He took her under her jaw, and she sensed a shiver of delight inside. She had to be nuts. She didn't like him. No, that was not entirely correct. She despised him. Every impulse, every thought, she received from him confirmed that. Why was it then, when he touched her... like that... she got... excited? It was crazy.
It's my inexperience, she thought frantically. That got to be it. The pressure, everything is just rising inside. *If I don't take care of it soon, I may give in to everything in pants, including the principal's dog.*
The principal's dog wore pants.

That image in her mind did help. She was snickering, but not because of Henry, as he led himself to believe. He thought she was an easy mark, who treated right, would give in to anyone showing more than a casual interest.

And he's right.

She just broke his grip and left him.

As she opened the door, she met Everett on his way in, visibly worried. How sweet of him.

– What happened here? He asked.

– He attempted to exploit the inexperience of little moi, and seduce me, but he failed. Don't worry about it.

– She's lying, they heard from the other side of the door. – That girl is as experienced as a ten dollars hooker.

Everett felt a pang of guilt. He had entertained similar thoughts during the course of the evening.

– Compliments, compliments, compliments, she sang exuberantly.

She took the hand of the man in front of her, staring into his deep, dark wells. He returned the stare, staring into himself. Perhaps it was at this point he said goodbye to his former life.

– No, she is not, he said half to himself, half to no one in particular. The emerging smile burned him.

They started to move, to move as one.

– JILL, hey, Jill!

They were on their way up the stairs, up a floor, when someone kept shouting her name, interrupting their task. It was Victoria and her loyal cohorts.

The bootlickers, blind followers, arselickers, Jill told herself.

Both she and Everett walked back down, to the assembled group by the stairs.

– We've heard that witches are allergic to salt. Victoria spoke up, dripping venom from her forked tongue. – And since we have an expert in the house tonight, we thought we should ask if it's true.

– What *nonsense!* Jill, suddenly dog tired of their shit, their transparency felt the stirring of bitter anger, of a shortened fuse. – I wouldn't make myself even sillier than you are, if I were you. I would say that you should have noticed that I've been eating your overly salted food the entire evening. Humans can't survive without salt. This is salt, isn't it?

She grabbed a saltshaker from the tray Victoria held out to her and held it high.

– Yes, Victoria exclaimed incredulously.

Jill stuck out her tongue and sprayed a thick layer of powder on it, pulling it back in, grimacing, swallowing it, in one, two, three turns, grimacing again.

The music stopped. No one was close to it, close to any switch. The music just stopped from one moment to the next. The room turned silent, the assembly hushed. The girl had the eyes of everyone present on her.

– We'll die if we get an iron stake through the heart, or one of wood, or silver. But I'll go out on a limb here and assume that this is something I have in common with everyone here assembled?

The fuse was definitely shortened. But she couldn't stop herself now, couldn't be stopped now.

A cross, a big one in silver decorated the wall, not far from where she stood. She took two steps forward and tore it down, held it up, without any visible effort.

– This has no «value», except as a symbol, a symbol of oppression, persecution, false play... What is valuable, truly important is the spirit, the will to Live and thrive in every Human Being.

The cross fell from her hands, dumped to the floor. Nobody moved.

– You're tired, honey, Meta said. – You're right, but still tired.

– Tired, Jill confirmed.

She didn't turn the music back on. The other girl, who did that, glanced suspiciously at the ON/OFF switch for a while, before collecting her bravery. The party got back on its feet, momentarily, quickly continuing on its spiral downturn. Everybody was looking at each other, second-guessing the others, uncertain about how to react and proceed. They had not yet completely adapted the older generation's «the show must go on» (no matter what) mentality. They were still young, not yet properly set in the mold, the form of their parents.

The party ended, as Jill could easily have predicted it would in Disaster. A small pain in the back of her throat stopped her from enjoying that fact.

But parties moved on, becoming nachspiels. This was unheard of on one of Henry's tubs, though. But tonight, it did happen. It died for lack of momentum, of nourishment. Henry himself was not to be seen.

Joan, whom they all knew from school as something of a joyride led on in the long walk off the Gyrich property.

– This shithole is so big. One is tempted to fear that it will never end.

Laughter. This was a mixed crowd. Some even had expensive cars, but most of the group belonged to the category that had not fled from the «attic», when things had started to get hairy. They had all taken a bite of the forbidden fruit... and they wanted more.

– Back to school tomorrow for you insensitive brats, she continued performing. They laughed harder, knowing fully well that she was indeed counted among the teachers as one of the «insensitive brats».

– That remains to be seen, Melanie said surprisingly (was it Melanie... how in the hell could one tell? Jill sure couldn't). – The night is still young, and a lot may happen.

Cars were parked not far from outside the gate, but everybody walked from there, a remarkably pleasant short walk to Oldtown, to Main Street, to Haldoway's Inn. The lights were on, and life was abundant. As they approached the entrance, they encountered a man, Gus Walters, as usual being thrown out of the fine establishment. Sharon took care of it herself. There wasn't a single mark on poor Gus, but he was clearly beaten senseless, even more so than the enormous intake of various spirits had made him.

– You're not closing, are you, Everett inquired, – this early on such a fine evening?

– Nope, Sharon was shaking her head. – Just removing some disturbing elements... Be welcomed and enjoy yourself.

– Asteroth is performing here tonight, isn't she? Jill inquired.

– She wasn't supposed to. Sharon frowned. – Not until tomorrow, but I was just as happy when she showed up tonight. Without her band, though, but she's just as... brilliant whatever she does.

– Is that allowed? Someone shouted from the back.

– She's allowed entrance as long as she's performing and not being served anything. Sharon shook her head in wonderment. – If I serve her a glass of soda, they'll close me down. Strange shit, right?

– So, she has to thirst or starve herself to death?

The woman smiled and raised a pointed finger.

– You know what, young man, you just hit on a major point there...

The lights and the fire embraced them. On a Sunday night, with it being a work and school day tomorrow, the place was a bit over half full. In Jill and Everett's eyes this was better. It was the evening for the politically conscious people. Quality before quantity. Jill had never liked crowded places anyway. She was grinning, grinning *constantly,* unable to stop herself.

Dark, minimalist music floated towards them from hidden speakers. The stage was dark, the candles only marginally brightening it. Sometimes there was a guitar, seemingly playing crazy, misty chords, spontaneous and Free. A voice, old and wise, young and fresh rose to include them all.

– «The surest way to corrupt a youth is to instruct him to hold in higher esteem those who think alike than those who think differently».

The tall, slender figure emerged from the darkness, just about visible in the shadows. She wore no makeup tonight, just a few markings and «jewelry» to point to her enjoyment of variety.

– Nietzsche wrote that, she said simply. – One more astute observation of a man who has been deemed crazy by the establishment and used as an apologist for and blamed for views completely different from his own.

– Mankind has, for some time now, used considerable energy in an attempt to control our surroundings, to «improve» nature. This, my gathering is at the core of the world we see before us today. Because, my friends, this «improvement» has most of all been a desire by the power hungry and their eager servants not to expand Life, but to narrow it, to break it down into nice little baubles to hang on hooks, hooks penetrating heart and soul, lessening, destroying everything making Life worth living...

With a few deliberate words she had gained their complete attention.

While listening, while the younger girl's words were piercing her being, Jill made a rather useless attempt at studying the mirage there on the stage. That was how she felt, as if... the girl wasn't really there. Asteroth was not like Laurie; she had no ability to «project», to add to her words with enticing images, no obvious paranormal ability. There were just the words, and an inborn gift of being good at communicating, a drive, a passion beyond words. In the manner of «talents», she seemed completely normal. Yet, there was something... Jill could hardly read her at all. And there wasn't a wall blocking her, as was the case with most people. A wall could easily be «bypassed». It was as if she wasn't there, not where everybody saw her. Jill smiled of her own confusion, realizing how much more even the concepts of what she was struggling with now would have confounded her just two short weeks ago. Gabrielle Asteroth was indeed present where everybody saw her, but to Jill, perhaps to all of them, she seemed to be present all over the rest of the room as well.

– Our thoughts and being must be stimulated, constantly challenged to not be dwindling. The coming of civilization has halted this process, narrowing down possibilities, narrowing Life, not enhancing it. Because of this, because of the «growth» of civilization, the human inner Magick has laid dormant, laid dormant for so very long. With the human self, our inner being suffering and suffocating under a blanket keeping us from breathing, the outer manifestations must by necessity turn Ugly... The ancient practice of honoring the dead may have led to the insanity, the blind madness of religion. The former smaller tribal nomads have become warring nations. Nomads are forced to «live» behind walls. Everything is distorted, turned upside down, in our brave new world, this... tournament of fear.

She slipped back into the dark. Music rose again, crawling beneath the skin, reaching the bone, by cutting, not cutting. There was no way to really determine how much time passed before her return. None in the audience had lost any visible interest when Jill sensed the first new stirrings in the air. The entity returning was completely covered in black and seemed like nothing more than masks, white translucent, bright colored masks dancing in the dark. More than one, moving interdependently, in a crazy air dance. And the thick layer of white make up, which might be or might not be her true face. Two hands, three, four.... five? When the sixth and seventh mask appeared, spontaneous applause erupted in the room.

Music faded with the applause. One creature stood unmoving on the stage, covered in black, white faced, ghostlike.

– I'm gonna explain humanity to you now, Gabrielle Asteroth said, her voice strangely undistorted by the mask. – One tiny part of the multitude that is us, that is Everything.

Noise faded, even the frequency stemming from active minds.

– We humans have always sought *something*. Picture this for your inner eyes, a particular group, *tribe* of ape-like creatures leaving the forest, wandering towards the endless, green plains and new forests, too many to be counted. Looking at them, there is nothing visible, nothing our eyes can see, distinguishing them from those who remained. But they *are* different. Like every group, every individual, every speck of life throughout history seeking beyond the corner. We, the Human Beings have hunted far and wide since then. Grown, Changed. This is a good thing. But lately, recently the Hunt has led us astray, sidetracked us, led us too far away from our origin, our core. So far away that we've almost lost touch with it.

Echoes, echoes from distant times. Diffused, distorted.

– There are people today, forces attempting to find their way back to the ancient wisdom. And there are people thinking they are, pretending to do so. We have a man calling himself the Bishop of California, stating that he's uniting old and new beliefs. He's one of many in the so-called New Age movement making that claim. New Age is not a homogenous «movement» per se, though, and has within itself many directions, many factions. But generally speaking, I would say that New Age, too, is about success, about money, just as much as the rest of the present-day world.

– In this town we have the followers of *Wicca*. Sorry, but that doesn't impress me any more than most of the so-called alternative movement. The supporters claim Wicca to be the teaching about Witchcraft, but it's really just more of the same, in my opinion. Wicca has its roots in the early ecological movements of the 19th century and is not an unbroken chain back to before the Burning

Times, as its proponents claim. And more important: It's a Religion like other religions, a system of set rules and set rules of conduct, with its idiosyncrasies, its ignorance and intolerance, isolating and ostracizing its more individual supporters. Besides, Wicca isn't only a diluted form of the older agriculture Magic, but the belief of the earlier agriculture societies is really nothing more than faint echoes of the older, far more powerful Earth Magick, that of the hunters and nomads of ancient times.

Jill sat there sweating. She was afraid to look over her shoulder, in case Laurie sat there with her condemning eyes, and that convinced her that she was already well on her way to being brainwashed. Instead, she found herself embracing the words and vision of the very young girl, the early teenager, there, on the stage.

– Wicca is at best, the magic of the agriculture society. The alienation had already started then. Agriculture means being stuck in one place, awaiting the harvest. It means cities, civilization, which by the way means «city states» or merely «living in cities», «city dweller». The Nomad, a major part of our Nature, became an outcast. We're nomads in our hearts, our core. A land without nomads is a land without Freedom. With agriculture came the cities and the notion that one creature, one life, was more worth than another grew to prominence. Preserved graves from the first city states clearly show ever more pronounced levels of discrimination, a distinct developing hierarchy, previously unknown. Previously mankind had seen itself as an integrated, humble part of nature. Now we, in our own eyes came to stand outside and above it. And mankind was separated into slaves, servants, carpenters, kings and priests, with gods at the top.

– The «belief» in the hierarchy, the pyramid, as a way of conducting a society has been one of the most devastating developments in human history. So has the belief in gods. Humanity has stretched itself too far outside itself, trusting outward appearances or concepts, relying on others to come and save them. What may have started as a celebration of dead ancestors has «grown» to the blind insanity of religion. Earthly matters are played down, in favor of the afterlife. How very convenient to any would-be tyrant.

– No, Life is fortunately far more interesting than this bleak, gray version of it. Physically, spiritually, mentally it's a world of challenge, Life and Fire, something to *embrace,* not detach oneself from.

To hear her speak was more than interesting, it was... inspiring! Jill felt the tingling inside grow to a rush.

What made humanity change from trusting themselves, being self-sufficient, to be increasingly dependent on the priests, on those «interpreting» the will of the gods?

The tingling and rush deep inside, encouraged by a story both known and unknown at the same time, a half remembered dream a few minutes after awakening.

Something had happened, perhaps over a very small amount of time, a day, an hour between the closing and the opening of a pair of eyes, perhaps gradually. One year, a hundred years, a thousand... But something had happened, a change, a wrong track, not just one single sidetrack. Ten thousand years had gone by and everything had just taken a turn, or hundred, for the worse.

Tingling of danger, excitement, possibilities, expectations...

(adversity, attraction)

Something had been gnawing at her subconscious

(since she was twelve)

and the dreams hadn't started in this place. She had had them

(since she turned twelve)

for very long. She hadn't really given them much thought. They were, after all, just dreams. But now she learned to give thought to such things, becoming aware of humanity's other half.

– And thus, we have the world of today, Gabrielle said. And now her words really seemed to come from behind. – A humanity ever further removed from the living, fertile Earth. We hear its cries of pain, but only through half-forgotten nightmares, and ever more stems from cold, heartless constructs. One cannot build on a rotten foundation, everybody knows this. But it doesn't matter. Because the Destroyers have the power, and they will continue to destroy everything making Life worth Living. The Earth and Life on it is ravaged and plundered everywhere, shit and Poison filling even the most remote wilderness. There are no more places left to hide. And I don't want to. Not anymore. We don't want to, any of us, the children of the midnight fire.

Jill turned then, at the same time everybody else did. Gabrielle had stood silent, but not quiet, in the open entrance for a while. Now she started walking among them, back to the stage, joining the silent figure covered in black. This time everyone was too stunned to applaud.

– We are the Witches, we are the Agents of Change. She stood there shouting, with a raised, clenched fist, glowing in anger. – Wherever our wandering takes us, we're showing the robots of civilization sitting in their coffins, showing them, no matter the blood, no matter the strife, showing people that the human spirit is still alive.

The music started up again. Low now, in the background, a rumbling cutting hearts.

Cast me a spell
In a confined space
Making it confined no more
If we're forced
To look at the world
Through a dirty window
Shouldn't we then
Smash it with the biggest stone
We can find

She started unwrapping the black cloth on the girl standing there. Brown skin started to materialize. Loeh was slowly revealed to the audience. Jason emerged from the darkness. All three stood and received the accolade.

– The present-day world is an illusion, the girl stated calmly, far older than her years. – Stop believing in it, and it will crumble to dust.

They bowed and curtseyed and the performance ended. A performance it was, but one cutting to the bone, inspiring wild hearts.

First and fierce in the queue of congratulators Jill took Gabrielle's hands.

– Congratulations, Jill congratulated her. – It was all so very, very impressive.

Then she turned and kissed Jason on the lips.

And the party moved on. This celebration was one that prevailed, and it was growing in intensity, not waning. The tavern was officially closed. No more people were allowed in. It was called «a private party» now, and was progressing in Sharon's apartment upstairs. Everybody had thrown money in a hat to pay for the drinks, all the drinks they were about to enjoy...

Music came from a disk now. It could play for hours without stop or repeating itself. The gathering seemed, within itself, from the very beginning, to have extra vitality and life. And no one more so, than Everett and Jill, who didn't really leave the dance floor and seemed to be ever more tightly entwined.

– We did surprise you all, now, didn't we…

Jason spoke to no one in particular, but it was Jill he had his eyes on.

– Congratulations, Jill congratulated him.

– We didn't really have time to practice, he went on talking, deliberately prodding everybody, – but it was no big deal. It was Gabi's show anyhow, and what a show.

Jill didn't really want to play games just now. She just smiled sweetly and turned to Everett once more, discarding Jason, smiling dangerously, dancing with swinging hips, dancing tight. Also with other dancers on the floor, even Jason, but she always managed, miraculously, without really looking, to find her way back to Everett.

Finally, it did come to the point where the loop ended, and the songs did start repeating themselves. They all looked at each other, scared of scattering this most fragile of moments.

– Listen, I must go, Gabrielle spoke up, hesitatingly. – I'll see you guys later.

– I'm indeed looking forward to that, Jason said. – I'll bet you have a lot to teach us, girlie...

She looked at him with the same happiness and apprehension she reserved for them all. Jill noticed the black rings around her eyes, the nervous, haunted look behind the flushed and happy face. She couldn't help but notice it.

– You don't look so good, Jill offered. – Is there anything we can help you with?

She looked a bit pale, paradoxically more so now, than with the white make up.

– I don't sleep well, Gabrielle replied. – I'm all right. I've had fun. Thank you all.

They all waved her off, as she disappeared through the door, down the stairs.

The music started up again. Jill returned from the short respite to her fevered dreams, the music inside, outside. Slow now. A different pace, but the same haunted quality. That was how she perceived it, anyway.

«Now, grab hold of the one you're dancing with», sounded the voice of the disc jockey on the disk, «and hold around each other».

The boy and the girl stood still for a moment, out of breath. The slow tune rose from the speakers, spread stealthily throughout the room, like wind through the windows, as the two kissed for the first time, forever and ever in the darkness. The melody ended. Another started. The same pace, the same haunting quality. The party finally took on a more somber mood, ending just a bit more, as people went home, as the various couples left the floor, left the room. Jill had discreetly turned off almost all the lights. Nobody but Everett seemed to notice anything. But they had really stopped looking around, rocking slowly back and forth, as they did, in each other's arms, forgetting the world beyond the embrace, no longer caring about it.

– Do you know there are no welcoming words for *night,* only «goodbyes»? She whispered, playing with the natural curls on his neck.

– No one knows what you're going through, but I do, he said softly.

There are no limits on emotions, he thought.

No limits on anything, she returned.

A stunned smile erupted on his face when realization hit him.

– Let's get out of here, he said, hardly able to hear himself think.

– Where? She whispered, with her lips close to his.

The longing made her feel so good that it almost made her feel bad.

– Somewhere. He had to swallow several times while she let him lead her off, far away from what they had known.

The air outside felt crisp, but not cold. She stretched her arms above her head, greeting the full moon, while bravely and playfully pushing herself tight to him. He wanted to catch her in his arms, but she laughingly swung away once more.

She ran off. He started chasing the flying cat and when he caught her after the short run to the city limits, they laughed in their rapture.

– I really am a virgin, you know... she snickered, somewhat somber. – So virtuous that I want to throw up.

– I must admit I find that hard to believe, he said stunned. – I mean... it must have been open season on a goddess like you?

– You're so cute, she said, licking her lips, licking her chops, while giving him hot glances. – Perhaps I wasn't a goddess then or that I've always been good at getting away.

– I'll have to be careful then, he said, – to not let you escape.

Her lips had become so sensitive, she marveled. Her entire body had. She had never experienced anything remotely like it, no matter how much the boys had cuddled with her.

Everything felt so natural between them. Later they would look back on this, awestruck at how easily it had happened.

She stepped forward, until she couldn't step any further.

– Feel, she insisted, conspiratorially.

And when he after some fumbling and hesitation managed to actually do it, he felt the resistance, and his cock rose hard and sore, he just couldn't help himself. She laughed viciously, throatily.

He couldn't move. Throat was sand dry. He finally managed to give voice to his desire.

– Where?

– There's a hut not far from here, she said. – A wreck really, a disaster in cold and rainy weather... perfect now.

They couldn't really hurry fast enough. The few remaining minutes until they reached their destination felt slow and trying. They almost stopped several times and wondered why not. They really wondered why not. But they kept on, as if driven. And they were. And there it was, in the forest glen.
He looked at her, as if he wanted to say something, but held back.
– It's all right, she said softly. – On a darkened Earth, one must be careful about opening up.
– No, I want to, he cried. – Who can I tell if not you?
– I... had a dream last night.
A truly Strange one.
– Lucky you. You... you dreamed about me, didn't you?
– Yes, he almost shouted in his excitement. – You had the head... the head of a black leopard, but it was you.
– You had the head of a jackal. She clapped her hands.
– That was what I thought, too, he exclaimed slowly, overwhelmed. – The dream was so whacky and real, so beyond detailed that I just had to believe in it, but I didn't dare. But it did make me more confident, confident enough to approach the goddess...
His teasing, the complete informality between them made everything even better. And the build up continued.
– Let me guess. She counted on her fingers. – You... spied on us, didn't you, on me? You didn't eat, you listened to Laurie, listened to us, doing what we did, eating what we did? Not completely, of course but close enough. You, too, went through the Spirit Quest... And avoiding much of the fucking hardship we had to go through, right? You slime!
He stood there and kept nodding, until he managed to pull his act together.
– You found your animal, you found yourself.
– Yes, he said. – We both found our Spirit Animal.
– Better, she whispered, – We *are* beasts, proud and fierce.
– Yes!
He didn't need to say more. That single word contained everything he wanted to convey.
The moon disappeared behind a dark cloud. They had both become used to heat such as this and bright summer nights. Now, close to the equinox, the days and night were equally long and nights turned darker.
They saw the hut, clearly in the Night. Windows were sorely lacking and there was no lack of holes in the walls. There were no stairs. If there had been once, they were gone now.
– It's so beautiful, Jill said breathless. – Just the way I've always imagined it.
Everett laughed. She enjoyed his laughter. It was so... warm.
He jumped in, jumped up, first, before helping her, lifting her into his arms. He managed, with a little effort.
There was a bed in the single room, a table and a few chairs, candles on the table. Not exactly a first-class hotel suite, but not bad. He let go of her and started pacing a bit, touching the bed with his fingers, reddening. Dry. Not a touch of humidity. She snapped her fingers to impress him, lighting all the candles at once. He blinked.
– Now, you.
He touched the bed, stroke his fingers along the fabric, wanted to say something manly, something silly. He kept his mouth shut. He touched the fabric of the bed, but felt like he was touching something else. While stretching out his hand, it was really his thoughts he was stretching.
– This is a well-used haystack, she confirmed with a twinkle in her eye, a singing voice. – A place filled with Energy and Power. Young lust, hope, rebellion has feasted on this place, creating lots of Magick.
He concentrated and he felt a blood vessel burst somewhere, and the pain was like fire, like a velvet curtain being pushed aside, transforming him forever.
– I feel it, he whispered. – I CAN FEEL IT!
– *Look at me,* she commanded.
He obeyed, and he didn't want to resist.
– What do you see?

– You!
– No, you *don't!*
A quick movement with the hand. Smoke rose from the floor, engulfing her. He kept staring at it. It dissolved after a few seconds, but by then she had... disappeared, vanished like the smoke. He had kept his eyes on her at all times, hadn't he? There had been no sound of steps. But she was Gone. It couldn't be! She had to be here.
She was gone!
– You can see me if you really try. Her voice came from somewhere in the room, out of nowhere, a voice full of need. – Hurry.
– *Lillith,* he said. The name appeared in his thoughts before he uttered it aloud, before flowing over his lips. – I see you.
She stood by the bed, nude, with her hands playing with her hair, shivering in desire, in expectation. She took hold of the hair, lifting it sensually above her head.
– I Knew you knew me, *Plat,* she said vividly.
He staggered, but kept walking. He walked all the way to her. The need burned in him. He could hardly think, fighting to hold on to his intentions of restraint.
– I don't necessarily believe that every maiden in existence is eager to let go of her virginity... but I sure as hell am!
So many... delays. She wondered about how many more times she could have delayed it, and the answer came immediately as a long and throaty moan: Not one single time more, not a second longer.
He grabbed her, tightening immediately his grip around her shoulders and back.
– Did you plan this evening in detail? He pondered.
– Not *everything...* she mewed.
Read my mind.
– I? But I can't...
Something gave in, and he was Changed.
Yes, you can, you're a Witch.
He was inside her. He was able to see all the lights, all the shadows in her thoughts.
She tore off his clothes. She hardly touched him, but tore them to shreds, tore them to shreds with claws of desire. He hardly noticed. She stood before him, nude and willing, shaking in fervor. He didn't have to be a mind reader to see that.
But he was. He was!
He had to sit down and luckily for him his ass hit the edge of the bed. She bent down and kissed him hungrily on the lips. One single touch and he lost his head almost completely. He grabbed her in haste, and shoved her on her back on the bed. In haste tracing the lines of the supple body, desperately attempting some sort of control. Tracing lines of limbs and skin, lovely limbs, lovely skin, lovely, lovely, lovely. Her outside, her inside, like a thousand wildfires. He could sense her thoughts like flames in the Night.
This is absolutely fantastic.
The remains of his clothes, the last few pieces of them fell to the floor and he stood nude before her. He felt his nudity, in a purely physical way like never before. Her longing, her fire exploded slowly within him, an unending flow of heat. «Reading» her thoughts, communicating so completely felt awkward at first, but she guided him beyond the hurdles, showed him how to open up, and in so doing opened herself up to him. He knew her discovery, her conscious use of the talent, was nebulous, too, and she had already learned so much. *All this... just really scratching the surface... how will it be when we're truly starting to master it?*
– You're so big and scary, she whispered big eyed, both apprehensive and attracted. – Aren't you?
He looked down at himself. He was already fully-grown, fully hard and more than ready, but he had to hold back. His hand caressed her forehead in a tender, but hasty movement. He lifted up her knee in a deliberate slow pull, kissing its point. That small gesture was enough to push a moan out of her. It wasn't hard for him to see that she was almost ready already. Thighs were moist, eyes were distant, breasts were swollen... and he could... he could smell her swollen cunt. He forced himself to be thorough. Didn't want to make it unnecessarily painful for her.

She stayed mostly passive while he was putting himself in position on the both supple and hard body, sensing that he couldn't really take any more encouragement just now. But it was so hard to wait. She needed him, she wanted him, this very moment. There was no later. Later didn't exist. There was only Now. She wanted to scream out to him, to make him complete what he had started.

You're right. I don't really know howIcanstandIT.

becauseyou'resosweetsofoolish... dear EvPlat

– Jill, he gasped.

Lillith.

He traced the roundness of hips, of soft skin, while kissing her above the navel. She put a hand in her mouth and bit it. He felt her reaction to that as an echo in himself. There was really no excuse for him to hurt her unnecessarily. He could more than sense every nuance of her emotions.

So strange, she noted, half beside herself. With the ever-increasing fever pitch her furnace had become, the sensitivity was increasing on every single point of her body. Every single touch was an experience. Every movement and thought like a cascade of passion. She could lie still no longer.

The involuntary movements started, as a flow, a flood. Fluid limbs, skin on fertile ground, Magick flowing like water. He couldn't think. His hips started rocking, pushing forward. She sat up and started kissing him, grabbing his hair, pulling him to her, and started kissing him, kissing him, again and again, pushing, returning his trusts. He penetrated her then, and the pain erupted, and the colors changed. He felt it, as she felt it, and stopped for a second. But she continued, burning in his thoughts. Pain paled. *Come,* she called. Come! He put her back on her back and slid over her body, back and forth, back and forth. She met his thrust, while holding his head close to her own. He felt her big, hard nipples scratching his chest. And wanted to touch them, to cup them. He didn't have time now... later.

TimetimeNowPlatNow

*Know you*KNOW US

– Lovely, he whispered. As the waterfall dragged them both away, making their fire inside burn stronger than ever.

He kissed her on the cheek as he lifted himself off her.

– Don't go. It doesn't hurt.

– You're lying, he said. – Besides, I must pee.

It hurt at first, his early leaving, but that feeling of abandonment, fleeting as it was, was virtually instantly overruled by the overwhelming she had just experienced.

As she stayed on her back, she could feel every wrinkle in the linen under her. All emotions and senses seemed to have grown to staggering proportions, so enhanced and enriched. She could smell the forest, she could hear its sounds, in a thousand ways she couldn't before. And even better, she knew it had nothing to do with her Talent, her Power. This was directly tied to what had happened, what she had just experienced.

She heard the sound of him peeing, saw his silhouette in the doorway, in the rays of the moon. She stood up from the bed and silently walked the few steps to him. Put her hands on his shoulders, her cheek against his neck.

– My head hurts, he complained.

– I can remedy that.

She pushed and pulled her hands back and forth through his hair, allowing the energy to flow. The pain, not so prevalent anyway, faded to nothing.

He had closed his mind to her. She couldn't tell if it was deliberate or caused by his inexperience. She fought to hide her disappointment, but she didn't want to close her mind, she wanted to be open. He still had his back to her. She was afraid to say anything, to shatter the moment, the most delicate silence.

– I could never have imagined it would be like this, she said, speaking low, akin to a whisper, allowing him to share the emotions, the Storm raging inside her.

And then he opened up, and his Storm was equal to hers.

– Neither did I. He turned towards her and gestured with his hands. – It... it was the most fantastic I've ever experienced. And the intensity wasn't really due to our... talents either, it was... us. The rest was the optional, spicy extra. Listen to me, during my entire life I've wanted, wanted to discover that I had paranormal powers and when it happens, the first thing I'm doing is to downplay it.

– Not the first... She smiled impudent.

He pushed his lips against hers and they stood like that for a long time, forgetting time, ignoring time.

She touched herself down below and then brought her hand to his lips.

– The Hunter's trophy, lord and master, she said throatily. – Accept it.

He licked the blood off her fingers, swallowing it, the taste of rust and dawn and deepest core.

– We're male and female, man and woman, she said, – such as it should be. Under the Moon's many faces, eyes stretching into darkness, I take you as my mate.

– Under the Moon, I accept, he said with a hoarse voice.

We're not alone anymore.

The Moon shone on them this night. They stood by each other's side, looking at the dark world.

He touched her left hip.

– Does it hurt?

He didn't have to ask or hear any reply from her. She shook her head.

– That's one nasty scar, he said carefully. – Must have been some wound.

– I don't remember getting it, she said slowly. – My parents say I fell down from a tree and cut myself on the lawn-mover. I remember… pain… and loss.

Quiet, so quiet out there, the whispers of the forest, the noise of civilization.

– I've felt something... for a long time, she said frosty. – Something close, inevitable.

– I can feel what you're feeling, he said, – but nothing on my own.

– You will, she insisted. – You will!

You shouldn't be afraid of the dark... you should be terrified of it... They returned to the bed, to its softness, pulling each other tight. *But not now...*

– You aided me, then I aided you, he said overwhelmed, as if something suddenly dawned on him.

– We shared mind, we shared body, she whispered in his ear. – Our combined fire banishing all fear.

They enjoyed each other's company, with a fever doomed to fade, but not now, not now.

– There's something strange about Northfield, the city and its entire area, he pondered, with an arm around her. – That's why I didn't seriously think about moving. I already lived in a place where there was much of interest.

– You were right, she confirmed. – I don't know if you've noticed all the tourists here. I have, in the short time I've been here. «Tourists»... Some have an inkling of why they're here, others haven't. This is a nexus of sorts, of people and... stuff.

– I saw you by the fire, he said, shaking his head. – Saw you by the many fires, saw you playing with the grass and flames. All my hopes and darkest dreams were manifested in that moment.

– You were *spying* on me, she said with a devious smile. – I should be quite vexed...

– But you're not.... He gave her his unbelievable, broad grin.

– Then I would've been a damned *hypocrite.*

She attacked him with a frightening ferocity. He returned in kind. The wrestling ended with her sitting on his knees, with her thighs tightening around him from both sides. She pushed his arms flat on the bed, completely in control. She licked her lips with her two-forked tongue, surveying him with a contemplative look.

When she sent him her thoughts, he felt it as if she was touching him with her lips, kissing him with a greedy mouth, biting him with sharpened teeth. She could do this so easily, after such a short time exercising her abilities.

He managed to turn his head, looking out, before looking back at her.

– Dawn is coming, he laughed. – Time to go to school soon. I think we should make our appearance there regularly. We have something to teach the poor sods.

– Yes, soon...

She moved, arched closer to his half stiff limb. It started twitching, growing. She was licking her lips again. And he couldn't really tell himself that he didn't find that disturbing. But great, too... Impatiently she briefly touched, caressed the hardening limb. Just the short while was sufficient. He stared at her with a wide-open mouth. *Now it's big and beautiful.* He felt the sweet itching fully, and bit his lips. She elevated her hips a bit, hesitated a bit, before lowering them on him. The penetrations this time was painless, effortless. She felt him deep inside and smiled pleased. She opened and closed her mouth once. A sound rose from her inside, and when she spoke it was as an extension of that sound.

– *You're real,* she mewed.

Their entire inner beings went on overload.

In joy he returned the growl.

And then he/they let go of the last vestige of control.

Chapter Eight: THE CITY THAT WAS NOT NEW ORLEANS

The book is old, decrepit.

NORTHFIELD: YEARBOOK 1993. 150. Edition (excerpt).

We, the citizens of Northfield are, rightfully so, proud of our history. Our forefathers were among the pilgrims making the dangerous, fateful voyage with the «Mayflower». They were first in the line of refugees escaping from persecution and poverty in Europe, seeking freedom in the new world. In 1630 they participated in the founding of Boston. And just a few years after that they set out once more towards unspoiled land. They founded Northfield and brought the word of God to the heathens. The Alui tribes were taught proper ways of living and many of their number left their sinful ways. The priest leading on in this important work was a forefather to our own, treasured priest, Joseph Parnell.

We took our deserved place in the America slowly emerging from barbaric origins. We were free to practice our religion and to keep certain undesirables away, as we're still doing. There are always the faithless, both individuals and groups, who through thoughts and actions desire to diminish the dreams of the first Americans. We must ever be on guard against the godless.

There has always been mutual respect and good connections between our city and our bigger neighbor, Boston, from both our modest beginnings to this day.

During the war for independence, we did more than our share. We took many refugees from Boston into our homes. To honor our way of life that no one can influence or change. And on that account, we've also contributed considerably to the process of converting non-believers, sending missionaries all over the world. The mandatory school-prayer has never been removed from our schools. Our children are taught to be good, God-fearing Americans. During the Civil War we showed people in the South proper conduct. Since then, no major groups have instigated rebellion in our beautiful country. One of our forefathers, Scott Thompson, belonged to the Abolitionist faction and was a very prominent member. Later he became an even more prominent man, both here in the Northeast, and in the country as a whole. His statue, a memorial to honor one of the city's great sons is raised in front of our city hall.

Our town is small, but not insignificant. We've done more than our share throughout American history. We've participated actively in the struggle for freedom and democracy all over the world. During the Vietnam War we made sure that there were no dodgers from our town. In this city no one was allowed to throw dirt on our values and our faith. Though we demonstrate our open minds and generosity by welcoming many students, from many faiths to our international school. The average grades achieved by graduate students are well above those of the national average. We're rightly proud of our teaching methods. They work and they're old and their quality is well proven.

Strangers have moved here and done well for themselves. Some may be a bit eccentric to our taste, but we accept them. People in this town are allowed a little leverage.

Our city is growing, with an ever more cosmopolitan character. Out of our glorious past will grow an even more glorious future. To the east Boston is awaiting us, waiting for us to join the rest of the region in a future Metropolis. It's the ultimate fate of humankind to subjugate the Earth and all its treasures. We've received the World Garden as a gift from the Creator and eventually nothing will stand in our way.

We've found our niche in Boston's manufacturing industry. Our entire industry, agriculture and trade are well adapted to the Boston market. We produce paper for the printing processes there and even if we can't guarantee what our paper is used for, we know that none of the godless, radical writings originate with us. We're spreading our righteous influence throughout the world, leading to ever more people recognizing the one, true faith. God stands above humanity, as we stand above the animals and nature.

WELCOME TO NORTHFIELD.

2

Stephen Bachman woke up next to his wife when the alarm clock roared at three o'clock in the night. Open eyes slipped, closed, opened painfully once more. A hand stretched through the dark for the switch to end the horrible noise. The wife turned on the light above the bed and he finally managed to locate the switch and turn off the sound. He allowed the head to rest on the pillow a few moments more. His only desire in that moment was to stay in bed until the morning light, at least that long... but he couldn't allow himself that luxury.

The dreariness came upon him, as it always seemed to do. Morning, the morning light seemed indefinitely far away. Further away for every crawling day. He forced himself to sit up in the bed and swing his feet off it, place them on the floor. Floor had always been ice cold during winter, but he hadn't experienced physical winter for what seemed like a long, long time. He couldn't decide, every day he fought on, whether or not he should give praise to or curse the infernal, eternal heat. At least it reduced their electricity bills to an absolute minimum. If they could have afforded air conditioner electricity bills would have skyrocketed. But they couldn't.

He attempted to keep his head in the normal position, but couldn't do it. The jaw kept pushing against his chest. He had strived, for a considerable amount of time to keep all the dreariness hidden for his wife. He could do so no longer.

– Do you have to meet at the factory this early every morning? She said tired, but with obvious understanding. It wasn't a question.

– You know I do. Thompson is personally supervising it all, to make sure we're all on time. If we're one second too late, his clock, he's pulling our wages.

– The work is so hard, too. All those chemicals. You've got sores and itches all the time now. There must be something we can do. We can't afford to move, but...

– But what? He dressed his skinny body. – You saw what happened to Luke and his «disciples». Thompson's influence is reaching far, to Boston and beyond. He's got the unions in his closed fist. He controls this entire city. He or people like him.

– Not the entire city, she said subdued.

– Don't say it, he exclaimed in distaste. – Don't even think it. It's out of the question. Got it?

– Yes, Stephen. She, too, bowed her head. – I'm sorry.

Stephen washed himself in front of the mirror. He would rather not, but there was a mirror above the sink, and he didn't want to remove it. That would've been one more admission, one more step down. He was only thirty, but he looked middle aged. The wife, dressed in morning gown, put food on the table. He envied her, because she, in spite of the sadness, still looked somewhat good.

– The water has the same, strange taste today.

Didn't it ever? What was wrong with her? She should've been used to the shit by now. One got used to everything.

– Tremayne was coughing again yesterday, still is today. No fever, he's just coughing.

He looked up at her. She had gained his attention.

– I'm pregnant, she said quietly.

In the light humidity of the hot night's heat, he looked through the mist-like fog at the pyramid. Surely it was one of the modern world's seven wonders, a glorious beacon in the dark. Lights were constantly on, throughout the building. One single broken lightbulb, undiscovered over a prolonged period of time would cause someone to be fired.

The Bachman house, and the houses of all the others working by and at the factory was on the opposite side of town. The walking distance was negligible. Four houses, a small, open space and he was there.

The queue inside was, as ever quite long. He «stamped» his computer card, registered one minute before the deadline. They were all moving through the «reception» hall. As ever, they could see Thompson, sharp eyed, all-powerful sit behind the glass in the control-room high above. The factory was big, with various production facilities and levels. Thompson preferred to have his entire Northfield production under one roof.

– GUS WALTERS, the cold voice sounded through the speakers. – Your credit card shows that you bought beer on the supermarket yesterday at 3.25 PM. You left work ten minutes early. You're fired.

Gus was virtually shrinking there on the spot. He didn't utter a single sound, just removed his working gear and clothes, and left. Everybody knew that Thompson would give him another job quite soon. One harder and with lesser pay. If he behaved.

Stephen's job was in the department for plastic products. He could feel the stench of chloride and PVC already. He hardly felt different. In the adjacent hall they made paint and pigmentation-products. Stephen couldn't decide whether he was lucky or not. They said it was worse in the other hall. But they probably said the same there, about this one. No matter, waste and leftovers were spread everywhere, both inside and outside the factory.

The constant noise worsened. The production machines started their daily run. The pervasive, abysmal sound echoed in the eardrums. Dust rose from the floor, from the machines, floating through the air. They were breathing it and got sicker with every breath. Stephen knew this, as it was basically common knowledge, but he was tied hand and foot. He had four children and a fifth on its way.

But what about the guys without families? They stayed, too. Did everyone quite simply search for a reason to stay on, instead of one to break out?

God in hell. There had to be something he could do, something that could be done. He bowed his head even more. One hand began to shake, as if to close.

– Speed up there, Bachman, you're slacking.

That was the «whip», the union man. Thompson couldn't be everywhere. He had people, deputies to oversee the details.

Damn, Damn, Damn. DAMN. What a crappy job. Fucked up job. Fucked up life. He couldn't take it anymore. He had stopped taking it years ago. And still he stayed on. He continued to bow his head, without dreams, without hope, while the cage surrounding him was ever shrinking.

3

The white limousine waited for Scott Thompson the moment he left the factory through the VIP door. The driver held the back door open for him and he seated himself.

– The Pyramid, he said casually. The other man had just about sat down behind the wheel.

– Yes, Mr. Thompson, right away, sir.

Thompson looked out of the one-way windows, as he always did, on the empty streets, soon to be filled with people, his people. The vehicle made its usual route, and after just a short amount of time it turned and drove down Big Road. That was the official name, anyway, but Thompson knew it was called Thompson Road among the subjects. Everybody walked it.

Just before the Pyramid the road made a turn. It stretched almost all the way to Oldtown and passed the old Civil War Memorial. The statue was pretty much a standard representation and didn't stand out much compared to the majority of such work. It showed a uniformed man on a horse, with his sword raised above the head. But the symmetry was broken by a little detail. The traditional hat was... missing. One could easily see the rider's face. As well as possible with a face remade in bronze.

The driver didn't join him on the way up. He held open the elevator door and was left behind downstairs in the private garage. The elevator lifted itself fast and silent, humming only slightly. It was big and comfortable, almost as big as a small room. He enjoyed that, having space around him. The elevator slowed down and floated as if on cotton the last few meters. When it stopped it happened so softly that it was hardly noticeable. The automatic doors parted. He walked out. The doors closed behind him. To make them reopen he just had to stand in front of them. He enjoyed it when things went smoothly.

He was once more standing at the top of his domain. The upper top of the Pyramid was one single room, surrounding the elevator shaft. Almost the entire wall consisted of one-way mirrors made of enhanced glass. The lights inside were dimmed, the lights outside blinding, reflected in the mirror, casting its glow across the city stretching out below. His city. He enjoyed looking at it, Master of all he surveyed.

It had taken him a long time and infinite patience. He had put his mark on this town in a way he could never have done in a major city. New York, Chicago, Boston, they were all too big, too uncontrollable. But he certainly had contacts there, and power. There and a lot of other places. Slowly, but surely, he would extend his influence.

He had excellent contacts in the harbor in Boston, where a major part of the nation's foreign trade was conducted, both officially and... unofficially. His control extended to the wool and fishing trade. He had excellent connections everywhere, above and below. The banks in Boston enjoyed his extensive share portfolio and he the services they could offer. But he had chosen Northfield as an operating base. It was a place to where he could withdraw, if he so wished. Many things were possible here, in seemingly contradictory ways that weren't really wise in the scrutiny the big city tycoons' fell victim to. Northfield had merely been just another hole in the ground at the time of his arrival. He had made a home for himself here, and made it his own.

The city was awakening below, as the September darkness gave way to the day. The planet approached the Fall Equinox, one of two times during the year where day and night, light and dark, were of equal length. And the temperature was higher than in July. The rather unpleasant thought was silenced and ignored. He concentrated on the sight of ever more ants running along below, below him. He ruled through fear. They knew he would rather trample them than not, and they strove for a life, an existence, as much as possible in anonymity, to not attract his attention. If they were lucky he didn't become interested for other reasons. His loyal, close associates, on the other hand, the ones he had handpicked through special means, they loved him, because he had handpicked them, made them love him. They served him enthusiastically. He expected no less.

He looked at his watch with a shrug. As expected, he had a bit of extra time on his hands, before the office day was supposed to start. His employed subjects would arrive On Time, neither before nor after specified time. He demanded uncompromising obedience and one of the set rules was being On Time. Without rules, without set conducts, chaos would rule. There were no other exceptions than his momentary whims.

The doors opened, as he placed himself before the elevator. He took two steps forward and he was inside. The lift sank only one floor, before halting. Doors opened to a darker, closed room. There were no windows. The additional door was hardly visible, even for him, who knew it was there. Around the bed stood nine shadowy figures. On the king-sized bed was a nude, young girl. She was seemingly sleeping, and her full body twisted and turned on the sheets. He saw, before his inner eye, as she was tracked and captured by his nine servants, the nine extensions of his own being. How she attempted to scream, but could not, how she attempted to fight, but could not. As she was led to a secret passageway to the Pyramid, led here.

– Hello, Joan, he said in a commanding voice. – Awaken, Joan.

Suddenly her eyes fell open, wide open. Her entire being had opened, had become a canvas he could paint as he wished.

She crouched on the bed, to hide as much as possible of herself. He undressed himself calmly, while she kept staring at him from the edge of her vision.

Let her, let her stare, he thought pleased.

She was afraid of him now, but soon she would love him. It was inevitable.

– You've slept tight, he grinned. – You'll sleep even more so.

4

By seven o'clock the sun had already dried what small amount remained of the night's moisture. Summer kept intensifying. Children were already playing in the streets. The heat made it increasingly difficult to sleep very long. Arid dreams made it worse. The adults wandered about with a strained, confused expression on their faces. They wanted to stay inside their cool, airconditioned houses, but they couldn't. Their daily duties couldn't, wouldn't wait. Teachers and students migrated to the premises of higher learning at Northfield College. Just a short walk through the sun, a trial of staggering proportions. Taking one step, forward or backward, was a strain.

Sometime, before that, before school, Jill and Everett were leaving the forest, yawning and with joy-filled smiles on their faces. He, with his clothes in rags. The ever-present wind whistled between the trees, and the tall, dried grass. Everything felt... different. To him, too, but absolutely so to her. She could sense the radiating glow around herself, she could almost see it. The very way the senses translated impressions, was completely dissimilar compared to before last night. She felt absolutely convinced that everybody could take one look at her, and realize, and know... what she had done. But she didn't blush. She felt slightly embarrassed, but what she felt most of all was pride.

They moved through the northern fields, heading towards the farm. He marveled most of all about his emerging telepathic abilities. Already he noticed that he no longer needed her aid, and it wasn't just from her he received emotions, moods, not even just from the humans they encountered, but also from a broader spectrum of the surroundings. Both within and without, he felt Life in deeper, more powerful ways.

Her steps, her very being, felt more confident, calmer, and simultaneously daring and wild, so wild, and her unbound lust, somewhat satisfied for the moment like an ember that could become a wildfire at the first contact with dry (but not dried) grass.

– If only we could have stayed in the woods forever, she sighed, glancing shyly at him. – But the world won't let us be, of course, and we can't stay away from society anyway.

– Perhaps at night, he said cheerfully, – if we were sufficiently... distracted?

Smiling and giving him a conspiring look, she hit him with an elbow in his ribs.

Perhaps not even then, since it's in that very moment we're most of all reminded of who we are, what the world should be, what it is.

She was humming both without sound and aloud, swinging herself in the dance, the Grass Dance. He joined her in that, too, further surprised by himself. They kept it going in the searing heat, until they reached the point where the grass was cut short. They stopped, sweating, resting hands on the knees, completely out of breath, straightening themselves, kissing hot, fiery kisses.

– There are things you must learn...

– I can do it, he said decisively.

– You and I can, like other telepaths, converse on our own, private «channel». She was holding his arms. – You must be capable of consciously erecting your own shield. If not for any other reason than to keep you from being overwhelmed by thoughts, the multitude of them surrounding us in a crowd. I was overwhelmed, the first day at school, and I couldn't shut them out. If I hadn't escaped, I would have turned... insane.

– I'll be careful, he promised.

As careful I can be in your company.

She threw her head back and laughed. She did that fairly often. Laughed. He couldn't get enough of the depth of her eyes.

Both felt their hearts beat faster at the sight of the main building. It brought a variety, a well of emotions. Not that of a home really, but close. And Everett hadn't so far even been inside the four walls.

She couldn't hide her ambiguity then, her fear of him being included in the coven, Laurie's Coven.

– What is it? He asked her gently.

– Nothing important, she replied, smiling sweetly and shaking her head. So easy it was, to deceive him.

She couldn't see anyone, but she could easily sense herself being welcomed. It was a more subtle version of the Embrace of the Goddess Laurie practiced, to overwhelm her charges. Everett could surely sense it, too, but he wasn't really aware of it, as Jill was, and couldn't defend himself against it.

The main building, the entire surrounding area, was a complete Whole, not only psychologically, but geographically speaking as well. Everything seemed flat, since everything, house, trees, exhibitions fit the terrain... perfectly. Everett was willing to take an oath, that merely fifty steps away there was nothing, nothing, except the wall of grass, untouched by human hands. You didn't see the path leading to the entrance, not before virtually stumbling on it. There were no people, no people anywhere. Not on the porch, not in the yard, not in the living room. Nowhere, until you happened to walk out on the terrace. The witches sat by the long table, all of them, including Laurie. They looked up at the newcomers. And then Jill felt the need to blush, convinced that her dirty deed, her emotions were exposed far and wide.

– This is Everett, she presented hesitatingly, seriously, cheerfully. – He has undergone trials, initiation and entered the Winding Ways. He accompanied us to the Crossroads and Beyond. He knows his Name... and he knows mine.

– I've wanted to wish you welcome to the coven for a long time, Witch, Laurie greeted him. – Let us greet him, witches.

– WELCOME, EVERETT, they cried out to him, him, in an overwhelming choir.

Echoing the far more powerful greeting he experienced inside, one far more powerful than he had ever felt. He «heard» Jill, too, distinctive and hot, keeping him from drowning in the multitude.

– Thanks for bringing him, little witch. Laurie patted Jill on the cheek.

Breakfast was served.

– There are things that must be done, Laurie said, – but let us eat first, replenish ourselves.

He discovered that he was absolutely ravenous, and he wolfed everything down, as they all did. Like everybody here he had gone hungry all his life, and was now helping himself to everything the table had to offer.

And afterwards, a dream, a memory, of times past.

Laurie had given him the robe, after he had made himself naked under the sun. He had swept the cloak around his body, around his mind. They all had their cloaks swept around them. The physical senses were turned off. But they were swimming in a sea of impressions.

His head hurt afterwards, but the pain was fast diminishing into insignificance. He did as the others, directing his attention at Laurie.

– Initiation is in the past, she stated. – Those of you living elsewhere will no longer spend the night here. The school administration has, thanks to me, ignored your absence these few days, but from now on, it will not be tolerated. Not from them, not from me. You will come here or to Square, when you're not required to be on the school's premises. You will not be late for school, not be late here. I've stressed earlier the importance of school to us, how important it is in several ways. Invaluable contacts are being made there, contacts, ties for the future. We will not reveal ourselves in brazen ways, but work in secret, influencing people and decisions.

Jill couldn't decide if she liked everything the teacher said. Didn't she speak about ties, about contacts, about manipulation? She was very manipulative, that's for sure.

They were all ready to go. The young woman stood before the mirror, brushing her hair, the thick, black hair. Everyone had been told to wear their school uniform, like good girls and boys. Anyway, she thought it strange to wear «ordinary» clothes once more. So much had changed.

She had wanted to wear real plain clothes, but Laurie had insisted that they should wear the school uniform (like nice boys and girls). Far from everybody did on this school, so why bother?

Because they were nice girls and boys, that's why.

She brushed her hair harder.

– You don't need to do that for my sake, Everett told her from the doorway.

– You're lying like hell. She pointed out the obvious with a short, dry laughter. – You just looove it when the dolls are dolling themselves up for you. Your thoughts on this are quite transparent, you know...

– Besides, you may relax. I'm not doing it for you, I'm doing it for me.

That was one of the things he loved about her, her ruthless honesty.

– Too fucking hot... she mumbled, and started to tear off her cute, little dress. She took off everything and redressed herself in a thin blouse and her dungaree «suit», found even the pants too uncomfortable, and after removing them, dragging the dungaree-shorts up her legs and thighs. It was tight around her thighs, but she didn't mind.

– Too hot, he confirmed and was rewarded by a thrilling laughter.

Barely outside, they felt the sun, felt its intense rays touch the skin. Jill put her black hat on the head and the eyes turned to shadow. And she was grinning, feeling the heat, welcoming it. She still enjoyed looking at the world with the hat on her head, but she didn't hide her eyes anymore.

– Let's go, Stacy said. – We don't want to come too late, now, will we?

She wore her «plain» clothes, too. So did Jason. Loeh and Rae and Kieron didn't.

They started moving. Laurie had already left. She trusted the «elders» to take care of things, but Stacy (the sneaky bitch) had done it for them. Andrea didn't look pleased.

– Well, back to school for you novices, Daniel growled, slightly humorous. He was the only one of the elder Nine who didn't wear his uniform. – You haven't missed much, if you ask me. It's hard to imagine the reason for the school's symbol to be «the Light of Knowledge». As one of the older, wiser students, I must tell you that I don't know if I can withstand the boredom… or if I can keep hiding my distaste for it.

– It's the same all over the heap, isn't it? Loeh shrugged. – School is school, no matter where we go, a preparation for «adult» life.

They all noticed the more than slight sarcasm in her voice.

– That's true, Stacy stated. – The question is what we're gonna do about it.

Nobody responded by verbally commenting on it, but they responded, nonetheless.

Others may be helpless to do anything about it, about everything, but we're not.

They entered the college park, such as it was, dried out, almost burned plants and lawns.

The onslaught hit Everett immediately. He was prepared for it, as Jill had aided him, by sharing her experience, but the onslaught of thoughts hit him, hit him like a wave on the beach. No matter the shielding, no matter the preparation, droplets of water... of whatever would always be leaking past it.

There was the sea of plain thoughts, background «noise» that he had adapted to, been able to identity, surprisingly fast and easy. And then...

There was the worry. Most of the stuff was mundane, general stuff, but these days, there was more. He heard, tuned in on voices, plain voices, identifying the fear, putting a name on it, somehow. A boy spoke to a girl a few steps away.

– I spoke to my grandfather today. He hadn't experienced anything remotely similar to this heat, this prolonged. And he claimed that his grandfather hadn't either.

Nobody had, that was the point. Everett allowed his thoughts to flow, let a minor percentage of available information to resurface, not certain if he was comfortable with it or not.

The Earth, or at least a considerable part of dry land on Earth, was suffering from drought. Reports from all parts of the planet revealed how strange the weather had become. Where there wasn't draught it was storming and raining. Extremities were found everywhere, in a global system obviously completely off-balance. In northern Canada the effects of heavy rainfall, corresponding with that of melting ice, caused floods on an unprecedented scale. Ice that had been there for an eternity, had been seen as eternal just faded away. In Siberia, the Russian Federation, the tundra, the frozen earth was about to melt. The inhabitants of Northfield, New England, United States of America had, as the rest of humanity experienced strange weather before, but never on this scale, geographically or timewise. Weather had behaved... strangely since the middle eighties and since the middle nineties, it had really taken off. And it happened all over the globe. It could no longer be written off as the overactive imagination of the few and anxious, of the Doomsayer and the crazed scientist. The old ways of soothing and misdirection didn't necessarily work anymore.

People were worried and their worry was reinforced every day now, no matter how much, how strongly they were told that things were basically all right. No matter the continuing official *sooth(e)sayer* policy, so successful in the past.

Jill more than sensed it, she experienced it, as she and the other witches entered the main building. She felt the rigid rules, designed to keep dissatisfied youth, non-contending outsiders and others in place, as chains around her body, her raging mind, felt them crack and break.

– Can you smell it? She said aloud. – Its scent?

– The scent of what? Barryman had heard her, as he stood in the door, «welcoming» his flock.

– Freedom, she said unafraid.

He gave them all twice the amount of work because of that. In his cleverness he didn't overtly state this, but he let it be known, in a thousand small and large ways. He was a teacher that didn't believe in personal, individual ways to wisdom...

And Jill couldn't avoid noticing the disapproval of her fellow students. Not the most insensitive person could've done that. And she was far from being one. For the first time since becoming aware of her talent, she despaired of it. And she almost shook with the helpless rage and hatred directed at Barryman. He had taken an instant dislike to her, during his initial «tutoring», and had probably just been waiting for an excuse to vent it. And she, like an idiot, had given it to him. Was that the price? Would that always be the price for honesty, for Freedom?

She closed her mind off to the others, didn't want them or anyone else to see her shame, her self-inflicted wound.

Later. They noticed, of course. Especially Everett, by her lack of usual exuberance. And they surrounded her in a healing embrace. She gave them a smile in return, not certain if she had truly enjoyed what they had done.

But her mood bounced back, as it usually did these days. And the wind played with her skin once more.

In spite of this and other smaller and larger aggravations, they made an attempt to fit in, to concentrate on schoolwork, because Laurie had asked them to do so. But it was hard. Not just because they didn't fit in, and didn't enjoy school. There was also the matter of all the distractions to a normal life Northfield had to offer. Their eyes, wary and simultaneously glowing with interest were often turned, pulled to the right, to the heights, to the Hill. The Presence of Frazer Hill was impossible to ignore for any of them. Even bathed in sunlight, like it was now, it seemed ominous and yet... there was something there, attracting them.

– Strange, isn't it? Jill ventured. – That overgrown mound is the only place in town with a «real» name.

– They put names on the Unknown and believe it will make it known, Everett replied ironically.

A smile crossed her lips. She rewarded him with a spontaneous kiss.

The sky was completely blue everywhere, completely free of clouds, as it had been for quite some time now, except for the immediate area surrounding Frazer Hill. Sun was warm. They knew it could easily burn, too, but just now it warmed them.

5

To many the early evening, the twilight in Northfield arrived just as unexpected every time. They didn't expect the sun to set at seven o'clock, while the summer was still hot and undefeated. In most of the town it disappeared even earlier, of course, behind Frazer Hill. But earlier they had always known it was there, after all. Now, they weren't certain anymore.

People attached to business in town didn't really have any reason to complain. Customers spent more time outdoors, used more money, especially during the evening. It was still hot, but definitely a breather, compared to daytime.

Then there was another matter, an almost unnoticeable... tendency during the recent weeks. Unnoticeable if one wasn't in the right places. Unexpectedly, many people had moved to the area recently. Most of them had moved to Oldtown, moved into the formerly empty apartments and houses there. Their choice of venue was frowned at by the traders and shakers in Newtown, but contributed only in minor ways to lessen expectations of higher profits.

It was a letdown that several of them had started businesses of their own, in Oldtown to boot. That they even pulled customers away from the modern shopping malls in Newtown, to the older (ripe for «renewal») part of the city. But it couldn't possibly last, could it? Not everybody enjoyed the fact that Oldtown had come alive again. It took the attention away from the important going ons in town. That, in addition to the fact that there were important people hungry to make a considerable investment, into turning promising, (for the time being useless) properties into modern, dollar-earning facilities.

But as it was, at the time, they already were, (sort of) they already brought money to a hard tried city treasury department. So that argument was also void. So, the important people bid their time, waiting for the inevitable Oldtown recession.

At this time, in the minutes and hour after sunset, Life really began on Main Street. People would say that the street came alive, but that was nonsense, of course. It was the people present who did that. From just after sunset, to the fading of the darkness close to dawn, they would fly like eagles (and crash like jumbo jets without wings).

And leave behind a mountain of money, Sharon Haldoway thought cynically, expectantly.

She was looking out of a window from her apartment on the first floor above the actual locale of her tavern, looking away from a fuming Gabrielle Asteroth.

– So, you're getting new people, and are just ditching me, is that it?

– I'm not «ditching» you, Gabrielle, Sharon said patiently. – At least not willingly. It's not like I really have any choice. My bigger, more powerful competitors would be more than happy to have me shut down, if I continue to allow a thirteen-year-old to perform in an «adult» establishment. You're a great performer, sweetie, and I'll come and see you, wherever you do your thing.

The tall, skinny creature crossed the room back and forth, wearing holes in the carpet.

– I can't believe you'll give in that easily. She stopped in front of the woman, studying her with her keen, uncanny power of observation. – There must be more to it. C'mon, girl, tell wise Gabi all about it, I'm no mind reader, you know...

The guilt was suddenly, undeniably written in the adult's face. She saw it in the girl's eyes, turning narrow and pointed.

– You shouldn't really be taking your emulation of the witches too far, you know. Sharon blurted it all out lamely to the girl, before she managed to stop herself. – They're not widely popular around here.

– So that's it? The girl's face was transformed by a triumphant, vicious smile. – Perhaps your reluctance isn't caused by you disagreeing with my *political* views, at all...

Sharon froze. The girl seemed to darken before her, the frame around the body to turn transparent, the tongue, wetting the lips seemingly stretching and pulsing. Sharon felt a rush of nausea flowing over her, surrounding her entire self.

Suddenly Gabrielle took a step back, her face frozen in bewilderment and terror.

– Forgive me, she cried out. – Please, forgive me.

She turned abruptly and ran frantic out of the room. Sharon could hear her descending the stairs in an arrhythmic discord.

Sharon leaned against the window, looking out of it, seeing nothing, nausea gripping her like claws and talons from the very air. Sweat made her cold in the searing heat. Sweat came easy, both the cold and the hot. Droplets of acid turned her skin into the very incarnation of gooseflesh.

She walked down to the ground floor without really feeling the steps under her feet. The noise, the ruckus from the bar started surrounding her, making her forget, making memory dim once more.

The dancers, the group of drifters sat by a table close to the bar, eating and drinking to their heart's desire, taking advantage of her generous offer of free drinks and food, the salary for their performance. She approached them with a slightly poised look.

– Careful now, boys and girls, she cautioned them. – Or your performance is shot to hell and then you'll be on the road again...

She didn't care about the hurt and disappointed look in their eyes. She was in control here, and if they didn't accept that... well, tough.

Erica behind the bar waved to her. Preoccupied, she waved back. Erica Reynolds and the other waitress/bartender, Cynthia Brandt had the right enthusiasm for this kind of job. So had the chef, for that matter, even if his skills (as a cook) left something, no, a *lot,* to be desired. But if she wanted someone better qualified, she would have to pay that someone far better.

Fortunately, people didn't come here because of the food. It was still a mystery to Sharon why people did come here, at least in such great numbers. Originally, she had planned a more... exclusive retreat, but that had changed pretty fast... with the clientele. She realized with a start that the reason people did come here, was because of the guests themselves, and that she had for once in her life been in the right place, at the right time. The undefined atmosphere, the one she couldn't name both attracted and repulsed her.

It didn't matter, she told herself, as long as they gave her their money, as long as she was in control.

She had been quite a drifter herself, through the years. Spending endless years, looking... for something. Nothing big, nothing more than the sound of meeting glasses through open windows and doors, a conversation over a meal, deeper than a smooth surface.

Gus Walters sat on a stool by the bar register, where he had been sitting for a while, drinking. Most of the day, if the truth should be told. He wasn't sipping as most did, but drank in big gulps. He didn't drink liquor, firewater, but the strong Guinness beer. Even so, it was as if he drank water, as if both the alcohol and the fat were burning up inside him. She was sensitive enough to realize, to know, that it was hatred, hatred against all and everyone that kept him going. She shuddered, stood there for a while, undecided. When he finally reached the talking stage, she was almost relieved. Almost. His tongue had loosened a bit too much. She didn't want trouble. She didn't bother anyone and wasn't bothered in return. An excellent arrangement. She wanted it to continue that way.

– ... we fought against the man and his dirty dealings for years, damn me if we didn't. His head was butting forward, while his loose lip was virtually touching his chest, the tongue slipping outside ever so often. – His power and influence just grew, while ours, we slipped to nothing. We didn't have any choice, but to give in to him, did we?

A guy by his side pushed him slightly in the side.

– That's enough, Gus, you're talking *too* much.

– I don't give a shit, Gus mumbled his response.

– Well, fuck you! This will be on our heads, too.

– I don't give a SHIT! The Guinness glass was shattered against the bar. Pieces of glass, beer and blood flowed everywhere.

Sharon was about to jump into the fray, when she became aware of four people walking through the portal. For a tiny moment the ruckus quieted. Four witches. Sharon knew them, would've have known them, even if they hadn't become a well-known sight in town recently. When walking to greet them, she made an effort not to treat them any different than other guests.

– Good evening, may I get you a table?

– Certainly, the intense, tall young woman granted her. Lights twinkled in green eyes. – We plan on staying for quite a while.

So young and so... forward, Sharon thought.

Stacy looked straight through the woman, to the emotion and boundless passion behind and around her.

I can feel it here, the pulse beating in the vein.

Stacy felt it all and she reveled in it.

She shared it with Jason, Travis and Loeh without thinking twice about it.

– As you may remember, my name is Sharon, the hostess greeted them, as she led them to a table close to the entrance. – I'm *delighted* to meet you again. If you would excuse me, there is something requiring my attention. There will be someone here to take your order shortly.

– I'm convinced you'll deal with whatever is requiring your attention... admirably.

Jason Gallagher shook her hand ever so lightly before releasing it.

He's so *young,* she pondered. He was at least ten years younger than her. She was pondering still.

The attraction hit her suddenly, violently. But she couldn't tell from his cold and indifferent exterior if it was mutual.

She made Gus sit down by a table, where he could be more manageable. It took some time, but calming him didn't require any major effort.

The dancers entertained her for a while, as they received accolades from the audience. They were really quite good. She had some knowledge of dance and could tell. And the audience enjoyed their performance. They hadn't been hired as much for their dance, as for their ability to create excitement and their performance was better with an audience than without.

«All Tomorrow's Parties» by Velvet Underground started flowing into the room. And what was flowing into the room wasn't only from the speakers, but from time itself. Stacy felt the gooseflesh, welcoming it, sensing the scent of the Sixties around her. And more...

She scented the perplexity of the dancers, as their movements enhanced the charged emotions in the room, the fear, the attraction (and more), as something deep within the room, within Stacy herself, enhanced the Dance in return. She gasped, closer to losing control than she had been in years. She stretched out her arms to both her sides, pressing the thumb and index finger together, straining to keep the other fingers stretched. Her three companions all reacted in different ways. Travis cautious, Loeh with frivolity and gathering passion, Jason... she saw behind, beyond his eyes, seeing the fire, hot and consuming, seeing him for the first time. She saw this, wild as it was, as merely the starting point of a Long Walk, stretching into infinity, eternity, as only a short prologue of what was to come.

After a time definitely indefinite, the dancers bowing and jumping, after the many dances, received the wild accolades from the participating audience.

– Thank you, one of the dancers gasped, out of breath, – thank you all.

One of each sex started carrying two hats around. Upon their return to the stage, both hats were almost full.

And the dances continued.

At some point, after several extra sets, one of the dancers held up his hand and managed to say something in a somewhat quiet room.

– I'm sorry to announce that the coming performance is our last dance for the evening. This day has been fantastic for us, folks, you can't imagine how much it means to us, but the simple truth of it is that we haven't learned more dances.

A new tape was put in Sharon's equipment. Music started rising, rising from the floor and up, music from the movie «the last temptation of Christ». World music, Earth music, rumbling in the ground, creeping out of the speakers. Loeh started swaying on the chair, swaying even more as she moved towards the stage, the group.

– Is it okay? She was asking.

– More than okay, after what I've seen so far, one of the men said, in a very hoarse voice.

– Okay then, Loeh said aloud to the entire gathering. – For maximum enjoyment of this we should go outside, crack some tables and chairs... if possible?

– My treat, Sharon said hastily. – I've wanted to redecorate anyway.

Outside, within the actual Circle, there was built a fire. The sky had been darkening for a while now, slowly being illuminated by a rain of stars. Eastern tones and sounds, with a further significance of World Music, spread and filled Circle as it had just filled one of its seven buildings and through the seven portals it spread to the street outside. Stacy could see it. Loeh had thrown off her jacket. Sharon feared that she would remove all her clothes, but she didn't. She kicked off her sandals, but kept the short skirt and the yellow blouse, revealing her navel. Skirt started levitating to her hips as she started to turn and dance. In the limited light it was hard to say what, if anything resembling clothing was underneath. She picked up one leg of a former chair, then one more in the other hand. The dance started with Loeh following the others' lead, but then she started from her own perspective, her own origin. She began what was clearly, to those familiar with it a Voodoun dance, but that wasn't exactly the style she was doing now. For a while she and the others moved completely different from each other, but then, suddenly they achieved a sort of harmonic disharmony that was quite striking. Loeh, the snake goddess was dancing in the grove, in the forest glen, and then, as the heavy drums started like thunder, *fire* rose from the sticks she was swinging through the air. She pushed sticks turned torches into the heap of wood, transferring fire and flames rose. Heat spread, from one second to the next, to the entire circle. Sharon discovered that her throat was dry. She sipped, swallowed beer. No use. Heat ravaged her.

The one they called only Loeh circled around the fire. Circled, circled, circled... The audience, the participants didn't notice it at first, but for each completed circle the flame grew. The dance had long ago turned raw, passionate, completely devoid of reason. The dancers were hardly recognizable, in either dance or appearance, compared to the excellent performance they had achieved previously. The accompanying voices coming from nowhere grew out of the music, kept flowing through the night as ghosts. Fire rose, protuberances pushing towards Loeh, caressing her. Her dance had a Voodoun origin, but it had very soon gone far beyond that, or even anything remotely familiar.

Embers were dancing in the air, feet drumming against the ground. First there was one body wriggling and twisting savagely, then there were more than one, then there were many. Loeh's movements seemed truly snakelike to them all. And alive, so damned alive. The fire, once flaming white, seemed eventually to shrink again, sagging (like a person). Like the eternal dancer herself, to an intensity equal to how it, she had been, before the firedance dance had started. Suddenly there was an explosion, a rain of ember and people screamed in enjoyment and worry. The Circle turned dark and full of Shadow.

Excellent control, wouldn't you say? Stacy sent to Jason.

– That was *marvelous.* Sharon applauded excitedly.

The dancers, frozen like statues, once more opened themselves up to outside influence.

– I've had some training, Loeh said jokingly, blushing, both because of the applause and the wonderful exposure of her own, heartfelt passion. – I first danced in *Bizango* - the Secret Societies, when I was five.

– I would like you to dance here regularly, Sharon said, committing herself. – Do you want to?

– I think it can be fun, if the others don't mind.

Sharon cast a look at the dancers. It was decided.

– Sure, one of the girls exclaimed. – We can learn a lot from this gal. She's *Hot!*

– I think it will be great, Sharon said, attempting to hold back a little, beside herself with excitement. – This was only the first time you performed together... Honestly, it truly looked like you've never done anything else.

– Like magick, Loeh said lightly.

Shaky laughter. Some weren't certain what to believe.

Stacy approached Loeh and put her hands on her shoulders.

– Hurting? She whispered into the other girl's ear.

– It stings a bit, Loeh admitted. – Flames were a bit close. It's okay.

– I can fix most things easily now, she was chastised. – But you should still be a little more cautious. A third-degree burn is attracting slightly more intense scrutiny, see?

An obedient nod and then she felt it, the almost burning heat moving through her body. Stacy stood close to her, holding her hands against the slightly singed skin, healing it. No uninitiated noticed anything. Stacy made sure of that. Loeh felt the power in her as a raging Storm, as she heard the inner voice:

When you cut yourself, you'll bleed. If you're poisoned, you may die. If I'm cut, I may bleed, but not for long. If I'm poisoned, I'll probably not even get sick, and I'll certainly not die.

Loeh had been fresh and spirited after the dance, but suddenly she felt weak and dizzy. Stacy led her to Travis and let her lean on him for support. Then she returned to the center of the circle, immediately stretching out her arms, catching everybody's attention.

I can feel the red flow. I can sense the dragon lines of the Earth.

They imagined she might be glowing as she stood there by the fire. They wondered. Could it really be the fire illuminating her like this? Even if the flame was growing again?

Suddenly, it was as if she was surrounded by Shadow, and they wondered where the darkness came from. They took a look around and discovered that somebody had turned off all the electrical lights. They scouted something akin to relief in each other's eyes. What had they imagined had happened?

Stacy Larkin stretched a hand towards the fire. And as she bowed her body, she pushed most of her arm into the flames and they imagined a stick flying into the hand. Her hand. It was burning, and as she held it with both her hands, the flames surrounded her lower arms. The audience stood there, gasping. She threw the torch back on the fire and fire stretched the entire way to the heavens. All material burned instantly to virtually nothing. The fire was gone and only embers remained. The witch picked them up and started spreading them, making a smoking circle. Smoke floated and blew around her, as if she was still burning. She kicked off her sandals and started walking on the embers. Some among the audience had seen this type of performance before, but never seen it be performed so straight-faced, so nonchalant. The spectators had forgotten her hands, so to speak. There was still smoke coming from them, but otherwise they looked fairly... *normal?*

Can you feel it, little sister, the sweet pain of burning?

She was dirty because of the soot... of course. Her feet, her smoking body emerged from the volcanic inferno underneath. Someone brought a washing tray. Nobody could later tell who. While she proceeded on washing off all the black, black soot, the people standing closest could see that her skin had turned pink on the places where the fire had burned her. As if it had just grown back. She was definitely more fair-skinned there than she usually was. Or was that, too, just their imagination, an illusion? A few minutes later there was no longer any discernible difference.

She had their complete attention. Jason smiled ironically.

– Most of us have arrived here from other places. She started her speech without introduction. – Even those of us born here have recently traveled far. We've come for different reasons. We've traveled away from something, but most of us have also traveled towards something...

And to something.

They saw images. At least they were thinking about them. With unusual clarity they imagined thoughts and deeds, leading them on their path here - and what made them remain… and right there, at the center of the visions stood Stacy Larkin. There were flashes in her eyes and everybody could see it.

– Her projections are far more detailed and sophisticated then Laurie's, Travis whispered to Jason and Loeh.

– Be quiet, now, Jason said. – This is interesting.

They couldn't tell whether or not he was serious.

– What happened when the prince braved the thorn wall and awakened the Sleeping Beauty? The Witch intoned with roguish eyes, smiling crookedly, characteristically. – She burned him to a crisp, of course, reducing him to a pile of ashes, for having the nerve to disturb her beauty sleep.

There were heard gasps and heavy breathing. The Witch smiled some more.

– Perhaps coincidence has led you here, perhaps not. Here you've felt vibrations of attraction and Hunger making you want to stay, making you want to flee, something Deep, fundamental. Call it curiosity or belonging, but you want to stay, to see what's going to happen. You know something will happen. A Change, one surpassing everything you've heard about and experienced. You have no «sensible» reason for this hope, but have come, in spite of the boundaries yourself and society have put inside you. Perhaps you haven't managed to express yourself in thought and words and action earlier, but you've come to this small, unknown place, this pinprick on a map. Such places have ever, by design or circumstances become instruments of Change. And you're right to be hopeful, to feel that wild burning expectation within. You've come to the right place...

For the rest of the evening and night, there were eager discussions and sparks were flying. Alcohol was consumed and enjoyed, but was far from being the fuel causing the sparks, the gleaming interest in everybody's eyes. Stacy thrived visibly in the commotion, excitement and expectation. She knew that even those who considered themselves only guests here would take everything with them, wherever they lived, wherever they went. If they attempted to continue their existence as it had been previously, they would indeed see it as it was, hollow and trite. They might not have realized it yet, but their lives had been irreversibly Changed.

Sharon kept company with the witches, sitting by their table, partaking in their experiences. No one saw anything strange in that, did they? Didn't she sit and mingle with the guests every night?

– Nice place you've got here, Travis said approvingly.

– Thanks, she merely acknowledged.

People approached Stacy like she was the second coming or something.

And she enjoyed it.

– How is the Change supposed to happen? One asked her. – Why do you think we can make it, where countless others have tried and failed?

She smiled to him, quite satisfied with his use of «we».

– Because this entire place is magical. Her reply was completely calm, measured, with dark and stormy passions underneath. – Here, humans can more easily be humans. Here, we're closer to what we once were and from here we will spread to all the people in the world. We will be Known and those with power will fear us.

Everybody else, too. But she didn't say that.

She circulated in the room, among the sea of faces, of thoughts, giving them reassuring and frightening smiles, tasting their emotions, their energies, excelling in it. She couldn't catch any discernible thoughts. There was too much «noise», too many people around, for her to listen effectively with her telepathic talent. But there were patterns of variance she was able to sense. Quite unnecessary really, right now, since she had no problems picking two diverging from the rest of the crowd. Two men closing in on Gus Walters caught her interest. They were dressed in gray suits, and among a certain type of people they didn't stand out at all. These were the eager servants of society, the ones serving people at the top, at the top of the Pyramid. She had no trouble guessing what was being said.

Gus had returned to the bar. He had continued to drink hard the entire evening. It continued to burn inside him.

– What do you want? He said sourly, he recognized the two men.
– Hello, Gus, Man One said nicely. – Not very polite, are we?
Gus didn't reply. Not in any words, taking one more swig of his beer.
– We're here to tell ya that Mr. T wasn't completely satisfied with the way your employment relation with him ended. We've got good news for ya: He's willing to forgive ya.
– He's willing to forgive ya, echoed Man Two. – As the goodhearted man he is, he's offering ya another job.
– Work and salary will of course be a bit less favorable. Your previous position is unfortunately already filled.
– I'll bet, Gus mumbled.
– What did ya say? Man One exclaimed, momentarily stunned. They weren't used to the sheep fighting back. Some needed certain... encouragement occasionally, but they were mostly running in the right direction.
– I think you should think this through very carefully, Gus. The warning was delivered in a slightly less friendly tone. – It may take a considerable time before you get such a generous offer again.
– Go to Hell, he spat in the most obvious manner.
– He's drunk, Man One shook his head in disgust.
He was drunk, but not that drunk. He had been worse off before. He knew exactly what he was saying.
– C'mon, come with us. After some time, when you once again are able to think clearly, you will have *learned.*
They attempted to grab him around the arms. He made an inpatient movement away from them.
– Don't make any trouble now...
– I think you should take your own advice, gentlemen...
They turned their heads. Sharon suddenly stood behind them.
They turned towards her, pleased. Before leaving the Pyramid, they had been given explicit orders to cause as much trouble at the tavern as they possibly could, if the opportunity should present itself. This was obviously such an opportunity. Lately they, and their brethren had been acting on many such offerings. And they didn't act with their former discretion either. There had been a time when they would have found that prudent.
As a single entity they reached for Sharon, a fluent, well exercised move. In a flashing fast move, she grabbed their wrists and pulled, pulled their shoulders off their sockets. Pain froze them. Suddenly they realized they were completely helpless, completely at her mercy.
– Tell your Master that I don't want any trouble, boys, she said while tenderly rearranging a curl on Man One's forehead. – But this is *my* place. I won't tolerate any interference here. Tell him that I've been taught by the best and that I'm more than capable of making my point, if he chooses to fuck with me. Are we *clear?*
They nodded, with faces contracted in pain.
– She's a cute little treasure, isn't she? Stacy told Jason. – Quite useful for breeding, too.
– Not bad, he grunted.
– Allow me to escort you off the premises, Sharon said darkly. – Do not return. You're not welcome.
She threw them both through the portal, as easily as she would have thrown cans of garbage.
– Now, what do you say? Stacy wondered, Stacy challenged. – Too tough for you?
– She enjoys power, he pondered, – while giving the impression of being a nice, cute girl. It will be ridiculously easy to make her submit to her darker, wicked nature.
While the feeling of trashing the two goons, the overwhelming rush of Victory was fresh in her, she walked to Jason and, with a patronizing snarl, invited him to a dance. He was just a boy, an inexperienced youth, aspiring to be a Casanova. She could handle him with ease, she was looking forward to handling him.
The dance ended. He wasn't a very good dancer. Even if he had the agility, he didn't have the moves. But she didn't really care about that. The fact that he hadn't really made a pass at her, any whatsoever, made her furious and that easily identified emotion, and its easily identified source, made her cringe with shame and fury. She heard his laughter, she heard it the rest of the night, no matter the distance,

the number of people between them. She attempted to ignore the strange way in which he was eyeing her, in vain. He still seemed completely disinterested in her... sexually. She caught herself in the wish that he would change his mind. Strange thoughts raged inside her. All the witches made her feel strange. Loeh for obvious reasons. Her fabulous performance. Sharon had never seen anything like it. Stacy Larkin was something else altogether. It wasn't her stage performance that stood out, but her... demeanor. She was so nice, so terribly nice that it was impossible to say no to her.

Sharon knew that Travis was interested in her. He didn't exactly make a point of it, but as an experienced woman she had no trouble reading whatever he was attempting to hide. Besides, he was among those people who could never hide much, from anyone. She danced with him and for him... as she did with Jason. Could it be that she wanted them to woe her, to even fight for her between themselves, to better wrap them around her finger? She couldn't believe this... this temptation rising within her. She remembered clearly now, what she so long had strived in vain to forget. This wasn't like her, it wasn't.

– We must go now, Jason said to her. They stood by the portal with Stacy, Travis and Loeh. – Regrettably we'll miss the remaining part of the party, but that is the lot of being nice little boys and girls, and not arriving a second too late to the first morning lesson at school.

– It was fun, Stacy said. – We will do it again sometime.

Stacy kissed her on the cheek. And they were gone, disappeared back into the Night.

Jason felt the fresh air outside, breathing it in with all the might he could muster. The game had ended, for now, the game he had always secretly detested.

He sensed something then, something outside, and he stopped.

Stacy sensed something, and it sent a shiver down her spine.

Suddenly Gabrielle stood before them, emerging out of the shadows.

– I was dreaming about you, she said with a pointed stare. – I know who you are.

The four older teenagers had to laugh, in shock, in relief.

– Shouldn't you be in bed by now? Stacy asked equally pointed.

– I was, then I wasn't, then I was here... Why do you ask?

– You... surprised us, honey. Loeh spoke with her most distinct southern drawl. – We're just worried about you, are you alright?

– Sure, the girl pouted, – why shouldn't I be all right?

They couldn't say if she was wearing stage make up, or if she had dark rings around her eyes.

She smiled then, innocently and enthusiastically.

– I saw your performance, and what a *wild* ride it was.

– Where were you? Stacy asked. – I didn't see you.

– I was there. I saw your wild, aggressive dance.

Suddenly she was darker, more somber again. They couldn't tell if she was referring to Loeh's literal dance or Stacy's more mental, indirect show. She was like that.

Deep.

– It's the Wild, aggressive part of us that is so liberating, isn't it? There she was again, both somber and a picture of joy simultaneously. – But also what may make it so easy to suppress others. Everything is skewed, is out of place in civilization. We're... we're so far removed from where we should be, so very far away from the natural life of a human being, so very far away from home. We're so very far away from home all of us.

– I think you're right, Jason said. – We are wild, we are hunters.

– The Horned God was the god of the Hunt. In older versions even the female aspect is a goddess of the Hunt.

– Our dear Delphi, Stacy saluted, not without a certain ambiguity herself.

The girl blushed instantly.

– Your collected knowledge is truly quite impressive, Travis said approvingly. – Where have you found everything?

– Oh, here, there and everywhere. A shrug, an uncertain smile.

– Why haven't you joined the witches long ago? Whether you're one in fact or name only, you surely belong among them... among us?

– That some claim to be Alternative doesn't mean they necessarily are, she said, turning away.
Turning back, with a half pained, half eager expression.
– It is an unfortunate trend that most alternative societies tend to degenerate towards being a cult. Instead of liberating itself from the chains of society, it's often picking many of present-day society's worst «qualities». It might be one person, the leader deliberately setting it up to be like that, or it may start out idealistic and turn «bad» later. Anyway, in my opinion members of any fledgling alternative movement should be on guard even before the signs are showing and signs will show.
– Wise little witch, Jason said appraisingly.
She was blushing again, no, more like flushing...
Embarrassed, but also...
The girl is frightened, Stacy realized with a start.
– I've got nothing against alternative gatherings, Gabrielle pointed out, coming on strong again, – but then they have to be *alternative,* not just a repetition of old mistakes, not more of the same, rotten shit.
– The way Everett was brought into the fold, for instance, is reminiscent of the Scientology Church. Usually it happens that way, through created emotional ties.
Stacy wanted to protest, but the quiet look the younger girl sent her kept her quiet. Stacy smiled amused. Did she feel aggrieved on Jill's behalf?
– I know, I know, that wasn't really her, Jill's intention, but intentionally or not, that was what happened.
And it was they who felt uncertainty gnawing, not the thirteen-year-old in front of them. They had, after all, experienced in full Laurie's methods of recruitment.
– I think Everett is too independent to be forced into joining anything, Stacy said sweetly. – So are you. But no matter, you should come with us now, it's getting late.
– You don't *understand,* the girl said with her hands half rolled into fists. – It has started already, and soon I'll be just as obedient and submissive as the rest of you.
– You're rambling, girlie. Loeh reached for her. – Allow us at least to follow you home.
– NO, I don't want to go with you.
And Loeh's hand went through the air as if there was nothing there.
The girl ran off then. They were too stunned to really do anything to hold her back.
And she was gone in the dark.
– Do you have bad dreams? Stacy called after her, receiving no reply, but silence.
Even if they all imagined they heard a mad, shrieking laughter from the darkness surrounding them.
– I don't know if I should be afraid for her or of her, Travis said quietly.
And in that they were all in complete agreement. Chilled to the bone, they stood for a long time, there on the spot, saying nothing, speaking volumes.

6

Blessed silence could finally ring pleasant in Sharon's ears. Downstairs there was hardly more to hear than the sound of glasses and glass rattling, the sound of her employees cleaning glasses, the floor, and everything. She was in bed, the big bed, in the living room, with a smile on her lips, seeing herself in the ceiling mirror with the thin blanket covering her naked body, the blanket already wet of sweat. It didn't make any difference that every conceivable window had been opened. Her body kept pouring out sweat and mixed in was also other body fluids. She was wideawake, but kept dreaming chaotic fever dreams. All lights were turned off. She felt the pain of their heat anyway. Lights reached her from the street outside, light enough or light less enough, for her to imagine a shape by her side in the bed. This shape did everything to her, everything she had ever imagined, everything she could ever possibly conceive of. And more... She was eighteen once more, awkward, inexperienced, and desire and expectations raged through her, and the body didn't feel like her own. A sea of hot water was drowning her, and she was floating away in its currents. She was so ashamed, but had no control over herself, no control over anything. What was *wrong* with her? She couldn't find an answer, only try to weather the storm, and even that was denied her, as the powerful, undeniable currents were sweeping her away.

The doorbell chimed. The sound reached her through a haze of red and low roaring noise, echoing ever louder through her brain. She jumped up and out of the bed, running in haste to the drawer. She was looking feverishly through the lower drawer for a bathrobe, a piece of clothing she hadn't used for years. She slipped it on, and it felt strangely comfortable. Tying it thoroughly in the front, she walked hesitantly to the entrance door.

It was a big apartment. It covered the entire floor, lots of space. Was it Todd again, with the keys? Her head shook itself. She had told him repeatedly that it didn't matter if he kept them to the next day. He was a little slow that man, but he should still be able to receive a message.

She opened the door. Jason stood there on the porch. The air she was breathing... it was hot, wasn't it?

– Hi, he greeted her.

– Hi, she mumbled. – C-come in.

What was the *matter* with her? She never s-stuttered.

Shaking, she had to ask herself why she had let him in. Now, it was too late. He had made the decisive move over the doorstep. He closed the door himself. What was wrong with her? This anxious behavior wasn't like her at all. She was a big girl and could take care of herself.

On the opposite wall she had displayed all the diplomas and medals she had won in martial sports and arts. She wanted to look at them, keep the eyes on them, but they kept slipping away. Instead, she could only see herself in the mirror, how the clothing seemed to be clinging to her body, her full-formed body.

– You should hire more people.

– Uh? Confused she made herself clear her vision.

– There will be twice as many guests tomorrow. You'll need more help.

– Thanks to you guys, she said sweetly. – Thanks.

– Rehiring Gabrielle would be a good idea, he said. – Her exceptional skills aside and the bad, bad way you treated her, she's a quite screwed up girl and could really need our help.

Music from a harmonica flowed into the room through the open windows. Some distance away the three witches and a considerable number of other guests gathered. She used the word «witches» without thinking twice about it. Somewhere in the crowd she could see Stacy Larkin, standing out. Everybody could see her, if she so wanted.

– I can't do that, she said coldly. – They would close me down in a minute, if they got the slightest chance.

– No, they wouldn't, Jason said. – *We* wouldn't let them.

– You're awfully sure of yourself...

One step and he stood close to her, holding both her arms.

– So, what is it? He whispered into her ear.

– I don't understand, she whimpered, looking at the floor, looking away.

– Is it so that you don't believe or to the contrary... that you do?

She wanted to force him to release her, to shake him off like she would a bothersome fly, but her moves counted for even less than a feeble resistance.

– He really did a number on you, Ted did...

She froze. In his arms, and deep inside.

– I don't think he wanted to, that he did it on purpose, but you were so thoroughly fucked up already then, that by «forcing» you to look within yourself, you got even further screwed up.

She turned on a smile then. A triumphant, sickening smile.

– I knew there was something familiar about you, she said softly. – So, you're another one of his bastards, are you...

He let go of her. She pushed herself even tighter to him, stroking a hand over his cheek.

– You poor boy, I don't envy you. It can't be easy, retracing his steps, can it?

He tried to grab her, or perhaps hit her. She showed his hand away, *easy as pie.*

– You don't look a lot like him either. Perhaps you're more the way he once looked, he once was... but I doubt it.

She walked away from him, giving him a self-assured smile. He was just a boy after all, insecure and as exciting as a piece of wood.

– You've got a big ass and huge tits, he said in a satisfied tone. – I like that.

– Excuse m-me?

She thought she had heard wrong. She had wanted to put all her indignation and disgust in her voice. But there were none. He stepped close to her once more, grabbing her, holding tight this time.

– What are you doing? She cried out, gasping in horror.

He untied her knot in the front, as he was pushing her to the wall. A slight pull with his fingers and he had completely exposed her breasts.

– I'll tell you one thing, he said darkly, with his mouth pushing close to hers. – You're just a sick bitch, in need of some serious readjustment.

He started fondling her breasts, with both hands, taking his time. He had let go of her arms, but they were just hanging there, by her sides, useless. She wanted to speak, to throw insults at him, but her lips were numb. Nothing worked. At least she couldn't make it work.

But he could. Her nipples hardened, and her body grew supple. She moaned and wanted to kiss him. He gave her stinging cheeks, first with one hand, then with the other.

– I'm not really doing anything to you, he told her, – except what you've always wanted somebody to do.

He exposed her shoulders and arms. The robe fell silently to the floor. And there she was, completely nude, at his mercy. His hands were investigating her then, evaluating her. She wanted to be angry, pull away from him. Instead, her longing and heat grew, by the second, to something alien, unrecognizable. She felt helpless, perplexed, utterly paralyzed. He returned to her breasts, fondled them harder and she moaned, eager to surrender... and submit. He stole a kiss from her. She responded helplessly. He dragged her after the shoulder-length, fair hair to the bed. He placed her kneeling upon it. She waited obedient and feared he would turn around and leave, leaving her alone.

She was more than ready for him by now. The pain and the pleasure so mingled that she couldn't tell it apart anymore. He took his time undressing. She was so weak. He was so terribly strong, and she was so weak.

– What are you doing to me? She cried in a low, whimpering voice. – What are you doing to me, what are you doing to me...

She saw his cock spring forth from its confines and released effortlessly another wailing moan.

He looked down on the firm, well-trained body of the strong-willed woman. She was his to do with as he pleased. He could hardly allow himself to feel any triumph, any abating of his gathering fury. For that it had been all too easy.

– Everything I want, he told her.

7

In mortal fear, that voice so clear...

Aside from having an unknown number of both elected and... *non-elected* positions in the community, Peter Barryman was a history professor, and taught it with an envious zeal. The way he saw it the importance of this subject was highly underrated today. What could possibly be more important than the *glorious* history of the forefathers and the other towering men of History?

He entered the classroom at exactly the moment the bell stopped ringing, not just closing, but locking the door behind him. A few of the scoundrels managed to trick him by sneaking in under his arm, but he would take care to make them remember that. There were others, just outside the door. They were left out. There were runners, just a few steps away from the finishing line. They were disowned. They would all be noticed and given notice by the hall guard.

The teacher placed himself behind his desk, a position he seldom left, taking in the (sorry) sight of the varied gathering. There were only a few carrying the required school uniform and there was no respect to see anywhere. During the sixties the youth had been released from their necessary chains and the damage was yet visible, two generations down the line. He had strived to reintroduce *discipline* in society during his entire adult life. A well-known local politician and city council board member, he had recently concentrated his efforts in the classroom and school in general, in the hope of bigger success on a smaller scale. It had worked badly here, too. The school had, unfortunately so, a reputation as a place practicing a liberal doctrine.

Still, one shouldn't despair. As Rome wasn't raised in one day, morals in ruins wouldn't be restored easily. It was even more important to work with impressionable youths, steering them right, making sure they weren't steered wrong.

His technique of revealing troublemakers was already famous. He didn't care about the obvious ones, really, they were easy to spot, easy to steer right. They had the brain of a chicken and were equally easy to turn around, making into useful aides. So were those with a certain, limited brain function, learning abilities, who were easy to feed information, proper attitudes and usually got good grades. They were eager to learn, and their brain wasn't going into overdrive. They were like tape-recorders. What they were fed, was exactly what they returned. No, the truly difficult ones were those having problems with authority, and had both an overactive mind and a passion... a passion to experience everything possible. They had to be taken down, and taken down hard.

He always spent one hour each week, during the first part of the semester, on a thorough examination of History and its impact on today, teaching the young scoundrels where his bite was. The majority behavior wasn't usually overtly disrespectful. Students want good grades, and they knew he wouldn't give it to them, unless they behaved themselves. Especially those on scholarships were usually easy to control that way. The snotty brats of the filthy rich needed a different approach.

Victoria Arness counted, as usual, among those who eagerly took notes. The twins Melanie and Meta also took notes, but he noted that they didn't do it both at the same time. They sat by the same desk, but still... Another fact irritating him about them was that they were identical twins. No one, and at least not him, could tell them apart. They dressed the same, had their hair done the same way. Their behavior was indistinct. And they were completely impossible concerning any sort of cooperation about it. They wouldn't be distinct from each other. He had had a very frustrating meeting with their parents about their unruly daughters, even suggesting they should be separated for a while. Neither the mother nor father shared his view. In his desperation he had placed a note to the local child abuse prevention center. His good friend, Doctor Lemegen had given him a very short piece of advice: *Let it go.*

Then there were Henriette Gallier and familiars. They didn't take notes at all, and usually did exactly as they pleased.

One couldn't intimidate them by threatening them with bad grades or with expulsion. They couldn't be expelled. Not as long as they continued to get good grades in other subjects and independent tests. Then it would be he who drew attention to himself, not them. He usually managed to deal with them in the course of a semester, but they were unusually many and promiscuous this year.

The witches were.

He would mention it to Laurie Isherwood the first time an opportunity presented itself. She wasn't an unreasonable woman. She knew the importance of discipline. She had demonstrated that.

– The world, as we see it today, then, he lectured, – is the preliminary result of a long, successful development. Humans have, in the relatively short time since the Stone Age, since they were nothing more than cavemen, made excellent progress to better their situation. We have put barbarism behind us and we're today closer to the Utopian society than ever before in History. We possess a lot of advantages that even our close ancestors couldn't even dream of. If the growth and development isn't halted or stopped, the future will guaranteed bring ever more wonders.

His eyes fell on the girl who sat there yawning and kept staring out of the window and he lost concentration and invaluable momentum.

– Miss Gallier, he cleared his throat.

No response.

– *Henriette!*

He was still completely ignored.

– Loeh, he uttered as he fought to stay calm, recognizing that he by given in, had lost the battle.

– Yes, teacher?

The disrespectful tone made him even angrier.

– You're here to listen and to learn.

– It's just that your one-sided version of History (laughter), isn't much to listen to, and we can certainly not learn much from it, except how it didn't happen, she said, *and she dared to smile.* – I, for one, believe that anthropologists disagreeing with the linear model have a much better foundation to base their theories on. History doesn't consist of a series of incidents where a development is better because it has happened later, closer to the present, not even subjectively speaking. There is hardly any textbook on this and that historical incident, the way you portray it. Everybody knows that. That you're a teacher doesn't give you any excuse to lie to people. «Progress» can't be measured by the twentieth century's narrow viewpoints. Ever more people will say, in contradiction to your bright version, that the present-day world is humanity on a dangerous sidetrack, at best. At worst we've already fallen off the cliff. Some societies were worse in earlier times, many were better. Civilization itself, the worst threat to Life during human existence is just ten thousand years old, hopefully an intermission in human History.

– Fifty thousand children are dying of starvation every day in this paradise of yours, Rae Morgan said angrily. – Billions of people suffer and die on its altar. We «dive» in a thoroughly unjust and destructive society.

He was about to reprimand her for the obvious reason that she hadn't been given permission to speak, but forced himself to swallow the bitter pill. He realized how little he had to win. It made him so damned pissed how these scoundrels kept opposing him, how well they succeeded. His victories were small and insignificant in comparison. They ignored him both professionally and personally. They dared to do tests contradicting his teaching. The worst was that most of their arguments could be seen as close to impossible to circumvent. As long as they referred to approved source material, there was quite simply very little he could do. About that. Last year one «witch» had complained about a grade and succeeded. The reputation of Peter Barryman couldn't take another such major hit.

– As stated, he started up again. – Our modern Civilization is the culmination of thousands of years' development, from chaos to Order. Order is a key word in our society. A major part of the Law is made to keep the public order. Without Law and Order, Civilization will crumble.

He noticed with satisfaction that Victoria and her like-minded friends had started taking notes again.

– Some world, Ivan Silvestri said sarcastically.

– Some order, Loeh said aloud. – Nature and Life are completely out of balance. The laws are made, designed for the rich and powerful, by the rich and powerful, to benefit the rich and powerful, against those who have little or nothing or less than nothing.

– That's e - nough, the teachers managed to push out of himself, somewhat authoritatively. He attempted to look into the blue eyes, into the radiant blue eyes in the bastard bitch's dark face, but had to give in, give up. – There are those who want to learn something here. Don't destroy their chance for an education.

– We're not, Stacy Larkin said. – You are, with your petty and envious ways.

– We're certainly not, how can you say that? The surprise in the voice was clearly assumed. It was Kieron Dane, the wild ni... – We only show them alternatives to the regimentation you keep forcing on them.

Barryman opened and closed his mouth without getting a word out. Eyes were bulging and he was in a sorry state.

– You should learn to relax, Loeh said worried. – To excite yourself like this isn't good for the heart.

– Come up here, he snarled, – all five of you.

– Why? Loeh hit him with. – Are you starting to realize how it is, being subjected to your own methods... do you begin to feel the *heat?*

– You slut, he screamed. – You come up here immediately, take your medicine...

Suddenly flames rose from the desk in front of him, flames reaching the roof, a wall of fire. With a shriek of fear, he stumbled backwards, until his back crashed into the blackboard, and he could stumble backwards no longer.

After the class the witches gathered snickering around Loeh. Both physically and mentally she experienced their comforting presence.

– I... lost control. She was slowly breathing in and out. – He makes me so furious.

– That's good, Stacy told her, told them all, – that's excellent. At the same time, he's playing on the team administrating the carnival, he's really serious. He means every word. He will burn us all at the stake... if we let him.

They all imagined themselves burning and they shuddered uncontrollably in the hot summer sunshine.

– He's *watching* us, Jill said in disgust. – I can feel his Lizard eyes on me, I can't *stand* it.

She stretched out her thoughts, her entire mind... *There.* He stood hidden behind the corner window in the staff room some distance away. *Go away.* He shook,

Backing away until he collided with a chair and nearly fell.

At the school staff-conference the morning after, he was visibly uncomfortable. His colleges were throwing him curious glances. This wasn't the old good old Pete «Iron Fist» Barryman. During the meeting they could observe his strange behavior firsthand. Among many examples of this, they noticed how he, in spite of the air condition, used his sleeve to dry sweat from his forehead. The sleeve got *dirty,* and there were the glances. He looked around, his eyes wandering constantly, at the slightest sound, at the slightest change of the light.

– They set fire to my desk. He hit the table with his fist.

The table cried out in pain.

– Did you hear that? He said, looking at all of them with wild eyes. – You did hear that, right?

– I must say I find that a little difficult to believe, Peter, the desk fire that is... Kelly from the administration said carefully. – Isn't every «witch» sitting in the back of the room?

– They have their ways, the former Iron Fist mumbled.

– What?

– They must have spread an easily combustible powder on the desk, he said aloud.

– Excuse me, Peter, but didn't you just pointed out a few minutes ago, that you had cleaned it merely a few moments before class? And unless they're psychic they couldn't possibly have known that the fire would start exactly during the critical seconds you ordered them to come forward.

And so it ended. Unsatisfactory.

The entire rest of the day, all over the campus, he caught the eyes of students allowing themselves to grin barefaced to his face. This and many future days. Not that he hadn't expected it. But it was still galling. Many years had passed since the last time he had been so openly defied. And it should be many years until next time. It wouldn't end like today.

Unsatisfactory.

8

Jill took the elevator «reserved» for customers and audience up the Pyramid. Sound, smell, thoughts flowed at her from all directions. She continued to look unaffected, while attempting to meditate and relax. Most of what she received with known and unknown senses was background noises. But high Above she sensed a mind separated from the others, separated by its goal-oriented approach, and a detachment, a cruelty making her shudder.

The elevator stopped and the doors slid apart. She stepped into something resembling a reception area. It was placed five floors from the top. Those who dared come here did it because they wanted the city's favorite son to lend them his ear. A woman sat behind the desk, the screener of this queue of men and mice. Jill ignored the long line as she walked straight past it. She hadn't come here to ask for or receive charity.

– Mr. Thompson is expecting me, she said tightly.

– May I have the name? The screener disguised as a receptionist asked after a short break, where she had decided not to ignore the girl.

A sensible decision.

– Don't be silly. Jill said softly.

The door to the private elevator opened. Jill had heard it was Thompson himself who operated it and only him. Some in the queue were on their way in her tracks, but were discouraged by the two big bouncers, the two unmoving portals Jill had passed through.

The receptionist divided her attention among the people in the queue once more and she told the man in front of it:

– Why don't you come back tomorrow? It was evidently an order. – And we're going to arrange a meeting with one of Mr. Thompson's associates...

The elevator floated almost soundlessly upwards, working as perfectly and efficient as everything in the building. As she ascended/descended she had a certain sense of worry, of fate. The cold, lifeless machinery closed in on her, and she found it difficult to breathe.

A smell of plants and green assaulted her the moment the doors slid apart. Plants in pottery, far away from their natural habitat. In space, in time, rearranged into something unrecognizable by human manipulation. Jill felt their suffering. It permeated her.

– How do you like the building? Thompson inquired. He stood behind the enormous desk, with his eyes on her.

– Cold, mindless machinery is giving me the willies, she said detached.

– You Englishmen, he laughed. – No sense of progress. Of efficiency, indeed, but not the imagination to go with it.

– Lack of imagination is a trait the English share with most of present-day humans, she countered. – Steered imagination is quite okay, but imagination running wild is not economically viable.

She could have pointed out that she wasn't English, but chose not to.

– You, too, saw the movie? I would have thought you're too young for that... DVD, of course. Director's cut? I have it myself. It's even better.

He moved, he didn't walk, away from behind the desk.

– I've been expecting you. The news of your short visit on one of my less... luxurious properties did come by me. And I've ordered a thorough research of you since then, and you're not uninteresting to me.

She didn't say anything.

– I'm a bit surprised, though. I and Laurie usually frequent the same establishments, the same circles, so to speak and we have a well-established tradition of solving minor disputes to serve the common good.

– I'm not Laurie, Jill pointed out a bit less cold than his tone of voice. In both, it had been cold in the translation of calm.

His smile was extremely... engaging. He seemed young to her, in spite of the graying hair by the temples. Physically he was like a mix between a basketball player and a wrestler. Tall, powerful build, without a heavy wrestler's collection of fat, and that was how she pictured him mentally, too. He seemed open, friendly, obliging and was extremely charming. She was so young, and he was so experienced.

He didn't take her hand. That told her something, even if she wasn't sure what.

He stopped by the window wall to the east. She stopped by his side, looking attentive up at him. He was one of the few she had met she had to look up at.

– Look at the view, he told her.

She looked down, down, down, layer by layer. At enormous steps made for gods. At the insignificant ants moving around down there. She moved her eyes over the city. His city. The Piper playing enticing tones. Fear was a weapon in his hands, and they let him play.

Her eyes stopped by the horizon, where the sun rose every morning. She knew what he wanted to say.

– I'll bet you can see Boston from here, she said knowingly.

He laughed.

– You took your time on your way here, he said.

– I was busy.

– With more important stuff. He nodded. – I can certainly understand that. Perhaps you don't really care about the rats in the basement, after all.

She felt the first pang of headache then.

– Actually, they, the *humans* in the basement are the reason I came to see you, she said, as if she told him a great secret. – They're living under horrible conditions and the house belongs to you.

– I've offered them aid. A shrug. – They've rejected it.

– It doesn't really surprise me, Jill said dryly. – If the offer is anything remotely similar to the one you gave Gus Walters. I guess it must have been slightly worse, though. For Luke to have remained in such a place with wife and children, I can hardly imagine the alternative. It must have been about far more than wounded pride, don't you think?

– Why don't they leave town, they and others, if I'm treating them that badly? He said teasingly.

– You've shown great skill, she praised him. – You've taken a succession of drastic measures to entrap them in your web. Perhaps they did once, but they no longer have enough money to leave town, and if they don't travel *far* away from your sphere of influence, they have no opportunity to get money. The few coins they manage to get hold of goes to pay the rent for their top dollar apartments... The work of a genius, I'd say. My compliments.

– I knew you were a smart girl, he said, he praised her.

– Why are you doing it? She asked impulsively, breaking out of the role-playing for a moment. – It, and everything else you're responsible for?

– This city is mine, he told her straight out. – I'm telling you this because I want you to learn something. The city is mine. Everything and everyone in it belong to me.

Fear burned through her, as she massaged her temples with numb fingers. She was convinced now about what had only been a notion, a suspicion. Someone, somewhere was doing something to her. Whatever it was, it didn't come from Thompson, at least not in a way she could determine.

There was pain, but also a growing sense of detachment, a need to close her eyes, to fall asleep.

– What about us? She asked him furiously, masking her sudden fear. – You don't actually believe you own us?

– You fit perfectly into the profile I want the city to have. An excellent «opposition». Most people don't take you seriously. And hear this... People who want there to be one... see you as a true opposition. Hilariously perfect, isn't it? And that the priest is thundering against you in his pulpit every Sunday is also just following the program, don't you agree?

Something there, something in his speech made her... made her wonder. And then, just like that, she had it, had it in her palm.

– Consideration, she said very loud.

– What...

– There are considerations, aren't there? She smiled broadly. – There are certain rules of conduct you must follow. There are certain things you can't do, including limits you've set for yourself for tactical reasons. You tyrants are as much a victim of the illusion of the system as the rest of us, aren't you? For the system to work, for you to keep your position, you also find it difficult to truly rock the boat. And then there are the other filthy rich, here, elsewhere. Publicity is important. Bad press gives you all trouble. You own the press and public opinion, of course, but you don't have complete control of it.

She jumped up and down, triumphantly, one single time, theatrically.

– Catch 22...

Now it was his turn to break the role-playing.

– Do you really have such a good reason to be sure of yourself? His eyes narrowing like slits.

– Do you? She countered. – So far you and your likeminded have decided the rules of the game, but they are about to be changed.

– So, you're being insolent, rebellious, he said, – Pity.

She couldn't truly penetrate his mind, but what she generally read from the surface, made her want to shudder.

– We, she corrected. – We will fight you, alone, if so be it. As I suspect you already know, our might is considerable. And we will get support. Not even your kingdom is free of worms. We will meet you with confrontation, if you so choose, but with an open hand, too.

– I can be so kind, so generous...

– A generous Master. She nodded. – I do not doubt it.

And she showed him a closed fist, how she dealt with pain. By introducing more pain. He saw how blood seemed to flow freely from the wounds she had inflicted on her own palm.

– And whatever someone is doing, it should stop now.

There was a loud crack, as if something shook the very walls of the building.

She felt the pressure ease up. He pressed a button under the desk. The audience had ended.

– You're an impressive morsel, he warned her, – but you can never be more than an itch in my side.

Just before entering the elevator, she turned for a moment.

– The branch you sit on is pretty thick, but that doesn't mean it can't be sawed off.

With an eloquent swing of her cloak, she stepped into the elevator, temporarily disappearing from his countenance.

He was making fists long afterwards. She could see him, and laughed out aloud and throatily all the way on her way out of the Pyramid and didn't care if he heard it. Everybody heard it, also his subjects and puppets. She hid small tears at the edge of her vision, still feeling the need to yawn, knowing that she had almost fallen involuntarily asleep, knowing fully well that would have left her at his tender mercies, under his spell. His or whoever was behind the attack. Because it had been an attack. It didn't have to be him. When she threatened him, he could have misinterpreted it for a general threat, and just been dismissing her in his usual fashion. It could have been Laurie, it could have been anyone, she couldn't tell. Someone had chosen a moment where she was occupied, vulnerable. She didn't doubt it was someone powerful.

But it didn't matter, did it? It didn't change anything. It was just one more factor, one more complication, in the new life she had chosen, she was fashioning for herself.

She held up her palm, looking at it as the skin healed in a matter of seconds, as she walked away from the building, but not from whatever she had encountered inside.

Rage shook through her… through the laughter, the fear, the elation. There was video surveillance here, but she didn't care. The wind was always blowing here anyway, blowing violently around the structure of the Pyramid. Garbage cans shook, paper floated in the air, windows vibrated. She let go of Control and enjoyed it thoroughly.

She had done what she set out to do. Met the king of the hill, getting to know him, and given him only shreds of knowledge in return. Everybody knew, now, that she had knocked her horns against the ax, and survived. They were equals now. And she had given him his chance. Beyond that she had nothing to say to him.

9

Everett thought it seemed strange walking around in the black robe. Even if he got kind of used to it after a while, it still seemed weird. Full of curiosity he started pondering both his own and others' reaction to what he was going through. People recognized him and stared. It was one thing dating a witch. It was another being one, or claiming to be one. He studied eagerly the faces of his acquaintances. His long-time suspicion was easily confirmed: He didn't have many friends.

Hot, so hot. Everywhere. And the temperature kept rising. People didn't have time to get used to one level of heat, before it spiked even further.

It was Saturday, the traditional market day in Main Street. The entire broad and long street was filled with goods, tables and tents. Shops moved out in the sun, from Main Street itself, and coming from within and outside the county, to buy, sell and exchange whatever was on the agenda, everything seemingly unaffected by the deadly weather. This was one of the few makings and dealings in and around Northfield Scott Thompson didn't have direct or indirect hands in. Like most influential persons he had left Oldtown several years ago, left what everybody had counted on was on its way to becoming ruins, of its own volition. It had been a mistake. He had, like others of the rich elite put his efforts into the Pyramid and other malls. Ten years back it might have been a good tactic, but not anymore. People (at least some of the traditional consumers) had started to open their eyes to alternatives, other «values» than efficiency and profit, and one of the results was a lesser migration to gigantic, cold metal buildings and for the assembly line products found there. Even the air condition in the shopping centers didn't seem to have that much impact on the choice of vendor spot. Oldtown had, during a limited time frame, turned from prospective ruins into a flourishing part of the city.

Enjoying ourselves, are we? He heard Jill through his inner ear, not the inside of the ear, saw her before his inner eye.

Indubitably, to quote Henry McCoy... He turned around and there she was.

He was still amazed by what had been dormant inside him for so long, that it was dormant no longer. So far, he had almost exclusively used his ability with Jill and only sparingly to interpret other thought patterns. He couldn't suppress the little sting of worry. The roar of Power was faint, but clearly present. He expected it to be inevitable. After all, every single human being was will to power, to grow beyond confines. The danger was to interpret that, as many did, in a too narrow a sense.

He realized now, why he had always been such an excellent Poker-player.

And now, he was even better.

– You must practice, Jill spoke softly. – How is the headache?

– Passable, he said truthfully. – It doesn't really bother me, except when we've kept it going too long and too often.

– Everything can be misused, Ev, she said, seeing straight through him, as usual. – The decisions we must take aren't really any different from those ordinary people must take every day and night.

– You're correct, of course. He nodded.

– Ok - ay, let's see... Her stone-gray eyes, so full of color, surveyed the crowd, enticing his to follow in her tracks. – There, do you see them, the three girls walking side by side, leaving School Avenue?

– Yes. His voice was hoarse.

– Now, what about the bombshell on the right? What is her strongest emotion for the moment?

He watched the girl among humans and heads. Watching, seeking beyond the well-done hair and the correct school-uniform, an intrusion, in spite of his clumsiness, she had little or no change of discovering.

– She harbors jealousy towards the other two, he whispered unnecessarily. – Because of their friendship, the unity they share.

– She still doesn't realize that any person needs to develop strength independently of others, Jill said, kind of pointedly. – She will learn. She's a little tough one. Let us do something even simpler. Make her scratch her ear.

That was simple. He just imagined himself to be her, scratching his ear. She lifted her hand to the ear and scratched away.

– Good boy. Jill kissed him on the «same» ear. He saw the girl's eyes widening right across the street. – We'll make a decent sorcerer of you yet.

– What did Udo want? He hawked.

– It was a message from Laurie, we're about to run out of stuff to sell and need new supplies, pronto, the girl said, with laughter in her eyes. – Can you believe it? The supplies used to be stored in Square, but because of low sales, they started to carry it out to the farm, and let people buy it from there. Well, anyway, we have been given the honorable mission of bringing more water to the desert...

– I guess the fact that we do need supplies is good news... But do we have enough? I didn't think Laurie had enough people for a normal production, far from an extended one.

– There are no problems, only solutions. The big girl dragged him off.

They took one of three wagons and put a horse in front of it. The two others had already driven off. Everett had absolutely not learned either to treat a horse or to drive the shit of a wagon. Jill had, to the extent that they managed to get moving.

It was a funny feeling sitting in the front of the wagon, in the small (tiny) seat, and look at streets and houses move slowly by. Pleasant enough, though, seeing the world move in slow motion. And it was a funny feeling listening to the horse, not just to its breathing, but also to its rhythm, its heartbeat, its walk, its breathing, breathing, breathing...

He discovered that he was breathing rapidly, matching that of the horse.

– It's strange reading the thoughts of an animal, she said brightly. – You can get seriously distracted.

It was strange, sitting still while moving. Paradoxically the effect was more pronounced than with faster, more «effective» means of transportation.

– Ah, here we are, she said, as they rolled the last few stretches to the storage room on the farm, – even in one piece.

She pulled a bit hard in the harness and they stopped quite abruptly.

– Instead of in pieces, he added innocently.

She gave him one of her best smiles.

The heat was there, all the time, no matter where they moved. Now, while carrying even the smallest of crates, they started sweating substantially more. They had to drink constantly to keep themselves from stopping the necessary sweating. It was so bad these days that they were carrying a bottle of fluid with them the entire day. Even at night they had to drink a lot not to dehydrate.

It turned out that Everett had been right. There wasn't enough of what they needed on the farm. They would have to get it from a wholesaler in town. That meant going to Newtown.

– This is embarrassing. Andrea expressed herself aloud and quite graphically.

– Only if we let it, Jill said with a voice as sharp as a wasp's sting.

– The farm is constantly losing money, Tamara complained. – It's a good thing that Laurie has a lot of it.

– She's providing for us, Andrea said, – seeing to our needs.

– Money is such a good thing, Jill said. – You gain power with it, and with power, you may grab even more money.

The dust and shit and waste of the city were blowing, surrounding them. But the wind was far from strong enough here, among the tall buildings, to give any illusion of fresh air. It was Rush Hour. People rushed from place to place, with cars, on their feet, rushing home. A short trip inside the most convenient mall or supermarket, then it was home to sleep. Tired, exhausted every day, every week.

- Wage slaves, Jill snarled. – Slaves.

The small group of witches had made a minor detour on Big Road, but after breathing exhaust and coughing constantly they reneged, and took a major detour.

Even here, away from the worst traffic, Jill had to dry running eyes. Laurie didn't go far enough in her criticism of the wrongdoings of the world. Besides quite blatant before their very eyes, the obvious, Jill sensed the fundamental *imbalance* all over the place. Here and in every other city, she thought. Not so much the merely physical poison, as the spiritual. The knowledge, the certainty that present day human life, was totally opposed to an environment where it was possible to thrive. As it was now, the human species could indeed be compared to the weed by the roadside. For a short while it may have felt like Lord of the world. But heaps of shit and poison had created a wasteland. The air was corrupt and acid rain was its milk, not fresh air. Humans stumbled through this landscape, a pale, broken figure, into the cold twilight's embrace.

Jill had walked here before. An ordinary street. Ordinary people with bowed heads.

But today… Today there was something… standing out, not really strange, but… brittle, a broken record not heard. Most broken records were heard.

She giggled, and the giggle had a touch of… of hysteria? Something was wrong. Suddenly she sensed an overwhelming wave of… of despair.

Everett stopped her with a rough touch on her shoulder. She saw the pained expression in his face and realized with a start that he sensed it, too. But none of the others did.

A man walked towards them, or walked the opposite way from their point of view. And she gratefully confirmed that it wasn't an attack, but her sensitivity, her and Everett's, acting out in close proximity to… to a worn-out human being.

The man was dressed in rags and mumbled over and over again:

– I'm okay. I'm okay.

And occasionally:

– I was okay, I was okay.

She couldn't «read» him, not deeply; she didn't even dare touch his thoughts with her own. His thoughts were like a bottomless well of hopelessness, of chaos and nothingness. He radiated it to such a degree that his aura was a sore, blackened puss of a wound. She thought she might have fainted for just a moment, as she leaned towards Everett to keep her balance.

– His name is Ralph, Everett said in a low voice. – He was recently released from… from the hospital.

– From *the* Hospital? Andrea paled.

– From the House on the Hill, Everett confirmed. – He was okay, more than okay, pretty cool in fact, before they came and took him away. Now he's just a shade of his former self.

Jill couldn't stand being close to him, she just couldn't, and they all hurried off, attempting to put as much distance between themselves and the man stumbling through the dust and the ash as possible. The shame and anger and self-recrimination raged through her. She couldn't control it, control herself, and her still nebulous abilities, and they all felt what she felt. She pictured tears running down her cheeks, but no tears came.

– I… She rolled her hands into fists, and it hurt as the nails dug into her palm…– feel so small. The hands were closed so tight that she hurt all over, as she leaned towards a wall, as she hit the brick wall with her naked fists, as she hit it with her knuckles and blood flowed from broken skin.

Completely exhausted she sat down, straight on the spot, on the dust-filled sidewalk.

Everett walked in circles, pressing a fist to his forehead.

The others couldn't stay still, so they kept pacing back and forth. Slowly, just slowly, slowing down.

Vulnerable, Jill thought. So fucking vulnerable.

She forced herself back on her feet, dragging herself up along the wall. Teeth-gritting dealing with the vengeance of a headache, looking at all her companions, with renewed fire in her eyes. She walked on and they followed.

Their Journey brought them into a narrow road, not really a street, but just a short dustbin of a path.

A beggar sat on his spot by the road. He didn't rise when they walked by, showed no aggressiveness, hardly moved at all. He lifted a shaky hand, not very far.

– Brothers, sisters, he whispered, – can you spare some food, yield me a cup of wine?

They all had met beggars once in a while. Jill had met many. It always made her both furious and made her feel powerless.

They had walked ten steps past him when she stopped, closed one fist again and turned back.

She knelt down at his side, pressing a ten-dollar bill into the dirty hand and looked deliberately into his eyes. A poet in rags. She was unable to do anything else than close her mind to the impressions emanating from him. It wasn't the same, wasn't as horrible as the complete and utter annihilation that had assaulted her in the meeting with Ralph. Here was merely sadness, resignation, a milder form of despair. It was enough. The impressions haunted her, she couldn't stand them. She had more money in her hands now than before, more instant security, but it was no use. What she gave him would always be too much or too little.

– If you don't mind having a fixed address for a longer or shorter while, come to us.

She released him, without really knowing if she had reached him, whether or not he had heard her words. She hoped he had sensed the warmth she had attempted to give.

After yet a distance covered, she mumbled:

– So much misery.

The others mumbled and nodded in solemn agreement.

– Why must everything be so *hard?* Her voice cracked. – I mean, it will always be hard to some degree, but why exaggerate it to this fucked up extent? Is it written somewhere? Who has written it?

They speeded up subconsciously, silently, coughing and suffering as they walked, walked away, reaching the storage facilities a few minutes ahead of schedule. Zachary, the owner, met them in the backyard, by the big door, where trucks left and arrived fast and efficient. The best that could be said about Zachary was that he sold to everybody capable of paying cash. Sometimes he added to the prices, depending on his mood. He was like Thompson, satisfied with their presence in town, as long as they were kept on a tight leash.

No aid was offered them. They had to carry everything out themselves. Quite a few of Zachary's employees were available, but they just stood there, snickering. The youths didn't mind just then. On the contrary, they welcomed the hardship. It distracted them from the painful thoughts hiding just below the surface.

In fact, they were so distracted that they hardly noticed when good ol' Zachy started behaving like a human being… being nice to them. He even lent them a platform truck, one without horsepower, one they would have to drag all the way back, but still… This definitely warranted a high level of suspicion.

Sweaty hands fought to keep the grip around smooth handles. Just to turn the vehicle around demanded major exhaustion of strength. But they persevered, gritting their teeth. And the good mood returned then, on a ride of pure stubbornness. They were great together, great while *doing* together.

When Udo stumbled and was about to lose a 50 kilos sack of flour and Tamara caught it and threw it over her shoulder as if it was full of feathers or something, they laughed. Not merely because it made them feel good, but because it felt good to Live.

Tamara placed the sack on the platform without exerting herself visibly. She got stronger. Something that wasn't hard to notice. She kept her undeniable female shape, but the strength in her limbs and muscles grew to an uncanny degree. And she was taller… wasn't she… The others had realized some time ago that the development, realization of her Power had to do with her physique. They were uncertain whether or not she had realized this herself - and if not - if they should tell her. The Change happened gradually and even if it was undeniable, perhaps she didn't see it or wanted to see it.

Zachary saw them off, even without demanding extra charge for the borrowing of the platform truck. They started on the strenuous trip back to Square. Everybody took turns. Still, they needed to have frequent breaks. Tamara did, too, even if she almost joyfully took longer and harder turns than the others. She obviously excelled in her strength.

When they arrived back at the place where they had encountered the beggar, he had vanished.

He probably ran directly to a bar, Jill thought, more than a bit down.

And why not? Didn't he, too, have a claim to some, occasional happiness.

Except it wasn't. She had sensed the moods of some drunks, Gus Walters for one, people who drank to forget rather than to remember. There was a tailspin of despair that made her more than uneasy. It provoked something in her that made her shudder. Alcohol could be a fine thing, but usually it served as just another way to control people.

She was the first noticing the other group about to meet them, meet them on a collision course. A much larger group to be sure. The front man, Tim Drake wasn't hard to pick. His walk, his entire demeanor came off as quite determined. The sleazy look was in place. Neither Jill nor her traveling buddies needed to draw a picture, to understand what was commencing.

Jill Stafford sensed something then, a rush, a heating of the veins.

– Leave everything to me, she said to her companions.

Drake had picked this place with care. Or so he thought, anyway. There weren't many people. He saw this as an advantage, on this occasion, since he and his group intended to do a bit more than pure harassment this time. Jill did, too, even if she wouldn't have cared if they stood at the center of Northfield Dome, with the entire town on the stands.

Drake walked in front of his usual little group. Jill easily noticed deviations from the norm, though. For one, Henry Gyrich wasn't present. That in itself would've given cause for alarm. *In others, not in me.* Jill could sense the fingertips burn with invisible fire. Suddenly she wasn't worried at all. Not even by the presence of other, total strangers in the pack, the pack of two-legged wolves.

The entire pack stopped a few steps before their leader. He walked the last few steps forward, before he, too stopped, towering over Jill.

– The goods you're carrying, they're ours, he said briskly.

– That must be a mistake, Jill said and played to perfection her part in the masquerade. – We've just picked them up and paid for them. We made the payment in cash to Mr. Zachary personally.

– They belong to us, Drake said sweetly. – Zachy should have put them aside for us, as we agreed to, days ago.

– I'm afraid this is something you must speak to Mr. Zachary about. A clear and present hardness had emerged in the girl's innocent voice.

– You should take great care not to be too difficult, sweetie, Drake's voice changed, turned coarse and unpleasant. – I'm a reasonable man, you know, and since I'm such a reasonable man, I'll suggest a compromise right away: Why don't we continue our discussion in more intimate surroundings? You're so eager to talk about naturals, and I must say I find that absolutely satisfactory…

He grabbed her jaw with a huge hand. *No, Tam, I'll take care of this MYSELF.* The big girl had been about to charge forward and attack the big man.

– You're such a nice and persuasive man, sir, the Witch told him with moist eyes, dark shadows in her face.

You're weak, she thought, while focusing completely on Tim Drake. You're unable to stand on your feet. You're stumbling. You're falling.

– Down on your KNEES, she suddenly snarled. – Crawl on your belly, like the *lizard* you are.
He was almost swooning on the spot, from one second to the other, too dizzy to stand. He fell on his knees in front of the Face of Wrath above, so far, far above, filling his vision, dominating the sky. Arms were like lead. He could just about keep himself from collapsing completely and really crawling in the dust. His eyes widened while he saw her stretch her claw-like fingers down towards him. She grabbed his hair and pulled up the head. Her face seemingly completely normal, but he knew better than that. By God, he knew better.
– You have hard tried my already hard tried patience concerning you, the fury said icily. – This is my final warning. I won't tolerate anything else from you from this point on. Get it? I hope you do, for your sake, or you'll *regret* it every single second for *the rest* of your life.
He nodded, and kept nodding. Tears flowed down his cheeks. He couldn't breathe. Far above the sun was shining, but the light didn't reach him, in the deeeep, black hole he sank into.
– You're afraid of the dark, aren't you, little Timmy?
He nodded and kept nodding, while desperately attempting to articulate himself.
– You shouldn't be afraid of the dark, my sweet boy. She made soft, comforting strokes on his head. He sniffed and for a moment he lifted his head and looked up with hope in his eyes… until she crushed it. – *You should be terrified of it.*
He cried out in despair, a despair so utterly Complete that there seemed to be nothing more.
Lift him, Jill sent to Tamara. Shake him.
– But I can't…
Tamara wanted to, eager like a dog in the leash, in the anger and fear she felt simultaneously, but didn't know if she could.
Do you DARE disobey me?
She charged forward, grabbing Drake's clothes and lifted him high above her head. Her hands whitened around the clothing as she shook him. She was directing all her anger towards him, to hide her fear of The Fury by her side.
– You make me sick, she raged. – I don't want to see your ugly mug anywhere close to me from now on.
– Drop him, Jill commanded indifferently.
Dust whirled as the big, hunky body hit the ground.
Those who had arrived here with him, stood frozen on their spot, pale and silent. They couldn't help but focus on the shaking heap on the ground. Some laughed, but there was no chance of mistaking the chill in the laughter.
– What Tamara so adequately expressed concerns you all, Jill spat at them. – Get moving, *get lost!*
The toughest among them, what was obviously hired help, hesitated a bit, but they faced the danger of being quite alone in their venture and after that moment of hesitation, they hurried after the others.
Tim wanted to join them when Jill snarled:
– Down, boy.
He once more turned into a husk, a crushed heap on the ground, wailing like a ghost.
She walked away, waved to the others to join her, ignoring him completely. In a joyful attack of seemingly arrogance Tamara started to pull the platform all by herself. And… She did it. Jill rewarded her with a smile, with a gracious nod. Tim Drake remained on his knees, alone in the dust, bundled and with sagging shoulders. Nobody cared to look back at him.
The group had wandered for a while in silence, when Everett decided to join Jill in her front walk.
– You can be unscrupulous, he said carefully.
– Yes, isn't it great, she laughed, and the laughter and the joking had a hard edge. – Blame yourself. The woman is more confident than the maiden.
Everybody laughed heartedly, of and with him, though with a slant of insecurity and fear.
– Tim has asked for it for a long time, Andrea said with obvious admiration. – It's just that nobody has given it to him before.
Shocked? Jill and Everett conversed on their private, intimate «mode». *Or are you like Andrea, shaking your tail for the strongest?*
I'm positive that you know quite well what I feel. What you did was… impressive. Drake deserved it unconditionally,

but I can't deny that what you did made me worried.

Each person is potentially many, she told him. *Usually there's no distinct division between them. The trick is to make sure one is the dominating one. Understand?*

He did.

Suddenly Tamara cried out, shouted in distress, in pain. She had to support herself on the rolling platform not to fall. They ran to her side. They did nothing but touch her, but still their touch hurt the distressed girl. She struggled involuntarily in their grip, and it made it quite difficult to hold on to the big body, but they managed to put her down on the platform.

– Pain… all over the body, she gasped. – EARS, oh…

They really couldn't make sense of the last word, but they did see that also her new garb was tight now. Jill attempted to lessen the pain by using her healing abilities.

– DON'T… It just makes it worse.

– Take deep breaths. Jill hesitated, stumbling in a minefield. – Breathe deeply. In and out, in and out.

Slowly, very slowly, the pain lessened.

– It's better now. Tamara put a hand to her head. – But it feels completely weird, as if I'm slowly burning or something.

– Just sit tight, Jill ordered her. The suspicion was more than a notion now, and she didn't want it confirmed in public. – We'll do the rest of the tour.

– Drag both you and the cargo, Everett completed.

– Sure, why not? Andrea ventured.

The sun was frying them, devouring their juice until they were no longer sweating. The muscles hurt. Andrea looked pissed. Jill managed a smile. Tamara wanted to get off and help, but they showed her back. They kept going. Tamara had to walk by herself. They still had to strain just to keep the wheels moving. Jill attempted to use her power to move the truck, to ease their burden. It worked for a while, but she quickly grew tired, and it was back to using muscles. She feared the sun would explode in her head. Children and also adults threw snide comments at them from the side. There was no mercy, no understanding, beyond the rudimentary, how to better hurt a fellow human being. Jill saw, in a mist of sweat (there was no sweat) how Tamara stumbled and fell. They put her back on the platform, and kept going. Going slightly upwards, towards Oldtown. And they didn't want to think about how far they had come, because then they would have to think about how far they had left to go. And they wondered if it was ever going to end.

They got help a few steps before reaching Main Street. The word had wandered, both in terms of good and bad. Kieron and Jason took over, finally. They didn't see them as more than two shadows, until they were less than a step away. Jill and the others stretched and whimpered. The relief was as welcome as rain.

– Free ride? Jason joked at Tamara's expense.

It was amazing. Jill realized it immediately. A moment's rage and she felt renewed, fresh once more. She almost felt gratitude towards Jason. Almost.

– She dragged everything alone a major chunk of the way, Jill spat poison. – She's tired. There isn't a law against that, is it?

– There is. Jason confirmed with a glee. – Everything not expressively allowed is forbidden, everybody knows that…

She's in the last stage of the Change, she sent forcefully to him. *She needs our support, not more chiding and scorn. Do you hear me, you fucker?*

Change to what? He seemed utterly unfazed. *She Hulk?*

– I'm not tired, Tamara insisted. – I don't need any help.

– You're lying. Stacy strolled to her from a table. – You're wrong. Now. Soon, very soon, you won't need any help from anybody.

– We wanted to drag the platform to square and put her to bed, Andrea ventured.

– An excellent suggestion, Stacy nodded.

People continued to stare, but they weren't openly hostile anymore, as the extended group of witches made it the remaining distance to their destination.

There was an eerie silence inside Square, compared to the street outside. The buzz, the noise, was muted, as if everything was further away than it seemed. Tamara fought her way up on her feet. Stacy took one of her hands, Jill the other, and they led her inside the house.

– You run along, Stacy told the others. – We'll take care of this.

– We'll join you shortly, Jill added.

– «Behold the Siamese twins», Jason recited in a false tune.

The house was as usual, cool and dark. The two led Tamara to the attic. She was sweating and staring painfully ahead.

– Hurts... she mumbled.

The bedroom was bright, too bright. Jill pulled the curtains tight. And the sharp light turned into a pleasant shadow.

– I don't need to be put to bed. Tamara shouted, turning 180 degrees both physically and mentally. Her eyes betraying her gathering confusion and irrationality. – I'm not a child.

– Look at me, Jill commanded.

In her voice, something in her voice. Tamara froze and looked at her.

– Look at us, Stacy said, in a dark, raspy voice.

That confused her. They had placed themselves on each of her sides. How could she look at both of them?

– *Look at us,* they told her simultaneously, in dreaming, haunting voices.

She wanted to shake her head, but muscles didn't obey her, eyes stared blindly at a fixed point somewhere on the wall.

– You will sleep, Stacy told her. – You will relax, you will sleep, and when you wake op, rested and calm, everything will have changed.

– *You will sleep, now,* Jill whispered, a whisper penetrating her entire being. – *Sleep.*

Eyes blinked. The big girl yawned.

– No, she whimpered. – No.

She didn't want to, but didn't have a choice. They started undressing her, treating her like a baby. And she was, in their hands. Eyes closed. She was already halfway into sleep as they lowered her body unto the bed. Still, she moaned and moved restlessly the last few seconds into sleep.

Sleep, Jill and Stacy sent to her. *Dream sweet dreams.*

Finally, she was still, breathing quietly through her nostrils. Stacy put a blanket over the large body. It didn't cover her feet properly and didn't quite reach the shoulders.

Jill turned abruptly, walking the few steps to the window.

– In a hundred years or so, they might know how to do this, she said irritated.

– As they did long ago, Stacy corrected her slightly, her irritation growing.

– She won't be better off when she wakes up.

– Yes, she will, Stacy insisted. – When that happens, the Change will start in earnest.

They both fell silent a bit, observing the sleeping beauty on the bed. Pity the sucker of a suitor who was unfortunate enough to awaken her...

Laughing a bit, ashamed, Jill looked out of the window, a bit distracted, at the market below. A fat, older crone smoking a huge, stinking cigar badmouthed Everett quite mercilessly. He, typically and stupidly enough, attempted to keep his polite, smiling demeanor. Still, he must have charmed her to death, because the old hag started «smiling», too (a startling caricature of a smile).

Jill attempted to penetrate the wall to the woman's mind. It was a hopeless task. There were too many people, too much disturbance for the girl's telepathic abilities to work properly. She truly felt like a girl then, so frustrated, so helpless.

She observed the fat crone fight her way to a bench, wheezing and blowing steam. Initially she had some company on the bench, but the others left one by one. After a while, after her having the bench to herself, a black man sat down by her side. The hag blew her nose again and moved a seat away.

Jill had seen enough. Anger flared inside and in a single burst of energy she pushed the disgusting lady off the bench. The blown, red face was a study in perplexity and everything about it seemed beautifully ridiculous.

But Jill didn't laugh. She grabbed her head with both hands, not because it hurt, but in astonishment, digging fingers and nails into her hair, wondering in a distant manner if she would notice if she pulled out any hair. Unholy shit, she had done what she had done so easily, so effortlessly, so naturally that it seemed like pure instinct. It wasn't as if the «lady» didn't deserve it, but… Jill was shocked, over her own conduct, over what she could do. It was the way she had done it, so self-serving and relentless. Was this how she was, that she would throw away all other considerations but her own?

The hand touching her shoulder startled her.

– She offended you. Stacy's sweet voice and words entered her ear like light oil. – She deserved much worse, didn't she? That she didn't realize her offense doesn't matter… does it?

– What are you saying? Jill asked, pulling back as she turned towards the other girl.

– Oh, stop playing the innocent offended one, dear. I'm fully aware of how you handled Drake. You have no secrets from me…

– That was just as easy, Jill exclaimed. – I made him fall by influencing his inner ear… as *you* did with Tamara the day at school. It made him fearful and susceptible about what was to follow.

Stacy allowed a flashing smile to take the sting off the other girl's poisonous outburst.

– And I understand you even better than that, better than you know. Green eyes met gray. – I didn't realize at first either, how right my treatment of lesser beings was.

Lesser beings…? Jill wanted to say something, something fierce and angry.

– You knew you were a witch before you came here, before you met Laurie. Jill could muster neither anger nor surprise.

– Long before. I've prepared myself, thought things through.

Jill wanted to say something spiritual and funny, but the voice failed her. Even thoughts failed. Numb, she felt numb. She «prayed» she would never become comfortably numb.

– Throughout history the powerful have reigned, Stacy pressed on, pressed hard. – Always taken whatever they've desired. In ancient times we made an indelible impression on what was then our present… and what was to come. We were gods then.

It was as if a giant veil lifted from Jill's eyes. Stacy took one step forward and grabbed her arms hard.

– YES! Stacy shouted excited. – *You understand.*

Jill couldn't think, didn't think at all, until she found herself completely elsewhere. The bedroom, with its charged atmosphere gave way to busy marketplace. Jill couldn't say how she had gotten there, but noticed that she was following in Stacy's tracks. She stopped. Stacy walked on.

Her right hand closed into a fist. She raised it to her face, looking at it for an instant before letting it fall.

Isn't this a wonderful place? She mentally cast her arms to the side. *All the people, the storming passions?*

She felt a strong urge to express her emotions.

It has its uses, Stacy commented «dryly».

She stopped, raising her arms above the head, and clapped the hands.

– Okay, she cried out. – Let's have a show…

She offered Jason her hand and he took it. Jill could see their auras spark and that the auras of the people close by were diminished. Stacy sent silent and invisible signals and the music started.

– *Bokor,* Loeh said by Jill's ear.

– Bokor? Jill said uncertain. – That's a word from Haiti, isn't it, representing the practitioners of black magic?

Loeh didn't say more, but followed Stacy around with her eyes.

As did Jill, with a dog eyed, frightened look transcending that expressed by Loeh.

Stacy was waving her hands, projecting her thoughts, daring her to take the challenge, the challenge not to accept the trinkets dangled in front of her.

The dance seemed to go on for hours. Jill stood still and had once more fallen into deep thoughts when someone grabbed her shoulder and shook her lightly. She turned fast as lightning, with all her spikes raised. There were sparks and there was boundless anger. She realized it was Everett and relaxed, smiling sheepishly. Feeling powerful, feeling ashamed.

– Jill, he said. Just that, nothing more.

She followed him the short walk back to Square. They both stopped before a smaller group of people.

A smile twitched in the corner of her mouth. Luke stood there, with his family and other tenants living in Scott Thompson's luxury buildings. The beggar was there, too.

The homeless man, she corrected herself. For all she knew he had chosen to live outdoors.

– A bird sang in our ears, that you guys needed some help, Luke said lightly. He seemed more devil may care now, far more so, than the last time she had encountered him, as she assumed he had been ten, perhaps only five years ago.

– Here and everywhere else, she said lightly. – Let it be known that you're all welcome.

– You should all join us at dinner, Everett said. – Afterwards there will be loads and loads of work for us all.

The sun descended behind Frazer Hill. The enormous shadow fell over Northfield. The day grew short, but the night was yet young. The marketplace continued to swarm with life. Jill felt the energy expand inside, inevitable, without any conscious decision on her part. She was like a sponge, sucking it all up, couldn't help it and it made her giddy, drowsy, happy, worried.

Around her there was gluttony of eating and drinking going on, especially among those not having properly done so for some time. She wanted to call their attention to it, to the dangers, but she couldn't find the energy… She laughed, an abrupt, shrilled laughter.

It didn't turn out to be a problem, but she knew it could have. Driven, impatient, moody she sought out the little girl, Luke's daughter. The girl was skinny and pale, but there was no trace of the disease remaining in the malnutrition-ridden body.

I've done some good.

She looked unseen at the vagrant (another word, negatively charged by society), half curious. He had long, black hair and beard with gray lines. But the eyes were clear, now, when he hadn't been drinking. He had refused anything containing alcohol.

Laurie was there, too, even if she wasn't seen. Jill felt her eyes, her mind, as the new recruits were taught the basics of market selling-techniques, her disapproval and anger.

But everybody in the street was having fun and Jill couldn't help but taking part in it. As the night descended, she felt better than she ever had done during the day.

Eventually there were only natural lights to be seen in the entire street. And all the torches had almost burned out.

– I'm thanking higher and lower powers that it isn't a school day tomorrow, Everett grunted. He was really tired.

And that convinced Jill about something: Even if they didn't take the school seriously, it demanded both their time and energy.

She herself wasn't tired. She felt refreshed. In fact, as she pondered the subject, she felt wide-awake.

While the torches were flickering in the wind and the last fires kept glowing in the night, she and Everett danced alone in the middle of the street. Alone together in the cold night. A night so hot that they had trouble breathing. They had put each other's arms on each other's shoulders, hands loosely closed behind the other's neck. She spoke to him, hot and excited.

Listen.

And he did.

Rae has fallen asleep with her Walkman on. Listen to the music through her ears. Then just listen… to everything. Listen to the Night. Look at it with the Night's eyes. It's Alive, isn't it?

He turned his head slightly, tilted it to the right. And the crescendo assaulted him from all sides. He stumbled. If she hadn't been there, supporting him, he might have fallen.

– I'm tired, he said frustrated. – Not just now, but all the time the last few days. I have slept, but it doesn't feel like I have.

– This is new to all of us, she said. – The excitement can probably be a bit too much for everyone.

– We should go to bed, he declared.

– The night is too exciting to sleep away, she suddenly burst out, irritated and impatiently. – I'm tired of sleeping.

He made an effort, opening his eyes once more, unable to hide a smile.

– Who said anything about sleeping?

Her eyes widened round and moist. Lips turned wet and the mouth opened in an expectant smile. She sensed her awakening Hunger, sensed it growing inside. Their dance turned wilder, but also more intimate, ever tighter.

– I'm sorry, he said, his face reddening a while later, in a room somewhere in Laurie's house in Square. He had her body close to his own and managed to feel nothing. – Seems like I'm really tired.

She had performed for him, used all her newfound sensuality, even used her hands and mouth in ever-greater skill, in vain. There was nothing there, no strength left.

– It seems like a lost cause, she admitted and startled he saw and sensed further determination in her, sensed and smelled her juices suddenly flowing. – To any ordinary girl it would probably be…

One of his newfound talents was the one of smell, one growing shockingly acute. Among all the shocking and wonderful things happening to him lately, that was almost one of the hardest to accept.

– Good thing you're not ordinary then, he managed to blurt.

– *Share my energy,* she whispered. – *Feel its strength. Share. Enjoy.*

She touched him once more, touched his not so sharp blade, his fucking useless cock. And he felt it, felt the energy, the strength and he cried out, in pain, in joy. Suddenly, seemingly from one moment to the next, he was big and hard, and he immediately pushed against her, and before he realized it he was pushing and pulling inside her. And the Power rose between them. She embraced him in a way he hardly could have imagined, far less believed possible. But it was true and he was swept away on a high tide, to the shore, where the soft sand waited.

The day after Luke and family, the homeless man and a considerable number of other malcontents were in place on the farm. More followed in the days and weeks to come. There was also a lot of talk in the city as a whole. A barrier had, if not been broken, weakened considerably. A dam was about to burst. A wall of fear, meticulously constructed through years and years. The eventual flood was inevitable.

Scott Thompson stood at the top of his domain, looking at it from above, as he often did. It was more of a stare, now, however, and it didn't give him the usual satisfaction. He could hear their whisper from down there. Some even dared to raise their voices. They had done so before, occasionally. In time the voices usually quieted on their own, without any effort on his part. He knew that this time they wouldn't. He would have to make them, personally. No disaster, really. His defenses could have a test run. The ants would be shown how their efforts were an exercise in futility, making them more pliable, more suggestible in the future. They would come even further under his foot and confirm for themselves that it was by far more pleasant under his foot than under his heel.

Paul Gyrich sat behind the desk in the library of his mansion. He didn't really enjoy it here. The reason for him being here, the reason for his discomfort, was that his private, special phone was here, and he had spoken a lot in the phone, that phone, lately. He didn't enjoy being contacted. He was the one usually doing the calling, when he wanted something done. Now it seemed that he was forced to, whether he liked it or not. There was unrest among the troops. As rumors would have it, the lemmings were on the move. Fools! They never thought beyond their wallet. As if a flock of lemmings on the move represented any true danger. If they had thought things through, they would have realized this. Wandering lemmings always, sooner or later, encountered a raging river. And they would continue forward, to their doom. Everybody using their minds knew what would happen to a flock of lemmings attempting to cross the raging river.

Laurie Isherwood stood on the porch of the main building on her farm, shuddering, as if a cold wind was blowing. She sensed the subtle changes in the air, in the mood of the city. The balance of power had shifted. Nothing would be the same.

Chapter Nine: STYX

A landscape like the moon, a beauty like raw, untamed Nature.

No, a landscape illuminated by the moon, the big, big moon above… more Shadow than the Night.

Jill awoke with a start in her bed in the boarding wing of the school. Before even opening her eyes properly she sat upright, wet and sweaty. Six o'clock in the morning and it was hot as the inside of an oven already. She was cold, someplace inside. By all false gods, as they all were, she desperately needed a shower. But they weren't allowed to shower anymore. Partial water rationing had been implemented three days ago by an eager, finally very eager city council.

In Fire Lake there was water. It was fresh and there was a lot of it. But no pipes went up there or to other reservoirs. No one had thought about the possibility that it someday might be needed. But what was really strange was that very few people went there, too. The witches did so every day. They encountered some other people, but not many.

Jill wanted a shower, but truth to tell she wasn't certain that she would have had one, even if she could. Not this morning. The sense of urgency, to the point of being overwhelming, made her forget all other considerations.

She dressed in a shorts and a blouse she didn't button, but tied loosely above the navel. Her feet she left bare. She walked more and more barefoot these days (and nights). The skin under her feet hardened to the point where there was hardly any discomfort anymore.

The door slid open, without her or anyone being close to touching it. She walked through and it slid close behind her. The key turned on the inside and she left it there in the hole. Nobody (but her, Laurie, Jason or Stacy) would be able to open it without kicking it in.

The hallway was a bit chilled, as it often was, (at least a bit less hot compared to everywhere else). There was a draft from the attic, as always, a strong draft, almost making it hard for her to keep her balance. She listened, with her ears, with her mind. With a few exceptions there was silence all over the campus. Most people were asleep. The cook and his crew had started the day. The principal, too. She was always early. And there were a few others. Jill checked on the witches. They were all in their bed, sleeping. Even Jason. He was the only one noticing her and he sent her an ironic response. But shouldn't Stacy be…

… she wasn't there. A split moment it had seemed like she was, but Jill didn't sense her in her bed, in her room or anywhere else. Jill speeded up her walk to the point of almost running. As she left the girls' dormitory, she could observe Jason coming from the boys' «quarters». The sun burned her face immediately. Without actually noticing it on a conscious level she started to fix her hair a bit, dragging her fingers through it, consciously straightening her body.

They reached the alley of trees simultaneously, meeting face to face.

– I got sick and tired of being stretched out on my back and sweating in the damn room, he said. – It's such a fine day. And it's got promise, too.

She felt the thrill of his words, her own unhinged expectations.

Little cute peeping she-devil, he acknowledged her. *I knew you had it in you. You just need to practice it a bit more.*

She didn't reply, saw no sensible purpose in denying the obvious. She had used her powers without any heed of others, of what they might think, what anyone might think.

– Don't look so glum, he laughed at her. – You look like you have been caught with your hand in the cookie jar.

– One who has the power has the right? She asked.

– That's common knowledge, the way the world works.

He gave her his arm eloquently. She pushed her own inside his and they continued on their way, their sense of urgency renewed.

They met a few people, people on their way to work. They met a few even more bowed, human-like creatures on their way from work.

– Poor creeps, he said, shaking his head.

They went straight for Square, not really expecting any problems or hurdles, but the moment they entered Main Street, from one moment to the next, a wall of dust rose before them, surrounding them. Jill didn't know what to do except holding her breath. The dust rose from between their feet, growing thick and deadly. Jason grabbed her hand. Contact was immediate. The Power burned between them, infinitely stronger than the sum of their parts. The dust blew away, burned, melted and fell harmless to the ground. The air cleared. Their eyes turned in a singular direction. Stacy sat on a branch in the closest tree. They hadn't noticed her.

– I thought I should wait here for you, she teased them, – so you shouldn't need to run in my tracks.

She jumped down, easily. The well-known flash in her eyes was in place. Jill knew it well. It was her own eyes every time she stared at herself in the mirror.

– We didn't discover you, Jason said dryly. – My salutations.

– Oh, I wouldn't make a fuss about it, Stacy snorted. – C'mon, let's proceed.

Laurie waited for them, at the top of the stairs.

– You're early, she told them evenly. They weren't quite certain what she actually meant by that, even if they had their suspicions.

Tamara had remained in the coma Stacy and Jill had placed her in the entire week, without the slightest move except for the regular breathing moving her chest. When the four of them entered the room, she was only in the early stages of awakening, but she was already twisting and turning violently on the bed. Andrea and Udo sat silent in chairs by the window. Laurie had ordered them not to interfere. Laurie had been just as unaffected, nondescript as she had seemed now when Stacy and Jill had told her what they had done. She had accepted it with a nod.

Tamara writhed, her body twisted in an impossible angle, awake and afraid. She looked at them with eyes clouded by pain. Nobody could stop it now. No matter what happened it had to complete its course.

– When will it… stop? Tamara gasped, heaving for breath.

– There's a way we might speed up the process, Jill said hesitantly, feeling as if she was moving through an exploding minefield. – The pain will be worse for a short while…

– Of course! Stacy exclaimed, – why didn't I realize it?

Jill had her own, cynical thoughts about that.

– … do it, Tamara whispered through pain and tears.

The two girls placed themselves once more on each side of the bed. Jill wondered frantically what could happen, if she should ask the others to hold on to Tamara's arms and legs. If the pain became completely unbearable the big girl could become violent and she was pretty strong already. Then it was too late, too late for regrets, too late for hesitations. Jill placed her hands on her. Stacy, too. It started. The rumble grew to a crescendo. Not through their ears, but through their other, more profound senses. For the time being, it was concentrated in Tamara's body, but also present in the house and the streets outside, all over the city. They used their healing power to speed up the body's natural processes. Reaction was immediate. Tamara cried out as she stretched her body. Or did the body in fact… stretch itself? Jill and Stacy could feel bones, muscles and skin move beneath their hands. It was creepy, though undeniably interesting.

Tamara gasped and continued to gasp in a seemingly endless time frame, pulling air into her lungs and kept gasping for more. Hands hit the ears quite a few times before resting there. Then she tore them away, as if she had burned herself. Stacy and Jill withdrew, no longer needed. The final stages of whatever would happen would be concluded swiftly now, without further aid.

Everybody could hear bones break and reset now. At least, that was how they imagined it, as her body, and perhaps also her entire being Changed.

It was accomplished. She lay still on her back, slowly spreading her arms, lifting them in the room with no sound. No problems… Nothing was… broken. She rose or rather jumped from the bed. Everything worked well, in fact so much better than before. With the single kick she had virtually thrown herself to the other, opposite wall. Perhaps instinctively, since that was where the mirror was.

After a while, she turned and looked, looked at them all. She hadn't really changed much. She had grown even taller, of course (of course), even more natural in her well-built body. Her inborn abilities had been actualized in the best possible way. She towered over all the boys now, but in a sitting position a given observer wouldn't notice any immediate change.

If not for her remarkable, pointed ears.
Everybody took the cautious approach while approaching her, even Stacy.
– Your hair is wet now. Andrea touched it carefully. – But it's usually so full and generous that it should be easy to hide…
– To not display, Stacy said. – If you don't want to.
– We should find some clothes for you, Laurie expressed critically. And thoughtful: – If we find anything useful.
– If we don't, we will sew her some, Stacy burst out, agitated, with obvious challenge in the voice. – That isn't any problem, is there? Almost all of us can sew or we can learn.
– No problem, Jason said lightly. And then even more cheerful to Tamara: – You may consider being a bit discreet. I don't think people are ready for giant elves… yet.
Yet.
Jill considered the further implications of Jason's words and the way he said them. She thought a lot. *We were gods then,* Stacy had said. *We can be so once again.*
The sun climbed from the fields in the east and sank behind The Hill. Day lasted twelve hours, though merely a blink in Eternity. In the wilderness behind the big mound, bathing in the rays of the dying sun, Tamara Farley stood in the center of the witches' circle. She, who had been less changed, had now walked further than any of them on the path they would all walk. It wasn't just the physical aspect of her Change they noticed, but also something in her eyes, behind, beyond the eyes. She was More than she had been.
– It *is* the mind as well. She frowned. – Something about how my brain works I can't quite grasp yet.
There was a Magickal creature standing there. The startling metamorphosis was far more than… than skin deep. What her brother and sister witches didn't see with their eyes confirmed that.
Helpful and eager hands adapted her new gown, cloak, hood and all, sewn in record time by her fellow witches in a cooperative effort. Everybody took turns. Most of them sincerely wanted to help. Most of them. Tamara herself, struck by the actual lightning, seemed to take it in stride. Seemed. Even for novice telepaths, even for non-telepaths, it was easy to see through her façade. Jill, among others, knew better. The Change had left her upset and vulnerable, as it had them all.
The support and warmth, given by the circle, could be overwhelming, but without it she would have been far more upset and vulnerable. She was the first among them with a physical characteristic marking her as *different.* Something she could never run away from, even if she wanted to.
She had *turned.* And they celebrated. The fire was lit. Yellow and red and dark flames stretched towards the sky, towards them. When they saw the fire, when they made their Circle around it, they were reminded of their dreams, The Other World, the world beyond, where it often took on another, more ominous meaning.
The entire Coven had gathered here tonight, not just the witches. It was the people brought in by Laurie, before the new arrivals, and the ones brought here by Jill and the others, the twins among them did attract more than a casual interest. Twins were, after all, quite a powerful symbol in magickal tradition.
– They're not really alike, are they? Jill shook her head. – Not in behavior.
– The Voodoun culture has always believed twins are the same person in two bodies, Loeh said, whispering once more in Jill's ear. – It stands to reason then, that they will exhibit different traits of the same personality.
Most of them took or were given a drug, something Jill suspected was LSD or related to it. She had taken it the first time when she was fifteen, while living among the sunworshippers. It had helped liberate her then, as it helped liberate her further now. But as she realized that Laurie had more or less planned this or was using the occasion, she decided to remain alert.
Drums. Somebody was beating a drum. Somewhere there was a drum beating. And by each hit or group of hits, the fire blossomed in the Night. The Shadows blossomed in the shadows.
– A man, a stranger visited us once, visited the Dance.
Loeh was rocking back and forth while reliving the memory.
Everybody listened intensely, to the Voodoun priestess, to their own inner being.
– His eyes were glowing fire and he grabbed us and took us with him to the raging river, the deep

waterfalls.

Jill could see it where she sat, not so far away. She was present, through Loeh, looking at, experiencing the Stranger. She lifted her hands. The flame of the fire grew, and the intense heat torched everybody. She laughed out loud. This was intense, this… She swayed back and forth, standing by the fire. And the fire swayed with her.

– Everything, she cried out. – I can see EVERYTHING.

And in that everything she saw a bird of fire, of shadow, saw it stretch its wings and rise from the smoldering ground.

Gabrielle said, surrounded by floating crystal balls, in a room without walls, without a ceiling, without a floor: He is rising, he is coming.

And then it started, the climax of the Journey: Time stretched out to Infinity. There was so much. You saw everything and you couldn't look away. This was the stage, Jill suspected, of an LSD-trip (if that was truly what it was) that some individuals couldn't take. Time stretched out Forever. You wondered if it was ever gonna end and it was fantastic, and you feared it would never end. It wasn't just like the entire Universe opened up to you, but an infinite number of universes, of realities and they were all equally real. A black hole opened up in front of you on your path, and it was just a tiny speck on a non-existing wall compared to the enormous universe behind. And that universe was absorbed into you and that universe was just a tiny speck of the boundless Entity, the God you had become.

This departed, departed completely from Jill's previous LSD «trips». Like a sea compared to a raindrop. Every gate on every Crossroads of existence seemed to be wide open and still there was more. Suns rose and fell. Fires burned down and burned again. The Shadow was a circle creeping on the ground, as the lights came from everywhere, there was no set direction, no fixed point. She had become every possible point in the air, in the ground, and she could see, hear, sense from all of those points simultaneously.

– I am everything, I AM EVERYTHING

And afterwards Infinity felt like just a tiny fraction of a second, and you wanted desperately to recapture that single moment, those billions of years and miles, but most of all you felt peaceful and you felt the fire burning inside burning stronger than ever.

Even if the candle burned on a low flame, even if only faint echoes remained of your godhood, of Eternity multiplied with Infinity Squared.

I'm he and he is me and we are all together

They sang, laughing, both crazily and heartedly.

– … *every* thought ever thought, every action ever done, every dream ever dreamt, she heard Jason mumble.

And there's more.

Passion is a fire.

Blood running like sap in the spring.

Total eclipse of the mind.

Mind restrained no longer.

The Human Being once more.

Drumbeat slowed down, or they thought it did. Hearts beat faster than it ever had. Like a Rock'n Roll melody going on the entire evening, like Mighty Quinn played to the max, slowing down to the chorus, in a never-ending loop. The Journey, the music of Existence continuing long after the audience has left the concert hall. It's just *now,* in the whispering Night afterwards that the music begins.

They sat there, clapping hands, singing and being more than a bit Alive.

Only slowly their attention was called to the nagging voice in their mind.

Laurie called to them, brought them back, as she wanted to use the opportunity to seize the moment.

– The Goddess has chosen you, Laurie declared solemnly.

– Nobody has chosen us. Jill stood up angrily. – We've chosen ourselves.

Sluggish on one level, incredibly astute on another, on many others.

– You're of course free to think so. Laurie spoke calmly, in contrast to the girl's juvenile outburst. –

But, no, you're wrong. The Goddess has chosen you, to do her work on Earth, in her garden.
– She has chosen you, Udo said. – And she has chosen Gabrielle.
Jill sat down, rejoining the anonymity of the Circle. Conversation died, relative silence descended on the circle.
– Now, that's a girl seriously fucked up, if I ever saw one.
Loeh's southern drawl was more pronounced (and sluggish) than ever.
– She needs our help, Laurie pointed out.
– Is she a witch? A curious voice from the night pondered.
– I don't know, it isn't always easy to tell, Laurie admitted, clearly frustrated. – But she's a bright girl and she will be a great… asset to anyone profiting from her talents.
Jill couldn't tell either, and usually she could. Just as with Thompson. That would suggest that she was, really, that he was. Did Laurie think in similar ways?
Or… did she know?
– We're gonna call her to us, and make her ours, include her in our protecting, comforting embrace.
And the protective, comforting embrace of the Circle sucked them in. On Laurie's request they joined hands. And the chant began. And the power grew.
And the various members of the Coven confirmed and reaffirmed their place in it.
– Night turns to day, day turns to night… Jill hummed as she did her exercise next morning in the bedroom at school.
As she moved her hands, her arms, her body she could still see, in broad daylight, the faint sparks coming from her fingertips.
The good feeling persisted. The ongoing struggle against Laurie didn't, couldn't destroy that. But it was diminished, devalued by it and by the general situation they found themselves, the world they found themselves.
Tamara giggled, spontaneously. She sat on the bed, eclipsing it completely.
– It was great, wasn't it, she said dreamingly. – Amazing, fabulous, indescribable.
– Indescribable, Jill nodded. – That's the biggest word there is, isn't it?
– But… the big girl sobered slightly, – isn't it… dangerous?
– The stories we keep hearing are usually propaganda, Jill said decisively. – I've taken it only four times in three years. There's no rush for more, no dependency. I don't know anybody who has had any problems with it, though I know they exist. It's important to remember that it's not a toy, but in my opinion the dangers are primarily to very repressed people. All their floodgates open simultaneously.
– I think you're right, the other girl eagerly nodded. – It opens up *everything*. To people who have closed themselves off from most of that, it must be more than a bit traumatic.
And the rest of us feel good, good, good. Jill danced and moved across the room.
– It's coming, she cried, declaimed out of the open window. – Night of Souls. All Soul's Night. Gone but not forgotten. A glimpse of the wild garden, not a garden, but wilderness ABUNDANT.
Both of them shouted wild cries, resonating in the hallways.
Just a bit later. Tamara tied (with regret) a headband over her very, very revealing ears and they went to eat breakfast.
– Hi, Jill said to those she met on their way. – I'm God. How are you doing?
And she said it with such utter conviction and calm that they all were left wondering.
- I, too, am God, Tam explained with great care, snickering wildly.
The two of them caused quite a commotion merely on their way to breakfast. It only escalated later during the day. They presented themselves as God to anyone they met…
And their laughter was full and hearty and content.
– How *are* you feeling? Jill asked her carefully, but candid in a quiet spot sometime in the afternoon.
– I'm much better already, Tamara assured her. – In fact, as you might realize by now, I'm feeling better than *ever*. And strong. I'm very strong…
She stopped, grabbed the couch within her grasp and lifted it above her head, everything in one easy, fluid movement. Her strength was greater than her awareness of it, though, and she pushed the sofa into the ceiling with a loud crack.
– Ouch. She put the miraculously fairly undamaged furniture back on the floor.

– We should test your newfound strength *thoroughly*. Jill managed to keep a straight face as she looked around for witnesses. No one was around, no one was close. – Until then you should be a bit careful. We don't want anybody to be injured, now, would we?

She combed fingers through the big girl's curly, spatial hair and touched briefly the pointed ears under the headband. Her friend smiled and shook her head.

– So short a time since our arrival, Tam said. – So much has happened and… I'm glad.

– Me, too, Jill said passionately. – I wouldn't have missed it for the world, not a single second.

Everything, an eternity of eternities, could, after all, be compressed into a single second. Life was… Joy.

Forever. Such thoughts she had to carry with her Forever. Bitterness should never be given the opportunity to strangle her, to smother her, in its tempting embrace. There had to be other ways. She had to use the rage burning inside, never allow it to use her.

The last weekend in September Jill and Everett made a prolonged trip into the wilderness. Weather remained the same, warm and dry, burning hot. Throat felt like paper merely after drawing breath a few times. Leaves on the trees had turned yellow, but that was certainly not due to any approaching autumn. Autumn was far away, if it would ever come.

Even here, far from all urban areas Jill sensed the fundamental imbalance, wrongness, physically and spiritually, in the present-day world. There was more than the presence of the poison that had spread to all the corners of the globe. The physical poison, though a horrible thing, was merely one aspect, symptom of many, of the actual disease. That it was focused on a lot wasn't surprising, of course. The present society, its population and its predecessors had a long history of attacking the symptoms instead of going to the heart of the matter. Not surprising at all… when the Disease was society itself.

It was so obvious and once she thought about it, it made more sense by the minute. She shook her head, both enraged and full of wonder.

They headed west, walking across the low hills, beyond Frazer Hill. The tree growth wasn't very pronounced the first stretch and the treetops, with their dry leaves, weren't very tight. They didn't really have the impression of walking through a forest. The heat just turned worse by the minute. It did help, though, when the growth finally turned tighter, and they could see nothing but the forest around themselves and just glimpses of blue sky above.

Their headbands dripped with sweat. Their scarce clothing was already soaking wet. They had brought one two-liter bottle of orange-juice each and had already consumed half of it. They had to drink, they knew that, or they would surely perish. But it made them sweat even more, more, more…

– Perhaps we should remove the last of our covers, he said jokingly.

– Yes, why don't we? She said brightly.

And grabbed the t-shirt and pulled it over her head. Her breasts fell from their last confines, unbound. He stopped, visibly shocked, he didn't bother denying it. As she pushed the pants down her thighs, she beckoned him to join her. He did, hesitated a bit before removing his pants, but he did so. It was strangely non-sexual, all of it. The moment contained something immediate and fresh, and very precious.

They kept their shoes on and proceeded on their way.

It didn't aid them much in their struggle against the heat, though, rather on the contrary. At least it seemed that way. And flies and bugs seemed to have an easier time sticking to their skin. And they started to look around in their vicinity for other people. There were no signs of any, but they felt like there were. They arrived at a minor clearing in the forest, an open area as big as their classroom. She started to slow down in her forward movement and then she finally stopped. He could literally see how she… how she seemed to fall apart, and all her old insecurities re-entered her at once. As if they had never really been gone, and they probably hadn't.

She pushed herself against a tree, halfway hiding herself.

He started to dress before she did. She sent him something resembling a grateful smile, but it was more like a rather strained edition. He felt down, too, unavoidable. They had no problems noticing the nuances of each other's emotions. Shame rode them like a mare. Because of their former nudity, enhanced by their shame because they felt shame. They both felt miserable.

– I used to s-stutter, she said. He was shocked by the nakedness of her face, of her mind. – A l-lot. I managed to get rid of it on my own, but it felt like dragging myself free from a quicksand t-trap.

She looked away, couldn't stand the thought of him looking at her.

– My self-confidence was pretty low before I got here, she said with a slightly haunted look, – and some of it remains, I guess.

– I would say it was pretty high even then, he said with conviction. – You broke away from and left a place you had lived your entire life. I don't know if I could have done that. I was lucky to be born here, or I would probably never have become a part of this.

– I was fat, she spat. – I ate rolls of chocolate and got even fatter and to compensate for that I ate even more chocolate.

– You weren't fat, he protested. – Generous perhaps, but not fat. And I quite like generous… even if I can see how you might disagree, even if I like you even better now…

He stopped, before getting himself into even deeper shit.

– Sweet boy, she said, with just a bit of the devil-may-care attitude he loved about her. – Lucky boy, sweet-tongued devil, lucky boy…

She straightened her body, looking at him once more, at least slightly more confident. The distant look in her eyes remained.

– I was clearly sexually inhibited. And sex, from I first experienced it fully, became a source of Freedom for me, of boundless release. I saw it as a liberation, so sweet, so much Life. But taboo as it is in most present-day societies, it's almost impossible to avoid the flip side of it, the shame and the fear. Sex worked as a liberation to me, for me, but it's difficult, so difficult to enjoy sex in this world of sex enmity, a time where any show of passion is considered an aggressive act.

– It would be funny, he conceded willingly, – if it wasn't so tragic.

They resumed their walk, more out of duty than of actual enjoyment. The heat had actually grown worse, and their spirit wasn't really in it, anyway anymore. Progress was slow and they arrived at the first intended break after several minor stops.

Is it so easy? She thought. Is it that easy, to just give up?

They ate and they drank hot bouillon from the thermos flask, hot fluid, to cool the body. She could sense, no, more than sense how her body worked to withstand a perceived hostile environment. It was almost, as if, just before the stop everything had suddenly seemed easier.

He seemed really out of it, though, as much as she had felt like being, just a few, short moments ago.

A rollercoaster, she thought inspired. Life is a rollercoaster. Or if it isn't… perhaps it should be…

– This is a bit of a strain, isn't it? She casually volunteered. – We should perhaps consider taking a shorter route?

– You're doing fine, he grinned dryly. – But you won't get any argument from me. I'm more than willing to postpone our exploration *many* days.

– You haven't seen, haven't experienced Fire Lake yet, she said rushed, very eager. – If we turn back immediately, we should be able to reach it before dark.

Eagerness rose in her, but it was more than that. Surprise rose in her, over how fast she in truth had recovered from the fatigue, the fatigue so prominent only minutes before. She recalled when she had dragged the wagon, with Tamara and the others. Then, too, she had uncannily fast regained the strength of her limbs. Except for the fact that it had happened faster this time. She had been even more tired, but had regained strength even faster. Something happened then, inside her. Nothing physical probably, but realization hit her. She didn't stop her walk, but she stopped in her mind, pondering, listening, making a fist with her right hand (and the right hand made a fist). Her…

Her healing power.

The incredulous smile lit up her sweaty face.

It wasn't the same as with Tam, a dramatic increase in muscle volume and size. But Jill, as realization slowly dawned on her, realized that she could exercise everything she ever wanted, without fear of (prolonged) injury or fatigue. Her healing power would heal her automatically and very, very fast. And - as she discovered this very moment: By concentrating she could make it happen that much faster, comparably speaking virtually instantaneously. She could actually notice it happening, there on the spot, just like she had with the wounds and headache.

She wanted to share it with him, wanted to share everything with him, but she held back, held back a couple minutes more, since she couldn't be sure how much his male ego could withstand. A bleak thought, she knew, but it was a bleak world. He wasn't stupid. He saw… and would eventually realize… that she «could take the heat» and hard exercise better than he could. Allow knowledge to be gained slowly.

The ever more cat-like body rose to full height. She smiled as she reached out one hand to him. Full lips touched his lightly. They held hands, hands locked on to each other, on the long, but familiar way back. Jill led him eagerly, persistently along, laughing and sparkling, in a sudden, abundant excitement.

– We followed Tam to the gym, Jill told him. – It was in the middle of the night, creepy and empty.

He could see it before his inner eye, experiencing it as she was re-experiencing it.

– She has grown so strong. We let her try a weight of the total of hundred kilos…

– Kilos…?

– Yes, you ignorant savage, we «Englishmen» have used the metric system since the nineties and it's about time you guys caught up... She smacked him lightly on the cheek. – Our Jennifer Walters lifted it in stride, with no visible discernable problems. She lifted it in one hand and put it back down, like she would a feather. We hardly heard it hit the floor.

– I've heard the talk about her sudden growth, her height and strength, Everett nodded. – It's hard to avoid hearing about it. How is she coping?

– We're... forming a protective circle around her, Jill said, as if probing herself. – Not that she needs it. She's tough and things are mostly all right. There are comments, of course, but she can take it. And it's almost expected of us that we're different. That she has grown ten to fifteen centimeters in a month is really incidental, compared to the fact that she dares to call herself a *witch*. We have in a way met the usual bullying halfway… if you get my drift.

– It works better than Laurie's «proven» methods then. Not very surprising.

They picked another route back. Without any conscious decision they entered a path leading directly to the Hill. They passed one of their Circles on the way up, the long ascent bathing in the merciless rays of the white heat. Everett realized that they were led almost instinctively to the place somewhere ahead. They had never walked this path before. It stopped being a visible path after just a few minutes, but they hardly stopped or even hesitated.

At the edge of the thicker forest, where there was a plateau, a momentary intermission on the steep climb, they stopped with their hands on their knees, gasping for breath. But then he saw it, was virtually observing how she regenerated herself, straightened herself, regained her inherent freshness. The little fallout there was, was pushed out of her muscles. He straightened himself by an act of will. They turned, looking at the valley to the west.

– So, this is how the sun looks like behind Frazer Hill, he exclaimed excitedly.

And he felt something then, something alien, something familiar, and a rush of strength, and he caught himself in wondering if it was purely a result of his will, of his imagination.

She placed herself in front of him, chest to chest, grabbing his hands.

– Come; let us *run* the remaining piece.

– Okay, I'm game, he gasped. – I think we should postpone it a bit, that's all, about a thousand years or so.

– I want to share everything with you. She spoke from deep down her throat.

…? He sensed it first in his hands. Eyes widened. Suddenly there was like sparks literally flew among them. There was pain, in his hands, in his arms and then the energy came flowing, into him. He had never felt anything remotely similar. The small samples he had received through her «warm» hands previously couldn't even begin to compare with this. It had hardly been more than a firecracker compared to… to… yes, an atomic bomb. It, she penetrated every pinpoint of his being. Her eyes glittered at first, before turning complexly white. The strength… his body was bursting with strength, to a degree that he feared that he would be completely released, severed from it… or really come into contact with it for the first time. Since…

Since

It was too much. He started fighting, fighting to free himself.

Don't fight it. Return… return some of it.

And even the white in her eyes started glowing. The ecstasy grew almost unbearable.

Then it was done. She let him go.
When she let him go she looked at least as healthy, as strong as he felt. She smiled wickedly, enticingly, and backed away from him, then she turned abruptly and started running into the forest. He started chasing her and caught up with her almost immediately, but instead of grabbing her, he ran by her side into the black forest.
Into…
The Crossroads.
Their surroundings seemed to melt, dissolve, into new and frightening and infinitely interesting shapes, scenarios. What they saw… they couldn't in any way make sense of it.
Your ability to see with your head, with your mind, with… everything is just as strong as mine. Knowledge is limiting you, limiting us, the twisted reason you, I have learned from birth and through adolescence.
YOU/I. He couldn't be sure if it was her «talking», if it was him, or both. The run through the forest would forever stand as a line of confused imagery to him.
Virtually everybody has forgotten who they are. Many have even forgotten that they have forgotten.
They stopped, just as they emerged from the tight growth into the natural circle by the lake, the sand by the shore. They were both breathing hard, but both pair of eyes glittered in excitement, as their breathing eased.
– This turned out to be a bit too chaotic, she said. – We must do it again, do it when we're better prepared. There's so much to learn. In the meantime…
She kicked off her jogging shoes and removed the rucksack, the backpack and then, without hesitation, she ran enthusiastically into Fire Lake. He hadn't really managed to regain his composure, before she immerged herself completely in the water and started swimming, except for the shoes, fully dressed.
Just as well, he thought. Might just as well wash our clothes. Better now than later.
She waved to him, winked to him. He almost forgot to kick off his shoes, (but remembered it at the last moment), before joining her in the water. He thought she swam like a fish, like a dolphin or something, but to his surprise he closed in on her by each heavy stroke. She dived. Feet rose in the air and her own weight pushed her below the surface, into the deep. She did it as if she had done it a thousand times before. He took a deep breath, bent his hips ninety degrees and by his own deed he was pushed down, down under. A few moves with his arms and he went even deeper. He could see her unbelievably well in the crystal-clear water. He realized that he had a rock-hard hard-on, that he had had it for quite some time, and he wasn't really surprised. Nothing strange about it, concerning the amount of time he had spent looking at her rear, her ass, her swinging hips. But for the time being he was more than happy to let the matter rest here, happy to just look and enjoy the sight of her as she floated through the twilight fields. He was savoring the hunt, in the certainty that the game was already caught.
She reached land a bit before him. Her hair, seemingly a dark cloud in the water, was pushed back now, tight against her head and back. He continued to stare at her… rear, as she wriggled out of her clothes and let them fall on the ground by the water.
– It doesn't really… *feel* like a house, does it? She said, clearly preoccupied.
For a moment there, directed by her words, he allowed himself to be distracted, of the imposing view above them.
– It looks like… something else…
– Yes, doesn't it?
He touched his forehead, suddenly amazed.
– How strange. Just now, it was like I was reading my own mind.
He turned towards her once more and realized that she wasn't looking at the house. She was looking at him… and his blood-filled rock-hard, pointed cock threatening to break out of its wet confines. A thin cover of fluid seemed to cover her eyes and he didn't need to stare to see how obviously excited, turned-on she had become.
– Do you see anything you fancy, My Lord? She said huskily, with a voice hardly more than a whisper, looking drowsily at him. – I've got no problems whatsoever flashing something I desire…
She fondled her breasts, caressing her belly, moaning then, and falling down on her knees. She started

tossing and turning in the grass, like a cat in heat. There was an old, dead smooth tree, without any remaining bark close to her. She crawled to it and on it, all the while keeping her challenging look at him. The female put one leg on each side of the tree, she did so slowly, deliberately. He swallowed hard. Hands begin to tear in his clothes, tear off the fabric by their own volition. He was still hesitating, without really knowing why, knowing himself. The swim had been cool, refreshing, but at this moment both his body and mind felt completely supercharged, overheated. Suddenly, both bodies were covered by thick, musk-filled sweat. His clothes were off. Unrestrained he threw himself at her, on her, placing himself behind her and he grabbed and lifted the already swinging hips. He started pumping almost immediately, moved fast and hard inside her, while stroking the smooth skin, the firm and yet voluptuous body, unable to stop or slow down the slightest. Was it even a marginal difference between him (and her) and a couple mating ten times a hundred generations ago?

The female body lay there gasping against the tree. Breasts, stiff nipples were pushed and slid back and forth against the dead wood. She felt every inch of his shaft inside, much harder than any tree or rock or anything. Their contact filled the entire her (the entire him) and paralyzed her. Every small movement brought forth sounds and gasps from them both, pushed from their depth and out between shaking lips. They understood each other through fever-hot thoughts (there weren't any thoughts). He came in a flow of pushes and pulls, of violent, insane trusts.

His/her senses returned slowly, painfully. His/her senses receded back into his/her primal self. He/she gasped and then moaned one last time. He pulled himself out quickly and sat down on the tree, beside the still writhing and hungry female, almost in shock, aware of even the smallest of details in his surroundings. He stared at the broad, brown back. There was only need in her eyes and nothing besides, a female wanting nothing else besides being covered again and again and again. Maybe there were thoughts there somewhere, in her, in him, but they were negligible, merely strays, leftovers from the explosion of passion and savage coupling. She lifted her head slowly, locked her eyes in his.

– Savage, Wild, she said huskily. – Not coercion. In case you're wondering, we were both equal partners in this…

He didn't doubt that. The doubt present was hardly more than an echo of his civilized upbringing.

She turned around and slid (like a snake) from the tree. Face was blushing in excitement, in need, of everything, like his own, like he could read through her thoughts. There was no pretense, no falseness, only a need, a passion brutally honest, now, and forever more. She crawled onto his lap and started «snuggling» (the word was hardly appropriate or sufficient), actively and demanding.

– No submission for any master, no subservience to cultural peculiarities, she growled.

He felt joy then, on a purely intellectual level, adding to the former purely emotional one (and they were all One). The apparent contradiction between emotion and reason was just one more idiotic aspect of present-day morals.

– My big and dreaded Master, she mewed.

– We don't own each other, he said tightly, unnecessary.

– I couldn't agree more, she expressed lightly, her fingers teasingly clawing at his neck, her sweet lips tasting his. And added: – But we do belong to each other.

She allowed herself to drop down on her knees between his legs. Eager hands grabbed his wet, half-raised limb. She looked expectantly up at him.

– I could have made this *wreck* able to rage the seas immediately, you know… I want to, but I prefer to bid my time.

Suddenly, evidently more insecure she let her lips embrace the throbbing head. It hardly mattered. The result was not in question. He felt it instantly.

– Do you do everything this good after just a few tryouts? He wondered. One of their advantages was that they could say everything to each other, without (too much) fear of repercussions. Now, it was his turn. – Clearly Henry can't have been completely wrong about you. You must have been a hooker in your previous life.

He fell from the dead tree. They rolled around in the grass. He moved inside her once more. She shuddered in ecstasy and closed her eyes. Her orgasm, delayed earlier, rode her fast and furious.

– Don't stop, she mumbled. – I'll come more, much more.

– … completely insatiable. He managed to shake his head. She laughed out loud. – To think you were a virgin just a short while ago.

– That's it, she said roguishly. – I've waited so long that I've got a lot of catching up to do. Besides... the custom of some Indian tribes was that the male warrior emptied himself first. Then the squaw, if she wanted more, had to work for it.

– You're doing a fine job, he exclaimed.

His movements increased in strength and intensity. He touched and fondled her, and she gasped in joy. She embraced him with her legs to push him as deep as possible inside of her. Deeper...Both started drawing breath faster, such short gasps that they hardly got any air at all and when they this time stopped breathing, it happened simultaneously.

Silence, in a vast hall without walls. They lay still in the grass and just listened to the surroundings, while enjoying the closeness of each other's bodies. The next hours, days, nights turned unforgettable to both. They would never be certain about how long a time they spent there, by the water and the house on the Hill, inside the black forest and they didn't care. They fucked. Many times. And they shared an intimacy that made it possible, without the slightest pretense. They talked. About everything engaging them. And they had fun planning all kinds of stuff.

They rested there in the grass, dozing off. Daylight had yet to fade completely the first day. She kissed him excitedly, without bashfulness, without holding back the slightest.

– Why do we have such strong urges? He said to the air. – Such heightened desire?

– That should be simple enough to understand, she said surprised. – You should know the reason for that as easily as I. We're closer to the fertile Earth. Therefore, we're even more creatures of passion than most people. This is both our strength and our weakness.

He patted the female, his mate on the chin and rose, stretching his body. He took his time, sensing, taking in the mood saturating the place, nagging at him, inside him.

Indescribable.

Here on this place of mysticism and beauty.

– I could stay here forever.

– Forever is a long time, she chided him lightly. – It's a great place to camp, though, while we're thinking things through.

– So much forgotten, he despaired, – So much lost.

– So much to do, she grinned, – so long time to do it...

She suddenly turned towards him, solemnly, intensively.

– I... heard a story once, she said dreamingly, concentrating, a distant look in her face, her eyes burning with a cold flame. – I'm not sure where I heard it, if I've actually *heard* it... It was about Styx, the river of Knowledge and Death.

– I can't even begin to explain how interesting that sounds to me, he told her. – The story isn't exactly the run of the mill Styx-story, is it?

– This is an older, ancient version, from the time before the monks burned down their own convents, in order to remove the knowledge of older times, perhaps even before the library in Alexandria was destroyed. I found it, read about it, a while after I had actually heard it... I think... in a book written by Martin Keller, the archaeologist. This is how it goes:

Did he hear music? He felt the ground beneath his feet, touched the air with his skin.

– Styx was originally the river of knowledge. In a distant past, the legend goes the knowledge of its whereabouts had been lost. Just a few managed the feat it was to find its shore and even fewer managed after that to find their way to its raging streams. Those very few achieved a knowledge and wisdom making them kings and gods.

Abruptly they experienced visions, a man approaching a glacier, insanity and hatred burning in his eyes. A woman danced inside a fire, with a big snake dancing around and on her writhing body. And there were others.

– But... the very truth of the matter is that Styx leads all the long way to the Kingdom of Death and a traveler who doesn't return to shore fast enough is doomed. A great king trembled because of this. He had seen in a vision that one day when the humans were as countless as the ants in the ground, they would return to the river of knowledge. But without the knowledge and wisdom to find back to shore.

Their clothes had been dry for some time now. They let them hang on the branches where they had left them. Night arrived with the same tropic heat they had experienced many nights before this one. The eternal wind didn't bother them. It caressed them and made the heat more bearable. They sensed it, as they had done on a distant continent in a distant past…

The hot wind is blowing. Hot wind is blowing…

Jill froze. Everett blinked once.

– Did you hear? She asked him.

– *Yes.*

He did hear something, and saw something, too, passing them in the air, a single entity first, then many. He experienced it also through her eyes, through her, her wonder, her tenseness.

There was the wind and the flapping of wings. Suddenly there were shapes all around them, flapping their wings. Black… black birds (not blackbirds) filling the air everywhere.

Ravens, he thought.

He could, impossibly enough see her shake her head, determined. She stood tall under the onslaught, hardly moving except by stretching out her arms.

– I'm not afraid, she cried towards the heavens, towards the depths. – I'M NOT AFRAID

It seemed to never stop. The number of birds continued to increase, to hammer against all their senses.

The ravens, all the ravens, settled in the trees, on the ground, the water. He saw her stand frozen. The darkness descended even tighter. All the trees, all the underbrush started moving at once.

The two rucksacks dumped down on the ground. Dry branches and twigs started flying out of the darkness. She did it, effortlessly. As she built a bonfire and lit it, she hardly strained at all. There were sparks and thunder, then fire. She built a circle of stones around the fireplace, to stop it from spreading. Water flowed from the lake, wetting the grass around the stone circle. Not a drop fell on the clothes or the fire. It seemed very much to him like her powers grew the more she used them. When she had completed her tasks, he sensed no fatigue in her.

– I am Raven, she said, eyes twinkling, as she stood with her back to the fire.

From then on, there were always some ravens following her around.

They ate. And they had never eaten anything that tasted better, realizing that the food hadn't changed from the very same type they had fed on days ago. The two of them had changed… and the surroundings. Everything seemed to be better up here. The air, the soil… There was a power and vitality present at this place that they hadn't known existed. This was a magickal place, newer, older, and so very different from any other on present day Earth.

Flies danced in the air around Everett to the point where they almost surrounded him. He didn't like that, a dislike growing stronger when he noticed how few of them were actually circling Jill. What she didn't seem to realize, that he had no problem seeing, was that every insect flying too close to her dropped lifeless to the ground. She didn't notice anything, it just happened without her being aware of it. He concentrated. All the flies flew away, and they didn't return. He smiled, quite satisfied with himself.

She caught his attention once more. He could never keep it off her for very long.

– Behold! She said.

She lifted her hands high above the head, to an impossible height, until letting them fall until she held them straight out to the left and right.

Dry grass was torn from the ground, many small pieces creating a form growing from the ground up and when they all were lit simultaneously a sword of Fire appeared in the night, visible far, far away.

– Excalibur, he cried out in excitement. – The sword of Arthur Pendragon.

Jolts of excitement and realization accompanied his statement.

The sword faded by lack of nourishment. But it would never fade completely.

She stuck a hand deep down in the rucksack and when she pulled it back up there was a book in her hand.

– A book? He exclaimed undignified. Then almost immediately, curiously: – What book?

– It sort of caught a ride, she said, almost apologetically, though her eyes kept looking at him with the same, amazing eagerness. – Listen to this, to King Arthur by Sir Thomas Mallory. *Listen!*

– «Throughout recorded history the strong have taken whatever they wanted. But a new day shall dawn when strength will not be used for own gain, but to protect the weak, break the grip of evil and serve justice».

– This is unbelievable, he said dumbfounded. – I've always loved that story. A bit corny, but…

– We're in agreement, then? She said soberly.

He knew what she meant, the further implications of her words, her purpose.

– Yes. Jeez. Yes.

She held out her hands to him, with the palms up. He met them, took them, with his own.

– We've walked through the Gates of Fire, she intoned. – We've taken the first, crucial step to regain what was lost.

Yes. Such was a worthy pursuit, something to reach for. He pulled the firm body closer to his own and kissed her frantically.

– Well, what do we do first?

– Now, we find ourselves a bed, she said softly, tempting him, pushing her hot body at his, stroking her lips at his, biting him in the soft shoulder tissue. – Now, we fuck.

He got a hardon immediately. They fell slowly to their knees while caressing the other. They sought intimacy this time, still loving fiercely, but movements were slower, more deliberate. They had had the day. Now, Night was here, for bad and for good.

They had satisfied themselves quite thoroughly earlier on. Therefore, they could do it calmer, more relaxed now, let the heat grow slowly instead of rushing it. He grabbed her breasts, led his mouth to them and started to lick them, suck them, bite them. She slid up and down on him while she sighed and moaned ever more intensively. And then the fierceness returned, abruptly and irresistible. She cried out, he gasped and growled while coming. World turned black, turned Shadow. They embraced it with fangs and claws, as they stretched their bodies on the ground, already halfway into Sleep.

2

In a dream within a dream the sea threw Little Jill back on the shore. She slept and didn't awaken with the sand's soft reception. The sand, the kind and nice sand, opened up and swallowed her whole, while she slept, started digesting her with nice, soft teeth. A giant wave hit the shore. It released her from her captivity, from her slumber, her peril, but she drowned, drowned, drowned. She found herself in a forest, running, running so hard that her throat felt raw. Her mate ran by her side. He wasn't of much help to her. She levitated high above the ground, invulnerable, invincible. There were lightning and thunder everywhere. And the wind… The wind rose to a terrible force. A lightning bolt passed straight through her, and thunder didn't harm her. The wind destroyed everything in its way.

Jill awoke with a start, with sweat pouring and eyes wide open. Before really fully conscious she shook Everett abruptly awake.

– What is it? He asked. – What's wrong?

– I don't know, she whispered, timid and scared.

She pulled close to him, shivering and paralyzed. He did his best to calm her, to comfort her, stroking her hair, her raven hair. It had been sort of dark brown. Now it was black. The fire. It burned still, even if it should have burned down hours ago. As he was staring at it Jill stiffened even more in his arms. Her eyes grew distant, empty. At first it seemed as if she was staring at empty air, but after what he would deem a monumental effort, he slowly focused on a figure standing upright a few steps away… a figure levitating at least half a body length above the ground. The figure was Jill, or at least one who looked like a perfect copy of her. A twin…

A Doppelganger.

– Who are you? Jill cried. – What do you want?

– I'm you.

– NO. Jill picked up a stone and threw it at the woman, at the ghoul. It went straight through her.

Jill gasped. She grabbed her belly with both hands and crumbled to the ground, her face contorted in pain.

– If you are her, then why are you doing this? Everett cried out in anger, without thought of the consequences. One moment he felt a pressure around the neck, but nothing more.

– *She must learn. We live in a predator world. She or he failing to see this will be devoured.*

The image, or whatever it could be, faded away. Jill straightened while she attempted to blink away the tears at the corner of her eyes.

– She's out there, she gasped. – She's coming for me.

– What was that? He asked faint, without really listening. – What… or who is she?

– A demon, sent to torture me, she replied with a snarl, in desperate puzzlement. – It grew out of a mirror and has been chasing me, bothering me, since I came to Northfield. What do you *think* it is? It doesn't exist. I can see it, but there's nothing there. I can't touch it, but it can certainly touch me. I don't want to talk about it, *okay*.

She crawled to him and with a viciousness that had always been a part of her, one that he had always dreaded she made him horny, made him want her, even if he didn't want to.

– What…

– Hush…

He gasped helplessly, as he started moving his hips, pumping inside her, moving to her tune. Kali, the Demon Mother, the giver and taker of life smiled to him, as she looked down on him, as she gave him pleasure, as she took pleasure, in a desperate, sickening need, as he was swept away by the remorseless tide.

– We can go away, she said dreamingly, a timeless time later, as she rested beside him with her head on his chest. – Far away. Enjoy life like hell, and never look back.

She kissed him on the cheek, a wet, comforting kiss. The full, swollen lips smothered his skin, seemed to embrace him, as her body slid off him, as she let go of him, as she fell asleep. He couldn't believe it. She had to have nerves of steel…

He lay awake for a long time, wondering about whether she had… r-raped him or not. He felt dirty, used, the image, the sight of the Creature hovering in the air terrifying him. It was the way he had always imagined a… vengeful ghoul, a revenant. Then he sensed a movement in the air, a presence, the overwhelming cold down the spine.

She mumbled something. He listened intensively.

– *I don't see her all the time, but she's there. She sees me whenever she wants.*

He almost jumped out of his skin and started shaking. She continued sleeping calmly. The cold abruptly took hold of his entire body. She had spoken in her sleep, unusually coherent. And her voice… had had a spooky similarity to that of
the creature.

He crouched above her, and even if he wanted to run and never look back, he decided to watch over her.

Her sleep wasn't exactly restful, though remarkably calm. If he had been her, he doubted he would have dared even closing his eyes.

He slept. They both had quite a useful night of sleep, even though they did experience moments more than worrying.

She could wake up screaming.

– She's coming for me. She'll never leave me ALONE

He attempted to comfort her, to chase away the ghosts plaguing the young girl.

– I remember, she mumbled in his armpit. – He's coming. He'll always come. *I remember!*

And as he felt a stab of pain, he saw it, too, experienced the nightmares, the images, and the visions.

By dawn they couldn't say if they had ever really been awake, been awake before. The potent, chaotic reality still imposed itself on them. They couldn't tell if they were awake, awake in the dream, or both. Or neither.

Reality dissolved wherever they directed their eyes, wherever their attention wandered, and giving way to the undeniable hyper-reality surrounding them. They submitted to it, resisting, groaning, finally giving in, as they were crossing hill after hill, through valleys and forests, struggling just to keep putting one foot in front of the other. The hills turned to mountains. A tiny group of human beings, hardly visible against the vast backdrop of a landscape, struggled on against weather and wind. Their clothes could hardly be called rags. The remnants of the group counted just a few women and children and even fewer men, none above the age of twenty. They were, and had been for a long time running from the «Viking» army of Olav Haraldson, called the Cruel, the White Christ's man in old Norway. A thousand years hence the memory was still vivid. After crushing their tribe using falsehood and superiority in numbers, he had ordered the decapitation of all men and boys above the age of five, and then taken all females as slaves. This little group consisted of the remaining few who had managed to escape in time. They had dwindled further in numbers since then. Olav's wrath had fallen on them because they had refused to submit to his White Christ and his wrath was terrible to behold.

North, ever north, away from Olav's influence. Olav continued to persecute them mercilessly. He didn't allow any viewpoint and way of life deviating from his own, and absolutely not theirs. They who didn't worship anything or anybody, but showed respect and reverence for all nature, all life. Jill and Everett recognized several in their group. There were people with blond and dark hair among them, but the majority had red hair. The two of them, a woman and a man led the tribe. They fought their way forward on a high mountain trail and had difficulty breathing. In the valley, far below they glimpsed men from the army chasing them.

The woman held a white knuckled fist around the amulet she carried in a cord around her neck. Forget. They must not forget. Olav wanted, above all to eradicate the very memory of them and their beliefs from the surface of the Earth. The decapitated heads served a number of purposes, but spoke mostly about Olav's power and served as a deterrent to others who wanted to resist his will. Women were taught, trained to be docile and obedient. They spent their remaining life as trophies, just as much as the decapitated heads. Their children were made thralls. They died bit by bit. The men had been lucky. That very thought churned and churned inside their heads, while they fell into oblivion.

Stine they had named her. Jill caught the name in a flash. She knew that Everett didn't receive impressions as strong as she did. Stine squeezed the amulet. It was their task to survive, so they could pass on their knowledge, from adult to child, down through the generations.

– We're independent human beings, she bespoke the small group around the protected, hidden campfire, – giving loyalty to none. We're few and our enemies are many. It doesn't matter. We will have our reckoning, our *revenge*... This is what we want. This is what we desire more than anything else... We will have it, even if we must seek it in the shattered lands beyond the *Dark River*.

Many years later. They had gained their revenge. The man the followers of White Christ called «the holy» had fallen in battle and they had been there when it happened. But the victory had come too late. Christianity had already gained a foothold in the land of the Vikings and was thus destroying them, destroying an entire people. They were running now, the few remaining faithful to the old beliefs. And thus it had ever been, it seemed, as far back as Memory itself, written and oral history. From what existed as living manifestations inside every human being.

– *Atavism,* Jill stated slowly, – cell-memory, the recollection of the ancestors hidden in every cell in the body.

He looked at her, a bit preoccupied, the powerful visions still lingering in his consciousness.

– And there is more. What we experienced tonight, what we experience this moment isn't a recollection of a distant ancestor, but *memories,* our own experience from a bygone age. We're learning to remember.

She and Plat stood by the Fire Lake. Flames licked the water and the air and warmed them, while they stared at an opening in the Black Forest.

Not the one in Germany.

The one here.

A young buck stood there, with his antlers up.

– I can make him come to us and eat of our hand, she whispered.

– We must kill him, Plat said. – We need nourishment.

Voice was sad. Lillith understood why, understood him.

– No, not now, she decided. – Perhaps later, but not tonight.

Sun started rising in the east. They didn't see it, but registered how the sky turned brighter. The morning mist floated above Fire Lake. Their eyes sparked as they kept them locked on the structure out there.

– We didn't sleep, he said in excited wonder, – but we were dreaming still.

Jill didn't listen. She was lost in her own thoughts. Stine, she knew, had wanted to kill Olav from afar (she could) long before the battle of Stiklestad. She had tried, but he was… protected.

– There must be writings, some history-books about what happened, she said distantly. – If not about any single occurrence, then about the king. No doubt colored and distorted by the victorious, but yet chronicles of the past.

Knowledge is Power.

Thin rays of sunshine reached them through the trees. There were flashes of light in the glass of the windows at the top of the house, blinding flashes thrown at them, enticing them with its secrets.

They found roots and herbs for breakfast and drank directly of the clear water.

– Such a treasure of variety, she ventured. – Plants and animals hardly found anywhere anymore.

– Rare individuals, looking for variety, usually find it, he bowed eloquently to her.

She acknowledged the implications of his words, her own joy with a nod, but she was clearly distracted. He could sense the power raging through her, like a Storm, undeniable. He sensed it in himself, but more muted. She stood indecisive in one spot for a while, before she set out into the forest. He saw her bringing the rucksack. She gave no sign that he was supposed to follow her, but he did so anyway.

She walked, sure on her feet, suddenly in a hurry. Caught by surprise he lost sight of her a few seconds before catching up with her by a little, dark pond. And he realized that reality still shifted and jolted around them. He saw only the white in her eyes, the mist surrounding her body.

He saw her squat in an easy, effortless manner. She brushed away the grass and upper, loose layer of soil to reach the red, iron-rich middle layer. Agile hands worked fast and confident and built a mound of the red soil. She used a finger to make a small hole at the top of it. Hands stretched and moved hesitatingly in the air above. She started mumbling, forming incoherent «words» with her lips. It resembled song in a way, but was more of a humming, sound pushed up the throat. He assumed it was a kind of concentration-exercise, one that each adept designed for his or herself consciously and unconsciously, to easier reach his or her inner self.

She sat down on her butt, with her legs crossed in front of her, around the mound. The right hand, her strongest, was placed above it. He drew breath hard when he realized that blood began to drip from the middle of her palm. Each drop hit the hole. Not a single one missed. The fluid seemed to expand down there, for a short while, until the soil started absorbing it. The wound didn't close until the mound had been visibly saturated and he felt the first stings of worry.

– It's all right. She spoke with a distant, detached voice. – It doesn't hurt. It's sort of nice actually.

The other hand pulled forth an in-advance prepared leather-chain, with a small pouch. She put it away and started to form the wet soil between her hands. Bloody soil colored the skin on her hands a deep red. She painted stripes and figures on her face and all over her body. Her left and right side were usually painted symmetrically, but also in completely asymmetrical patterns. It was done with a precision showing more than mere skill, as if she could see her own mirror image and almost immediately after completion the figures seemed to… start dancing of their own accord on and off the skin. He couldn't be certain if she indeed did look at him with only the white of her eyes showing, but pinprick sensations on his own skin told him she was. But there was also more, movement under his own skin, possible changes within him, and notions he never had given much thought started surfacing.

He had noticed it almost immediately after she had given him one of her health baths. They had speeded up processes in Tamara's body. Why not in his?

She formed the remaining clay into a ball and put it in the pouch. It fit perfectly. After tying the fabric around it she hung the chain around her neck. The pouch came to rest between her breasts. Her eyes turned normal, as she rose and once more focused on him.

– This must be done by everybody on their own, she commented. – It's a very personal action and the progression may vary from person to person and time to time. That's what makes the magick so potent. It's a Totem, a representation of our most private self, our core, everything we are and may become. It can give a certain protection. Though it can also represent a danger… if the belief in it grows too strong.

– Protection? He cleared his throat so hard that it hurt. She stared at him with the special look again and he felt small. – Against whom?

– Against… enemies. I don't think there will be any lack of them, do you? Against enemy Covens. Against every fucking person on the planet and beyond, if they get in our way. I've made my amulet. Stacy and Jason have or will make their own very soon. The three strongest, the most potent Magick. Laurie has carried hers under her blouse all the time, haven't you noticed?

– You're a bit too cryptic at times, he snorted.

– You've tasted my blood once, she smiled. – Once is enough.

I'll share everything with you. Isn't that enough?

And he takes her hand.

They ran into the water together, until they reached its depth, and they started swimming. Both drew deep breaths and dived, dived into the deep, so easy and effortlessly. They enjoyed themselves immensely down there. She used her telekinesis to make them «float» in the water. They didn't need to swim. She pushed them while they «stood» upright. They looked down and could see the lake floor. At least before she signaled him, gave him a moment to prepare, before pushing them even further out on the vast, endless deep.

We've been under for close to a minute now and we still don't feel any real need for air. How come?

It's called aquatic breathing. Quite a few people have that ability to partly switch off the need to breathe under water and ours are probably stronger than in most. We are Witches, you know. And we've turned far more physical the last few weeks… or haven't you noticed?

Suddenly she was close, her lips touching his. Two mouths opened… and… they shared air. Almost paralyzed by surprise and sudden overwhelming lust he forgot to breathe for a moment. She didn't do anything. He knew she didn't. After a night, after days of…

«…the thirst of desire is never filled nor fully satisfied.»

Cicero? He was right, damn me…

A teasing smile, a pull, and she was gone. In a wild underwater dance, she started performing for him, a breathtaking display really threatening to take his breath away.

What if I will be able to do this in air, too, she marveled. *Fly like a bird above land and sea.*

We can fly on the wings of thought. He wondered about this euphoria, whether or not it was caused by lack of air. *We may talk anywhere, at any time. When we're together and when we're not. No one (or very few) is able to listen in.*

They reached land in the middle of the lake, where they really had been heading all the time… and almost opened their mouths in astonishment. They saw stairs, carved from the stone, partly overgrown, but they started deep down and continued all the way to the surface. They checked it, circling the islet. There was one set of stairs on each side, four… no five in all. Of course…

He pointed at his mouth and then up. She had anticipated it for a while and had already stopped using her powers. They floated and swam upwards to the surface, with fast, powerful strokes.

He stumbled and fell in the grass, coughing and breathing hard. She floated the last stretch as through a warm current and stayed floating with her head just above the water. While he was looking, she started to rise straight up in the air. Chest, hips, thighs above the surface… until the momentum stopped. The water reached to just above her knees then. She dropped back into the water.

– Did you SEE that? She exclaimed excitedly, flying to shore and throwing herself at him, her arms around his neck. – I almost made it.

– A typical scientist would have insisted that you must have stood on something, he said dryly.

– Oh, you silly boy, she laughed. – He would have insisted on calling it a mass hallucination. That's the safest bet, covering most possibilities.

– You're right, of course. That's their last recourse when countless people independently of each other have observed the same, «unexplainable» «phenomenon». In other words: Everybody has experienced the same hallucination. That's of course the least satisfying explanation, but they don't care.

– The «Phenomenon» can't be explained by current science, she mimicked. And then desperately: – «But there must certainly be a natural explanation».

They supported each other while shaking with laughter.

– They haven't even realized that the word «supernatural» and related words are a contradiction in terms. Everything within nature is a part of it and can't, by definition, stand above or outside it.

This morning, like countless previous mornings, the air turned from hot to desert hot. They looked at the house, looked at each other. They didn't see any openings on the back and hurried to the front. The sun shone straight through the portal now. The dusty floor in the hall seemed to become alive. Before they had time to regret anything they stepped over the threshold. She had been here before, he had not. Everett immediately sensed… a differentiation, a well of emotions. This was a place of countless possibilities… and dangers.

– I started my tour on the right, she said cheerfully, hesitatingly. – And never got to explore the left side.

– Then we go left…

He was rewarded with a flashing smile.

While leaving tracks of wet feet, they penetrated the fortress of knowledge and death and life. He turned his head and looked back. The tracks didn't disappear or anything.

On a wall, in a passage, where the sunrays never reached the house displayed to them a row of paintings, haunting images of… of a world gone insane.

Inside the first frame, there was only a short text, written in big, deliberate letters:

> «To the witches following me on the path to madness: This is this centennial, as I see it. Young friends, young rivals, beware of the future hidden in your depths, beware of the beast inside».
>
> Alan Rachine 1904 AD

– I've heard about him, Everett said. – Another infamous sorcerer…

The first painting was a self-portrait (sort of), of the clearly brilliant, but disturbed artist. The disturbed part was clearly evident in the way he had placed the eyes, nose, ears and mouth. The eyes were the mouth, the nose was the eyes, one ear was the nose, and the twisted mouth was one ear.

And the remaining ear was a car. It wasn't a gimmick, it was real. Everett stopped attempting to describe the remaining image to himself, sweating cold drops from every point on his skin.

And the car was a modern Corvette, not the «simple» cars available in 1904.

In the right, lower corner was scribed: Self ar 1904.

All the other paintings had scribed «ar 1904» in the lower left corner.

– Jesus, Everett was shaking his head. – This guy is beating the other surrealists to the ground.

But it wasn't really one style. Labels were completely wasted (as ever) on this guy. He had many styles and his own, unique expression. It was more Rembrandt than Surrealism really, but it could also be said to be more Surrealism than Rembrandt. It was Reality, more vivid than reality itself. That wasn't possible, of course, but that was how the two of them saw it right now.

– It could be one hell of a deliberate hoax, of course. Jill panned her right hand along the paintings, without touching them once, shaking in joy, in terror. – But I don't think so…

Their attention halted by the last two paintings in the row. They were not placed in any particular order or sequence or anything, but the last two in the row caught their eye… perhaps because they seemed even crazier than the others: One showed a haunting image of an expanding mushroom cloud, something completely unknown in 1904. The other was of an enormous garbage heap, of a magnitude and consistency also unknown in 1904. There was a plane-wreck, one Saturn 12 rocket and a lot of assorted goods from the late 20th century.

– Catching, he commented dryly.

– Isn't it, she nodded cheerfully.

The sorceress and the up-and-coming sorcerer continued their exploration of the house, fortress, castle and its many-faceted moods. Time started to lose its meaning. Place started to lose all meaning.

– It's a trap, she said suddenly, with her ghostly voice, – a seduction… if we allow it to be one. Its resident power may both aid and devour.

Yes, before humans were Fire, and it had always been both their curse and blessing.

– It's so *old,* he exclaimed.

She nodded knowingly.

They passed the major living room and finally arrived at the smaller one. It was exactly as she

remembered it. Some more candles were gone, as was to be expected.
– Do you know what? She said mischievously. – I can sense them, but I can also *smell* them.
– It's funny, he laughed. – I can, too, to the point of the… uncanny. Now, that's strange, isn't it? For us to use the word «uncanny» about anything anymore…
He cried out. It happened so suddenly that it startled them both.
– What is it? She was by his side in a flash. – What?
– I felt a… contraction… in my arm. He held around his right wrist. – It's gone now.
– How are your ears?
– That isn't funny, you know.
– Oh, I think it is. She danced away from him. – I think it definitely is…
The door to the stone castle inside was closed and locked. She unlocked it and unclosed it with an irritated nod. Less easy it wasn't. It didn't creak this time either. She teased and called to him as she led him inside. She was the snake, the temptress, who wanted every human to decide on its own what was right and wrong, good and evil.
– I can make the pain go away, you know. I can make any pain go away.
– I think you rather shouldn't, he said.
– What is happening to you will happen, sooner or later, with or without my contribution, she said wooden and testy.
He wanted to give her a very testy reply, when he stopped thunderstruck. There were tears running down her cheeks. His hand got wet immediately in a clumsy attempt at sweeping them away.
– I'm s-sorry, she sniffed. – I know I'm being unreasonable, but I've had some friends I've seen destroy themselves because they didn't want to be themselves.
Tears in the night were often not seen, only heard, as a sad sip in the soul. People created a shell around themselves. They gave everything to it to make it glimmer and strangled what shone inside.
– People show too little of their real emotions, he said with regret. – I'm glad you don't have that problem.
– You're so *sweet* that I want to devour you, she said, instantly smiling once more.
And he, instantly worried again, withdrew a bit.
– What about hatred? He wondered.
– That is, by its very nature a quiet emotion. She looked away. – One we're hiding and carrying year by year. It's growing for every new denial, growing in silence. And isn't that natural? Because hatred is the most powerful emotion there is, much more so than love. It can hold out through ages of silence, to suddenly emerge anew.
– Love… He said it as if it was a foreign word… – also endures death after death, life after life, even if it may be a bit more despairing.
She held the door open this time, didn't allow it to close, not until they ascended at least halfway up the stone staircase to the floor above. They didn't hear the door actually close, only saw the light below disappear. The temptress smiled some more.
– Don't worry, she whispered loud. – We're not giving in to the house, but to ourselves.
And she grabbed his hand.
Can't you feel my heart? How it's beating, beating with everything that is, everything we are?
They entered the great hall, where the mirror awaited them. Light just barely trickled through the cracks in the window shutters.
– Wouldn't it have been *great* if everything was *open* here? She stretched her arms to the side, including the entire room in her embrace.
And he felt the prickling all over his body. Her power, it was…
– Allow me to put it in more bombastic terms. He grabbed her hand, only slightly startled by the claws subconsciously tearing at him, at the skin. – In this place we shall take the first decisive steps away from hatred.
They embraced. He smiled in spite of the pain, but she didn't. She looked solemn at the wall behind him with a face he couldn't see.
And towards it, she thought. Thoughts she didn't share with him. Not the least towards it.
She licked the blood off his hand, healing it in an instant, brushing off the sadness he sensed in her,

as she rolled close to him with her indomitable energy.

Kiss was wet and hungry. Quiet as hatred desire had grown in her over time. As it started burning in her, it did so without delay in him. He felt a bit… weak, but he wanted her very much. Of course, he did. They dropped down on their knees, and she put him on his back.

– Look here, she said with the tongue between her lips. – What a boy…

His cock had grown long and broad and hard. He closed his eyes. She lowered her hips, descending on him. Delight spread like rings in the water.

Time lost all meaning.

Shutters fell from a window. He just saw it, didn't hear it. The thunder as it hit the floor was utterly silent. Space had lost all meaning. They conquered, saw and came, as they learned more about each other, about all places, a flood of knowledge, undeniable. About all places, but most of all about this place, about here (wherever that was). There was so much here, a mountaintop, a forest, beyond the horizon, not just the horizon itself.

But the mountaintop was so steep, so steep. He would fall, fall.

He rested on his back. Vision was muddy. He saw her stand before the mirror. She was so sweet and so diabolic.

– Power corrupts, he mumbled.

Lillith.

They stood at the top of a mountain (or was that on the roof) and beheld the world, a journey full of mountaintops, with valleys and horizons aplenty, as they exposed secrets and learned truths. There were ever-new mountaintops to climb. It was they, in a distant past or future, days of future past. They weren't Jill and Everett, but they were Lillith and Plat. She kissed away his tears and he understood her.

They stretched on the flat roof, sunbathing and happily satisfied, in a cocoon of warm air and pleasant drowsiness. The hot and cold wind didn't, couldn't reach them here, in the eye of the Storm. Here, they could prepare for the trials awaiting them. Only fools waited long before starting such preparations, but here, just now, there was peace, on this bridge over the raging river.

Chapter Ten: PYRAMID

Awakening

Sunrise. Colors like rust and blood

Jill sat on her naked ass in the dusty loft, her feet crossed in front of her. Focusing. Emptying all thoughts. Concentrating.

Leave the body, she told herself. Allow the mind to roam free.

The Witch opened her eyes. She didn't blink. They slid open and remained open. She sensed the carpet, the bed under her, the ceiling, the walls, and the floor surrounding her. Head turned to the side. Tamara lay crouched in the other bed. Jill swung the feet outside the bed and put them on the floor. She rose, stretching her body full length, enjoying every move. Eyes wandered casually through the room. The room itself had gained a bit of a personality by now, as they had decorated it with some personal stuff. Tam had the big teddy bear. Jill had put the mask from the carnival on the wall and a candle from the cabin where she and Everett had shared passion for the first time on the bookshelf. And just yesterday they had, she and Tam, procured a new poster.

They had put it up on the door, a large, dominating and yet full of shadow poster of the rock group Mystic. A haunting image of Magick actualized. One's eyes were pulled towards it, inside it. It wasn't an ordinary poster with many and strong colors. There was indeed something… haunting (yes, that was the word) about it. She couldn't really tell whether it was a drawing or a photograph. Whatever, the artist… responsible had to be… Jill was absolutely wildly fascinated of what she saw in it. She enjoyed the group's music, but it merely mirrored their lives. Reality surpassed any fantasy. The art mirrored reality. Jill was beyond any degree fascinated by theirs.

The members were all stated members of the world encompassing radical organization Phoenix Green Earth. A name making her innards move when she had heard it mentioned several years earlier in connection with them for the first time. She had been more than familiar with the legend of Phoenix for as long as she could remember.

There was no sunrise to see through this window. But it didn't keep Jill from seeing it… as clearly as if she was standing on the opposite side of the building. She casually dragged a single t-shirt on before opening the door to the hallway and then to the room on the other side. Without looking to any of the sides she walked to the other room. She made certain that the two girls slept soundly in their beds, without having any qualms about it. She didn't want to be disturbed. There was the window. She walked closer to it. There was the sunrise, exactly the way she had seen it.

The sense of dislocation didn't leave her, though. That rather pleased her. She had for years now carried with her similar notions, unrealized proof of being different.

Did she truly leave her body, was that what happened when she saw something she couldn't possibly observe with her eyes? Or did she quite simply… move through time? Or could she do both? The thoughts brought a thrill to the fore of her consciousness.

She had never done it consciously, never even attempted what she had seen as an impossibility. Feet returned her to the hallway. Excitement and undeniable desire, Hunger kept her moving. Eyes stopped by the shadowy stairway leading to the attic. Without really thinking about it she followed the irresistible pull of something within. There was privacy there in the shadow. She would be able to do… whatever she wanted to do, without risk of being interrupted.

Nude feet stepped quietly on each step. Having reached the door at the top, the only path leading further on, she looked back a final time, as if she would never return. There was no one there. She walked through the door, closed it and walked further up. The staircase took on an even more spiral form. She reached another door. It was locked. She sniffed in contempt. Locked doors represented no hindrance for her anymore. A hand against the lock, a click, and she could effortlessly open the heavy steel door. She hurried through it, and closed and locked it behind her.

One single window attempted to illuminate the entire one-room attic. The window, covered in dust and cobwebs only let through dirty light. Everything had been cleaned out here. There was no furniture, nothing, from wall to wall. One single electric light hung from the ceiling. There was no advance warning. Suddenly wisps of smoke and air seemed to attack her out of nothing. She waved it all away in bursts of rage and not to be denied panic. And it did evaporate, returning from the nothing from where it had seemingly originated. She had prevailed, but it had all left her with a terrible nausea and she threw up bubbling, acid stomach contents. She wanted to run away as fast and hard as she possibly could, but she caught herself in time. There was a moment when she could hardly stand on her feet, but she recovered, gathered her strength, and sensed it well up in her once more. Eyes glared in triumph. With a look she knew would have more than worried Everett, she dried vomit from her lips and lower face.

He doesn't know himself, she thought. But I do. I will.

This place fit her needs. There had been a… gate here, and even if she had destroyed it, the borders between worlds stayed weakened.

Knowledge came to her, thoughts from ancient human life, like life fighting to reach the water surface, eager to breathe.

She wanted to leave, her instincts told her to, but she made a fist and allowed her anger to have free roam. So much remaining energy here and she sucked it up. Bloated with it all she sat straight down in her own vomit. There was nothing left here that could harm her… now.

The place had what she'd been looking for.

She crossed her legs and pulled them to her. Power. There was Power here for those who could make use of it. She didn't believe the added juice was needed in order for her to leave the body. She could probably have done so at any quiet or silent place. But this happened to be perfectly… perfect. She licked her lips as she drew a circle in the dust around her. Not the strongest of protections, but she wanted to rely on her own power anyway. The barriers of time and space were weakened here. She didn't want a long trip. Just long enough, sufficient enough to know what it was like.

Concentration - realization wasn't imminent. She remembered sitting for hours attempting something like this, without success. So much had changed now.

The Witch opened her eyes. Everything looked the same, or almost like before. She thought she had double vision for a moment there. But no, she couldn't be positive. Damn. Concentrate. This isn't like meditation. Meditation allows, virtually encourages thoughts. Here you must empty your mind, remove all conscious thought. Focus your energy. The thought is free. The thought is free. The thought is…

There had been a nightmare, a specific one, haunting her from the age of twelve.

On the night following her twelfth birthday she had had the first nightmare about the fire, a nightmare haunting her often after that. Her parents had sent her to a shrink, in vain. As time went by she had learned to hide her inner thoughts from them and they didn't bother her anymore.

Memories.

Her cat had been hit by a car, and she knew who had done it. A man in the neighborhood. He had driven off the road a few weeks later and hardly survived. He had to stay in the hospital for months and his recovery had been hard and painful. This was something she definitively hadn't mentioned to her parents.

Thoughts blinked out.

Her mirror image: She had played with it when she was little.

One last thought before oblivion: The heavy realization that this, this room had been a trap, a magick trap, specially designed for witches.

Awakening.

As if she turned lighter. Arms and feet seemed so far down. One moment she seemed to have double vision. Then she was Free. Some call it Psyche, others call it soul, or aura or astral form or a thousand other names. One thing was certain: It wasn't matter what rose from Jill Stafford's body

She stared down at herself. She seemed so small, so vulnerable. The body's blank look stared into the nothingness. She experimented by stretching herself and the body remained in position, as it would stay until she returned to it. Her attention turned to the door. It seemed natural to her to use the door, so she did, though without bothering to open it. She slipped just straight through as the spirit she was. Thoughts kept rushing in, from what had been the edge of consciousness, now being the center. Everything at once was the center. She remembered so much, details, so much, memories flooded back in. Too much! With an effort she managed to push it into the back of her head (her attention), as she had to. There was both fear and joy there, but she had in no way the experience necessary to deal with it yet.

Floating before the mirror. She discovered she could be both visible and invisible. By wishing it, concentrating extra hard she could look exactly as she normally did, with colors and everything. She floated out in the hall, down the hall. The doors opened as she passed them. It was funny. She laughed. It sounded like an echo from a seemingly infinite ravine. She passed Stacy's room, stopped, floated back and decided on a tour inside. She floated just under the ceiling above the bed. This time Stacy didn't notice anything, but continued sleeping soundly.

Jill resisted the temptation to attempt anything more and moved on.

People had begun awakening and rising from their beds. The level of activity increased steadily. The spirit was assaulted by honest thoughts and not quite as honest speech. It irritated her. Quite a few observed the phenomenon with doors opening by themselves, until she agreed with herself to stop it. There were some claims later (in closed company) that there had been laughter.

Pull yourself together, girl, there will be more than enough time for play later.

Or perhaps not.

Outside she welcomed the rising sun with open arms. There was no sense of movement in the wind or anything else physically, like heat, but it felt good anyway.

She could look directly at the sun, and it was like she saw it and everything else for the first time. Wind blew straight through her, but she could effortlessly decide its path. It moved in a half-circle around Frazer Hill, and she decided to follow it on its path.

Momentary darkness, immeasurable, and she discovered herself high above the American inland. The name Wyoming came to her easily, without her having to search for it in her mind. Below her humans were chopping down trees wholesale. Men with ever more efficient tools and machines left huge open wounds in the landscape. One such wound, on a long, steep slope was already in motion as she watched. This was what had attracted her to this place, this disaster.

It started almost gentle, with just a few pieces of mud and small stones, but as she watched it grew to a full-blown landslide. Loggers and others ran desperately for their lives, completely out of luck, out of chances. Horrified and fascinated simultaneously Jill couldn't tear her eyes away from the horrible happening below. She could do little or nothing about it. Most of it had already been done. Big machines had torn the trees from their sockets over a vast area. And then it had been raining for weeks. There was nothing left binding the soil, making it stay in place, making the erosion and the slide other than inevitable.

Initially she had no intention of involving herself. That changed when she discovered a little boy running, while screaming himself hoarse. Perhaps he knew he had no chance whatsoever. During one fraction of a second, she wondered if this was or should be any concern of hers. Hadn't they brought this on themselves? Didn't they deserve whatever fate their own stupidity and chains of coincidences had brought on them?

She sighed. Who did she attempt to fool… Thought and action one she suddenly found herself down before the raging fall of landmass. She could actually sense the air pressure in front of the slide, a hungry beast, swallowing everything in its path. She grabbed the boy, a split second before it would have taken him, and lifted him up, as high she could come. She succeeded and howled in triumph, as she hurried away with the tiny body in her lap, as the landmasses raged on below them. The boy suddenly stopped screaming and an expression of ultimate surprise quickly turned to wonder, transforming the dirty face, as he floated towards the crowd of people a safe distance off. She wondered whether or not she should reveal herself. If she didn't, they would certainly be content with a simpler (harder) explanation. What the heck, people needed a good shake up now and then (a lot more often really). Besides she wouldn't really be revealing anything.

Arms were raised, fingers pointed. She lowered the boy into the mother's arms. The father died at that exact moment, buried under tons of water, dirt and rock. The mother and the others were obviously at a loss to explain what had just transpired. Fear and joy warred within. The boy had virtually floated into their care, saved from certain death.

– The air pressure, the woman expressed uncertain. – It must have been the air pressure from the slide that miraculously saved him.

Mumbling agreement and nodding accompanied her words. Nobody mentioned that the pressure had hardly been noticed where they stood. Naturally it was more powerful closer to the slide...

– Nature can be gentle, a man said.

– This... It demanded a certain strain for Jill to be able to speak. But when she made another effort, it went like clockwork... and the voice... the voice was that of the female creature from Fire Lake. People gasped. – This is a tragedy in more ways than one, especially since it could have been easily avoided.

The frozen and frightened humans first heard only a voice from the empty air. It slowly took a shape, a form they could relate to. Eventually they could observe the entire, full-bodied woman float in the air above them. Jill could well imagine how she looked to them, shimmering, ethereal, powerful and divine. Many of them wished to and did attempt to run away, but she didn't allow that. A dramatic wave of a hand and they were frozen in place by the mighty Goddess. She knew she could make them worship her, it would be so easy, and the thought itself was infinitely seductive and tempting. Power corrupts. She repeated it in her head like a mantra.

– You're exploiting Nature, destroying it and thereby yourself. Behold your harvest.

– I know what you're gonna say. I know your thoughts as if they were my own. She descended in their midst, concentrated and grabbed a huge, powerful built man around the jaw. – You're driven hard by the foreman. He's easy to blame... especially since he's buried under tons of soil. You may blame the greedy administrator. That makes more sense. It isn't the first time he has forced you to do life-threatening work. But what you should remember from this moment on, that you've failed to, in the past, is that each and every human is responsible for his own actions, her own life. You're Human Beings, not dumb inarticulate sheep, puppets on strings. Nothing says you're gonna Obey. Nobody can force you. You can only fool yourself into believing they can.

The man was injured. Blood flowed freely from his right arm. She held him in her grip, pushing him down on his knees. She started glowing as his shoulder started twitching. They cried out in fear, more than one was screaming. But they couldn't move. They couldn't move their feet.

He lifted his arms in wonder. She let him go. He didn't bleed anymore. Only a pale memory remained of the wound. He touched the slightly inflamed skin and looked up at her with wide-open eyes. She knew he wasn't strong enough to stand up. Neither he nor anyone else knew that even if she had healed him, she had taken more from him than what she had given. She let go of them all and virtually everyone approached her to touch her. It was like touching air, but not for her. She bathed in their energies, as she took from everyone close to her, strengthening herself.

– You, like most others, are asleep, «living» your «life» in a stupor, she said enraged, voice thick with disgust. – The power hungry have, long ago taken control over the world, over the human part of the world, and kept it. To keep the power is their only aim, their only thought. Everything rocking their position is seen as dangerous. They're opposing all changes that could weaken them and their hold on the world. And they don't care who is pushed off the cliff with them, in their insane venture. And as good sheep, you keep accepting every indignity, every injustice with a bowed head. And you have the audacity to blame others for your misfortune? And you claim to be Human Beings? Are you a pale, broken figure stumbling into the twilight?

– Who are you? One burst out. – What are you?

– I'm Lillith. Suddenly the voice had changed, turned almost normal. – I'm Wrath, I'm the returned Power. Fear me.

Silence. They remained frozen like ragged, wet dolls.

Promising, the witch thought.

– She's a creature of SATAN, a man in the back cried hoarsely. His voice was thick with feat and hatred. – Who knows? She might just as well have caused the slide.

– She saved me. The boy spoke up in silent rage. – And there's no need for her to have shown herself at all. It's to our favor that she did, right?

More silence, heavy and charged.

– My great grandmother told me about people like you, an old woman cackled. – She called you Djinn, the magick people. Her take on it was that you were special people, but with all the weaknesses of the rest of us.

– Your great grandmother was wise, Jill said.

The boy looked at her admiringly.

You're a smart kid. He froze, but didn't really look too surprised. He understood that no one else had heard what he had just heard. But more than a score naïve, though. When you've learned about life, learned a lot, come and seek me out. I won't be hard to find.

– We would welcome change, a man said carefully, – but people who have spoken up publicly before have been fired, the most eager blacklisted.

– You think it's your lives here I'm talking about? Her voice, as good as normal now dripped of venom. – The Earth is about to become one giant garbage heap and you can't see beyond your petty small-time problems?

– What shall we do then?

– I don't want you to go off and kill your superiors, she said teasingly, provocative. – That would only get you in immediate serious trouble and accomplish nothing… I know what you think. You think I'm one of those damn radicals and you're quite correct in that assumption… Except that I'm far more radical than you to this moment have been able to imagine.

She kept looking at them with her direct, penetrating stare.

– I'll take care of Richardson and the pyramid above him, one step at the time. The rest is up to you. Life isn't easy.

They didn't quite get that about the pyramid, but they accepted it, as they accepted her, as they would accept a storm.

– You're so young, an older man spoke up. – How can you be so hard and unfeeling?

Perhaps because I have to. She had once more levitated high above the ground, high above them, floating further down the valley, turning invisible once again. This time everybody heard her voice inside their head. The world and their view on it would never be as it had been. They had witnessed water turn to wine. Now they could close their eyes and still see. They could no longer avoid it. And the fear, something ephemeral until this morning turned tangible and compelling.

Nathan Richardson was still sleeping. The Witch tore off the blanket covering him, shook him out of his rather pleasant morning slumber.

– What the hell…

He jumped out of bed, amazingly fast and versatile for someone so fat. The witch pushed him tight to the wall and held his shoulders in a painful grip. He stared at the Fury, at the living nightmare manifesting in front of him.

– Listen up, lackey, she snarled. – You're gonna change. You will stop taking cuts of the workers already lousy salaries. From now you'll start treating them as human beings.

She dropped him, suddenly and painfully. He raced to the closet and pulled out a giant shotgun. He fired. The only result was a giant hole in the wall behind her. He fired again. Another hole. She tore the shotgun from his grasp, turned him around and pushed the barrel deep into his cheek. He wanted to run, then, run until he couldn't breathe anymore, wanted it so bad that there was hardly room for anything else anywhere inside him. But he was held in place by an invisible force. He peed on himself and made a big mess on the floor. And there was no way he could tell whether or not his desire to cry followed from the humiliation or because he was scared shitless.

– I could've killed you. It would've been so simple. But if you continue as you've been doing, it will be a true pleasure to do far worse things with you. You're a creep, Nat. Your only consolation is that there is a lot of room for improvement. A lot!

– YES, WHATEVER YOU WANT, WHOEVER YOU ARE

– You know what I want, Nat. She put the shotgun back in the closet. – It will be hard on you, this; to turn your back on 50 years of thoughtless egoism and backstabbing and scratching of backs. But it is, as they say, never too late to become what you could have been. Who knows, perhaps you'll even enjoy it?

She turned and floated towards the wall.

– Wait, he shouted and shrank as eyes emerged at the back of her head.

– Don't be worried of reprisals from your former masters. I'll deal with them. They'll be quite busy and won't think about bothering you.

– I can believe that. He sat down on the bed. – I have to admit it. You've managed to give me a bigger shock than anyone I've ever encountered. My sincere compliments. I've never believed in such mumbo-jumbo stuff like telekinesis and psychic energy. You've convinced me. Something that proves I've made major mistakes during the course of my life. I see before me enormous possibilities for profit and power…

– Fear me, Nathan. Then she was gone.

– I believe you, she heard his distant voice. – One of my advantages has always been the ability to interpret others' behavior, to easily see if someone is telling the truth. You mean every word.

The echoes of his words haunted her, above the dry cornfields of the Midwest, through flashes of cornfields all over the world. The desert was spreading all over the planet, gaining foothold in previously lush and fertile areas. The night still held dominion over California. In just another flash she had appeared above the desert in the southern parts of the state. She could virtually see it growing. The widely infamous Death Valley continually extended its influence to new areas. This clear fact didn't stop the wholesale forest clear-cut in the immediate vicinity. It would not re-grow. Wind came and swept away the remaining fertile soil, one of many actions highlighting human unreason.

She observed the same name on the machines here as in Wyoming and other places, Eternity Inc, another subsidiary of Garrett Industries. Brian Garrett, the man she had taken this little detour to meet.

Richardson had met him. The memory had been crystal clear in his mind. He had been… scared. Therefore, Jill had attacked him harder, more ferocious than she had planned, really let go. She was still not certain whether he was more afraid of her than of Garret.

The Golden Gate Bridge appeared below. She moved further up the San Francisco Bay (on her broomstick, he he). The city awaited her below. She was able to look at the world with a wonderful and terrible clarity. So much bad, so much great. The cities… the cities… are Death. Life covered with death, a garbage heap with just a few remaining jewels. Life today was jewels covered in garbage.

My awareness serves me well, so well.

And the bitter aftertaste was there, spoiling the fresh drink.

The Sun had yet not caught up with her. Here, this far west, the night still held back the day. She «landed» in the middle of a busy shopping street. The stores had already opened, or they had been open all night. The big city was more than a bit overwhelming to a simple country girl…

Suddenly in a very playful mood she flew fast and furry in and out of stores procuring a simple poncho and a pair of shoes. She landed in a dark alley and made herself turn visible. It took some doing, but she managed to create a telekinetic field around her astral form, mimicking a body. She let the poncho slip down on her, landing on her shoulders, making only the «head» stick up, through the small hole in the middle of what was essentially a square blanket, a wide one, reaching down to her thighs. The shoes she used to walk natural, or as close to natural as possible. Before she left the alley, she made sure her hair was blond and her features changed to someone unrecognizable, without, within. She didn't really know why, but it was certainly a prudent move.

It felt right. No, more than that. Like a necessity.

The streets leading down to the harbor and Oakland Bridge were already crowded with people and life. The heat was even more pronounced here than in New England, the famous chilly coastal fog completely absent. Most people dressed in modest and light clothes. She experienced the heat through the people she passed on her way. After fighting it for some time, she let go of a giggle. It was kind of funny that a ghost walked in their midst, and no one noticed. She had a great time as she saw places she had only seen in photographs and in movies. She had heard it be claimed that San Francisco could be counted among the most beautiful and alive cities on Earth. She wanted to return once, as flesh and blood, to confirm it in person.

She hailed a cab, the first one showing up. It was empty of passengers, but not available. She didn't have time to wait. Irritation almost exploded. Smiling she recognized the fact that her temperament always had been over the top.

– The Eternity-building, she told the driver. Seats seemed pleasant enough and she leaned back. To her it was evident that he knew the place very well and not merely knew of it, but everybody would have realized this on the merit of his reaction, and the conviction in his voice.

– You're one of them, ain't ya?

She gave no reply or any indication that she had heard him. He expected to be ignored.

He drove recklessly, as if life itself was at stake (and perhaps it was), but she had seen other drivers speed up even more than this. He talked endlessly and she let him. The drive lasted no more than two minutes, tops, before reaching what indeed seemed like the end-station. Shadows in the streets and in the air grew and turned colder. A large, major and modern office-building came into view, reaching for the heavens. She wanted to shrink in its shadow… or grow high above its head.

–… bet on it. I've had a lot of you in my cab. I don't know what it is with you guys, but there's something. Something in my innards tells me… Tell me, I don't know if I recognize you. Are you new?

– I've been away a long time, Lillith said. – I'm on my way home.

The music of the night started playing for her. She heard it, but more so she sensed it beyond any sense. It told her what to do. A black cat howled outside. A cheerful grin spread throughout her being. She dug her claws even deeper into the man in the front seat.

– Drive by. Don't stop.

His face turned into a stiff mask. He drove two blocks beyond the entrance and parked outside two ramshackle houses.

– Good. You never did this trip. You've never seen me. You fell asleep. The meter doesn't work.

Sparks erupted from the meter and the entire taxi turned dark.

– Fell asleep… no trip, nobody… doesn't w-work.

– Sleep, she commanded, and he did.

She allowed the body to lose its coherence once more. The Poncho and the shoes remained in the car as she floated out of it. She checked on the sleeping man one more time. This had probably happened to him before. He would be confused when he awakened (she wasn't sufficiently skilled in this yet). He would probable adhere that to the place, not far from the Garret building. He would fill in the blanks on his own, at least the major parts. The human brain was truly something remarkable.

The cat sat at the top of a garbage can. She scratched him behind the ears, and he was purring energetically. It didn't surprise her that he had noticed her before she touched him. Perhaps cats were a domestic animal, but they had yet to lose their touch with the wild, the deeper levels of existence.

The building seemed quite ordinary from the inside. Offices, offices and more offices. The entrance hall was an exhibition window, of course. And there were some meeting halls, for gatherings and parties and businesspeople. Jill didn't have much knowledge of the business world and the ongoing dealings there, but everything seemed just a bit unusual. In a way the space was ruthlessly used, with many and small offices (the way of the future), but still, the place didn't seem to have all the necessities and characteristics of a modern corporate building. One example was that nothing was rented to outsiders, smaller companies and/or firms. Jill knew it was very unusual in buildings of this size and the conclusion was clear: They didn't want anyone looking in. Jill moved ever more cautiously in her further search. If things were like she suspected quite strongly by now, that Garrett was a mighty witch, she had every reason to proceed carefully.

The people here were as much a part of the façade as the concrete itself. Garret had a huge and luxurious office on the premises, but he hardly used it. He made all his dealings from his villa up in the mountains. There was a secretary, a woman, guarding the office. Jill got the most of her information from her. She had to be even more cautious now, since Garret would realize it immediately if the woman's mind had been tampered with.

She hurried on. There was a time limit to how long she could stay outside her body. She had no idea how long that was. She didn't notice anything yet, a warning of sorts, and she thought it was supposed to be something like that… but she didn't know.

Before her was the mountains and the plateau where she would find the property with its chateau and many adjacent houses. The woman had traveled up here countless times and had clear memories about the way. Jill enjoyed the fabulous view, enjoyed every aspect of her inborn talents. Everything she had experienced since she had met Laurie in the small, closed in room in London seemed like a dream, a true dream. She harbored no fear about her awakening one morning in Wales, discovering that it had all been a hopeless fantasy. She would always be grateful to Laurie, who, whatever the reason had brought her here.

Here.

The California Valley disappeared behind her. The extensive open area between the mountains and the villa almost blinded her enhanced senses. The property was so enormous, stretched so far, that it seemed impossible not to discover it.

A tall concrete wall encircled it, one with three holes, three gates. There were no visible guards or visible sentries of any kind. There was no need for such, since there surely were quite a number of hellhounds with steaming maws inside. A cold overwhelmed Jill. She reflected a bit over this, how real it felt, almost as if she walked around within a solid, material body…

And then she reflected no more.

Her senses howled

danger GET AWAY D A N G E R

and it wasn't words at all, but an instinct older than any civilization. What is asleep, what rarely or never awakens in present day humans.

Heart hammered in her chest. Wherever else came the thundering, hammering sound from? A wall, a field, a dome-like force-field surrounded the property and she was convinced that it didn't originate with any technology, but the mind-power of people, witches inside. It sucked energy like a sponge, hers, too. She went into shock. Cold and heat shot through her. Panic petrified her, but it also made the energy boil within her. She had to get away from here

get away.

COLD

Someone would come, come to get her. She had definitely outstayed her welcome in this place. Shit, what a lousy attempt at gallows humor. The threat was real, realreal. Panic exploded in her.

GET AWAY NOW

White light, daylight. A crowd, more than a crowd. She blinked without eyes. This place, the scene below, below tall trees. She recognized it, recognized what happened, what had happened. This was the Mall, Washington DC, United States of America, in summer, Fourth of July 1992. It happened during the celebration of the 500-year anniversary of Columbus' «discovery» of the American continent. The Indians, the American natives, protested against it all, the celebration and its origin. They and supporters had arrived from south, west and north, from all over the Americas. Two huge crowds, masses, one in favor, the other not stood against each other on Pennsylvania Avenue. It was never pretty when nationalism, the modern, distorted version of the old tribal sense of belonging was challenged.

The vision faded and she suddenly found herself high up in the air, higher then when she had crossed the Atlantic Ocean in an airplane. She looked up. Space was really black, eternal darkness, between the too many to be counted bright points. She looked down at the Earth, blue and beautiful. Directly beneath her feet, it seemed was the Gulf of Mexico. A giant storm gathered strength down there, growing in strength and size as it moved north.

She had actually seen satellite photos of «Hugo», «Andrew» and «Katrina» and other giant storms devastating the southeastern United States the last 50 years… and this was nothing like them.

It was bigger by far.

Darkness. Something was wrong. The darkness lasted so long, long. Cold. Was this the eternal night? She feared that she had stayed outside her body too long, that she was about to turn into a ghost, a real one, a permanent one. The darkness surrounded her shining astral body, smothered it, strangled it, took it in, swallowed it forever…

LIGHT. Heart hammered in her chest. In her chest. She gasped and gasped wildly, drawing air in heavy breaths. Head rested against the chest. Saliva flowed from her jaw. Attic was so bright. How could she ever have imagined that it was dark here? In a circle on the floor around her and on her had dropped a crowd of dead insects. Sweat made them stick to the body. She fought to stand up, in vain. She was exhausted, more tired than she could ever remember being.

A strong hand was held out in aid, Stacy's hand.

– You should be very happy that it's I. The power of your hunger would have made empty husks of anyone else.

Jill attempted to strengthen herself on Stacy. It had no effect. She managed to stand up on weak, shaky legs.

– Brian Garret, she gasped. – He… he is…

– I know of him, Stacy acknowledged.

– What did you see in the park, in the Boston Common, in his acolyte? Tell me!

Shaking hands attempted to grab the other, in vain.

– I saw nothing, Stacy said with a distant look in her eyes. – There was a wall there, nothing but a wall of normalcy. He was… laughing at me.

And in the distance, deep within her eyes there was fear.

Jill nodded, fighting to stay on her shaking feet.

– We must prepare… strengthen us…

– We shall, Stacy insisted. – Trust me. We shall!

And then she bathed Jill in her energies and Jill could hardly move while the strength of a thousand suns once more swelled within her.

– Thank you, Jill gasped, infinitely grateful.

– Oh, it was so little. Stacy made a very deliberate shrug.

Jill wanted to lean on the other girl's shoulder, but discovered that it wasn't necessary anymore. She had Changed, everything was different, all her senses more astute than she could even comprehend right now. She realized that her trip had… had shattered the veil, whatever had blocked her perception. The Spirit Quest had increased her abilities. This had brought her one more step further even beyond that. And there was more, more, more… to come.

– We shall, she said.

And Stacy smiled.

And there were shadows on the window, dark wings making their presence known. As the two girls made their way down from the attic, three or four had made their way inside, resting in shadowy spots in the hall. The ravens would always be there.

Jill realized that she hadn't really been gone that long. Most of the students were still asleep. Her clothing or rather lack thereof caused a few stares and insults. She could easily have kept them from seeing her, but she didn't bother. It was just a short way to her room anyway. Just as she opened the door (using her hand), the t-shirt quite literally fell apart. Its remains loosened from her body and fell to the floor. It had been new such a short while ago («real» time). Now there were merely rags left.

Tamara looked up from the book she was reading, greeting them both with a smile.

The wind is blowing from the open window, blowing extra hard for a moment, making the pages of the Book of Shadows turn rapidly and chillingly.

Reality is shifting. Reality is shifting constantly, that's the way of the Path; it's never the same.

The Witch, having gone through trials stands before the mirror, and it is as if she sees herself for the first time.

– This is unbelievable, she says. – I must have lost 5 kilos.

– Guys, the big elf says.

– You must have lost almost ten pounds, Stacy says.

– Look at this, Tamara says, and shows them the book.

This is the account of a Witch…

First of all: Everything can be read in these pages, the end as well as the beginning.

Eternity beckons, from Eternity we came and we're on our way back.

I'm not really writing in this book, as much as experiencing what I'm writing.

From eternity we came, we came from eternity, from the infinite Void we come, filling the Void.

They skip pages to quickly reach the end, but the end is far, far away.

Vision is skewed, slightly off center. They look at themselves from behind.

And there are many pages, telling itself. Lillith stands in the small room reading her own mind, just a few of many possible selections, turning the pages of the Book of Shadows.

She looks up, more than startled, more than shocked.

– This is a chill, she says aloud. – I've never really understood that phrase until this moment. The cold trickle down my spine is a raging river, the River Styx, gathering strength, touching its bridges.

And her words are a choir of multitudes, echoing through the Void.

Tamara looked at the two other girls, as they were finishing their reading, as they all were looking at the pages of the book, putting itself to rest for the moment, as the last few words appeared on the old paper.

– This is your writing, Tamara said. – … Right?

– It is, Jill said, getting dizzy. – But I don't understand it, how can I?

Stacy looked at the book, smiling.

– But I do. It's easy. We're writing our own fate.

– Yes, Jill said. – We are.

She looked in the mirror again, at her naked body. It didn't bother her anymore. So that was how it was or could be. After a while at least, she had started using the energy of the body and as she understood it, it had happened fast and violently. Just a bit longer and she would have disappeared into nothing, to forever roam the world as a ghost.

And fear made her shake and throb.

The muscles clearly showed now, her newly developed muscles. She wasn't skinny, as most people would've been, but the last of the excess fat (too much chocolate) she had carried for years had virtually disappeared (from one moment to the next). Her breasts were as large as ever, her hips and thighs very distinctive and generous, but the skin was now tight and smooth.

– I kinda like it, she said with a near whisper, – but this is one treatment I won't recommend to anyone.

Laughter. They all laughed in a hopeless attempt to normalize what couldn't be normalized. They were not that much different from other people.

– It wasn't necessary, anyway, she said with regret. – I feel… cheated somehow.

– Some people are never satisfied, Tamara grinned.

– You're right, Jill replied. – They're not.

– Yes, Stacy said. – You will be okay.

– Yes, I am, she said.

She took a long, prolonged shower, fuck the regulations. The bug acid, all over her body burned, making it less of the pleasure than it otherwise would've been, but afterwards she felt rested, sated. She realized that she didn't start sweating immediately after the shower, anymore. Yet another effect of having moved up another level, grown in Power and Stature.

– All my clothes are too big. What the hell, I can always go naked.

– You can have some of mine. My parents shipped two suitcases the same day they shipped me.

– You will do that, for me?

– Why not? Another deliberate shrug. – As I said, I'm not exactly lacking in the clothes department.

For her to fetch and bring the clothes and for Jill to try them on was a fast and satisfying exercise. All three had fun with it, Tamara almost most of all. For Jill to find herself in the new clothes felt strangely tedious.

She lingered, before leaving the room, even more than she used to. The school day was about to begin. First the very nutritious breakfast, then a long day of trite and boring «learning». She even dreaded the upcoming physical exercise she had come to revel in, on some level, because of the fixed routine when doing it directed by the teachers. The energy, the joy surging through her, helped a bit, but not as much as it should. Damn it! Regimentation, conformity was a powerful tool. It could crush even the strongest spirit.

– Come now, sister, Stacy called from the hall. – Idle students don't get to go anywhere.

– Coming…

She stood before the mirror again, looking at the stranger there. It wasn't just the clothes and certainly not the face. The skin had darkened visibly, and the cheeks were somewhat lesser in terms of puppy fat, but it was the same body. The change was something beyond appearances. The clothes did the rest. She looked at a confident and elegant young Lady.

The three of them stopped a bit on the long stretch to the classrooms, where pictures of cute and smiling girls decorated the red brick wall. She noticed immediately (as she did every time) the small piece of melted chocolate on her cheek.

Looking at the picture of the entire class, taken the day of the arrival, there wasn't really anything obvious, nothing on the surface, separating the witches from the rest. They all looked normal enough, like normal well-adapted, unremarkable kids.

– What a bunch of yahoos, Tamara snarled grinning.

The other witches greeted them when they entered the classroom. Loeh looked a bit funny at first. Jill, first of the three in the line to receive hugs and kisses was the center of close scrutiny, even if there was nothing overt about it. All of them had learned discretion recently.

– Hell on wheels, Miss Potter, exclaimed, – can we start soon, please? Do you do this every time you meet again after a night away from each other?

Jill's calm wasn't shaken the slightest. She said lightly:

– We're taught to touch and caress each other. It's important for humans to touch and be touched, as it is encouraging harmony and its absence is one proponent for disharmony.

– I want to be initiated, a boy cried.

It took some doing for the teacher to make the ruckus die down. The class she had set out to start in time got profusely delayed, and her foul mood didn't exactly improve.

Wounded pride and all that, Jill thought and sent to all her co-conspirators. And the rich content of her thoughts went with it. Speech was a barrier.

There were gasps and loud laughter and hands pressed to the mouth to keep it from opening.

– New threads? Loeh whispered quite loud from the other desk.

– Stacy was nice enough to let me borrow them.

The teacher brought the point of her prod several times in contact with the blackboard.

– Now let's begin. Jill, can you come up here and answer questions from page 36 to 56?

– No, I can't do that, the girl said calmly, – I haven't done any homework today.

The room turned silent. Several interested parties turned their eyes on her.

The teacher brought her hands together in front of her face. She looked very pleased.

– So little Miss Stafford has scoffed her duty, has she?

Something snapped inside, a lock, a barrier, and the girl felt freedom. She longed to use her powers, but she wanted to do what she was about to do even more without using them.

– You see, Miss… Potter, what I did in Reality during the weekend, Jill said, in the same, patronizing tone as the teacher, – was so much more interesting than whatever goes on in this bad dream. And we all know what happens after we awaken from a dream, don't we?

Jill waited a bit before delivering the finishing touch.

– You forget them.

That shut the «teacher» up. She stumbled in words and hesitated during the remaining of the class.

And Jill had really done very little. She wanted to do so much more.

There was a flapping of wings, scratching noises from outside the classroom. Four ravens held court on the cornice, just outside the window. She didn't need to see them or hear them, to know they were there. And it was a tradeoff. She could always trust them to read her mood, her agitation.

Miss Potter looked at the ravens. She looked at Jill, then back towards the ravens and at Jill again. Jill returned her stare with a very smug expression. The ravens flapped their wings. One of them screeched. The sound cut through everyone present. Jill sensed the warm, pleasant breeze inside and crouched pleasantly in her seat.

She couldn't get rid of her agitation. Not during the remains of the day at school, not during the physical exercise class or in the streets of Oldtown afterwards.

The exercise was hard today. She had less bodyweight to move, but was clearly exhausted even before she began. She had healed. Skin had pulled back tight over loose leftover skin from… from her ordeal, but she realized she hadn't really recovered yet. Death had touched her.

The coach had a comforting word or two to offer.
– I've never seen such remarkable progress as you've had since your arrival, the older woman told her while touching her shoulder. – You were obviously highly motivated and that always helps. But progress always comes in a touch and go pattern. After weeks of seemingly racing, you may imagine you're standing still. But you're not, you know. Your body is just catching up, adapting to its new reality.
– I did use to walk mountain trips at home, Jill offered. – That may have given me some foundation. It wasn't sufficient to take care of the chocolate intake, though.
She looked at the teacher, managing to fake a grateful smile.
– Just go easy on the diet, okay. You'll need more food now, not less, a lot more. I've seen people increase their intake four- or five-times during periods of hard exercise. And… I've also seen both girls and boys stop eating altogether.
Jill got a new respect for the coach. Anorexia and Bulimia wasn't stuff generally talked about. It had been and was too connected with social prejudice for that to happen.
– Don't worry, the girl sniffed. – I plan to eat a lot of all the free food the school has to offer. I intend to start working on my shoulders/upper arms next. For that I need a lot of protein and such.
She showered again, still jittery and worse. She could imagine during fits of neurotic thoughts that the bugs had penetrated her skin somehow.
After rubbing herself with the towel, rubbing herself a lot, far away from her new clothes (she didn't want them to get wet), She took them in her hands, touching, feeling the fabric. Stacy had grown up with this. It didn't occur to her how special it could be.
– Great stuff, a girl said, both envious and nice.
– Yeah, Jill offered. – Stacy helped me out in a rut. She has two suitcases of it.
It did occur to Jill how vulnerable a young girl she was, after all, how vulnerable they all were. If someone wanted to hit her where it hurt right now, they could just do damage, any minor damage to the clothes, and she would fold, break like any dry twig.
– You know, exercise can be good for you, but you should always remember to buy new clothes while you're at it.
Jill looked at her, inside her, but there was no malice there.
They were all looking at her with new eyes, some with respect, and others with malice.
– With new clothes and a hot new body, you kinda look a bit like her, another girl cried from the opposite side of the room, not friendly. – You even have the same scar on your hippo.
Jill touched the scar on her left hip instinctively. The hens of the local henhouse had mentioned the ugly scar before, but it been incidental then, when there had been a substantial number of other «faults» to point out.
– Hers is on the other side, she said preoccupied.
– But don't you think that's one hell of a coincidence?
Jill looked at her with the most «evil eye» she could muster.
– Not particularly, no. «Coincidences» like that are as common as grass.
The crafty girl paled, at least inside. Jill could've done more. She wanted to.
The streets of Oldtown were hot, dusty as ever, but the wind wasn't hard enough to damage the clothes in the short term.
Laughter escaped through lips pressed tight together, a harsh, bitter sound. Even the Queen of the World had to «worry» about sprains and dust in her clothes.
The rollercoaster went up and down and up and down again. She realized one more thing. Her experience this morning didn't only play havoc with her body, but also her emotional and mental state. It was to be expected, of course. No one could play with fundamental forces of existence without repercussions and certainly not an inexperienced novice of a witch. Her powers had saved her. She had been lucky. Fear played an evil tune in her gut.
She sat down on a bench in the shadow under a tree. A raven cried from a branch. She couldn't see it, but didn't need to.
An old metal sign had been left two or three steps away, in the tall grass. After sitting still a minute or two, a second or two, she stood up from the bench and walked impatiently the short distance to the

sign. She picked it up, studied it, without studying it. She didn't need to, didn't need to read the crafted letters.

PYRAMID INC
A division of Thompson Chemicals

Even this hadn't been removed. How long had it laid there? It was dirty and rusted with age. She could still smell the chemicals on it. Raising her head a bit, she could see straight across the river to the factory. She squinted her eyes slightly, even if she didn't need to. The ugly production facilities, with their many poisonous fumes brought downwind across the river imposed themselves on her enhanced senses.

The song of the ravens turned insistent. It wasn't really one of warning, but more informative, and really completely unnecessary. She knew who was approaching.

– My shadow is chasing me, Jill cried out in misery. – I can't escape it.

– In Voodoun, «soul» and «shadow» are the same word, Loeh said softly.

– I figured that one out for myself, thank you, that I am, in fact, having an inner conflict, Jill snarled, abruptly changing, turning… turning scary. – You have every reason to be proud of your ancestors…

She turned towards her friend, and she couldn't tell, had no idea, why her rage chose this moment to manifest itself.

– You're nothing to me, she said icily, – You're nothing more than a tool to be used and discarded.

Loeh stood rigid, completely helpless, with a blank look in her face. Jill walked close to her. The girl's terror manifested as flames uncontrollably leaping from the skin on her bare neck. Lillith caught the flames on her fingertips, in complete control.

– Do you know how insignificant you are, compared to absolute, utter Power, do you have the slightest inkling of an idea?

The sunshine turned away. The wind turned cold.

Loeh attempted to move her lips, to make her tongue and larynx work, in vain. Her eyebrows moved a little, like fluttering of a moth's wing, in the dark world she had entered.

– Sure, beg for mercy, like the sniveling baby you are.

And Lillith left. Loeh fell on her knees and stayed in that exact position for a very long time, shaking with horror and the sum of all her worst fears.

Jill kept the shield, as she hurried away. She didn't walk fast, but she hurried still. She knew how she looked, or at least how she would have looked, if most people had been able to notice the sideshow of living scarecrows in her peripheral surroundings.

She stopped at bit, her sensitive eyes easily noticing the shift, the shift towards evening, and as ever the sense of marvel and shame warred within her.

There was a sense of movement on the edge of her vision. She looked down. A little girl stood there. Her mother had gone to a newsagent, to buy a newspaper. Jill realized with a start that she could probably make the mother forget about the girl, and leave her alone.

That was an absolutely frightening thought.

– Are you a raven? The perceptive little brat asked.

– Perhaps I am. Why do you ask?

– Are you a carrion bird?

Aren't we all, to some extent, she thought.

– No, just a bird, honey, flying free.

Another evening came to Northfield. Daylight gave way to darkness, as it had for billions of years. The shiny lights from the Pyramid made pale the stars high above. Or so it seemed. Scott Thompson wanted it that way, this evening included, when inviting the haves and potential haves in the city to a grand Gala in his extensive domain, his modern castle.

Laurie was invited and therefore, by default her brood.

Under Laurie's strict supervision they had been trying on dresses and suits several days in a row. She had *sent for* salesmen and tailors, made them come all the way from Boston, bringing their entire shop with them. The grand living room on the farm had been chosen as and transformed into a try-out and failing place. Clothes in all sizes and forms hung from the hangers and were tried on and discarded, and left on the floor in quick succession. Servants picked them up discreetly and made them disappear just as easily.

– If she wanted to impress us, she has succeeded beyond words, Rae stated with twinkling eyes.

Tam concentrated on standing still while they took her measures. With a slightly humorous smile she looked down at the rented help that cast her nervous glances. They could see her ears, of course, and she discovered that it didn't bother her half as much as she thought it would. Everett strained to seem unaffected. He didn't enjoy being coddled. Stacy and Jill stood side by side in front of their personal full-figure mirror, the lower edge of their dress brushing their legs. They shook their head, and the dresses were promptly dropped on the floor. The discarded clothes were removed, and they were given new ones in due haste. This time the lower edge was far higher up. They smiled, but then Jill raised her left brow once more.

– Hello, there. Yes, you.

– Miss? One of the girls hurried to their side with a nervous expression painted on her face, even more exposed to their sharper senses.

– Why are the two of us always given exact matches? Jill inquired in a slightly agitated tone.

– It s-seemed appropriate, Miss. You have similar built and posture, and are excellent as a pair… esthetically speaking, I mean.

– Does this notion of conformity include a rule that everything must be an exact match? Gray eyes flashed. – It should be possible to change at least some of the design and use a variety of colors. Don't be so fucking clueless concerning creativity.

– Yes, Miss. The girl pulled back, curtseying. – No, Miss.

Jill closed her eyes a moment while struggling to contain her temper. She had always taken easy to anger, but this… She could have burned the poor maid to death, transformed her into a pile of ashes, before being able to stop herself.

– What conceited crap, she mumbled. – Why do we put up with it?

– But it is fun dressing up once in a while, Stacy insisted. – You should learn to relax, to enjoy it. Trust me, I've learned a lot about these social events. They're a sign of our stature, our elevated place in society.

Laurie is seducing us, Jill thought, seducing us all, Stacy most of all.

– I thought you had had enough of this shit?

– You never get enough of this shit, Stacy said dreamingly.

Stacy's light brown hair was fixed to stand up in a top. Jill insisted on having hers as it was.

The girls were let out in the winter garden in pairs as they were groomed properly. They were met with applause from the boys, snide remarks from the other girls.

– You must have come to the wrong place, Everett remarked. – Two such goddesses can't belong among us mundane mortal folks.

– Thank you, good sir. Stacy curtseyed before him, giving him an extravagant wink. – You're too kind.

The stab of jealousy Jill felt couldn't tarnish the joy of the moment. This was what she really had been missing her entire life; companionship, tight relations, understanding from friends seeing the world in much the same way that she did. Seeing Loeh pulling back a little didn't change her happiness, her joy of the moment. She preferred not to dwell on the things the sight of Loeh reminded her off.

Laurie is seducing us, Jill thought, seducing us all, me most of all.

Or perhaps… we're seducing ourselves?

Gabrielle's words about the tailspin inherent dangers of alternative movements echoed through her mind, but it was faint, without impact.

– Behold… the Raven, Jason welcomed her in his arms, kissing her on the cheek.

She looked up. There were at least two of them on the glass roof. She hadn't noticed, perhaps because she had started to take their presence for granted.

The wait was pleasant in a way. There was nothing to be done, no chores awaiting them. They could think and explore.

Laurie had really collected all kinds of stuff during the years. She even had a weapons collection:

Swords, bows, crossbows, rifles, knives, spears and a lot of unclassified stuff. Jill passed by a curious looking knife sending chills down her spine. She picked a Katana, a light Japanese sword from the wall. Her hands moved it through the air, easy as pie. She couldn't lift the bigger, heavier broadswords. But the Katana was so light, so maneuverable that she easily mastered the first initial strokes. But that was it, of course. After a while she didn't know how to proceed, got embarrassed, and returned it to the hilt.

The television was on. The television was always on, mostly CNN and such. Laurie wanted them to be updated on world events. It was a giant modern 70 inches monitor screen, hooked up to the Internet on a permanent basis. They could, at any time check out anything their heart and mind desired. Jill had been quite the web-freak, before coming here, but hadn't really kept it going since then and didn't really miss it.

She could at any time find a thousand long link list of the disastrous result of industrial pollution, though, and that would always be useful.

Then she saw him, Brian Garret, on the screen. She had seen him often enough, of course, in pictures and on the front page of magazines, but this was the first time she saw him live. His public appearances were rare, even if he wasn't considered a reclusive like Howard Hughes and such.

And she had seen him through other people's eyes and experienced him through their emotions, their fear. He was seen as the classical illusionist and many would've claimed he had even invented the term, if there hadn't been many in line before him.

She heard his words. The volume of output sound was quite low, but she tilted her ears, her head and she could hear him.

– … humanity is indeed on the cusp of a great revolution, a major change. As you all know I've devoted my life and effort to aid this development, this leap of consciousness. I'm one of those lucky few who have been fortuitous and fortunate enough to be one of the front-line assemblers of this our glorious future…

He was a speaker at a major convention. The people sitting in a great hall listening to him, ate up his words, licked them up as gold on the ground.

– He's a great man, isn't he? Andrea had come up beside her, as she gradually had closed in on the monitor. – He's the living embodiment of Laurie's thoughts about participation and change. It is possible.

– Laurie isn't connected to him, is she? Jill commented in a casual manner.

– Unfortunately, no. Andrea laughed. – She has a few shares of his stock in her portfolio, but that is hardly closer than virtually every stock market participant in the world. She says people like him and organizations like his will start emerging all over the world, all a part of the consciousness of the New Age.

– Shiny eyes, diluted pupils, Jason said to Jill shortly afterwards. – Yep, she's definitely qualifying to the title of devoted cult-member of the year.

– The so-called «new age» is about money and success, Stacy stated, – like everything else.

Jill was watching the play of the kittens. Malvin got trashed by one of his smaller sisters, but a few minutes later he, too, got his licks in. There was something precious and straightforward here, as they were tearing into each other. Jill saw a lot of straight, honest malice... but there was nothing malicious.

She was fully aware that the how's and why's in other animals couldn't be directly transferred or compared to human relations, but cats both alone and in their interplay with others, had an inherent freshness that most of today's humans seemed to lack.

The witches traveled to the Pyramid in style, in wagons pulled by horses, old classic, comfortable coaches. It was in many ways a very peaceful and relaxing experience, and as often had been the case Andrea was far from being the only witch with shiny eyes.

They arrived fashionably late at the Gala, but as quite a few as usual saw this as a prudent course, some commotion had to be expected. Dressed up servants opened the doors of the various chariots.

– I feel like Cinderella, Tam heaved.

– Let's hope a younger version of Hulk Hogan shows up tonight then, Daniel said.

Tamara was blushing, but did laugh with the others. She didn't take offense.

– Hulk Hogan? That dwarf?

Please, let me not be dragged in, Jill thought, as everybody laughed their hearts out. Let me keep my… my sense of perspective.

But she was already there.

They stopped a bit outside by the water fountain, by the statue of the man on the horse, one of three in the city.

– Gosh, people, Rae spat. – I do believe he has made sure the statue is made more to honor himself than his ancestor.

The bronze face did look like Thompson, but that wasn't strange, was it? Some of the traits of the ancestor had to have survived to present day. Jill shrugged. The bronze made it hard to distinguish between facial features anyway.

The shopping mall, big and impressive as it was didn't really stand out among hundreds of similar malls across America and throughout the world. Strictly functional, without… soul. Though it was clear there hadn't been spared any expenses during its construction.

The real thing was upstairs. The children's eyes widened as they used the marble stairs, ascending the Pyramid and reached the enormous, generally not open for the public reception area and the even bigger hall, on the third floor. Scott Thompson used it only each time he held his Galas. Curious, hateful and envious eyes followed Laurie and her protégées from below, until they disappeared from sight.

As above so below, Jill thought.

– *You're being looked at, scrutinized, assessed,* Laurie had told them. – *Get used to it. It's the way of the world.*

– Their staring is understandable of sorts, Andrea giggled. – We've never had the honor of being invited here before.

There were five water fountains in the reception area, in a narrow pool stretching the entire length to the massive (opened) doors ahead. Along the walls built-in Egyptian lamps cast fire over the walls and the water. Jill had seen similar stuff in the Egyptian department at Boston Museum. She also recognized more stuff she suspected had been removed from the museum and placed here for the occasion. One could get the idea that Thompson harbored an obsession towards Egyptian artifacts, but Jill didn't think so. She thought it had a superfluous quality and to her the exhibition seemed more like expensive ornaments than a sign of more than indifferent interest. A show window, another part of the ongoing façade, sham. Just like the game he and the others city rulers played in the city council and other public forums. They fooled people into believing important decisions were actually being made there, while they in truth made them inside dark rooms, behind heavy curtains.

They saw no employees receiving the guests, no guards out here, even if they didn't doubt there could be sentries on a possible spot of unrest on a moment's notice. Everybody simply walked up the stairs and into the major hall. The illusion concerning lack of security was evident.

A few steps inside the great hall they were discreetly met by an aide.

– My name is Martina Gardner, she greeted them with a pleasant, professional smile. – On behalf of Scott Thompson and Pyramid Inc I wish to welcome you to tonight's Gala.

– Thank you, Laurie said formally. – We're glad to be here.

– Mr. Thompson has asked me to extend his wishes for all his guests to enjoy the evening, Martina said. – I've been informed that he will be with us shortly. Now…

– Are you from Eastern Europe, Martina? Stacy asked her pleasantly. – I thought I heard a flavor in your accent.

– I am originally. The woman's eyes lit up like a jewel-decorated Christmas tree. – I was so lucky to be chosen for Pyramid Inc's exchange program. Now, if you'll excuse me?

– Certainly, you just run along, dear. Stacy gave her a merciful dismissal. The woman left, obviously on a schedule.

Stacy had cast one look at Martina's dress and decided it in truth cost more than every cloth Laurie's progeny wore, and far more than anything Stacy herself had ever worn. She shook her head and didn't actually bother with it. She denied the entire line of reasoning. Money wasn't the only measure of Power in this world. Not anymore.

Many started mingling. There was a lot of space to do so at, no sardine in a box here, no, sir.

Eyes showing both disgust and interest, and the whole specter between studied Laurie's cohorts. The youths walked through this Hawkworld within as they walked it without, with caution and undeniable curiosity. Too little of one, too much of the other would destroy them, they knew that, they had learned this, both before and after their arrival in Northfield. Even more than most people they were walking this razor's edge.

– *And there's no center, no balance, except what we're throwing away.*

Stacy and Jill turned towards each other and realized that none of them had spoken.

A man met Laurie and took her hands. It was his honor, the mayor himself, who always strived to lay his eggs in the softest bed.

– I see that your students have once more increased in numbers, he grumbled.

– That's the way it goes, she replied lightly, – since they're students for life. So far nobody has flunked.

– I don't mind, he pointed out quickly. – The new seems to be as… fabulous as the rest.

His eyes surveyed Stacy and Jill, the two girls standing closest to Laurie at the moment. Had Laurie planned it, made it happen? Jill knew that spittle flowed into his mouth and the usual heat rose in her from top to bottom. *Pull yourself together, you damn bitch.* Sometimes she wondered about herself, she really did, whether she would react this way to any man desiring her. Stacy in contrast, returned his scrutiny with a calm and steady look.

Thompson entered the room. No ceremonies, no effects. Very effective.

– Welcome to my Gala in this representation of a glorious future, he said in a short speech. – Pyramid Inc may be my smallest company today, but it's one for the future. A bright and profitable future, ladies and gentlemen.

He gave them assurances, confirmations of their view on existence. They gave him applause and accolades.

The party could begin. People started mingling in earnest.

The youths did, too, breaking up in smaller groups, trying to keep themselves from being intimidated. And they acted with impunity, as if they owned the place. The assembly looked at them with disgust and in clearly patronizing ways. It made them even more eager to hold their heads high. They couldn't be ignored.

Everett glimpsed his parents in the crowd. He didn't approach them. There was nothing he could think of, to justify an approach, nothing he could or wanted to say to them. Instead, he looked at himself and his brethren in one of the major wall-mirrors. Under the moon he saw them, and it was a truly enjoyable sight. They could look homogenous at first sight and without a closer scrutiny, but one who wanted to look beyond the obvious, would see that many of them had something that made them stand out from the rest. They dressed similar, something not surprising since this could be said to be Laurie's preference for dressing, not their own and Everett had noticed that all the other upstarts had made their own amulet…But individuality revealed itself in minor ways. Rae wore two big golden earrings. They would seem a bit too big, which certainly was the point of the exercise. Tam used an extra wide headband, covering her ears. Practical girl. Jill wore her hat and simple bands around her midsection and her left thigh. Kieron had a ring of plants around his lower waist. Living plants, if Everett's vision hadn't been too impaired by recent events. And Everett himself had made good with sunglasses… where one glass was missing. They were all great. He grinned.

Tamara counted clearly as a candidate as the most unsettled among them. They guarded her in their circle, to a certain point, but not so much that anyone should notice. She had to learn to deal with it and the resultant pressure.

To Jill all this seemed very mundane, close to too normal after everything she had experienced. She sipped a glass of wine while allowing her eyes to wander in more than a speculative way over the assembly. The speculative eyes dwelled often on Stacy. The green-eyed one nipped to her own glass of wine in much the same fashion that Jill did. She enjoyed herself as Jill did. Her eyes had turned just as speculative. They had a lot in common. Both were chameleons, capable of inserting themselves into any given and desired environment. And contrary to the chameleon… create their own. They had its advantages, but not its drawbacks.

An interesting assembly, Jill thought.

There weren't many interesting individuals here, but all the influential people in the area had to be present and several from elsewhere. It both attracted her and repulsed her simultaneously. She had a sense of being home, but more of being overwhelmed by a sickening and disgusting impression. They decided a lot here, the creatures discussing and whispering in dark corners. Property, not necessarily values changed owners. Decisions made here influenced billions of people. Still all those people had no say over those very decisions. Jill felt it prickle inside, of the excitement the sense of power created in her, and also in disgust.

– We're so very vulnerable right now, she said to Stacy. – In the process of throwing away established truths, what we've so far taken for granted, and still far from certain what direction we should choose.

– Laurie spoke about it, didn't she? Stacy winked. – But in a strangely ambivalent way, especially when touching upon what she called the Path to Power.

This congregation enjoyed all the power it could possibly amass. Jill didn't need to convince herself of that. Why had Laurie brought them here?

To learn perhaps. But learn what?

Jill and Everett danced tight. Fast music, slow music, they held hard around each other.

– Did you know that Joan is serving here? He asked her.

– She does? He nodded. – No, I didn't know that.

Everett left her with a mischievous smile and set course for the restroom.

Jill started wandering and she did so alone. There wasn't truly anything to do in here, except observing and listen in, so she did just that. She looked for Joan, but couldn't find her. A lot of maids and servants walked about. Jill found a certain relief in the fact that Joan didn't work with them. The girl she had known, albeit briefly, wouldn't have fit in here at all.

Then she saw a similar light-clad figure coming out of the kitchen, in the shadowy parts of the hall, and walking up the stairs, the stairs used by the servants, to the next level of the pyramid. Jill hurried after her, chased her all the way up and into a corridor, where there were a lot of doors, a lot of rooms.

– Hi, she called.

The girl in the servant uniform turned around. Joan turned around.

– Hi, what are doing up here?

– I wanted to talk with you, Jill said. – You disappeared on us. You haven't attended school for weeks. I even called your parents and asked if you were ill or something. They… denied it.

What a strange word to use. «Denied» felt a lot less appropriate than «said no»… or something.

– I've quit school, Joan said proudly. – I finally got fed up.

– That's great, Jill commented a lot more enthusiastically than she actually felt. – But why start working here? There must be a dozen other, better places in this city alone to start.

– I had to do something to satisfy my parents, at least temporarily, Joan said a bit defensively. – Working for Scott Thompson is seen as a secure post in this town.

She seemed quite all right, quite normal, (whatever that meant), and Jill told herself that she had no grounds for worry, nothing to point at or base the reason for her persistent fear on.

She seemed so much herself, so much not herself that Jill got gooseflesh all over.

Jill had known her for a witch by the first glance. Her aura had been quite distinctive. Now it was muted… cold. But Jill couldn't get a fix on her mind. She closed her eyes as much, as long as she dared. To her mind, her mind-power it was as if she was alone up here. And it felt absolutely horrible, because she knew she wasn't. She realized that someone could come at her from behind and she wouldn't know it. Her powers had been a cause for joy and safety since she had become aware of them. Now she started to look around. She had known she had limits, she just hadn't been made this aware of them before.

– You must go, Joan said.

– Yes, go, Jill said in a hollow voice.

Joan scared her, and she hurried back down below.

A crowd had a lot of fun just below the stairs. She recognized Anton Berkowitz, one of the senior teachers at school. She heard him and his words cut like a knife, a razorblade inside. She knew no one could see any blood, but she bled anyway.

– The paranormal can't really be considered a part of science, he said in his witty, light tone. –

Psychology perhaps, but not as one of the heavier sciences… I mean, no one in their right mind would believe that witches ride a broomstick at midnight, would they?

That's right, she thought. No one would. You bastard!

The crowd, his court laughed heartedly, or so they probably thought anyway, his wittiness rewarded.

– Or sit in a distant cabin somewhere in the woods, mumbling curses at people…

The laughter turned hysterical.

She wanted to confront him. She wanted it so bad that it hurt. But she would only lose on such an incredibly stupid act. He and his like held all the cards.

– There are, of course, certain *phenomena* worth investigating and that is being done. Nothing has come out of it yet, but that doesn't mean there never will. We must continue to investigate all parts of nature, disperse all shadows one at the time.

Jill left. She stumbled on, hardly conscious of her whereabouts, and the alarm clock cried ALARM, ALARM in her chaotic mind.

– You're crying, Everett said astonished.

– Not anymore, she said, as she looked him in the eye, as the burning in her eyes dried any tear away.

She went to the ladies' room to, as they say, «save her face».

Stacy had already arrived, waiting for her. Jill stopped.

– You look like a snotty baby, Stacy said.

– And you still look like a painted doll.

The dark one walked to the mirror, stopping there, looking at herself.

– Make me one, she said. – Make me a painted doll.

– Trust me, Stacy said. – I'm an expert. You'll feel like a new person, you'll *be* one.

Stacy took her lightly by one arm and led her to the stool by the door. Jill sat down as the bright one opened her purse and found her brushes and pencils.

– This will be a bit of a rush job, the painted doll stated reluctantly, – but we'll make the best of it.

Jill felt the brushes and pencils on her face as light as feathers, like the sting of needles. Stacy's claim of being an expert could easily be defended. One might claim that she had done this her entire life and one would probably be right.

The dark one stood close to the mirror studying the face there. Her newly sharpened features had been softened once more, while other areas of the face had been highlighted. The skin could hardly be seen through it all, only imagined. Stacy's hand rested on her shoulder… comforting?

She looked like a painted doll.

Her smile, always an effort took even more to move.

Half an hour later she danced with Scott Thompson. He had taken the initiative a short while ago with a smile and his scary, intense eyes. At first, she had been furious at herself for not refusing him instantly, but when she managed to cool down a bit, thought about it she realized it would be an excellent opportunity to learn more, get to know the enemy better. She touched his neck with her cheek, but this time physical contact didn't improve her readings, not in any way. If she wanted information, tactical data, she had to talk to him, get him to open up.

– I'll bet you love my modest home even more now, when you have had the opportunity to look closer at it, he said in an even more than usual arrogant way. – A fine castle, don't you think?

– The building is okay, she replied with a shrug, as if they had just started discussing a rock.

– This is merely the beginning, he continued unfazed. – Eventually I'll build another Pyramid, one a lot bigger, where people can live and work, a controlled environment, one without such distractions as distance and outside provocations.

– That isn't surprising, she told him in quite the cold manner. – I've always known you were a control freak. You're creating illusions to more easily fool people into letting you do as you wish. Too bad you won't realize that control is the biggest illusion of all.

– So, you won't quit your rebellious crap? He didn't hide his anger now. – I can't believe you'll bother.

– If we're not a threat to you and your equals, why are you so afraid of us?

– You're dangerous, he said. – Sand in a machinery working to perfection. You're turning water into wine, open doors that should stay shut.

– You're turning all wine to vinegar, she said quietly. – Closing the eyes of those that still can see.

They finished their dance with sharp, correct steps. Something had bothered her about him since their first encounter. It had just been resting, hibernating uselessly in the back of her head. She was more experienced now, knew more about her capabilities. It had dawned slowly on her for some time, but the realization still came as a shock.

She could read him emphatically, receive his emotions and also surface stray impulses… but no deeper thoughts. She could hardly hide the shock. She didn't believe he was a witch. He couldn't be. Nobody had the capability to hide themselves that well, had they? But his mind read like a wall, like layer upon layer of concrete and steel, impossible to penetrate. The glimpses she received didn't really make her desire more. She got sick of the splinters of his thoughts.

In spite of his brilliance, he was clearly narrow-minded and full of hatred and fear. Whatever path she decided to walk, she didn't need him.

The dance ended as it started, with polite distance. When she left him, she couldn't resist the temptation to throw a challenging observation at him.

– That a branch is thick is of no help if the entire tree falls.

She circled, mingled a bit more, while passing and studying Joan Davis and other servants, hosts and hostesses. They didn't approach Jill and she didn't approach them. They acted very servile towards Thompson, as if he should be a god, Thompson the Almighty. And they entertained his important guests to an even more unsettling degree.

The girl took her sweet time, but she circled in on Laurie very much like that black panther in the forest had done its prey.

Laurie had another conversation with the mayor. They seemed to be best pals.

Outside, Jill yelled in her head. Laurie swayed slightly.

I can hear you, girl. The reply was admonished as a reprimand.

– Is something the matter? The mayor inquired eloquently. She shook her head, excused herself and hurried off.

The hall welcomed them in its animosity, huge and empty. Jill could still hear voices, not only from the inside, but from all over the place, from outside, from far away, not with her ears, but with her enraged mind. She stamped her feet at the floor while rubbing her fingers against her forehead. There was no pain, only rage… and Power. The huge windows shook from the onslaught and any piece of wood within the range of her Fury started smoking.

– Pull yourself together, girl. Laurie grabbed her arm.

The windows stopped shaking, the wood stopped smoking. The rage remained.

– Thompson *knows* about us. Jill tore herself free from Laurie's grip. – He knows what we can do and has learned how to raise a shield, keeping his thoughts from being read. *A shield!* I can't do that. *You* can't do that. Why didn't you tell us, why didn't you warn us?

– Was that necessary? A slight, teasing smile. – Come on, now, a local king?

– *You* have never managed to stop him in anything. The girl's eyes twinkled like ice.

– In my eyes I'm doing quite well, Laurie stated rigidly, suddenly on the defensive. – To move too quickly can be worse than anything.

– Don't be so modest, Jill said sarcastically. – You have almost as much money as he has.

One moment, one eternity they stared at each other with pure hatred in mind and eye.

– He lived in the Far East for years, studying under a master, Laurie said eventually, looking away, unable to keep meeting the girl's intense stare. – I don't know who it was. I don't know what he learned there. Something is haunting him. I don't know what. He hates us. I don't why.

– Perhaps there isn't any «why», Jill shrugged. – There are some people who don't need a reason.

– Whatever, you must listen to me, all of you, and listen well, the older witch insisted. – We must not, cannot move too fast. What you did at school was careless and you've challenged Scott by inviting his tenants. And that you visited him the way you did, that was very stupid.

– His tenants…? Jill's eyes softened and widened. – Unholy shit, you don't have a clue, do you?

Her anger left her and she couldn't keep it from happening. She wanted to keep it, but keeping it was so hard, so hard. Calming down had always been easy. Keeping the anger would always be hard.

– I prefer the hare before the turtle, she snapped, – and I assure you I've got no intention of falling asleep by the roadside.

She left Laurie there and the woman seemed to fade away in her tracks.

When Jill re-entered the party hall, she experienced the powerful wave of thoughts flooding her mind and she could take it. It strengthened her. The Power sounded like a song within her and above it all she sensed Stacy, her agreement, her approval.

The dark one met Everett, or sought him out, she couldn't tell. She looked inside him, at the wounds opening every time he glanced at his parents. Amazement and pity mixed inside her. There was a raven on his shoulder. She was on his shoulder, was the bird flashing its wings, rising in the air, easily leaving the room through the big doors. The two-legged raven approached him.

– This… She searched for words. – The Pyramid is destroying the world.

– So much misery all over the world, he said sad and angry. – So extensive that it has become the rule instead of the exception.

– So much to do, she mumbled with her head resting between her arms resting on his shoulder. – If we should choose that path.

– It does seem hopeless, everything? He said exasperated. – The journey towards the Kingdom of Death, the nothingness has been going on for so long that it seems inevitable. But there is no choice, is there?

No choice? She smiled. Poor, naïve, innocent boy. It flashed through her mind, the story about Styx, the river of Knowledge and Death.

– There is so little knowledge, so few stories surviving from «pre-historic» time, she said. – We need a map, some guidance. But awareness is distorted. All the details are gone. It can't always have been as bad as now.

It can't.

People floated around her. None of them seemed to actually touch the floor. They looked insubstantial, desaturated, lacking flavor. But not her friends, not her fellow witches. She clung to that image, that mirage, for the small joy it gave her. And she knew that Laurie smiled somewhere, gaining strength once more.

But there was something…

She saw Tam. The big elf emerged into her view, a smaller group of people, witches and others surrounding her, all of them comparatively dwarfs. The giantess had called them to her, and realization dawned slowly. Tam grabbed her headband. Did she really intend to… Jill wondered briefly if she should stop what was about to happen, as a rush of excitement overtook her, made her Live. Tam smiled broadly in a devil-may-care attitude the others knew so well within themselves by now… and pulled the headband off.

The Winds of Change (I)

Phoenix - Arizona August 15th 2002

Desert-hot, arid air. Phoenix during summer, worse than ever. The thick dust made it even harder to breathe. Asthmatic people had long since run from the city, those who could afford to, that is. The rest had died. The old and the young didn't go outside without breathing aid and a lot of oxygen. The word *arid* was no longer in any way sufficient in describing the air quality in this hell on Earth.

Perhaps it was no coincidence that the global protests against this year's G8 summit went beyond even «riot-level» here. The Governor had declared martial law and curfew two days later. Units from the army and the National Guard had yet to regain control and order within city limits. While Putin and Bush and the other world leaders had one hell of a time somewhere in the Canadian Rockies their eager servants had a hard time in several hotbeds across the globe.

Brian Garrett approached the city in his private jet. He watched the rebellion on the wall screen, even though he didn't need to. He didn't have to close his eyes. Just by concentrating slightly he was down there, in the heat and utter insanity. He had always preferred it this way, descending into Hell from above.

An aide entered the cabin. She carried a tray with food and soda.

– Is everything okay, Brian? She spoke with a fluent, pleasant voice, the way she had been taught in one of his centers for behavioral studies. – Do you require anything else?

– Everything is okay, Lucy, he replied. – I won't need anything presently, thank you.

Flustered she managed a courteous nod. They were so easy to control, so easy to manage.

He pushed a button on his remote and the images on the wall shifted. He watched his own, televised speech a few days ago.

– … and I've always been convinced that the way of things is to heal. We will, given time, heal the wounds, the divisions in this country, in the world at large.

The applause rang a bit false in his ears, but then it always did, even when it wasn't. This was already being mixed with the footage recorded in the streets of fire, in Phoenix, across the globe. His publicity people were working overtime to complete it all, to coincide with his appearance at the Rocky Mountains summit.

But first his unique expertise was needed in the hell below. At least the appearance of such. He grinned, as he looked out the window, at the seething heat far below. He could see the heat, the heat erupting from angry people.

– It was a great speech, she marveled.

– I agree. The grin widened. – Both the wording and the timing were excellent. Give my regards to the public relation department, will you?

– Of course, Brian.

He felt it, had felt it for some time now: The time was nigh. As one by one of the old prophecies were coming true, coinciding with his own, numerous re-occurring, ancient visions his time was approaching, and approaching rapidly. It was about time. He had waited long enough.

He closed his eyes briefly. Opened them again… and stiffened in his seat. Something…

Something down there, something he couldn't see. He closed his eyes, concentrating, as sweat broke out all over his body. In a flash of panic he was convinced that Lucy would be able to smell it, smell his panic scent.

It moved down there, the monster, chasing his tail as it had done for so long.

Flash! He saw a hooded figure walk on the desert road, a figure without soul, mind, eyes and body. It walked relentlessly towards him, a demon without form and substance. No matter what direction he might take, there she was…

She was coming.

And down there was It, a terrifying Beast flaunting its claws and fangs.

– Give the order to turn around, he ordered, fighting to keep his outer calm. – We're returning to base.

– Certainly, Brian, Lucy smiled. – You've decided upon another approach, then?

– Indeed, he replied, slowly relaxing in his seat.

She hadn't sensed anything. She was so easy to control. They were all easy.

He kept his eyes open, as the Hell of Phoenix and the dragon he had sensed down there was filed away in memory. He would deal with it. Sooner or later, he would deal with it all.

But not now.

He had all the time in the world.

His time was near.

Chapter eleven: STACY AND JILL

The silence and size of the public library in Boston made the streets outside grow even more distant. One heard the sound of steps on the wooden floor and nothing but. One could see pages be turned, but didn't hear it. The ceiling is stretched so high above that it seemed like the sky. So much knowledge gathered under this ceiling, treasures not appreciated. On the contrary, there were a lot of people fearing and hating it and what it represented. Too many.

Jill remembered almost too clearly, the memory burning inside her, the absolutely frightening vision she had had concerning a possible future, the smell, the sight, the sounds, the horrible stench of mixed weeks-old sweat and blood, the flames licking the walls everywhere, the sickening fizzle from the burning treasures, the ultimate triumph of those who wanted ignorance, intolerance and one singular view to rule. One part of Jill couldn't help but wondering if that was reality and this the dream and that she would awaken at any time in chains and collar.

It took some doing, but eventually she found a copy of Snorri Sturlasson's tales about the old Vikings. She confirmed to herself what she knew well from her earlier, fairly superficial studies. They were hardly more than fiction with documentary elements, more like a modern novel than actual history. Snorri had, after all, lived a couple of hundred years after the events he described. But he had done a good job of collecting information and a lot of his stories had a basis in fact.

– Interesting book, isn't it? Stacy spoke over her shoulder.

– We weren't supposed to meet, yet, were we? Jill told her. – There are still thirty minutes left until our decided rendezvous. How did you know I was here?

– I always know where you are.

– You do? Jill queried interested.

– Well… Stacy looked almost embarrassed. – It isn't really necessary for me to know your whereabouts. We think very much alike, you and I. This time I must admit I wasn't really up to par. I came here on the same errand as you…

– You did? Then you must have had the dream, too.

– I certainly did. A gracious nod. – I thought we could study it together, the two of us. We have *so* much to talk about.

She seemed uncharacteristically eager, almost like another person. Jill decided to allow herself to be carried away.

And she was. They looked through the book full of eagerness and with something close to joy, taking turns in turning the pages of the book. So smooth the interrelation proceeded that they moved like one person and they enjoyed every moment of it.

– I didn't see you there, Jill said suddenly.

– I didn't see you either, Stacy said in her usual mysterious manner.

– HERE it is, Jill cried pleased, – immediately distracted from the path her thoughts had taken. – Listen… Olav Haraldson - «the holy». He lived from 995 to 1030 and ruled the last 15 years. «Receives the main credit for christening Norway. Christianity had existed for a while within the kingdom's borders, but he won the decisive battle against the heathens. After his death during the battle of Stiklestad, where he was murdered by the vengeful, he was canonized. Among several miracles linked to his person, there is the fact that his hair and nails grew for several weeks after his death».

Jill looked up, visibly furious. Stacy maintained a cheerful expression, unconcerned in her acceptance of accepted lies in the world.

– History-books filled with propaganda are always making me pissed, Jill snarled. – Everybody knew then, as everybody does today, or ought to know that not all body functions stop when life does. It says here that his body remained on the battlefield for weeks. What about all the other bodies? According to this… this fallacy their cheeks should've remained smooth.

– Look at the lifespan of all these kings, Stacy chuckled. – They didn't exactly live to see old age these guys.

Jill sent her an exasperated look.

But in spite of their ever-decreasing admiration for written history they left the old building in a hopeful and cheerful mood. The substance of their dream had been confirmed. They still had a link, however uncertain, with what had been. They allowed themselves to enjoy the eternal sunshine.

– It's memories, Jill insisted. – Not imagination, not visions, as we may ordinarily experience them. Memories, like childhood in… this life… only even more distant. It's real.

– Yesss, Stacy pondered. – Not this life, but pieces of our eternal existence.

– Think about the implications. Jill's face had been lit, like fireflies in the night. – Think about the possibilities.

They walked a bit further before Jill spoke up again.

– It could be projection, of course. That we're projecting a solution, a salvation to our own fear of death, of non-existence… but I don't think so. I don't believe that at all.

– I really appreciate your enthusiasm, Stacy said suddenly.

– Get out of here… Jill turned red. She had never been very good at handling praise.

– Don't underestimate enthusiasm. Stacy patted her on the head. – You swept Everett off his feet with it and you wooed Laurie into endorsing your little street market. We can always use such a gift…

– Thanks… I think…

Their official reason for traveling to the big city would be to buy Tam new clothes. But even if it could be said to be a secondary objective, they meant to complete it.

At least one of us does. Jill turned her attention wholly to Stacy for a moment. She invested no small amount of venom in that look.

They did window shopping, and visited many stores and enjoyed themselves, now, when they had more than sufficient funds. They didn't buy anything. Nothing found acceptance in Stacy's critical eyes. It was perhaps just as well that she made the decisions, since Jill felt both detached and distracted from it all. She was worried about Everett. He had seemed unusually tired, virtually exhausted last night, and it had merely been the culmination of a several days' downward spin. She had more than once given him of her healing energy, but it helped less and less.

She worried.

They went to John's shop close to Bleeker Street. No one had bombed it yet. Inside they could still experience the joy of woodwork without paint. They could experience John. They realized he played up to most people's view of him, their prejudices, challenging them.

– Long time, no see, she greeted him, before he opened his mouth to speak.

– Not that long, he assured her.

– A lifetime, she said.

She knew he noticed the changes in her, both within and without, the way she moved, her newfound self-awareness, her entire demeanor.

– We've traveled to this far land to find suitable clothing to our little sister from our last meeting, Stacy said lightly. – She has added shall we say a lot of growth lately, and her old rags don't quite cover it all anymore. Her wardrobe has become rather light, I'm afraid. We thought about you instantly.

– You don't say, he said dryly.

And proceeded to shoo all other customers out of the store. Very soon they found themselves alone with him in the quiet rooms, alone together with his overwhelming presence. He was… attractive. Jill wanted to… fuck him, but she sensed something as surprising as reservation in Stacy and held back herself.

– Now, ladies, how much would you say that your good friend has added to her growth since the last time I saw her?

– She's well formed, has a powerful build, and is taller than any man I've seen.

– Dear me, the big man whistled.

Stacy didn't move. Clothes started to levitate. All kinds of clothes, floating towards the middle of the room, forming around a shimmering form in the air, a human figure. The clothes were torn and ravaged.

– As you can clearly see, these are too small…

– I've got bigger, coincidently, he informed them with the smile still in place. – They were bought for basketball players, men and women. With minor modifications they should fit her well.

– Basketball-players, we should have thought about that, Jill said critically, when they surveyed the clothes in the storage room, clearly designed for big people.

Perhaps we should consider getting her one.

– How come you couldn't sell this? Stacy wondered. – There aren't really that many Big-People stores, are there? They should flock here.

– I sold some, he grinned, – but young and naive as I was, I didn't realize that the big companies sell wholesale to sport-teams.

They had fun and joked among themselves while searching through and picking from the heap of clothes. But there was something… keeping them from… Even if everybody knew that everybody knew much, everybody wasn't certain what everybody knew. The girls behaved in an unusually meek manner. They let him pick suitable rags without commenting on it and they didn't respond to his half-hearted advances.

– I met Laurie once, he said, – during the native conference in Washington DC in '92.

– Before or after the ruckus began? Stacy asked, really noncommittal.

– After, he said darkly. – All illegal aliens had been declared undesirables and deported. But there was no sense of defeat among us who met afterwards. We had expected a show of force, of oppression. The struggle had just begun.

– Just begun, Stacy stated.

In her eyes there was an implication of a promise that Jill both liked and disliked, disliked and liked.

– Perhaps you haven't heard how Laurie damaged her foot? John continued. – They did it to her during the major demonstrations in Copenhagen, Denmark, the fall of 1988. Police officers smashed the demonstrations… and her foot. The doctors didn't have a clue how she managed to stand at all, even less walk. I didn't see her again, but I heard she changed after that. I guess she had already changed when I met her, even though she was still a part of the movement. She had never been very interested in money. She managed on her teaching salary. During the following years, however, she built one of the fastest growing fortunes in the world.

– That's right, Jill nodded. – No one talking about it understood how. She had never showed any financial talent before.

They all smiled their roguish smiles. The girls looked at each other, through their thoughts. He didn't notice. The two of them felt a certain relief.

– Come visit us, John, Jill offered when they were about to leave. They carried bags filled with clothes in both hands. – I think you'll enjoy yourself.

– What do you think? Jill asked Stacy after they had walked for a while, a good while. – About me inviting him.

– That's okay, the other shrugged. – We can always use one more stud.

– But why… holding back in there, then?

– Ah, you hot bitch. Stacy laughed hard.

They walked a bit more.

– He's a *man*. Stacy stopped a bit. – And one who wants to have his way with us, *his* way. We're not ready for that yet.

– I… understand.

– I know you do, honey, I know you do.

They were humming together as they left the gray fog and entered the green fortress, the green lung inside all the gray. The park didn't seem the same now, during daytime, the city's presence, the taming of the wilderness that much more evident. It felt good to know then, that the wilderness wasn't dead, only sleeping, and often opened its eyes.

– Laurie, too, only wishes to use us for her own purpose, Jill said, bitterly.

– Laurie wants a lot of obedient little soldiers, Stacy confirmed.

– It's true! Jill almost shouted. – Just look at how she's attempting to tame… domesticate us, form us. School is one example of that. To go there is an obvious mistake. It's doing nothing more than crippling us.

– Laurie lacks what she needs. Stacy's voice and eyes turned intense. – We don't.

They walked through the park in slow, lazy moves. There was a considerable amount of people present, even though it was far from being crowded. They attracted both interest and envy. The two girls bathed in it, very conscious of their tight dresses, with the straps on the arms, with their naked shoulders. Jill was black and Stacy white. And as ever Jill wore her hat. In spite of their light clothing, they seemed innocent enough. And the two-legged wolves closed in on them.

– I can't forget Joan, Jill said frosty and in a low voice. – I know… I know well it's possible to change overnight, but I still think he did something to her, destroyed her will, making her thoughts dark and horrible, making her *his.* I can't imagine what she must have gone through, what he must have done to her.

– No matter, he's just one man, a pawn in the game, Stacy commented cold, unconcerned. – What is needed is to change the game rules. Then the world gets rid of millions like him. He isn't important. I find our visions from the Viking Age far more disturbing.

– Yes… the king had protection against «sorcery». Who protected him?

– Who do you think? Surprisingly enough there was a slight tremble in Stacy's voice. – That should be clear enough, even to Sleeping Beauty?

– But it couldn't… Jill nodded slowly, ignoring the other's sarcasm. Her thoughts had traveled the same path. It was clear. The day suddenly turned cold.

Thoughts raced through the mind.

The scope paralyzed them both, making them shiver all over.

Youths, boys and girls sat together, and they joked and laughed in the sunshine. Jill experienced the well-known flash of loneliness, one that had faded in bits and pieces since her arrival in Northfield, but not vanished. It would never vanish completely. She was special, even among witches, they both were. Laurie had realized this. The question was *when.* If she had known about it all the time and sought them out because of it, or if she had gotten more in her lap than she had counted on. Whatever, the restlessness prevailed. Both the girls tended to cast long, nervous glances around.

A girl and a boy snuggled in the grass, quite unconcerned with their surroundings. Clothes were only loosely attached to the hot bodies. Eyes glassed over, distant. Both wanted to throw the dice, have it fall where it may, but didn't dare, not in public. Jill sensed expectation in Stacy and «spoke» up.

Don't you dare. Let them have the freedom to decide for themselves.

– As you wish. Stacy walked on, unconcerned.

Then they passed a bunch of boys and men, sitting in a circle under a rock. Their age was from the late teens to close to thirty. Jill wanted to go to them, but held back.

– Let's move on, Stacy said, slightly less unconcerned. – They'll come to us.

– Not if we disappear in a fast and determined manner, Jill spoke hastily, in complete opposition to her desire, her almost to be action the second before. – Fast, but not suspiciously so.

– Time to make up your mind, the other girl grinned. – You've chosen a man. He's a good choice. He is, as you well know, He Who is Dwelling in the Tomb. The good Everett doesn't know his own Power. Not yet.

– But there's no reason to just keep to one fish, is it? Variety is, as you well know, the very essence of Life.

– There's… a lot of fish in the sea? Jill said hesitatingly.

– Excellent, sweet sister. Excellent. You're learning.

Two of the older males in the circle broke away and started stalking the two girls. They shortened the distance fast, but not strikingly so. The designated prey felt both fear and exhilaration. The girls had reached one of the park's exit gates when the two men overtook them.

Jill and Stacy stood on a mountaintop, surveying the endless fields below.

– It must be hard for you to carry such heavy bags in this heat, one of the males said without introduction.

The girls stopped, looking uncertain at each other.

– It's okay, Jill assured them. – We're pretty strong.

The wind was blowing. There was no wind.

– We can see that, the other man joked. – But I'll bet you've kept it going for quite some time and must inevitably be both hungry and thirsty. We've got a cool place just around the block, where you can refresh yourselves. We would be delighted to carry your bags that short way.

– That's very kind of you, Stacy said innocently. – It would be so nice with a place where we could cool our heels for a while.

Jill discovered that she was indeed hungry, realized startled how hungry she really was. It dawned on her that she hadn't eaten anything, anything at all, since early in the morning. She was starving, ravenous.

They were led to a big, abandoned storage building, in truth like sheep to the slaughter. If it wasn't for the fact that they were really wolves in sheep's clothing. She giggled and noticed that Stacy did, too, simultaneously. *We're still not beyond the star-eyed, giggling young girl stage, a fact that doesn't escape those who believe themselves predators.* All four of them smiled in expectation.

For Jill to enter the well-equipped, luxurious former storage-room was like stepping into Hell itself.

The men found food from the well-equipped refrigerator. The girls started digesting huge amounts of sandwiches and cola.

– Jeez, you gals were really hungry.

– We're used to health food, Jill said without anger. – But sometimes I get so hungry that I can eat anything.

The two men almost laughed out loud then. A moment or so she wondered if she had gone too far, but their suspicion lasted only that small moment. They were used to young girls being dumb as flagpoles.

It wouldn't have mattered if I had. I'm at the top of the mountain and the wind is blowing.

The two well-muscled males sat down next to each of the girls. Their bare chest and thick arms seemed overwhelming.

What are we going to do? Jill sent, panicking slightly. *They'll never let us go voluntarily.*

Relax. Stacy's sending was relaxed, comforting. *Enjoy it.*

– I must say I'm thoroughly enjoying your tight dress, one of the males said carefully. The inexperienced young females had to be handled with care, at least during what the men had dubbed first stage.

– It's hot, Stacy excused herself, and blushed hard.

Jill couldn't fathom how she did it. But it was easy to see she wasn't wholly pretending anymore. She was far from unaffected by the men's presence and Jill had never seen her this subservient.

– You don't have to be modest. We like what we see…

– We should go, Jill attempted. – We're about to meet our parents shortly.

– I don't believe that. You big girls are alone in the big city, at the mercy of its hunters.

He grabbed Stacy by the hair and pulled her tight.

– You'll need protection. The other bent slightly forward to kiss Jill.

She pulled away from him to the outer limits of the sofa.

– Don't be like that. You're so horny that your pussy is dripping wet. So, stop kidding around.

It was true. Jill closed her eyes. She could sense the draft close to the inner wet thighs and her breasts with their stiff nipples pushing against the boundaries of the cloth. She was once more at the mercy of her heightened desire and found she didn't mind, didn't care. He kissed her, so dominating, so sure of himself, so sure of his power over her. He lifted her up and pulled up the lower edge of her dress.

– No panties, he confirmed grunting.

She got a hazy look of Stacy and the other one who had exposed her swollen breasts. Stacy also sat there with her eyes closed. Head was bent back, and the mouth was open.

His arrogance was virtually without limit. The impressions flooded her brain. These two were merely the first assault line. After an appropriate time, the others, all the others would come running and take what they wanted, whatever they wanted. And after that the training would begin, as it had with countless girls previously. He was so confident, so intensely sure of himself, that he, in his mind, was already there. It annoyed and irritated her enormously. These men hadn't met any resistance to speak of in their endeavor and didn't expect any now or in the future.

– No more delays now, she heard the other man say. – We know very well, all of us, that you want it and that you're gonna get it. You're not virgins. You know what it's about and from now on you'll learn not to be obstinate. But eager and obedient and attentive as women shall be.

– Yes, Jill whispered. – Yes.

With a cute smile she started to fumble open his zipper. There was dizziness somewhere. She hardly knew what she was saying. Irritation boiled over completely. Until an eternity of a moment later the boiling in the brain halted, and was supplanted by cold anger. She grabbed hold of him, kissed him on the lips and held him frozen in her grip. He had insulted her, and he would suffer. Suffer. She heard a wild, savage growl and couldn't tell whether it was Stacy or herself, or both. He made a feeble attempt at resisting her, in absolute vain. Their lips were like chained to each other. This was real. The Power was Real. It moved and touched inside her. She could kill him, she knew that, but also knew that it wasn't worth the effort. He tried to strike her, push her away then, finally realizing that he had made a fatal mistake, concerning who was the hunter and who was the prey. The once powerful arms fell along his side, powerless. He attempted to kick. Feet were paralyzed. Only her now incredible strength held him in position. Impression flooded into her, uncontrollable, from him, everything he was, his every thought, his every action, everything he/they would've done to her, to them, if he/they hadn't been stopped. It was a horrible chain of images, impressions. She held on to them, to him. When she finally pushed him away with a snarl filled with contempt, he was literally pale as a corpse and the broad chest moved only marginally up and down. She was breathing, drawing breath, deep and full. *Life filled her*. She felt absolutely *wonderful*.

Indescribable. The biggest word she knew.

Wide awake. She saw, noticed Stacy correct her dress and her hairdo, remake her make-up, aided by a small pocket mirror, brushing and cleaning. Her aura, both their auras sparkled and expanded until they completely dominated the room. The man by Stacy's feet was like a mirror image of the wreck camping by Jill's feet.

– J-john, Jill stuttered.

That got Stacy's attention. Her features also froze in shock.

– Yes, *John*, she said pondering, hatefully. – He was behind this. He set it up, in the hope of accomplishing an easy victory.

Jill's thoughts whirled in chaos and conflicting emotions. She «saw» John meet with them, saw him instruct them, even if they might not have recognized him themselves, in the fog he had cast over their mind.

– He showed us a complete façade, she said enraged, fearful, hurt, – without us suspecting a thing.

– John, she mumbled, touching her forehead. – Why…

Rage and disgust warred within her.

– He fooled us, Stacy pondered, raging. – We were on to him and still he managed to somewhat roll us over. That sneaky sack of *shit*.

– We should f-find him. Jill's voice trembled. – M-make him p-pay.

– *Yes*.

And they did try, try to find him. He shouldn't be that far away, but they didn't find him, couldn't sense him at all.

– We're bursting with power, and we can't find him. There was a slight tremble in Stacy's voice, too.

– Then let's go and find him the old-fashioned way. Jill snarled, unable to hold back.

She had started moving when Stacy stopped her, with a hand, a thought.

– No, she said decisively. – No… He knows us. We don't know anything about him, we know that much. He might have made another, far more dangerous magickal trap for us. He may not have the raw power to beat us in open struggle, or he may not think he has. But he's dangerous. My instincts were correct earlier. We aren't ready for someone like him yet.

– Yes, you're right…

She stared around her, at the carnage. Eyes moved back and forth over the bodies thrown across the floor. She touched her lips, looked at her hands. They and her entire body quivered of powerful energies, pulsating and expanding endlessly. Bile rose in her throat. The man there on the floor. She had hurt him - and enjoyed it, she still did. This gasp was one of pain and she ran off blindly. Eyes were open, but she didn't see anything. She just managed to reach the outside, before she was forced to lean against the wall. Her stomach content returned the same way it had come just recently, like an angel of vengeance. Vomit decorated the wall. Pain made tears jump from between tight closed eyelids.

Time passed, immeasurable. She looked up and to the side, seeing how Stacy stood relaxed close by,

how her aura continued sparkling with energy.
– That wasn't very hard, now, was it? The impressions you receive will fade fast. They always do.
– What did you do, did we, d-did I?
– Don't play dumb, darling, it doesn't suit you, doesn't suit you at all. You didn't do anything else than what you've done to a lesser degree for some time now. Look at poor Everett. Who do you think is to blame for his fits of fatigue, the shadows under his eyes? Do you want three guesses?
– Damn you, don't try to play *games* with me. Jill Stafford turned in anger towards the other witch, discovering to her joy (and horror) that The Power hadn't been weakened the slightest by her throwing up. Her own inflated energy-field pulsed and interacted with that of Stacy, so similar.
– You're absolutely correct, Stacy laughed out loud. – Not if I know what's good for me… right? You know what you can do to people opposing you now. See how easy it is, Witch…
– No, NO. Jill looked down in despair. – I'm not like you.
– But you are. It was said softly, sneakily, convincingly. – You're exactly like me. It's really quite simple, little sister. We exist and we exist to rule.
Jill looked away.
Jill dried saliva and vomit from her lips, looking at the other with a pointed stare.
– I'm waiting. Stacy stated challengingly at her. – We can do this. We've got time.
– You are wrong, Jill said pressing her teeth together. – There's nothing new in what you're saying. «They who have the power have the right». Such shit one may hear everywhere. I've decided to not live like that. I'm not saying that the two inside didn't… deserve what they got. I'm not saying that at all. But that we did what we did, what does that make us?
– That's an excellent rhetorical question. Stacy smiled so broadly that she seemed to illuminate the entire street. – They will survive if it bothers you. In a few days they're good as new again, at it again, filled with stronger hatred than ever. I believe the one you took care of actually was the worst. He'll be the one most eager to expand upon his engagement in the business. How many young and ignorant girls do you think have gone through the treatment meant for us? Well, that isn't important, is it now? It wasn't his foul deeds that made you do what you did, but his behavior in your presence. He didn't treat you with the proper *respect*, the respect worthy of a Queen or Goddess or *Homo Superior*. But when push comes to shove it doesn't matter what he and any other does or doesn't do, now, does it? It's just your opinions and actions that matter. And that's something you want to make extremely clear…
– Stop, STOP. Jill knelt down in despair. – Please s-stop.
– You poor girl, Stacy said in a comforting tone. – So coddled, protected you've been, after all, from life's realities.
Come to me.
The crying girl crawled to the statue standing there before her and the statue helped her up. They left the place together, not really thinking, only doing. Stacy discreetly made sure their bags with clothes floated in the air for a while, until Jill was able to carry them in her hands. Jill leaned over, resting her head on the other's shoulder. She felt relaxed and restful in a way she had never before experienced. She was present on this spot, but also elsewhere. The power-surge had made everything easier. She could see beyond… beyond… She knew it wasn't permanent, but also that it *could* be.
They passed the hilltop and there, walking towards them was the gang, the collection of pimps. The boys looked at the two girls, first incredulous, then slightly worried. They saw, but didn't really fathom the floating bags.
– Hello, boys. Jill called to them as she straightened her body, looking blindly at them. – We kinda hoped we would be running into you.
Music rose from her Deep. One or two of the men raised their arms and started pointing. They were still twenty, thirty steps away when they stopped. The two in front turned first and started walking back in their tracks. Jill smiled. She knew a bit of what they saw. Their own imagination added the rest. All of them had turned, walking away from the two girls now. They started with a slow, uncertain walk. Before long it had turned into a disorganized, desperate run.
– You're such sweet boys, she told them dreamingly. – I'll be visiting you, visiting you often. When you're alone in bed at night I want you to think of me and long for my sweet touch.

Two of them ran over a road without looking. A car promptly hit them. Their comrades didn't stop for a second, but continued their panicked run.

Stacy just looked at her. There was fear in her eyes.

– It was easy. Jill laughed hard.

– This is good, Stacy told her, a comforting whisper. – You've started to look beyond the thin black veil. Don't worry, No one shall any longer be able to govern us or decide what we shall do or not do. No one! We will be that powerful.

– I don't know, Jill said, back to her doubting self, her features changing remarkably back and forth with her moods. – Shouldn't we begin to think things through while we're doing it? Everything is so confusing… I feel like I'm flying blind in the middle of a storm. I've got no idea where…

– Isn't that what you truly *hate?* The sound of that word, so seductive. – To be at the mercy of forces beyond your control? Won't you rather create your own fate?

Than forever play the victim?

There were other people in the street. They had a general idea that something had happened, but didn't have a clue as to what.

The witches left the area of storage buildings and back alleys and entered the broad street of mundane reality once more, where there was more than a score of people. Jill let the hands catch the bags and Stacy followed exemplary her example.

Yes…

– Good, Stacy said.

2

Jill sat in the highchair on the porch of the farmhouse. She scratched Malvin on his back. He who had only been a tiny, black ball of hair the first time she had seen him and was about to turn into a real *beast* of a male cat. He pushed himself towards her hand, purring soundly. As usual he was extraordinarily pleased with himself, that bastard.

He didn't jump into her lap and after a short while he ran off again. Perhaps he was smart enough to see what nobody else could see.

Everett sat on the upper staircase. He wasn't pleased. She had tried to keep up the pretense since her return, but it was hopeless, of course. Without being able to determine what was wrong, he knew there was *something*. He was searching himself for whatever he could've done. So sweet and so stupid. What would he do when he was told the truth?

She couldn't tell how long they had been sitting here, silent and unmovable.

They were practically alone here. It was their turn to guard the fort. They finally had a change for some quality time together.

– I'm a psychic vampire, she said flatly. – I'm sucking life energy out of everything living, feeding on it, strengthening myself, weakening others. I've done it with you and probably with everybody around me without knowing what I was doing. Now, I know.

He stood up, straightened himself, turned, turned back.

– So, we can't… can't we still…

– You would do that? She asked, her voice dripping of sarcasm. – You would sacrifice yourself… for your Queen?

– Don't DO that, he protested. – That's Stacy's line.

– Is it? I'm not so sure anymore.

– I can't control myself, Ev, she continued. – My Power, all Its aspects, it's like a storm, a force of nature, within me… an independent creature. Sometimes I feel such *Hunger*, Ev. I can't be human.

– We Human Beings are Hungry, he said, something catching in his throat. – And we, who perhaps aren't Homo Sapiens Sapiens, even more so. You're like the rest of us, both more and less than human.

– I'm nothing like the rest of you weaklings, she told him.

No more words were spoken. She closed herself completely off from him.

She turned her head, looking at a faraway point. When she turned it back, he was gone.

3

She sort-of went through the motions the next couple of days. She went to school and then to the farm or to Square, and back. The trip went back and forth. For a while, those few days, she had the distinct, suffocating impression of standing completely still. And there was no way she could live like that. In a way she realized this even more pronounced, now, realized it more than ever.

Early the next morning she ran alone all the way up to Fire Lake. The sun had not yet risen. The castle stood there still in its moist twilight. She swam in the dark waters. On the forest boundaries she stopped and looked at the city. The rising sun blinded her. She waved her hands in front of her face, in an effort to shield her eyes. She had done various experiments these days, being alone, but none of them had really led to anything. Her power had not waned significantly. What she knew she did even easier than before the last trip to Boston, but when she attempted something new, she came up empty. She lacked knowledge. Even simple information would do just fine at this stage. Earlier she had progressed through a process of luck and instinct, nothing that was forthcoming right now.

She had tried meditation, she had tried fasting, everything short of Malaysian dance… with no result to speak of.

– It's my power, she said aloud. – It comes from me. It should do what I want.

Perhaps that's the answer. Maybe in her case simple wish fulfillment did work. All the trappings, the dancing, the circles were needed to focus the power, but it shouldn't be necessary for accessing it. In principle it should be as easy as telepathy and telekinesis, and lighting fires, which were, after all, merely outward manifestations of something more… of something far more.

– *Death might bring Life.*

– What… she turned, but there was no one there.

– DAMN you, she shouted. – Show yourself.

There was a slight breath of wind, then nothing.

– You're chasing me, she mumbled. – Not giving me any peace. Damn you. Damn me.

She started running again, didn't care if she got her clothes all sweaty once more. To sweat was healthy, not the bad skin nightmare girls were told. It allowed the skin to breathe, allowed the runner to breathe, and she needed to breathe, needed it badly.

Her recent power-increase hadn't directly improved her physical prowess, but she could better draw on her inner resources to hold out longer. Now she started running flat out and she kept it going on that full speed as she left the city behind and ventured into the wilderness. It started to hurt and she kept it going. She wanted to know what her limits were. She wanted it badly.

And she did know a few minutes later when she knelt on the ground with double vision, nosebleed and a hammering heart. She did throw up again, as she slowly, slowly regained her strength within and without.

She had felt nausea on other occasions also lately. Outside the downtrodden storage building in Boston hadn't been the first time she had thrown up either. At first, she had believed it was morning sickness, but a speedy pregnancy test had excluded that possibility and she had breathed a sigh of relief.

She was still breathing hard, when forcing herself to stand on her feet. How many times had she done this in the course of her life? How many times could she continue to do it? The world was like a beast, ready to swallow you at any turn. Her eyes burned in her pale face, a stubborn streak refusing to give in.

A family weakness her cousin had called it. But it wasn't a weakness, but a true strength.

Her vision cleared, as she dried vomit and saliva from her lips and jaw. There, just before her, in the forest glen, she recognized the ramshackle cabin, where she and her current chosen mate had affirmed their union. Slowly, very slowly a smile transformed the young, vulnerable face.

She walked to it. It looked different in daylight (even more ramshackle), but she felt it. She couldn't avoid feeling it, what she had felt the first time. Her senses had been many times enhanced since that first time, and it pulled her to it like a beacon. She felt Passion, the drive making Magick possible. Nothing very significant compared to what awaited them on the Fire Lake, but diluted, mellowed as this was, it fit perfectly at the present time. She picked up a stick on the ground and started to beat it at the ground, the mix of forest and open field floor.

The stick turned to a sledgehammer. Around her people started to appear from open air and it was both the present time and the future. The future was now. She beat rhythmically on a flat-stone and moved it bit by bit by each strike. Little more than a week ago she had started using a minor sledgehammer and discovered how great an exercise, what an excellent strengthening of both her upper and lower arms, and her shoulder-muscles it was. Now she used two of the sort she hardly had been able to lift then.

And she was elsewhere, swinging the Katana sword and even the heavier broadswords. One swing, two, three, and she got the hang of it, improving with every stroke. What had been hard and next to impossible turned easy. And she was back by the cabin, back to wielding the sledgehammers, and the swords were still in her hands, in her grasp, cutting the air, her memory, opening her recall of the forgotten past, the smile brightening her face.

Her brothers and sisters in spirit, both witches and others, had joined her out here a few hours earlier. It hadn't taken any serious persuasion. Her enthusiasm and mood had made them join her without any real swaying taking place.

They cleaned and sort of decorated inside and outside the cabin. They didn't chop many trees, just sufficient to make a circle of tree-stumps in knee-height around the cabin. The cabin itself didn't look any better in daylight… It gave away exactly that sense of age, excitement and worry they wanted. This was a place of «worship» as good as any. They fixed a bit without overdoing it. Branches and bushes were attached to the walls, covering the worst holes. The area within the ring was flattened. A huge, flat rock put between the stumps. Wood and stone, humanity's protection against the power of the Storm. They polished and brushed the top of each stump, made it easy to sit on. If one person sat on each stump, they could hold hands and complete the circle easily. The ground inside the circle and the floor in the hut was covered with red flower petals. They flowed with the wind while Toni and her brother and other girls and boys pulled them from their bags and released them from their hands. All the children looked curiously at the somewhat improved hut and the older among them, those around the start of their teens, giggled and sent each other lewd looks when sprinkling the cabin floor with petals.

– This is one of our special places, Everett said aloud, calling their attention. – Our first of many around here. Young people have used this place. They have met here for their first close contact with another human being or for their first union with a new mate.

– There's something special with the first time, Jill said, a bit hesitatingly, as she discovered that he held out his hand to her, as she took it. They held hands. She patted the bed and there was laughter. – This is our shrine to desire, to united passion, to the Litany of Sin, to desire without force, submission. If that happened here, it would be the ultimate misuse, distorting, destroying Magick.

– There's so much hatred in the world, Loeh stated.

– Emotion, passion dominates the world, in all its myriad variants.

Jill created a gush of wind, signifying the forces of Nature.

– How's that? One spoke up. – I can't see the connection.

Jill's voice washed over them like a fresh spring wind.

– We need it, crave it, both when giving kindness and spite, no matter how we reach out to the world. It's a part of us we can never remove or ignore.

Stacy granted her a sarcastic smile. She understood the hidden implications of the statement.

– Love isn't the dominating force in the Universe, Jill said. – Life itself is… in all its myriad of variants. All emotions, all passions. Humanity is a tapestry of the dragon, an entire ocean. To just believe and act as if we're only one single wave on that vast ocean is to make the Human Being so much a lesser creature than what we are. We're feral and wild, passionate and rational simultaneously. We can't cut out one piece of a painting and claim it's the same painting, can we now?

She understood now, even as understanding eluded her. At the very least she had taken one step closer to awareness about her own inner and outer workings. She looked at Loeh, she looked at Stacy, she looked at Jason, and she looked at Everett. He looked away. Stacy sent her another sarcastic smile.

– The horrible and the tolerable go hand in hand.

The crowd dispersed reluctantly, but they would be back. Jill waved to Luke and his family. They all waved enthusiastically back, except Luke himself, who was a bit reluctant.

– Nice speech, Stacy commented.

– Thank you, Jill said calmly.

– Offering an explanatory model for human strife in just a few sentences might be a bit too ambitious. Though who can say, perhaps life really is that simple.

– And that complicated, Jason pointed out.

– I love it, Jill said passionately. – I love it all. The bad, the truly bad occurs when people are attempting to limit Life.

The four of them walked towards town. Everett didn't say much.

– I loved people's reaction when you mentioned the Litany of Sin, Jason said approvingly. – They knew, they understood.

– And they felt their juices flowing, Jill winked.

They crossed the cemetery before actually reaching Cemetery Park.

The Shadow of the Hill was cast on them.

No, that isn't true, Jill thought. We're entering it voluntarily.

– I feel her in my head, you know, Stacy said suddenly very, very frosty and rigid. – It was gone for a while after Boston, and I thought I had surpassed her, but now it's back. Laurie is in my head all the time and she won't let go.

– I don't, Jill said surprised. And then uncertain: – At least I can't tell if she's there.

– I can feel her, too, Everett said curtly. – She isn't doing anything, but she's there.

The four of them stopped. The three others turned to Jason, inquiringly.

– Okay, he said irritated. – She's in here, too. Sometimes I wonder if she ever sleeps. Perhaps a part of her doesn't, so what can we do? She's light-years ahead of us in experience.

– There has to be something random, Stacy said, – something unexpected she can't easily defend herself against.

They started walking again, cowed and despairing.

Just outside the school area, between the park and the old town, there was a slight rise, a mound in an otherwise flat area.

Jill stopped and she started talking in her ghostly voice.

– They died here. At this exact spot they were burned to death

And the day seemed to turn dark. *Dark*. Nothing had really changed, but to them it was as if an invisible blanket had been pulled from somewhere, like a filter casting a strange light over the world. They all felt it and shared it, as if time itself had stopped.

– Death might bring Life, Jill the ghost said.

– What did you say?

Jason froze, staring first at the corporal Jill and then at some other indefinite point.

And then they all saw it, the ghostly flames, day turning partly to night. First only on the mound, then forming an incomplete pentacle around it. Holes in reality itself. Strains of fire and shadow.

– I heard it earlier today, as I attempted to penetrate the fog clouding my mind. It… started or at least grew more pronounced after my… empowerment in Boston. I felt such clarity, but also confusion, both… emotionally and… in other ways. I remember talks I know I've never had, events that never took place. Sometimes it is as if time is switching back and forth, as if events are repeating themselves and conversation becomes a fucking jigsaw *puzzle*.

The cold wind blew, heating their veins.

– And now it's happening again.

Stacy stood there, just as pale, just as shaken. One fleeting moment there were just the two of them there, and then all four again.

– We're… vulnerable, Everett said, – and she's taking advantage of it, damn her.

There was more shimmering in the air, both confusing and not.

They looked at each other, intensely. Stacy raised a fist to her face.

– We must do something. We *will* do something. We don't exist for her to use as she sees fit. We're not Laurie's playthings.

– No, we're not, Jill spat in anger. And the Rage rose in her, welcome as rain.
– It must be something big, Stacy stated. – We need to protect ourselves… against many things.
The two boys didn't understand the add-on, but Jill did.
– We must prepare, openly and hidden, Jill told them, told herself. – We'll be searching for and awaiting patiently what is to come, what will come, what we decide here and now.
And they touched each other, skin to skin, thought to thought.
– It's a kind of a… wish fulfillment, Everett said astonished.
– That's right, Stacy said intensely. – And contrary to most people we have both the ability and the power to actually do it. We're not sheep fit for the slaughter.
And in a flash, they felt the heat of the sun on their skin again.
And they found themselves crossing the schoolyard, parting company.
Jill found herself in her room at the dorm, dancing. She looked out the window. Stacy had placed herself before the mound, stretching her long snake-like arms over her head, panning her hands in the air, writing on an invisible wall.
Wish fulfillment. Jill wrote in her diary. *We're witches. We make true what is Shadow.*
She sat by her desk before the open window and the open window spoke to her in whispers.
The pages of the Book of Shadows are turning rapidly in the wind, in the gathering Storm.
She stretched her arms above the head, yawning. The day, time today flowed slowly, as if days had gone by without anybody knowing. The girl froze, looking down. Her right hand moved down, opening the lower drawer, grabbing the other book, the second Book of Shadows, hesitatingly opening it, reading it.
There are two books, she read. *One written by the witch and one writing itself. They're different and they're the same. Though the one written by the Shadow will always be more detailed, more clear, more clouded.*
She turned to the last pages, no longer the same she had read earlier.
The nebulous witch, still hurting, still raw, is sitting in her poorly chosen sanctum, reading about herself sitting in her poorly chosen sanctum, reading about herself.
And just the page before:
The major four, lacking one to be the major four, are conspiring to free themselves from the Goddess' yoke.
And the last page, a new line, writing itself as she looked.
This day is flowing slowly. Time is stretching like water and the Book of Shadows is growing.
Suddenly many more pages were added or there were many pages to the end, at least. She started turning the pages rapidly. She skipped to the final page, suddenly panicking.
And the Dollmaster is storming the witches' citadel and making it his, making them his.
Jill closed the book with a thunderous crack. She put it away, putting it back in the drawer, feeling the horrible nausea wash over her. And she sat unmoving in her chair for a long time. Days and Nights passed by as she failed to move, failed to act. There was anger then, finally, at last, making her rise, making her move, rise from the chair, move out the door, into the hot sunshine. There was a barn there and there were other people. They seemed familiar to her, but it had been so long. She hardly recognized them.
She met Olivia Norman, one of the more positive, liberal teachers in the hall.
– Hello, Jill, she said.
– Hello, Olivia, she said cheerfully. – What can I do for you?
– I've wanted to talk to you for some time, the teacher said, more than a bit taken back.
Jill stopped and said, even more cheerfully:
– Okay, I can spare a few seconds…
Olivia's ability to speak failed her and she stood there, undecided.
– You're a bright girl, she said finally. – I've never understood why so many of you throw away your chances the way you do.
– Chances to do what, specifically?
Olivia opened her mouth to speak, but no words came out.
– Poor Olivia, Jill told her. – Don't you know your own mind, know yourself, about anything?
And she was gone, like the wind.
She sits in her poorly chosen sanctum, writing her Book of Shadows.

The book is changing as Time itself is changing, flowing like water.

Luke swallowed hard and shook his head, suddenly overwhelmed with emotion. He felt both such warmth and such an overwhelming sadness. The one threatened to wash him away and the other to suck him down into the vast Abyss.

– Alone together or together, Jill spoke with conviction. – We'll all return here.

The cabin. We're back by the cabin.

Luke was only wearing shorts. Nothing special about that. He was always dressing casually and light during the summer. No, for the first time in ages he was fully able to sense the wind, the air, Life inside and outside. Something had slept inside him almost since childhood, now awakening to full strength and the cold wind surrounding him for so very long had turned hot.

– We're walking the path through the twilight summer, the shadow lands, Stacy said. – We can never leave it, but Freedom is ours to find somewhere ahead.

Toni jumped and danced with the other kids in front of the procession, on the way home to the farm. It was hard, if not impossible to look at her and realize that she had been sick, on the verge of death, just a short while ago. Even if Luke knew Jill didn't wish it so, he felt indebted to her and the other youths surrounding him.

– I can help you, too, he said, she heard him say, – help you to avoid my mistakes. Experience can be very hard earned sometimes.

She saw the barn straight ahead, the old, ramshackle barn.

– This old barn, for instance… I've wanted to do something about it since my eyes first fell on this miracle of still standing architecture.

They laughed with him, not at him.

– We'll need a bit more equipment, though.

– *I'll get it,* Jill and Stacy said simultaneously. The others were so used to them speaking as one that they didn't react in any particular way to it.

– We'll get it, Stacy said calmly, with a slight smile. – The rest of you guys should start on the job. That way we may finish this before twilight sets in.

What she said should have been ridiculous, but wasn't. He had a notion of why, too, but he still wasn't sure.

The tool shed was on the other side of the main building. Stacy and Jill weren't interrupted on their way there, nor while they were there.

– So you do believe that every action is fundamentally selfish, Stacy commented pleased. – That's wise.

– Yes, Jill replied in a neutral manner. – I don't necessarily see anything inherently wrong with it either… unless it becomes totally self-serving. It's typical for you to ignore the positive aspects of what we spoke about.

– I worry about you. Stacy shook her head. – I really do. Anubis can be of enormous use to you, to us, if you're playing him right. But you're letting his weakling old self get to you.

– I did play him, Jill said. – It was so easy, so tempting. Don't ever expect me to enjoy it, okay?

– But I do expect you to enjoy it. Stacy stopped just by the wall where most of the tools hung. – We're gonna rule Homo Magi, little sister, and thereby the world. There's no room for squeamishness in such a scheme. There's a rebellious streak in you. You need to prove something to yourself, I can understand that, but now it's time to put such childishness behind us. This is our fate. Can't you feel it?

Jill stood there with both her hands rolled into fists.

– I know you can. Stacy nodded to her.

– *Shut up!* Jill said enraged.

– Are you telling *me* to shut up? Stacy turned *white* from anger. The last words she spat so fast that they seemed like one. – You impudent, little…

A box filled with wood rose in the air, thrown against Jill. She barely managed to direct it away from herself and it smashed into the wall behind her. Her mouth twisted in a snarl. An axe flowed with murderous intent towards Stacy. The moment before it reached her, its path seemed to bend and actually drill itself into the door straight by her head. Nails started to fly from the small cardboard box. One was… fired from empty air and hit a board under Jill's right arm. Almost simultaneously another ripped Stacy in her sleeve and flew out through the half open door. A host of nails started flying through the air then. They crossed each other halfway and hit the wall on both sides with a lot of small bangs.

The storm calmed. The unused nails fell to the ground. The wood smoked where the nails had penetrated it.

– You won't get it easy attempting to beat me into submission, Jill told her curtly. Eyes turned normal once more. – I'm just as strong as you.

– Fortunately for you I don't need to. Stacy laughed the confident, poised laugher. – You have already joined my cause. In time you will do so eagerly. The difference between us isn't raw power, that's true. You're still lacking the essential will to use the Power. That will change. I could have killed you, but chose not do. With my experienced cruelty it would have been easy. I'm patient. You will join me, with all your heart and soul.

– One virtue? Jill said teasingly. – Virtuous Stacy, take my hand.

Take it.

And Jill grabbed her hand, took her unprepared. It wasn't shaking hands exactly, merely a touch, a struggle. They held on to each other, in forceful cramps, wild touches. The contact suddenly turned unbelievably strong, powerful. Jill discovered, realized what had earlier escaped her: The barrier Stacy had raised around her thoughts, to hide whatever she wanted to hide. Jill attempted to smash it, break it down, but couldn't do it. The resistance was too strong. She knew, like she knew the other had access to her inner thoughts and emotion. They let go of each other, but the contact, the one that had always been there, would never be broken again.

Materials, nails and tools, rose in the air at their command. They smiled and wandered through a landscape of milk and honey thinking dark thoughts. They knew that the struggle wasn't done. Not between them and in no way the one they should wage against the rest of the world. It was about to start in earnest, everything, everything they had waited for, for so long. From their own personal starting point, viewpoint, both equal and unequal to the other, they threw themselves into the Storm.

4

The four of them went to Everett's former home, the place he had lived with his parents, a fairly big place, but just a house, nothing like the giant mansions elsewhere in the city.

They didn't meet his parents. The house was quiet, just as they wanted it, a sort of temporary safe house, neutral territory. They couldn't be certain *she* wasn't with them, with them wherever they went, but at least this place wasn't hers.

Everett's bedroom was exactly as he had presumably left it. And more importantly; the computer and Internet access was still in place. Evidently the filthy rich didn't care much about their children's whereabouts or their actions, as long as they remained in the fold or didn't cause a scandal (or something).

– It shouldn't take too long to find it, Everett stated with a clear undercurrent of excitement in his voice.

So, Jason, Stacy and Jill sat down and watched the screen while he did the search. He had basically the same set-up as Laurie, but not as fancy, of course.

The news was on, and he let it. Jill sat there without really listening or watching, until the word of the most recent hurricane came on. There had been a substantial number of them this year. The news announcer's voice started to penetrate her screen.

– The hurricane Wilma has now reached the Southeastern parts of United States, wrecking havoc in its wake. After devastating major parts of the Caribbean our quite angry Lady has set her eyes on Louisiana and Texas and is expected to cause millions of dollars of damage. People have been evacuating the coastal area the last two days, after an early warning from our excellent weathermen.

– They have used up all their names, Jill exclaimed incredulous.

She studied the offered satellite photos. Was this the Storm she had observed from Space? It didn't look like it, but then she had been in quite a different state of consciousness at the time, so she couldn't really decide. Her entire body tingled, and she let it happen.

– Wilma is the 21st hurricane this unprecedented season, and is thereby completing, for the first time in history, the system used by the National Hurricane Center in Miami. All the hurricanes are given names, and this means they have to start all over again before the season is done… Usually the list of names is only repeated in the six-year loop the center is practicing, but it looks like nature has thrown a monkey-wrench into any human made system this year, folks…

– They're treating it like a joke. Jason shook his head.

– And now sports. The Lakers will…

– I got it! Everett cried. – I got the recording.

His reaction seemed a little excessive, but they understood why. The same maggots of worry and gathering desperation haunted them. They felt hunted and couldn't be sure if it was real or blatant paranoia. The true fear was that they would never be sure.

They sat down, watching intensively. The Mystery Hour program they had viewed a while ago repeated itself… with a twist. They hadn't known then, what they had heard through the grapevine that far more had been going on after the ordinary broadcast had ended.

And it had been recorded and broadcasted up and down on the Internet ever since.

– … creatures of passion. Wild, savage animals roaming the forest.

Ted Warren's voice, so passionate, so enticing.

– Isn't that more than a bit… extreme?

– I don't think so, Gayle, Warren grinned. – On the contrary, I find it completely natural. It's the way we «live» today that is unnatural.

And so it went. Gayle Tadero, the interviewer turned visibly excited as the interview progressed. Ted and Liz, too, even if they had been very passionate already from the start. They touched each other constantly and it seemed to be very hot in the studio.

The official broadcast ended in a basically calm manner. But even so it had gained infamy status even before… the juiced-up copy had started circulating on the Internet.

Gayle walked straight to Ted and started kissing him, kissing him passionately, very flustered and very eager. Liz stripped, casually and hotly both.

– Okay, boys and girls. Ted waved the audience down from their seats, pulling them to him. – Time to get the show going.

Some ran down. Some left the auditorium.

But most walked down to the stage in a sort of excited daze.

The four watching the recording sat there, not really believing their eyes. They had witnessed many incredible «incidents» lately, but nothing that could possibly compare to this.

– They're doing it, they're really *doing* it. Stacy clapped her hands.

– They're doing it, Jason stated.

– We must show this to everybody, Jill said weakly. – We must show it many times.

And the Storm gathered and gained strength. The four felt it, and they, too, felt strengthened. Darkness descended and everything previously was thrown out the window.

5

Planets circle stars. They are remains of the stardust that created the star an infinite time in the past. These remains may have a form like an asteroid the size of a football field or a giant planet close to a star's mass. Planets are known to contain Life. General human theory is stating four conditions for development of Life in Cosmos:

- **The size of a star** - The original mass determines potential lifetime and how long time Life will have a chance to develop.
- **Its lifetime** - (Not necessarily connected to its mass. Disasters of Cosmic proportions outside the star system may impair its function in fatal direction.) Directly determining the life of any satellite.
- **The planet's size** - Planets' size is measured according to Terra's size (not surprisingly), which is given the relative number 1. It shouldn't be significantly smaller since that would

cause gravity to be too weak to hold onto the atmosphere. It shouldn't be significantly bigger, since such planets, if experience from our solar system holds water, become gas giants.

- **The planet's distance to the star** - Terra is close to ideally placed, in the so-called lifebelt. Just a little bit closer to the sun, like Venus, and it becomes inhospitable hot. Lead melts on the surface in the thick atmosphere. A little bit further away from the sun, like Mars, and it becomes too cold. The Martian atmosphere is too cold and too thin.

Life is valuable…

Memory can't precede consciousness.

What was this? She sat in her chair, her head resting on the desk. She must have fallen asleep. It was so strange. She was fully aware of this being a dream. This was… fantastic. She had to remember it all, write it down.

The Universe, they say, began 15 billion years ago in what must have been the biggest explosion ever. In what has been described as a pinprick of a needle (even if all measure was meaningless then, at least then) an enormous expansion began. The number 15 billion is just that, a number. No human can imagine such a long time, such a time span. In other words: The Universe is supposed to be 15 billion light years big (without that helping comprehension any). Light moves with a speed of close to 300 000 kilometers per second. In other words: The distances in Cosmos are so monstrous that we're unable to comprehend them. Observers from Earth, through their machines, are able to «see» 10 billion light years into Space. The charming problem concerning this is that we're not seeing the place we're looking at, as it is now, but as it was 10 billion years ago. Will we one day be able to see the beginning of the Universe?

What is Time and what is Space? Are they merely labels, hooks and pegs to hang things from?

Well, as the scientific creation myth goes, «once» in a timeless time when all matter was one single mass of infinite density, something happened. A sudden, expanding explosion from one «central» point. Everything that was this mass became the Universe. Now, excluding «dark matter» and such, the most typical place in existence is empty space. If a person has been teleported to a random spot in the Universe, the chances of getting close to a star or a planet will be close to microscopic. But there are within star systems consciousness is evolving.

Memory can't precede consciousness, can't precede existence, can't reach back before the dark nothingness before Life's ember. Still, perhaps this is memory, these flashes of the Universe slowly cooling after the Big Bang, these Shadows on the edge of consciousness. There is no thought, no eyes or ears. They say that in the future it will be possible to store information on a molecular level. One single nucleus may contain billions of bits of information. Perhaps it will be similar to all other technology, a discovery instead of an invention. If information truly is stored on a microscopic level, then all that information, back to the beginning of the Universe is present… in us all.

Even today, all (known) matter is 99 percent Hydrogen and Helium, the two elements created by elementary particles in the fireball after the explosion. In the newborn galaxies, when Space was one billion years old, stars developed fast and ended fast in supernova explosions. This was the first generation of stars. The waste they released was heavier than the Hydrogen and Helium that had created them. There were Carbon, Oxygen and even heavier elements. Carbon, when mixed with Hydrogen, is a necessity for what we call organic compounds.

Billions of years later these compounds are present in the creation of new stars. This time the development is happening at a slower pace. The stars are more stable and have a longer life span, as is the case with the planets circling them. On at least one of these planets, perhaps on more than one, in an atmosphere of Hydrogen and subsequent Methane and Ammonium, powerful lightning flashes across the sky and the earth. Without eyes the boiling soup is seen. Without ears the rolling thunder is heard in the scarred landscape. The first organic molecules, simple and more complex are emerging in this seemingly life-hostile environment. Perhaps there will be Life on this planet later on. The stars are bathing the planet's atmosphere in ultraviolet radiation. The heat leads to lightning. These energies are creating the complex organic molecules that may lead to the emergence of Life.

Without thoughts there is the realization that it won't happen here. The process leading to Life started too late on this planet. The star has turned old. It has consumed all its fuel of Hydrogen, turned it into Helium and the helium is turned into Carbon and Oxygen, and even heavier elements like Silicon, Iron and Uranium. The star expands to a red giant and eventually devours its inner planets. Dust and matter from this star system spread far and wide throughout the Universe during the following eternity.

Our, the Earth's star is a third-generation star. It and its surrounding systems contain far more complex and heavier material than previous generations of stars. Terra, third planet from the sun is like all the other planets bombarded with material and meteorites. Some of these meteorites contain inactive organic molecules, molecules enjoying great evolutionary possibilities in the heat and the lightning of Terra's primordial atmospheric soup. They say the Sun and the Earth are approximately five billion years old. Barring a close cosmic disaster this star will continue to burn «steadily» (the Sun is fluctuating wildly) for five billion more years. Humanity has more than enough *time,* hasn't it?

The Sun is an average, «typical» star (there are no typical stars). There are those that are smaller and others of gigantic proportions. The Life emerging on Earth couldn't have happened if it was a little smaller or a little bigger. Our star system isn't typical, even if the star is. They say that 98 percent of the Galaxy's local systems are double or triple stars, or stars in clusters, all probably unable to contain Life.

If not before, The Universe has on Earth developed consciousness. An existence coming to pass by a number of coincidences, but nevertheless is able to see, hear, feel, think and Live in the infinite emptiness. On the brink of space humanity faces its decisive test. It must make peace with the planet giving birth to it, if the exploration of Cosmos shall not be more of an escape than... an exploration.

Life is valuable.

First part (excerpt and summary) of:
«Observations on evolution and development of Life in the Universe».
Observed by Gabrielle Asteroth, born 1992-02-29

CHAPTER TWELVE: Freedom Road

Once started on the path one must continue on it, or all is lost.

What's the difference between humans and animals? Is there anything, anything significant at all? Intelligence, many will claim. But given the current human state of affairs many will disagree and with good reason. Especially if one is mixing intelligence and wisdom.

The hands perhaps? Though the apes have hands, too, and use them in similar ways, using tools quite effectively. Some scientists claim that apes can never surpass a three-year-old human, but this is a test measured for humans, by humans, using human standards. Can anyone cry preconception here?

I agree with those who say that we're still apes. The similarities are simply far bigger and more extensive than the differences. There are those claiming we have an ability of abstract thought lacking in animals, but I'm not so sure. That ability is something wonderful, but exactly because of this there's no need to lay any single claim to it. Even if that ability has led us from a perpetual state of Freedom to the stone cities, to the verge of self-destruction, a tailspin suicide run, it has also given us a richer life, by giving us a sense of Self. Or perhaps so…

But when, how did we become… humans? What, if anything caused it, caused the change whenever it happened, making us the human subspecies of the ape family, instead of «just» apes? What makes a creature leave its usual environment and seek what's different, what's Unknown? Probably the same as ever: A chain of coincidences and a never diminishing curiosity. One group, a small one, seemingly less adapted to the surroundings than the majority, leaves or is left behind by the majority. Perhaps left or driven out to die, banned from what had been their home. It's then that their latent abilities bloom in full. What was just a hunch, a notion becomes something fully fledged and pronounced. During just a few generations they've become the norm. Mutations are happening constantly. Most are damaging to the offspring, detrimental to further Life. Some are just plain useless… but some very few cause an individual to be better adapted to its surroundings, to what might be a harsh environment. It's merciless, but that is Nature. As merciless as it's generous. Except the generosity has a limit, but not the mercilessness.

We know that now.

Or perhaps we don't know it, now, what once was a given, what our distant ancestors knew as a truth as obvious as that of the sun rising every morning.

The evolution from Ramapithecus via Australopithecus to Homo Erectus seems almost painfully slow, stretching over millions of years. Personally, I don't believe much happened in «the dark age», the one without preserved skeletons, other than that nature took its time. Any other explanation to describe human evolution doesn't seem needed to me.

Time. Time created the human being.

Australopithecus is called the first humanoid, the forerunner to the first human, Homo Erectus, the erected man. Legs, ankles, head and pelvis in H.E. were completely adapted to the use of an erected body. And they used fire. But 500000 years ago, there was still little art or recognition of self in water mirrors or smooth surfaces.

But now there's only between 200 000 and 300 000 years to the next stage. The first Homo Sapiens, ancestors to all present-day humans, emerged between 500 000 and 200 000 years before the present. This relative explosive development led to Homo Sapiens Sapiens… and to Homo Sapiens Magi. The thinking, creative animal had arrived, and the planet would never more be the same.

She sat by the window in the classroom, she was certain of that much. She was breathing the air of both a distant and a close land. Her immediate surroundings distracted her. Factory pipes spewed smoke and poison, unnatural to nature and all life in it. Within the poisoned walls humans toiled under the whip. Outside protesters knocked their heads against the fence. The first ones in Northfield in living memory. She experienced Scott Thompson's distorted features inside his world of glass. She saw eager and rebellious passions mirrored in the faces of those who dared to oppose him. Humanity hadn't forgotten. There was hope.

Once more she breathed the air of the distant land. The veil of Space and Time faded away…

… Three hundred thousand years. So far, so short a distance in time. There is a legend… many… about a woman. In present day language she had as many names as there were languages, but the best known was… In present day speech it sounded something very much like Gaia. The meaning was as varied as the many names.

The Earth. The World. The Well of Souls. Eternal Life. The First One. *The first to live on,* instead of merely die.

The waterfall marked the end of the plains with the still major sea. Both were clearly diminished. One could see evidence in the terrain that both the waterfall and the sea had once extended far beyond its present boundaries. It wasn't that long ago either. *Victoria Falls,* the girl by the open window thought. They looked very much like they do today, but with far less water, a drought unheard of, both before and after.

The female stood upright on the rock growing out of the hill. Arms were stretched to the sides. She spoke a flow of guttural sounds, a singing not singing. They flowed over the land around her. The ancient Africa, the great eastern plains where many on present day Earth theorize human Life began.

Her body was in a natural state, nude and without any form of ornament. The constant heat every day and night of the year made clothes unnecessary, and this was a long time before vanity played any part in human life. As her contemporaries she, too, had hair on certain areas of the body. Her forehead was short. Her face, even if free of hair, was coarse. The bones above her eyes were thick, protruding. Body was short and had a heavy build. She generally looked like her contemporaries and tribal members, those who had cast her out.

But… and she knew it herself… a closer look revealed minor, evident nuances between her and the rest of the tribe, also compared to her sisters and brothers, the others born of her mother. Her forehead was longer. Her face not so unmovable and her body was definitely taller. She was as tall as the tribal males. And she… behaved differently. Her behavior deviated clearly from the rest. Something that in the close, tight bonds of the tribe was noticed far more clearly than any physical deviation.

The tribe had arrived at the land by the big pond many births ago. The times had been good then. The tribe had enjoyed painless growth. The fire-keepers, through their more extensive vocabulary of signs and movements, knew more than the others and found pleasure in telling them about the time before the arrival at the green and pleasant land. They had all made use of its sweet rewards.

But the flowing water arriving from far away, giving the land - and them - Life had decreased slowly, almost imperceptible over the years and suffering, almost vanished into Legend, found the tribe anew. First, they were able to keep a balance of sorts. As many died as were born. When new life was born the oldest had to leave to die. This was an old custom, virtually inborn and there was no aggravated grief. But soon, very soon their situation worsened. Those who «had to move on» got younger and younger.

The tall skinny female had lived ten full seasons, fully grown now. Many were older than her, but she was childless, barren.

The day after the blood had flowed from her loins yet again, she left the only place she had ever known. She walked until she could no longer see Life's Center anymore, to the Bones' Pond, where all the old and useless went to seek death. She brought no weapons, no tools. She had no more use for such things.

In and by the dry pond, the river of sand, there were countless bones and skulls, some recent, most dissolved by time, and heat, and sand. Gaia lay down, to once more become one with the vast Earth below her. Parts of her would remain on this spot. While their siblings, the four-legged ones would come to her and spread all they could eat of her throughout the endless plains forever.

Clouds black and gray drifted across the mountains, touching her unmoving body. She felt the pains of hunger in her stomach, a short while, and then it ended. *She knew dreams.* They came to her now, unwanted, disturbing her wish to become one with the land, sending her awakened thoughts in directions never before experienced. The body lay still, but something was stirring inside her, both part and not part of the flesh and the blood. Something that had always belonged to the shadows twisted and turned and pushed, and wanted out. She recognized the feeling, even if she had never experienced it, never thought she would ever experience it; that of a birthing mother.

Suddenly she found herself high up in the air. She gasped and snarled in fear and in the wish of being afraid. But she sensed a calm, strange and familiar, new and ancient. And a word, a concept she had never thought before. Something timeless. *Time*... What was on her mind? What thoughts did she think, out here, in the shadow land? Suddenly, with a pull, a shock, from one moment to the next, she moved one step further away from her former tribe, her former life.

Everything... flowed around her. The land changed without changing, A changeless Change. The four-legged ones remained the same. The Water of Life spread anew, and trees returned. All plants cried in Joy because of all their new siblings joining them. A... forest of growth came to be around the Big Pond. And in its proximity, she could observe tall, upright ones... not the same. They hardly resembled in any way her old former tribe members, but she knew she was there herself, even if she couldn't see herself.

She sat up, moving easily up on two legs. Darkness had fallen. The wind rattled all the dry bones. At the top of the hill, just a few lengths away, stood a beautiful long tooth unmovable. But Gaia didn't fear that its claws and teeth would be used to tear her apart. She knew now that those who had been her people were doomed. Exactly why and how wasn't clear to her yet, but she knew that she herself wouldn't die. She ran towards the long tooth. The wonderful hunter waited until she was almost there, and then made an enormous jump into the night.

And Night jumped, too, as it did in these parts of the world. The cloak covering the mountain that once in a distant future would be called Kilimanjaro shimmered in the lights from Little Sun. Little Sun, merely a pale reflection of the One Who Gave Life. The two-legged female stretched her body on the rock. She realized now, why the people she had belonged to, why they would die. Its waves differed ever more from the land. The land changed. They didn't. Even in a new, flourishing land they would succumb.

The female could recall her own birth now. This was like experiencing it anew. And it didn't just happen to her. Everything around her had suddenly changed. The land... was dead, its Shadow not... alive. It swarmed with Life. But none of its countless creatures had any living shadow. Except her. What she sensed in herself was lacking.

Everything necessary was present... but form without content, as if the land itself hadn't been born yet. It lacked a consecration, something to give it birth, make it come alive. Until now. Now the world was about to be born. It had waited all this time... for her.

Her waves flowed in unison with the land, and they were one.

The heavyset, big teeth bit into animal flesh, pulled and tore at it, chewed it to bits. The fire warmed both her and the Shadow, warmed Her. She had made new tools, new weapons. She was alone. In the entire world nobody knew her name. She didn't really know for what, but she, too was waiting. Fire from the sky had given her her own to carry and care for. She moved across the plain, while ever seeking the best shade, the best hiding place. Constantly casting glances around her, seeking enemies, fully aware of her vulnerability, that she was prey to every possible tribe, including the one that had been raising her. She didn't belong to them anymore.

She strived to become one with the land, made the attempt several places, before she found the special rock. There had been... touch, a flicker of a shadow, but it was a temporary and traitorous feeling. Most of the time she felt half in, half out. The sounds she released through her mouth were meaningless, at least at first. The first minutes, hours, days. She gave them meaning. Lights, sounds turned many. A stone turned and under it was a flash of shadow. An animal cried her name.

(I can see the rainbow, the multitude).

Her waves moved in synch with the land (and they were one).

The shadow changed form as she was running. Four-legged, two-legged, a two-legged winged creature...

She stopped abruptly, scenting the male before she spotted him with her constantly seeking eyes. For a prolonged time, they stood there, a safe distance away from each other, in mutual distrust. He was ragged, bleeding from more than one place on his skinny body and seemed generally as if he had wandered alone a very long time. He was an outcast like her. Her sex grew heavy and wet. He sniffed heavily several times in the shifting wind. But then he didn't waste any more time. He stormed to her. She crouched on all fire with her hips, her sex stuck up in the air and widespread legs. One single thrust and he reached deep within her, rocking back and forth.

I can feel him. Not just his rock-hard cock, but all of him.

His wounds were… they were mortal. Nothing she could do could save him. When he left her he was already dead. She grieved, grieved far harder than if it had been one from her old tribe. Not the least because she sensed that what had always been dead inside her now was blooming. She didn't really dare believe it, until her next moon-time failed. Then she had confirmed what she already knew in her shadow's shadow.

She followed a small river up into the mountains, seeking ever higher as the moons came and went. The land turned colder, fertile. She kept the skin of her kills, making covers. In a water mirror she saw her face and she noticed the special twitch in the peculiar face. She had seen it a few times earlier in her features, mostly the last few moons and recognized it as a sign of her… enjoying herself. The loneliness was hard to deal with sometimes, but since she wasn't any typical flock-beast she survived where others might have just laid down and died on the spot. She had strength to survive on her own and soon she would no longer be alone. And something more than a notion convinced her that it wasn't just a matter of the little one, but more.

Time… flowed. She sort-of noticed its passing and in quite different ways than while still living in the village, though still only from one incident to another, a break in the routine needed to survive and thrive. She gave birth to her male child some time into the dry season, in the shade of the giant icecap covering Kilimanjaro. She had some idea about the distance up there, even if her eyes fooled her into believing she could just raise up a hand and touch it. The sense of comfort and belonging, however, both for herself and the child, as he grew to manhood, made her quell her curiosity and remain. The dry wind from the plain below created a constant temperate climate where they lived, making it a good place to thrive. Hard and difficult to find, but the reward made it all worthwhile.

The male quickly grew taller than her. She had gathered almost immediately after his birth that he would grow up to become quite different from both his parents. They mated as soon as he was ready for it. It didn't last many moons until she sensed new life within her. The waiting had ended.

Other outcasts, seekers or wanderers eventually came to follow in her footsteps. Mostly from even further away, but also from what had been her tribe. They came from the entire ring around the Mountain That Cut the Sky. They found the rock first, just a few starting, setting out on the seemingly endless journey. Most of them stayed there. Just a very few followed the tracks of her shadow and merely a very few of them again succeeded in finding her. The rest were killed, lost the track or stopped.

Gaea's female child had been born when the first two found them, a female and male together had arrived. Afterwards there were more. Never many, never more than two or three, either together or alone, each full season. Sufficient, though, over moons and full seasons, through births and new travelers, for them to become a minor tribe. Gaea birthed many children, far past the time it should have ended for her. Her children birthed many of their own. She grew older, but only very slowly. Many she had seen born, not related to her died. Even her firstborn grew old and died before she did. Not many followed the river up anymore, coming to them from the outside. Their number increased to the point where they dared started taking trips down to the plains once more.

They noticed it all of them, realizing it long before they actually started expressing it, how other tribes seemed to disappear even from the plains. Nature made ever better room for them, without them actually doing anything. They had to hunt there, too, now, but there were very few clashes with the remaining tribes. And then the last few two-legged ones just seemed to die along the land itself. The mountain people still happened to encounter other tribes, but they had grown to become the biggest one in a vast area. They were shunned even more after that.

The children of her children started to die of old age. The first from the fifth generation had been born and grown up to have children of their own. There were still tribe-members who weren't of her blood and among them people from the fifth generation had started to die of old age.

She was old now and wished to wander, walk away. But they kept her from doing it, friendly, but firmly. She started to tell them about the coming times. It was impossible to tell how far into the future her visions would become reality. She, they had no words to describe it, no thoughts to comprehend it. The images, the emotions told her, told them enough, though, more so than they ever wanted. Cold… so much terrible… alien, alienated. Drought everywhere. Stone, nothing but stone.

You must move on, she told them during her last days. Never be like the plants and take root in one

single place. We're Nomads. Without this in our lives we'll rot inside and eventually fade away and die.
Gaia's first daughter held her. This woman was still young. The years worked on her even less than they had on her mother. And she had given birth to many children. She would give birth to another any day now. Gaia touched the round belly and the special twitch they all knew so well moved her face again. It looked more like how anyone from the older tribes would have expressed themselves, but it didn't bother those who surrounded her. She had been the first in many generations to seek new land. And the mountain people didn't feel contempt or anger towards the older tribes. They knew that without them they wouldn't have existed.

The frail creature on the ground blinked once. Stones, rocks, soil flashed in lights and colors. Gaia blinked one last time with her tired, old body. She felt so alive. Suddenly the lights and the colors started dancing in the air… and the Shadow dancing in the middle of it all was her. She looked back down at what had been her body. And then she sought within, seeking what the frail shell had contained, now, when she had become so much more than she had been. She couldn't tell for sure when this new, this Change had happened: In her youth, well before this body had drawn its last breath or in exactly that moment. She stretched her «arms», spread her «lap», herself, embracing her children, stretching herself to all the places she had wandered while she had been among the living, now when she was more alive than ever.

They left her there, on the spot where she had expired and moved the camp somewhere else. Next morning when they went back there, she was gone. The land had claimed what it had once given. Many years passed. No one forgot. In addition to all the stories they experienced constant reminders of her presence. Sometime distant, sometimes right there in their midst. The time came when they left the mountain and wandered out into the world. They left torches there, burning wet and hot, to easily find their way back, if they one day should so desire. They kept on wandering, the eternal nomads. Sometimes she had a form as a human being, sometimes as a shadow, but in the mists of time and shadow her absence rarely lasted long. She was never really gone. They - and she - spread across the world. When they needed her, wherever they wandered, she was with them.

The stories about her grew and changed, as she changed herself, as Homo Sapiens split and spread across the vast continent, the vast world. Homo Sapiens - Thinking Man. This species was the forerunner to all the following subspecies: Homo Sapiens Neanderthalensis, Java, Solo, Homo Sapiens Sapiens and Homo Sapiens Magi (among many). Legend became hard to separate from fantasy, but they still felt as they were honoring her in a way. The stories differed, but the core of it all remained the same. She was the origin. Without her they wouldn't have existed. They gave her many names, many origins. Though there was one that stuck, one used more often than others:
Mother Earth.

Third part (excerpt and summary) of:
«Observations on evolution and development of Life in the Universe».
Observed by Gabrielle Asteroth, born 1992-02-29

2

The girl sat by the open window. Wind blew hard through it. It didn't alleviate the heat that much, but it still felt good. Air was so *dry*. Ever more grains of sand tore themselves off the ground and rubbed against each other in an endless disturbing low hum. You no longer heard just the locusts in the evening, but the ghostly whispers of the sand as well. The sand penetrated everything. She sat in the classroom, trapped by the imbalance and injustice everywhere and hating every moment of it.

– Gabrielle…

She looked up. It was Miss Chapman, the history teacher, making her voice heard. The *corrected* science project was dumped on her desk with a silent snarl.

– In your defense I must say that there's nothing wrong with your ambitions, the teacher expressed herself in quite a patronizing way. – But part three of your work has the same, pretentious, circumstantial «quality» as one and two. The very least you should do to improve upon it, is to do a substantial trimming, not do all those distracting detours…

Words, spoken and written, swam before Gabrielle's eyes. She saw the letter «C» and little more.
– That you're narrow-minded is your problem, the girl prompted. – You shouldn't attempt to bother others with it.

The room turned silent. Even the wind and the sounds from outside and the low-level talking seemed to fade.

– What are you saying? The teacher seemed pleased with herself. – We've got some extra time today. Why don't we hear our little genius elaborate further on this?

– Well, it is common knowledge that I'm a pagan, a very active pagan, Gabrielle shrugged. – And that you, as a *devoted* christian and otherwise are pretty much opposed to pagans anywhere.

– Now that you mention it… Miss Chapman bent slightly forward, leaning over the girl. – Your heathen ways, also visible in your work, are indeed troubling. You're on dangerous ground with your blasphemy, girl.

– I don't believe in God, or in any supreme being, Gabrielle exclaimed impulsively. – And the American constitution gives me the right to believe in whatever I *want.*

– You're a minor, an irresponsible brat, the teacher replied coldly, no longer bothering to hide her hostility, – clearly not sufficiently mature for this class level.

– One thing is intolerance, Gabrielle continued unfazed. – Another is your blatant ignorance. The general rules for projects such as this can't be interpreted by you. They state clearly that you can only judge the work on its own merit. We're asked to speculate, and I wrote myself in as an observer to make it easier for others to access the story. Then it's your writing skills and by default your ability to interpret others' work. The story is, by *my* definition, one about humanity and the Universe itself, or at least one tiny chapter of it. It can't and shouldn't be narrowed and trimmed. «Indigestible» bits and pieces can't and shouldn't be left out, without lessening the whole. Your «opinion» is nothing new, you know. I'm usually told to leave something out, to lessen it in scope and ambition, «to get a leaner, more streamlined story». After reading through it I always end up adding *more.* Pretentious, you say? Well, that is, as ever, in the eye of the beholder.

She didn't shout, but it seemed that way, as if every word was released close to everybody's ear, both their ears. She spoke in a leveled, modulated tone, every word hitting like a brick. Where she sat she seemed much older than her physical age.

– That's it. Miss Chapman turned demonstrative away. – I'm going to recommend that you're moved down a level on the next board meeting. I want you to know that I'm only thinking about your own good… and that of your immortal soul.

Gabrielle let out a burst of laughter, more of a bark of hysteria. The teacher continued on her quest back to her desk. The girl rose so suddenly that she knocked over both her desk and chair. Teacher and pupils stared at her with wide eyes. She had hit her knees on her desk, but hardly noticed the paralyzing pain.

– It's the sex, right? Low-keyed snickering erupted in the classroom. She heard the inevitable catching in her throat and hated it. – That's what you're really objecting to, the showing of true passion?

Miss Chapman blushed, red as a tomato.

– You won't claim that one can write a story of some length without describing sex and sexual intercourse and still claim realism, will you? You're not that… stupid?

Julie Chapman charged then.

– I need you to help me out here, Gabrielle, the Principal appealed to her. They were having a «confidential» conversation in his office. – Your behavior lately has showed a steady decline. Care to tell me why?

– Let me see if I can get this straight. Gabrielle counted on her fingers, very deliberate. – Julia attacked me, and I get the blame.

– Most people would say that she had more than sufficient provocation…

– No, that's wrong, that's utterly and completely incorrect. The girl sat in the chair with a slightly bowed head, her eyes burning into the man before her. – After she had attempted to provoke me for several minutes, without really succeeding, she reacted badly to getting a sample of her own medicine. And teachers aren't allowed to strike the students, anyway, far less *assault* them. I could press charges, you know, and win easily.

– Your parents don't see it that way, he said, shaking his head.

– You've spoken to… my parents, without speaking to me first?

– They do agree that you're a bit too… headstrong, for your own good.

He spoke to her as if he was a kind, old uncle. It irritated her to no end. Her head and cheek hurt where the teacher had hit her, before she had been getting her own licks in.

– I can't believe this. She threw up her arms in exasperation. – You're all conspiring to censor me and you even have the audacity to claim you only want what's best for me. I can't believe how you can call yourself a Historian, how you can pretend to support true inquiry. Hasn't it occurred to you that the mind *must* be free from all limitations… that everything is meaningless without that simple rule? Can't you see that, at least?

The last sentence was delivered in a quiet, almost subdued way, more in despair than in anger. Not that it helped any. As she had feared, expected he continued his rant, as if she hadn't really spoken at all.

– You're one of our most intelligent students, Gabrielle, he said insistently, patiently. – It isn't a coincidence that you're placed two levels above your age group. So, will you please tell me what's wrong?

– You could have placed me at the university without it making a difference, she shrugged.

– Oh? Uncle Principal exclaimed, not so uncle-like anymore. – How come?

– Julia and you are both excellent representatives of society. The girl gave him her most flashing smile. The principal smiled, too. – And there's a major difference between society and me.

Good ol' Uncle Principal sat there with his mouth wide open. He didn't smile anymore.

– Didn't I tell you that your dreams would get you into trouble? Maeve Curry told her later that day. She spoke in a cheerful, joking tone, with merely a slight edge of worry.

Maeve was in the same class, two years older, but usually felt a lot younger, a feeling shared by other older children and even grown-ups.

– It doesn't really matter, Gabrielle replied. – Not anymore. It is as if school and everything we're told is… important in our lives… isn't, and means even less each day.

– What else is there? Maeve innocently shook her head.

They stopped at the top of the long and broad stairs leading back at the school. The first call had already chimed. Before the second chime they had to be present in the classroom. If they were found in the hall after that, without a hall pass, they would be reported.

Gabrielle stretched her neck, looking at Frazer Hill, but also at the streets below it. She had done so many times, in prevalent curiosity and fear. Maeve saw it, too, looking where she looked.

– Are you serious? She said shocked.

Gabrielle nodded stubbornly, while struggling to smile. It wasn't far to the Hill, the farm and to Oldtown. She wanted to go there. She couldn't.

She had a valid reason for her fear her friend lacked, and it all seemed farther away than ever.

– You don't want to be seen with them, do you? Maeve asked.

And as Gabrielle met her eyes and stared her down, as the other girl looked away, the young witch felt lonelier than ever. She couldn't go there, she couldn't stay here. Where could she go?

The two of them never spoke again.

Things didn't improve at home when she attempted to talk with her parents later that day. She had always obeyed them, been the nice daughter, but now it dawned on her that they had never given her the same consideration. They weren't any worse than the people at school. They weren't any different either.

The two of them sat in the sofa. She sat in the chair. They gave her the same look they always gave her, as if she was an ornament they evaluated. There wasn't a thing in the house there was anything *wrong* with. If one scratch or fault was discovered, it was removed and exchanged with a faultless supplant. That wasn't an option this time.

Had to be very frustrating.

– We've always been compliant to your special… interests, her father began. – We've allowed your fantasies to flourish in the vain hope you would grow beyond them.

– You were always such a nice girl, her mother appealed to her. – What happened to you? Our little girl didn't lack respect for her elders like we heard from school today or what you've said about the nice Mr. Thompson.

– I'm growing up, mommy…

– Don't you dare being impudent, young lady, her father warned her (father knows best). – You shan't talk back to grownups.

– But I wasn't…

– SHUT UP. I told you to SHUT UP, didn't I?

– Yes, daddy, she sniffed. – I'm sorry daddy.

– Perhaps we should send her to Dr. Tomlinson…

– I don't need a fucking SHRINK. She jumped up from her chair, couldn't keep herself in check anymore. – His only solution is for me to *adapt.* He keeps claiming that what I really want is to be like everybody else and that's *bullshit.*

– That's ENOUGH. The father rose to his full length, walked around the table and slapped her in the face.

She stared at him in shock. Her cheek burned. It didn't really hurt. But she virtually shrank from his wrath. He had always had that effect on her. She started crying in big, gasping sobs.

– Since you refuse to show your parents the proper respect, we, your mother and I will discuss what must be done without you being present, he said sternly. – You're confined to the house from this moment on and until we've decided the appropriate action. Now I want you to go to your room immediately.

– Yes, daddy, she said, standing before him with bowed head. – Now, daddy.

When she walked sniveling upstairs, she heard them talk, he with his usual, confident drive.

– What did I tell you? The young don't need anything but a firm hand to steer them in the right direction. With strict guidance they'll soon enough learn prudent behavior.

3

The ravens were gone. Jill felt a flare of panic. She couldn't see or hear or sense them anywhere. They had been here… hadn't they? She tried to think, remember where she had seen them last. It was difficult, since she had become used to always having them around.

She… had been in Laurie's house in Square, with Andrea, picking up baskets of fruit for the market. Now she found herself out by the farm, wandering, wandering aimlessly, heading for somewhere. But where she couldn't say. There were voices somewhere, but she couldn't tell where. She could smell the apple-trees; see the rosy shiny apples, as she walked her predestined walk.

Laurie and Udo stood by the barn. It seemed that they were arguing about something. But something was wrong. The barn looked as bad as before Luke had fixed it the other day. And Udo's hair was longer, not so well done as it was *supposed* to be.

The girl hid behind the wall of the barn, trembling, looking without looking, without being able to look away.

Laurie said a word then. Jill couldn't really make it out, but it had a profound effect on the German boy. He gasped and sank to his knees, completely without strength, without will. And when the other witch roamed his mind at will, he couldn't do anything to resist. He was helpless. Small droplet of tears started to trickle down his cheeks.

– You see, Laurie said triumphantly, – what a complete control I have over you. You believe that, now, don't you?

– Yes, he sobbed. – I do. I do!

– Then we won't have any more displays of rebellion, of insubordination, of disobedience, will we?

– No, I'll be good, I'll be good, please.

– Good boy. The older witch patted his cheeks. – I'm convinced we'll get along much better from this point on.

Much better. She left then. He followed.

He walked subdued by Laurie's side.

His name, his animal spirit. She knew his name and through that she had gained access to his most secret being and thereby gained control over him. This was the past. It had probably happened almost a year ago, just after he had arrived here. Jill trembled. She couldn't stop trembling. Everything dissolved around her, and she was back in Laurie's house in Square… Laurie's *Sanctum*… and she realized with horror that she had never left.

Andrea had left. Laurie had sent her away with a wave of a hand.

– I'm going to show you something, Laurie had told her. – Show you how I deal with rebellious whelps.

The ravens outside had cried and flapped their wings. One move with Laurie's hand and they had dropped out of sight, flown away. She had cut their connection with the girl.

Laurie stood behind her left shoulder. Jill couldn't stop trembling.

– Yes, I know his Name as I know yours.

A whisper in the ear and the girl froze completely.

– I had to deal pretty decisively with his insurrection, though. I won't have to do to you what I did to him, will I now? He did become quite the lackey after that, you see, and hardly much more. I would hate to have to do that to you. You'll be so much more use to me with all your blessed ingenuity and power intact. But I will stop all signs of rebellion cold from now on, do you understand?

Jill wanted desperately to shake her head, but she couldn't move, she couldn't send. Nothing worked. She could receive, but do nothing actively.

– I know you do, you're a bright girl. And it's for your own good. From now on you'll obey me in all things, instantly obey the orders I give the moment I give them.

Something… a release, and Jill could move again, think again.

– Do not raise your shields. Laurie raised a finger. – Not against me. I will have complete access to your thoughts at any time.

Shields? Did she have shields?

She obeyed with bowed head.

– Yes, you have shields. Though rudimentary I have to concentrate to get through them and that is darn annoying, and I won't have it.

– No, Laurie.

– Yes, I know you understand, child. A hand under her jaw pushed up her head. – And you'll understand even better as time goes by, when I've taught you the proper use of all your wonderful gifts. There's so much inside you, so many treasures…

– Yes, Laurie, thank you, Laurie.

Suddenly she was frozen once more, easy as pie. The monster by her side snarled at her.

– I meant it when I said I wouldn't tolerate ANY disobedience from you. And there was clearly a hint of irony in your voice and thought I didn't much care for. Yes, I know you're sorry, so very, very sorry for this is the only reprieve I'll ever give you, is that *clear?*

She could nod again, and she did, with tears streaming down her cheeks.

– All of you are mine to do with as I wish. Only I know what's best for you.

– Yes, Laurie, thank you, Laurie. The girl spoke evenly, respectfully. She didn't dare do anything else.

– This time there was no trace of rebellion. Well done, my dear. I know you fear me now, but though regrettable, it's for the best. In time you'll thank me.

Laurie turned away. Jill remained on the spot.

– You'll continue as usual, of course. Even though the others may suspect something, they can't be sure. They have been mine, too, anyway, for quite some time, without consciously realizing it.

Jill hadn't been told to speak, so she didn't. There was pain somewhere inside her, stabbing her all over.

– Gabrielle's parents called me. Seems like the girl is more trouble than they can handle. But no matter, this is an excellent opportunity for us. I want you to go over there and fetch her, and bring her here. You will use any means necessary, but I know how bright you are. It will be an easy task.

Jill stopped before the mirror in the hall. Everything worked again. The fog in her eyes had gone. She was herself again. She would never be all right again.

Laurie saw her off.

– I know you harbored some secret hopes that I was some kind of real-life Charles Xavier, bringing peace and harmony to the world. But that isn't how the world works, child. I'm sorry.

– Don't worry about it, Jill said hoarsely. – I'm a big girl and I can handle it. I'll serve you, giving you everything you've ever wanted and thereby giving me everything I've ever wanted.

– Yes, the older witch said pleased, – use your anger. That way you'll only serve me better.

She was outside the house. The ravens returned. The streets hadn't really changed. Everything else had. She almost got run down by cars twice and was angry with herself. The Snow White of Northfield. Everything was her fault.

Jill Stafford walked around a corner in Newtown and entered a quieter, more protected area, a typical middleclass neighborhood. Before her she saw row upon row of pretty houses, pretty gardens… At least the gardens had been pretty once (middle class definition), she gathered, groomed to perfection. Now, the lawns were brown and large parts of them looked like they were covered in ashes. Now, no one but an arsonist could call the area pretty. She giggled hysterically, stopped in her tracks, and raised a closed fist to her face. She listened to the voice from the wilderness, the mirror image, but everything was silent. Her powers remained in place. Everything remained in place. How much use was that, with a *shattered* will?

Lawns had turned brown ashes. The trees were about to die from the longest drought in the areas' living memory. Watering plants had become a felony in Northfield. The city council had gritted their teeth and passed the law with a minimum of preparation and waste of time. The fact that the entire Metropolitan Area and legislators in major parts of the Northeastern American continent had done the same the day before made it that much easier for them.

The news was overrun by tales of drought or floods and torrential rain and landslides. News flooded them from the entire planet. Some places it wouldn't stop raining. Here there was not a single cloud in all of the pale blue. To her inner vision however, it was so dark that she had trouble looking through all the charcoal in the air.

– I see the poison mist in the east, she sang. – I see big trouble brewing.

It was comforting in a way, a form of Mantra enraging her, keeping her from falling into the deadly gray calm. Was Laurie truly aware of the boundless Fury, the Beast within her?

The gown, cloak and hood embraced her, both as a prison and liberation. She looked at the world from under her flat-brimmed hat. Her body felt cool under the cloth. People she encountered were sweating like pigs (if pigs did sweat). She didn't really encounter many, though. The heat didn't encourage outdoor life. These houses had air-conditioning. They stared at her, not so much when passing her on the street, but from their kitchens and living rooms. She had thought she had grown used to the staring, and perhaps she had, but earlier today all her anxieties and insecurities had returned with a vengeance, exactly as Laurie had wanted.

She would've found the house easily, even without the address and the fact that thick bars had been put before one of the attic windows. Something ominous and present up there scared her to the point that she didn't dare send out her thoughts to check on it. But that something also pulled at her, caused by curiosity, compassion. And by emotions, moods and passions for what she had no name.

Everything looked so *normal,* like she herself on the outside, even what was normal for *her*. She feared the others, even Stacy wouldn't notice anything different about her. Not so strange perhaps, since she hardly noticed any changes herself. Laurie's method was so insidious, so cruel that everyone she used it on was tempted to, and easily fooled herself or himself into believing that everything… everything was all right.

The doorbell chimed discreetly somewhere inside the entrance hall when she pushed the button. As she had expected, typically for Gabrielle's parents, what she knew of them, there wasn't any shrillness in it. The door opened. A nervous, tired woman showed her head and hardly anything else.

– Please come in, she whispered quickly. She looked as if she was about to pull Jill inside. Jill hurried inside. Door was closed instantly behind her.

The husband, the father towered in front of the entrance to the living room.

– I'm Joshua Asteroth, he said curtly. – I called Miss Isherwood on the phone. This is my wife, Blanche.

Jill offered them her hand. They took it hesitatingly.

A loud crack from above made the entire house shake. The mother jumped, very jumpy. The father, too, did indeed jump, even if he didn't show it openly.

– Gabrielle is upstairs, Blanche pointed out, quite unnecessary.

– Some tea, miss…

– Stafford, Jill Stafford. She curtseyed, as she knew Laurie would want her to do. – Thank you.

They sat in the sofa. She in the same chair she suspected Gabrielle usually sat.

– Our daughter was confined to the premises of the house three days ago, Asteroth said very factual. – She went to school the first day, but upon returning she went straight to her room without eating and has since then not come out. She has pulled more and more inside herself, away from the world and us. During those first critical hours we considered foul play on her part, that she was indeed sulking, but we abandoned that consideration fairly quickly. She grew more silent and ate less. We haven't actually succeeded in getting her to eat and drink much of anything and we've been forced to feed her. We canceled the confinement and her face remained impassive. She lay on her back in the bed, staring blindly at the roof. That was when we decided to call in a… a shrink.

During the entire duration of his narration, he had served Jill the details impassively and in the dry way of a senile professor, but when uttering the last sentence something had changed his voice.

– It was then… it started. The wife looked at the ceiling, as if it was about to attack them. – It had developed into a full scale… it had started *in full* by the time Dr. Tomlinson arrived.

– He stayed in the room no more than two full minutes. Asteroth giggled, completely out of character. – He came charging down the stairs as if the devil himself was chasing him. It was almost hysterically funny… in a way…

Mrs. Asteroth gave him a strict look. He closed his mouth with a snap. Perhaps he wasn't the true boss in the household…

Jill enjoyed herself so much that she almost forgot why she was here. Almost.

– I'm interested in her monthlies, the hooded girl said. – Am I correct in assuming that they started quite late?

– That's right, the mother replied. – She has only had two of them, perhaps three. There's a connection, right? I *knew* it!

– There's a connection, Jill said calmly, – but not the way you think.

– In what way do I think? The woman cried after her.

Jill didn't reply with words as she started climbing the stairs to the next floor. The two of them followed her, carrying with them a many-faced worry. They were like open books to her.

Her toes sometimes reached outside the sandals and touched the carpet. Since her senses were even more sharpened than usual at this time, she imagined she could feel every hair in the soft surface of the stairs, the floor.

Carpet is of excellent quality, she thought. The Asteroth couple has spared no expenses.

She wanted to giggle, but she failed in the attempt. Her heart hammered. This would have frightened her even under the best of circumstances and this wasn't anything near it. She, a puppet dancing in strings, was about to enter a paranormal hot zone. Did… did Laurie want her to fail, to be crushed to dust by the forces, the Power present here, or didn't she dare to do it herself?

Jill felt a little better, a little worse.

Father and Mother Asteroth followed her in her exact footsteps up the stairs. She didn't laugh. Her entire body had been covered in sweat. She feared she would pee, spoil herself and break like a dry twig in the storm.

Her eyes locked on to a drawer at the top of the stairs and a photograph there in an expensive frame. Yes, yes, she told herself. They spare no expenses. She snapped it out of thin air. The Asteroths froze in their tracks. She ripped the frame to pieces and grabbed the picture itself, pushing the palm of her left hand against it. Raw Power immediately flooded her body and being.

– Alone, I'm alone, she mumbled. – The heck with it.

The girl on the picture had rumpled, bright hair, healthy fair skin. On the picture there was yet a bit puppy fat left, something not evident the times Jill had seen her in person. She wore jeans and a college-sweater. Her body had just started forming itself. She smiled openly and trustfully to the world. Jill wanted to kill the parents and everybody else in the world that had set out to destroy the girl, who had created the *monster* waiting inside the door.

The door waited there merely a meter or so away (three feet or so, she thought absentmindedly). She would've known it was the right one, the only one, in a hall of thousands. The door grinned at her, pushing at her like a wet blanket weighing her down. Cold, humid smoke leaked through the keyhole and from the opening by the floor. She pushed down the handle and pushed open the gate to Hell. Smoke and cold flowed, surrounding her, sticking to her like angry bees. Mostly by the floor, but there was a thin mist everywhere. Small objects and remains floated around. She walked inside.

The girl sat on the bed. She had her legs pulled up, so the front side of the head rested against her knees. Her arms embraced her legs to such an extent that they seemed like tight ropes. Eyes were open, unmoving, completely without expression. There was a strange darkness in here, almost night, even as one saw everything inexplicably clear. The sun shone outside, but it didn't shine in here. The image of the world outside, the window was like a painting, a children's painting, simplified, unreal. The girl sat in the middle of the shit and the stench, a stench more than mere smell. Everything physical in here was… enhanced to something that wasn't matter, as if it was broken down, as if it was being broken down and … digested. The girl's hair might have been fair once. Now it had turned brown and dirty. She had painted herself with feces. The face was sunken and swollen. She had kept her clothes on, but there were hardly more than rags left of them. She had scratched herself several places, long, bloody tears down both sides of the body. The room and its very texture seemed to change and shift constantly, as if it was about to vanish, be wiped out. This was a Sanctum, a Place of Power, a truth evident in every detail (the truth is in the details).

Gabrielle ruled here. Within these walls she was Master of all she surveyed.

– Hallo, Gabi, Jill greeted her, from one witch to another.

The name, the baptizing of a Witch, resonated in the room.

A slice of the wall shook loose and was thrown at the older girl. About an arm-length away it stopped, as if against an invisible wall and was thrown back. Jill stood her ground steady and somewhat calm. She couldn't really read the other's thoughts, but she sensed surprise and then danger. Good. All kinds of objects floating in the air suddenly and shockingly raced towards her, a violent, virulent attack. She could feel the pressure on her shield now, but everything glanced off it.

The creature on the bed lifted the head. Eyes colder than the moon stared at Jill now. The bigger girl, low on confidence and inner strength, just a leaf blowing in the wind, strived to keep that from the other.

– *This is my place. Get out of here.*

No, I have no intention of doing that, Gabrielle.

The Monster shook. She snarled. A tablecloth slid straight through Jill's force field. It didn't have any greater speed or force than the previous projectiles, but Gabrielle had *changed* it. It didn't have any substance without her wishing it. Jill lifted her arms in a dramatic gesture. The cloth dissolved in flames and heat. Jill's hands continued to glow. No flames, but light and heat. The mist started to evaporate.

– Oh, you're *warm,* all right. The Monster's mouth twitched in a *demonic* grin. – Not so strange that you can satisfy Anubis, that you need him. You can keep him in check, and he can survive your full, consuming desire.

– W-what… Jill was thrown off balance, of resolve.

And then she felt it, a low hum transforming the entire room.

– Get out, she shouted to the parents. – Get out NOW

They ran. The door closed after them, closed so hard that it was almost thrown off the hinges.

Jill couldn't stand anymore. She floated in the air. There was nothing to stand on.

– I'm Queen here, the Monster rasped. – Everything in here is subject to my whim.

And Jill realized something. She recalled something from a dream of hers. And the little girl in the bed really resembled or rather reminded her of her dream monster from her childhood. She couldn't remember any details. There was only the realization of a terrible memory. Panic struck her as she was lifted up, fighting the numbing paralysis in both mind and body. She attempted to steer it with her own power, but it had no effect. Suddenly, without the slightest warning, she was thrown at the wall. The shield she had surrounded herself with, held. Gabrielle grinned wickedly and threw her at the opposite wall. It hurt this time, but the despair hitting her, hurt far more. Useless, she was useless.

She looked at the monster and she saw something else, something not necessarily having anything to do with Gabrielle at all. Cold started penetrating her skin. She felt heavier, even if she kept floating in this eternal wetness, this vast world of nothingness. No. Eyelids turned heavy and she started having visions while still awake. She saw herself as an unmoving statue, an exhibition in Gabrielle's aerie. No, she couldn't, wouldn't allow that to happen. In the nightmare she saw tendrils, tentacles grow from the monster's body stretching, stretching towards her as flakes of skin started loosening from her body and the pain made her want to scream, but she couldn't utter a single sound. Everything in her was *frozen, frozen, frozen…*

Heat erupted from her entire body. The way she experienced it, imagined it anyway, every cell in her body started burning and she cried out in release. The mist evaporated and her feet stood on the floor, on solid ground again. Her eyes snapped open, staring, confronting the monster and she sent her burning thoughts deep within Gabrielle's mind. And she saw immediately revealed the childish needs of a wounded, deeply wounded young girl.

Rule, rule. I want to decide, I want the power, I want, want, want

No, don't you see what you've done here? Don't you see how lifeless you've made everything, made yourself? It's a manifested expression of a creature totally devoid of mercy, of emotion, of anything but the cold, senseless need to Control.

There were other ways Jill could have fixed this. She wanted to. She wanted it bad. Inside her shaken, shrinking self-image she wanted to strike out hard and fast and *punish* the little brat for her transgressions, for the fear and ruthless exposure, but then Gabi would have become *her* thrall, and she didn't want that.

Not if she didn't have to.

An eternity passed and without anything happening.

The girl collapsed on the bed. She gasped and started sobbing in full, painful bursts. Relieved to the point of exhaustion Jill allowed a smile to emerge in her face. She sat down by the girl's side and her glowing warm hands began touching the cold and skinny body. The cold and the vicious darkness let go. The sun and the heat from the outside reached them. The girl's body slowly stopped shaking. They sat there, holding and embracing each other for minutes.

– I was so lonely, *alone,* the girl sobbed, holding on to the other witch for dear life. – I couldn't take it, I just couldn't anymore. I can't, I can't.

– I know, Jill said with trembling lips. – I know.

She was still afraid, still wanted to crush the small form in front of her. Even if she had felt mostly in control, it had been too close, a moment where she had almost let go of everything and Gabi would have gained the upper hand, forever, becoming the monster from the nightmare.

The child gave away a tiny, muffled cry of joy and clung even harder to the woman. Jill held her softly, while talking to her in a singing voice, oiling the distressed mind. To sit like this felt so peaceful. One could sit like this forever, but that was no good. She made herself hard and whispered into the girl's ear:

– We've both found a bridge over the raging river. But you must cross it alone. We all must do that.

The crying stopped in a few decisive drawings of breath. Gabi sat up on her own and dried her face in quick, heavy strokes.

She looked like a normal girl again. A very dirty and wet and sick girl, but normal. Jill froze as images of the monster, the nightmare, haunted her.

– You need to clean yourself up. Can you do that alone?

Gabi smiled and nodded, putting up a brave front. Jill refrained from mentioning in passing that she could see straight through such false bravery.

– I haven't healed all your scratches completely. You need physical proof for a while, reminding you what you did to yourself.

Gabi smiled bravely. She stood up on weak legs and writhed out of her rags, tearing them off. They dissolved even more as she did it, making the shrunken heap on the floor little more than bits and pieces resembling clothes. She ran to the bathroom. Jill heard the sound of the shower and sensed the cleansing water soak the skinny body. She kept the contact, the rapport she had made with the child, just in case.

The door to the hall had opened again. Her attention turned very slowly to the shrieking sound of the door turning on the hinges, to the parents, their heavy breathing, their insecurity and fear.

– Perhaps we should withdraw to the dining room? The missus suggested weakly.

The witch picked up her hat from the floor and brushed her slightly dusty cloak with her hands, following the happy couple cautiously back down the stairs, constantly on guard for whatever unexpected might occur. As she couldn't really read Gabi, she also had a hard time gathering information from the minds of the parents. Some were born with natural shields. For all she knew they planned on having her for dinner… Her nerves stayed jittery, she couldn't help it.

And there was satisfaction, to a point, at least. She thought that Laurie might have made a tactical error sending her here. Nobody, not Laurie, not Jason, Stacy or Everett would know the jewel upstairs as well as she did.

– Your daughter was well on her way to a full-blown catatonic condition, she told in a hard-edged tone of voice. – In this case the fact that she's a witch made a bad situation worse. If you had waited until tomorrow to call for help, it could have been too late. Very soon she would've pulled herself so deeply within herself that the ailment would've become lasting.

– Witch? What are you saying? The father held on to his head, as if he feared losing it. – What is it she can do then? What did she do? What is she capable of?

– This is new to me, too, a lot of it, Jill admitted willingly, – but I believe that Gabi's special talent is that she can make the world of the mind, what we call the Shadow World visible, make it physical and thereby influence her surroundings. The opposite is also true. The result is pretty much the same. She can pull the physical world into the Shadow World, create her own part of it. In earlier times people like her were called *Dreamweavers,* since this is where we go when we dream. She achieved control over everything within her room, everything that stayed there for a prolonged period of time. She lived through a nightmare and if she hadn't been stopped this nightmare would have spread to the rest of the house, to the street, to an ever-larger area.

– Dreams… My God. He sat straight down, coincidentally exactly on the sofa. – Can she make thoughts real, is that what you're saying?

– Yes, Jill replied. – Perhaps. At least to a certain point. The thoughts that have become part of the Shadow World. In time she will be able to do much more, if that is her desire.

Would she have any choice? Did the Power give its wielder any choice?

– What can *you* do? Aside from that neat fire trick, I mean.

He was being sarcastic, showing deliberate, over the top skepticism, but it was an act. She knew she had to thread carefully here. Something had awakened in the man. She sensed, the way she interpreted it, something new about to emerge to his conscious mind: The realization that he had bet on the wrong horse, that by treating his daughter the callous way he had, he had left behind a fantastic tool to use in his quest for improving his standing in society, as he saw it.

– I'm a Multi. I have many talents, but I can't do what your daughter can. May I have an apple, please?

An uncertain nod. She held out her hand in a dramatic gesture. An apple from the bowl on the table jumped up in the air and into her palm. Their eyes widened. She took a huge bite of the fruit. It tasted delicious.

– I should point out an obvious fact: It's a major advantage that Gabi is a witch, after all. If she wasn't she would've been on her way to a hospital now, to a padded cell, the way you've made a habit of treating her.

– What can we *do?* The mother cried out weakly.

– You must let her go with me. For the moment and for the unforeseeable future she needs to be surrounded by equals, by like-minded in thought and action. This must happen without the slightest interference from you. You must hand over custody of her to me, to me personally.

– But you're no more than a child yourself? This outburst, this predictable shit, was the only thing the wife managed.

Jill smiled. She knew she had won. And not by using her power. By her force of will alone, so much stronger than theirs.

– I'm much older than you, she said absent-mindedly, – Why not do something that never has occurred to you? Why don't we ask Gabi what she thinks?

– What if she says no? Asteroth asked, his anger burning on a low flame.

– I see that as a sign that she's strong enough to remain here, Jill stated unconcerned.

– I want to go. Gabi stood in the opening to the hall, chewing on a piece of meat. – I'm okay, but I am suffocating here.

– You're MUTANTS, Asteroth exclaimed. – You really exist.

– So are you, Jill grinned, – mutants, that is… So, I would be careful with the racism if I were you. That's why you've managed to hold Gabi in check as long as you have. You have a certain ability of persuasion, to make people see things the way you want them to see it. I noticed it the minute I met you today. Calling us mutants, by the way, is as good a definition as any.

– You're bluffing, Asteroth said hoarsely.

– The truth will soon enough reveal itself, won't it? Jill Stafford laughed aloud.

Jill and Gabi didn't keep their eyes on each other, but they had contact. Jill looked at her.

– I'll just pick some stuff I want to bring, the child-witch said eagerly.

She disappeared in a rush up the stairs again. Lillith nodded slowly in acknowledgment. After a while of fattening her, she wouldn't stay a child for long.

The girl returned jumping and dancing. She carried a small shoulder bag. She was fully clothed now, rather simplistically in bare feet, a shorts and a thin, green shirt, tied above the navel. The cap on her head completed the picture. She smiled unconcerned, an amazing recovery, change from just before her previous walk up the stairs. Gabi knew now, beyond doubt, that she wasn't the only mutant in the world.

– I'll be visiting, Gabi Asteroth told her parents halfway through the door

Then she closed it, closed it behind her.

4

Young body, young mind, starving for so long, bathing in sunshine. She jumped and danced side by side the towering older, experienced girl. A real forest witch, if she had ever seen one. She giggled.

– What now? She asked curiously.

– The first level of business, Jill declared, – is to start feeding that starving body of yours.

Gabi looked very guilty when looking at her belly. The stomach's rumble was quite telling.

Jill dragged the girl with her to the first café she could find, an old-fashioned one at the corner of the neighborhood. There weren't many people present this time of the day, but Gabi… Gabrielle knew most of them, both children and adults, and was deeply ashamed over the shame she felt.

– Do you have asparagus-soup? Jill inquired cheerfully.

The speechless lady behind the counter managed a nod.

– I don't need such weak stuff…

– Two deep plates of asparagus-soup, Jill ordered, decisive now.

They sat down by the window. Gabrielle strived to overlook all the badly hidden glances.

– No, don't do that. Jill told her.

– Don't do what?

– You may ignore people looking at you, but never try to fool yourself into believing they don't exist.

– Ok-kay. Gabi turned a bit in her chair and waved to a group of girls she knew.

They didn't wave back, but they stopped staring. Gabi made a point of shaking her head. The group of girls had been, or had seemed to be, one of the more positive ones. They had dressed a lot like she had and even shown up on some of the band's concerts. But they didn't want to be seen with a witch.

She wondered about the guys in the band. They hadn't called her lately, not even after she didn't go to school, after she got… sick. They hadn't called. Her parents couldn't claim responsibility, at least not sole responsibility, of keeping them away. She had listened in on every phone call in the house. It hadn't really registered in her misty mind, but she would have known if anyone important had called.

– Among many things I'm a Healer, Jill said. – That makes me responsible for your health. Food and its connection to health is one of the first things we learn.

– At the witches' school? Gabrielle said jokingly.

– Quite so, Jill nodded. – You must probably run to the toilet the first three or four meals whatever you do, but that isn't so bad. You get to cleanse your system of the remaining waste.

Gabi slurped the first taste of the soup. It tasted so great and that showed on her face.

– It hurts, she said after a while.

– That's to be expected, Jill nodded.

They sat there, silent for a while.

– You said you wanted custody. What is that about?

– An insurance, against interference. A lot is threatening us. I want you to experience Freedom, to develop your Power, to Live your Life. *Dream a dream and what you see will be.*

The big girl's words, both through her mouth and her thoughts, both worried and pleased the young teenager. She sensed a deeper, unseen part of the floor below, the table they sat by and their very surroundings.

– Did someone… do this to me? She asked low and frosty.

– I don't think so. Jill replied uncertain. – No, I didn't sense any direct intrusion. So if you don't count the entire local community I would say you did it to yourself by surrendering to the inhuman pressure you've been exposed to.

– Yes, Gabi said, still frosty. – I, too, think it is a wise decision to blame myself. I have a right to be angry, but not to blame others for me giving up. Right…?

– You're a spunky and wise kid, Jill joked.

Gabi couldn't take her eyes off the other girl. She could still feel the heat from her warm hands, her burning red-hot hands. An eighteen-year-old girl very changed from the person she had first met in passing just a few weeks ago. And she had helped Gabi out of her cage. The cage put there by others, but which she had walked into with all her eyes shut tight. Jill's dark-skinned face was an ever-shifting mosaic, changing in daylight, twilight and night, the shadow in her eyes dancing like fire.

– Jill, she said abruptly, – why did we make a stop here?

– I told you. Jill shifted uncomfortably in her seat. – You needed food.

– You know… The pointed stare froze Jill somehow, just as much, if not more than the girl's power had done. – I've come to realize that I've actually used my powers for some time now. I've mostly used it during my performance, and I've used it… to listen. I thought I had extremely good hearing or something. As you've no doubt heard, that I've also said in public, I know a bit of Laurie, about her intentions. I warned you about her.

– Yes, you did. Jill couldn't keep up the façade anymore and bowed her head in shame.

– And she still screwed you over. Gabi seemed like the oldest now, the wise big sister. – But you shouldn't feel too bad about it. After all, she had and has experience on her side.

– She has been after you for a long time, Jill moaned. – She could just as well have orchestrated what happened to you. She could be listening in right now. I can't even tell whether she's fucking with my sandwich or not. I can't be certain of anything. She could even be behind my spells, my occasional dizziness.

– There are stories of powerful adepts suffering from nausea during their transitional period, Gabi told her softly. – One is changing rapidly. One is even changing reality rapidly. One needs time to adjust. Some never do. I've heard them turn stark raving mad.

– I've read a lot, she added blushing.

– There's a shadow chasing me, Jill complained bitterly, fearfully. – I can't get rid of it. It has attached itself to me, leeching my energy, my Self. That could also be Laurie.

– Loeh told me something about that. In Voodoun Soul and Shadow are the same words, the same thing, inseparable, forever dynamically relating.

– So, you mean… Jill's face, consorted by grief and pain changed in wonder. – No, that can't be it, can it… The thought has crossed my mind, but it seems too much like wish fulfillment…

– Without acceptance of Self there can never be any true growth, and you make yourself open for other undue influences. We know this, don't we?

Jill stared a bit. Loeh could have spoken those words. And Loeh seemed to be there, with them, for just the slightest moment, before vanishing into the shadows.

– We could run away, Jill sniffed. – I don't think Laurie would actually be able to stop us.

She wouldn't want to, because she would've won, and could pick them up, their scarred shells, any time she wanted.

– Can you read me, Jill? Gabi, the self-assured cocky youngster asked.

– No. Jill shook her head, wondering. – Only general surface emotions.

– I know you penetrated deep within me, but can you scan me or influence me in any way with your mind powers?

– N-no, not directly. The older girl shook her head. – I had to shake some sense into you. That was the only way I could have stopped what was going on, without harming you.

– Thank you. Gabi grabbed her hand with both her own. – This is the way I see it: If you can't I'm willing to bet Laurie can't either. She'll have to use guile to win me over and I will know what she's up to. We must beat her. Laurie cannot teach us anything more now, nothing that we cannot learn for ourselves. We already have our own Coven. Let's keep it that way. Whatever we decide to do with our powers we don't need her.

Poor girl. Jill looked at her. Believing she's so cynical, so clever. Jill, fearful and ashamed, kept silent.

Gabi smiled, feeling good over being able to lift Jill spirits.

And she felt pretty good herself.

The music, the surroundings seemed to reach for her, and she let it happen. Suddenly she could listen in on any conversation she wanted in the room, even on the street outside. No preparations, no concentration and yet she experienced it in so much more detail and fullness than before. It was no longer possible to mistake the power for mere good hearing. She could… move her attention wherever she wanted in this place. Like she was… somewhere else… By the pinball machine, outside on the parking lot, inside a dark closet where a young couple was fucking. She reached it all… through the Shadow World. It was everywhere. She was everywhere…

Then she sensed… Her smile vanished abruptly.

– He's coming, she said in a hollow voice. – The Dollmaster is coming.

Jill stiffened.

Fear embraced her and she couldn't speak.

– What do you… see? She finally managed to ask.

– I'm in a room full of floating crystal balls. The child's voice came through a thundering buzz no one could hear. – He's coming. I can see their faces.

– Is it more than one? Jill asked insistently.

– He's coming. I can see their faces…

She trailed off… And then terror struck her face as if she had been hit. Jill could just about make out some random thoughts among her horrible silent screams.

The King of the World… The Wastelands… The kings of Death… He wants nothing more than Everything. He's coming. HE'S COMING

The images, the horror haunted Jill, even if they didn't actually scare her. She ignored the temptation to let it, whatever happened, continue. It touched something horrible, something shameful in her. As sudden as Gabi she had been covered in cold sweat, and she feared she would be slipping away any moment. She put her hands on the girl's shoulders and *stopped* the use of her power.

– This is incredible, Gabi marveled, after a while, as cramps threatened to bend her over and terror shadowed her face. – I've never before dreamed while being completely awake. And so intense.

– Are you okay? Jill asked worried, while fighting to keep control of her own, hammering heart.

– I'm quite okay, now, Gabi assured her. – You don't need to worry. It's just the stomach making itself unruly, that's all. You may stay here.

She ran to the toilet. And Jill, just as shaken by the unexplainable fear didn't manage to whip up concentration sufficient to use either her mind or her body. Perhaps just as well, since in her present state of mind she could have executed any act needed without thought of the consequences. The room hadn't… existed for her these few seconds. Another reality had completely superimposed itself on this one, and it had been impossible for her to decide which was real. Slowly, painfully slowly she once more grew aware of what went on around her. No one here knew that something unusual had been going on.

The paralysis in her limbs let go. She heard it then, the silent scream. Just a few seconds, no more, until she reached the toilet, but she had no idea how she managed to keep the calm, or an illusion, a reasonable facsimile of it.

She found Gabrielle in the cubicle, the stall farthest from the door. The girl hadn't closed the cubicle door. Eyes stared blindly at some point out there in the void. Jill put her arms firmly around the child, *shaking* her. One blink, two… *contact.* Lillith shook her thoughts as she had done her body.

– I'll not be doing this again without a lot of good reasons, little child.

The lights and heat flowed through the scared little girl. She sighed deeply and crouched in the big girl's arms.

Some minutes later she stood upright in front of the toilet mirror. Eyes were sparklingly clear. She stared into the mirror, touched the smooth skin where the remains of the scratches had still revealed themselves just a few minutes earlier. Now, they were gone.

– Your entire being is strengthened, Jill said softly. – I can't keep doing it. I take at least as much as I give. It will demand an increasingly growing contribution from you. Eventually it will only make everything worse. Do you *understand?*

Gabrielle the child nodded. The physical wounds had been healed and they wouldn't leave any scars. But wounds on the soul never disappeared completely.

– We shall take our time. Jill kept talking softly. – We shall learn where magic flowers are growing, on the mountain, in the forest. And then we'll see what image the dreamer is weaving. Just don't… fear me.

– I can never fear you. Gabrielle swallowed hard. – I know you'll never harm me.

You retain a child's innocence, don't you, little witch? That's both good and bad.

– Come, she stated coldly. – Laurie, our Queen is awaiting our arrival. You'll learn to serve and obey her as we have.

I know you're just saying that because you fear she's listening, Gabi thought.

Jill led her out of there, but she didn't hold the child's hand. They walked through the café. People had already sat down at their table. Not that it mattered. They would never return.

They strolled out of the neighborhood without making haste. Gabi saw people in their kitchen windows, staring and whispering among themselves. Contempt flashed within her, and she approved of Jill's slow walk tactic. Let them see, let them look at free beings parading between the cells.

She soon realized what route they were taking to Oldtown, and a rush of expectation flowed through her.

– That's one of the advantages of living in a smaller, close-knit town, she whistled. – You can easily walk between the attractions…

They noticed the smoke and the gray air long before they actually saw the factory itself. Thick, black smoke erupted from the pipes. The building loomed, even in the «might» of the gray fog. Barbed wire surrounded the entire property. The group of private guards and police officers had placed themselves inside the barricades. All of it looking like complete overkill compared to the small group of people sitting in the middle of the road, in front of the main gate. They were forcibly removed every time a truck or a new group of workers arrived. Not many minutes later they returned. They kept returning. Most of them had already lost everything because of Scott Thompson anyway. He couldn't hurt them more than he had done already. He was unable to hurt them anymore, except perhaps murder them outright, but a few of those present would consider that a blessing. To them prison with its regular meals and softer beds, had to be considered a step up the ladder.

And there were others, new arrivals in town, who hadn't come here to hide.

Ivan, Rae, Travis and Loeh sat in the middle of the tight cluster of people. They waved and Jill (and Gabi) waved back. She sensed the warm, aggressive joy from them and the other protesters. It strengthened her, empowered her, making the elements already in place coalesce and burn.

She and the girl stopped in front of the gate. The girl looked uncertain at her. She looked back and nodded.

– See the House spitting Poison, the girl shouted, with a voice loud and powerful after years of singing. – Tick tack tock, the mad dance continues. Girl, Boy, Man and Woman doth protest this insanity and what happens when they protest this insanity, what happens when they're attempting to talk reason with the unreason? They're bullied, beaten and bruised. The mad dance continues.

– First step is the questions you ask when you don't accept what you experience in your neighborhood, Jill shouted, filling people's mind as she did so. – If you don't find satisfying answers, you're slowly realizing that something is seriously wrong. You start appealing to people's reason and are met with indifferent hostility. Then there's *action* and then the problems, the hostilities start in earnest. By showing open and true disagreement with the forces ruling society, you're exposing yourself and become vulnerable, making yourself a target for their complete attention and retaliation.

– Yes, there's exposure, a man nodded. – But if you're prepared for it, it isn't so bad. And being an obedient little sheep isn't a guarantee against random attacks anyway.

– Most choose to forget this point, Jill nodded. – They don't want to realize that it's far easier to tramp on ants crawling on the ground.

– HI, YOU BITCH. A commanding officer shouted to her. – Nobody has given you permission to hold a speech.

Jill turned to him with a strange smile on her face, a face contorted by Rage.

– So, we have permission to stay then? Thank you very much, but you see, we don't need permission for anything. You are the criminals here, breaking the law of Life. You think the people pulling your strings are powerful, don't you? Well, then, you-and-they-have-no-idea-what-Power-is.

Everything he was about to do, to lift his arm, to give the order for the troops to start the assault was stopped, interrupted. His sleeves started *burning*. He screamed and ran away. The flames already licked his upper arms.

I can do so much more, she thought. Why am I not? Why don't I?

– You won't lift that cute rifle against me, will you? She laughed scornfully. – Will you shoot down an unharmed woman for open camera only because a man has been careless with some of the numerous chemicals on the premises?

One of the other men shook his head and lowered his gun.

– Anybody else feeling naughty? None of you will participate if you're asked to *clean up* here, will you? *Will you?*

Some shook their head. No one said anything.

I have them now. And it was so easy. I can do so much more.

She turned to the protesters, easily recognizing the admiration and the bit of fear in their eyes.

Come, she told the four witches. We're expected.

Ivan, Rae, Travis and Loeh rose and left the cluster.

– We'll be back. Jill smiled dangerously. – We'll all be back…

– That was FANTASTIC, Gabi said with stars in her eyes, as they were leaving the plaza.

– It was stupid, Jill said tightly. – Too much for being careful and too little to be of use. We must stop holding back if we're ever going to achieve anything.

– *The road to Freedom is paved with pain and hardship.*

Jill turned towards the empty air, where the voice had come from.

– Thank you for telling me, she screamed in a high-pitched voice. – Are you sure you don't have anything more obvious to tell me today…

Vulnerable she thought. I'm so vulnerable.

– We all heard it, Loeh told her softly. – It's not in your head. Not in the way you fear, anyway. Your Shadow is emerging fully, attempting communion, attempting… integration.

Gabi's eyes widened.

– «In Voodoun soul and shadow are the same words, the same thing, inseparable, forever dynamically relating».

– The same being, Loeh confirmed.

– And Voodoun is one of… how many thousand religions on the planet? Jill countered bitterly. – What if they got it slightly wrong? And I've seen what happens when the *Loa* takes control. There isn't exactly much left of the original personality.

– *You* are afraid of *me?* Loeh said perplexed. And then, after a while. – No, you're afraid of yourself. That means you're afraid of everyone and everything. I've accepted my Loa. Every time it takes control it's strengthening and enhancing me. All the popular culture movies and books get it wrong. I wasn't erased, but grew more *aware* than I've ever been before, and afterwards it didn't leave me, but lingered and continued to grow inside me.

She hesitated.

– That was A, Jill said sarcastically. – How about serving up B as well?

– I saw a demon, Loeh said in a voice clearly trembling, – with long raven hair and black eyes. She joined us in our dance, embracing us all with her many arms.

– *Us?* Travis said.

– Us. I saw you all. You all joined me in the Bizango when I was twelve. My brothers and sisters in the secret societies changed in the dance, changed into you. I knew you before I ever met you.

Jill continued to walk in front. She said nothing more.

– You don't understand, any of you. I received my Loa. My brothers and sisters did not. They were overpowered by something far more powerful. I was shunned after that, driven out.

– We do understand, Dancer, Gabi said softly. – We all have scars. You were isolated from an intolerant and oppressive society. But it brought you on a Journey of self-discovery and contemplation. It brought you here, to limitless Freedom.

– Your words are soft as petals and dripping with honey, Dreamer, Loeh replied, a bitter taint in her voice. – Laurie is right; you are valuable.

The walk brought them inevitably closer to the old city, to their destiny. They entered from Main Road, entering Cross Street. The church appeared in their line of sight, inevitably, as they reached the avenue leading to Main Street. Joseph Parnell, the priest, coming from a long line of Parnells, stood there on the stairs, as if awaiting them. He was a demagogue and only thirty years old. Jill didn't fear him, but he filled her with disgust. She noticed that Gabrielle sought closer to her.

– SO, he roared in sick triumph. – Street trash, blasphemers and Satan's spawn have found each other. I can't say I'm surprised.

Confronted with what seemed like his absolute certainty, Jill wondered if he could be right, at least in her case. She knew better, but the doubt remained.

– If anybody is Satan's spawn here it's you, old man.

Don't fear him, little girl. She calmed the shaking figure by her side. *He's only a fossil pretending to be human, filled with intolerance and hatred. He's tolerating no other views than his own.*

She didn't reveal how sick it made her just to marginally touch his mind, his surface thoughts. His hatred and intolerance had grown to a wall, to a point where it defined everything about him.

No! She pulled herself together, steeling herself, her weak knees. Don't reveal your weakness. Two-legged wolves are always prepared to exploit it.

– You're all DOOMED, he screamed hysterically at their backs. – Your only recourse is to kneel before the Lord and beg his forgiveness.

The invisible shadow of the church reached for them. They hurried away from there.

– I'll never get used to people like him. Ivan shook his head. – I mean… they're all fools, but they make me sick.

– Clearly an advantage, Gabi said, somewhat good-humored, – considering the alternative.

– I totally agree with you, My Lady, he said eloquently. She was flushing. – The day I *don't* feel sick concerning Joseph Parnell and his equals, I'm truly fucked.

The dust in Oldtown's streets began blowing around their feet, rising ever so slightly, as if warning them not to proceed further. But the legs carried Jill further and the others followed her lead.

The walk wasn't long, to the house inside the Square.

They walked through the gate, up the stairs, surrounded by their own honor guard the moment the gate closed behind them. The door closed behind them. Jill couldn't remember noticing if it had actually opened. Gabi looked around her with skeptical eyes, with the excitement of a child, of innocence.

Laurie sat in her big chair in the deep of the living room. The entire place was completely different from how Jill remembered it, or could remember remembering it.

Jill took the girl by her shoulders and pushed her gently forward.

– There you are, child. Come here.

And Gabrielle the girl ran eagerly to the commanding presence awaiting her.

Jill felt herself being overwhelmed by a stark raving terror. She wanted to run, but Laurie held her in her grip and wouldn't let go.

– Let us all experience the blessing of the Goddess, Laurie cried out. – Let us welcome our new sister, give her a taste of the moon ceremony tomorrow, her initiation.

Welcome, Gabrielle. Feel the touch of the Goddess, feel her warm embrace. Blessed be.

Like a valve, a snap of the fingers, the embrace of the Goddess overwhelmed them all, not the least the young girl. She cried out in joy and fell to her knees before the woman in the chair.

– BLESSED BE, everybody cried out aloud, Gabrielle loudest of all.

She looked up at Laurie with tears in her shining eyes. So easy, the child had been seduced.

– That was *fantastic,* she sniffed. – I feel such happiness, such Joy that I fear I shall burst. Thank you, Mother.

– You're welcome, child, Laurie the Queen said, taking her hands.

Jill walked to her and knelt by her side. Bile rose in her throat, and she wanted to puke, but she wasn't allowed to.

– Thank you for bringing this jewel to us, my precious.

– As you commanded, Jill said resting her head in the Queen's lap.

Laurie turned her full attention to her, sighing.

– I know what you're planning, but it won't work. Let it go and join my vision, join me, fully and completely and I'll lead you to a glorious future.

Jill felt a peace then, a serenity, as Laurie patted her head, she knew then she had always longed for. In a state of total bliss, she let herself be submerged into Laurie's light.

– Yes, Mother, she mumbled.

She thought she got a glimpse of the shocked expression in Stacy's face, but she couldn't say for certain. It could just as well be her imagination as with many things, since she had arrived in Northfield. Terror faded like an old, half-remembered dream. She wanted… she wanted to see the look of betrayal in Gabrielle's eyes, but saw nothing, nothing but a happy kid.

A giant had placed herself in the path, blocking everyone who wanted to proceed.

5

They ran up the Hill, through the forest, the four of them. One scared young girl and three other anxious youths surrounding her in a protective embrace. They felt the Freedom of their limbs, the beginning of Freedom in their minds. The four didn't just escape from something, but also to something. They felt it, the embrace of the forest.

Jill sat in the chair in the library, in the living room. Gabrielle took one book out of the shelves and started reading in it with the same sort of enthusiasm she did everything. Her eyes were big and shiny, like a little kid believing she had been given the keys to existence itself.

She was a little kid. Jill pulled up her legs and started rocking back and forth in the chair.

– Have you looked at all these books? The girl said excitedly. – It must be one of the largest collections of arcane knowledge in the world.

It was as if she didn't or couldn't notice Jill's burning shame, her deep, dark mood, which in turn made her even more susceptible to the occasional ever stronger, ever more frequent waves of invasive thoughts recreating her. As she weakened the other force grew stronger and more persuasive.

Jill stumbled in a root, in her own feet. The three others pulled her back up. She cried out in despair, in gratitude, overwhelming her guardians with wet, smothering kisses.

– Can you feel her now? Jason asked her sharply.

– I don't think so, she howled. – It seems like she's gone or further away, fading… I don't know, I just don't know.

COME BACK. SNOTTY LITTLE…

She howled again, like a lost soul.

– I must go back, she shouted. – I must, I must

The tree of them had stopped it, stopped the message from reaching her fully. Her legs kept running, her mind kept fighting.

Jill stood up from the chair and rushed into the hall. Stacy waited for her there with a pained,

shocked and also a strange… scared expression painted on her entire Self.
– She did this to *you?* She… she asked.
Jill nodded, blinded with tears choking her voice. There were no visible tears, no outer signs of distress. She nodded and couldn't stop herself from nodding.
Like a puppet, she thought angrily, like a slave.
– We must leave, now, Stacy said.
– Yes, Jason said, appearing out of nowhere, from nothing, with Everett by his side, opening the door.
The girls tumbled through the door, out in the yard, with the boys right behind them. And there was resistance, like they were walking under water, like the air was mud, but they managed, and they moved, out through the gate, to Main Street, around the corner, setting the course.
– Do my mind, she urged them. – Fill it up, making no room for her.
And their presence was like a valve on a never closing wound.
They left the forest, reaching the shore of Fire Lake. The moon, with just a slight notch away from being ripe, bathed them in its silver rays, as the dry sand-dust rose in the air.
– You must heal me. Jill coughed hard. She rushed to Stacy, supported her entire weight on her. – Permanently remove her corruptive influence.
– And do you want me to baby-sit you… every time you get into trouble? Stacy replied teasingly.
– No. Jill turned away from her, the strength of resentment dominating her once again. – No, you're absolutely right. I will fix it and heal on my own.
– We'll guard you. Everett said. – We'll all be within you, knowing if anyone is attempting anything.
She sank down on her knees. Their perception changed, attuning itself to hers, and they knew how dangerous that was, wondering if that was what Laurie had planned all along.
– I want to return, run back to her, she sniveled there on her sore and bloody knees, – crouching in her shadow, s-sit in her l-lap while she tells me bedtime s-stories.
With an effort of will, crying out in pain, she fought her way up again, brushing her lip, drying off her blood. A bit of her tongue was clearly missing. It grew back as they watched. They realized stunned, when she spit out the bitten off part, that she had done it on purpose.
– Let go of me now, she said.
– B-but. Surprisingly enough Stacy was the one who objected.
– Let go of me, now, but stay on guard. We can't be sure if this was where Laurie wanted us to go. We can't be sure of anything. There's a child in the grip of a manipulative tyrant of a witch in the house down there, because of our weakness, our inability to take control of our lives, and it's time we put a stop to it.
She ran into the water and started swimming, using her powers to augment the force of her strokes. They joined her, following her. Everett was sagging behind, the one unable to use anything but the force of his limbs alone. She ran into the house, as he completely out of breath, feeling strangely good fought his way up from the water. He had really built a substantial amount of muscle lately.
They found her in the kitchen. She wanted them to. They wanted to shout while she found a knife in the drawer. A very sharp knife, shiny and sharp as new.
She stabbed herself straight through the lower left arm, crying out, as she purposely knelt on the kitchen floor, pulling the blade out. Lifting the arm above her head, droplets of the blood landed on her outstretched tongue. There wasn't really that much blood and the wound closed itself as they watched.
– That wasn't so bad, was it? Jason said a bit shaken.
With ice-cold determination she stabbed herself in the belly.
– AIIIEEEE. The scream tore into them.
Stacy didn't say anything. She stood there, pale as milk.
Jill Stafford fell on her side. With hands wet and slippery of all the blood, she pulled the knife back out and to really make a point she hacked away at the major vein on the thigh. Blood gushed from the many wounds like a fountain.
The knife slipped through her fingers, sliding far away on the floor.
– You're not HERE, are you? She shouted. – For some reason you're AFRAID of this place, fearing

its Power, its Mystery, its Horror. You're *weak!*

The wounds closed. If it wasn't for all the translucent, shimmering red fluid, they would've been tempted to believe there had never been any.

– Weak… The Witch repeated as she rose from the floor. – I cast you out. I condemn thee to walk the wastelands, the nothing.

And they all imagined they heard a scream somewhere.

Stacy's already torn dress had spots of blood on it.

– You did that, she said accusingly. – You hit me on purpose.

Everett and Jason glanced at their own bloodless clothes, as if excusing themselves for their lack of spots.

Jill smiled pleased, a sensual intense grin.

– You know now what I'm capable of, she said triumphantly. – You'll never forget.

– I'll never look at a drug-withdrawal attempt in quite the same manner again, Everett tried to joke.

She kissed him. She kissed them all on the lips, taking from them without asking.

They stood outside, taking in the moon, taking in the Night.

– We should restore this place to its former glory, Stacy commented dryly.

Even in moonlight they could see its age, its decay.

But it was still here, after 100 years of non-use.

– We must never underestimate Laurie again. Jason wandered in circles like Uncle Scrooge, making drawings in the sand. – She has had a lot of time preparing for all this, subverting the will of the older eight. And for all we know she may have faked her low power levels, too, to lull us into a sense of false security.

– We must protect ourselves, Everett growled. – From her, from anyone.

– Yes, that's what we're doing, Stacy purred. – That's what we shall do. We'll use pure positive emotion, pure negative emotion… to purge ourselves.

– There is some power in duality, Jason agreed. – Especially when using it against its benefactors.

– We'll use the power of duality… to move beyond it all. Jill clapped her hands in excitement. – To move beyond the open hand, the closed fist.

– It's quite a simple procedure, Stacy grinned.

– I can't see how, Everett shook his head.

– It is, as with all things, about the manipulation of Energy, Stacy said. – About creating a massive flux of it and…

–… *moving it around,* she and Jill ended the sentence together.

The two of them looked at each other, as was their way. They looked at Jason. He lifted his left hand, meeting theirs in mid-air.

– Stand still, he told Everett.

Stacy raised the right hand, her free hand, the open palm and it pointed at him.

– You're the guardian of the tomb, she declared. – You're he who guards the gate to the Kingdom of Death.

– Why? The big boy asked. – What are you two…

He screamed, as smoke rose from his chest and huge parts of his upper body, as he, too, fell to his knees. Sweat poured from his brow as he stared astonished at the markings covering his chest and belly, at the inverted, smothering pentacle on his abdomen.

– Yes, focus on the pain, Stacy commanded. – Embrace it.

He attempted to focus on her, through layers, hazes of pain.

– I know what, who the Dancer saw, Stacy said mysteriously. – It's pretty simple really…

– Care to share it with us? Everett said sharply, gasping.

– In time, Anubis, Stacy hummed. – In time I won't have to.

Jill shook as if struck.

She staggered, and would have fallen, if Stacy hadn't supported her.

– You're still weak and we can't have that, sister. Even you can't draw on your reserves like that, without tiring. And Laurie had already brought you low. As we shall bring her low.

Jill focused on her faintly.

– You need a healing sleep. Stacy looked intensely at her, still mysteriously scared. – You must heal fast. We need you tomorrow.

– I think you're right, Jill nodded. – I need to prepare, like we all do.

This had brought them closer together. This had strengthened them. It had brought them an intuitive understanding of each other, of a world they shared.

Jason started throwing logs in the water, setting them on fire as soon as they hit the surface.

– There are things known and there are things unknown, and we're outside it all. Everything is unknown. Everything is known.

As smoke drifted on the water Jill chose a place, half adrift already, half awake. She sat down, crossing her legs, her eyes sliding slowly shut.

– I can see the forms in the smoke, she said sleepily. – I can see the mists of Time and Shadow.

– Yes, I know, Stacy whispered excitedly. – I know. We're so close now. After so many years, after millennia we're almost there.

Jill turned over, resting her head on a dry mound of grass, moaning.

– Sleep, Kali, o'mother of gods, Stacy soothed, in fear and boundless anticipation. – Create and destroy… dream the world.

And the body slept and dreamed, and the soul dreamed, losing itself, finding itself, and what was Jill Stafford was ascending into a black hole, cast out into the Void, never to return.

"I don't know if God exists,
but it would have been better for
his reputation if he didn't»
Jules Renard

«We are forces of chaos and anarchy.
Everything they say we are, we are.
And we are very proud of ourselves».
Jefferson Airplane

«And anyone not found written in the Book of Life
was cast into the lake of fire»
Gideons' bible Revelation 20:15

«And all that is hidden
Everything repressed
And forbidden
And more
All that is inside
Erupts to the outside
And more
In the dance of life
Commencing on Fire Lake»

Amos Keppler - **Fire Lake** 2002

CHAPTER THIRTEEN: Masks - the Face of Death

Skeletons hung from trees. Children danced through the streets, singing fiery songs, painting, decorating the walls. The preparations for Halloween started early this year. But not that early really. Most people hardly noticed, noticed the subtle changes in the smallest things, in the details of Life.

The drum sounded somewhere in the distance. Ivan sat in their midst, playing. He was far away, and so were they.

There was the drum (the drums?). With the drum, its rhythm was the sound waves, the vibration in the air, the ground below, wisps of smoke calling.

The four had called the Drummer and he in turn had helped call the rest. All were called, but not everybody heeded its beat.

The Gathering assembled on the Hill, by the edge of the forest, just a short uphill distance away from Square, Laurie's Place of Power. There were houses between them and it, but it still felt uncomfortably close. What had started as an escape to Fire Lake and its fiery temple had turned into confrontation as the only possible outcome. Stacy felt boundless Freedom as the anger and fear and determination of the others mingled inside her.

People could see them, if they looked, see the ceremony of desecration, the rejection of all things previously.

– Tonight is the dancing moon, the full ripe moon. The Samhain is upon us. This is his first night. This night and every night until the Fall, until the gathering of the condemned.

– Aye, Jason, said closing both his fists. – We're the Dead, living Life in all its myriad of variants, *unbound.*

– We're in agreement then? Stacy looked at each and every one of them.

– Aye. Jill stood with her back to them, but her voice was frighteningly clear.

– We already have our own Coven, independently of Laurie, Jason said calmly. – Let's keep it that way.

– Aye, Everett growled.

– Aye, Daniel said.

– Aye, Ivan sang.

– Let's do it, Gabi spat.

The child's anger both shook and inspired the others.

– Yes, Andrea called out.

– Aye, Travis agreed.

– Aye, Tam shouted.

– Aye… Rae said hesitatingly

– We must, Kieron repeated.

Daniel and Andrea were the only ones here of the older generation. The other six had remained within Laurie's «protective» shield.

– I can still feel her, Andrea said hysterically to Stacy. – She's sunk her hooks in deep. I don't know if I can keep her from intruding, from disrupting me, making me disrupting us.

– Shhh, Stacy told her, as she held her and Daniel in her healing embrace.

Something happened, something impossible to describe. Their eyes… cleared.

– Thank you, Healer. Daniel said in a voice thick with gratitude. – THANK YOU

It is a stopgap measure, Stacy thought. But it will work. It will work now.

They stood there with the rest of them, standing tall, shaking like leaves.

Everyone gathered looked at the Rite Master.

– So has it become, so it *is,* Stacy cried. – We bind ourselves forever to darkness, to the shadows of the Earth and the Sky, to the boundless Other World. There is no other world, only this one, this boundless one.

They undressed, casually, eagerly. They did stare at each other, with hungry, sultry eyes.

There were people walking off and on by the end of Main Street below. Some saw it and pointed, looking away when they saw the huge, burning eyes upon them, heard the dark, challenging laughter.

The Dance began. They were all peeing where they stood upright, not caring where their body fluids went. And then their shit followed, surprisingly easy, like a waterfall in spring. Their thighs and feet turned dirty as everything flowed from their lower openings. Everybody was moving back and forth in their own path, moving in their own and others' body fluids. Only Jill and Loeh stood still. The others started touching their thighs and started smearing each other, started consuming the discarded pieces of themselves. Ivan kept playing while smearing himself, playing his body. His soiled hands kept playing the drum and the beat thundered from the Earth. The others threw it around, in a circle, in an impossible to define, pre-destined pattern. Travis stood a bit away, just by the edge of the Shadow, sucking up rays from the sun and his body started glowing.

– Desecration is in the eye of the beholder, Jill sang, still with her back turned. – Desecrate the Queen. Fill her with slurping tongues. On to the Hill. Find the hood under the face. Shine the Moon.

Asteroth the Maiden started turning, round and round and round, calling to the ground below, brushing her hair with her fingers, making it brown again, shit filling her mouth, flowing from her mouth, through her brown lips, filing between her small breasts.

She giggled.

– You have no idea how therapeutic this is, she mumbled, her eyes turning huge and strange. – A child voluntarily undressing herself in front of baaad naked adults, digesting her own waste in a satanic ritual… that will never do, will it, though? My teacher will go *bananas.* A story like that will never be accepted…

The others didn't stop, but it was as if time itself paused.

– Well, to HELL with it, she shouted. – We're human beings, not scared tiny mice, hiding from the cat. We are the cat, the predator, looking for a snack.

The drum thundered, and the Earth itself shook under their feet.

And they danced, as the air itself started shimmering in her immediate surroundings.

And they laughed, and they felt good, as the laughter rippled in the air between them, empowering them further.

And she recited:

The day is a worm
Devouring your soul
A cage of hens
A playground of sheep
A bouquet of flowers
Are rotting on the spine
Dying on the vine
Total eclipse of
The Fire inside

Loeh started shaking her head, started nodding. Eyes turned all white, as she started swaying, as she started dancing.

– *kali,* she mumbled, in a humming, in a song.

And the name sent chills down everybody's spine. They all knew it, recognized it. Most of them had studied mythology and the various ancient pantheons since they were children.

– Kali, she cried out. – I was not born into your service, but you took me, took all of me, made me yours. Speak to thy humble servant. Why did you call me then, why are you calling me now?

Jill turned and everybody froze completely in their tracks. Her face was both not changed and changed at the same time. It had turned night in the middle of the day.

The many-armed creature flowed towards Loeh, dancing her mad dance, twisting the threads of reality. And the fluids and feces emanating from her made the plants grow visibly in her path.

– *It was my will. Your siblings were tasty morsels, Dancer. But they were hardly more than snacks. They weren't worthy of you. You shouldn't grieve because of their fate.*

– But I do, I do, Loa whimpered.

– *That is of no consequence. Only your subservience is.*

The dance turned wilder, the mood turned even darker, as the two of them circled each other. The only relief in the dark was the Shadow.
Loa started calling out in Tongues. They couldn't make out what she was saying at first, but then suddenly, it was clear as glass, a splintering of pure, terrifying daylight:
– KALI, GIVER AND TAKER OF LIFE, HOW MAY I SERVE THEE? MY LIFE FOR YOU, MY LIFE FOR YOU
– I accept, godling. I will fill your vessel with my own essence, my will.
Jill's voice turned almost normal by the last two words, but still it was as if there were two speaking, or even more than two, layer upon layer, a legion of complexity.
Loeh cried out in terror, and she fainted on the spot. She fell to the ground, and lay there, unmoving.
There was silence. They heard nothing. Not the sounds from the far city, not the sound of their own breathing.
Everybody turned to Jill, to the demon, creating Shadow in the midst of the day.
– Hail to thee, creator and destroyer of Life, Stacy cried out.
The others repeated her words, mumbling, speaking loud, in reverence and fear.
Rae sank down on her knees, throwing up violently.
Jill turned, in a whirl of wind and stone, and she walked away, disappearing into the forest, into the shadows.

2

She knew this was a dream. She was Lillith within and without now, in the Shadow World, tossing and turning and sweating in her bed. Here on the Astral Plane, where everything was Now; past, present and (possible) futures. The moon shadow originated from her. She moved through the streets of the city, walked, flowed, levitated. The set course was to the Crossroads. Northfield turned foggy, dissolving around her.
The Crossroads couldn't be found in the Market this time. The rainbow on the gray trail had an infinite number of colors. There was a place of gathering, though. She didn't recognize those she saw there, but several of them seemed strangely familiar. A woman with stinging eyes of fire. She didn't know her, but knew of her. But the one she was pulled towards was a woman in leather garb…
She floated above the North American continent, where humans had arrived last, the last land on Earth receiving the human spirit. During ten thousand years the land and the people living on it, had been one. The last five hundred years the land and its people had been ravaged and plundered in countless horrible ways. Humanity's tailspin suicide run had begun in earnest.
Africa. She saw lights and colors spread from a single point, from what had been the cradle of mankind.
Everything happened so fast. She knew this. Time was against her. To compete in a run against time was a lost cause for everyone.
ImagesandImpressions cleared. Tall mountains. She had returned to Norway, during the age of the Vikings. The young girl, Stine, lay hidden in the ruins of what had been her village, her people. She had laid there for several days and nights, frozen in body and soul, terrified of what she was witnessing.
Olav the Cruel and his men had assaulted the village and butchered every male and older female. They had partied and enjoyed… the fruits of victory quite thoroughly since then. Skulls put on poles encircled the village now. It, the land itself, was desecrated now.
Gudrun and her daughters, Stine's mother and younger sisters, were taken before Olav and his court. The children clung to the upright, proud woman. But her eyes were foggy, as if she didn't really believe what she saw.
– I am Gudrun, daughter of Gudmund and Tara, witnessed and guarded by Unni and Roald, she said loud. – Why have you committed this… foul deed, Olav Haraldson?
– We have taken possession of this place, Olav declared arrogantly. He trampled to a pole, pulled it from the ground and stuck the skull at the top in Gudrun's face. The children screamed and Gudrun backed off. – Here you have your Satan's Gudmund, what's left of the ungodly bastard. The others are

all here somewhere. They will serve to remind people of the power of White Christ. They are nothing. You are nothing. We have taken you as our thralls. As our property you are nothing more than the price we at any time choose. Show us your worth, Gudrun, daughter of Gudmund.

– No, she cried, backing off more. She was pushed forward again.

– Remove those rags, woman.

– No, never, she shouted.

Olav signed to one of his men. He grabbed one of the daughters and pulled her away, carrying her within Olav's grace. Gudrun cried out in protest but a paralyzing blow from a stick kept her from moving.

– This is your second oldest tramp, is it not? The King held her by the jaw. – Where is pretty Stine, who we have heard so much about?

– I don't know, Gudrun replied numb.

– You know what? I believe you. He told her this in a gracious and pleasant manner. – We have all heard that Stine is just as quick in the head and on her feet as she is strong and pretty. She has managed to slip away. There is always a hole a fish may slip through. The King gives her his regards. Marte, here, is an excellent compensation. She is also widely sought as a future bride.

He pulled off her dress in one move.

– … and all the rumors about her value seem well-founded indeed.

The still wind carried the wicked laughter back and forth on the plain.

– Be kind… merciful Master, Gudrun begged. – I will do it… whatever the merciful Master wants…

She stepped forward. The children were held back. She started to pull in the strings keeping the cloth in place. The heavy dress dropped to the ground. She stood still keeping her eyes down, her head bowed. The huge man of Olav's Guard grabbed her and held her hard by the long, thick plaits.

– Gudrun has born many children, he commented grinning, – but she is evidently not any worse for wear because of it. I believe she has many more births ahead of her.

– Like mother, like daughters, Olav laughed. He sent Marte a look filled with thick desire and started to remove his clothing. He struck out his hands, invitingly. – Tame them, they are yours.

Stine lay hidden, trembling in fear and rage and full-blown hatred. She wished to attack and tear apart the king and his men, but fortunately, as she may not see it her fear won.

Gudrun's desperate protests faded when they brutally squeezed her huge breasts. They beat and kicked her into subservience. They put her on her back and had their way with her, one by one. Olav gave the young maiden his special and unabridged attention. She started struggling, a few, useless moves, before he had her under his complete control. Her eyes were already red after the helpless sobs. He started to digest the irresistible maiden, the Lord King. And when he had finished with her there were many others, waiting in line.

Some of the other women and families quite enjoyed themselves, since Gudrun and her line hadn't been well liked by everybody. They forgot for a short while the heads of their own men and sons on the stakes surrounding the former village. They laughed scornfully witnessing the fate of Gudrun and her brood.

Until their number was up.

For three days and nights Olav and his faithful men celebrated their victory. All women and older girls were taken repeatedly and received their lessons in the life and blind obedience expected of a thrall. Some fought, others attempted to save themselves by giving in voluntarily, others again begged to be spared and some begged for death. The end result remained the same.

Stine's pain had grown steadily, into a horrible suffering. She had hardly moved her body or closed an eye during all this time, all this time in this horrible, evil place, where skulls and dead eyes stared accusingly at her. She wanted to end it, to join the long, long line of those without independent thoughts.

The girl had felt… strange when Gudrun, broken and crushed, had knelt by the river before the priest of the White Christ and he had splashed water on her head. Something happened. It didn't make her feel better, but different… and worse. An emotion inside from her inheritance almost burned her up. Eyes were pulled up, to the highest mountains, between and beyond the low, misty mountain clouds. Something visible to all whom could see. A man, a creature with gray hair in one tail, plait down his back. She saw him… and felt fear.

Lillith felt fear on more levels than she could imagine.

He seemed to… to *feed*, on whatever happened here. He stood motionless with closed fists stretched to each side of his body. The energy flowing into him wasn't visible, as far as most eyes could sense, but Stine saw it. She had thrown up many times, silent and with an iron-hard self-control. What she felt had long since passed beyond ordinary fear. Passively and paralyzed in thought and limbs she awaited the end of the game and that they would come and fetch her, to share the others' fate.

But no one came… Could it be possible… A notion more like a treacherous hope than anything remotely realistic entered her conscious mind… that he didn't either, the Almighty, see her or know where she hid. She had sensed his suffocating presence, like a blanket that keeps air from the sleeper. Whatever, sooner or later, if she stayed, she would catch his attention. She had to escape, find others, warn them, gather them. The White Christ's Power was irresistible if one played his game. His pawn, the king, had to suffer. But what would she do afterwards? What?

She sneaked away during the deep darkness, from what had been her home, from what had been transformed into a tomb. Stiff and frozen, she had to struggle just to keep going the first steps towards eternity.

But soon she ran wildly, into the eternal night, filled with an ever-growing hatred.

Later. She led the refugees from many tribes over a shaking bridge. The last in the row didn't make it before an arrow hit him in his back and made him fall into the abyss. She saw Olav Cruel and one of his bowmen congratulate each other far below and she heard them speak.

– I got him, the bowman howled pleased. – Did you men see that shot? It was one of *them,* one with knowledge. One natural rebel less.

– Excellent, the Lord and King praised him. – This way we can deprive this people of memory itself, until they're nothing but a tribe without a name.

Later. Many years after the battle of Stiklestad. Their allies had betrayed them. They had been betrayed by power hungry men without loyalty, and they had to run once more. Stine had realized that she merely had been his, White Christ's tool, like so many others. Everything she had done, or almost everything, had only served to strengthen him and his campaign. She had told her tribe to go north, keep going north and leave her. And after a heartfelt discussion they had done her bidding. They had left her by this little cabin by the river, with just a minimum of provisions. Old as she was she had little use for food. She awaited Death.

He walked all the long way up. She could see him, from deep below in the valley, to the turn of the road just below her, and the last stretch. The trip had taken the old, no older man, hours, in what must be his infinite patience. She saw that he wasn't old and that he hadn't really aged at all since she had seen him as a young girl.

– I've been expecting you, she told him. – I've been waiting for you.

– You're no good to me anymore, he said with regret. – And I've wasted enough time and resources chasing you.

– You haven't captured me, she snarled. – You don't know who I am.

– Something has always bothered me about you, he admitted graciously, pressing his brows together. – It's about time I got my curiosity stilled.

– I know you, she spat. – I know the secret name of God.

He got distracted and shook to the point of losing concentration. The grip in which he had held her, loosened. She directed all her attention inwards and instantly every cell in her body disintegrated in blinding fire. It happened from one moment to the next. The ash rained to the ground.

– You lied, he said enraged. – You don't remember.

– I will, a hollow voice told him from thin air. *– I'll remember and I'll get you. One day…*

– You will pay, he swore. – You are hereby cursed. Your lives will be scream and suffering, until the day you kneel by my feet.

And she sensed it, the horror and truth about his words, how time and space bent to his will, how she was cursed to forever suffer. But it wasn't anything new. It had ever been thus.

He seemed so small and insignificant from where he stood, from where she saw him. But she knew how big, how small he really was. Through guile and time his shadow spread its poison across the

Earth. He had made her his tool, again, as he had done with so many, so many times. Never again! She still didn't know for sure if he had actually seen her in the village that time, those horrible days and nights long ago, but he had been aware of her existence. Always. While her knowledge of him had turned vague. But that served to her advantage, too. She was so changed that he didn't know who she was. He had used her, as he used everybody. She would never allow that to happen again.

I swear…

Clouds parted. Many times. What she received on her Journey turned unclear once more.

Somewhere else. Much later. She heard singing, choir song in an enormous cathedral. Young boys. Boys for life. A young nun crouched in a dark corner, frightened and cold. Why did she ever have to freeze?

Nun? How could she? Hide, hide in plain sight, that was the only way. She had no choice.

The church bells called. Not to mass. They had had mass today. It called for an assembly in the courtyard, a declaration or a punishment or… anything. She trembled. The bells had called for a while, without her moving. The number of nuns passing outside began to thin. She hurried out and joined the line. One of the first creeds one learned in the monastery was to be neither first nor last. Never call attention to yourself. Live out your life in humble service.

The one nun among many found her place out there in the large courtyard. The young priests in training arrived from the opposite side. This was a large monastery, where males and females studied God's word not completely segregated, separated from each other. From opposite directions from the central point, they stared shyly at one another. They stared at the Judgment Circle, where punishment was executed and witches burned, at the center of the entire area, in front of the towering cathedral. A pre-pubescent boy knelt there today, nude and with his hands tied behind his back. Big droplets of tears landed in the sand, and everybody easily heard his terrified sobs. The mass of faces remained expressionless.

The echo of the last chime was fading. The head nun and priest led a procession heading for the center point, all of them wearing masks of strength and solemnity. Only the head nun walked close to the child, as if he was contaminated by the vilest of diseases.

– You were chosen to the honor of singing praise to the Lord, she shouted dramatically. – But you chose to throw away the gift He has given you and even if His mercy is considerable, you must be punished. You must learn that nobody can escape God's Wrath. As must we all.

– AS MUST WE ALL, all the nuns and priests, and would be nuns and would be priests repeated.

She bent forward and held fingers under his jaw, lifting the tear-wet face so he had to look up at her.

– Your brothers will live in their Paradise on Earth. A hand indicated six other nude, hairless boys. – They will be honored, because they will honor God with their Heavenly song for the rest of their days. But you're born with the brand of *Satan* and have even shown by your deeds that you wish to serve the False Prince.

– But… you will learn, will you not, repent your sins?

– Yes, Sister, he sniveled. – P-please…

– Don't you fear, little songbird. She smiled, a shadow in the corner of her mouth. – You will be *saved.* You will forever sing the Lord's Praise and therefore you will never be cursed by the diabolical powers sleeping within you. Your reward is awaiting you in God's Heaven. The Lord appreciates even more those who suffer in his name.

The boy couldn't stand, couldn't walk. They dragged him to the platform and chained him to it. He would've had major difficulties moving even if he wasn't paralyzed with fright. The choir started singing and the song rose from the cathedral, a hellish buzz of boys' voices that would never change. One of the priests pulled forth a knife. Rumor had it that he had been responsible for the horses in his younger days and developed an expertise based on many years' experience. He pushed the boy's legs apart, grabbed the genitals and performed a quick and simple cut. He raised his hand so everyone could see with their own eyes what he held in it.

– Open your mouth, boy, the head nun commanded.

He obeyed. The scream had been locked inside him, forever. The priest with the knife pushed his entire handful into the open mouth.

– That's right, boy. Chew. And you don't dare stop until I give you my blessing. Not if you want redemption from eternal damnation.

The song filled the air. Lillith experienced it both through the young, frightened nun and her present perception. The jaw, moving up and down, seemed to grow and grow until filling her vision, until it was all she could see. She screamed, but there was no sound from her larynx, no sound anywhere, but inside the dark confines of her soul. She screamed herself hoarse, but no one heard any of it.

Clouds parted again. Even the veil of the future parted. She saw herself, or someone looking very much like her, years from now, cross the school's plaza, a young confident woman, wearing a jacket, a skirt and a tie and high-heeled shoes. Her hair seemed to be just done. Lipstick enhanced her thick, Slavic lips. Carefully made make up showed a modern, sophisticated woman, someone she had always wanted, no, yearned to be.

Sometime later she taught one of her classes. She had them in her pocket. They ate out of her hand. There were many young witches there and also quite a few mundanes. They laughed when she wanted them to laugh, taking notes when that was her desire, with an energy and sense of duty making her proud.

From the other room she could hear and see Gabi, the adult Gabi, excel in the teaching of impressionable youths. The school had grown considerably in size and importance the last few years, after the mutants had taken over. Many of Laurie's major subordinates served on the administrative board and took active part in the development of the teaching.

It was all absolutely terrifying, and she couldn't wake up, and the conviction that this had become real, was real, haunted her increasingly hard.

She and Gabi, Jason and Everett left the school together. They walked straight to Square, to Laurie's Sanctum. Inside the house, in the eloquent dining room Laurie's sat on her throne. They knelt before her, the four of them.

– Greetings, children.

– GREETINGS, MOTHER.

– So how was your day? She asked them during the dinner, while the servants were about to serve the main course.

– It's great, Mother, Gabi said eagerly. – The students are so attentive, so eager to learn, that it's a Joy teaching them.

And the silent scream grew and grew, and no matter how loud it grew, nobody could hear anything. In the Spanish plaza, throughout time and space the singing continued. She saw the mouth chew as energetic as ever. And the sound of the chewing made the ears hurt and blood flow from the nose. And still not a single soul noticed anything.

Jill sat upright in her bed, sweating and moaning and she wanted to scream her ears off. The air trembled and trembled. *Vibrating* might be a better word. Alert eyes were pushed wide open. She was sweaty and nauseous, but didn't really feel weak or sick. On the contrary. *Wide awake,* rather, alert and ready.

It was still early night and very, very dark. The dream had more than probably started immediately after her falling asleep. Tam had awakened, too, more timid than Jill could remember her in a long time. Had the ceremony during the day frightened her? She lay silently, unmoving in bed. Jill slipped out of the bed and walked to the window. It had truly turned dark. Electricity had failed all over the campus and over major surrounding areas. The light she could hardly do more than glimpse came from Newtown somewhere, suddenly so far away.

«One step forward and two back».

What? Who? She listened, stretching her mind.

– I didn't say anything, Tam said nervously.

– What is it, big elf? Jill said kindly.

There was something.

– You look different, really different now, not like today. I can see straight through you. Your eyes are *white.*

– I can see well enough, Jill wondered. – But there's something...

She could easily have looked at herself through Tam's eyes, but chose not to. From within came the certainty that there was no need for that. She stretched out her arms, stretched them wide. Suddenly her hair blew straight back from her head, like a halo. The air sparked in front of her.

Tam's eyes widened when she saw another Jill rise from the bed, rise from the bed again.

Jill saw herself as Tam had seen her. She saw herself rise from the bed, herself float in the air. Tamara pushed her big body at the wall.

– You're me, Jill said numb. Then her lips and that of the shadow moved in synchronicity, in union: – *I'm me.*

She moved towards her body. When she touched her hands, she started to fade, until she could be seen no longer. The part of her she hadn't always known of, but always had known. And now she knew of it, too. She knew it and was Whole, so much more than she had been.

Jill blinked. In that blink there was an eternity of lives. That to Stine and Vyla, and many others. King Olav spoke in a whirl of water and wind: «This way we can deprive this people of memory itself, until they're nothing but a tribe without a name».

She saw the globe from Space. She observed colorful shimmering threads between the Earth and the Moon's orbit. She stared down at the Gulf of Mexico. An enormous amount of air in uproar, a Storm gathering strength making Katrina and all other storms the last ten, fifteen, hundred, thousand years seem like a small child compared to a heavyweight champion.

To follow Laurie is to take one step forward, two steps back.

She was able to see, with absolute clarity Ivan sitting upright in bed, with his head tilted, as if he was listening. *The drum,* she sent. He found it without looking for it and instantly, without preparation he started hitting it in a slow, rhythmic beat. His roommate woke up and uttered something intelligible. It drowned in the beat of the drum. The sound started spreading from his room, through the building, across the Plaza, until everyone within the school's premises heard it. The drum seemed to come alive in his hands. His talent was control of sound. Sound could penetrate anything. Its unheard vibrations could break into vaults and people's mind. Now it was seductive, comforting and activating simultaneously. It awoke humans from their slumber, evoking forgotten emotions, forgotten dreams, awakening the land itself, making it come alive again.

Jill pulled a t-shirt over her head. Tam did the same.

– Come with me, Jill ordered her. – From now on you're my personal bodyguard.

Someone knocked at the door and the giantess fell easily into her new role, her new life. Jill stopped her easily with a denying thought. Without moving she pushed down the handle and opened the door. Two unusually uncertain identical girls waited in the hallway. Melanie looked through the cleft to see if anybody hid behind the door. She and the twin sister looked worried as they exchanged glances.

– Hey, what's happening? Meta asked Jill. – What happens at school?

– No electricity, Tam informed them. – Grid breakdown.

– Grid *breakdown,* how likely is that? Meta said doubtfully, and then lightening up. – That's *great!*

– Come with us. Jill said lazily, as much as she could be that currently… the way she looked.

From down the hall, Stacy the Witch came wandering, approaching them. She had the same shining white eyes as Jill. The same power raged in her.

– Good, then I won't have to drag you out of bed…

It wasn't exactly like Loeh's the day before. They were more intense and almost translucent, it wasn't just that the eyeballs had turned inside the sockets.

The two of them clasped hands, touched each other and remained in physical contact. Jason started walking on his hands from his room, down the hallway in the boys' dorm. Every door he passed was ripped open with a loud crack.

– You guys wanna see some action? He asked.

– You guys wanna see some action, he pondered.

– You guys want to see some action, he told them.

And his head sat on his back and the boys that didn't follow him ran off in complete and utter panic.

– I can hear drumming, one said.

– I can hear singing, another one said. – I can hear chanting. So much noise and I can't get Toby to wake up.

The other boy, Toby slept through it all. As did many others.

They were present in each other's head the four of them, even Everett who slept in his bed inside

Square, and then Gabi was there, too, in a way. She stretched out her arms, as if testing the very air around her, and then her nails scratched, scratched a hole in the very fabric of reality. She floated up through that hole and didn't disappear, and smiled excitedly.

Messages went back and forth, so fast they could hardly comprehend them, in what they would later call Speedlock. They walked by each other's side. They were seen walking by each other's side. The full moon…

The full moon was red.

– In Space, Jill and Stacy intoned. – Nobody can see you bleed.

Meta laughed out aloud. Melanie was silent.

All the witches present within the school's area joined the increasingly considerable processions, they and many of the ordinary students, more of them than expected. Victoria stopped the girls by the Plaza exit. She was fully dressed.

– What is going *on* here? She asked sternly. – Why are you not… sleeping?

– For the same reason you're not, Vicky, Meta said without a trace of respect. – We intend to have fun, fun, fun.

– Something woke us all up, Stacy said with authority. – Allow us to throw some light at everything for you, Vicky.

She (and Jill both), held up both hands. There was no fire now, but they started glowing. Gasps of excitement echoed through the main hall.

– We're just gonna have some fun, Vicky. Jill put one hand on the other's shoulder. It warmed, but didn't burn. – This is something rare, you see, a night of opportunity. Why don't you join us outside?

– Why not? Victoria sniffed. The usual perfect demeanor had some very profound clefts. – What kind of stuff have you used on your hands, by the way?

– Phosphor, Jill replied good-natured and comforting for delicate souls.

Stacy turned a bit impatient and in a dramatic gesture she threw open the doors. The big and heavy doors were thrown off the hinges and landed on the ground outside, several lengths away.

Meters.

Yards.

It turned silent, silent as death. Somebody ran to check the hinges and the doors. They looked bewildered at everybody. And then they took an extra good look at Stacy and Jill's eyes, which could hardly be painted with phosphor.

Sound of the Shaman-drum came closer, and it turned louder. Jason and Ivan led the procession from the boys' dorm.

– Can't you *hear* it, girls? Rae whispered roguishly. – Can't you hear the Night, how it moves, how it lives…

They did listen and the night did breathe and speak to them. Some of them breathed in and out as if they had never done it before. Just a very few kept back when the witches led them outside and most of them also followed when they saw the number of others follow, outside in the mist, in the unknown night.

You see? Jill sent to Stacy. *We didn't have to force them.*

They're still young and impressionable, Stacy pointed out. *They have yet to set in their mold. Besides, mysticism is so integrated in the Chapters that this isn't really that much of a stretch. They see it as an adventure. Like most they reckon they'll be productive members of society after just a few years of rebellion. The sooner they reconsider the better.*

They giggled and laughed both of them, so pleased with themselves, so nervous. The others looked curiously at them.

Jill continued receiving images and impressions from the very air surrounding them. And she scouted for Laurie, determined to defend herself at any cost, to not give an inch. She moved her feet over the tarmac here, as she, the immaterial part of her, if such an insufficient explanation sufficed floated above earth and waters. She saw Samhain, Lord of the Underworld, with his fire-eyes, sitting on his throne, scrutinizing his subjects, stirring the living and the dead. There was a corruption in the land, and he couldn't find its cause. His was the Kingdom of Death, but he was Alive and so was the land.

And corruption, a sort of living death, invaded all lands, all «kingdoms». She could see them, the armies of poison, the walking dead. They were merely pale shadows of what they had been. They had been human once, but were hardly recognizable as such now.

Samhain, the man, the god died screaming, in rage and disbelief.

Above waters and present-day Earth now. The corruption was virtually everywhere. The North Pole, the South Pole. The holes in the Ozone Layer were permanent now. Lichen in Norway, in Greenland, in Canada withered and died in the middle of the growth season, one of the more pronounced signs of the damaged Ozone Layer everywhere. Humanity waged chemical warfare against itself. Dioxin and a host of other man-made chemicals made horrible changes in animals and humans. Males were born without penises. Females with them. Horrible diseases born out of civilization ravaged and destroyed. Lillith stared blindly, stared enraged at it all, and saw Life on Earth die slowly, painfully. She heard a voice she now knew was Gabi's speak in the void between worlds. «Everything has ended here, even those that never began…»

– It's about time, she mumbled, – about time we're doing this, doing everything.

– Gabi feels strongly we need protection, she said aloud, – against open and hidden threats.

– Yes, against everything, Stacy nodded. – We're like insects emerging from the chrysalis, to be insects no more. We're vulnerable. Experience has shown us that.

She turned to her sister witch.

– You know, I must congratulate you on your find. She's a true jewel. We'll find many uses for our little Oracle.

The two groups of young men and women met at the center of the school property, close to the mound between the park and the parking lot, melting into one in joyful expectation. There was a low hum, a song seemingly originating from the ground below, from the Earth itself, of pain and pleasure, intermingled, interchangeable. Stacy and Jill turned their hands, leaving traces of themselves behind in the very air and the others inhaled it with the air they breathed. Ivan continued to beat the drum, and everybody moved to it. He rotated slowly; he was the axis the others moved to. As if on a signal a circle was formed wide and tight.

The wind was blowing, as it always did. And ever stronger, while time crawled. Jill heard it speak to her, but couldn't tell if it really did, or if it all came from within. She recalled herself less than a month ago, a fairly innocent young maiden, ignorant of what lurked in the shadows. What they were about to do tonight… It was still true that they stumbled through the dark, one step at the time (not two backwards). The still uncanny abilities she and Stacy and Jason had to communicate with their minds tied all those present together, and the communication also happened on an even deeper level, an understanding of nature and their surroundings, more instinctive than conscious and strictly rational. The wind brought knowledge about the hidden and the forgotten and an indescribable Power.

– Gabi, our historian, our Oracle, told us a bedtime story earlier today… Jill spoke calmly, with a cheerful taint. – She's the youngest among us, but her Power is strong. It goes like this:

She pushed her mind inside all present, making them share her thoughts along with her words.

– 100 years times four ago four witches held a ceremony on this place, on this exact spot. They were interrupted and captured by the first Joseph Parnell. In another ceremony he «cleansed» this place in a service honoring his god. He sacrificed the four witches, burned them at the stake. This is one of many «incidents», a word *popular* in government circles by the way, making this place and the entire Northfield area something special, a cauldron of untapped Power. In Death there's Life.

And during the last sentence her voice changed again.

– You can all feel it…. I know you can.

– I can feel it, a boy almost shouted. – A… t-tingling in the skin, as if I can notice my blood moving in the vein.

That was exactly how Jill herself felt, except to her it was a thousand times stronger, more potent.

– Good, she said, closing her eyes briefly. – Very good.

Everybody sat quiet, listening, captivated by the story. They moved even tighter together. They saw nothing extraordinary and heard only the voice of the one speaking, but imagined the movement of shadows in the dark and imagined hearing their pained whispering in the wind.

– Violent actions and incidents leave traces, Travis said. – They may weaken the borders between the physical world and the shadow world. Or perhaps there are no borders? Perhaps we're merely imagining their existence? Anyway, in the world that may be divided from the physical world, there is no Time. Actions and incidents are preserved there, throughout Eternity. What we do in Life echoes in Eternity. Perhaps there is no shadow world? Perhaps there is only One? But no matter: Extreme emotions and violence may be better preserved, easier observed.

The witches parted the circle itself and moved further within it, where they made a smaller version of the bigger without. They stood still for a while, concentrating. The wind increased, coming from all sides. The first, smaller dry twigs fell from the darkness above. Then there was a rain of both twigs and branches, dead a long time ago from lack of water and nourishment. The rain seemed to slow down just above ground, laying itself to rest quite nicely in the fast-growing heap at the center of the circle.

The uninitiated mundane students held their breath. They understood most of them that something fundamental was happening, something that, according to their accepted teachings was fundamentally impossible. It happened. There was no way around it.

It happened.

More floated in the air above, thousands of tiny dry blades of grass. They realized this when the grass ignited at the top and worked its way down to create a cone, a cone of fire. There were those among them that jumped to their feet and ran away from there as fast as they could. Ashes fell to the ground. The heap of twigs and branches caught fire, and they all felt as if they sat inside it. Somebody, somewhere photographed it all. Jill smiled. She was herself, she was everybody else. Imperceptible, with waves of pulsating energy all the images were completely overexposed. It would seem like the digital film had been exposed to constant, unfiltered daylight. Unity faded. Jill blinked. It felt like both a death and birth each time a unity faded. This was the technique Laurie had used with such skill to seduce every nebulous witch who had entered her coven, one that had grown in strength with each new arrival, to something irresistible. The only recourse left to them was to shatter the unity, shatter the coven, and build something fresh, something new from the ashes.

Jill and three other witches left the inner circle, placing themselves between it and the outer one. Jill, Stacy, Jason and Ivan placed themselves in one corner of a square each. Everett could have taken Ivan's place, but they had decided upon another approach.

– Tonight, we're gonna chase Death away, Rae cried, as she, too, left the inner circle. The flickering light from the fire gave golden hair and skin a further quality and she looked like a goddess. – Not the final, inevitable death of the body, the shell, but the one that may befall a person while he or she is still walking and breathing.

Rae Morgan placed herself between Stacy and Jill stretching her arms towards them. Something happened then, something even more disturbing than the twigs and the branches and the fire. The ground straight under the open palms started… moving, started stretching upwards, two thin rope-like lianas, until it touched those palms, surrounding those hands… and it started thickening. Rae released a soft cry of pain. Startled gasps of shock sounded as the people in the outer circle realized that her skin, both that on her arms and the nude feet, started turning gray. More geysers of ground erupted straight from the ground all the way around the inner circle, connecting to Rae in shoulder height. Her entire body stiffened, slowly… slowly turning to stone, to living stone. Jill and Stacy stiffened, too, as that living stone attached itself to them, drawing upon their resources. They knew, they had known that this would be a desperate act, one that, once started would be beyond the point of no return. What they had hardly more than glimpsed in their atavistic memory, became an inevitably reality. Magick was *real,* was a potent force in this world, was the potent force they had always imagined. One learned only by doing and they needed learning, needed doing.

Andrea, Tam, Daniel, Kieron and Loeh dissolved the inner circle. All but Andrea held a cup with a smoking brew in both hands.

– We need four virgins, Andrea said in a joking tone of voice, – two of each kind. Anybody volunteering? It's nothing to be ashamed of, you know, but if you wish to hear my opinion in the matter, it isn't anything to hold onto either. C'mon, first come first served, you know.

The cheerful mood loosened some of the worst fear, but the dispersed laughter died pretty quickly, as the air and mood tightened. A girl jumped up. It was Victoria.

– Ah, a brave soul. Andrea exclaimed without sarcasm and clapped her hands. – Come forward, brave maiden.

The maiden ran to Andrea as fast as the feet could carry her. She stood still before the imposing mutant with bowed head. Andrea grabbed her around the jaw and made sure she held her head high. And then, with a defiant stance, she did.

A boy stood up in a fluid, confident move.

– Forget it, Andrea told him immediately. He grinned and sat down once more.

See how she's standing there, proud and defiant, Stacy sent to Jill. *Doesn't that serve to show how complex human nature is? The best of it all is that we haven't really done anything to persuade her.*

She has longed to liberate herself, Jill parried. *There's every reason to feel joy because that's happening now, isn't it…*

– Isn't it typical that a girl is the first to volunteer to something like this? Andrea chided. – Come on, boys… the world may end by the first light tomorrow. This may be your final change to get lucky…

A tall, skinny boy straightened to his full height, hesitated just a bit more, before stepping forward. Merely a few seconds afterwards a couple, holding hands stepped forward. Jill recognized them as the couple from the bus stop. They hadn't departed, not until now.

– Behold the four. Andrea spoke muted, easily distinguishable from the roaring wind. – They're from the fertile planet, as are we all, as we are a part of it. This is a fact. A time span bigger than we can imagine has led to the boundless variety in fertility and Life we know today. It's nothing more than a wasted effort to claim that this is because of any supreme being. The planet is a living organism, and we give it consciousness. Tonight, this very moment, we will celebrate our contact and relationship with everything that lives.

The four of them watched her with a nervous wait and see attitude. She had their complete and undivided attention. She sent them a cheerful look and no more was needed to make them undress themselves. Victoria slipped out of her cream-colored blouse and pulled her t-shirt above the head. Her hair, always in such an excellent order, was thoroughly messed up. She pushed her pants down her thighs. A slight hesitation and the panties followed suit. The quiet, half admiringly mumbling from all around her, was strangely satisfying. She had always known that she, objectively speaking (whatever that meant) was attractive, but had never been able to get rid of the arrogance painted in her features, even if that had been her desire for as long as she could remember. It had been so hard. Her parents, her relatives and acquaintances expected a certain conduct from her, a host of non-derivative acts.

Now, the situation had been turned upside down and she realized how much she had disliked standing on her head all her life. When the skinny boy (she didn't even know his name) navigated his underwear off his hips and exposed his stiff, blood-filled cock she joined the silent humming. The sound was nothing her ears could hear, but it was just as distinct. She wondered how it had to be for him… for men. They all had obvious signs of the same excitement boiling within her.

Everything was quiet. Only the wind blew. She had never thought about that before, but it always did.

Tam stepped forward, holding the cup with the smoking brew in both hands.

– What is it? Victoria and the other girl and boys asked in a perfect chorus.

– In simplistic terms? Loeh said lightly. – It limits our cognitive and rational abilities. Similar potions have been in use during fertility rituals for tens of thousands of years, bringing forth our most fundamental urge.

– I don't n-need it. Victoria shook her head decisively. – I'm already so hot that I'm b-burning. I swear.

– We know that and it's good. Quite visible, too. But you shall be so hot that you can think of nothing else, until you're nothing more than a vessel for the energies ravaging you. Your need will be unbearable and from then on it will double in intensity every second, until you're nothing more than that need, a female beast crying for the male's hot sting.

Victoria didn't look at Andrea, but her eyes were locked on Rae… on Morgana's cold deep blue eyes, alive within the frame of the frozen features. She accepted the smoking brew from Tam, pulled the cup to her lips. The brew wasn't hot. She drank, emptied the cup, felt the fluid burn down her throat. The other three drank, too.

– I don't feel any different…

– Come here, maiden, the strict Morgana commanded her, and her voice didn't sound that altered. – Come to me all of you. There are yet more preparations to complete.

She released herself from the stone circle, but stayed in contact with it. Flakes of gray and metal and stone and dirt and tarmac danced in the air within her immediate sphere of influence.

In a stupor Victoria saw the butt of the boy in front of her, tight and firm. He saw her, shaking hips, glimpses of a face filled with drowsy excitement. They stood still. Morgana Rae stood before them, her bare feet subbing the tarmac, never really breaking contact with the ground. Ground started moving again. Strands grew from it and as they grew, they were tied together, forming thicker, rope-like bonds. They tied themselves around four pairs of ankles. Victoria moaned.

This wasn't like the substance penetrating the skin of Morgana, Jill and Stacy earlier. These were just ropes, capturing the four ceremonial sacrifices.

– Don't be afraid, Morgana breathed to them softly. – These are the bonds tying you to your former lives, caging your emotions, your passion. They're about to fall.

Bonds captured waving, but weak arms, tied themselves around wrists. The bonds were shortened. All four of them were forced down on their knees. Arms to the side. Bonds wrought itself around their neck. They couldn't move in other ways than tiny pulls and twists.

– What have you done? Victoria just barely managed to lift her head, to look at the imposing figure above.

Morgana knelt smiling by her side, comforting her with soft touches on the chin, as a few tears left her eye.

– I have the power of the Metamorphosis, she explained. – I can influence, change and control my surroundings. Relax now, little Vicki… relax… Now we're just gonna paint you a little, and then we're ready to go.

Vicki blinked. She didn't see the witch, couldn't see any of them, but could feel hands all over her body, as they drew lines on her skin, circles around her nipples and arrows pointing to where she suddenly felt the first contraction. She attempted in despair to pull her thighs together, but the chains keeping them apart made that impossible.

– Link with your arms, the ceremonial mistress, Morgana Rae, told those in the outer ring. – The ring must not be broken. The spell will be so much more potent then.

Loeh scrutinized the four with burning eyes.

– Light by dark, she chanted. – Dark by light. That's good, that's great.

– Vicki, Morgana began. – Charles, Lori and Keith. You and your guardians in the outer circle have started on your Journey to the Shadow World. The non-physical world, existing side by side with the physical. Once you enter this land you can never leave it.

She waited. No more people left the circle.

– Excellent… *Maestro?*

Ivan hit the drum for the first time, a sound reverberating through the air through the ground and hot, hot bodies. Vicki felt it come through her bonds. The first wave of raw lust ravaged her. She gasped. She knew that Charles was behind her, even if she didn't see or had seen him there. She felt him, deep down, where we're all in contact, felt him twist his body and shake the chains. When beat followed beat and the witches' throaty chant started. How his hips shook back and forth and semen shot from his blood-filled limb, from his, from that of the other boy.

The chant rose in the air. Travis stood in the middle of the stone circle with his hands stretched above his head. A… shimmering mist seemed to grow out of the thick air, from Stacy and Jill, from Morgana, from the four hungry souls chained and locked, hungry for Release, from all and everybody, seemingly passing through Ivan, pausing close to Jason, gaining strength, penetrating the stone circle, surrounding Travis… and then he seemed to absorb, digest it all, bathing in it. He started glowing. His hands suddenly pulsed *violently,* and a broad energy beam shot upwards towards the night sky. Vicki and Lori moaned in ever-greater need, despairing because the boys had spilled their seed on the ground and not inside their hot nests. The ones comprising the outer circle started moaning, too, but they couldn't move, locked to each other, now, in an iron spell. Nobody could move, nobody could leave the circle, nobody could break into it.

– I want you to imagine a ball of fire, a big, big one, above the fire embers. Liberate your energy, set it free…

Everett awoke with a start, instantly wide-awake, more awake than he had ever, ever been. He rose from the bed. His feet moved over the floor, but he was in a completely different place. The body was completely naked as he stepped out in the hall. Gabi ran to him. She embraced him, pushed her smaller hand into his. He got an erection merely by observing the flashes of light on the half-grown body. She stared at him, her mouth wide open.

Distant thunder, closer than a heartbeat called to him. Gabi nabbed him in the elbow without nabbing him in the elbow. He gave her a self-assured smile. Shadows formed behind and before them. He recognized Laurie and her remaining pack of older witches. Distant powers, closer than a breath called to him. He recognized the tomb surrounding him. The powers were also his own, hidden far below in the deep, below many layers, many lives - rusty, unused for so long. He was no longer only Everett Moran.

– They're doing it, Laurie cried terrified. – They've no idea what they're doing, no idea about the consequences.

– They're DOING it, Gabi cried in excitement.

The rebel witches had come, earlier that evening, following the ritual on the Hill, throwing shit at the walls, in every room of the house, desecrating the place. Laurie had stood still, shaking in rage and helplessness.

– GET OUT, she had shouted. – GET OUT!

And they had eventually all left, except for Gabi and Everett. Laurie had tried to touch them, physically and mentally, but it had been like touching pure electrical currents. Udo and the others had started to clean the house, mechanically, robot-like. They had washed everywhere with strong soap, but the smell, the stench remained.

Risk was an important part of the ritual. So they had all parted, parted to gather again later. They had come from all over the world to this place of antiquity and power. From far away they came. They came from far away.

Again. They started it all anew. They.

Energy flowed into Travis, submerging him. It started to hurt. The beam broadened. Somewhere up in the air it started to split, once, twice, spreading all over the city, its entire length and far more than its width. A fair chunk of the land around was included. Hot and cold streams prickled inside Everett. He got scared. He wasn't in the circle, but everywhere outside it, within the wide wider circle encircling the town. He was in a tomb, a burial chamber. Death and Life surrounded him, swarmed in his presence.

This must stop, Laurie's cry sounded in everybody's thoughts.

Her connection, her faint connection with the circle was cut like a string with a scissor, brutally excluding her. Two giant razors met and parted. Laurie shook and screamed short and sharp.

– I won't stand for it, she shouted hysterically. – Damned disobedient little…

– Whatever control you had over them, over us, is gone, gone and gone. Everett told her. – You did it during their Spirit Quest, didn't you, when they were at their most vulnerable, made a path to their inner self, to take command over them if you deemed it necessary? Well, you took on a bit more than you could deal with, I guess…

– It was, is necessary, for their own sake, she said strict and hard. – They don't know evil, what's right and wrong in this world.

– There is no right and wrong, he responded. – And those finding pleasure in deciding what others shall think and do, governing their thoughts and acts are the evil ones.

The necessary rock-hard concentration made him sweat. He expected an attack at any time. They could still access the circle through him, through the girl, disrupting its purpose. He was tied to what went on there through his power, whatever it might be and so was she. Because nothing could keep her out… from anywhere.

– Give me the girl, Laurie commanded. They attacked like a gestalt, all seven simultaneously. All their power belonged to Laurie. They were her weak-willed puppets.

– Don't take me for an *idiot.* He sensed the older witch' thoughts on the edge of his own, but he managed to resist their combined power.

He did.

– Beware, Gabi warned, – you insane cretins, daring to pit your puny powers against he who is Anubis… He Who Guards the Crypt. I would beg forgiveness if I were you.

Something… broke just then. The pentacle on his abdomen started to *glow*. Waves of power emanated from him, pushing Laurie and her underlings away. Suddenly he had access to everything the circle could give, even if he needed merely a fraction of a fraction of it to dismiss the weak and poorly executed attack on his person. The Name meant something to them, to Laurie. That was clearly the case. But more to him, because he began to realize what it entailed.

– Come to me, child, Laurie attempted. – Join me.

– No, I won't join you, she spat. – I was fooled, was seduced by the Call of the Goddess, but you missed your chance, and now, without your key puppets, the Call of the Goddess, your *drug* is only a meek echo of what it was, anyway.

He heard the four most potent voices, Jason, Ivan, Stacy and Jill, saw them and their all-white eyes glow in power. He saw Shiva and Vishnu in their infinite dance of destruction and creation, and he saw Stacy and Jill. Why? In the mirror he saw his own eyes, darker than the deep of Space.

– Come, let's leave this place, he said in utter contempt.

They walked to Gabi's room and the air started shimmering, and to the others they seemed to fade away into nothing.

And they materialized outside the house, outside Square, outside Laurie's place of power.

– I used to do this all the time, the girl said eagerly, – without being consciously aware of it. I could be at home and suddenly find myself outside the tavern or other places. It was more a subconscious thing then. Now I can control it much better.

With nothing more to keep it in check the Power swelled within him. Sweat started flowing. Lori, Keith, Charles… Vicki (Victoria) pulled senseless in their bonds, in the harness keeping them chained. The Need had long since passed the point of reason and rational thought and it kept building. And they would have reached the releasing climax minutes ago, if they hadn't been kept from achieving it. He heard their desperate moans and begging wails. The energy saturated the circle now and all the negative aspects of it they didn't need they poured into him. He leaned against the brick wall. Flashes flared for his inner eye. They (what they hadn't done) making a doll of clay, binding it with Laurie's hair, burning it, dissolving it to nothing. Loeh dancing throwing the doll into the air, until it disappeared, faded from memory. He saw what they had done. During the moon ritual earlier this evening Laurie had acted insecure, not her usual self at all. All her insecurities, all her fear had emerged and haunted her for all to see.

– Where *is* everybody? She had asked irritated. All had been gathered around her. – I can smell shit.

– And there's a lot of it around, isn't there? Jill had told her.

Laurie had looked up, seeing her former charges, puppets approach, seeing the still wet waste in their hands. And then the group had gone inside, completing the desecration.

Laurie had completed the ritual, but nothing had really come of it. No power, no satisfaction, nothing but the hollow promises she had always tempted them with.

He leaned against the brick wall, not to gather strength, but to collect it, focus it. He fumbled in the dark as they all did, but what they did was not unknown. A terrible, frightening Power grew within him, and he had never felt better.

– You need a place to relax, Gabi whispered. – Shouldn't we get away from here?

– There's no need, he grinned grim. Even the voice was hollow and dark, dark, dark. – This just makes me more dangerous. They know that and have crawled into their corners to hide. *Perhaps you should do the same, little insect.*

She knew what one did with insects. One crushed them under the heel.

– Tell me what to do, Dreaded Master, she begged him. – Please.

Dance, ancient dance. In the forest. In hiding from the dry, hot sand. A thousand small lights. Prayers to He who dwelled in and guarded the Crypt of Eternity.

A young priestess approached the young Anubis in his lair, offering herself to him, before his transformation, during the time of the beast. His loins, his entire being were filled with the darkest power.

He pulled himself together with a major effort, achieving some sort of control over what clawed and roared within.

– You may give me heat, slightly alleviate the pressure, he said a bit kinder to the half-naked, scared little girl.

– Heat... I don't know.... I've never done it before.
– You've never made the attempt, he explained, fighting to stay calm, calm, calm. – You radiated a physical and metaphysical cold because it was your state of mind at the time. You're not that person now. You can do it. Let yourself go... slowly, carefully.
The dark and the shadows trembled and moved as if alive around them. She sensed his pain, because she had contact with everything if she so desired. And his pain radiated from him for all to see. She concentrated, attempted to do as she had learned, calming her mind, harmonizing her inner being.
It started as a... quiver in her fingertips, a humming somewhere in her mind, not with numbness as before. Why the hands? She knew that the high number of brain-cells used to analyze impulses from them, as shown on a «Homunculus», led to a higher degree of control... She stopped analyzing, and started Doing. The dark surrounding him turned partly shimmering bright, but she couldn't overwhelm it no matter how hard she tried.
– Thanks. He touched the underside of her jaw, and she grew enormously aware of his blood-filled Thing, still seemingly pointing at her. Her blushing spread instantly to the entire body. She turned very self-conscious, and all her wits left her.
She could hardly move. Legs felt like jelly. The sudden, shocking pain between her thighs made it difficult to stand. She had heard it be *whispered* about among the older girls, but the expectation could in no way compare with the reality.
– I can help you... more, she whispered. – Please allow me, Dreaded Master.
He realized that she wasn't joking, not completely. She knew more about him than he did himself. He would have shaken her knowledge out of her if he hadn't sensed that it originated in her subconscious more than her conscious mind.
– I wouldn't mind, he said hoarsely, cursing himself for being defensive. Hadn't he stopped caring about society's stupid rules yet? – It's bad timing. I must keep it inside for a while longer and it must fall on the wayside, you know that.
– Yes, of course, she whispered. – Please, forgive me.
They started moving, a hurried walk, soon changing to running. They passed the church and charged into Newtown. The ever-increasing pain and the ever-stronger cramps forced Everett to take frequent brakes. It *hurt*. What was always both pain and pleasure had now become only a dreadful pain. In his fever visions he saw only shadows around him. Trees breathed their last along Main Road. There was hardly more than dust where there used to be green lawns and fields. He easily noticed the well-groomed green garden on the Gyrich-estate. Trees full of leaves closed off the view of the gloriously bright estate.
The transport of water had to take a major chunk even out of the Gyrich budget.
He saw the fire; he saw the circle through Lillith's eyes, heard through her ears, through leaves rattling like snakes on the ground. He didn't need her ears to hear the drumbeat. It penetrated his being in ever more painful waves. The smell of his own dead sweat and their fresh sickened him. *May Satan take them!*
A burst of icy wind almost put out the fire. Shock and fear flowed through him.
Hold out, my love, Jill comforted him. *It won't be long now.*
His senses, both the physical and the hidden, approached their ultimate potential now. They had to, the way they overwhelmed him. Three... streets to the left three cute little girls tortured a dying grasshopper. Suddenly he was the little bugger, indifferent, stoic, distant, who had given up on life. Just as suddenly he had become the three torturers. Indifference, emptiness... A violent Hunger after something they couldn't name and it bothered them, it bothered them terribly. *Life is the Blood. Blood is the Life.* He smelled the sweet (not the salt) taste of blood. Something had pinched his lips, pinched them several places. Fangs, long pointed... He heard Gabi's scream, heard it, even if not a sound escaped her. She remained close to him, unmoving, paralyzed and the eyes were foggy like crystal balls. He smelled quite a few people in the empty streets, but he didn't see anyone. All of them far away. This place was silent and safe.
Why didn't it *happen?* He had never been very good at holding back before. He realized that she had done this to him, somehow. The bitch!
He directed his entire attention to the girl by his side. He was able to see it all for his inner eye. How

he emptied his dark seed in her, how he filled her with his essence. How she changed, becoming his creature, his eager servant, doing his every bidding. Skin darkened, hair darkened. Everything about her turned dark. She looked at him with her excited expectation, looking forward to any one of his biddings. And just by looking at that future, a few minutes from now, it threatened to become real.

– What are you DOING? Olivia Norman walked close to the circle and attempted to push herself inside. She didn't even come close to it. Something kept her away all the way around. She ran off, crying hysterically, shouting totally terrified. – WHAT IS HAPPENING, WHAT IS HAPPENING?

The bonds holding Keith pulled him backwards, until he lay there, stretched out on his back. Morgana Rae, the priestess of the gods held her arms high and hands, thumb and index-finger together. Vicki and Charles were lifted up until they stood there on shaky legs.

She's good. Stacy was quite pleased… with herself. *We made an excellent choice.*

Jill didn't comment on that (even if she wanted to). Everything had proceeded as planned so far and now only the last, critical juncture remained.

Charles and Vicki pulled ever closer to each other. She couldn't turn around and see him, but knew he was there. Aside from that she didn't know much or didn't think much anymore. She existed only as emotions now, as boundless passion. As if in an endless dream she noted that Tam lifted the liberated, senseless Lori and carried her to the equally liberated and senseless Keith, lowering her at his hips, the desperately raised hips.

– Dark on light, Morgana chanted. – Light on dark. *Let it begin.*

Lori parted thighs wet with sweat and cunt flow and Tamara Farley lowered her down on Keith's cock. At exactly the same time Charles had finally fought himself close enough (Vicki the reborn, Victoria no longer, felt his hot breath in her neck and cheered) and pushed his cock deep within her. There was *pain.* The potion had softened, but not removed it and it wasn't supposed to. The pain was an important part of the ritual, the liberation. She leaned forward in her bonds, as he took her. Lori's hips moved up and down, up and down, while Keith writhed and gasped below her.

The beat drummed faster and faster. All movements quickened.

The fire flickered and grew. The incomprehensible chant turned slowly into words, even if no one was certain they heard words form in the four witches' larynxes or if it only seemed that way.

– Bound love, one-way passion, liberate thyself. Emotions chained, locked inside the deep cellar, emerge. In stars' night and shadows' day.

Then… it happened. The fires seemed to grow, no, to erupt, rise in the air. A ball of fire grew to rise from the fire on the ground. Quivering of energy where it hung a human height above the ground. The bonfire faded, but the ball kept burning, independently. It kept rising in the night and kept growing. It continued its ascent until its path crossed the beam from Travis' hands. Gabi saw the black seed erupt from Everett's seemingly overgrown limb and she shook in her first orgasm.

Bonds loosened. Charles put his arms around Vicki, and she arched back her head, finding his lips. Keith pulled Lori down and she showered him in wet kisses. A tidal wave rolled in from the sea and brought them with it. Huge enough to make their feet wet, to make them drown in the infinite sea.

The fireball *exploded.* All the gathered energy spread to the four winds, penetrated the city and the land as a blanket, removing all blankets, removing what kept people from breathing. The final part of the bonfire (that didn't burn), the remains of the wood burned to nothing, and the fire died. A bit of additional smoke rose from the circle and then there was just the scorched tarmac left, to suggest that anything had ever burned.

Stacy and Jill, once more able to move their bodies, experienced how any stiffness they had ever suffered vanished like smoke, floated away like Lead on Venus, as they were soaking up the energy in the ground every time their feet landed on another piece of the warm, warm tarmac.

Everybody realized suddenly how quiet everything had become. They raised their head and while listening they could hear a faint echo of the final drumbeat. They sniffed in the air, the fresh, refreshing air. And all fatigue seemed like blown away. Awareness penetrated their being, like ice-cold waves on the beach a burning hot summer day.

Crimson dawned slowly in the east. Yawning and happy youths danced in the streets. They whispered and spoke aloud among themselves. Whispers abounded everywhere. Temperature exceeded a hundred degrees Fahrenheit early in the morning. The burning sun rose in the sky above the flat and scorched land. Energized whisper continued. Something was wrong… or did one merely more easily discover whatever was wrong? The sound of audible discord had definitely increased.

The number of protesters outside the Thompson Chemicals production facilities doubled over night, so to speak. A clearly bigger part of the population stared at the Pyramid and didn't care much for the view. They cast long, distrustful looks at the building housing the city council and at police officers in general. There were people who felt… unwell wherever they found themselves within the city and in spite of it being a working day many families took off for the wilderness.

And the rumors of what had been going on the previous night had already been multiplied and distorted beyond recognition. Angry and hateful stares followed the witches and their Circle wherever they went.

– You should be ashamed of yourself, an old, fat woman cried to them from the sidewalk.

– Why? Jill replied, shot back at her. – Ashamed for being Human, you mean?

They had bothered to dress before leaving their ceremonial mound, but only casually, very casually. Jill felt the sensuality penetrate her very being, every single move she made.

They all did. It didn't take enhanced senses to realize this. After a giddy, promiscuous walk through town, they re-entered the school-area, entering classes in droves. They sang and had a jolly good time about it:

«There is a place not fit for Life
FUCK SCHOOL
There is a place
Everyone Alive is shunning
FUCK AT SCHOOL
Come on
Do you think a place
Feeding you garbage
Can ever be a place of learning»

Olivia stared at them and now her Good Samaritan thing had been supplanted with confusion and fear. Jill didn't feel sorry for her. Her hypocrisy had always been apparent.

Time passed as school did, somehow. And the fact that they were bored out of their skulls didn't matter anymore, because now it was really true that they weren't really there.

The Sun vanished behind the Hill. The shadow the Hill cast over the city seemed even more pronounced now. Most ordinary people didn't really notice, though, not on the surface. Cars still filled Main Road. The beams from the lights exposed the dirty air in full, well before twilight had set. The river running by the factory was still yellow and people would continue to ignore it. People coughed and the water they drank gave them diarrhea. They had been warned not to drink it, but the general consensus on that was that everything seemed to be dangerous these days. Besides, right now, they had no other options. Those with money could import water and build a private stock. Important citizens, the finer restaurants and some stores sold it at heavily inflated prices.

Laurie had two deep wells on her property. The witches who had been her young charges gave people who wanted it water for free, from an outlet in Square. Not too many took them up on their offer, in spite of the fact that the market in Main Street had attracted a growing number of customers lately. Most were in denial. They didn't want to admit that their ordinary supply was… tainted. If so they would also have to admit to a host of other things in their lives… that weren't quite right. They would rather blame the witches for everything… and they did.

Among those in the population who had accepted them, however, under the surface, the witches noticed a marked improvement. They were generally in a better mood and definitely more rebellious.

Jill enjoyed herself in the crowd of people coming here to enjoy themselves. Still, in a major part of her mind she was *constantly* on guard, constantly in contact with Stacy and they checked the others frequently for anything… suspicious.

They often caught a glimpse of Laurie in the crowd, but they couldn't get a firm grip on her. That worried them. Sometimes they had her in her vision, sometimes not, but they felt her wrath. Any hope of her accepting the open hand faded. They hadn't attacked her with deadly force. They could have, but had chosen not to and instead focused on doing a liberating ceremony, freeing themselves, not one causing others harm. Perhaps it had been a mistake, a possible fatal one and fear gripped them, as they realized that Jason had been right: Laurie didn't hide herself anymore and she was much more than she had previously revealed.

Every one of them had jumped off the uniformed deal. Now, variety in clothes had become the norm instead of the exception. Jill still dressed mostly in black, but she had cut the length of the dress. It no longer reached below her knees, but just to the middle of her thighs. She had removed the sleeves on the arms all the way to the shoulders. Only the cloak had been left intact and using it, she could still cover her entire body if she wished.

They easily caught the sound of distant thunder with their enhanced senses, tremors in the Earth and the Sky.

No one who had participated in the ceremony had actually slept. They didn't feel sleepy, not in any way. On the contrary. They felt excited and awake, and ready for anything, realizing that they had to be. Awareness was a two-edged sword. The innocence and naiveté of childhood had left them behind. They had left it behind.

Perhaps Everett had slept. He hadn't been seen since he had brought Gabi to them at dawn. Jill had sought him, slightly panicked, but except for a general impression of his well-being, she hadn't been able to locate him. No one could find… *Anubis* if he didn't desire it. She realized astonished that this was the first time she had thought of him by that name. She reflected on it and over what she herself, had said about previous lives. It was indeed worth a reflection or two.

There, she discovered him, she saw him, on his way down from the Hill. The three of them felt him join them in their wake. His light, his colors, his darkness joined theirs. One of the first changes she noted was the amulet he carried around his neck. He had finally started accepting his powers and being. Both because of necessity and need, as had they all. He used the increased strength to block her from his thoughts. It hurt her, even though she refused to let it show. Her own power had grown to such a degree that she didn't need to strain herself whenever she wanted to block him.

Now, has Laurie made any move yet? He inquired, still far away in a physical sense, with an impatience completely uncharacteristic for him. He spoke to her, even if he didn't shut out the others.

He's scared, shocked, as are we all, she thought.

Not yet, she replied, *but she will. She will crush us like insects, if she gets the chance. And she will. We gave it to her, gave her one more shot, with our stupid flower-power stance.*

The bitterness rose in her like poison, and unable to hide it, she sensed the hatred rise, too, shocking and paralyzing and liberating.

– Hallo there, Vicki said brightly and haughty by her side. She had waved a hand in front of the witch' face. – Now you were far away…

– Not that far away. Jill forced a smile.

– Such a wonderful day, isn't it? Vicki clapped her hands. – I want to take the opportunity to express my appreciation of your costume. The design is clearly improved, and the somber quality is gone. Well, see you later, huh?

Jill followed her with the eyes as she danced and jumped down the street. There remained merely ever so little of her old, inflated personality. She had virtually changed overnight. As had Charlie. He stood a short stretch away, courting Meta and Melanie. It wasn't that apparent with Lori and Keith. They had just come even closer to each other.

Vicki's increasingly chaotic hair moved back and forth in the erratic wind. She wore a headband, but that served mostly to keep the mane away from her eyes and as a declaration of her newfound independence. As the clothes. They were far from being cheap, but far from what were expected from a «well-bred» young lady. The loose blouse revealed more than it covered of her upper body and the tight leather pants didn't reach below her knees. A disaster in waiting, as her old aunt would have said.

She waved to Everett and ran to meet him, making her intentions quite clear. For her sake Jill hoped the discovery of the wolf hidden in the lamb wouldn't come as too much of a shock.

Jill searched her own feelings and realized that she wasn't jealous. At least not in the usual meaning of the word. That rather pleased her.

And then there was Morgana. She worked with clay outside Sharon's place. So strange that they had thought of her as Morgana less than a day. Now it seemed like she had always been Morgana Rae.

The new names, the name changes, were, of course, only a result of the more profound changes within.

Many of the new arrivals were present here today. People who had for unfathomable reasons decided to move here this autumn… this fall (she grinned). This place had been known for a while as a place where unusual things happened, like Pluckley in England, which she had known of before moving here. Pluckley was called «the Village of Many Ghosts» and attracted travelers from all over the world. So was the case with Northfield, but there had been nothing like this convergence earlier.

They obviously enjoyed themselves and Jill wanted to, too.

Something kept her from doing so and she couldn't wholly blame Laurie.

Something made her… hurt. It had been hidden a long time, she knew that. But now, with her expanded consciousness, everything rose to the fore. Awareness was and would always be a double-edged sword.

We're children of fire. Fire can both burn and warm a person.

The fire was within her now, as always, desire, cheerful and dark, even if it burned with a low flame after the previous night. After the senseless orgy following the celebration of Life. An explosion of lust, an unconditional surrender to the deeper instincts in us all. In some way it had served as a confirmation of their chosen path in Life. Others had been shaken to their very foundation. It forced them all to rethink the life they had lived to this moment Now.

The remaining daylight faded into twilight, into darkness. Stars turned themselves on, from horizon to horizon, above the city. And the moon slid across the heavens, distant and cold.

Torches, lamps and candles were lit in Oldtown's streets and houses, in windows and on tables and walls. A lover's quartet of four, having just moved into their spacious apartment invited to a wiiiiillld Masquerade and before anyone knew it, the idea had spread through the entire Main Street and the surrounding areas. The mood turned even more informal, reckless. Most of the new inhabitants of Oldtown, and that was almost everybody present, painted their faces or put on masks and costumes. The members of the newly established coven, too, but they didn't forget. They could never forget.

Not all of those present put on masks, but that didn't mean they had any less to hide. These people had come here from all corners of the globe, and they were among the most interesting stock present day humanity had to offer.

Packs of humans had spread throughout Oldtown, but were mainly concentrated in two places, not far from each other. Inside and outside Sharon's place in Circle and in the octagon-formed (no longer) abandoned warehouse across the street, where Adam, Kate, Madeleine and Trevor had opened their big doors wide.

– Good evening, folks, Adam spoke into a microphone. – Good evening, wanderers, nomads and similar… and a hearty welcome to you all.

His words easily reached everybody in the building and also many well outside of it.

How peculiar, Jill thought, as she and Stacy entered the premises side by side. The mask feels like it's become my face.

And it was indeed as if it moved when she moved her face, as if it had been given life and turned to skin just for tonight. Her pale face in the mirror reflected everything, all the light, all the shadow hitting it, but gave away nothing on its own.

The two identically dressed witches danced to the rhythm, to the mad beat and their every step was identical. And when the werewolf entered the scene, to the delight of the others, the pair of mannequins met him with a totally equal response. They were like one engaging the beast. Two eager females doing the mating dance in an ancient dark forest.

– I can feel your lips, Dark One, Stacy recited, – the pressure of your teeth, the sharp fangs penetrating my skin.

I love the opening for the lips, she sent in a laughter filled with fevered desire.

Her lips full and filled with blood tonight.

– Grandmother, grandmother, what grand teeth you have, Jill recited, encircling the beast, appraising it, as a possible future consort.

Laughter rippled through the room.

A tall, slender figure dressed in rags wore a clown's face, or rather more precise that of a mime. The ancient «silent art» taken to the extreme. She removed one mask, threw it away. The one beneath was exactly the same. And she removed one more, and one more and one more… She threw her faces away and as she threw them, they disappeared into thin air and never landed on the floor. She paid each and every one of the guests a visit, posing in front of them, with her stiff, doll-like appearance. Until finally she had removed her final face… and they saw nothing there, but a black hole. She still had hair and a neck and all, but no face. Everything turned quiet, utterly quiet and the silent art dominated the scene, as it had done in ancient times. She grabbed the air then, pulling back one of her faces, putting it back on. Sighs of relief filled the room.

A ball turned in the air, in the open air. The mime grabbed it and started juggling. And suddenly there were more than one ball. She juggled five simultaneously. At least that was a fair estimate in the heated discussion afterwards.

Then the balls just faded away to nothing. And the mime stood there on the spot without her head. And more than one, both men and women fainted on the spot.

She will be trouble one day, Jill thought. It's inevitable.

The mime stopped in front of Kate last. Kate, with half of her face disfigured, who had sworn never to wear a mask.

The two Queens of Spades walked to Kate, too, surrounding her, as if the mime had pointed to her, marked her for extinction. They moved like stiff puppets, playing the game, because it was expected of them. Only a few knew who they were, but they weren't certain if they would've have cared even if the whole world had seen their faces. They had challenged the ruling elite last night, issued a declaration of war, and they were glad.

The mime touched the disfigurement in Kate's face, while the Queens of Spades prepared and tested their subject. And then, as the mime vanisheded in a twinkle of rainbow sparkle, the astounded Kate felt light and sleepy.

Yes, relax, Kate, sleep Kate, feel joy, Kate.

And they grabbed her head. Adam attempted to charge them, but was held in place as if by invisible hands. Kate cried out in pain.

We considered waiting, Kate, but your pain was so great, Kate, we want you to embrace Life, Kate, and not sing our praise.

Adam wasn't held anymore. He stood frozen, unable to move. The mime appeared once more with a mirror. Kate stood still, shaking like a leaf. She saw, disbelieving, and believed. She knelt before the three figures in front of her, but before she could say anything, could utter a single word, they faded away, vanishing before her eyes and the only thing left to mark their passage… was her face.

Stacy and Jill sat in a corner in Sharon's place. People looked at them, pointing at them, pointed at all the witches, but most of all at them.

– *Look* at them, Jill giggled. She had ingested such staggering amounts of alcohol so fast that the ability her body had to heal itself hadn't been able to catch up yet. – They're already seeing us as *gods*. We're already put on the pedestal in stone and bronze.

– We can't perform public miracles and not expect some sort of admiration. Stacy shrugged. She drank, but only beer. – We lived among our worshippers once. We can easily do so again.

Sharon counted money, a lot of money. She could hardly believe how much it was. When Erica approached her, she hardly acknowledged her presence.

– We don't have more clean glasses, Erica told her both happy and nervously. – And if this rush keeps up, we'll surely need more help…

– Fix it then, Sharon told her with a slight edge in her reply. – That's what I'm paying you for. You are the manager, right?

– Yes, the other woman swallowed. – Right away, Miss Sharon.

– Did you see that, Stacy pointed out to Jill. – How easily she dealt with a disgruntled employee?

– I did. Jill shook her head. – I didn't care for it much.
– Party pooper. Stacy blew a lot of hot air.
– I'll be gone for a while, Sharon told Cynthia. – You take over for me.
Cynthia wanted to point out that her break wasn't over yet, that she still felt exhausted, that she had worked her butt off all day.
She didn't.
Sharon Haldoway walked up the stairs, to the place she had seen as her home. She opened the heavy door, so finely made that it seemed like it was an integrated part of the wall. In the soft, flickering shadows it was even more difficult to discover. Jason relaxed on his back on the bed, not very dangerous… threatening.
Nude.
– What are you doing here? She screamed at him.
– The bed is soft, he said. – A willing female is on its way, and everything is great.
– What are you doing to me?
– I? I'm not doing anything to you, except allowing you to do everything you've ever wanted.
His cock rose big and hard. She gasped and went down on her knees on the spot, her hands attempting to be all over her burning body simultaneously. With weak fingers she attempted to drag off all the clothes separating her from him, from his touch. Her big, sore breasts were uncovered. She pinched and squeezed them. Half-closed eyes turned foggy, dreamlike. She felt she was being lifted up and carried to the bed where he waited. He received her and easily removed the piteous, remaining cloth.
– I'm liberating you, Sharon, liberating the side of you you've always wanted to stay hidden. It's much easier than I thought it would be. I'm just practicing a bit on you, you see, to see if and how I can develop it all.
Her entire body, her entire being shook in her need, her longing. He took pleasure in exploring the firm body. She was strong, physically and mentally, but was like putty in his hands. He removed the last piece of fabric, pulling the white lace panties down her strong, wet thighs.
He kept her levitating. A demanding task for sure, as desire started to overwhelm him, too. Her body stretched and spread legs wide. He took her standing up, allowing her to move her hips, to throw and twist a bit, release tiny, involuntary sounds, but not more than that. He pushed forth his hips one final time and roared triumphantly. He lowered himself into the bed with her. She crouched close to his body, still moaning and whimpering.
Somebody entered the room silently. He recognized the thought-pattern, but didn't stop Sharon from jumping up from the bed and at the intruder.
Jill stood calmly by the door. Sharon froze in mid-air. She hung there, fighting in vain to free herself from the giant invisible hands holding her, fighting a few seconds. After that Jill didn't allow a single show of defiance. The big body went limp. A drowsy look clouded what seconds ago had been sharp and alert eyes. Jill stretched the catch to its full length and rotated it slowly, while studying it with a cold, dispassionate curiosity.
– Such a sweet toy you've found, dear Jason…
As she studied herself, her powers. She saw her aura surrounding Sharon, overwhelming Sharon's own. To keep the heavy body levitating and paralyzed took no effort at all. What she had needed to concentrate hard to do as late as yesterday, she did diabolically easy now.
Jill stretched out her hands and touched the nude body in a way she had expected to be… trying, but that wasn't the case. In fact, it came off as so easy that it felt as if she had done it a number of times before. Instead of only one.
The buzz began. There was no rage this time or even strong emotions, only an ever-growing sense of well-being. The energy flowed into her. Sharon whined in helpless pain. Then the emotions flowed, too. Jill felt bathed in strength, and it made her feel so good, so very good. A terrible and violent joy surged through her. And she had complete control. She released her prey passionlessly, mercifully. Sharon landed on her feet, but went instantly down on her knees, pale and shaking, powerless. She had enough remaining strength to keep herself from falling on her side. Jill thought she should be grateful for that, knew she was. The witch had accessed all the woman's thoughts, one moment she had been

her. The Hunger in Jill had already subsided. She felt full, satisfied, lazy… and horny. And powerful. It boiled and sparkled within and without. Her eyes sparkled in white.

– Sleep, sweet puppet. We don't need you at the moment. Sleep, *sleep*…

Sharon had closed her eyes even before the hypnotic voice had started on the end command. She had fallen asleep before she had lain herself down on the floor.

Jill assessed Jason with a speculative, hot look.

– *Succubus,* he said, and it was more than an underlying hoarseness in his voice.

She smiled seductively. The remarkable sense of wellbeing brought an unrestrained sensuality. She wanted him, she wanted him, and she wanted him. They had time, more than enough time, before what should begin tonight would begin. She was ready for it. The Power pulsed and flowed within her. But she could always use more. She posed for him, undressing slowly, joyfully. Flirting, teasing by taking her time, knowing fully well she was irresistible, that he couldn't have resisted her, even if he had wanted to. But he didn't. Their similarities made her worried somewhere, but she ignored it, giving herself wholly to passion.

– Strange, she reflected, and looked for a short moment back on the unmoving Sharon, – how we're emulating, repeating the mistakes of the old world.

– That doesn't matter, he teased, chided and tempted. – We can do whatever we desire. The world exists for us. It's just a dream we may live, as we want.

He lifted her up in the bed and gave her a kiss on the neck, full of hunger. She straightened and stretched her head backwards. He attempted to hold her. She slid easily out of his grip, even if she remained in his lap. Like a snake she danced and writhed, like a snake she smiled. Teasingly she allowed his hard part to rub between her thighs, before pulling away. He caught up fast, catching her wrists in a firm grip and putting her down on her back. They struggled and he kept her under him while giving her an appreciative smile. He pressed a knee into the softness below. She released a loud moan and stopped struggling. He bit already hard nipples. She stared at him with eyes clouded with an unbearable need.

– I for one believe we're Agents of Change, he said, exposing his teeth in a wide grin. – We must become an irresistible force, because that's what we have against us, right?

In an unexpected, quick move she had pushed him off her, pushed him down on his back and put herself on top.

– Yes, she whispered virtually silent. – Yes…

She moved her hips slightly forward and pierced herself on him. He pushed himself up, deep into her.

– We'll *rule,* he stated smiling.

– No, she mumbled through her lips. – *No*…

She let herself sink forward and kissed him with wet lips. Many times. She kissed him in despair. Her hips moved up and down. He moved as she moved. How he didn't know. Thoughts turned indistinct. Flames from the candles flickered and grew, grew and flickered. A union of flesh, but to them certainly also one of thought. Perhaps they wanted it that way or perhaps mental walls broke as instinct turned dominant. During these moments they lived in the Now and just Now, in flashes of heat and passion, they were one.

The bell, the old one at the top of the ramshackle city hall, started on its twelve strokes. Midnight, Dark Hour. Jill sensed a draft when opening her eyes, a gust from the black poison well the world had turned into and from the bottomless hell it might become. It lasted only a moment, but when she rose and felt the heat of the summer night on her sweaty body, she knew that it hadn't been… wasn't… her imagination.

Jason stood by the window. Darkness sparkled around him like soft lightning. He was shadow. And would've been like a wild beast, if not for his obvious sophistication. It was with intelligent hunger he watched her, stared pointedly at her, as she moved around. He had sensed it, too. She saw it in his eyes, his entire demeanor.

– It feels so good moving around naked, she smiled.

– Very liberating, isn't it? He confirmed. – In the cage most people exist within, they can't appreciate that.

– Not a great environment for anyone to grow up in, she said frosty, – and certainly not for mutants.
– That's what's most lacking, he raged, seemingly relaxed. He could just as well have been talking about the weather. – The encouragement to seek, to become something different from the norm. Birth isn't enough. A society with a justified pride in itself and its work must not merely accept diversity, but encourage it. In the disgusting, oppressive current world many may live an entire life without realizing that they're special. Discovery, realization of our abilities, of any ability is dependent upon circumstances and an added strength of will is needed to use them, to use them *well.*
His words burned within her, making the heat rise high once more.
– Being born into, growing up in this society encumbers us with so many blocks, she stated sad and angry. – Well, they don't have a habit of burning us at the stake anymore, that's something.
– They're strangling us slowly instead. And don't you think they'll eventually do the worst again… if we let them?
She walked to him and took his hands. They held hands and stared into each other's eyes.
– We will be tigers and not let ourselves be butchered like lambs this time, will we, now, my fanged tigress?
– No, she said sharply, and her aura sparkled and spread.
– Then we must become the irresistible force and we must rule. There is no other way.
– Oh, yes…
He kissed her on the lips for the first time and stopped her yapping. His two hands explored ruthlessly her hot nest.
You bastard, there has to be a better way. There has to…
He wanted to tell her one last truth, one last ironic remark. She grabbed his rising cock, took him in a firm grip and all words were lost. His turn on was as sudden, as explosive as hers. They were children of nature, immediate and impulsive like the storm. And as they fell hard to the floor in countless fiery embraces, they quickly grew equal to the hot night.
Everything intensified after twelve. Peculiarly enough everything seemed to grow quieter, but this happened only on the most visible part of the surface. The mood was tense, without most people being able to tell why. There was dancing, but for once during these great, promiscuous times, it could be said to be muted, or at least not excessive. There were rumors and knowledge circulating that made everybody wide-eyed with curiosity. A secret was often like that, one that no one and everyone knew of.
People gathered indoors, inside the tavern, pulled there by a seemingly irresistible force.
– You won't believe what I've heard, one boy whispered to another. – What we'll hear is, according to a friend of mine an alternative history lesson to end all alternative history lessons, profound and wild beyond belief.
– The victorious alter and author history to suit their purposes, the other shrugged. – Everybody knows that. It isn't exactly news.
– But it's even more than that, his buddy continued, as if the other had hardly spoken at all. – These people know what they are talking about… and they are *for real.* They don't practice stage magic, but true witchcraft. They…
He stopped, holding back, shaking his head in embarrassment. The other looked indulgent at him.
– Hush, a girl hissed excited, unnecessary, without malice at them.
A man stepped forward, a dark man, dressed in cloak and hood. He appeared ancient. Everybody imagined they could hear the quiet sound of their own breath. After just a few more seconds… or rather moments silence reigned in the room, in the building and entire scenery.
– Time itself has, for a very long time been a mystery to mankind. He started right away, without introduction. – Now, tonight, my friends, you will experience something unique, a glimpse behind its curtain, its thin veil…
– He is sincere… isn't he? The girl whispered to the two boys, having momentarily forgotten her earlier call for silence. – He truly believes what he's saying.
There was something about the entire setting, something very, very convincing, adding to tidbits most of them had experienced since they had arrived in town. Even the professed skeptics among them stared stunned at the hooded man in their midst. All guests sensed the fundamental in the

coming happening. Some, incredibly enough were stupid and frightened enough to leave, but in most curiosity clearly won over fear.

I'm ready, they heard a thin voice from somewhere.

Slowly everybody realized that the flames on the candles were growing. The initiated instantly discovered the energy shift in the room, but for the rest it took time. The growth *accelerated.* Within the span of a second all the fires rose uncannily high and suffocated because of lack of nourishment. Only the oil lamps remained to illuminate the room and there weren't that many of them. Still, this wasn't the exclusive reason for the darkening of the room. Even the air itself seemed to darken. Darkness… blinding. In a cloud of smoke and light a shape took form, a shape dividing itself into three. Stacy and Jill covered one with their respective cloak. They heard the clock on the wall of the old city hall strike once. The cloaks parted in something akin to a single movement. It was like Gabi materialized there and then, appeared out of nowhere to nervous applause. The three of them curtseyed eloquently in an excellent act of comic relief.

The moonbeams didn't reach them. Stacy and Jill's eyes had once more turned completely white. Gabi reached only to the chin of the well-grown eighteen-year-old girls, but was still tall for her age. She had dressed in a simple white dress with ornaments for the occasion. It had become evident to all that the young witches were well on the way to move away from Laurie's strict dress code.

The three of them had placed themselves by the only available table in the room. No one had sat down there. Why, no one could really say. They accepted it, though, without too much worry, since it was only a minor detail compared to everything else strange going on in town, what was becoming an ever more normal part of their life.

– The hour after midnight belongs to the dead, Gabi spoke with a high-pitched, clear voice. – Time has passed One. Time to begin. Tonight's story will begin as soon as the final preparations are done. During this night and this night only, we must close ourselves off from the world, which has both eyes and ears.

She sat down by the table. Jill and Stacy sat down on each side of her.

My compliments, Stacy sent excitedly to Jill, *with this girl. And you've obviously enjoyed the round in the barn with Jason, too, the way you're glowing.*

He's a good lover, Jill replied embarrassed, *and he had some quite interesting arguments concerning our situation, to boot.*

He sees himself as Magneto. A mental shaking of the head. *He… has read too many comics.*

The slight hesitation didn't pass Jill's scrutiny.

– You're right, she exclaimed. Gabi looked nonplussed at her. *That's weird, I didn't think of that and I read comics as well.*

That's because you're unable to see the whole picture, my dear… But I promise you, you will…

– HEY, little Gabrielle, someone cried from the spectator's corner, one of her classmates, – you're only thirteen. How did you gain access to this sordid spot?

By right of birth, she wanted to cry out loud and proud.

– I'm three years and twenty moons, friend Jerry, she countered quickly, laughingly. – Or rather two years and sixty-eight moons. I've always been early.

Laughter. Swelling pride because of nods from Jill and Stacy. Then she regained her composure, nodded. Nodded once more, decisively. They had practiced this several times today and tonight. It wasn't hard, not really. The two grown girls took her hands.

A young girl sat in a dark room, stretching her arms, clawing at the air.

She sensed the heat in her hands, recognized it as the healing power, the charging of batteries. They did for her what they had done for Morgana, boosting her power, giving her both less and more control. The heat in her hands spread up the arms, to her entire body. She concentrated on making her power grow, grow stronger than she had ever been close to achieving. It started, slowly at first, then the flow increased to something undeniable. It wasn't that her body started glowing exactly, but that it shimmered, turned indistinct, in shadow, in silver and cold, and hot colors. And it, and she spread throughout the room. She sat in her seat, as she expanded and could sense the room. Stacy and Jill were already surrounded by it. They sat there calmly and let it happen.

– *You'll sense a certain unpleasantness, discomfort,* the witch-child told them, in a hollow, spacious voice. – *It will pass soon enough.*

The oil-lamps on the wall glowed like lanterns in mist. The girl could sense the room, its walls, its boundaries. She embraced it all, filling it up, took it into herself. When the silver shimmer had expanded to the entire place, they all felt it. A quiver, as tiny electric shocks on the most sensitive spots on the body. The room's colors faded. Nothing they could explain. To something resembling black, gray and white, but a more varied, richer texture. They realized that the color hadn't really faded, only that their perception had increased to make their old perception of color a pale imitation of the true thing, *what they saw now,* as the colors «returned», more varied, a richer texture than they could ever have imagined. It dawned on everybody, also the people who weren't witches that they no longer saw with their eyes only and that this was just the beginning. Those among them who had done acid, recognized certain similarities, but this was even more intense, more pervasive. This was what they had only glimpsed through all their various previous attempts at altered states of consciousness.

She fell into a trance. They could see it, noticed the further ghost-like change in the room. Her body turned rigid, her features contorted, almost frighteningly relaxed.

– He's coming, she said, looking at them with a blank stare.

– Who is coming, dear? Stacy asked her gently.

– I don't know, she replied. – There's a room full of floating crystal balls and I can see him coming.

Stacy and Jill soaked up the excitement in the room, poured it into Gabi and the excitement grew further, and the Power grew. Jill studied the spectators, corrected herself. There were no spectators here. Everybody contributed, even if they didn't have any conscious knowledge of it. Both Jill and Stacy felt… high. It was as if they had skin-to-skin contact with everybody present. And everybody present felt at least some of what they did. Waves of panic and joy intermingled with an ever-growing curiosity among those who suspected what was happening. But the panic never surfaced, but remained below the surface as worry, as thrilling fear, enriching their lives, not lessening it.

Not even among those who looked out the window and observed a man on his way to the tavern, how his walk, his forward momentum slowed down to virtually nothing. He was clearly headed for the door, but he slowed down to a point where he seemed to be standing completely still. Like all the other people outside he looked like a mannequin in a street display. Observed from the tavern it would take him years to reach the door. Jill herself experienced a thrill of both fear and joy. There was a pull strong as a tug. They had arrived.

Gabi emerged from the trance, but not completely. Her speech was still slurred and slow, her eyes still clouded, but she was fully aware now.

– I've always experienced strong and detailed dreams. They didn't just hear her with their ears anymore anyway. It was as if she was everywhere in the room and even inside their head. – But after my first bleeding the previous month I have been able to dream, to see that much clearer. I've received impressions I knew were far more than random composed images. The burden nearly broke me, until Jill helped me accept my burden and joy in Life.

And she Changed again, as she ventured deeper into her Power, deeper within herself. Stacy and Jill observed it, looked at each other in awe and fear and recognition. This was familiar to them. They couldn't say why, but they knew the Power for what it was.

– I'm a Dreamweaver, one of several throughout human history. I have access to Styx, the river of knowledge and death. We're riding its raging currents right now. In the land not a land, that humans through time and space have created beyond what most of us experience as real. A place not a place with many names and an even greater variety of descriptions. The Shadow World, Hinterland, the Astral Plane, the Land of Twilight Summer, the Kingdom of Death, Elysium, Valhalla, Nirvana, Heaven, Hell… It's where we go when we leave the body or don't have any. The usual rules of Space and Time don't apply here and Dreamweavers who gain a certain control over the Astral Plane may ultimately also control Time/Space.

Tonight's story is about a Dreamweaver. He wasn't the first and not the last, but he has been one of the most dominant forces on Earth the last ten thousand years, what official historians love to call historic time. His age… they who saw him grow to manhood… knew him as *Jahavalo.* Other tribes that later escaped the most immediate consequences of his influence, called him *Goht,* their word for *Enemy…* It had been a rarely used word, but turned out to be an often-used name.

Jill knew. Explosive, almost uncontrollable hatred rose within her, a paralyzing cold descended her spine. Memory still failed her. She couldn't remember why it was, only that it was. Memory failed to emerge as anything more than splinters of a vast puzzle. She didn't sense any… presence after Gabi had said the secret, unmentionable word aloud, but a cold draft was clearly noticeable when it penetrated their tiny hiding place. If the real thing or their subconscious use of their power had caused it, they couldn't say. But they did shiver and it was far more than a mere emotion, the realization that fate had caught up with them.

4

THE FURTHER AND INDEPENDENT WORK OF GABI, BORN 1992.02.29
(christian, western time frame)
Part 5

The small group of humans fighting their way forward over the enormous plain was one of many escaping the destruction of Atlantis, the land that had sunk below the sea. The old and the tribe's storytellers told many stories about and from Atlantis, as the generations went by. No one alive had experienced it firsthand. Not they and not their grandparents grandparents grandparents grandparents. That was as how far back the Storyteller had somewhat reliable information from, not mixed too much with Legend. But they knew it was an unthinkable long time before that, that their ancestors had returned to a simpler way of life. Other tribes they met, and sometimes mingled with, had their own stories to tell about and from Atlantis, that they again had heard partly from others. This tribe, with its line of storytellers, had always been on their way towards Sunrise, but so much time had passed. They had met tribes headed in the opposite direction, too, telling stories about and from Atlantis. Tracks crossed and crossed again. They were hunters and gatherers, and happy with that. But it did so happen occasionally, that they sent their thoughts to the distant Atlantis, distant in space and time.

Jahavalo was born (or perhaps reborn) in a cave by the Konya-plains in the present Turkey. The boy showed an early interest in the old stories. He himself belonged to a long line of storytellers, but they wondered at how much better he was at presenting details in the old stories than any of his recent predecessors. His words seemed to come alive through his mouth, the images he created seemed alive and true to them all. The ancient city he spoke about appeared real. They didn't just become convinced of its existence, but also… that he had been there, that he had been a god among gods. The legend of Jahavalo began growing already in his early adolescence. The details could vary, but the core of events persisted. In hindsight one could safely claim that he was as if possessed by what he called the Vanished City… if it wasn't for the fact that it soon would be very, very dangerous to state something like that. To claim that Atlantis had never existed (which some, Weavers and others of good humor had done occasionally) turned out to be equally dangerous.

He had heard about gatherings of huts from other tribe's storytellers. But people hadn't lived permanently in these places and that was what he desired. He wanted control, to be Lord and Master of everything he surveyed, and he surveyed ever more. His persuasive nature, his ever-growing powers and what became more and more clear; his complete and utter ruthlessness gained him ever-stronger influence. Words like «Master» and «Power» had been rarely used earlier and they hadn't had quite the same meaning and significance. What had started, as minor, innocent inquiries about minor favors grew to something quite different and more ominous. A Storyteller had traditionally, to a certain degree, been favored and a few dead storytellers honored beyond death, but this was something more and dramatic.

By his decree, the First City, Catal Huyuk, was raised towards Sunrise on the fruitful Konya-plain. He constructed a society of walls, boundaries where none had been before.

– I don't know… Much is hidden. These aren't my memories and I have to rely on what was said centuries later or miles and miles away. He was born with a long life or he made it so later or a combination… But he hasn't managed to cloud everything. He did so much horrible, so much deliberately horrible…

Those who found themselves at the tavern in Northfield, and on the raging river Styx received images, impressions from ten thousand years before the present. They saw stones soiled with blood, from sacrifices, from executions. Memories, it is memories, the cry exploded in Lillith's mind. Jill bent forward.

The entire tavern shook. Or perhaps it was the boat, shaking on its foundations…

– Move on, Stacy gently commanded Gabi.

The first permanent «homes» were hardly more than ordinary huts and were easy to dismantle. He didn't want that. The closed in buildings where the access way was through the roof were built in stone and clay. As he formed the clay, he formed his people. The future revealed itself to him and he grew ever more convinced about what had to be done. He stayed young while new generations were born and died. Eventually there were only those in Catal Huyuk who worshipped him and didn't fear him. His Power had already grown beyond Konya and now he mercilessly strengthened his chains. Moving further, ever further, in his quest for domination, for control. His subjects multiplied and moved, and he moved with them, dominating more and more land. There were those who… opposed him and there were setbacks and obstacles. But he was immortal and could wait. Only the times he fought others with godlike powers did he meet any real resistance. But it helped him realize that his present methods had been used about as far as they could go. He started to realize how patient he truly had to be. His great work took form. The plan that would come to fruition in ten thousand years.

– Worship is the key. He's sucking power from it, gathering energy. He will remove people's ability to dream, and make everybody crawl for him like the ants on the ground.

The time came when he had complete control over a major area. His enemies had run to places where he couldn't reach them with his Power. All his subjects either worshipped or feared him or both. He confirmed for himself that he had indeed reached the limit to his current influence, in this Age. The world was large. The methods he had used to this point turned out to be ever less effective.

He had laid the foundation. The time had come to make the leap from Lord and Master to God. He arranged his own Ascension. It wasn't hard. Just a bit illusion and special effects. He knew what time and the storyteller tradition would do to Jahavalo's earthly life.

A stormy night he ascended, rose from the city, glowing like a star, a gargantuan figure that could be seen far away. A thunderous crack and he was gone. The paralyzed gathering remained on the spot for days and days. Many would starve to death. He left Catal Huyuk, the Stone City, a place finally rivaling the fabled Atlantis in size and number of inhabitants. Ten thousand people, the privileged classes lived within the city walls. Many more, the hopeful and the lost lived in camps outside, all over the plains. One day Atlantis should be rebuilt and then there would be a place for them. The Lord their God had told them so, that so it should be by his return to Earth.

He left his possessions, the land many were convinced was the entire world and wandered south. The name Jahavalo, the unmentionable was forgotten, but not he who had used it. And many stories were told about him revealing himself in distant lands and among distant people. For a few hundred years the stories told about his wars with the other gods, then they ended. The old gods were gone, slain by the One God. He (He) lived many lives. Sometimes as a devil, sometimes as a god, but he was always devoid of mercy, both against those who worshipped him and those who hated him. The number of cities on Earth grew steadily and humanity grew in numbers, grew fast in his tracks. There were those who opposed him and his will. He has broken many, but not all. There are still a few who are opposing him and all his works. A few that may stop him. But everything has blurred in the vestiges of Time. He became a figure without form, face and saturation. During countless conflicts he chose the side that would best serve his interests, but during an increasing number of these, as the years flew, he participated on both sides. On many occasions he instigated the conflict from the very beginning. A conflict, once started, could easily be kept going, during centuries, millennia. And he sucked up strength from them all and his Power grew. He dominated an ever-larger part of human life and death.

– He has taken many names and been called… is called… even more. The hundred names of terror… many of them… if not all… belong to him.

– He's known by a thousand names. Many are familiar to us, the best known… He's Yahweh, God, Satan, Allah, Ahriman, Dollmaster, Apocalypse, the Eternal, Decay, Time, Legion, Death… his influence has spread to all corners of the globe now. He's everywhere, the enemy of everything alive.

– And destruction and despair follow in his tracks…

5

Poisonous dust is blowing. Everything is soaked in gray. All strong colors have faded away. Spirit and fire have faded away. Everything valuable has vanished like smoke. Dreams have turned to fever and nightmares. Life has become little more than existence, breathing without awareness. People gasp constantly in their misery, their unending suffering. Moving has become nothing but one step in front of the other. There's no thought of tomorrow or even today.

Everett shook. He had had his first truly, spontaneous waking dream, nightmarish images from a sterile, joyless future. The room seemed deadly black around him. He looked out the window in desperation. The man outside, who had seemingly stood there for an eternity, human flesh turned stone… didn't he move an arm… a foot? Slowly perhaps, incredibly slowly. If you studied him and all the other statues out there for minutes, you might convince yourself they were moving. As it was, they looked like props in an absurd theater, where the gods sat on an invisible row and watched. Several hours had passed within the tavern's four walls and merely a few seconds outside. If… the Dollmaster had discovered this séance he wouldn't have time to take action before it was done. But he would know that a new Dreamweaver walked the Earth.

The Power waned. Jill sensed it. If there had been a moment where it could have gone over the top, that moment had passed. Gabi gasped, as her control slowly slipped, as the room returned to normal. They crawled back onto the shore of the river Styx just a bit below where they had started on it. Gabi and the two who had helped her the most, dragged the boat back up, well up on the corny sand. The shimmering air turned once more to air. They all made use of their stiff limbs. Time returned to normal. The people outside moved as was expected of them. The man that had been on his way forever walked through the door. He and the others behind him couldn't possibly avoid noticing the alienated, peculiar mood. Everybody sat there astonished and looked at each other with wide-open eyes. There was fear, and also anger, as if they had just been told something important, something essential, very close to the truth. Stacy and Jill exchanged looks, for once not poised. Perhaps what they had heard wasn't exactly the truth, but a sort of metaphor, or partly a metaphor for what had happened, but it felt very right, and it made them sick to their stomach.

Everett wandered through the streets, alone and in a miserable condition. He had rushed outside, couldn't stand being inside anymore. He strived to avoid it, but he caught glimpses of his face in the windows. Tiny droplets of sweat formed through his skin and every single one seemed to hurt. It wasn't cold sweat, but glowing drops of lava, leaving a trace of unpleasantness while drying. Couldn't they see it? No, not those around him. So many people in the streets tonight and they were clueless to all the things going on in the world. They wandered into Oldtown to get a taste of the exotic, not more than a peek, standing on the outside looking in.

Time is a funny thing, Everett thought.

So short a time had passed by since he left the tavern, and already it could just as well be another lifetime. Each new place, each new scene was another time as well… because inedible events would seem distant and hard to remember.

He plunged deep into Newtown. The plunge had no purpose really except for the need to keep going.

Cold light, empty darkness, he was uncertain whether or not he wished for something else. Because he sensed the colors in the light and everything crawling in the dark. There existed… a quality in the air not there before, or he had been unaware of before, joy and threats on every corner he turned.

Eventually he ended up in Fun Street, the so-called entertainment area in Northfield. The façade had a few discos and bars. Most of what went on here, went on below the surface, though, as it usually did most places. Even here there were more people than usual. Home certainly turned out to be too small for a lot of people tonight. They did their utmost not to look directly at him, but he heard their whispers, their voices like noises in his thoughts. He couldn't gain sufficient control over himself to close them out.

The day ended and people desperate to erase it from their experience, cast themselves into the night. And the next morning most of them would desperately want to erase the night. The day world, as it was had no place for the night. All this hypocrisy, the evident sadness did nothing to improve Everett's mood. People went to work every day, said their prayers, existed under their yoke, yearning for something more, but did nothing to break their chains. On the contrary. They did all they could to reinforce them, in themselves and others.

They went to mass every Sunday, many of them, living under this enormous deception, enduring hell, so they could receive their reward in the afterlife. Or there were other valves, other incentives of reward and punishment, stick and carrot, while the cycle repeated and repeated itself ad infinitum…

– HELLO, old boy, longtime no see…

He turned and saw Henry Gyrich, with Tim Drake and everybody approach him.

It wasn't that long ago.

– Nice to meet, isn't it? He didn't mind meeting them, even though they hadn't changed, and he had. He smiled.

– I see that you're out of uniform…

– We've stopped using any sort of uniform, he said and felt strangely detached from himself.

– Some show you all did last night.

So far only Henry had spoken of them. They walked closer. Drake towered over Everett.

– The entire town is talking about it. Yes, I would go out on a limb here and claim that it's the main subject in any conversation right now. My compliments.

– I'll tell you what, Everett grinned, suddenly very calm. – You don't need to be a mind reader to realize that behind these words of flattery some clearly wicked intentions are hidden.

Henry's grin was wiped out on the spot.

– Are you really saying what I believe you're saying? Hank is uncharacteristically gawking at him.

You bet, Everett is telling him without speaking.

– What are you doing here anyway? Drake the thug couldn't rein himself in any longer. The game's foreplay had taken a bad turn. – Aren't the chicks you've got your hands on *professional* enough for you?

Nobody *saw* the hand moving forward, only the movement. Anubis grabbed the other boy's throat and held it in an iron, paralyzing grip. With his free hand Everett hit him in the abdomen, hit him hard. Tim Drake cried out in pain and sank to his knees. He hung, like a sack of wet clothes, in the other's grip. The others froze. Everything had happened so fast, inducing such powerful paralysis. And then there was a question of the face, the face he knew as Everett Moran's. It seemed perfectly normal, in every way he had learned to know it, but… few words fit worse.

Everett forced himself deep within the thug's consciousness, penetrating deeper than he had dared with anyone, he felt strong enough for that now.

It was a silent and sickly dark place. Insecurity, distrust and contempt dominated there, fear of many things, not the least of not being accepted. Moran wanted to stop then, but something made him continue, something cold and moist in his own consciousness that until this moment effectively had been held in check and only expressed itself through random dreams and nightmares.

– You're a weasel, Timmy, a spot on the ground, always following the leader, attempting to hide your subservience behind cardboard scenes. Poor little Timmy. You're an excellent soldier and that is all you are.

A slight push and the big boy fell hard in the dust. He stayed there, crying like a wounded beast.

Everett straightened himself, breathing in and out, making his eyes rest on the group in front of him.

– Some performance, Henry said appraisingly. – I would bet that you've changed in major ways, old sport.

Everett penetrated for a moment the other's thoughts. There were no major disturbances in Hank's Self. There was strength and belief in that strength. No evident weaknesses or cracks. Anubis knew he would find it if he sought long enough. Everybody had something soft somewhere, making them vulnerable and exposed. He could do it, but had lost interest really. There was nothing for him here anymore.

– Those who dare may join me, he said in a matter-of-fact manner. – We can never be too many.

Two boys left the group. A group split. Two of the new cells were so different from the rest that they walked a new and separate path.

– Don't get in my way, Everett told Hank.

– Come, he told the two boys, and they followed him.

The heat from the neon lights changed to the warmer lights in Oldtown. Everett didn't look back. He didn't have to, to know the two boys were there, to know where everyone in close proximity was. All his exceptional and unexceptional senses had suddenly grown even keener.

He heard Ivan playing his guitar somewhere, trembling, torturing chords echoing deep within the soul. The music conveyed a sense of… of urgency. At least to him. Everett couldn't say if it was really the music or he himself interpreting it that way. Asking Ivan would be next to useless, since he was the one among them that perhaps lived most in his subconscious. Everett felt the restlessness inside, as something solid, tangible. Jill had used similar wording to describe the suppressed part of the personality, which simply put had to express itself now and then. What did the French call it? Yes, «the Dark Monster». Everett smiled. Sometimes it was hard to understand how far he had come the last month, so far in recognition of Self.

But this was something more. He wasn't… an ordinary human being. Nor was Jill for that matter. But it was something physical about this that seemed to (literarily) crawl beneath his skin. What had happened last night had liberated something, released his final inhibitions. He, too, was a Multi, the fourth among Laurie's newest brood of witches. She had truly bitten off more than she could chew. Had she really believed she would be able to control four of the most powerful beings on Earth?

Where the last thought originated from, he didn't know.

Then there were the others. They had merely a single ability each, but one that gave them a myriad of user possibilities. Then there were others still, the witches she had picked last year and held in her grip that could well carry hidden depths within themselves. They could no longer presume that she had told the truth about anything. They had to presume that she hadn't.

A woman stumbled across the street.

– I'm okay, she howled. – I'm okay.

He didn't know her, but she made his skin crawl even more.

– I *was* okay, she insisted. – I was.

The sound of the guitar, its vibrations increased within and without.

He led the two boys in through the backdoor (it was closest) of the tavern. Gabi waited for them inside, blushing and slightly trembling. She still wore the white dress, but it, like her seemed to shimmer and Change on the spot.

– I knew you would come here, she said, – so I went here to greet you, as I knew I would.

He looked at her, afraid for her, afraid of her.

– I'm so much more than I was, Anubis, she said. – We all are, and more is added every second.

She turned to the two boys, bowing slightly.

– I'm Oracle, she greeted them. – You know me, you know me not. I'm your guide and I bid you welcome.

– The Oracle of Delphi? One of the boys burst out.

– Perhaps, Everett grinned.

The two boys were fifteen and had been in the same class level at school as Gabrielle Asteroth. She had been unlike all others then and was even more so now.

– We start life with a name given to us by others, she said. – We, too, do that, but we choose as some do, our own, signifying our Change, our initiation into Magick. We choose different names for different reasons. Everett here is called Anubis. Come, and I'll introduce you to others.

They ventured further into the tavern. In the corridor leading to the barroom, they saw a girl with golden hair and dark skin draw lines in the air and change the very walls she touched.

– This is Morgana Rae, Gabi said. – She used to be Rae Morgan, but isn't anymore.

Smiling Everett saw that Morgana already was well on her way to changing her environment. The corridor had been decorated with mystical, non-pattern patterns. The boys stared wide-eyed at the witch who made matter obey her will. Everett was ready to intervene and calm them if they should display signs of panic, but they didn't. Wonder and awe showed in their features. He hadn't been mistaken about them.

The excitement in the bar was sort of subdued, but it was excitement. There was a buzz, but one quite lower in volume than during ordinary nights. This night couldn't in any understanding of the word be deemed ordinary.

They sat by one single table most of them, most of the key players. Gabi placed herself behind each of them as she presented and introduced them, called their name.

– This is Jason. We call him jokingly Samhain.

– Not just jokingly, Jason said.

– This is Jill. She is Raven.
– Hallo, Raven greeted the boys.
– 'lo, they replied hoarsely.
– This is Tam. She's Tamara no more.
The names… the Other names had come, came to them easily, as if they had always been there, at the tip of the tongue.
– This is Loeh. She is Loeh, she is the Dancer.
– This is Ivan. We call him the Drummer or just the Player.
– Call me Pan, the player said.
– This is Travis. He's Apollon.
Gabi stopped behind Stacy, about to grab her shoulders.
– This is…
– Moonstar, Stacy completed. – I'm the Hunter's Moon.
– Andrea is Olympia.
– We have all chosen or will choose a name for our Self.
They were walking through another corridor, unknown yet familiar. All the guestrooms were located in this wing. Everett didn't really know what they were doing here. Gabi walked a few steps ahead of them, light-footed and shimmering. She turned a corner… and when they turned the same corner… she wasn't there anymore. They could see nothing but a long row of doors, doors, doors.
A door slid open. A door numbered 13.
As far as he could remember there was no door or room numbered 13 in the building.
The number 13 was generally avoided.
– She has an excellent flair for the dramatic, doesn't she…
They walked through the door.
They couldn't really have imagined the room inside. Morgana had been here, too, but here she hadn't done more than the first bits and pieces of the foundation. This was the Dreamweaver's Place of Power and Gabi had transformed it beyond any recognition. Her fantasy, her dreams and will, ruled here. Everett couldn't really see the end of the room. It wasn't even a room anymore. They walked through a Greek setting, mixed with any other imaginable and unimaginable element. As big as it had become it should have reached well into the street outside. But he knew that if he went outside and checked the wall would still be there, be where it had been. Gabi had expanded the room to the Shadow World.
– Greetings, Gabi said formally. – I bid you welcome to my Aerie.
She stood before a table. She had transformed almost completely from the person they had experienced just a few, short moments ago. Her clothes, her hair and she herself had Changed. She was dressed in a (simple) top and skirt. The hair from her temples had been bound in tiny plaits. She had decorated herself with jewelry around her neck and arms. She seemed far more confident. The shimmering was gone. He knew she couldn't be that much older, but something had indeed happened.
Something resembling glass pellets, perhaps her version of the crystal ball, levitated around them. They could glimpse images there. Glimpses. Nothing more. Mist rose and floated in the air. Mist and something resembling transparent cloth, sheets, pieces of cloth, making the room change and interchange constantly. Gabi sat behind a table (suddenly she sat behind the table) of an ever-changing reality of light and shadow and color and non-color. Somewhere behind her was a staircase seemingly leading Nowhere. On the wall there was a painting of a castle, an old haunting fortress, perhaps not a painting. Nothing was solid or real here… except the Oracle.
There were a few steps, a few flagstones from the door to the table. The boys looked nervously at each other. They wondered how far down it could be… if the steps should suddenly vanish beneath their feet.
Everett studied Gabi with ambiguity. She had made a quantum leap forward in the reach for her potential. And she was far from being the only one. This night had been a major motivation factor. They were all preparing for the meeting with the Face of Death. But… what if it already was very much present in their midst?
– I'm a Witch, Gabi replied to the question the two boys were unable to vocalize. – Like Everett and

many others here. Before the start of the Human Time, the Earth was a soulless place. What we do more than anything is filling out the darkness.

– Gabi will be your Guide, boys, Everett said lightly. – She will show you the sights and give you a history lesson you'll never forget.

Not too fast he hurried back out in the corridor, the hallway. After closing the door behind him, he lent at the wall. A sharp pain somewhere in his stomach or its immediate surroundings forced him to bend forward. He took one step forward and it felt as if the foot twisted in all directions at once. He dried the cold sweat the best he could and returned to the barroom in a way seemingly calm and composed.

It seemed like a long time had passed since the last time he had passed these shores. Only one of the tables was filled with people now. There weren't many people present. He saw only a few witches. Jason, Morgana, Tam and a few others.

– Have you seen Jill? He asked. – Or Stacy?

– Not for a while. Tam looked at him with her incredible blue eyes. – You know them. They come and go like shadows.

He left without a word, closing his fists as he stopped briefly right outside. Blackest hell, he shouldn't have left them. He should've realized that the slippery bitch would go somewhere. She always did. He hurried on, increased his speed almost without realizing it. He didn't know where he ran, but he knew in whose direction:

Hers.

Surroundings turned indistinct. He couldn't believe the strength in the legs and thighs. The speed with which he was running made his blood boil. Feet drummed towards the ground at first, but his moves soon turned fluid, instinctive. How fast did he run? People looked incredulous at him. He would've enjoyed the speed and the run if it wasn't for the pain. While passing Square he saw Laurie in her Place and he snarled at her. She shook. His pain and bewilderment echoed through air and soil. He turned towards the Hill and ran along it further inland. What unbelievable strength he showed. He had shaken Tim Drake as easy as he would a dry blanket and now he ran virtually effortlessly through a fairly rough terrain, a run differing dramatically from the one he had made with Jill. She would've been unable to keep up with him now. He had never been a runner, even if he had enjoyed running now and then. But now he did run, and it seemed like he had never done anything but running.

The sense of urgency grew ever stronger. Something seemed to be gnawing at him, at his back… eyes staring, hard, unblinking… creepy. He halted his run abruptly and looked up. Why up exactly he couldn't say, except perhaps on other levels than where his mundane consciousness resided. He looked up and something returned his stare. Unable to scream he froze in his tracks. A creature, a vision worse than any nightmare levitated in the air above. A face, a body more demonic than he could imagine. Or at least that he could imagine he could imagine. The ghoul scowled and grinned down at him, if it could be said to have eyes or features at all. If demons existed this was how they had to look. No demons, only demonic persons his grandfather's father always told him. Young Everett had believed him. Now, he wasn't so sure anymore.

Whatever it was it… expanded, and attempted to surround him. He screamed and jumped away in wild panic, like a frightened animal. He achieved nothing except closing himself off in a corner. No way out.

He snarled and it sounded so much like a beast that he almost feared himself more than… the ghoul. There was a kind of build up inside him, now also in his brain, a violent pressure between his eyes. Something that couldn't be seen, that possibly couldn't be measured, but was his collected mind power in one powerful burst directed at the disgusting creature and dissolved it in thousand bits, making it fade to nothing.

Nothing there anymore. He had done it. He.

An eternity passed. He couldn't say how long. He started breathing and slowly realized that he felt… good. In spite of the pain, the increasing pain. The pain made him feel good. When he attempted to run everything turned worse. What he had done hadn't weakened him, but on the contrary dissolved the last vestiges of walls in his psyche, liberated him. Still, something was wrong, missing. He had to find her. Had to!

He looked up and he saw her. Between the trees, at the top of a big rock, she stood upright. Just a slight slope and around a bend

and he was there. She had moved and was nowhere in sight. She had turned invisible once more and he panicked. It took him several attempts and a big effort to push the word from his throat:

– *Lillith.*

There she was in the moonlight, in the forest glen, bathing in the moonlight. He knew her so well. Her face, its form, its features, the bodylines, very visible, in spite of the wide gown. The hairstyle. The hair, always reminding him of raven feathers.

– Very few people dare to look too strongly at the shadows of eternity, she said softly. – They're afraid of what they might find.

He did it instantly, looking first at the shadow on her right. She stood there, too, or rather levitated. But what he saw when staring at her left side made him pause. He saw himself levitate and suddenly he understood.

The spirit did in general look like him and didn't seem immediately threatening, like the demon ghoul, but in several ways, it scared him more.

She took one step towards her mirror image, and it did the same. Two steps, three… They integrated, became One. It happened with such ease that he realized that it wasn't the first time. Not the first time it had happened consciously. His own mirror image, his soul floated closer. This was *Plat,* everything he was, body, mind, the physical and spiritual.

– I accept you, he said aloud. – You're a part of me.

It dissolved and he felt it return to him, to its body and for the first time he was fully conscious of the process. He felt a tremendous clarity.

You did arrive in time.

She smiled to him, as seductive as ever, lovely, irresistible.

Pain ravaged him everywhere at once. He was frozen in an upright position without being able to decide if she held him in her grip. Something… happened. It happened *now.* Clothes suddenly felt enormously tight and just after a few seconds he grew so big that he shredded them like they were paper. Muscles bulged and waxed. He couldn't stop staring at the hairy arms and the claws emerging from the point of his fingers. He saw what happened through her eyes and more and more incredulous he wondered if it could really be himself he looked at. But the incredible (and horrible) transformation continued unabated. His jaw and the lower part of his face expanded until he could see most of… hell… the snout with his own eyes.

He stood upright, still completely two-legged. Perhaps a wolf would have looked like this, if it had had a basically human form. But he was wilder than any wolf, bigger than any man. All his clothes were gone. The body covered in thick pelt-like hair from top to bottom. The face had… The face mirrored human emotion, but no expression could describe how he felt. He could smell the entire forest with his nose. The scent was so complete, so textured that it was like a map, a living, breathing map. He threw his head back and howled. The howl of the Wolf penetrated the forest, penetrated well beyond its confines. Primal passion given voice describing everything he felt in that exact moment. His anger, his lust, his sorrow, his joy. How could the stupid assholes do it, claim that the animals had no complex language? One single howl and he had just given voice to everything he had never been able to describe using tens of thousands of words.

He stood there before her, heaving and breathing, Anubis finally revealed, in all his glory and he felt pride. The female didn't give away any fear-smell. On the contrary, the smell completely overwhelming everything else was that of her swollen sex. She started to undress, in slow, deliberate moves, at the very least as wild, as primal as he.

– Come to me, Anubis, she called and with his large ears he registered every nuance in her hoarse voice.

He had grown below to something at least comparable to his other growth. He sensed his heavy cock hit his thighs as he wagged forward, feeling so vigorously alive. Had he truly been alive until this moment? Only in what had been forgotten dreams in his early teens. He towered in front of her, not so much taller perhaps, but his presence was certainly overwhelming. Both to her and himself. She pushed herself close, smelling his pelt, stroking his pelt, smelling his sex, sliding away, going down on the ground, rolling on it, behaving very much like a wolf-bitch. She rose with glassy eyes. He grabbed hold of her and held her in his grip. He feared he would tear her apart, leave her like a wet spot on the ground. But he needn't have worried. The wolf knew and when instinct took over, when the Wild overwhelmed them both, it might be rough, but it was a long time away from turning lethal or even violent. There was no kissing, no caressing, only the wild dance. Even if his conscious mind hadn't adapted to this new body, a part of him acted as if he had always had it. The female went down on all fours, smiling in lust and hunger. He went down after her. He smelled her submission the moment it happened and howled in triumph and joy. The echoes came from all over, as if there were still wolves left in the area. He howled again, and again, giving voice to the voiceless, filling out the void. The last vestige of even involuntarily resistance vanished in the female and then, in exactly that moment, he possessed her. He held her in his grip, as she continued to writhe under him. Claws drew blood, inevitably, but the wounds healed and vanished after merely seconds.

– Oh, you my big and furry beast, she breathed.

He snarled and his thighs hit hard her sweaty buttocks. The smell, the overwhelming scent of his fur drove her completely insane.

– Big, big, big, she moaned and howled.

He held her head by her raven hair, bit through the hair, to the delicate skin below. He didn't penetrate very deep, but the taste of blood made them both lose the final cognitive thoughts. They were just male and female now, mating in the wilderness.

And all the time… something felt wrong. As it had all the time since he first saw her on the rock, in what was the deep of his rational thought. But it felt right, too, ever more right, and that was what was wrong. Nothing happening later, whatever his suspicion was about, had strengthened it, but in spite of this the meat grinder turned and turned in his head. Wrong… wrong… wrong

6

… *wrong. Everything was wrong.*

The same night. The same Moon. Laurie called her eight original students to her. Andrea and Daniel didn't want to come, but couldn't resist her siren call. Nobody heard their cry for help. Nothing escaped their muddled minds. Laurie had carefully planned for and chosen this moment. She and her eight loyal subjects should regain what was lost.

Preparations were made in haste and under pressure. The group had returned to Square. There was nobody else present.

Andrea attempted to speak.

– Silence, deceitful bitch, Laurie whispered. – There will be no more betrayals, no more willful resistance. That's my good girl, my sweet child.

Andrea stiffened. Eyes turned distant, turned to glass. She sat down by the table with the others.

– This is *my* Place of Power, Laurie breathed. Her place, the room where she had accepted all her charges, also they who had betrayed her. – They'll never be able to overcome us here.

She lit eight huge, black wax candles, each placed in front of each of the witches. She put wooden bowls filled with a smoking potion before them.

– Drink, she bade them, and they drank.

Daniel hesitated a bit but drank. Andrea held hard around the bowl, but didn't drink. She fought her way back from oblivion once more. She sensed the pressure from Laurie's will, but fought it.

– Why won't you tell us what you're gonna do? She asked weakly.

– Such a precious, precarious girl, Laurie breathed. – You've always been willful, sweet one, but your willfulness has come to an end. Now, *drink!*

Andrea had lived too long under her influence, under her spell, to resist the hypnotic command. She drank in big slurps, the young witch, and her body and eyes once more stiffened, to join the other seven.

They saw nothing else, heard nothing else then the one they had submitted to and her dominant Voice.

– I take you as mine. By the depth of blood, by the loyalty of mind, I bind you. By the inexperience of youth, by the

experience of age, I bind you. Frozen you are, frozen in my service you are. I take your service, in the other world and this one. By the power of the God, by the power of the Goddess, I make you mine. I bind thee, I bind thee…

– And bid you to turn yourself over to me.

A tearing sound rose from their depths, from a horrible pain not visible in their faces.

The final step commenced. She had prepared so long to take complete control over them. And through them more would follow. She had waited long enough. An expectant smile crossed her face. She sensed their energies, sensed them being bound to her. It worked, it really worked. Soon she would be in complete control of them and all their precious powers. It was for the best. She knew best… She…

Smile vanished. She blinked. There was another… presence in the room, but she couldn't for the life of her see anyone.

– You knew. A hoarse, hateful voice cried at her from the Abyss. – YOU KNEW!

– Who are you? She demanded. – Show yourself. Who…

– We came here because something was missing in our lives. You used that, exploited it like the worst tyrant. You'll not exploit our vulnerability anymore. I will not allow it.

She recognized the voice, but couldn't place it. It was distorted, not sound through a larynx at all, but just formed as waves in the air.

– What are you *talking* about? Laurie Isherwood stated incredulously. – I brought you together, brought you here, to serve me. You're here to do my bidding. You won't be told anything more than what I deem necessary, what I decide you need to know.

Laurie felt as if she was wandering through a desert, as if she awoke from a deep sleep. And a dark figure was chasing her, a hooded creature without blood, face and mind. All the power she had amassed left her. It happened as easy as if someone had snapped their fingers. *No.* Everything she had stolen returned to the eight sitting around the table. All the illusions, all the deceit she had so carefully crafted for herself evaporated, exposed to the dark sun in her presence.

– You've outlived your purpose. You're hardly more than dead wood we leave behind.

She sensed the presence as something physical then, a dark mood, claws growing out of the night. In a flash she realized how wrong she had truly read the situation and underestimated the danger. She backed off, until she stood frozen pressed against the wall. In a howl of rage and disappointment and protest she was pulled into the air and thrown across the room and into the opposite wall. She hung there, like a ragged doll. Body was paralyzed, but she could still feel. She was ravaged by a rage reducing her own to a breath of wind compared to an autumn storm. Knives of fire and cold penetrated her, tore through her a thousand times. Her death cry was sensed by every sensitive in Northfield. She was dying, but didn't die. Not before she had… she had… she had screamed herself hoarse for an eternity. Not until Udo finally managed to scream, screaming his lungs out, no longer able to hold back the pain stifled for so long. He started crying. Great, heartbreaking sobs. The shock washed over the eight, tearing into them, as they regained their faculties, their free will.

Eventually the bloody, torn, ragged doll was discarded like garbage, thrown into a corner where it lay still. Lay still while cooling and hardening. Silence descended. Death had come to Northfield and the nightmare began.

Chapter fourteen:
DAYS AND NIGHTS
(in the city that wasn't New Orleans)

Police cars were the only motorized vehicles regularly traversing Oldtown. By the end of this night, they crawled all over the place. Outside Square and every other inch of the area. And even in Northfield as a whole there was a police presence beyond any normal night (or day). The rumor that Laurie Isherwood had been murdered spread like wildfire in the dry grass would have done. The police Chief feared riots and had given orders to his subordinates to under no circumstances provoke further… unrest.

The blue and red lights blinked and blinked. Within the walls of Square, the investigation had already started in earnest.

– Okay, let's go over it one more time, Lieutenant Hugh O'Keefe sighed heavily. – From the beginning, please.

– We came here to go to bed, Jill Stafford explained, still tense, obviously shaken, vulnerable. – It was too late for us to return to the dorm, and we have an agreement with the school board, allowing us to sleep here. We found her. We called you. Then we found weapons and searched the premises. There was no one here. No one has left the house since we arrived.

He studied the others: Stacy Larkin, Everett Moran, Jason Gallagher, Andrea Natchios, Udo Beyer, Daniel Webster. Hands that had been clutching weapons still curled into fists and caused knuckles to whiten. Especially Beyer looked skittish. They all did, but he looked especially bad. O'Keefe didn't hold that against him. He thought about his conversation with the coroner.

– There was more than one, the pale man had told him. – Two held her, while one or more stabbed her repeatedly, cut her to pieces so to speak.

– What about a ritual killing? He had asked.

– In my opinion you can exclude that, the reply had come dryly. – This wasn't a planned act. In all my years in the profession I've hardly seen any clearer signs of affect-killing. Whoever did this must have been filled to the brim with pent up rage and hatred. This wasn't so much a murder as a… *destruction.*

– I've seldom seen anyone this mangled, O'Keefe carefully told the youths. – You must have very irreconcilable enemies.

– Enemies usually are, Stacy Larkin pointed out.

– One last question, the lieutenant said a considerable amount of time later. – You don't happen to know who her heirs are?

– Of course, Stacy said ironically. – In case racism and hatred towards what's different isn't the murder motive, huh?

– She showed us her will, Jill said softly. – Everything goes to our collective leadership, everybody she initiated to the Coven. Everybody is specifically mentioned by their full name in the will.

That was it. A sense of unreality persisted in them. The bloody piece of meat they had found had been moved off the premises now, but that, it was just a… piece of everything. The witches left Square in quite a joint fashion. Everybody kept quiet until being far away.

– You did good. Stacy praised Jill. – We were all good, but you were great…

– Spare me! Jill replied sarcastically.

– She attempted to enslave us permanently tonight, Andrea stated frostily, – but somebody, something, someone stopped her.

– You didn't see… anything? Everett asked insistently.

– We were totally Gone. Udo shook his head. – We were left with a general sense of Wrath. And realization, not the least, of how she had exploited and treated us.

He had practically become another person now. Now that he was no longer a puppet, but a human being.

Every step they took, every time they drew breath realization hit them all the harder.

We're Free. *Free!*

Unreal. Jill hadn't really been following the conversation. The pressure from above was gone. They were Free. Everything had changed - again. Reality hadn't changed, but her perception of it certainly had and it was as if she didn't live in the same world anymore. But she did. They didn't live in a dream. Reality surpassed fantasy through and through. As if in a dream she reached out with her mind and for fun lifted her arm towards the iron-gate in front of them. One heavy pull and it shook loose from its hinges. The immaterial Jill lifted it high up in the air and twisted it around and around, until the metal had been reformed to scrap iron.

– Brava. Stacy applauded. – You might wanna consider a career within modern art?

This time Jill curtseyed and smiled enigmatically.

They walked on in silence. No one wanted to be the first to say something. Not until they got the farm in their line-of-sight Daniel finally said:

– So, have anyone given any thought to Gabi's story about the… Dollmaster?

– There is an ancient muddled eastern legend. Andrea spoke quickly, carefully. – People who gave him that name knew him for what and who he was. A related legend tells about Thalama, the Goddess of Destiny standing against him.

– But the story, Daniel exploded, – is it true?

– True? Stacy said teasingly, frosty, unable to hold on to her usual aloofness.

– There is something to it, Jill stated. – We all know that, don't we? But as Gabi herself told us: Her knowledge is limited. She wasn't there and therefore couldn't speak from Memory. In other words: The story was second, third or fourth hand. Oral tales delivered down the generations. She didn't dare seek too deep or use too long a time. But that doesn't shake its foundation. We all felt it, didn't we? Details may vary, but the core remains.

– Quite a genius setup, Stacy admitted gritting her teeth. – First, he creates a setting of injustice, inequality and segregation. Then he promises all the lower classes a society, a paradise where everybody is equal.

– The story has a certain backward logic to it, Everett said darkly. – What I find most unbelievable about it all is that he has spent ten thousand years destroying everything in his path. It's completely and utterly… inhuman.

– The thought about the hierarchy's justification is dominating the world. Daniel made a fist. – The thought about religion's justification is dominating the hierarchies.

– He's far from alone in his attempt at turning the world monogamous, Jill swore bitterly, – but his contribution can't be underestimated.

– His goal is nothing more than complete control, Stacy challenged them thoroughly, – and he will destroy any opposition. But he has encountered some unexpected problems…

A grinning Jason picked up on her cue.

– Think about it. He started the Burning Times to remove the last of his… competitors. But he found himself in a dilemma. To not obstruct the industrial revolution too much he had to allow some room for independent thought and creativity. I can imagine he attempted to steer science, allowing it to develop into a new religion. And now he has lost what little governing power he had. He wanted Control, not a world without subjects. It's ironic in a sense that he has succeeded too well in developing civilization's «potential».

– And then… there's us…

– We're the returned Power, his equals. He has pushed a giant snowball down a steep slope to the precipice for so long now, creating an irresistible force. The only thing that may stop anything like that is another, equally irresistible force. We fit well into his darkness because we can fit in anywhere.

– Yes, Jill said quietly, – that's our strength… and our weakness.

They stood there for a while without looking at each other. Nothing more was said.

2

The grid supplying electricity to major parts of northeastern USA failed the next afternoon. Several hours later it became clear it would be a prolonged failure. Even redundancy systems took a fall. And other grids had a breakdown as well. While grids not yet broken had to be shut down because of certain upcoming overload. A system so long taxed beyond endurance collapsed. Finally, «overnight», one brick made the entire wall fall.

Among all the numerous disasters and problems this created was the rapid decomposition of bodies. The remains of Laurie Isherwood were delivered in haste to her heirs. The coroner's office in Northfield did not have an independent power supply.

Before the word got out, before too many offers of «taking care of the funeral», they acted. They put the body in a canoe early in the morning, stuffed the canoe with dry twigs. Morgana lit the fire and with one hard push sent it floating out on Fire Lake. Smoke and embers mixed with the morning mist and created a special mood at the dawn. By luck and the aforementioned circumstances, they had managed to keep it a private ceremony. Only the witches were present. And they kept the ceremony short and sweet.

– Why are we doing this shit at all? They all heard Gabi. – Isn't it just a little bit hypocritical?

– We're not mourning her. Jason shrugged. – We're burying her.

Morgana was the only one doing anything, saying anything. The others stood pulled back in the forest glen. Fire rose to full strength. The remains, the shell melted away to nothing in the searing heat. The canoe itself burned quickly to a cinder and would sink soon. It was on its way down the river Styx.

– She made many mistakes, as we all do, Morgana cried out. – But without her we would never have come here. She gathered us. We came here because something was missing from our lives. She brought us here to look for something we may never find. If not for her sake, then for our own, let's never stop searching. May our paths cross again under happier circumstances.

She chose the Path of Power, Jill thought frostily.

But what about me, have I chosen?

That was a question haunting her. On the Hill, while she slept and dreamed a few hours in the house on Fire Lake, on the farm and during a random, idle walk through this city of stone. It was early afternoon. She heard them whisper, in the erroneous belief that she couldn't hear them, hear their yapping, that they were safe merely because they put some distance between her and themselves. They should have known. What she truly was, what she could do to them.

She sat down, to more easily concentrate on… pulling herself together. She had been close to doing something very nasty to those people. Her temper had always been hot and fiery, but now she felt like a cauldron, not merely like she lived in one. And then there was the flip coin that was really a flip coin. Many times, when she had been composed, in control of herself, hadn't she shown herself to be at least as dangerous?

Laurie was gone. The path lay wide open to an unimaginable Power. Stacy sought it. Jason, Scott Thompson, even Everett, even if he didn't fully realize it yet. If she should compete, join the race she would have to use all the means at her disposal. And somewhere out there awaited them the Great Manipulator. He and thousands more.

She had to do what everybody was doing. Gather allies, building her power base. Do everything necessary.

A man with shiny black shoes rose from the bench. So much dust there was these days he couldn't have walked far. He enjoyed a young woman's company. She wore high heels and leaned heavily on him for support. He had spoken patronizingly about Jill earlier. Now he did it again. About «the lazy bitch sitting on the lawn with her head between her knees». She put his shoes on fire. He screamed like a stuck pig and ran off, jumped over the fence, to the dried river. He managed to find a pit deep enough, but even then, the fire wasn't put out immediately. Panicking he started jumping up and down, screaming himself hoarse, sinking down on his knees in despair while crying and sniffing, his face bloated in tears while dust and steam rose to cover his shaking body.

Jill rose with a weak smile. Was this what constituted a rational decision?

The Sun wasn't visible in the streets between the tall buildings. But instead of cool shadow this created an even worse enclosed heat. Jill felt it, too, even though her physical surroundings influenced her far less than it had done. Besides… this was definitely more psychological than physical… so familiar. The Cage was present wherever she walked or wandered.

Question: What was the wolf's reply when Little Red Riding Hood asked for an honest answer?

The reply wasn't: «So I can more easily eat you».
Answer: «I'm always lying».
Q: What is the Almighty's reply when he's asked about the illogical in god's existence?
He exposes his beautiful fangs and replies: «He's an accomplished liar».
Little Red Riding Hood dies ignorant.
The end of the world comes as a thief in the night. It's so hard fighting against it, so damn hard.
The old, blind woman sat on a small bench, staring at an uncertain, but known point a place ahead of her. She spoke to the air with a rough, cracked up voice:
– Is it true that the Beast has awakened?
– «It» has never slept, Jill replied bitterly. – It has just fooled us into believing that it has.

3

They moved fast to take control over Laurie's accounts, her vast estate. There was potential trouble awaiting them all along the spectrum. Distant relatives eager to oppose the will. They were persuaded to drop any filing of cases. If asked about why, they could never give a satisfying answer. Those in the legal system attempting to delay the proceedings were stopped in their tracks. All potential trouble was dealt with instantly and decisively, often before any visible objections arose at all.
Udo showed them everything on a computer-screen. He had been her trusted aide. She had made him so. They looked at it in awe, as rows and rows of numbers and acquisitions rolled over the screen.
– She wasn't as loaded as my parents, Stacy whistled, – but she was getting there, and during a considerably shorter time.
Even Gabi had been listed as one of the beneficiaries… a week before Jill had brought her «home».
– As you can see, I was one of the witnesses, Udo said. – Laurie had a very take-charge attitude about her. If she wanted something or someone, she fixed it or them.
They heard the thick bitterness in his voice. They couldn't fault him for that.
There was a lot here, a lot to take in, a lot to take care of.
– It seems like we did the right thing, after all… when we pussyfooted around the Goddess' humble priestess.
Daniel engaged the assembly without introduction.
– We were lucky. Jason said in a tone dripping of sarcasm. – Somebody else did the job for us.
Nobody commented on it.
– There was somebody else doing the job… right?
Still no takers, no comments.
The first sessions Jill, Stacy, Jason and Everett held with Udo could easily be described as frustrating. He was shaking already before they started and a nervous wreck afterwards. They couldn't say for sure if they would ever be able to help him or if he truly needed help.
– Just come to us if you feel you need us, Jill said sweetly. – Come immediately.
He nodded and left.
– We're not exactly trained as therapists. Everett shook his head.
– And what about it? Jason said ironically. – In my book that's a major advantage, both for us, and the people we're helping. We learn by doing, not passively repeating the words and actions of others.
They all nodded, fully aware of the fact that he wasn't referring only to the current case.
– You're incredibly wise sometimes, Stacy said appraisingly.
He was blushing. They stared dumbfounded at him. He was actually blushing.
Stacy dragged him off, stars and heat in her eyes.
She waved a quick goodbye to the boy and girl left in the room.
Jill looked around the room, what had been *her* room. All the blood, all the stains had been removed. The entire building had been redecorated, cellar to roof. That was one of the first things they had used money on. There was nothing left of Laurie here. Nothing physical, nothing spiritual. It wasn't a consecrated place of power anymore, just a room, just a house. Jill sensed nothing from it and she was able to relax more.
– Is anything wrong? He asked.

She gave him a pointed stare. Damn him. He wasn't supposed to be able to read her like that. It had to be the body language. She had certainly not given away anything in other ways.

– The scar, the scar tissue is… hurting, she gasped. – I can't remember that it has ever *hurt.* There has been discomfort, but never anything like this.

– Hasn't it slowly been fading? He asked carefully.

– It has, she said exasperated. – And there's nothing visible lately that has changed that. I've attempted to speed up the process, but it isn't working. There's nothing wrong with my power. It's working every other place on the body. It's even working on the area of the scar tissue, but not on the tissue itself.

He could have reminded her of a conversation they had a short while ago. He chose not to do so.

They heard Stacy's screams of delight from the attic. Two broad smiles crossed their faces, before fading once more.

– Your succubus power…

– Yes? She straightened, looking at him.

– Can you control it? Can you consciously make yourself not doing it?

A mix of frustration and delight was visible in her features.

– I… don't… know. At least not when I'm fucking. Then every kind of control isn't only slipping, but… vanishing completely.

He grabbed her carefully, intensively.

– No matter. I can take it. I can take it *now.*

She kissed him on the cheek. He released her.

– I believe you, she said.

Perhaps she could be hungry, without starving.

Perhaps.

The witches, the entire eighteen piece gathering, sat in one of the boardrooms of what had been Laurie's solicitors; Albert, Albert and Roberts Inc. The talk was high and excited. They didn't care to pretend to a shred of a somber mood.

– New experiences can be incredibly… fresh, Andrea said more than a bit subdued. – To undress in front of everybody was… To undress without actually having sex was actually great… Nudity is completely natural, isn't it?

– Jesus. Stacy rubbed her forehead. – Let's all head for the nearest nudist beach…

They laughed and it felt good to be alive.

An impeccably dressed man entered the room. His hair was impeccable. Everything about him suggested that he had come to them straight from the assembly line.

Jesus, Stacy grinned (to them all). *Here is indeed room for improvement.*

Kieron bent over and let out a loud bark of laughter. He managed to stop himself before it turned too wild and caused too much a disturbance.

– Hello, everybody, the man greeted them, in an unintentional parody of a jovial greeting. – I've met Mr. Beyer and Miss Stafford before. To you who haven't met me my name is Frank Thorne. I've been your attorney for some time and I'm the executor of the will.

He found his papers, a thick pile of paper hidden in his briefcase.

– First of all, I can tell that Miss Stafford's temporarily adoption of Gabrielle Asteroth has been approved. With the biological parents' assent and special nature of the case you, Jill Jasmin Stafford born 1987-04-30 is granted a six months' custody of Gabrielle Asteroth born 1992-02-29 after which a final decision will be made.

– That wasn't bad, Travis said approvingly.

How did you manage that feat? His pointed look asked her.

Thorne said a lot more, about tight surveillance among other things that drowned in the buzz.

Then he pulled an even thicker pile of papers from his hat (his briefcase) and the buzz quieted.

– You, all eighteen gathered here today, are equal beneficiaries in the will, all of you mentioned specifically. You don't own one of eighteen parts in the various holdings and companies owned by the late Laurie Isherwood. You own everything collectively. There are many things that must be considered here. It isn't just a question about your legal rights. They're unquestionable. But also about whether or not you will be able to actually manage the considerable fortune.

– Udo has done that in fact, Stacy said, – for a *considerable* time already.

Laughter. And the young lawyer reddened. Perhaps the honorable Albert, Albert and Roberts wouldn't send an errand boy of a junior partner the next time.

– As I said there are possible snags, but they shouldn't present any significant problems. The will is quite clear and seventeen of you are of age. Miss Asteroth's share will be managed by Miss Stafford until she reaches the correct age. There are a number of decisions you must take, concerning the ongoing operations and such, but we will go through them with you.

– I think I speak for everybody here when I say that for the time being we're pleased to let things continue like they were when Laurie owned it all, Everett said. – We'll let you know if and when we desire changes.

– Okay, Frank said. – Are we in agreement then?

Murmurs of agreement drowned him around the table.

He spoke at length, and they listened. This was, after all, to them, another unknown part of the world they needed to know and learn about, in order to survive and thrive.

Smoke drifted above the water. Fire Lake reflected the Sun's few, remaining rays. Fires were lit in the forest glen and encircling the castle in the middle of the water. More canoes were pushed from land, carrying materials and tools. The hammering and redecoration kept going for most of the day stopped for a while. The darkness was a time of rest and play. Cooking and eating, music, dance and a variety of other activities relieved work. Jill could see it all from above, how the light from the Hill was seen and felt far away, how it slowly pulsed, expanded. The place had an aura like a living being and it was about to awaken now, after a prolonged dormancy. There was power here and therefore dangers, but it wasn't sick or dying like the world outside.

– Are you all right, honey? Jill asked the blooming teenager playing with Malvin.

They rested on hammocks outside the main building on the farm.

– Yes, Gabi replied upbeat. – I was down for a while, but I used your method, albeit not in the drastic way you did, but it was so *inspiring,* Raven, and I was inspired. I confronted my… problems, made them turn back on themselves. Standing naked in front of other people and consuming your own waste? I'll recommend it to *anyone…*

The tall, skinny girl ran to the older, bigger one and embraced her.

– And I couldn't have done it without you. You brought me here. I love you, Raven, I will do anything for you.

Something stuck in Jill's throat, and she was unable to speak.

The emotional moment ended. They could feel the wind again, the world again. Even stronger, even more. Even Now.

Gabi dried her tears with both hands. There wasn't any more of them.

– Are you sorry Laurie is dead? Jill asked her carefully.

– Of course not, I'm *glad,* Gabi said calmly. – The creed that children are nice little innocents is one more stupid present-day illusion. There's a quality to children cruelty that most adults have left behind. And why shouldn't I be glad? She wanted to enslave us, to use us for whatever sick purpose she had in mind. She enhanced all my insecurities and played on my longings to make me more pliable to her needs. When I heard your call and the beat of the drum it was as if I had awakened from a drug-induced sleep, and she did that only during a few hours. Hell, I'm exalted.

– She could do that, because she used your power to do it, as she used your power against yourself.

A few seconds passed, a bit of ticking of the clock.

– I'm glad, too, Jill said. – No, more than that; I'm *pleased.* She was our Enemy and we vanquished her.

Things happened so fast and as they sat there, events were speeding up to an even more uncanny degree. The pages were turning in the book of shadows.

– So, you're ready then?

– Ma'am, I was born ready, Gabi replied in a somewhat to be desired imitation of a southern drawl.

The wind, yes, the world, yes. Jill took it all in. Humans were creatures of emotion, of passion.

The future was already here.

The future was now.
She stood in a boardroom, in one end of the long table, dressed as a perfect imitation of a young female executive.
– So, we, the owners, she concluded, – have decided to turn our investment portfolio a bit, towards more desirable projects. Therefore, we will, quite frankly, starting now, sell our interests in Thompson Chemicals, Pyramid Inc and all similar grand polluters and abusers.
– That may seem more than a little rushed, don't you think? A man sitting close to her spoke up, after a prolonged silence among all the resident board members.
Gabi took one step forward.
– The chairman recognizes the Union's representative in Thompson Chemicals' board of directors, she hailed with more than faint mockery in her voice.
– It so happens that I am and also a long-term member of this board. So why should you be worried, the man from the union pointed out, – when the workers are not? Doesn't it tell you something about the precautions taken to ensure everyone's safety?
– Oh, it most certainly does, she said dryly. – It tells me about the value of the Union and its men.
– But even if you weren't thoroughly corrupt, even if «your» workers weren't a sack of sheep, it isn't just about you. Even if you truly accept being run over by any would-be tyrant there is, allowing yourself to be slowly, inevitably poisoned, that choice does have consequences for everybody on the planet. By your acceptance, your inactivity, you're just as guilty in the destruction of Life, of the world, as your «employer».
– We workers usually find ourselves between the rock and the hard place in the struggle between the environmentalists and the corporations.
He was good at this, his punctuations, phrases and choice of words more than suggested that he had been schooled and groomed by certain parties. Gabrielle saw how people nodded and grunted in agreement, including many of those who saw themselves as neutral.
– I would say that people claiming to be neutral, to not interfere, are nothing of the kind, she said, in a slightly higher pitch. – They're the servants of tyranny. Can we continue as we have been doing for so long, making compromises concerning health, humanity, Life? Are the polluters and destroyers at all interested in doing anything really useful? Of course not. They're hardly interested in anything beyond what color their next swimming pool or giant bathtub shall be. And their eager servants have even lesser needs. To them it's sufficient with a pat of recognition on the head, a few dollars more in the bank, while their kids are suffering and dying because they've been drinking polluted water or eaten food filled with poisons or genetically engineered ingredients. Humanity is already fucked for generations thanks to these highly moral people.
Jill smiled.
– There you have it, people.
A woman bent forward.
– But even if you sell these highly valuable stocks, you still have a lot left you may find unpalatable?
– We will indeed have a lot of polluters and people cooperating with polluters left, Gabi said. – You can say we're starting at the top. Or the bottom, if you will.
– It seems clear that the new owners have irreconcilable differences with the board, the man by the end of the table commented, no doubt attempting to scare off «impressible youths».
Jill had felt it from the start, easily, how they had attempted to intimidate the two girls, a move certainly not unexpected.
– We have talked about this, too, among ourselves, Jill told them lightly, smiling innocently. – And you're right of course.
– Perhaps you would be better served to move forward with a bit more restraint, the man by the end of the table offered sympathetically.
– We thought about that option, too, though not for long. There are indeed irreconcilable differences between the new owners and the board. That's why we've decided to do a Geribaldi.
The room turned very silent.
– A... *Geribaldi?* The man at the end of the table said astonished.
– Precisely. I know you all will support this excellent move...

And on that note the meeting was adjourned. The words she spoke, where she told them to go, what they could do to themselves, afterwards were unnecessary, really. But she clearly enjoyed it.

Her brilliant gray eyes would follow them deep into sleep, into nightmare in both days and nights to come.

Smoke drifted above the water. Day turned to night, while relative silence descended on and around Fire Lake.

– This place is OURS, Jill cried from the rooftop. Everybody saw her as a creature dancing on the precipice between light and darkness. – We don't own it. Nobody owns anything or anyone. But here we can create something lasting and make it into something for others to follow if that should be their desire.

She was fully aware that only her face was visible towards the dark sky, the flickering lights from the fires, and the effect of it. Glowing skin on a face without body and form and substance. She saw Stacy by one of the fires nodding in satisfaction, in approval. The witch swept her cloak around her and vanished from their sight. Somebody applauded. Stacy looked indulgent at them.

Jill walked down the spiral stairs, to and through the bedroom in the attic. She heard it almost immediately, his play on the old piano, a sound so full and spooky. Sound and music, like everything else surrounding them lately were enhanced. She stood at the top of the stone stairs, looking down. The old oil lamps oozed a bit yet, but it would stop eventually. They cast a soft and pleasant light. To eyes, to senses, to all shadowwalkers. He started singing when she was halfway down. She knew that he knew exactly where she was and that it wasn't only because he was a telepath. He had a powerful ability to scan people's… depth. She wondered if he realized it, if he was able to observe the shadow in himself.

The witch enters the forest
And I follow her
Through fire, through shadow
Her deep eyes are haunting me
From head to toe
And I'm Changed
In a wisp of smoke, she is gone
In a wisp of smoke, she is There
The Mystic is dreaming the world
Creating everything from nothing

The door to the living room stood wide open. The empty fireplace in the library gave way to that full of Life in the outer room. She knew the pull, the draft from it and the pull, the draft from the spiral staircase leading down and down, far below the Earth. Fire flickered in the wind. She kept the door open and danced through it, into the warmth of the others, embracing the soft glowing candles. Many sat close, listening to the clear song and the music surrounding them in the twilight shadows. His eyes twinkled while he turned them at her. She smiled to him.

Outside was the same really. There were no longer any discernible differences between being outside and inside. The wind blew as hard, as quiet here as it did inside. The water surface was like a floor in a room without light. One wanted to walk on it, to enjoy its familiarity, but was afraid of suddenly finding oneself on traitorous ground.

Gabi sat by one of the fires. Gabi… that was her name now. It fit. She felt like a new person, far more than a new name. A stranger had found herself a home among other strangers. She didn't need the fire to stay warm anymore. When she waved to Jill it was in a burst of pure joy.

– We sure showed those pricks, didn't we? She shouted.

Everybody laughed. Jill nodded as she waved back. The girl's excitement left her with a warm, boiling river inside.

The wind chimes on the veranda played up from time to time, making them listen, making them wonder. It sounded so natural, like the whistling of trees, as if they were actually speaking, communicating in a foreign language.

Silence descended slowly, ever so slowly on the assembly. They slept there, indoors, outdoors, slept with impunity, and as they slept, as they did not, night turned to dreams. And between the fire and the forest, they dreamed the world.

4

The city could be an exciting place. Or there could be places within the city that could be exciting. Northfield had, as the majority of the population saw it, been luckily spared such embarrassments. In the days to come the future appeared, a slow, decisive Change from the peaceful and safe, as the majority, as they had been raised, preferred it. In many ways the change from day to day happened so slowly that it was hardly noticeable, while in other areas people couldn't help but noticing.

Dust rose and fell constantly. The most obvious physical change was the dust. Water rationing had been imposed on the entire Metropolitan area yesterday. The local city council had expanded its partial restrictions to all aspects of water use today. Nobody really understood why they hadn't done so the first time. The first restrictions had basically covered the use of water in gardens and such. Now, showering was practically banned. Water could be used for washing bodies, the old-fashioned ways, but washing of clothes was strictly prohibited. People wearing suits and dresses not stinking of sweat were at best frowned at, at worst looked at in a more than suspicious manner.

The witches had been present in the streets for some time now, a fact that had caused a lot of irritation. Now, they seemed to take over wherever they moved. Even where they weren't visible their presence was felt, and their few supporters increased in numbers and bravery. They had lost their position within the hierarchy, but had gained their own, by their own power.

The apathy dominating the stone city didn't let go, but loosened a bit. People in the streets were patronizing, but curious in spite of themselves. Two women carrying a heavy load in their bags approached the Marketplace on the previous parking lot.

– It's further than I thought, one of them was breathing heavily. – It's too far without a fucking car.

– Perhaps we should have stayed away. I've heard that the witches are more than present here. They're everywhere.

– Laurie Isherwood bought the farm, I hear. Someone finally took care of her.

– Her students put her body in a canoe and burned it all. A snort. – What a strange custom. I thought it was only in India they buried people in boats. And I'm willing to bet those youths were normal, nice boys and girls until that witch caught them in her web.

They walked along the fruit-stalls and tables with woven clothes.

– Scandalous clothes, they snickered.

They paid for two scarves and put them in their bags, before hurrying on. They hadn't come here to buy anything. Their eyes moved, as they themselves moved to the small tent on the opposite side of the Market. As they walked there, they felt people's stares.

Two men took part in a heated discussion not far away.

– I'm telling you there's no use going in there. The two standing guard outside the tent put it there. I saw them. There is no one else inside. No one. The two outside never go in.

– There have been people inside, the other one objected.

– But they've come out again, and fuck me if I know what they're doing there.

The two… guards, they had to be guards… were one Amazon with… pointed ears… and Everett Moran. They knew him or rather his parents. They had encountered him regularly during his early childhood and previously a month ago, just before he moved away from home. They hardly recognized him.

A poster said:

WE CAN'T SOLVE ALL PROBLEMS,
BUT WE MAY BE ABLE TO HELP.

Both the elf-princess and the boy smiled in a warm greeting. When they didn't feel threatened by her, why then made the sight of his exposed canines them nervous? His face had in strange ways become like a remote, alien landscape, but it was the teeth that really did it.

– Welcome fair ladies. He bowed. The day was bright and fair. It did no good. His expressive face reminded them of Dracula, as they had seen it in the movies once upon a time. – What brings you to our humble castle?

They giggled like young girls. What an eloquent, polite man. He really reminded them of Christopher Lee…

– We seek advice, said the one.

– And aid, said the other.

– You may pass. He grinned and took one step to the side. The opening to the inner parts of the tent revealed itself. One final hesitation, before they pushed each other inside.

«Forsake all hope ye who enter here». The thought crossed their minds, as the darkness embraced them.

Silence surrounded them. The rays from the Sun didn't reach them anymore. Their eyes adapted only slowly to the weak, weak light. They had to stare ahead a long time, until compact darkness gave way to a sort of charcoal crimson dawn.

Staring so hard that their eyes hurt, they finally saw a woman. They saw the table she sat behind, but they didn't see the chair she sat in. They heard a rumble in the ground, faint cries in the night.

– Hello, Hester, Doris, she greeted them. – How may I be of service?

A hand (probably hers) indicated the suddenly appearing chairs on their side of the table. A *pentagram,* Hester realized enlightened. They hesitated a bit, wondering where, how… the witch had gotten their names. They sat down, sat down in the very, very comfortable chairs, the very, very safe chairs.

– I wish to stop smoking. Hester cleared her throat.

Such a relief to get it off her chest. It melted off like a wet sack covering the body.

– Are you sure? The witch asked. – You must want to, or I can't help you.

– I want to, Hester said decisively.

– You want to, the woman confirmed.

She rose, sweeping her cloak around her body, like a veil covering her face. There was no wall between them anymore, nothing keeping Hester from seeing everything of the face filling her vision.

– Follow my finger, the witch commanded.

Hester obeyed. As the robed creature in front of her moved the index finger back and forth.

– Follow my finger, the witch commanded.

And there was another index finger. Of course, how silly of her. Everybody had two index fingers… didn't they? The two fingers moved simultaneously. Confused Hester attempted to follow both the fingers. And then she saw a third, and a fourth, and a fifth. Her rapid eye movements slowed down. Eyes and body stiffened.

– That's good, Hester. Relax. Close your eyes.

She believed she closed her eyes, but they remained open.

– Yessss, your eyesssss are open now, Hester. Open yourself up to me, open your deepest, most secretive thoughts.

She walked alone in the dark night and black eyes followed her wherever she went, holding up a mirror where she could see herself. She swam in a warm sea and there were no places to hide.

She blinked, opened her eyes wide. The witch sat on the same spot and so did she. She couldn't tell how much time had passed, if hours had passed or merely seconds. A look at her watch revealed that she had been sitting here for thirteen minutes. She had no problems anymore keeping her eyes open. Usually the eyelids always felt heavy, even in the middle of the day. Now she felt rested, refreshed.

– What did you do? She asked with a clear hint of worry.

– Not much more than recommend and prod, the witch smiled, grinned wickedly. – I placed you in a meditative trance. It makes it all… easier.

– I don't feel any different…

That wasn't completely true, but not completely wrong either.

– That's the entire point. A shrug under the cloak. – I gave you a crash course cure, I didn't brainwash you. You'll find out whether or not it's effective soon enough.

– What happened? Hester asked Doris.

– Nothing, you just sat there…
– Look at it as a dark magic spell, the witch told her cheerfully, with a sinister grin. – Perhaps that will seem more natural to you.
– How much do I owe you? Hester said tightly. She opened her purse.
– Pay what you think is appropriate outside. Go now.
– What about me? Doris asked wondering and slightly irritated.
– Yes, what about her? Hester reacted instantly. – Her reason for coming here was just as good as mine and can't I stay while she…
– What she desires costs more, the witch replied softly. – And desires no witnesses.
Frost raged through Hester. She suddenly felt an extreme desire to once more experience the sun on her body.
Hester had left. The two of them sat there, face to face, without distractions.
– You're concerned because your husband is fucking other women.
Doris shook and cast a nervous glance back towards the opening, the glimmer of light she could no longer see. She bowed her head in shame.
– How *could* you know that? I haven't told anyone about my… my suspicions, and it was merely a coincidence that we at all came here.
– I've got telepathic powers. The bird-eyes of the predator stared pointedly at Doris and froze her in the chair. – I read minds. I'm an empath. I have access to emotions and desires.
– But Hester had to t…
– People's minds are a chaotic cauldron of confusing, contradictory notions and it wasn't instantly evident what Hester wanted. Your wish, on the other hand is more than obvious.
– Yes, I want him to *suffer*, Doris exclaimed suddenly, passionately. – I wouldn't mind seeing him *dead.*
The echo of the last word thundered through the air. Doris stared thunderstruck around her.
– We don't do that. The witch kept her good spirits. – Not as anything but a last resort. There are a number of methods available before killing.
– I'm willing to pay whatever it costs. I'll give you anything, as long as it *works.*
Claws grabbed her from the darkness, like a cat playing with the mouse, a voice hoarse and filled with venom.
– You shouldn't be so *eager* to promise. Someone may take you up on the offer and what you pay might just be yourself.
Doris realized what she had said, and sank even deeper into the mire of her own shame, even easier to twist and turn around any finger. The claws let go, but she felt them still.
The nightmare of images and possibilities lasted only a fraction of a second. She knew what she had almost given away.
– Do you love your husband? The witch asked suddenly.
– What…
– Do you think he is a monster? How is your life together?
– It's okay, in a prosaic sort of way. Doris bowed her head. – But we're not making love much anymore.
– In other words, you're not fucking as often as you would like?
She nodded. Didn't trust her voice.
– You're an attractive woman. Once more the statement came sudden, unexpectedly, bringing her out of balance. – Why don't you take lovers? I know one thing and that is that *variety* has saved a lot of couples from breaking up.
– I know that you're practicing polygamy, Doris said tightly. – It's okay for you, but in our circles it quite simply isn't done by a woman.
– But it's quite okay for the male to do it? Poor me, I thought the world had progressed just a bit…
– I just want back the intensity we once had, the woman whispered. A small tear revealed itself in the corner of one eye. – We've become like strangers to each other.
A hand covered her own.
– Then we've established that he isn't a piece of shit asshole, right? That's a bit of progress there, don't you think?

– Y-yes…

– *Okay.* First a warning: I can't assure you that you will want to return to him when we're through with you. You see, the important is what you want, not family and friends.

– Can't you tell me my fortune, sorceress, so I may more easily reach a decision?

So trusty, the sorceress thought, so naïve.

– I'm not the Oracle, she said, a bit pulled back. – She might be found in the Green Rose in Main Street.

– What are you then? Doris lent eagerly forward. – Who?

– I… The name others gave me is Jill Stafford. My sister is Moonstar. She casts light in the dreary night. I'm Raven. I cast shadow in the ruthless daylight.

Her eyes turned distant for a moment, as if she was watching something far away. She seemed to ponder a bit, before once more turning towards Doris.

– Come. Come with me. She reached out her hand. The older woman took it.

At one time the voice had been stranger than ever. Doris pondered. Almost as if there had been two talking simultaneously.

Raven led her deeper into the tent. The tent seemingly so small seen from the outside. She realized startled that they moved through something that had to be a passageway, a tunnel. There were no walls. At least she was unable to see any. The passage wasn't long, but it led them… away. Instantly they arrived in another room, a room that couldn't be inside the tent. Doris felt drowsy, light, as if she was dreaming and levitated through… through the Void. A huge room, without boundaries. It might end somewhere, but there were no walls (even though the walls had pictures). Certainly not. A dark place, brightening ever so little after a few seconds. Within its boundaries, far away, close by Doris could just make out three-dimensional circular, transparent shapes floating in the air and within them images constantly shifting and changing. By this table sat a young girl, a child. Doris recognized her. A child, in appearance, but a second glance, below the surface suggested otherwise. Doris stopped before her.

– I'm Oracle. Enter willingly and without fear, the child greeted her, – and know that you're welcome.

– This woman is in need of your talents, Dreamweaver, Jill said formally.

– Of course, Raven, the girl nodded, gesturing to Doris. – Come and sit down.

Doris put one foot ahead of the other, moving forward. Feet sank into mist, but reached solid ground (or at least something resembling it). She sat down in the chair, a chair appearing out of nothing. Raven remained standing.

Oracle pushed her elbows at her sides, reaching out with her palms. The air shifted and moved, and changed. One of the many floating balls started to pulsate slightly, to glow, as it sank towards the table and it expanded as its descent stopped between the girl's palms, now turned 45 degrees. The ball grew until it reached the palms on both sides, now clearly resembling a crystal ball.

– Touch it, Doris heard in the distance.

– What? She had to blink, like in the morning after a long night's sleep.

– *Touch it. With both hands. Not hard, but hard enough to feel it push against your skin.*

She did as she was told. Merely that act alone, between everything else here was indeed a strange experience. The mist-like, indistinct surface on the smooth ball had a kind of sticky solidity. But every time it pulsated, when the misty forms within moved too fast to be seen, it was as if… it wasn't there at all.

– *You can remove them now. Lean back in the chair. Watch, listen, feel.*

The faster than light movements slowed down. An image appeared. A bedroom, two people, one man and one woman, in a hot embrace. More than an embrace. One rough, primitive, but loving. Doris reddened from head to toe.

– This is one of your many possible futures, Jill Stafford told her. – It may become reality, if you truly want it to be.

– I do, I do, Doris said out of breath. – What must I *do?*

Raven stretched her hand into the dark void. A cup of wood appeared in her hand.

– Give blood.

Ravenhair grabbed her wrist and placed the cup under it. Doris felt a sharp pain. Blood flowed into the cup, filled it to the brim, fast as a river. Doris looked terrified at the huge wound and feared that all her blood would flow away before the wound closed. Then the strong, brown hand started to pale… to glow. The hammering pain was supplanted by one sharp and sweet, then that, too, disappeared. Doris pulled stricken the hand to her. There remained not a single mark.

Jill drank of the cup. Then she passed it on to the other witch, the child-witch. The girl hesitated a bit, before drinking with eyes filled with trust. Both painted their lips with the blood.

– But… do you dare?

– You're healthy as a fish, Jill said. – As a wild mare.

The image in the crystal ball shifted and changed again, to an office. A man took a woman from behind. The same man, another woman. Both were as good as fully dressed. The woman stood there with her butt stuck up and her upper body sprayed over a desk.

– That bastard, Doris exploded. – To fuck Whitney Clarke like… that… like he has never done with me.

The witches exchanged cheerful glances.

– This is something happening right now, the child-witch informed her somberly. – Do you still wish to fuck him?

– Fuck him? I'm gonna fuck that bastard to death, Doris swore both pissed and swallowing hard. – I'm not gonna let him out of the house until he's completely drained.

– It was something like that we, too, had in mind, Jill, Raven said cheerfully.

The image shifted once more. An apartment this time. Doris recognized it as the one she shared with her husband. She saw something on the living room table she didn't recognize. A large cup, so beautiful that it took her breath away. It twinkled and glowed and pulsed.

– Is it there now? she asked in awe.

– It will be, Jill said. – Its content you will mix in the food and the wine in the opulent meal you will prepare for your mate, the meal you'll enjoy together. I guarantee mindless fucking for the next three days.

Doris already sensed heat spread all over her body in a way it hadn't done for years.

– W-what do you require in return?

– Once, somewhere, sometime, you'll return the favor. The girl spoke from her throat and the voice seemed hollow. – What we ask of you won't be impossible for you to do. We have drunk your blood. You're tied to us forever.

She's only a child, Doris thought unfounded. But when I look at her and she at me I'm the child.

– You will be Changed, you will Change. Nothing will be as it was, or has been.

The nude woman, dancing full of life in the forest shade was clearly different. Her cheerful schooldays were merely a faint echo of what she saw herself as in the crystal ball. She attempted in vain to observe Frazer Hill, the Hill there in the background, the Unknown, the forbidden… so tempting…

– I'm prepared, she said bravely.

The crystal ball… Christ… that she at all could imagine something like this, a dream… like distant butterfly wings. She heard the flapping of dark wings, imagined them on the back of the Raven standing above her. The dream, the reality rose in the air, shrinking to the size it had previously, expanding to fill the room, her own mind, previously so small, so vast now.

She noticed, could not help but noticing the close contact between the witches. They communicated without words. The girl rose and walked from her chair, from behind her seat.

– Come. Follow Those Who Fill the Darkness and be Reborn.

Another passage, another path, through shadow, through fire. She sensed it wasn't the same she had walked earlier. What did it matter? Often the thought came to her that they hadn't really moved at all, that everything had happened in her head, that this was a place where everything happened in Thought. A shadow path stretching an infinite distance ahead.

Very, very conscious as she was of her surroundings, she sensed more than she saw how the «ground» itself under her feet changed. For every step she took

– So bright…

everything changed. An image before her… then more… seemed to grow out of the air itself. Everything she had learned so far in her life, what she had been taught had no meaning here. Had it any meaning, anywhere?

She once more felt the weight of the body, its full weight. They stood in the middle of a cluster of green grass, in a wide, withered area. Somewhere ahead a young boy, nude under the sun and their glance, stood a step within the circle of tree stumps. He didn't move, clearly in deep meditation.

– A boy, full of life's fire, Jill said. Mystical, wonderful Jill. – A Phoenix merely waiting for the spark lighting his flame.

– He'll follow you home afterwards, the girl giggled and seemed almost human. – He will be eager to do everything for you, slave for you, to be allowed access between your tight thighs.

This is the starter, the first course. Young, uncomplicated joy. She heard the voice inside her head, and it didn't worry her half as much as it once would have done. *Enjoy it, it will dissolve your tight and sore knots and what follows will set you free.*

The two *witches* left her. They turned around and disappeared the same way they had come, into thin air. They faded away, already a distant memory and when she for a moment wanted to follow them there was nothing there, except air, grass and ground.

Head, eyes and body turned towards the boy. He hadn't discovered anything yet, discovered her. She smiled and her feet led her to him. She loosened her hair, the stiff hair. She removed her clothes, clothes stiff for so very long. Shoes were kicked off and she felt the ground under her. The female entered the circle, cast a glance at the cabin, and smiled expectantly, before directing her complete attention at the young David. So stiff he was, so needy, so very needy.

She spoke to him.

Hester looked at her watch for the umpteenth time. She observed people come and go from the tent, but no Doris.

– What are they dawdling over in there? She asked irritated and stared up at Everett Moran.

– I can't say how long time they'll use, Hester, he said shaking his head (his hairy head). – It might take the entire day. The most sensible you can do is to go home. I'm sure Doris will have a whole lot to tell you when you meet again.

Hester snorted and left. But she didn't leave the place. She wandered around, lurking between the stalls all day and hardly took her eyes from the tent. Armed with her (in)famous evil eye she checked it out from all possible sides. Doris didn't come out and neither did the witch.

The number of people dwindled around the stalls. Light faded and lost its power. Sky darkened. Hester kept close. Stalls and tents were disassembled, packed and carried off. She hid while Everett and the Amazon did their own disassembling, packing and carrying. No one could at any time hide in the thin roll of tent and everything was… empty where the tent had been assembled. She ran to the place and started digging in helpless frustration. Nothing.

Dust drifted just above the ground, around her feet. Otherwise… nothing. Hester had hands dug into her hair and looked about her with an insane expression in her eyes. She stayed thus. She remained on the spot for a long time.

5

The school's education area usually remained silent and abandoned during the evening. The laboratories and the department for natural science, too. Except for one room. If one looked carefully, one might be able to spot a light in there. Then again, it could just as well be the reflection from the city or somewhere else. Two of the teachers occupied the deep corner of the room. The younger, Felix West connected the gathered, advanced video player with the equally advanced computer equipment. Lights of artificially stored knowledge came to life, illuminated the room and created the strange effect seen from the outside. West pushed a disk into the player. He rested a finger a moment on the play-button before pushing it. The disk played. No words were exchanged.

The recording started with the two processions meeting by the mound. West had heard the sounds of Ivan Silvestri's drum and been lucky enough to be able to observe what happened. As a moderate scholar in occultism and rituals he recognized the scene below. He had seen similar ceremonies during visits to primitive tribes and people.

He sat behind an almost closed window a considerable distance away from the action. The entire area had been cast in darkness and only the powerful lanterns in Stacy Larkin and Jill Stafford's hands made it possible to see anything. Sometimes the image turned fuzzy because of too much use of zoom and subsequent bad focusing, but usually there were no problems seeing what was happening. He didn't have a sufficiently powerful directional microphone at hand and therefore he heard merely fractions of what was being said. Everything he could discern, though, was immensely interesting to an amateur anthropologist like himself. Sometimes during quiet moments down there, he supplied his own comments. The lights from the lanterns faded or were put out. Hissing sounds were heard in the dark and the night. He felt a cold trickle down his spine. He really did. At first, he couldn't believe it. He had always thought it was a myth. Something seemed to move very fast through the air. Then someone lit the beacon. He backed off and almost dropped his camera. The fire grew and cast its sharp light over the cold landscape.

Time had passed, he had no idea of how much, when Victoria Arness undressed. A fertility ritual, *here*. His throat dry as sand he hardly managed to shake his head. Four had undressed now, completely nude, walking forward, displaying themselves for the circle. Something *happened*. Ropes of a sort tied themselves… were tied around ankles, wrists and necks. The four were painted and decorated, made pleasing to whatever god waited in the wings. He had to shake his head again. This happened here, in a modern city, in the twenty-first century. And the participants were educated, highly intelligent people, though young, but still…

The drumming started up again. An unbelievable loud choir filled the air, his inner ears. In the darkness, between the turning off of the lanterns and the lighting of the fire, *what had he seen?*

The videotape revealed nothing of consequence. The two men stared at it all the six times they viewed it. They saw Travis Nichols use an even stronger lantern and direct it at the sky. They saw Olivia Norman make her failed attempt to penetrate the circle. People pushed her back, in quick brutal anger. They saw the orgy begin and the ball of fire rise from the grounded flame and up in the air, where it exploded in a violent expression of energy.

– Some performance. West strived to hold on to a cool professionalism.

– Indeed. Anton Berkowitz didn't have to go out on a limb to agree wholeheartedly. – Whether they're taking advantage of a random, natural phenomenon or have planned it all from beginning to the end. Laurie managed to teach them well before taking off.

They kept silent for a while, still kind of overwhelmed.

– They're clever. West kept shaking his head. – They convinced everybody present.

– They're dangerous, Berkowitz stated emphatically. – And they must be exposed. We must proceed with caution, though. They've already become a considerable, unofficial force in this city. Before we strike, we must be covered on all sides. We must have in our possession undeniable evidence of their fraud and how they're seducing this city's youth.

– It's strange, the younger man said tentatively. – Their influence has increased after Laurie's death, not decreased.

– Only apparently so. They're vulnerable now and if I'm correct forces are conspiring against them at this very moment. The foul heathens will get their due punishment and we can publish our material without risk and forever mark them as frauds.

Anton Berkowitz looked very pleased with himself. West had to admit that the fanatical light in the other's eyes bothered him a bit.

A bit…

6

Dreams. A dream. She understood that instantly now. A Witch she was, a legendary Sorceress for whom no gates were closed. *Images.* Some had no more substance than a flickering thought, while other incidents in time and space had left a lasting impression. She wandered in a churchyard, the one in Oldtown, by Deep River. She realized she had been there before. Jill had never been there before, but she would be. This was her future (how could she know). Her hair… the style was different.

She was older, she sensed that (therefore she knew). Perhaps not many days in actual age, but a lot measured in knowledge, in what might be deemed wisdom. The door to a burial chamber stood ajar. The black within compelled and repulsed her. She walked inside.

She crossed the same churchyard, but it didn't look the same… now. All the statues, the sculptures worn down, downtrodden at the start of the third millennium, so new… now. The door to the crypt stood wide open.

Via Appia, Rome. *The first Christians hanged crucified in endless rows, further than the eye could see.* Jill crouched like a fetus, floating passively through the air. She recognized this scene, too. She was here, hanging on the cross in the searing heat. Caesar Nero had burned the city and blamed her and her fellow suffering martyrs. Why did people believe him? How could they?

She re-experienced her own history that was also an important part of recent human history. But… why only suffering and death? Was there nothing else? Generosity instead of cruelty, something beautiful in contrast to all the horrible? Or was she drawn to all the bad as the legendary Pariah? Or did she learn more that way? Perhaps she had to learn. The subconscious, the third eye was a bottomless well of information and creativity.

Rome. Nero was dead, the support for his beliefs shattered. The people of Rome embraced Christianity. Perhaps not immediately, but inevitably. She stood in the high halls of power with other servants of the One God. As One they watched him ascend the stairs below. The Living God honored them with his presence.

Lillith wandered the Shadow World, her spirit floating above land and sea. She observed two young lovers by a pond. She saw them grow old. A quiet, peaceful life, a short respite from the Storm.

She floated above a dry, ragged landscape. By the foot of the mountain a man levitated high above the ground, above a kneeling crowd. He spoke furiously to them. Jill heard the name they whispered in fear and awe: Zarathustra. This was the old Persia, close to three thousand years before the present.

– … *and one day the One God, Ahura Mazdah will return to judge the living and the dead…*

Zarathustra - the Prophet. She had read about him. A person with an enormous influence on recent humanity. His teaching about duality (Good and Evil) and his prophecies about Judgment Day had spread to Judaism and from there to Christianity and to Islam. Judgment Day, the final hour, when all sinners, supporters of foreign religions should be punished and Ahura Mazdah should reward all his faithful worshippers by granting them a place in his just and shining kingdom, the eternal Heaven.

The man didn't have his eyes directed at his subjects. He seemed to look directly at her, and it dawned on Lillith that he was truly doing so. In a flash she was even further back in time, when he gave her the knife and she used it to stab the little, defenseless girl. He saw her and read her like an open book and a triumphant smile crossed his features. Her presence confirmed his success. He knew that he would be close at succeeding, that three thousand years from now his grip on the world would be very close to how he desired it: Total.

She recognized him, the old and the young man. Ahura Mazdah, Zarathustra, the man she had spotted in the Norwegian mountains, the Dollmaster, Yahweh, *Jahavalo.*

Smile turned threatening and then, by the thought of the last name it vanished completely.

Lillith fled.

7

Jill found it strange to once again experience the wind in her face. It felt so long ago.

On the brightest day she, Stacy, Gabi and Loeh wandered around inside Churchyard. It didn't take them long to locate the particular door, crypt. The door was closed and locked. She unlocked it easily enough with her mind, she hardly needed to concentrate. The door slid open. She did feel something as they entered the crypt, but just a flicker, a tiny part of something much bigger. There was nothing inside. None of them sensed anything.

The door itself, though, had ancient carvings and symbols on it. They seemed strangely familiar and such realizations no longer surprised her. The intimate tingling each time she encountered something from her Total Recall.

– For a place I've never been it looks very much like one I remember, she said, satisfaction very present in her voice.

– Yes, Stacy agreed, very full of herself.

They left withered flowers and dry soil. For a while they wandered along the river, certainly not deep anymore.

– Strange, I had expected to feel more in a cemetery. Jill raised a brow.

– Everything has usually happened to people before they're put in the grave, Stacy pointed out.

She waved cheerfully and left them, setting course for the school.

– What's going on? Jill asked sarcastically. – Have you suddenly become duty-bound and eager to absorb their absorbing teaching?

– Just a small errand… She waved again. The secretive smile was in place. – I'll be back…

– I don't understand her, I really don't, Jill said a while later.

Loeh hesitated a bit.

– She has two heads and four eyes. A nervous glance at Jill. – That's her secret.

Jill pondered this, later, while being alone. Impossible as it was to avoid noticing it, she had noticed the brush of insecurity and fear in Loeh's voice and demeanor. Stacy could be frightening, but this…

Suddenly her feet… tickled. She looked at them, looked incredulous as green, fresh rope-like branches crawled up her feet and thighs. Just seconds later it had tied itself around her upper body and lifted her up in the air. It tied itself so tight she feared she would black out. She concentrated on even breathing while waiting patiently.

Kieron appeared in her view. He grinned skewed at her.

– I have you now. To get out of this you either have to harm the plants or me, and I don't think you'll do that.

She concentrated slightly and more than that slight effort wasn't necessary for her to take control over the plants. They put her respectfully back down on the ground and pulled back in a very respectful hurry.

She replied to his silent query:

There is nothing you all can do that I can't do better.

He ran off like a scared rabbit. She didn't feel sorry for him.

She had so much anger inside. Where did it all come from? Did it originate with the world itself or was it something more personal? One incident or several? The most probable was a kind of combination. Something had happened, something she was unable to recall. She had had dreams about it since she was twelve. The memory felt so close, but every time she went for it, it slipped away, returned to the murkier parts of her mind.

And she hadn't been angry just now. On the contrary. She had been deadly calm, cold, relaxed, efficient and that terrified her possibly even more. She found herself inside the circle of mushrooms behind Frazer Hill, shaking in rage, fear and despair.

All her pent-up aggression combined and exploded in a violent outburst. Stacy, on the other side of the Hill, was struck down. Jill's face of Fury appeared above her.

– *You're hiding something,* Jill spat. – *I want to know what. You will tell me everything you know.*

– You've come far, Raven, my compliments. Stacy rose, with her sarcastic smile intact, cold, relaxed. – Yet you've still no idea how little we've developed of our potential. Tell me, what will you do if I refuse to obey the Queen's Royal command? Will you *punish* me? Let me pay for my insubordination?

The face sobered and started to fade.

– *You're not yet ready,* Stacy said. – *You will be.*

Then she broke contact. Jill fell down in the smoldering grass in the circle, exhausted and more frustrated than ever.

Stacy sharpened her concentration slightly, turned and sought Loeh. There, *contact.* It was time. From this moment on she would never let her go. Loeh didn't notice anything. Neither did anyone else. Stacy, though, could easily register the other girl's constant worry. It had been there for a while, not subsiding. Stacy had chased the game long enough. Time to take it down.

Darkness set, once more a bit sooner than the previous day. Branches bent and were pushed aside by the chasing hunter in the forest. Stacy approached the tavern. There had been a red streetlight in front of the building. Someone had changed it to a green. Eyes lurked in the charcoal night. Stacy smiled and walked inside. She had waited long enough. Other witches in the room waved to her. Loeh did, too, but not very enthusiastic or convincing. The sharp-eyed Voodoo-priestess knew too much about many things and that was the reason she had to be subdued first. One of the reasons anyway.

Stacy walked directly to the bar. The glass with Guinness beer stood there, ready for her. She raised the glass to her lips in a mocking salute and took a huge sip. She swallowed the fat, tasty fluid and it quenched her dry throat. She was fully conscious of her position in the room. She dominated it. She dominated everybody present. They knew she was one of the four, one destined to rule. They knew… almost as clear as she did herself. She drank the glass empty. Alcohol weakened a witch's power, but not hers.

Neither Jill nor Jason nor Everett was present. Loeh had almost always kept close to at least one of them, but not now. She had believed herself safe here. Stacy had put that idea in her mind. And she was never far from Loeh's thoughts. Loeh feared her on the verge of panic. She was so frightened that she dared not show it.

Loeh couldn't take her eyes off the raven in the corner of her eye. Her vision seemed to turn misty. Sometimes Stacy seemed to close in on her, while she the next moment wasn't there at all. Loeh jumped to her feet with a beating heart. She went to the bathroom with fast, fluttering steps. Stacy remained by the bar, so very relaxed. Henriette Gallier closed the door hard behind her and started running. She chased by the toilets and continued towards the exit.

Stacy blocked her way. Henriette wished she could scream. She stopped, staring blindly and paralyzed at the terrifying creature.

– *You belong to me, Mambo. Have no fear. I intend to make good use of you.*

– I'll burn you… burn me… swear…

– *… no fear… relax… assured that I won't have any of that. From this moment you'll never light your fire without my permission.*

Come with me, child.

Her will left her, as she obeyed, as she heard nothing else than the insistent voice it didn't occur to her to resist. She saw nothing but the lucid face, like a sun illuminating the darkness of the condemned. Where were they headed? Oh, yes, she brightened. A place where they could be undisturbed. A sofa, they sat on a sofa. The mist cleared and the rest of the room slowly appeared in her vision. She focused on Stacy. It seemed that that was all she was able to do.

– I can't move. Lips moved slowly and she had trouble making the sounds sufficiently comprehensible and loud.

– Of course not. You're not supposed to. You will sit perfectly still while I operate blind obedience and loyalty to me in you. I've decided that you shall be my maid, the first of my many enthusiastic servants.

Take my hand.

– No, no, no… no… The mumbling lost its power after the first attempt, and she obeyed the irresistible voice.

Stacy pushed her free hand against the other's face. Fingers at the forehead, palm at the full lips.

It began, a vibration skin to skin. Loeh experienced a horrible weakness spreading both in body and mind and moaned from a soulless darkness.

Stacy turned the key in the door as an afterthought.

The energy flowed into her. She held the prey's hand to the mouth and sank her teeth in it. Dark brown skin broke like a thin membrane of a fruit and blood flowed. It tasted salt and delicious, delicious. The sorceress licked her lips and let her head bend backwards. She felt great. Everything… cleared. The Power, her inheritance expanded within and without and inside the mind of the prey, where she was headed for the core. Defenses were bypassed easily. She didn't smash them, but quite simply removed them. In spite of the fear Loeh's inner being wasn't paralyzed. She fought the intruder with every ounce of her considerable power and skill. It wasn't even remotely sufficient. She hadn't overestimated the danger, but badly underestimated it. She fought with a desperate stubbornness, but gave in inch by inch before the overwhelming Power of the creature invading her entire being.

You're good. That's great. You'll be a great trophy.

Stacy had visited people's inner mind before. It resembled the Shadow World, but was less random, more focused. She was bombarded by energy, impressions. She easily rejected all of it. If she had been overwhelmed, Loeh could have gained control of *her*, but there was no contest, only conquest. The Storm quieted and Stacy reached Henriette Gallier's Core.

This was the image Loeh had of herself. Her Self was strong, just like Stacy had expected. Stacy had merely weakened it marginally with the initial softening.

The Astral Form, everything Stacy was and more, floated through the landscape of Loeh's memories. The streets in the French Quarter in New Orleans, where she had grown up. The nocturnal ceremonies where she had been initiated as Mambo - Voodoun's priestess. Stacy circled the forest where she could glimpse what she sought, the Self, the girl's All. But she couldn't reach it. She had to. Or her control would never be more than superficial. She circled and circled, as she continued her search.

A man, a counselor treated her badly. Stacy easily sensed the shaking in the surroundings. He had struck a serious blow to her confidence, but this wasn't what Stacy sought. Loeh had prevailed against the man's attacks and perhaps been strengthened by them, after liberating herself from his influence. Stacy knew she had to probe deeper, far deeper. Incident after incident in a mutant's life passed by in her world of the mind. Stacy wondered how much people actually remembered of such memories. They never disappeared, but they faded, for many reasons, from the upper consciousness.

Heartbeat. Rapid, like in a mouse captured by a cat. The shaking in the surroundings turned to visible fear. Sky darkened. Stacy smiled.

GO AWAY Awayayay*...

A final act of defiance, but with a simple thought Stacy kept it from expressing itself.

Your resistance is even less than expected. You have always secretly yearned for this, freedom from choices and responsibilities. I will capture your «Ti bon ange» and you'll be my devoted slave.

There was more than one way to go, choices to the inevitable end. Stacy took her time in her final search... There... she felt something crucial. Yes, that was *perfect.* Her smile broadened.

A scene formed by the small forest. A little girl stood crying behind a gate while her mother left her without looking back. Perhaps it had happened like that, perhaps not, but little Henriette remembered it that way.

– MOTHER! She screamed howling. – Please, come back, MOTHER.

She remained alone, completely alone.

Stacy slipped into the image of the tall, distant woman, and turned and walked back. She opened the gate, and the joy-filled child ran into her open arms.

– Mother, the little girl sniffed.

– Mother, Henriette gasped in Stacy's embrace.

A broad, bright path formed into the woods. All hurdles vanished.

– Hush, Stacy whispered into a sore ear, while softly caressing tangled hair. – Don't despair, you'll always be with me, little *Cha.*

Henriette Gallier stiffened like a doll for a moment, and then she turned very, very pliable. She moaned in helpless despair, hopelessness.

– P-please, she begged. – Don't proceed any further. You don't need to. I'll be obedient, serve you in all things. I surrender to your mercy, Mistress.

– You should have thought about the consequences when you chose to oppose me, Stacy Larkin said in a crushing blow. – It's too late now. I've already bound you to me by unbreakable bonds and I'll never let you go, beautiful *Cha.*

Stacy grabbed the other's lucky charm, the totem amulet around her neck and pulled hard. The leather necklace broke and she held it up in triumph, crushed it in her hand. Loeh cried out in raw, deep pain.

– I'll take care of this. I'll make a fine, new one you can carry around your neck, the visible sign that you belong to me fully and completely.

Stacy grew to a giant in Loeh's inner world. The giant lifted her up to an open mouth. Stacy knew that she could devour Cha now, forever disintegrate her personality, but she wasn't interested in an empty shell. Instead, she chained everything that was Henriette Gallier to herself with unbreakable chains.

– Your wishes, Mistress? Henriette mumbled and mumbled. – Your wishes, Mistress? WisheswisHESWIShes

– We will come back to that, child. She rocked the crouching form back and forth. – Come to me, my child, let me nourish you.

She exposed one of her breasts and led Loeh's mouth to it. Loeh held her eyes closed. The pouting mouth found the nipple and the child started sucking. There was nothing sexual about the scene, but rather something sinister beyond words.

– You're mine and you'll be an obedient and devoted child. I'll protect you and teach you, give you direction in life. Sleep now. When you wake up, you'll be reborn to a life in my service.

Stacy looked at the wall, smiling slightly. She had no need to look at Henriette to see her, see the glow surrounding her. She felt heartbeats, ancient drums, ancient ages in the child's body and her own. It was good. She frowned. They were like children, all of them. She had to teach and lead them. They had to learn. What she had started so long ago had to continue. They were like putty in her hands, but even more they would be so in *his*. She sharpened her concentration… and then she dreamt Loeh.

8

Jill sat up inside the circle. She had slept. The enormous expense of power had made her fall asleep of pure exhaustion. But the rest had been well spent. She felt fine now. Actually, she felt good. She rose effortlessly. Limbs felt supple and muscles vigorous.

The sense of danger, urgency descended on her from out of the deep, threatening dark. She gasped in horror. It dawned on her that it had been there all the time. She had dreamt something, but couldn't for the life of her remember what. Eyes, senses pointed her eastward. She let the body follow in a frantic, powerful run. The lights from Oldtown soon surrounded her. It was as if she had brought the city to her, instead of bringing herself to the city.

A woman on a hill was dancing on a twilight day. Dark, long hair covered her face and a lot of her body. Dancing, calling down the sky, raising up the earth.

Jill found herself in the city. With people around her on all sides she had to concentrate, concentrate hard to not become overwhelmed by their thoughts. Tam, always eagerly at her service, waited outside the Green Rose. Raven was always in contact with her on a fundamental level. But now she needed her physical presence. She needed protection provided by her chosen bodyguard.

Ivan sat inside Square and played the guitar. A pack of known and unknown people sat in a circle around him. The shaman-drum stood by his side. He never went anywhere without it. Good. She nodded. So, she had seen it and so should it be.

– I want you to beat the drum, she told him. *Now,* she sent.

He nodded slowly and put away the guitar. He smiled to the others as he offered his excuses, something that was totally unnecessary. Eyes twinkled in interest all over the place.

– Yes, stay, Raven ordered them, as the moonlight was reflected in her eyes. – I want you all to dance, dance your mind and reason away.

She sat down in front of Ivan. A nod from her, a nod from him and he began beating the drum. One of the first beats was deep and spread through the Earth to all those who had started swaying and moving their feet. Sound filled the old city streets and spread far beyond them. Many people not hearing it with their ears heard it still. Tam joined the ring of dancers. Dance turned wilder, more instinctive. The released violent energy strengthened Jill. She bathed in it, and she knew that this time there would be no problems Traveling. She sat with her legs crossed and rocked back and forth a while until her movements slowly stopped and she sat still. It started to twitch in the corner of her eyes. Her reality split in two and three and four… and five… What she saw with her eyes didn't change, but she noticed things she couldn't see with her eyes. Little spaces in white turning black. The black turned glowing white. Colors increased in numbers and variations. The sound of the drum was the only constant in a veritable buzz of sounds. Reality on the edge of consciousness slowly but surely became the dominant. Surroundings turned indistinct. Whirling legs and arms changed to patterns of energy.

Everything turned dark and silent. She rose. The city was here still, but quite unfamiliar compared to the one she knew. It belonged even less in the twentieth century than Oldtown did. She looked towards Newtown, and it wasn't there. She found herself in a small village, a settler's township, Northfield in its first years. The sound of drums reached her, and she sat the course towards them. Transfer happened instantly. She cast a glance at the schoolyard. She knew there was one, even if she couldn't see it. She saw the Witchdance, men and women of various ages moving within the circle, joyously wild and undisciplined.

Surroundings shifted again. She shifted them. She could steer her Journey, now and in addition to her own power she bathed in that from those dancing in the circle surrounding her unmoving body. They had all seen what wasn't matter rise from Jill's body and a sound had escaped from the depth of them all. Those who saw it for the first time were filled with both awe and fear. A few ran away like scared rabbits. The dance continued.

The young girl dancing in the whirling circle froze. She saw the specter hovering over her. For a brief moment their eyes met. Jill moved inside her, was her, knew everything she knew, what she already knew, what she had always known. And Northfield wasn't Northfield anymore, not even the settler's township, but something far older. For a very brief moment in time Jill saw a city, not exactly a city, a place old as time, before being yanked away.

The dance stopped. All the others bowed down before the girl, Vyla. The first, the second, the third Vyla? Like the two first wearing that name she was doomed to die, to burn in agony and tears and rage.

Jill thrust herself further on her Journey, looking for whatever she was looking for… so important to remember. Wind raged around her. She experienced it as real, so real that she was swaying for a short moment. Then she found herself in another woman's body, in a Norwegian mountain valley. Long before Olav the Cruel emerged on the stage. Even before the god-kings. And it was real. She could feel, taste, smell… *remember.* Jill had heard people say if there was really anything like reincarnation it had to be a terrible thing. Each new life, each new memory, each earlier life remembered had to lead to ever more dissolution of the personality, one's Self. Such an idea didn't in any way pass muster. The more Jill remembered the stronger her sense of identity became. Instead of dissolution there was enrichment.

But whatever she sought she didn't find here. Somewhere in Time and Space something existed that could bring relief to what haunted ever-larger parts of her life. What was the rush? The smoldering anger made her move on. A mystery leading her to the edge of the Abyss.

She stood by a bridge, an old, derelict bridge. It stretched from the high mountain cliff and far into the mist, into *Muspelheim.* She walked on a bridge. Muspelheim stretched into infinity, eternity before her. She walked and walked, but got nowhere. The mists of time prevented her further Journey. More power. She needed more from the whirling feet, the sweaty bodies. She wasn't worried about taking too much from them, not as long as they didn't touch her physically. But it was pure crystalline rage that made the mist dissolve and brought her further. She howled in fury and impotence as the mist solidified into a wall. She floated in the air above the Salisbury-plain, above the stone-circle Stonehenge, in both new and old times. She observed an endless row of slave labor pulling the large, heavy stones. She returned to the Norwegian mountains. Jahavalo hadn't arrived there yet, but he would.

Whirling feet slowed down, until the first dancers fell to the ground, completely exhausted. The circle broken the Journey ended. Jill rose easy enough. She didn't have to use her hands. Something she could dedicate to both her recent physical and mental prowess. It made her feel good. Her eyes sought among the tired, but happy and laughing dancers. Children, most of them were like children. Innocent, naïve, helpless.

Through an opening in the circle Loeh appeared. She walked inside and walked to Raven's side. In her hands she held out a cup of smoking brew. Raven could easily smell its content well before she saw the hot, boiling blood. The cup was half empty. She accepted the offering and swallowed every drop in one gulp. Greedily she sucked the content into her mouth. She needed strength and it spread to her entire being giving away a smoldering heat. The torches in Square flickered, and then the flames rose, taller than ever.

She had no need to look around with her sparkling clear vision. She saw herself through a dozen pair of eyes, glowing, aware, ready and it was like sunbathing on the hottest of summer days. Energy, everything was energy.

Life's fire had hardly been anything but embers for many years, for centuries. It had hibernated an eternity in the valley of the shadows of death, while awaiting the kiss of awakening. The torches in Oldtown burned down. The bonfires shrunk. Most of the party-animals returned to their dens. But the fire was kept alive. It would never more be embers.

Never again!

9

She was back in the Asteroth home, its attic, the girl's bedroom, her aerie. Everything had turned cold and wet. She couldn't understand it. Everything had turned ugly. She had thought she had put it behind her. Gabrielle attacked her with her full, unrestrained, irresistible power and she was frozen, frozen. She hung there, suspended in the lifeless Nothing, while her body and mind weakened. Eyelids grew heavy, limbs grew heavy. The cold penetrated beyond her skin, paralyzing her. She hung there, unable to move, unable to think. Suddenly the Monster appeared in front of her. She couldn't recall having seen the little girl move from the bed, but suddenly she was close, so frighteningly close. Fear gripped her. She wanted to scream, but couldn't utter a single sound. The emerging panic felt dull, useless. She was at the girl's mercy, God help her, help her, help help help

– Welcome to my aerie, Little Jill. Gabrielle spoke in a hoarse and spiteful tone. – I'm so glad you decided to visit me. I don't want you to ever leave.

Jill stared at her in horror. That was all she could ever do.

A little move with her hand and Jill started turning, slowly, round and round and round. Jill knew she turned as she could feel the centrifugal force, but she couldn't see anything except the demonic face.

– You know what… merely your presence… is strengthening me, making me think in ways that never before occurred to me. Let's see now…

Another wave and the turning body stopped. And then the captive could only watch in horror as tendrils, tentacles started growing out of the girl's body stretching towards her. Her entire body shook as they attached themselves to her legs, arms and head. And then, instantly they started sucking, draining away vitality, heat and Life. The Monster started glowing and the wide, ecstatic smile made her face even more demonic. And then… she grew horns on her forehead. Flakes of skin loosened from Little Jill's body, and she couldn't scream, not even in her mind, as the pain became her being, the only life left of her.

The tendrils pulled back, all the way into Gabrielle's body, but she had Changed in dramatic ways. She looked older, but worst of all was the horrible expression in her eyes, of intelligence and cunning.

– I could just dispose of you now. It would be easier than scratching my cheek. But I don't know if you were aware of this, but you're like a living battery. And don't worry. I'll bring a lot of outlets you can recharge on, and I will be able to recharge on you for all Eternity. And don't worry. You'll soon enough forget your old life, in favor of the endless one in my service.

She turned slightly, waving her hand and a huge, dark gate opened in the wall. Jill floated through it, followed by Asteroth, the Queen, the terrible and omnipotent Queen.

Using only seconds with no more effort than it would have taken her to snap her fingers the Queen created a throne-room, a dark and mighty hall worthy of her statute.

– I know that this isn't very appealing to you right now, but it will be, believe me. You will come to love it, to look forward to every moment of it.

A row of exhibition blocks grew up from the floor on the left side of the chamber. Queen Asteroth placed her on the first, closest to throne. The first of many she would store and raise from the living dead each time she needed them. Greek statues, tokens of her Power. Jill felt her limbs freeze even more, freeze completely as the demon finalized her work. All senses worked sort of, but she couldn't move, couldn't use anything, only passively receive. She was a statue, only a statue, serving her Queen's pleasure.

Jill woke up with a hammering heart. Happy awakening from a dream, from what she fervently desired was a dream. But could she ever be certain anymore, of anything? Was this only the demon toying with her, showing her the futility of her resistance and possibly everything happening since then a cruel trick? Had that truly been Gabi, sweet, kind (but dangerous) Gabi, or someone masquerading as Gabi in Jill's mind? Was it a memory, a premonition, what? She didn't know, but she would guess that many witches and all precognitives had problems occasionally deciding what was dream, what was reality.

Dreams. She knew that for most people it was exactly that feeling of being stuck. To her it had always been a sense of flying, of limitless Freedom. But now she was stuck and not for the life of her could she manage to grab hold of any of it. The more she reached for «it», whatever «it» was, the more it slipped away. The sense of being powerless was like a crushing blow. She cried hard and howled in her bottomless despair, but no one listened. They forced her to listen, giving her no pause, and she faded away until she just as well could be invisible and the scream from her depths never reached the mouth, and she was nothing but numb.

The Winds of Change (II)

Berlin August 16th 2005

Nicholas (Nick) Warren looked absolutely fabulous where he sat on the dark floor, as the light from the candles softly lit the room, shadowed the room. His shoulder-length black hair, his fireeyes and the words he spoke glowed within everybody present. The approximately thirty youths sitting there on the floor with him couldn't take their eyes away.

He didn't stand above them. He sat there, in their midst, speaking to them as equals. This was one of many similar meetings, held in relative secret, attended by the Warrens this year.

– None of us has so far gone far enough, he stated. – It's about time we did. We should never be afraid to go too far because in that way lies truth. There's a change in the earth and the sky… and *we* are making it happen.

He was rumored to be a hundred years old. Surely, he couldn't be, looking like he did. Afterwards, the only thing Sally Regehr actually recalled was many of the other girls, about to faint in his presence. She felt contempt for them, allowing themselves to disgrace themselves, *failing* him.

Several days later she, Peter and Lena sat back in a car headed for an unknown destination. They looked at each other, a bit surprised because they didn't wear blindfolds.

It didn't really matter. She saw nothing anyway, nothing but the goal in front of her.

They had left the car hours, days ago. He led them through thick forest. They had long since passed the moment of exhaustion, the point of no return. The sight before them, that of many men and women exercising and fighting, training with a lot of silent weapons made them shake their head. Not in denial, but in excitement, and the undeniable fear. The skill revealed made them gasp,

He stood just a bit in front of them, giving them his complete attention, bathing them in his heat. And they all knew that was incidental.

They were here, finally.

– Lena, Peter, Sally… welcome to Phoenix Green Earth.

CHAPTER FIFTEEN: The house on the (other) hill

She crouched in bed in her room at the school, sweating. The thin blanket she usually covered herself with lay folded by her feet. She was able to observe a drop of sweat form at the tip of her nose. Infinitely slow, like slow motion. Heart hammered as in frightened prey.

The door was kicked in, thrown off the hinges and flying into the room before settling in a cloud of dust between the beds. A crowd of monsters, both female and male stormed into the room. Tam jumped from the bed in full defense mode.

No, Jill sent, calming her down. *Not now.*

She had no idea where it came from, this ruthless rational ability to measure odds, to realize that the enemy had the upper hand. She had known before she saw all the guns pointing at them.

– Don't even think about doing any tricks, one of the police officers, a woman said hoarsely. – I assure you you'll *pay* for it.

Jill easily noticed the raging frustration, insecurity, the plump confidence behind most masks. They didn't really fear the collecting of these troublemakers would result in any trouble, but a slight fright lingered still. Their general confidence wasn't really that high.

They forced Tam down on the floor. Jill saw that in a flash before she herself felt hands painfully crush her limbs. Then they sprayed something in her face. *Teargas.* She coughed hard and her face was flooded in tears. Cold metal closed around her wrists, ankles and neck. *Bracelets and chains.* They weren't content with mere handcuffs. Bastards. *Bastards.*

– Cover them. Remember we're on a schedule here, people.

They were dragged on their feet and a simple poncho was slipped over their head. A cloth without arms, as made for use with chains.

– This is the worst I've seen, an officer cried out. – The entire room is crawling with illegal substances.

He held up a small plastic bag containing a white powder… cocaine. Jill wanted to open her mouth to speak, but she couldn't stop coughing.

– What I can't understand is how they've managed to hide it from the school's principals, a young, green officer wondered.

Somebody laughed. The boss looked hard at them. The laughter died.

– They have, of course brought it here tonight in the erroneous belief that it was safe.

Jill and Tam were harshly pulled on their feet and then dragged and pushed away. The familiar halls and hallways were in no way familiar anymore. They experienced it like descending into a nightmare. Jill realized that now, now, she had awakened. Reality was a slap in the face, a harsh snap of the whip.

There were two long rows of police officers there, standing rigid along the walls. The other students, the other witch-students got the same treatment as Jill and Tam. They were all being led away in chains. A few of the other students had fear written all over their face as they looked at it all from their safe rooms. Those among them who had shared room with a witch stayed in bed, unmoving and wide-eyed.

They didn't want to see what happened, but they couldn't avoid it.

The stairs suddenly seemed extra steep and threatening. They had all been chained hands and feet, but their keepers still pushed them brutally hard forward, downward and they fell and stumbled almost as much as they walked. Loeh hit her head on the wall with a damp sound they heard strangely well in all the noise. The police officers kicked and hit her a few times before it became clear even to them that she was unable to stand up or even move. One of the really big bruisers in uniform threw her on his shoulder and continued unabated. Jill wanted to help her, but the moment she broke the line she was dealt more than enough blows to make her stay in the place they had assigned her in the chain.

We can't put up with this. Whatever the consequences. When push comes to shove consequences don't count.

She waited for the anger to come, for it to once more rise above the paralyzing numbness, and it did. It sparked. Eyes were filled with hatred. All of them should burn. *Let them burn. Body and soul.* She concentrated on every uniformed person she could see. She had problems sensing them around her, but…

It didn't… work. Nothing happened. She concentrated. Her facial features contorted in rage and puzzlement. A sharp pain cut through her, cut deep. She howled and fell, bringing with her several others on her way down and they were laid out on the next level below, moaning in confusion and fear. They stared bewildered at each other. Jill fought to ignore the searing pain tearing her body apart. She read the same pain in the others' faces. Realization dawned slowly, as more uniformed servants joined them, bringing among others, Stacy. She had a swollen cheek. The newcomers joined the chain. The procession continued. Jill leaned her head on Stacy's shoulder. Because she needed support, badly, but also to come close to her.

– What's happening? She whispered. – What have they… done to us?

– It's the chains, you know that. Stacy said bitterly. – They're breaking, «short-circuiting» the energy in our body.

Numbness descended as a heavy, wet blanket on the rage, strangling it. All kinds of thoughts raced through her mind, none of which she could recall afterwards.

And she cursed herself for not fighting, come what may, when she had been able to.

As the girls arrived at the plaza, the boys, too, were pushed and pulled under threats and spiteful words and violence, to the waiting cars, in a parody of the ritual the witches had performed some nights earlier.

She sensed something then. Something tearing into her, tearing her apart. She gasped. The… Book… The Book of Shadows. Suddenly she had returned to her room. The book burst into flames, consuming itself and its environment like hellfire a cold winter night. She could see it through the desk, just before the desk disintegrated in a violent burst of Fire. The remaining policemen started burning, too. Then the room, then the corridor. Students ran nude from their rooms. Most of them escaped, but not all. As everyone down at the plaza stopped, as they all froze, flames erupted from the school's roof. Something *happened,* a tear in the fabric of reality, a change in the earth and the sky. What had been was no more. She SCREAMED as those forces cut into her. Something had Changed, irrevocably and she cried out in PAIN.

– Holy Mother of God, one of the uniformed men shouted. Several of them crossed themselves.

In less than a minute the building had been engulfed in flames. They heard distant sirens, closing in from the fire station not far away. Far too little, far too late. Some of the other students stood frozen, naked and vulnerable, looking at the completely unreal horrifying spectacle. Others just ran, scattered in all directions of the winds.

She and several other witches knelt on the ground, gasping for air, sweating and nauseous, weak as kittens.

The Book was gone. The Future was gone. She couldn't stop shaking her head, as she mumbled a denial, something intelligible.

– Okay, let's keep going, the boss, the seasoned pro barked.

Slowly, glassy eyed his crew grabbed the witches anew and with renewed anger and brutality pushed and pulled them off.

They were thrown like slabs of meat into the back of the vans, packed tighter than sardines in a can. Heavy doors cracked as they were closed and locked. Every single move felt like a strain. So hard to breathe. The close proximity they usually enjoyed, they usually found comforting now felt choking and horrible. This was the intention of their captors. They were supposed to suffer and burn forever.

Demonic carriages raced off, surrounded in exhaust, penetrating the walls to the defenseless inside the cages. They coughed and howled their plight, even if they knew very well that any prayer would find nothing but deaf ears. They saw nothing but blinking red and blue lights, all they heard was suffering. The blue smoke suffocated them, the red mist forced on them undesired thoughts of pain and blood. The four riders of the Apocalypse ravaged the land, boiled the sea. Jill pulled in her chains. She had twisted her body so much that the iron tightened around her throat and face. The more she struggled the more it hurt. She neither heard, saw, sensed in any way, smelled, tasted the others around her. Only silent, mumbling and threatening shadows…

Lillith screamed, HOWLED in misery and insanity.

She sat on a floor with her legs pulled up, the arms around her legs, the head pushed between her thighs. Gray and wet air surrounded her. She sat in a naked cell. Smooth floor, smooth walls, smooth ceiling. A place she couldn't reach, beyond the ceiling somewhere a lamp cast the gray, pale, dirty light at her. The chains *hurt*. Her entire body, the entire her hurt. There was no one else here. The loneliness had made her scream her throat raw. There could possibly be others in the neighboring cells, but she had no way of proving that to herself. And she needed that now. She needed it badly. Her eyes worked in a way, but not well. Nothing worked. All her senses had been torn from her. She crouched like a tiny animal in a cage. She had always been one. Frightened beyond words, paralyzed without any will of her own, will to move, even if the door should suddenly burst open.

She had to get up and get moving. Do something. Nothing moved. Not even fingers or lips. Black thoughts swallowed her, as if she fell through vast Space. Someone had thrown her into a deep, deep well and then forgotten everything about her. She fell to one side, stayed there on the floor, twitching and turning. It hurt, no matter what her position happened to be. Dozing. Sleeping. Even when awake. How long time had passed? How many hours, minutes, seconds since they had thrown her in here?

After a while she stayed in one position, on her belly and one cheek at the cold floor. The mouth pushed forth like a snout, paralyzed, half open. It was like being to the dentist. The entire side of the face was paralyzed. She couldn't move. How long she lay that way she had no way of telling. The door opened eventually. She hardly registered it when it happened. She heard feet dragging heavy boots and she felt pain when being kicked in her ribs.

– Get up, lazy bitch.

She stood up on shaky legs. It hurt, but getting kicked in the ribs hurt more. A hand grabbed her tight around an arm and dragged her away. Only a few steps outside the man holding her pushed her at the opposite wall and pulled a hood over her head. It covered it on all sides, down to the shoulders. The only hole was a small one, at the mouth, for her to breathe through. Another jerk and they dragged her further into the black world. She heard familiar voices around her, heard moaning and suffering. She wished that they had filled her ears with cotton, too, as they had filled her mind. Her power hadn't vanished completely, not the empathic aspects of it. She could sense people around her and general emotions from the man holding her. But that made everything worse. She got nothing from him but impressions from a mind filled with a dark basement of brutality, insecurity, mixed with contempt and a sick need to dominate. He enjoyed fully his own role in the scheme of things, both as participant and observer. He made her shake in the hot night. Was it night still? Yes, it had to be. Black, cold and without the slightest mercy. She cursed the fates, allowing her to keep her sensitivity. Why couldn't that have been taken from her, too, like everything else making her Special?

– Where are we going? She recognized the voice of one of the boys, but couldn't for the life of her remember his name.

He got beaten up badly, rewarded for his loose lip. Jill felt every hit as if they had hit her.

– You will shut your mouth, a man shouted brutally. – You will all keep your mouth shut, if you want to avoid major pain.

They were packed like sardines again, in something that had to be a big truck. Their hands forced above their head and chained to the wall in a horribly uncomfortable position. Placed very tight they couldn't really move, but only push uncomfortably at each other. How many were they? How many had been… taken? Surely not everybody? Some had to have escaped the snare, if just a few. So hard to think. Had they been given something to dull their minds? Their present guards differed from those who had captured them. These weren't police officers, at least not ordinary police officers. These people walked in higher spheres.

Mask had to be extra thick, especially around the eyes. The drive seemed to last an eternity, an eternity of seconds. Suddenly the car ground to a halt. She realized why they hadn't been gagged. Their guardians wanted somebody to speak up, to… *punish* him or her, conveying a message to the others, about what would happen to anybody speaking up. They were being… trained. Was that the right word? The knowledge made her shiver. Trained… in the s-service of someone? It made her shiver uncontrollably.

Doors opened with a shriek. They were pulled out on a cold, very cold floor. Needles of ice stabbed through their body. They heard no sounds, none not fitting in, not necessary, rational. Then they were brought through several doors and locks and the insanity started in earnest. The choir of voices rose from the depth of consciousness. Even if they first and foremost heard it through the ears the young and defenseless prisoners were positive that this… this all living beings perceived, on a plane independent of any physical senses. They saw without eyes, heard without ears, tasted without tongue, smelled without nose, sensed without skin the horrible happening around them. They heard the penetrating screams. They would have done so even if the ears had been covered in wool and lead, and everything. They realized where they had been brought. Jill noticed she was shaking her head, as if she didn't wish to admit the truth.

They had been brought to the Asylum, the House on the Hill, a place behind wires and fences and tall brick walls, where unwanted and noisy individuals from the entire Metropolitan area were locked up. Very few got out and those who were released weren't the same anymore. The spark of life had left them. They who refused to adapt, the careless and unlucky easily ended up here. Memories of ruined, mindless people stumbling through the streets of Northfield surfaced in the thoughts of the prisoners. The shudder started. They couldn't stop shuddering.

Long, dark corridors. Hallways, badly lit. Jill saw the world only through the eyes of he she had skin contact with, and it was a horrible experience. Her paralysis, the obvious enjoyment in him. He belonged here. Not the poor bastards howling their suffering from cells with smooth walls, the «patients» ruthlessly strapped to beds made of thick iron poles. She wanted so to express her bottomless despair. A primal scream rose from her depths. The sound emerging from the throat was stifled, without strength. As was the case with her body. She felt as if she had no control over her body anymore. The young, scared girl felt trapped inside it.

The guards threw them into cells and left them there, alone. The heavy door thundered as they closed it, screeched as they locked it. They had left her alone in the dark, blind, blind, blind. She had wanted an end to sensing and now she could not sense anything but the cold, cold floor. The dark enveloped her like a cancer, no longer her friend. She crawled around a bit, feeling the walls with her hands. Nothing here, nothing but the walls. She lay still. An immense time later she realized she had shit herself. She started to cry, big, sore sobs drowning in the silence of her cage.

Someone said «food» and she crawled to the door. Someone said «eat» and she obeyed, using her fingers to put the sticky glue into her mouth.

She drifted off. She drifted off again. And heard voices. And saw pictures. She shook her head in denial and then the pain came, horror-wrenching pain making her howl in despair. Listen, the voices said. Watch. Good girl, *good* girl.

The spacious room had a bright and blinding quality. She sat in a chair. Even with dark glasses her eyes hurt, and the bright light made her eyes flow with tears.

– Hello, Jill, a man said.

– Hello, Jill said.

The man greeting her sat behind a big desk. He wore a white coat and looked very stern and impressive.

– I'm Doctor Allan Renke, Jill. I'll be your personal friend here.

– That's good, Jill uttered distantly. – I like having friends.

She bowed down to her hands and took off the glasses. The tears had stopped flowing. Her eyes seemed to clear from one second to the next.

– What am I doing here? She asked.

– You're sick, Jill, the doctor said softly. – You need help.

– I'm not sick, she protested.

– That's what they all say, honey. A woman sitting in a chair on the right side of the desk caught Jill's attention.

– This is Doctor Sara Holcroft, Jill, Renke said. – She will be responsible for your day-to-day treatment.

– I'm *not* sick, Jill insisted. – I'm wet and horny, but I'm not sick.

– Let me tell you why you were brought here, Jill, Holcroft said. – You're a girl with a seriously warped view on sexuality and you're suffering from very dangerous delusions. You burned down your school, killing a lot of your fellow students.

She looked at them with burning eyes. The shock burned her. Hard, so hard to think. Everything felt woozy, misplaced. What had they done to her?

– Release me from these metals and I'll show you delusions, she spat ironically.
– Metals? Renke looked puzzled at her. – Jill, you're not chained. You've screamed about it since you arrived here, but that's simply another one of your paranoid delusions.
She looked down in her lap. There were no chains, not even any straps. She stared at them, sweating and terrified.
– What have you done to me? She whispered screaming, in vain attempting to raise her voice.
– We haven't done anything, Jill, Holcroft said soothingly. – You have done it to yourself, your family and your friends. We keep you sedated for your own good.
Renke leaned forward a bit.
– Relax. Here, have a chocolate. In his hand was a big, juicy chocolate plate.
– No. She shook her head with wary eyes. – No way!
– As you wish. SISTER
Jill turned her head, and a big woman approached her with a syringe in her hand.
– I'm sorry, Jill. Renke shook his head. – I'm forced to conclude that you don't want to improve yourself. I'm afraid your recovery will be a long and strenuous one. But don't worry, we'll do everything in our power to help you. We've helped many and given time, we'll improve you, too. Don't you worry. It's all in the attitude, you know. The minute you decide for yourself you want to get well, I'm convinced we'll see quick signs of improvement. You just wait and see, girl.
She strained and writhed in the chair, but the muscles wouldn't obey her. Both her limbs and her will felt dead and weary. The nurse grabbed her arm and immediately set the syringe. The way easy way the needle penetrated her skin showed great skill.
– We'll talk more later. Renke dismissed her. – For now, I want you to relax and familiarize yourself with the surroundings, your new home.
She wanted to speak, to protest, but whatever they had given her worked fast and decisive. Her vision clouded, everything clouded, fast and fury, fast and furry.
Everything just… left her. She could sense the movement of the chair as the nurse pushed her forward, but not much more. They had put her out of commission and now they were going to stow her away, somewhere out of sight and out of ears. But not out of reach. To them.
Darkness. Listen, Jill. Watch, Jill.
Daytime. A room full of nutcases, screaming and howling insanely. She caught a glimpse of herself in a mirror and wished she hadn't. A face with all muscles working… wrong. She sat in her chair drooling. Saliva dripped from her constantly open mouth. She looked just as nutty as everybody else here. Was this how all hopelessly insane people experienced life? Completely sane on the inside, but unable to express it?
She laughed. She knew she did. But it came out as a shriek, a howl of despair and fear.
– I must get out of here, she sniveled into the darkness. – Let me out of her… please.
Holcroft sat before her, smiling reassuringly.
– You're making progress, Jill. There are finally some initial signs of you wanting to get well.
– I don't belong here. Please let me out, please, please, please…
– Calm down. Holcroft towered above her, with a hospital sheet in her hands, cool, efficient, the very image of professionalism. – What I want you to do is watch and listen, okay?
– Ok-kay…
– Good girl. A pat on her cheek, making Jill feeling so good, so good, so good. – And if you're really good you'll get the reward. You want the reward, don't you?
– Yes. Jill brightened. – Oh, YES!
– I think I'll give you the chocolate right now. Just a tiny bit, but I want you to think of it as a promise of future delights, okay?
– Yes, Sara, please, Sara…
She opened her mouth as a polite little girl and Sara (nice Sara) placed the bit of juicy chocolate on her tongue. A broad smile emerged on the tear-filled face, making the tears dry. It melted in her mouth and tasted lovely, so lovely. It melted her. She melted and floated away in a pool of fluid, drowning in the still, still river.
The horrible sounds, masking as screams grew distant. She couldn't sense her feet touch the ground,

not in any way. The mask had been removed. She could vaguely recall a time when it hadn't been an integrated part of her face, her head, such a long time ago. Lights shone in her face. She struggled to move her eyes to get away from the blinding lights, but they blinded her wherever she looked. Slowly, slowly her vision cleared. She found herself strapped to a table. The table slanted a bit, making the feet closer to the floor than the head. Her vision clearing slowly, slowly caught Stacy and Everett, strapped as her, defenseless as her. She stared with eyes growing wide and wary. Wires, electrodes were attached all over their bodies, the majority on and close to the head.

– Wave to Jason now, girl, a voice commanded her.

But Jason wasn't here… was he?

But then she saw him, on a fourth table. Of course, she did. She waved to him, even though her hands and arms were still strapped to the table.

Perhaps it had been yesterday she had first seen Stacy and Everett on the table. Confusion kept riddling her. She kept shaking her head. The cobwebs and confusion persisted in haunting her. They must have been here for a very long time now. An hour, a minute, a year.

Women and men in white coats walked back and forth in the room, studying a number of computer screens. Or they sat in front of them, hardly looking away. A man, an older one with gray and white hair approached her with a… syringe in his right hand. Fear riddled her mind, but she found no outlet for it, unable as she was of moving any muscles except some in her face, a stiff mask expressing nothing. The man… she recognized him… Anton Berkowitz.

He smiled confidently to her. He gave her a trustworthy smile. The smile appeared huge and warm. Why did it seem as if he stretched his hand towards her from miles away? He patted her on the cheek. He leaned over her from far away (his smile filled her view) and spoke to her in comforting voices:

– You're dangerous, all you freaks of nature, but don't worry. We have the means to turn you into useful, productive citizens here.

Freaks? Had he said «freaks», used that word? Or had she just imagined it that way?

– The other one has awakened, too. A voice tuned in from the side, Holcroft's. – Their energy consumption is truly remarkable. Whether it's poison or anything else is generally digested and dealt with in an incredibly efficient manner.

– It doesn't really matter. Berkowitz had straightened to his full height again. – We just have to administer the doses accordingly. In fact, this makes it easier for us to speed up the Program.

– You know the others may grumble? There might be… repercussions.

– I don't give a damn about their careful and cowardly ways. These are mine. The minute the binding is completed our esteemed partners won't protest… They won't dare.

Jill saw the syringe be lowered. She saw it lifted again. Empty. She expected her vision to cloud once more. It didn't. But the sense of detachment, alienation, even with her own body grew. It wasn't hers anymore.

– Do you hear me, Jill? The smile once more filled her entire vision. – I want you to answer, little impudent girl.

– *Yes.* Her lips seemed to move by themselves.

– Good. Now I want you to listen carefully. From now on, from this very minute all your senses will only perceive me and me alone, unless I tell you different. You won't perceive anything that I don't tell you to perceive.

She fought, she did, but in vain, all her effort useless. Darkness descended. Sounds faded. Everything faded.

Sense-loss complete. Alpha state complete. Fast and problem-free.

She found herself on her back in a bed. She knew that, in spite of the utter darkness surrounding her. The soft and light sheet surrounded her. She was alone - and scared. Not a fear striking her with panic, but a numb ever-present never disappearing, insisting. She walked hastily away, fast and furry, fast and furry. No matter where she walked, wherever she escaped she never got anywhere. The darkness smothered her, threateningly… and insistently. So, she remained on the bed.

A small streak of light grew… so far away. A door opened. The light flooded the room, blinding her. She couldn't close her eyes, couldn't use the hands as shade. A man entered. A shape so big that it had to be a man. His shadow reached all the way to the bed, making her shiver. He turned on the lights,

one lamp on each side of the bed. Door was closed. They were completely alone.
– Now, how is my little girl?
– F-fine, d-daddy. She felt very small and defenseless where she lay.
Unprotected.
– Hello, Jill, the deep, male voice sounded in the room. – Say hello to daddy, now.
– Hello, daddy, she said weakly, hesitatingly.
– That's my little girl, he praised her. – Polite, attentive as you have learned.
A huge hand grabbed the blanket and dragged it off her. She sensed the cold draft while being completely exposed to his scrutiny. She saw his eyes gleam in recognition and hunger, and it scared her, but she knew she couldn't move, because she had been told not to. Daddy ruled. Daddy ruled all. She was a polite, attentive girl. All polite, attentive girls did as they were told, as adults and especially daddies said they should do.
– Please, daddy, I'm frightened…
– That's the way we do it, to easier achieve control, Jill. We're supplanting one trauma with another. Ours.
– You're into… behavior control and… modification? It was so hard to think. – Yes, you *are.*
– You're such a remarkable girl. The man seemed to shrink before her eyes. She fought herself to sit up. – But disobedient and strong of will, too and that isn't good, not good at all.
The man was Anton Berkowitz, but he seemed so much younger… His hair kept the black complexion and… He was smaller, suddenly, not so imposing… the wrinkle on his forehead seemed to grow, GROW
Her eyes opened with a start. She was back in the laboratory. She was in the laboratory, period. They had just fooled her into believing she had left. They screwed with everything she was, *brainwashed* her.
– Incredible, she just lifted her head.
– Give her another injection, she heard Berkowitz commanding voice. – And increase the dosage.
He bent over her. The strict smile bent over her. The room faded on her, faded to black. She desperately wanted to scream, but managed nothing but a pathetic moan.
– She's projecting an incredible amount of alpha-waves. They all do. These are operating on a completely different level from the rest, also in areas we have no clue how to observe.
– But it is the two girls who have the extremely effective immune defense system, another assistant pointed out. The voice was clinical, chemically free of emotions.
– Everything is going to be okay, you'll see. Strict Smile with his comforting voice. – We're going to take extra good care of you all.
The little girl soon to be teenager lay in the bed with thick linen covering her. The lights were lit, but subdued. The door opened. She pulled the linen well over her head.
– Now, now disobedient little girl. He locked the door. – Be good girl, now, or you must be punished. All disobedient girls must be punished for their own good.
Fearfully she pushed the linen forward.
– Hallo, Jill, the man who seemed to fill the room said.
– Hello, daddy, she greeted him with a hopeful smile.
– Rise, he bade her strictly.
So she did. Reluctantly she let the linen go and stood unmoving with lowered head. He grabbed her under her jaw and pushed up the head.
– Lifted head, lowered eyes, girl. He gave her a light, but stinging slap in the face. – You will learn.
– Yes, daddy, the girl sniffed subdued.
– Kneel, now, in *position.* She obeyed with lowered eyes.
– This is the way you will always sit when daddy enters the room, until I bid you differently. Is that understood?
– I understand, daddy, she replied subdued.
– Good girl. Rise now and give daddy a kiss.
She obeyed hesitatingly, shy and reddening, but daddy rewarded her with a pat on the cheek and she blushed in joy.
He proceeded to fondle her breasts, the small breasts and he kept stroking the large hands over the

They walked in the park. Daddy had bought her a new dress and a hat surrounded by flowers. He was so elegant, so manly in his broad, blue suit. Nobody could match him.

– Tell me something, he commanded.

She pondered for some time, realized what he meant, what he sought. He wanted her to tell him something he didn't know.

– I was very little, the girl told him enthusiastically. – I believed I saw myself in the mirror… until I realized that she sat in the chair, and I didn't.

Cold cold cold

Jill sat in a chair in a room filled with machines and instruments. How she had come here… she didn't know. She remembered a dream, but couldn't recall its content. Everything was indistinct, the surroundings virtually faded. Was there more? She couldn't see it.

She's primed.

– Rise, Jill. *No, no, daddy, please.*

She obeyed, mechanically. As mechanically, emotionally detached she registered that she didn't wear her chains anymore.

– There is a wooden box five steps in front of you. *Yes, I see it, daddy.* – I want you to lift it for me. Lift it without moving.

She sensed the excitement and expectation in the strict man's voice. The same emotion flowing through her, because they allowed her to show them what she could do.

The box lifted from the floor. It stopped in its ascent approximately half her full length above the floor. It remained there. The captive audience felt as if they were observing a feather kept floating by the wind. Except for the fact that the box didn't change its positions the slightest. It hung there, as if frozen. Jill had a wireless metal band fastened around her head. It glowed slightly in the three LED-cells on her forehead, but that was all.

– *Alpha-waves level increased only marginally.* The technicians had a hard time hiding his excitement.

– Now, clever Jill, I want you to light fire in the corner closest to you.

A tiny flame erupted virtually instantly, grew a bit, but didn't spread. Members of the audience stared wide-eyed at each other.

– The Alpha Wave reached out in a straight line for just a moment here, the closest technician reported.

– Her energy field is manifesting itself ever clearer, another reported. – To me it looks like she's two places simultaneously.

– Good girl, Berkowitz whispered. – Good girl.

He noticed that her nipples hardened and grew under the white fabric and smiled triumphantly.

The flame spread to the entire top of the box. It happened from one moment to the next, so fast that it could hardly be measured. Suddenly the fire surrounded the entire box.

– Alpha level fluctuating, the technician reported nervously. – It passed the danger level… there.

– I want you to stop, Jill, Berkowitz commanded. – Put the box down at the floor.

The smoldering box hit the floor. There wasn't much left of it and the flames turned to insignificance. The guinea pig stood just as unmoving, but it flashed wildly on her forehead.

– Alpha level fluctuating wildly, the technician cried.

– Flies? One stated amazed. – I've never liked… f-flies.

Berkowitz realized that he, for the first time in years, had a stiff penis, one insanely rock-hard.

– I see spiders, one howled in panic. – Huge, bad SPIDERS

– I see three of her now. NO, four, no five. The woman clawed herself bloody when she dug sharp nails into her face.

– TURN HER OFF, Berkowitz screamed. – GET HER GOD DAMN NULLIFIED.

An operator managed to pull himself together long enough to punch some keys on the board. At first it didn't seem to be doing any good, but then the presence in the room finally brightened significantly.

– Level descending, falling towards lowest level.

– Energy level on all wavelengths down, third technician reported.

Second technician wasn't capable of saying anything.

They usually kept her drugged. They had to do that, considering how drowsy and dull she stayed all the time. When awakening, sort of, next time she lay on her back on a table in a blinding white room. The chains were back on. The cold metal smothered her skin. They had also used the leather straps. She was hardly able to move anything but her head. Stacy lay in another bed by her side. On her Jill could see the metal headband she only sensed around her own head. There was no one else present. No sounds. In Stacy's eyes she saw how dull her own eyes were. Above them, above the beds their captors had placed bags of fluid. Fluid flowing into their veins through tubes stuck in their arms. Wires attached to their skin led to machines with wires leading out of the room. Every impression they received enhanced the notion of a resting room in a hospital. But they weren't sick, were they now? Stacy's eyes closed. Jill strained in vain to keep her own open. She attempted to speak, to say something, anything. She managed only inarticulate sounds, drowning in the silence the room impressed upon them.

She lay on her back, with hands strapped along her sides. It made her feel deeply ashamed, to despise herself, but she was grateful for the chance to close her eyes, to no longer be blinded by the white ceiling.

Her head shook back and forth, as the heat continued to rise in her. She floated in a sea of desire. Moans constantly escaped between numb lips. She was wet all the time, a dull, continuous, unsatisfied lust. She saw that Stacy's thighs were just as shiny. There was no door to the hallway. Everybody had the chance to observe their shame. Male and female nurses passed by all the time. They didn't enter, but stopped sometimes with lewd, scornful grins.

Day or night, it didn't matter. It was all the same, a continuous flow of reoccurring patterns. For all they knew nothing existed outside this place. All their memories, every single one could be one sick dream, without foundation in reality.

Two pair of eyes struggled to open. Two heads strained necks and turned so they could see each other. The girl saw her mirror image move her lips. Strangely enough she understood what was said. No discernible sounds erupted from the quivering lips. Perhaps they both spoke and spoke the same.

They think the Hunger gives them another weapon against us. They're wrong. Don't fight the Hunger. Give in to it. It's our only remaining weapon.

And perhaps that's just what they want us to believe.

The girl twisted and turned on the table. The mirror image did the same. Pushed the thighs tight, pressing them at each other and then spreading them as wide as possible. The louder moan of desperate need emerged completely natural. And the enhanced hormones spreading through the air multiplied the lust. She had found herself in a state of heightened desire for a long time, now, but it was nothing compared to this. Wet in eyes and corners of the mouth she struggled to focus the vision, to establish contact with those leering in the hallway. They came then, both the girls. The hot water broke. It was a miracle. The lethargy diminished in noticeable ways, and it kept doing so, while the Hunger increased, rebuilt itself, stronger than ever. It worked as a kind of focus. To them, anyway. She allowed herself a silent laughter. What was this, if not sexual energy, power? The dullness didn't disappear, but it had lightened a bit and she was ready for what had to be done.

– *Those bitches are horny as loons.*

Did she hear anything? Steps in the hallway? Time drifted anew. There was nothing she could do to prevent it. Why had they placed her and Stacy together? Perhaps they had all been placed in pairs. She had a vague sense of Jason and Everett… of seeing them together, too. She knew it had to be them, even if she couldn't see their faces. A face floated closer once again. *His* face. And it felt horrible. It wasn't just the fact that she had no way of stopping it, but also… she didn't fight. She wasn't able to make a fist, no matter how much she tried to.

Eyes slid open. Had she been dreaming again? So tired… so hard to think. They moved. Someone moved them, moved their hearts like trinkets. Down to my knees in pain, kneeling in blood and despair, so hard to move, to be. Someone pushed the beds forwards, backward, down, down, down… Doors opened and closed in an infinite number, in a gray night without end. Dr. Berkowitz and his team waited. The Smile didn't fill their view like before, but they were dragged to it. They had been… bonded to him. Jill felt sick to her very depths; a place within she couldn't reach.

– Welcome, girls, he greeted them.

– Thank you, Dr. Berkowitz, they greeted him simultaneously, weakly.

– Good girls. He gave them praise and they turned warm all over.

The staff started the preparations fast and effective. Hypodermic needles were changed. Their chemical balance was changed. Instruments activated. The girls' use of their limbs returned. Chemicals, keywords, electricity to wake them, chemicals, keywords, electricity to make them sleep, to make them move, to make them lie still.

So grateful, (we're so grateful).

– You won't… operate on us… will you? Jill asked with shaking voice and mouth.

Berkowitz stroke her hair in a calming, patronizing way.

– Don't worry, good girl. We'll take care of you from now on and you're much too valuable to us to risk tampering and possible damage. We have, for quite some time now, been able to utilize other, more secure methods to ensure your cooperation and unconditional obedience.

– Don't crawl for them, Stacy sneered. – Don't give them the satisfaction.

The doctor *looked* at her.

– Now, you were a *bad* girl, Stacy. The girl shrunk visibly and was unable to meet his eyes. – Don't you know what happens to *bad* girls?

– Y-yes.

– They get *punished,* right?

– Y-yes.

– But that isn't a problem here, now, is it? Because you wish to be good, don't you? You want to be good so much that it hurts. You will accept our aid; learn to be good all the time?

She nodded energetically where she lay. He patted her on the cheek and dried a tear from the corner of her eye.

– I knew you would.

Jill lay frozen and silent while chains and straps were removed, and while Stacy very slowly emerged from the mire of fear and darkness he had pushed her into. When he could do it *that easy,* to *Stacy*, he could do it to anyone.

– Sit up, he bade them, and they obeyed with lowered eyes, fearful and ashamed. He continued in the same hard, strict tone: – I assume you've become very aware, now, of who's in charge. We can turn you off whenever we wish. Fortunately, it's a major advantage for both parties if you realize that unconditional cooperation is the only path remaining for you.

– Well, as long as it's a matter of cooperation… Jill didn't manage to stop herself until it was too late.

– RISE, the Doctor snarled.

The girls obeyed instantly, without thinking. They stood like soldiers, ready for inspection. Eyes turned foggy and facial expression froze.

– *Kneel for me.* The last remaining will left them, and they did as they were told, mechanically and mindlessly. At the back of their head where the thoughts were still free, they asked themselves a question they didn't want an answer to: Could they have refused the order even if they had wanted to?

Dr. Berkowitz walked in a minor circle around them.

– You belong to us… we *own* you, all of you, he said in a horrible, controlled wrath. – Property doesn't demonstrate independence or stipulate terms. We will use you, in any way we may desire. Your only concern is to obey our commands and live the way we wish you to live. As long as you're good girls, you won't be *punished.*

The last word made them both cringe. *I'll be good, daddy. Good, good, goodgoodgood*

They hadn't been told to speak and therefore they stared silently at the floor.

A while later they sat at each other's side in a broad chair, surrounded by wires and instruments. Boxes lifted. Fires lit. But nothing more happened. Satisfied nods from the staff.

– Jill, the doctor called abruptly. – Can you read minds?

– Yes, sir, she replied.

– What did first technician have for dinner today?

– Steak… well done, with peas, carrots and ice cream for desert… with strawberries.

She hesitated, as if she wondered about something, if she should continue.

– Yes? The doctor encouraged her impatiently. Once again, he had to irritate himself over an erected cock.

– And he had his wife, the first time on the kitchen table. The voice was even, as if she was a waitress discussing the menu. – Then he brought her to his bedroom, tied her up and whipped her bloody, before having her again. He enjoys subduing her. She is his slave. If she displeases him the slightest, he punishes her. He enjoys seeing women in chains and nothing is better than when they're kneeling and shaking by his feet. His view is that all women are born inferior and…

– That will do. Berkowitz waved her off. Jill stopped speaking instantly. It was completely unnecessary to ask the technician to confirm the truth. One look at the red face spoke volumes.

The doctor noted that Jill smiled. She was proud as a little child of her talents. Good.

They had merely begun to map the talents of these two, of them all really, he was convinced of that much. They were like open wells that could be explored and exploited - by him.

– Eh, alpha level rose just slightly, but returned to her normal almost immediately, the technician spoke through clenched teeth.

It worked. He could control them. They belonged to him. He would own them more and more for each new day now and eventually… soon… they would be his completely. For the moment he could barely begin to imagine the possibilities, but they were *endless.*

– New fire, he commented. He didn't realize at first that he hadn't specified any location.

Two fires started in the very air. He stared as hypnotized at them, and he wondered for the first time if he had overestimated his ability to hold the tiger's tail. Panthers, night black panthers.

– Put out the fire, he ordered hoarsely and then he stared mute.

The fire vanished, as if it had never been there. The only trace of it was soot particles in the air. They confirmed it by using microscopes on the general area. What had really been burning? Tiny dust particles… or *oxygen-molecules?* And the fire hadn't spread in any visible way. He mentally dried sweat from his forehead.

– Tired Jill and Stacy? He had driven them through many repetitions, but they stayed unforgivable healthy and fresh. He grabbed them around the jaw, in a comforting touch, ignoring the begging eyes.
– Yes, you're tired, he stated, suggestive. They blinked instantly. – I think we'll have a break, now. Sleep, good girls, sleep. *Sleep.*
Eyes closed. He removed his hands and heads fell. Jaws hit the chest. Jill sank into a state deeper than any sleep, a state without dream, without existence. None other than what was imposed upon them. Jill couldn't understand how she was unable to hate them and still despise herself.
She lay stretched out on the bed in the white room, in straps and chains. They both did. What had they dreamed this time? Did the treatment manage to supplant their usual dreams in their complex minds? Or… were they going mad? She laughed, an insane, ice-cold shriek of laughter making one of the passing nurses shake in fear.
Movement again. Or the filth they filled their minds with to give the illusion of such. Had they developed an advanced type of VR-technology on this place? The government had to be in on it. Even not a bunch of the filthy rich could easily finance or get away with something like this. There was a high probability that both public and private funds were used. *Listen up, bad girl.*
The fearful voice interrupted.
Yes, daddy, I'm so sorry, daddy. I'll listenlisten
– *Awaken.* She awakened, but didn't move. – *Open your eyes.* Eyes opened, without seeing, distant and empty. – *Look at me.* She saw a tall, dark man with a strict expression in his face. She knew she could deny him nothing. *Good girl, you know Allen, don't you? He, too, will be among your teachers.*
– Rise.
Chains were off, Straps were off. She obeyed. Stacy, too. He carried their chains while they walked behind, obediently followed him, wherever he went. Their faces had an eager glow. They looked forward to what they should do, whatever it was.
A sound, a banshee wail was thrown back and forth among the walls, the horrible living walls. They bathed in it, but felt nothing. They found themselves in a circle of pain and felt only numbness, as their Master wished. How long had they been here? The sense of haste burned in them, burnedburned burned
BAD GIRLS A flash of two little girls frightened and tight in a bed and a giant towering above them.
Darkness. A sense of falling. Heads hitting the floor. That was all.
– *Awaken.* She awakened, but didn't move. – *Open your eyes.* Eyes opened without seeing, distant and empty. – *Look at me.* She saw a tall, fair-haired Allen with his strict expression and knew she could deny him nothing.
– *Rise.* Chains were off. Straps were off. She obeyed. Jill, too. He carried their chains while they walked behind him, obediently following him. Their faces glowing eagerly. They looked forward to what they should do, whatever it was.
A light, a thin line through a small opening. It seemed dirty gray at first, but then it turned into a bright, shining ray, giving them tears in their eyes. Allen led them into a room full of computers and surveillance screens. Doctor Berkowitz stood with his back to the machines, facing the two girls. They lowered their eyes and fell on their knees before him, they couldn't help themselves.
– Rise and sit down, he said kindly. Kind daddy.
They sat safely in their chairs, and he bade them to look up, calling their attention to one single screen.
Look, he told them.
The other screens turned black, pitched black, but on the one they saw a girl lying alone in another white room. They recognized Morgana, her skin so pale, the girl so quiet, unmoving. Her chains and straps were in place, and she wore the same clothes as Stacy and Jill.
– I want you to look at this as one step further in your education, the good Doctor said. He held up a DVD.
– We recorded this a week ago. The first part is speeded up slightly compared to real time.
A week. Courage failed them even more, failed deeply. They saw the good doctor put the DVD in the player and push the play-button.
The image seemed to remain the same, with the exception of a bit of flickering at the start. Morgana

lay there, pale and quiet, a representation of how Jill felt. The camera started zooming in on details. For a while the chain around the wrist filled the screen. At first nothing visible happened. Then it started *bubbling*. Slowly at first, then faster. One single bubble grew to a number of small. The camera zoomed out and all of Morgana appeared once more. What happened showed clearly at this time. The metal headband, the chains, the straps, the white fabric, the bed, everything she was in direct contact with fell apart. The bed collapsed from under her. She fell through it, to the floor below. When she rose and the dust had settled, she stood there nude, free. The first steps had an uncertain feel to them, but she speeded up quickly enough.

She stopped. The facial features froze with the body. The entire body… stopped and fell, completely paralyzed and… turned off. The head hit the floor. The girls heard the sound as a cry of horror in the Void. Morgana lay still. She hadn't uttered a single sound.

– We have designed an extensive loop-program into your indoctrination, the Doctor explained and couldn't quite keep the excitement out of his relaxed, professional voice. – Whenever any of you without explicit permission step outside the parameters in thought and behavior we're teaching you, all voluntary functions are disconnected automatically. I don't need to go into detail about this. You're bright girls. You know what I'm talking about, don't you?

They nodded, mute, deaf, numb, sick and queasy.

– Please don't enslave us, Jill begged gasping, finding it difficult to breathe. – We'll cooperate, be g-good g-girls.

– I'm certain you will, my dear. The Doctor patted her on the cheek. She sensed small bursts of energy she sucked up from him. It was no conscious act, but it was there, hungrily, uncontrollable now when she had been turned into such a passive puppet.

The alarm went off. For a fragment of a moment there was silence, before the screens were turned back on. All the screens made up one single, large image. The girls stared at it in helpless fascination.

What they saw was an enormous, hairy Beast, a wolf-like creature, tearing apart security guards and physicians in a red fog of murderous rage, its claws making bloody signs in the air. It filled the emptiness in Jill, and she stood there mute, staring, warming herself in its rain.

The angle shifted to another camera. The red fog captured the image there, but five seconds later a woman cut both her thighs' veins on the beast's claws and the blood splashed the lenses.

–… me a fucking report, Berkowitz gargled into the comm system, the sophistication blown from his behavior.

A face sweaty and scared appeared on a monitor.

– We entered him through a series of differentiated tests. Everything appeared to be in order, but suddenly he, the object started to grow aggressive. Whatever we did the adrenaline level rose further. We decided to turn him off. It was then he attacked and changed before our eyes. Most of team 11 was erased, sir. Just now he's engaging team 16. I personally observed him being hit by enough sedatives to stop an elephant and it only made him more aggressive. At first, he showed some humanity. He was content with tearing to pieces only those directly in his way. Now, he's tearing apart everybody.

– Why didn't you gas him? Berkowitz barked.

– He quickly broke out of sector 11, sir. We couldn't and can't gas him without risking contaminating the entire building.

– Okay, put a stop to him, the Doctor sighed. – By any means possible.

– I'm not sure I get you, sir…

– Kill it, the good Anton snapped. – Kill the fucking beast. Beat it to death if necessary. Unless you see clear signs of the sedatives working. Is that clear enough for you, Thorsen?

– Yes, sir, clear as day, sir. I assume we can always fall back on cell and semen samples if the worst should happen, huh?

Doctor Berkowitz broke the connection and turned to the three others in the room. The girls shrank from his wrath. They were unable to do anything else.

– Get these two as far away from the animal as possible.

Allan didn't waste any time in voicing a reply. He was used to following orders. He chained Stacy first. She didn't resist. Jill, too, stood still. They had no choice, no more than puppets on a string. Jill once more felt the horrible cold from the chains.

– Go! Allan walked so fast that they had to run a bit to keep up. That was the way they were taught. Always predict and follow the masters' wishes.

Senses had sharpened now. While running down the corridor she «heard» what happened far away and it was sinister beyond words. She sensed the beast's rage, the pain, the boundless fear in those who were butchered. They hardly managed to give expression to it all. They didn't scream, they didn't cry. Jill bathed in it all, in a passive way. She knew she should have been beside herself with rage, that she should have shared what was emanating from the… from the animal, but those thoughts belonged on the logical, intellectual level. She was more like a machine receiving signals, impulses. She and all the rest of them, indoctrinated to serve a purpose, nothing else. By all false gods. All gods were false. The thought came to her from far away. It felt right, but still brought a violent fear and self-recrimination. Among other things the Program also included a good, Christian training, a fact that didn't escape her. They didn't have complete control.

Not yet.

She stretched out a hand as they were running. Stacy grabbed it tight.

Silence. Deadly silence. The troopers charging into the room of torn up bodies stopped, uncertain. The Beast they had come here to find, which scared the shit out of them…

was gone.

– Satan, he must have entered the ventilation shafts

– Impossible, with its size

– Eh, with its agility

Just then Lillith started smiling.

Allan led them impatiently through a door instantly, automatically closing behind them. In a long, dark hallway going down, down, down a number of doors closed behind them, sealing them off from the rest of the complex.

The inner room was a well-equipped living room, big and… luxurious? Was that the right word? Jill wondered. Wall to wall carpet. A sofa so big that it reminded her of a bed. Extensively furnished. Probably huge amounts of food in a freezer close by. A bomb shelter.

Two men, even bigger than Allan, waited for them.

– Sit down, Allen commanded. And to the two men: – Don't let them out of your sight, not even for a moment, understood?

They nodded, relaxed and confident.

The girls sat down in the sofa. Jill strained to smooth a wrinkle in her skirt. The single touch was sufficient. She saw Holcroft before her, how the repressed woman had spoken aloud about their «fucking pushing sexuality». One light touch and the sweet, wet warmth below turned to pain and heat. She began caressing herself, back and forth, up and down. The first moans started, growing to moans of helpless, desperate need.

– Passion is our strength, she said clearly and darkly. – Not our weakness.

The two guards looked at each other and then at the door where Allan had disappeared.

– We need you, Stacy said low and throaty and seductive. – What are you waiting for? We can make it good for you. It's a part of our training.

– Please… Jill begged them.

She moaned as she breathed now, as if she no longer had any control over herself. The two men knew she hadn't. They knew perfectly well what their training dealt with.

They ripped off their clothes and registered in satisfaction how their cocks rose to point straight forward.

Allan returned. They stopped uncertain.

– We may have to stay here for quite a while, he drawled. – I see no reason why we shouldn't entertain ourselves, shouldn't find something to pass the time.

He stepped straight to Stacy and dragged her on her feet, gave her a brutal kiss. She moaned longingly and he registered with enormous satisfaction that her arrogant smile vanished. He grabbed her breasts and squeezed hard, then harder, until she screamed, fast and sharp. He tore off the little she wore of clothes in small pulls and eventually in one single pull. The two others placed Jill on all fours. One penetrated her from behind, while the other instructed her to take him in the mouth. She had this drowsy girlish look while doing it and he turned harder than he had ever thought was possible. She gasped, fully aware of what he thought of her, how he looked at her. Her thoughts almost an extension of his. She had trouble distinguishing between him and the man behind. And then she got the first orgasm and then she didn't care anymore. Allan pushed Stacy on her back on the sofa. He lifted her hips and took her. She experienced the third orgasm the moment he came, the moment he pumped into her. Jill couldn't tell how many times she had come. Allan walked to her, holding her up by the hair.

– Now, did you enjoy that, little cunt?

– Oh, YES, she exclaimed. – It was so good, so good. Please do it more. Please.

– So good… Stacy mumbled with her mouth to Allan's chest. – More, more, more, please. Please remove the chains so we can please you further.

He slapped her so hard that the head was seemingly thrown aside, loosening from the neck and the blood splashed on the floor. She didn't rush any of her hands to the mouth, but remained in the same, docile position. Her face was locked in the doll-like smile, in happy servitude. He enjoyed that. The Program surpassed his wildest expectations.

– Be glad I choose not to punish you, he admonished. – Don't be stupid, understand.

She nodded eagerly and performed for him, writhed her sexy, to-eat-up body like a snake.

– But you like your women eager, don't you? She said coquettishly.

Everybody stood, lay or knelt on the sofa now. The large pillows had been removed and there was more than enough room.

– We like it when you're chained, one or the other of the guards said patronizing. – It makes you even more attractive.

– We know, Jill said shyly. – It pleases us.

She writhed back and forth on the body of one of the men and used her hands and mouth on him, while the other entered her from behind. He who fucked her from behind came for the second time. As he came, he moved fast and hard and seemed filled to the brim with energy…

But shortly after the ejaculation he seemed to lose all power and collapse. He collapsed like an empty sack of something and ended up lying still close to the girl.

– We'll make it good for you, so very good…

– Are we not good, Good Master?

– Very, very good, good girls, Allan/the guard moaned in unison agreement. – You… shall be… rewarded.

– Thank you, Gracious Master, thank you.

Allan thought the girls had switched places, but he wasn't sure. He fought to get up, but was unable to. He lacked the strength to pull it off. The simplest of acts and he couldn't do it.

The girls sat down on the men, placing their legs on each side of the body beneath. They started rocking up and down on the stiff, sore shafts, keeping continuously eye contact, while grabbing the men's shoulders. It… *felt so good.* The power they took from the men flowed into them, through the loins and hands to their entire body. It was

NOW OR NEVER

Nails dug deeply into flesh as they gathered all the concentration they could muster for the moment. There was PAIN, but it *happened,* the almost unconscious use of the Unknown in their depths. There were the sounds of opening locks and the chains fell off. The loop-program impregnated as a safety valve was blown to pieces. The metal headband started glowing and sparking, before burning out. And then it was torn off the girl's heads, as if by an invisible force. The men moaned and cried in misery and fear. They attempted to lift their arms, but it had become a small matter to keep them down, to keep them in place. Jill was strong now. Stacy was strong now. Deadly strong and the masks of death stared down at their victims.

Then Jill sensed it. It felt at first as if she had burned herself. To this point their bodies, their flesh had operated independently of the mind, because the mind had been paralyzed, without a will of its own. Now it awakened, now Jill welcomed the power, The Power she had denied. She embraced the joy of it, the joy of Power.

They had hurt them, hurt them all. They were going to pay, *pay*.

It… started… as a quiver up the spine. The confusion, the spell the masters of this place had used to darken their minds was like blown away, from one moment to the next. While his power was at its strongest, the moment he ejaculated inside her, she took everything away. He *squeaked,* hardly audible… and died.

She turned her head almost indefinitely. She watched the walls, beyond the walls. The room vanished before her eyes, turning more real, not less.

– My Goddess, she heard Stacy utter time and time again. – My Goddess!

A SOUND, unidentifiable even to her, rose from the depths of her being. Such a terrible, beautiful sound impossible to forget. She remembered and understood. The ancient hunting instinct of the predator awakened abruptly. A growl erupted from her larynx. She licked her lips (her chops). The third man screamed in horror and jumped off the sofa like a terrified fallow dear running from the predator. Jill and Stacy were on him, caught him instantly. They shared him, took all his energy, his blood, his flesh, tearing him apart bit by bit with fangs and nails and long claws of mind power. Stacy pulled out his heart while it was still beating. Every piece of him was alive while they digested it. Stacy offered the sister the remaining half of the heart and Jill accepted enthusiastically. So right all this, so right, so right, so right…

They stood there, facing each other, heaving for breath, breathing easier than they had ever done. So good, it felt so good. The power, the POWER

Stretched and burned, crushing walls of limitation. Jill blinked. Stacy blinked. Reality shifted… and shifted anew.

Flash: Jason sat on a throne, surrounded by his subjects.

Flash: Jason lived among his subjects, as a living God. He was Death, but also Transition.

Flash: In another tradition, in another time and place, in colder territories, Everett was also Death, the Keeper of the Flame, the Guardian of the Kingdom of Death, the Fenris, but he was also the Guide, the Ferryman, in the hot sands of Egypt, of pre-Egypt.

They were many. We're all many, we're Legion.

Stacy stretched her arms, her snake arms above her head and her eyes, her Gorgon eyes burned. Jill didn't freeze, but burned with her own fire. They bathed in each other's fire.

– My compliments, sister. Stacy acknowledged and there was only a weak echo remaining of her former sarcasm. – You play the defenseless, sweet innocent to perfection. It's a role you're born to play.

– We're complementing each other, Jill said. She discovered incredulous that it was true, inevitably and added: – We're so much alike.

The visions continued unabated, information, knowledge and perhaps understanding and awareness. And Hunger, a Rage not abating but increasing by the second.

Stacy was covered in blood and guts and flesh. Her face had a satisfied, content expression and still she sparked of energy. Jill knew that she looked exactly the same herself and it didn't bother her at all. The Energy penetrating every shred, every cell of their body had grown so strong that also others could easily see it. What would have happened if they hadn't… started out from such a low point, if their body and mind wouldn't have needed much of the energy to repair itself? Jill didn't want to think about that right now and filed it away.

She had never felt so Clear, so sure of herself. Nothing was beyond her grasp, nothing. It was a good thing that this had happened. The monsters at this place had done them a favor. They had subjected them to another trial in the Burning Court the witches had to endure in order to survive in a harsh and ruthless world. They had been so close, so close to being enslaved, enslaved forever. Never again, they could never allow it to come close to happening again.

The Burning set Court in 15th century Barcelona. She burned. The young, innocent witch Vyla burned for her crimes against the Holy Roman Church, burned for no other reason than that she existed. She burned. A twelfth century bishop watched while burning her. Just before her spirit flew, before the pain grew too horrible, she saw a man, a warrior, charge the bishop, killing him, cutting him to pieces with his sword and any other weapon in his hands. She saw the bishop's guards rush in to save him, in vain, their spears penetrating the warrior's body from all sides. He stood there and bled to death, while the bishop breathed his last by his feet.

It started as a low rumble in the ground. Everybody noticed it. The various doctors looked up from their important work. The guards grew visibly astute. A… presence suddenly penetrated the entire building. Anton Berkowitz kept council in Surveillance and studied the monitors. In every room where there were sedated subjects… they opened their eyes. He had just about sufficient time to clench his fists, before all the monitors turned black.

Jill and Stacy didn't look at the other when leaving the room. They didn't need to. The sealed door before them slid open and once more disappeared into the ceiling. *Technological gadgets are so easy to control, are they not?* They moved forward, driven by a deep and strange savagery. Both sensed strongly the fundamental rationality behind it.

Doors slid open in a seemingly endless row. Everett waited for them outside the shelter, the building within the building, snarling and spitting. They did recognize him with their mind, even while the eyes saw what could be any beast (any Huge beast not existing in ordinary reality). His fur was covered in blood and guts, and he growled and howled insanely. Strangely enough his rage had a calming effect on their own, but fortunately not much. They wanted to keep the rage, the drive as long as possible. It wouldn't last. The problem as they had come to see it, both here and in the outside world, was keeping the anger, not gaining it. In a world where any emotion, any passion tended to be slippery like water.

– Greetings, Anubis, Stacy said. – Be welcomed to join us in our Hunt. There is more than enough prey to go around.

They observed how he calmed down. He fell on his knees, howling in pain. They noticed his raw paws, the blood on the metal wall and torn off claws on the floor. He had attempted to dig himself through the walls to them.

– Oh, you poor beast, Jill purred. – You must let us help you.

Softly spoken words to calm the wild beast. He stood on his knees before them, but still he towered over the two girls. They put one hand each on the damaged paws and one hand each on his head, pushing their bodies at his. The paws healed, claws re-grew. Bullets were pulled out of wounds and the wounds closed. He started to shrink before their eyes. His face changed to something resembling a human expression. He straightened himself and the intelligence of Homo Sapiens Magi illuminated his entire being. He didn't seem any less dangerous.

They continued on their way. Stacy walked on his right side and Jill on his left, all three holding hands. They walked straight forward, unafraid. The girls' hands, too, had fingers bent like claws. They moved soundlessly, unnecessary as hunters closing in on their prey, and they noticed the approaching guards practically simultaneously. There was no eye contact. The guards moved through an adjacent corridor around one of the corners ahead. But they knew. Of course, they knew. The pack leader carried a mobile instrument able to register and track the unique energy they, Homo Sapiens Magi radiated. Jill kept feeling wonder over how clear everything had become. Not clear-cut perhaps, but clear, right as rain.

The leader stopped and signaled *contact,* then showing three fingers. Guns already pointing forward were raised a bit further and the troops steeled themselves ready for action.

The instrument was torn out of the leader's grip. It rose up in the air to the ceiling and remained there, in a fixed position. Raw nerves exploded. One of the male soldiers fired his weapon. He shot the instrument to pieces. The man kept firing. The bullets went in all directions. Another fellow soldier struck him from behind with his gun, while shaking his head in irritation.

The machine guns were abruptly torn from their hands and smaller firearms pulled from jackets and holsters. Many uniforms seemed to tear themselves apart. Firearms and knives, and everything levitated up under the ceiling, well out of reach.

The door ahead opened. Fifteen, twenty steps away they saw three entities emerge. The male and female guards saw one of the oldest human legends come to life: The werewolf, accompanied by the at least as dangerous witches, demons from humanity's riddled past. The draft from the open door was like a gust from the blackest night. Darkness danced around them in spite of all the bright lights. They made the darkness dance, they made it move, made it dance and spark in ebony. The soldiers stared helplessly at the werewolf's steaming mouth and red, burning eyes.

– *Dream the nightmare of the condemned,* the Beast growled. They couldn't for their lives understand how they could understand him (it). It*It.*

They fell asleep in their tracks. But long before their bodies had actually hit the floor, they had experienced one million years of horrors and no matter what they did, no matter how much they wanted it they couldn't wake up. They were in His crypt, His waiting room and there was no way out. Not after a billion years and they had become His creatures long before that. They threw themselves from high places, breaking their bodies on impact. He brought them back with a contemptuous snarl. Death couldn't save them. Life couldn't save them. They belonged to the Jackal God, forever. Insanity claimed some of them, as they crossed a line they had been close to for a long time. A very few managed to drag themselves up by their hair and run away completely beside themselves. The three let them. It would only contribute favorably to the panic, chaos and confusion.

Gabi crouched on a bed. The room was that of a typical, ordinary teenager, completely disgusting in her eyes. She was able to take small steps, move «freely» around the room, but was chained hands and feet. The headband was impossible to remove. The pillow she pressed her face against wet of tears.

Awaken. She jerked her head up, but saw no one. *Awaken, little Delphi, it's time.*

Then Gabi saw Jill float in the air above her. Even if she differed in major ways from the Jill she knew, it was clearly her. The girl felt happy, but confused. She was awake, wasn't she? She wanted to ask Jill about this, but Jill had disappeared once more. Gabi sat up in the bed. Something made here look at the wrists and ankles. The chains had fallen off. The headband, too. It remained on the pillow, blackened and useless, so fucking great useless.

She rose and looked around, hesitatingly reaching out her arms, twisting the bare feet. The half forgotten, suppressed emerged from its hiding place. Was this how it felt, to be blinded and then once more be able to see? She watched in joy as sparks flowed from her fingertips, saw colors spark around her toes. Hands glowed hot as she dried her tears, angry, stubbornly. She, Gabi wasn't an innocent little girl anymore, but a big, bad witch. One who didn't have her equal in the entire world and not one to fuck with.

The parents quarreled and had the audacity to leave her the fallout, in order to easier endure their own, worthless lives they, themselves had partly created. By accepting and willingly enhance and support the intolerable in their surroundings. Then, when she after a long struggle finally got help to break out of her confines, an old geezer came and told her she was a danger to her surroundings, him and other insane men and women chaining and locking up living beings for study, use and ruination.

Colors darkened, but she fought to keep all the colors of the rainbow. She smiled bravely, as her attention directed itself at the door. The mighty power flowed from her being, her power, under her control. She didn't need Jill's help anymore.

She turned transcendent there on the spot and the transcendence spread to the room at large, the very air. The door seemed to disappear… fade away to nothing. She walked through the opening where the door had been, half dancing, half floating. It would have been okay for her to wait for the older witches to come and get her, but her mood didn't call for patience. She carried a strong urge to put a scare in someone.

The building, at least this area of it seemed completely deserted. The girl passed many open doors, looking into empty rooms. She was alone.

gabi

She stretched her senses, hesitatingly, beyond these walls, the level she now found herself. The floor, the walls, before her, behind… *Easy.* It demanded no effort, no effort at all. A door was kicked off its hinges and three men rushed at her. Ugly guns shot black darts. She knew what type, what they were. If they hit the mark, they would make her docile, compliant. Similar drugs had been in use during the heyday of the Burning Court. This was the true Hammer of Witches. Drugs sedating and dulling the witch (or anybody), making her or him confess to whatever the captors wished of them.

Gabi didn't have to lift the arm, wave her hand, but did so anyway, as a dramatic gesture. The darts vanished in open air. At least it seemed that way for the aggressors, until they appeared in the air behind them, with the same speed and forward movement, hitting them. They fell like chopped wood. More guards appeared. They wisely avoided firing their guns, but advanced forward with due caution. Gabi continued to advance, too, seemingly straight into their lap. They smiled, confident of their ability to adapt to the unusual circumstances and snare their prey. She smiled, too, vowing to show them who was truly the prey. Another gesture and the floor beneath their feet lost its substance. Nothing appeared to have changed. As far as their eyes could see the floor was still there. But they slipped straight through it. Those remaining stopped abruptly, swiftly losing any desire to advance further. But when they turned to run, they literally lost contact with the ground and started levitating on various levels above the floor. Gabi kept advancing, as she had done continuously.

– What's HAPPENING? A man cried out.

– You're in my kingdom now, Gabi declared softly. – Here my every wish becomes real.

A woman floating by attempted to stab her with a dart. The only thing she achieved was to stab a colleague, several lengths away. Her arm faded away and it, without the body appeared a completely different place. The blatant aggression in the woman's face and stance was supplanted by fear and incredulity.

– You witch, what did you do? She pulled back the arm and it was as good as new. She seemed unable to quite believe her good fortune.

– You're a fine one to complain about mistreatment, Gabi said, slightly more threatening. – You may call it poetic justice if you like. You do want to keep your arm, don't you?

The woman terrified, instantly started crying.

– Yes, please. Please don't hurt me. PLEASE

– Then you don't mind becoming my servant, do you, Gabi said consciously cruel, making herself hard. – My obedient and humble servant?

– I would be honored… Honored One. The sobs were hard and heart wrenching. – I am… yours.

– How easily you give up your independence, your will to others, Gabi mumbled surprised, pondering.

An expression of curiosity crossed the young/old face. She looked closer at the female. She was young, too - and strong, at least physically. Gabi let her eyes wander, searching among all she had in her power. To this point it had mostly been a game. Now, if it still was, its nature changed dramatically. Cruel, predatory eyes stopped by a young, powerful built male. She pulled him to her, placed him by the female.

– I accept your declaration of servitude, she declared. – You'll be the Virgin Goddess' Temple Guards and a part of the Anubis' elite sentries.

– You crazy cunt… She stopped him by a single gesture, took away his ability to speak. And it would be even simpler to return it to him, if she should wish it so. It wasn't very likely, though. He, they lived only to listen, anyway. That's what they had done so far and that's what they would keep doing.

– Such an outburst won't do, she pondered. – You'll have to be punished, of course. You have to learn.

She gestured. His body twisted and turned in horrendous pain. He couldn't scream. Only muffled sounds erupted from his mouth. As sudden as the pain had started, it stopped. She looked at him. He started crying, half insane with fear.

– Now, are you ready to beg your Goddess' forgiveness?

He attempted to speak, but no matter how much he desperately needed to, he was unable to do so. Panic dominated his face, his entire posture as he nodded. And nodded. And nodded.

She comforted him, patted his head as she would a dog. He sobbed in relief and gratitude.

– It's all right, she whispered. – Know that your Goddess forgives you and accepts you.

Shining silver strings grew from her fingers and surrounded the two. *They're evil, they don't deserve better.* The strings surrounded the shaking bodies, tightening hard and mercilessly. In just a moment Gabi, *Delphi* had sucked out almost all their juice, sucked it inside herself. And her Power grew.

Gabi.

She made the strings retreat, but left a silver collar around their neck. They breathed easily enough, but were tied to her. Now, Forever.

GABI

Jason? She lifted her head, dividing her attention away from this place. *You're not… inside. You weren't taken captive? Where are you?*

The load of information Jason instinctively sent with his words was far too extensive for her to take in, in her immediate, conscious mind. But for her inner eye she saw how he had awakened on his room at the school and quite simply thrown himself out of the window (the open window where hot night air flowed in) from the top floor. He hadn't landed softly, but the panic had practically given him wings and he had landed far more softly than he would have, if he hadn't half way flown, levitated down from the high point.

I'm outside a tall, electric fence. I can easily break through it, but the place is crawling with guards and for some reason my telepathy is completely useless against them. Their helmets must somehow protect them. Fetch me.

– Ok-ay, she spoke aloud, weakly, hesitatingly.

She saw more. They had hunted him the entire time, but he had hidden in the depth of the castle, and they had never dared venture even close to it. Only at night, while going out for food he had been close, and slowly he had pieced together what had happened and why… and where.

She let the two guards float away, ashamed. Jason… There had been some initial contact with him, but after a while she had sensed things about him that had kept her away. Now, though, he had come here, putting himself in danger. She concentrated, searched. Outside Jason rose from his hiding place, to full height. A hole in the air, the very matter of existence appeared before him, a shadow, a light far brighter than that of the emerging dawn. The guards started shouting to each other, started shooting, pulled the trigger for all they were worth (and they were worth a lot), but there was no one there anymore. Jason Gallagher had taken one step forward and disappeared into what had seemed like ordinary air. Gabi smiled in anticipation. The contact between them had made this even easier. He approached her through the wall. She threw her arms around him, shouting in pure joy.

– One week? Jill cried subdued. – We've only spent one week in this hellhole, and they still managed to so much to us, almost turning us into good little slaves.

– That's modern brainwashing techniques and behavioral modification for you, Stacy said equally horrified.

They moved instinctively all of them, without any real conscious thought, to the center of the building. They gathered there and for each new arrival they gained strength. The moment they touched Jill and the others waiting, they felt, finally as if they were about to awaken from the nightmare. The nightmare that would stay with them forever, that wouldn't fade in daylight. They wouldn't allow it to ever fade. The results of the brainwashing and the torture, and even most of its traces faded during the contact with their Unimind, but not the memory. Never that. To forget was to die. The suffering would help them build the armor they needed to protect themselves, from the world, in the world.

The guards were either taken care of or escaped to the furthest reach of the complex. Gabi ran into Jill's arms, shouting happily.

– I've had quite a strenuous task while you were enjoying yourself here, Jason said dryly. – Except for me, everybody was taken. Nobody slept on the Hill that night and they knew it. We opened ourselves wide, people. We could hardly have done it «better».

– *It will never happen again,* Lillith sent/spoke. – We'll make our own fate.

Is that possible? Gabi wondered.

As she had often repeated: She was the historian and she wondered if even they, with their possibilities and abilities to influence their surroundings could escape from the claws of the past.

I, too have grown, Jason sent to Lillith. *The energy of the crypt is within me, finally.*

Anton Berkowitz breathed somewhat easier. The techs had finally managed to get the surveillance system back online. That had to mean that order was about to be rest…

He gasped for air. The monitors showed empty beds everywhere… and in the central gathering facility he saw the Witches and also many of the ordinary patients. He wasn't sure what he was seeing. The sight seemed too incredible (to be credible). He had read reports during his years in the business, heard shocking reports through communication systems… but this…

– External, he barked.

Outside was even more unbelievable… and worse. All vegetation seemed to be moving. Long branches caught the guards. All resistance was useless (of course). Almost preoccupied he looked at the smaller monitors, showing the internal corridors where the few, remaining free guards had run to. Animated walls, ceiling and floor attacked them. Some accepted what happened in a catatonic calm, others struggled insanely against the raging reality attacking them. The end result remained the same.

– Use the gas, damn it, he said aloud.

Before anyone managed to react and actually get to it, he had walked to the large, blinking panel and hit the button with a clenched fist.

A thick, yellow gas flowed out of the walls, into the major gathering room, and also in adjacent halls and corridors. Eventually it would infect every non-protected area in the building. It couldn't be helped. With the funding this project would enjoy after this he could set up five new modern, top facilities. A possible problem was that all this could be too much, that his superiors would suspect him of having hired a special effects crew to receive major funding. No, he already had a visual recording and undeniable data in his suitcase. Not that there was any need for having the suitcase easily at hand, but…

He wasn't certain of what he saw. The large monitor showed the witches forming a circle, a huge circle. In the thick smoke they seemed almost transparent… No, not smoke. The air itself thick of silver and ebony. And the gas vanished… into thin air. As soon as it flowed out of the containers it was *gone.*

– Ask Bush to hurry to the roof and get the chopper started up, he roared insanely. – Instantly, you hear.

He pulled the last disk out of the player and threw it into the suitcase. And he was off.

– Tapper, Holcroft, you're with me. The rest of you burn and destroy everything you can think of.

The two followed him, obviously relieved. The others remained, shaken, but disciplined. They had learned about and been trained in the workings of hierarchies since their first breath.

They hardly managed to take one step forward. The door had just closed, when a creature of light appeared in front of them. The light blinded them, paralyzed them as completely as any sedative. They fell to the floor and a soft, comforting voice sang to them, sang them a lullaby. Travis Nichols faded away.

Berkowitz, Doctor Berkowitz and his aides, ran the last, few steps to the roof. The roof shook, the air itself seemed strange to them.

– I can't take it anymore. The male aide wiped his face and neck constantly. Sweat seemed to pour from his skin. And he scratched himself all over. He grabbed the doctor by the collar: – This is your fault. You've given me something. Do you think I *believe* this? You must be out of your mind. I'm not an idiot, do you hear? Do you think I enjoy being a guinea pig, you… you…

Berkowitz pushed him away. The Doctor and Holcroft proceeded to the flying machine ahead. The roof itself seemed to lose all coherence. They jumped aboard a split second before a deep ravine opened up behind them. Tapper managed to drag himself in at the last, possible moment.

– Take off, he screamed to the pilot. – Get it airborne, OR I'LL FUCKING KILL YOU.

The machine lifted off the roof, the ground, whatever, so easily, easily, humming and strolling above the beautiful New England forest. Berkowitz leaned weakly back in his seat, looking back at his hospital. He felt bad, he felt horrible, almost physically ill. It looked the same as ever, a building like any other building (in the beautiful New England scenery). Well, that was that. A small setback in a way, but many steps ahead in others. Infinite possibilities revealed themselves. Infinite.

Holcroft smiled to him. Her face was flushed, and she looked downright weird. He gave her his famous eye, but she didn't seem to notice, to notice anything.

The building grew distant behind them. He leaned back, relaxing a bit.

Holcroft and Tapper sat close together, holding each other.

– They're so sensual, she mumbled. – I couldn't stand it.

Tapper had opened his fly and started jerking off. His enormous cock pointed at the roof. Berkowitz felt strangely detached from it all. Tanner and Holcroft started fondling each other in a hot embrace. Berkowitz looked incredulous at them. What the fuck…

He looked back at the building. Excellent land value, he had seen it from day one. An excellent place to retire. A cabin by the sea, a fishing rod, a big fly zooming back and forth. The building disappeared in the horizon.

Or… did it? Did it Really? Didn't it seem… closer? He blinked and looked down. Forest had given way to plains. In spite of this the building they had left *grew* in his field of vision. The machine abruptly did a 360-degree turn, everything was spinning, spinning, hallelujah, no a 180 degree turn.

Everything had grown dark, so dark.
– What's up? For some reason he himself thought of the question as meaningless. What was happening to him?
– Up is down, sir. Holcroft giggled. She sat on Tapper's hips, rocking up and down on his big shaft. And she sang: – Down, down, down
– We're returning to base, sir, the pilot reported. – Trouble with the engine.
– What the hell do you mean, you ASSHOLE. The good Doctor screamed at him, his voice cracking. – The engine is like a clock, damn it.
Instantly the engine stopped roaring and started ticking instead. The pilot turned his head… turned it on his shoulder. As far as his body was concerned, he still had all his attention directed forward. Berkowitz gulped in fear. He saw not a face, but a skull, nude, devoid of flesh and it spoke.
– You chose the wrong man, it cackled, – bet on the wrong horse.
The horse cackled, no, *neighed.* What was wrong with him? A horse didn't cackle… did it?
– WHAT'S HAPPENING TO ME? He screamed in utter despair, from a deep, bottomless darkness.
A fire erupted close to him, a pyre where bodies burned. A young, innocent looking girl looked down on him where he crouched.
– You're dead, old man, she told him, – and you've gone to Hell.
– No, NO, he gasped. He strained and crawled towards the innocence so far ahead. He wanted to touch her. Only touch…
He touched her hand and the fingers turned to claws. She opened her mouth and a forked tongue spilled out. Her eyes turned evil, EVIL
– NOOOOOOOooooo
He lay on his back in the central gathering room surrounded by a ring of people. Jill Stafford sat on her hind legs by his side. He looked feverishly around. Where was the chopper? It had to be here somewhere. Inside the tiny, tiny box on the fireplace, perhaps?
– Problems with your perception, Doctor? She said sweetly.
Her eyes flashed roguishly and more than implied something dangerous.
– Beats the fuck out of your meager VR, doesn't it?
He looked at her, shaking his head in denial.
– That's right, she smiled. – The slumbering witch has awakened and a lot of it is due to you. You should be proud. Allow me to thank you.
She lifted him up by the collar with one arm, shaking him.
– Give us your confession, old man. We know everything already, but we wish to hear it from your sordid mouth.
He started talking, he couldn't stop talking. It felt good. Confession felt good. He hadn't visited a confessional since early childhood. He hung in her grip like a sack of bones afterwards, completely exhausted. Her bones, her property dug up from a cemetery to serve her eternally.
Holcroft sat on the floor, smiling. Tapper had his head buried in her lap. She patted him on his head.
Suddenly there was a sharp pain in Berkowitz' chest. *No,* he who was in such excellent shape. He had gray hair, true, but otherwise he didn't look his age. Well, perhaps it was just as well. This way they wouldn't have the pleasure of making him pay, of taking him out.
– Oh, no, you won't get away that easily, dear Anton, Jill mumbled intensively. – There's so much you shall do for us, Anton.
He felt it then, a heat hotter than he had ever before experienced. A heat that should have reduced him to cinder, that only warmed. Almost only. The roguish look was clearly present in her smile. But the pain in his chest disappeared and he felt more peaceful than he had for many years. He started laughing and he didn't stop. The laughter was hard, accentuated and ironic, completely devoid of warmth and emotion.
– *Sleep, Anton, sleep, you damn asshole.* He closed his eyes and fell asleep. Her rage sent him into sleep and the laughter reflected the walls in the blackest night.
Jill straightened. Everybody noticed. The raging force binding them together dissolved and slowly faded. They let it. They had to. Such an intense contact couldn't be sustained for much longer, not

by a single human. And it was no longer necessary. They wanted to be themselves. On the previous occasions their minds had joined it had been very short-lived. It hadn't diminished their sense of Self, but strengthened it. This time necessity had made them sustain it too long and the river had grown to a waterfall threatening to pull them away. It had been very seductive and treacherous all of it.

Jill frowned. They would continue to learn and grow, but at their own pace and of their own volition, in all areas of life. No one should pull their strings. No one.

– So, what now? Jason winked. Jill didn't know if it was to her or to Stacy, or to both. His Power had also grown. He was hiding something.

– They say that confessions are good for the soul, she said, as she kept smiling her roguish smile, looking down at Berkowitz. – We shall see, we shall see…

2

Sunset in the big city. Boston. A taxi stopped outside the public entrance of a police station outside Chinatown. A dignified, elderly gentleman emerged, followed by three younger people. Everybody was impeccably dressed and walked through the main entrance in a thoroughly believable way. The older man removed his hat and walked to the desk, while discreetly as ever avoiding the pieces of garbage and paper on the floor. His three companions found a somewhat clean bench and sat down. They were tight these three, two men and one woman. Their faces seemingly constantly flushed, they looked very distracted, all of them.

– Good afternoon, sir, the man by the desk said politely.

– Good afternoon, the desk sergeant slipped astonished, attaching a slight question mark. – Uh, is there anything I can do for you, sir?

Even if he had already experienced his share of crackpots visiting the station, he saw something truly unsettling in this one.

– My name is Anton Berkowitz… Doctor Anton Berkowitz. My colleagues and I are here to report a series of heinous *crimes*. My colleagues, the doctors Tanner and Holcroft, and the pilot Bush, will confirm my statements and also give their own, unique view of the events in question. We go back years, they and I, and have a lot of interesting tales to tell. First and foremost, though, it's necessary for me to come with a statement.

– Okay… the young, newly appointed desk sergeant signed discreetly to an older colleague. He had harbored a suspicion right from the start and now his stomach buzzed in a strong, strange sensation.

– I, Doctor Anton Berkowitz solemnly declare that I know of my right to have an attorney present, and the right granted me by the law to not have to incriminate myself and that all I say can and will be used against me in a court of law. I hereby deny myself these rights. Is anything unclear at this point?

The police officers shook their heads.

– It's also necessary for me to point out that most of the transgressions happened in other counties, all over the nation and indeed the world, dating back years, the most recent in Northfield, a considerable distance away. Distance is a general, necessary precaution, since participants in the before mentioned crimes include countless highly placed local and national and international officials. Many prominent citizens in Northfield, for instance, among them Scott Thompson and the Chief Commissioner are involved. Other important precautions of ours include DVD - recordings, older videotapes and documents and copies of documents posted and spread on the Internet and sent to the media in this state, New York, other cities in the United States, Canada, Europe, Asia, South America, Africa and Australia. And we've spread our confessions to a number of police districts in the Metropolitan area. Our esteemed colleagues are there right now… how do you put it… spilling their guts. We all feel this is necessary, since local, federal and international authorities have an even stronger interest than usual to keep a lid on this kettle. There's also a matter of powerful private interests with major investments to protect. This is the major league, young man. They will either give you a medal for this… or shoot you.

The sergeant just sat there, gaping.

Half an hour later all four of them sat in front of witnesses and recording cameras, making seemingly endless confessions. Very detailed, very accurate, very astute. The senior officer looking at it all through the one-way mirror hardly did anything but shake his head.

– We can't make them shut up, sir, the young sergeant said brightly, excitedly. – They're yapping continuously, to the point where we just about can slip them a few questions now and then. And everything *fits,* sir…

Slowly most of the present policemen started smiling. Expectant, hungry smiles lit up the observation room.

3

– This will be big, Jill said, smiling uncertain.

– Yes. Stacy smiled in her usual solemn way. – We'll be celebrities in wide circles. It was the only way we could protect ourselves… in the short term.

They sat in a car on the other side of the street, watching while journalists with pen and ink, cameras and microphones gathered before the local chief commissioner.

He stood at the top of the stairs looking very nervous, but also very determined.

– The policemen here will surely pursue this case to heaven and above, Jill shook her head in conviction. – They have been pushed and trampled on for so long and are so proud of their independence that they would have done it, even without the media coverage. But in this case the fourth, supporting estate is making it easier for them - and us, to cover our ass. It's so very, very funny all of it.

She laughed and laughed so hard that it became impossible for her to stop.

– Don't be such a child, Stacy joked and poked her good humored in the ribs.

Shaking in laughter, unable to hold back anymore Jill collapsed in her seat. The car shook so much that its movement was almost visible on the other side of the street.

CHAPTER SIXTEEN: Masks - the Festival of Life

In the heat of the night, in the heat of the day the move, the migration to the Hill, to Fire Lake began. Drumbeat filled the night as the fires stretched to heaven, burning deep below the ground. Garments fell from bodies, into the fire. Bodies emerged from garments, into the fire. Everett was the first, in swift, furious movements, then Jill, Stacy and Jason. With obvious contempt they threw their coverings on the hot furnaces surrounding the lake, the house. All the others present followed suit.

The highchairs were raised. Stacy was the first to take her place in one. She surveyed her kingdom proud and fierce.

Scene: Daylight, outside the courthouse in Northfield. Scott Thompson, handcuffed and enraged behind the relaxed façade is escorted inside by an army of police officers and lawyers. An even bigger army of curious bystanders forms two rows on both sides of the street. Even more than outside the police station when he was arrested and registered, fingerprinted, DNA-tested, retina scanned and so on. Rich people are usually beyond that sort of thing. The commoners present can see his mood. They're used to seeing it. His entire presence is like a dark cloud a sunny day.

A large monitor is on in an exhibition window. Lots of channels send news these days, send news often. Huge speakers are placed on the wall outside and people can easily hear the sound. The sound is good.

The news anchorman is coming on-screen, presenting his expressionless face.

– And then, once again we will see and hear Anton Berkowitz.

– *We did research in behavior control and modification, advanced and very sophisticated. Funding was no problem. Various private and public governments have shown an increasing eagerness in the matter of funding. Governments need to control the population. They need to know how to deal with rebellion and with groups critical towards society. Make no mistake: They're not really worried about these splinter groups per see, but of them gaining popular support. Corporations need to have consumers keep buying their products even though the danger of using and/or eating these products is common knowledge. We offered our help in a broad spectrum of areas, in both direct and indirect brainwashing. Test-subjects were no problem, even initially, in the groundbreaking early days. When there was lacking in sufficient numbers of those who were somewhat legally committed, we removed from society those that prominent citizens had on their list of being difficult and bothersome. Our skill and knowledge increased, to the point where we, with luck could return many to society as well adjusted and often also productive people…*

Doris and her husband moved through the crowd. They weren't really lacking in space to move in. No one was, except the people occupying front row. They stood sufficiently close to the screen to see okay and hear well enough what was being said. Once again, the network repeated the showing of the laboratory tour with Berkowitz as the guide.

– *We've accomplished much. We can make people see persons and things that aren't there. We can induce memories. We can do countless «impossible» things. Jason Gallagher had escaped our clutches. We made them believe he hadn't, even if more than one had witnessed his escape. For the best possible result, it's important to instill in the subject a deep sense of despair. After a while even the strongest person grows receptive to our influence. And the teaching can begin…*

And they could all watch subjects undergo treatment.

– Less than three hours since the arrest. Doris stamped the ground. – And he has made them convene the preliminary court-hearings.

– Couldn't it be that the authorities for once have acted swiftly to wrap it all up?

– Both statements are true, she said in a crushing blow.

Her anger was evidently not directed at Evan, and he let it pass.

Every time one channel stopped sending news about the scandal of the day, the shop owner switched to another. Other news was ignored. The president's daughter had been busted using heroin. Yet another storm gathered momentum in the Gulf of Mexico. Terrorists had blown another American public building to bits. Everything was ignored in favor of the News of the Day. It seemed like every channel in the world had something about it. But the news-hunters from this particular network had been very thorough. They had gotten hold of a copy of Berkowitz's interrogation.

– … *connections to the authorities,* they heard the voice of the female police interrogator.

– *I've given you documents, names, places, times…*

– At this time, we're more interested in the Top Man. You talked about messengers, agents. Who did they report to?

– I didn't talk to him more than a few times all these years, but he was always masked. Berkowitz continued in his dry, lifeless voice. – He wore different faces every time. But I recognized him. One always knew it was him. I had the impression that most of the agents… that most of them had it the same way. They didn't know who he was, but they knew it was him… if you know what I mean.

– Your witches should almost feel gratitude towards the good Anton, Evan said half cheerfully, half cautiously. – They will have far more room to maneuver in regards to Thompson in the immediate future.

– Almost, Doris emphasized.

– I mean… he will certainly be released on bail, but he will be busy.

As if on cue Thompson emerged from the court building, without handcuffs, surrounded by his police officers, lawyers and bodyguards. State of the art new limousines awaited them by the end of the stairs. The ominous, impressive company disappeared inside, and the luxurious crafts cruised off. A few minutes went by, while the crowd remained, indecisive. Then people started to wander off. Most went home; secure in the conviction that nothing ever changes. Passive, like sheep. Doris sensed a very pronounced chill down her spine. Just a few days ago she would have been one of them.

She turned impulsively towards her husband.

– Let's go to the Hill right away, to them, she suggested eagerly. – We won't have missed too much of the Witch Castle initiation.

He pulled back, visibly.

– I'm still not convinced I want to go there at all. You say we can learn so much from them, but they're so young…

– Young in age, old in wisdom, she whispered seductively, pushing herself at him. – Or have you forgotten…?

He still could hardly believe the changes she, they had undergone the last few days. Hit by lightning from the clear blue sky everything else had become insignificant. He had returned home from work, expecting nothing, hoping for nothing. She had been happy as a bird, singing instead of merely talking, as in their younger days. But she hadn't made anything of it, just silently and laidback served dinner and he hadn't really been suspicious. He had thought it was just another of what he deemed her phases.

They hadn't left the apartment in four days and four nights.

After the first, wild night she had quite simply told him the entire story, told him what she had done. He had astonished realized that he didn't mind that much. Not when considering the overwhelming result. And when he realized that he couldn't remember the name of his secretary he found that he didn't mind at all.

He looked stealthily at Doris, the woman by his side, while they walked arm in arm towards Oldtown, a place he hadn't even visited in years. Even if her freshness had a somewhat mature content, she seemed wilder now, than she had ever been in her youth. He himself felt better than he had in years, free, irresponsible and bursting with fighting spirit. Emotions that in no way lessened when they passed a car with open windows, stuck, frozen in place in the daily major queue on Main Road.

– I see that the documents go far back… the woman leading the interrogation said hesitatingly, *– but the… research doesn't begin to… yield results until spring 1980…*

– … q*uite astounding, I know,* Berkowitz grunted proudly. *– The work, the impregnation we did on the subject Mark David Chapman, ended on quite a happy tune. This in spite of it being obviously nebulous territory. As there's always ways to improve one's work, one is never completely satisfied with any result, no matter the outcome, you know…*

2

One single tone, a single guitar string seemingly vibrating forever. Then Ivan struck the Shaman drum. The flute and the rest of the «orchestra» joined in. Kieron struck a battery of drums, slowly at first, increasing the speed to the point where his hands moved too fast to see. They stood in front of the broad entrance to the castle on Fire Lake. Rhythms hung heavily in the air and the music flowed across the water, through the forest. The song seemed to both originate with and target those who did and didn't sing, from a place within.

Stacy and Jill, Jason and Everett sat in their highchairs, thrones of woven wood close to the eastern wall, turning towards the beach and the stone pier. They didn't wear a single piece of cloth on their body. Not even the minimal loin-covers many of the others wandered around in. The four wore some feathers, simple jewelry and ornaments tied around arms and legs, nothing more.

The Sun had risen as high as it was about to, warm and on a cloudless sky, as if in summer. But it was October and its rays hit them sideways, throwing both light and shadow in their faces.

Wind was blowing from the west. The wind was blowing from the north. The wind was blowing from the east. The wind was blowing from the south. Like in the legend of the Four Winds, the Winds of Change coming to blow away the Gray Fog. Janus, the many-faced god of the Crossroads and the Four Winds were present in their whispers.

He is coming, Delphi whispered in Jill's ear.

Red flower petals whirled through the air. The children threw them around, covering the path from the broad, main entrance to the shore, and from the shore on land and on three paths to the forest. People trod on them and felt their soft fabric beneath their feet.

The Change was palatable, both in each witch and how they related to one another.

In the night and the fire each of them walked to all the others, in a whirl of simultaneous motion.

– You're not my enemy, Stacy said to Jill, – you're my sister.

– *You're not my enemy, you're my brother.*

And it continued like a chant through hours and hours of sweat and dance.

Their Change had been taken one step further. The house (on the other hill) had thrown them through one of many gates of fire. It had abruptly and effectively ended the rivalry among them. They realized that only by uniting their powers and skills they would have any hope of halting the march aligned against them, the monster's ball pushing at them from all sides. They had indeed started the process of throwing away control now and breaking the invisible chains of society. And it made the pressure increase even further. Both the possibility of reward and risk increased.

Jill reminded herself of what Berkowitz had revealed to them, that Thompson was merely an insignificant pawn on the outskirts of the spider's web. It didn't take any great mind to realize that he was only a local minor king of the hill anyway, not even truly a part of the Great Game. Someone... knew of them out there. More than one someone, more than one group of someones. All the publicity would inevitably lead to the point where their existence got revealed to a host of people, in spite of the bit of blurry image they had made Anton present (of them), including those who would recognize them for what they were. People who, through experience knew that their talents included far more than picking the right herbs, who knew them for what they were.

She and Stacy, Everett and Jason kept in constant contact, kept constant vigil. While they earlier had only occasionally scanned peoples' minds, they now did it regularly, scanned everyone crossing their path, everyone close to it. They should never more be taken unaware, never be taken, period. They should never more be *unprepared.*

The party, the celebration continuing from the previous night had started anew not long ago. The Dance, the Play, the Life. The twins Meta and Melanie danced wild, energetic, uncontrollable, but even to those who made a thorough study of the girls it seemed like one of them was studying her own reflection in an invisible mirror. Golden hair sparkled in the wind and the sunshine. Even the way their hair moved was virtually the same.

Others danced and added to the beat by clapping their hands. Some were satisfied by clapping their hands, while others just sat quietly in the grass and on the ground relaxing. They participated in a variety of activities, but were One.

All the witches and virtually everybody who had so far joined their Circle were present. And the guests, those coming to this place for the first time, were on their way. From the town below, passing the burned-out school building, up the hill, through the forest. They followed the sound of the drums, or Drum. The sound seemed to come from everywhere, from the very air, the plants, the ground, flowing towards them from somewhere within themselves.

Jill looked pleased at the celebration, at her siblings, at herself, how former shaking insecurities and inhibitions had been reduced to insignificance. How it was muted in the new arrivals. She surrendered to the hypnotic, magickal mood. Hypnotic in the sense that it made her more aware, not less, that it instead of chaining her set her free, releasing the inner instinctive, impulsive human being. The primitive, wild creature she, too, had denied so long. *We can all be what we once were.*

The children had completed most of the... of the deflowering (Jill giggled) of the ground. Some remained on the mainland to deflower the people, the pilgrims emerging from the forest. The others started swimming, crossing the lake, the sea, to the land of the Gods. They ran wet and wild to the throne of the Four.

Flash: Everything shifted. Suddenly she sat in a massive, gigantic hall. She received her acolytes, as was her right, as a Queen Goddess of Egypt.

The children of Fire Lake did kneel down before her, as would Egyptian temple children, as they had done then, in a mix of deference and fear, and she couldn't say she didn't enjoy it.

She nodded to them, a bit impatient for them to rise, recalling how she had, as the Queen Goddess of Egypt, ordered flagellated a boy not kneeling properly. She had licked his blood from the sacrificial stone afterwards. It had tasted sweet and hot.

All of these knelt properly enough, though, as if they had never done anything else. Some of them, with thoughts transparent as glass, harbored rebellious thoughts, but those were faint, easily dealt with, if necessary, not really present in their body language. Toni, daughter of Luke knelt closest to the throne before the Queen Goddess, leading the other children. Lillith nodded pleased. In time she would become an excellent servant.

Lillith heard them, heard the pilgrims, both the children and adult children. She heard them move through the dark forest, as she moved with them.

– The forest is still humid, even wet, Evan said astonished to his companion.

For some reason Jill was unable to hear her reply, but she sensed it in her body language and joy of them moment.

Kate and Adam walked up on the beach surrounded by a lot of their own acolytes. Lillith saw it happen, as it had already happened several times in Kate's mind.

One Kate became many. Somewhere a book formed out of nothing, turning its pages, somewhere that same book was burning, and Jill couldn't tell which Kate was which, which Kate was real.

The group stopped before the quartet triumvirate.

They all fell on their knees, silently like dust. To Jill it seemed to happen simultaneously, countless times.

– Speak! She bade them.

– Hail to the Giver and Taker of Life, Adam cried. – We humbly submit to Her mercy.

– We come to serve Her as She desires. Kate's lips trembled. – Her will, Her Cause is... ours.

The regal figure turned her head slightly, before climbing down from her stature, easily and agile of limbs. A silent choir rose from the ground, the water. She walked straight to the black-haired kneeling woman, grabbing her around the jaw. There were tears in Kate's eyes. Jill could understand that. What the Goddess giveth she could taketh away.

– And what, pray tell, is that cause? Jill heard herself say.

– Anything... the girl cried out. She was like a child. They were like children, all of them. – Command and we will Follow.

The images and emotions Jill received from the poor girl spoke volumes. She had become nearly hysterical with religious panic during the days following the healing. During the witches' incarceration she and her fellows had wandered the streets, speaking of the Queen Goddess. They had actually used that name. Given time they would have turned into a full-fledged cult. Jill looked around, also at the onlookers. Not only those kneeling had listened to and taken to heart Kate's words. Their miraculous escape from the Asylum hadn't improved matters. The stories told in the media, had grown one or two notches more in whispered rumors and fevered minds.

She observed Doris and Evan reach the shore of the castle, approaching them, approaching her, seeing in their minds a readiness to kneel, to bow like the rest.

– No, she said flatly. The woman by her feet looked startled at her.

They would use that, use the momentum, its horrible Power, but not like this.
– Know that the Goddess, that I… she cried, – that *I*, Jill Stafford want Human Beings in my midst, not sheep.
She turned to the three others. As the murmur grew loud enough to hear, they had already descended the woven wood.
– That would make us Masters, she shouted. – And we're not. And all Masters are slaves themselves.
She turned to Jason, eyeing him.
– And we're not…
– I'm not so sure about all that, he said dryly.
Neither am I. She thought.
– I saw you, she spat, – on your throne. You were bored out of your skull.
And the murmur grew to a crescendo.
She signed for the kneeling congregation to rise, smiling and shaking her head, as did Jason, Stacy and Everett. No pyramids, tear down all the pyramids. They could play a bit with ceremonies and rituals, but they had to look out, for it to never becoming anything more. Or was Jason right? That they couldn't leave out any method, any means to become an invincible, immense Force? Jill saw herself keep struggling with these thoughts, this inner turmoil during the eons to come. Toni looked at her, finally daring to, nodding once. She understood. Children understood, when push comes to shove so much more than adults.
Lillith heard them. All the Human Beings, of all ages. Heard them move through the dark forest, through the Shadow. The flower petals whirled through the air. Lips moved simultaneously, identical.
– What did you say? Jill and Stacy asked each other.
Stacy smiled a beautiful smile, she really did.
Pilgrims broke out of the forest, already happy, filled with expectation. They wandered into the water, starting the swim to the world beyond, the center of the Storm. Perhaps they had waited for, fought towards this moment like the salmon swimming up the river, the eternal sea to seed new life. And they wouldn't die, but Live.
Doris and Evan were among the first in their group to walk ashore. Her face glowed in joy as she, grinning eagerly pushed him with her the last few steps to the Witches' Castle. Jill and Stacy, Jason and Everett met her halfway. Doris ran the last few steps and grinningly grabbed Jill's outstretched hands.
– I bow to you, O'Mighty Sorceress. The middle-aged woman stood straight with mischief in her eyes. – I will follow you sharp-eyed beyond the gates of hell.
– What she said, the man by her side said, while clearing his throat.
Jill smiled when hearing the silent sharpness in his voice.
– Doris and Evan, I'm especially glad for having you here today. May your Journey bring much pleasure, not too much grief.
Music halted for a while. The flow of new arrivals finally ceased.
They all gathered before the house, before the witches.
– I'm warning you here and now, once… and never more, Jill said loud and proud. – Once and ever more, your perspective will be Changed. You'll seem like Strangers to who you were. There will be no return to the life, somewhat, you knew. We greet you, welcome you, as Free men and women.
She knew they stared at her, didn't need to see it to know it. It didn't bother her anymore. She hardly knew shame anymore and enjoyed that immensely. She enjoyed everything about it. Two clicks from the Stone City gates the shame had been inflicted upon her. Ten thousand years she had struggled and suffered on her way back.
– Free men and women, she repeated, – on their Journey. As you may have realized by now, we don't want slaves. We demand more of you, far more.
Without coyness and with swaying, sensual moves she and Stacy turned and walked inside the house, into the shade… and the Shadow.
– Please join us inside, Jason offered. – We've prepared a modest meal, as a start of our feast, our celebration of Life.
They all walked inside, through the broad Gate, into the brighter shade. Jill and Stacy waited for them in the great dining room, watched them enter with pointed, penetrating stares.

– I've thought about something, Jill said hesitatingly, causing the other to look at her, – concerning Berkowitz and his… deeds. I wonder if Laurie… knew.
– She knew, all right. Stacy spoke in a burning whisper. – You can count on that.
– Then let her *burn,* Jill whispered.
– Yes, Stacy said. – Yes!
Wide-eyed people looked around. The house had seemed big from the outside, but nothing like anything approaching its real size. A table was set, one with one, single bench all around it.
– One hundred plates, one hundred cups, father, Brian, son of Luke said in a factual manner. – Are we one hundred?
Luke shook his head. If he wasn't very much mistaken, they were exactly one hundred.
A moment of silence baffled the assembly, as even the less sensitive among them noticed the pervasive… pressure from the house. Just for a moment they were overwhelmed by the nondescript impressions the old walls gave away. They gave away *something.*
It had grown stronger since Jill first had visited these halls.
They sat down. The witches casually, randomly, as the others slowly found a place. Slowly one hundred candles started burning. Smoke rose from them at first. Then the flames cast their orange light on faces across the room, dimming the light from outside.
– It's the time of the twilight, time of the wild dance, Ivan cried, his voice carrying all over the building, and outside, above the lake, into the dark forest. – It never gets completely dark. It's twilight. All the blood, all the open wounds, all the joy is there for all to see.
– And with these words, my friends, Everett grinned, – I declare this banquet opened. Start chewing till your heart's content.
It was a modest meal. Vegetables, fruit and some pieces of meat. There were those who looked nervously at the plates. The meat looked distinctively… raw? And the glasses were filled with water? Well, they thought. The witches had a reputation for modest living, not for gluttony. That explanation satisfied most of the guests.
Stacy and Jill rose. They placed themselves back-to-back halfway turned, seven to eight positions from the oval end farther away from the exit, close to the heavy door leading into the deep recesses of the castle.
«Castle», «house»… they constantly used both words, without being able to decide which they thought suitable. One of them? Neither? Both?
When looking at the two girls, women everybody found themselves changed once more, also from the person they had been outside.
– We're form, Stacy spoke with her usual flavor and stinted smile. – One great imperfect form. We're form out of Chaos, but we're also Chaos itself. It's *logical,* is it not? It might seem like a contradiction in terms at first… But not after we've given it some thought. Don't you agree?
Nods and assurances of agreement around the table. She smiled ironically.
– As we go within ourselves, we know there are no contradictions. This we know, as we know many things, from the moment of our birth. Later we forget. The immediate and genuine is replaced by hypocrisy and deceit. We must be constantly reborn not to forget. He who isn't busy being born, is busy dying. Together here, elsewhere we'll travel towards the identical doors of heaven and hell. I don't know… perhaps it's the same door? *Anyway,* we're gonna confront the extremities of our existence. We're gonna Travel on Styx, the River of Knowledge and Death, to its very end…
Jill looked at her from the edge of her vision, looked at herself, freezing down her spine. She met the eyes of Charon - the Ferryman, and he nodded.
– We'll go to infinity and Beyond, Stacy continued. – There are no borders, no limits or limitations. We're just taught to believe there are, to make it easier on the tyrants. Well, from now on there will be no more such bullshit.
Some cheered and applauded. The intensity of her words stirred something inside of them. It wasn't just words. They sensed her utter sincerity and they rejoiced.
Something within responded. They did.
– Before we eat, Jill took the lead, – let's have a toast, do an initiation, or the start of one. You'll awaken and perhaps you'll realize that you've been sitting like this, in a place such as this many times

before. Give us just a moment please. Give us Eternity.

The two raven-haired females reached out one arm each, in a ninety-degree straight line from the body, one her left, the other her right. Closed fists opened above each their glass. And then - many gasped - a wound opened in the palm of the hand. One single drop of blood appeared and liberated itself from the skin, falling into the glass, into the water. It spread instantly and violently, in a raging, racing speed through the clear fluid, to the point only seconds later, where the fluid wasn't clear anymore, but blood red. As if there had been a cascade of blood, instead of a single drop. The level rose in the glass to just below the rim, but didn't reach critical mass. Everybody stared as transfixed at the glasses and at the two witches circling the table, sacrificing one drop of blood in each glass they passed. The same repeated itself. The very modest amount of red «overwhelmed» completely whatever had been there before. The two met halfway, stopped a moment, before crossing each other's path and quickly returning to their seat. Or had they been trading places? Perhaps, to drink of each other's blood. That was what had happened, wasn't it? Evan and Doris and other newcomers exchanged confused looks.

The girl covered in the thin fabric of a dress rose, joining the two older girls. The people of the gathering knew her, most of them. She was Delphi, the present one, the presence, the collector and whisperer of truth.

– The food we're gonna eat, the animals and the plants, have given their lives for us to live, she spoke. – Not voluntarily, for sure, but still, the fact remains. What is needed more than anything in the current unaware, unconscious technological society is an increased awareness. The broth before you will strengthen both your body and your mind and soul. Accept the blood, the Blood of the Witch and throw yourself into the Dance of Life.

She took her glass and lifted it up, to the height of her mouth. Most of those present did as she did. A few left the house with fast, panicked steps, and they would never stop running.

– I would like to make a toast to Freedom. Jill lifted her glass (for the second time?).

– TO FREEDOM, everybody cried.

– To Total, uncompromising *Freedom,* she spoke, she swore. – Beyond any niceties and speeches.

And they all drank.

– *Blood is the Life,* Jill said, Stacy said. – *Life is the Blood.*

And they kept talking, as One, a hypnotic litany of Night and Fire. Forever!

– As we struggle, as we throw off the chains of tyranny, as we're rejecting The Pyramid and its fundamental injustice, we're looking back… at what… and who we once were. Deep in the ashes of our own fire we give birth to ourselves… *Forever…*

– *Life is the Blood, Blood is the Life, the others repeated.*

– FOREVER

Jason was the first drinking. As the others repeated the litany of blood and led the glass to their lips, he lifted his glass ironically to the Two and emptied the glass in one turn.

Some drank with caution, though, until pausing in amazement.

– This *is* wine, Evan insisted to Doris, in case she wanted to contradict him. She just nodded and kept smiling.

– Yes, she whispered, nudging his arm. – Wine mixed with blood. A broth long time ago baptized the Blood of the Gods.

She leaned heavily towards him.

– Can't you *feel* it? She whispered even lower. She had emptied her entire glass and the huge eyes were bright and clear.

– Yes… He emptied his own glass in a quick burst of energy… and then it was as if the content *exploded* in his stomach, as if the energy itself expanded, spreading like wildfire throughout his body, as if the fluid expanded in the body like the blood had done in the glass.

He felt *something.* All his senses turned sharper, everything turned that much sharper. He heard the birds sing outside and also far away, deep in the woods. The smell, he could smell the food. Until this moment he had never thought he could ever smell much. He started eating, they all did, and it was an experience. Evan was willing to swear he was able to tell how much less poison it was in this dish, compared to the bland food he usually consumed. A tear formed in his eye. A moment he became

overwhelmed with grief, and it was such a powerful emotion that he felt enormous, total Joy.
– It tastes great, a woman said, not many places away. – The meat, too, scratch me.
The meat was prepared in a way. It wasn't exactly like eating raw flesh in the wilderness and it originated from a domestic animal. Still, it was as if they… felt the animal, its resistance, its unwillingness to die, its Life. They imagined the plants stretching towards the sun.
– My teeth are drowning in spittle, Luke exclaimed.
He couldn't rein in his excitement, he didn't want to. He felt Alive. Many years had passed him by, since he had even approached a similar joy. It would continue, he knew that, long after the traces of the broth had faded.
– What the Blood gives you will eventually fade, Stacy told them, unusually soft, – but we're bound now, Forever.
Jason sat there, watching, as his arm started fading. He had no control over it, but he had anticipated the result and didn't fight it. He disappeared completely. The bench empty where he had been sitting. The girl by his side screamed.
– So that's how he escaped, Jill said smugly, very pleased with something.
– I can't read him at all, Stacy said. – It's very frustrating. He isn't just invisible, he's *gone.*
– But I'm here, they heard his voice from open air. He touched her. Everybody witnessed how the skin on her left arm seemingly contracted of its own volition. She swept the air with her claws. Nothing. Teasingly he said: – I can touch you, but you can't touch me. Not without my consent.
He reappeared, indistinctively at first, then once again clearly, normally.
Delphi started to shimmer, but she got it under control quite quickly. Others started to exhibit new, until then unknown talents. Andrea moved her arm very fast. Moans of pain escaped her lips as her body changed on the spot. It wasn't anything like what Tam and especially Everett had gone through. But her muscle mass increased significantly and her strength probably even more.
Others didn't or didn't want to exhibit what they suddenly found out about themselves.
What Stacy had said, hadn't been completely truthful or correct. The new they had discovered wouldn't go away. It would, on the contrary increase in intensity and complexity, as a plant in constant growth. And it felt completely natural, as a natural extension of all the changes they had experienced earlier in life and after arriving here.
Jill didn't focus on those she knew. Her attention was drawn towards two, a man and a woman, sitting quietly on the bench holding hands. Their aura had been approaching normal the entire time since their arrival outside. Now it flared completely erratic. Jill started sweating hard on the spot, something she hardly did anymore. She nudged Tam carefully to not reveal her worry to anyone else, and sent her to fetch the two. Jill herself and Stacy closed in on them from both sides.
– Would you please come with me? Tam gave them a pleasant, but decisive smile.
There was no attempt on their part, as Jill or Stacy could register, to read Tam's mind. What were their powers?
They rose hesitatingly from the bench and followed Tam. The heavy door to the castle's interiors slid open. Jason and Everett walked in first, then Tam and Loeh with the two newcomers, in the rear Stacy, Jill and Delphi. Lamps flashed on, fire rose from candles the moment everybody had walked through the door, and it had closed silently behind them all.
– We should have known we couldn't hide anything from you, the man shrugged.
– Dreamweaver, Jill ordered, – we need to isolate ourselves.
Shimmering light spread fast from Delphi's body, surrounding them all.
– We're totally isolated now, she reported. – No contact out, or with the rest of the Shadow World.
– What did we do wrong? The woman said. – What's happening?
– We received no thoughts from you, Jill said in a crushing blow. – No deep ones and just a few surface notions. That made us suspicious. And you know perfectly well what's happening.
– We come here from a Circle in Boston, the man said. – The others sent us here by vote. We will tell you everything you wish to know. There's no need to force us. We are, after all just messengers.
Stacy and Jill circled them with hard, vicious smiles, touched naked skin with long, black claws.
– So cute, they choired. – Their juice is like nectar.
– You're the cute ones, the man said abruptly, authoritative, – and I, for one want to devour you all.

The two halted, astonished and confused. Then he touched them, and it was as if their mind… clouded. Everything stopped working. Jill moaned, in despair, in fear. She wanted to move, to act, but she was paralyzed.

– That is also true for you boys. The woman had walked over to the already frozen Jason and Everett. With a triumphant look of ownership, she touched their cheek. They stood there like statues, with glassy eyes.

Pheromones, Jill thought dully. They're spreading them through air and thus take control over others, he over women, she over men.

She was unable to even access a shred of her mind power, no matter how much she struggled.

The male signed to Tam, and she walked to him, paralyzed, enthralled. Gabi stared dog eyed and devoted at him while blindly obeying his every suggestion. Loeh looked fearfully at Stacy, but she got no help there and she quickly knelt before him.

Gabi performed for him, as he gave her instructions with his waving hands, like he would an orchestra. Finally, he seemed content and grabbed her around the jaw.

– You're truly a cute little witch, he said harshly. – Are you really a Dreamweaver? Answer me, you bad, disobedient brat.

– Yes, sir, she replied fearfully and respectfully.

He smiled triumphantly and cruelly, as he could hardly believe his good fortune, holding back his ecstatic excitement. What a find!

– Whatever you did, brat, undo it.

Gabi didn't move, but the shimmer in the air faded. They all felt the draft in the air. But only the man and the woman could move.

– That's good, brat. After a while you'll learn to obey instantly, without the slightest hesitation. You will all learn.

Jill felt sick somewhere. She would have closed her eyes if she could, in grief and rage, in her pathetic impotence. These witches were older than they were, at least ten years and they had evidently gained a very precise control. Powerful witches with a finetuned control. She wanted to swallow, but she couldn't even do that. She noticed dully how saliva ran from her mouth, from all their mouths.

The woman grabbed Jason and Everett's hanging cocks. They grew instantly hard and throbbing. She kissed Jason softly on his cheek, clawing at his chest.

– What a charming specimen, she purred. – You won't disappear on me, will you now?

– I will not, he replied, his voice and stance filled with servility.

She rewarded him. His hardness expanded even more, contracted and expanded, and semen washed the rock floor.

She pushed herself close to Everett, without letting go for a minute the hold she had on him.

– What a beast you are, she spat in disgust. – You're a beast, are you not? Show me what a lowly animal you are.

He changed and grew huge before her. She smiled. Steam flowed from his chasm of a mouth. But there was no rage this time, only dog-like servility, eagerness to please his Mistress.

– Down, boy, she commanded sharply.

He went down on all fours.

– Yessss, now it's almost right. She pretended to think it through. – But I desire a true four-legged creature…

Jill stared in horror how the change proceeded further, to the point where something very much resembling a wolf stood there. An enormous wolf, but still a wolf. It wasn't the change itself terrifying Jill, but the sovereign control the woman had exercised over it, the sovereign exercise of ownership as she combed the ragged pelt with her fingers.

– You're such a sweet, four-legged animal. I must remember to get you a fine collar. You'll enjoy the kennel where we keep our other beasts.

A snap with his fingers and the male made Jill and Stacy turn towards him. He made them turn his entire attention towards him.

– You're such beauties, such prime specimens, he bragged. – You'll come to contribute to our cause in major ways once your attitude has been turned in a more suitable direction.

He did with them as he had done with Gabi, Loeh and Tam, smearing a fluid version of the pheromones on their skin.

– From now on you don't have powers anymore. He spoke with such confidence, such… finality. – We have removed them. Such you'll stay until you're found worthy of your birthright.

– You I want to keep as you are, sweetie, the woman whispered into the wolf's ear. – Keep you forever. You'll forget what you were and come to serve me enthusiastically.

Jill noticed it already, how her mind darkened. The inner voice, will faded, as the outer had done.

– Yes, that's right, he confirmed. – Everything is just chemistry.

– You're strong and hard, the woman said. – You received us quite honorably, with the cat's hunger for the mouse, but you weren't *prepared.* You hadn't prepared an in-depth defense. You'll pay for that.

– Come with us, sweet pets, the man ordered.

They obeyed. Not merely blindly, but also eagerly. Followed Master and Mistress back out in the dining room. Where virtually everybody sat frozen or lay unmoving on the floor, or stood there like statues. They who still moved were easily dealt with. They licked the woman or man's hand, and they were done.

He spoke into a cell phone, just a few words she couldn't make out. It was evidently a signal.

– You Multies, he laughed scornfully. – So varied, no focus, so easily distracted.

She drifted off than. She didn't move, didn't sleep, but just drifted off. Time blinked in and out. Next time the sensations of sight swept over her it had turned markedly darker. There was the sound of rotor-blades, as the choppers landed. Unable to turn her head or even see, she heard. The sound of many people running overwhelmed her weak faculties. She scorned herself for her weakness, in vain. The prisoners might have walked out on their own, might have been carried away like cordwood, she wouldn't know. The Man made them exhibit themselves like the catch they were. They were inspected by grinning and expectant soldiers in full uniform. Not any uniform she had ever seen or smelled, but a uniform, nevertheless. A private army. Of mutants? She and the others had been reduced to *things,* a trophy fit for nothing but exhibition and servitude. She looked at the Man full of gratitude. He had shut her down, her down - down - down - down. Somewhere in the core of her being something stirred.

but the surface was so far above, and in the attempt to swim the long way up, she lost her breath and died time and time again.

down - down - down

They sat in the chopper, moving through the air. Choppers arrived and left during the dark night where no one saw, no one heard. Their disappearance would be another unsolved mystery, nothing to be worried about. They had taken everybody, not only the mutants. She and Stacy sat close, holding each other's hand. They concentrated so hard that it hurt, wishing for the Power to awaken. Nothing happened. Master and Mistress had conquered them, made them their obedient slaves. They wondered why the humans had been taken, too, but it wasn't their lot to ask questions.

There was pain, as she penetrated deep within herself, deeper than she had ever needed to go. She might have screamed, but she recalled no sound.

The birds not radiating the slightest light lifted off the ground in the lightless dark, taking off for an unknown destination. She remembered so little. Why couldn't she recall... who she was? A huge hole had supplanted her thought, her mind, her emotions, her Self. He had torn it out of her. He had turned

her

Lillith blinked. Two pair of eyes opened and closed. They once more met the eyes of Charon across the table. Jill couldn't tell if it was her eyes or Stacy's or if it mattered. What had just happened here? Charon, Anubis, Plat, Everett's deep frown shook them. They saw how he shook. Paralyzing fear and berserker rage warred for dominance in them, but what remained were the cold rage and the calculating fear. They saw Jason fade in again, saw him fade out. Gabi was crouching on the bench, with her arms around her, about to lose herself again. They had… returned to the dining room? What had just happened? Had she… and Stacy (Jill and Stacy) experienced a dream while fully awake, a shared vision about the future? They had experienced something similar before, but never this immediate and terrifying. Or had they quite simply returned from the immediate future… to keep it from happening? Whatever had happened, the howling sense of DANGER persisted, one they couldn't or wouldn't ignore.

Fade. It was a redundant message. Jason had already started to fade once more.

Their attention was in its entirety directed at the couple at the end of the twenties, holding hands. Rupert Lee and Priscilla Utheridge. Jill suddenly knew their names. Like she with her increased awareness was able to observe the pheromones flowing from their skin, into the air, into everybody sitting here. She remembered now. They had closed the door, and no one had reacted. *Hell.* Jill felt with a sickening feeling inside how what floated in the air influenced her already, sneaking, dangerously. They didn't have much time.

Tam was sent to them once more. Again? Jill and Stacy rose, but remained. Jill relaxed a bit. Her body, her will, now, while being fully aware of the threat, fought even harder against the intrusion.

– Would you please come with me? Tam sent the couple a friendly, but decisive smile. She didn't fathom what was happening, but had sensed the intensity in Jill's mind.

The couple rose hesitatingly. They looked at each other. The heavy door to the castle's interior slid quietly open. Everett walked first inside. His back was slightly bent. Tam and Loeh led the two newcomers inside. At the rear followed Stacy, Jill and a shaking Delphi. The door closed behind them all. Lights turned on and candles lit themselves (as if) by Magick. Jill would have smiled if she hadn't been such a boiling cauldron inside.

– We should've known we wouldn't be able to hide anything from you, the male said in regret. No emotion, no passion, only a dark hole of malice.

Rupert Lee was an amazing actor. Was there a slight shaking in his voice… this time?

– *Dreamweaver.* Tight lips quivered.

Shimmering light had already started to spread from Delphi's body. The fluorescent mist first surrounded her, then the woman and the man.

– We're isolated, Delphi reported. – We're isolated from them.

They all registered how whatever floated in the air vanished the instant it left the two bodies. The fair-haired man and the black-haired woman screamed as the mist cut into them. They wanted to move, but except for toes and fingers, they were unable to. They floated in the air before their predatory captors.

– What's h-happening? The woman gasped, stunned, as if unable to realize they had been conquered. – What did we do w-wrong?

- We didn't get any deep thoughts from you, Jill scorned them. - No deep ones and hardly any surface thoughts. That made us suspicious as hell. Not too bad for a multi, huh?

The two stared at her with a bland look of utter incomprehension. She fully enjoyed the moment. She knew, but they never would.

- We gave you a gift of the Blood. Now we're rescinding it.

Shimmering silver threads grew from Delphi's fingers, entwining those she had in her power, binding them to her. She sucked the Power out of them. Their skin turned pale, and their bodies were sagging. Delphi started glowing. She released them, pulling her strings. They fell on their knees, completely powerless in mind and body.

- You challenged opponents several levels above yourself, Jill said, dealing the crushing blow. - That's all you need to know.

The bottomless hateful rage couldn't be denied. Stacy and Jill jumped at them, dug long, dark claws into them, pulled even more power and knowledge from the already exhausted bodies, sucking juice from thought and mind and soul. Pricked the skin, drawing blood.

- What's reality and what's fantasy, can you tell me that? Jill snarled and slapped the man in the face with her left hand and hit him hard with her right. She pulled back a bit… to hit again.

She attacked the woman, too, hit and kicked her, hit and kicked both, until they lay unmoving on the floor, unbelievably enough still conscious. She made sure of that. Stacy stroked her back, embraced her, kissed her on the chin, calming her. Both knelt and surrounded the two bruised ones on the floor in a healing cocoon. But they made sure it hurt and they forced every possible iota of information out of them.

It felt marvelous. They didn't dare go deep in the others' minds because of possible pitfalls put there by another telepath. They were inexperienced yet, but they were familiar with the concept, knew that something like that could be done. What they did was to force deep thoughts to the surface, sucking them in. The flow of information was… staggering, a lot more than they could remember there and then. They wouldn't have been able to protect themselves like this, like they had to, if not for the rage running like lava in their veins.

In a flash they saw a woman with burning eyes, with fireeyes. Rupert and Priscilla's Lady and All. She smiled to them, horribly, expectantly. As fast as the vision had appeared it faded.

Jill stumbled to the stairs, hitting the stone painfully with her left calf. She remained there, with her hands on the head and the head between her knees. Gasping, alternating between despair and rage.

Gabi looked at her, indecisively. Jill looked up with eyes full of tears.

– Do it! She nodded with a decisive snarl.

Delphi walked close to the two prisoners. This time simple thicker silver threads grew from her hands, turning into collars around their neck. The collars would be invisible to most people, but they gave Delphi control, as much as she wanted. And their energies would always strengthen her. She felt shaken, torn up inside, between conflicting emotions. She was fully aware of the fact that she wasn't the first Dreamweaver to have used her power this way.

– They're yours, Anubis, she said respectfully.

– I don't know. Everett hesitated. – They never managed to do much.

– They would have, Stacy said hotly. – If you doubt that, you doubt everything we are, everything you are.

– They will be excellent Temple guards, Anubis, young Delphi said, not without a visible pride. – They'll seduce all intruders, leaving them as horny wrecks in the dust.

– Rise, Anubis said harshly, in a hollow, horrible voice, as if he shed a skin for a while just then.

Delphi had seen him like that before. She trembled in awe and fear.

Rupert and Priscilla rose with empty eyes, shaking like leaves. They stared at the Fenris Wolf, begging him with their eyes, not daring to open their mouth.

Not even when the tiny human fangs grew in the mouth of the man towering above them, did they utter a single sound. He pulled Rupert to him first. The long, pointed teeth punctured skin between the neck and the shoulder. Powerful jaws bit through. Everett sucked the salty blood into his mouth and swallowed it. So easy, it was so easy. He didn't suck a lot, just a mouthful or two. He let go of Rupert and turned towards the female. She released a tiny squeal when seeing the hunger in his eyes, what he had only marginally sated. Enough to not devour her completely. He sank his teeth into soft skin and drank greedily. He sensed her surrender before that and for every passing second, he bound her closer to himself. He had bound the male, too, but the will behind the act, the drive to go through with it was so much greater, in him, concerning her.

He remembered. The memory would ache in his consciousness for centuries, millennia. For perhaps the very first time, if only for a moment, he wanted to *be* Anubis… the Jackal God.

Silence descended on them. Pain raw and vengeful turned on them all.

Jill raised her head slowly. Eyes emerged. Two open wounds with a light glowing ever stronger. The memory of what Rupert and Priscilla would have done to them and what they had done in return kept haunting her. She wouldn't stand for it. Already tight hands tightened slowly, consciously into a fist. She refused to let the world make her… make her hard. She wouldn't allow it. Never!

Jason. She sent, in a way not to misunderstand. She saw him appear only two steps away. He had been here all the time, that careless, disobedient idiot.

– This - changes - nothing, she hissed low and hoarsely. – Nothing. We are what we are. We're seekers, but we're not like a boat sinking at the first sign of bad weather. We're born to stand against the Storm. This won't make us turn in either direction. *Do you hear me?* If anything, it should only make us even more dedicated to the path we've chosen.

She looked at them one by one. One by one they nodded.

They straightened once more, but not completely. The ambiguity in Jill's words didn't escape them. Gabi attempted a smile and succeeded in a way, allowing the shimmering mist to evaporate around them. The wind was once more blowing hard and strong. The way they felt this moment, this ambiguity, this was the way they truly were, fighting and free… come what may. They challenged the

Storm… come what may… and their wild hearts beat.

3

The wind chimes above the gate played to everybody who listened, within and without the castle walls. High or loud, far and near, one always heard them.

Stacy stood below the chimes. The always well-done hair whirled in the wind. She studied Jill as she sat down with Delphi, entertaining a group making a circle down by the Lake.

Drag yourself up by the hair once again, Lillithsister, she thought. Dig deep in the mud for your humanity. Try once more… to get it right.

Stacy felt the wind, felt its soft caress from all sides and laughed. There was another fresh burst of air, another breeze of Life. Women, men and children laughed spontaneously, as they charged forward. The mood was exuberant and wild. They knew nothing of the horrifying destiny that had almost befallen them. The celebration continued. Stacy stepped down from the porch. For just a minute she allowed herself to be immersed in the surroundings, the dance, the life.

A single silent accord in the shimmering air and it was as if… everything… as if everything let go. Some of the hundred went straight from walk to dance. Gloriously spontaneous and dangerous, dangerous. Stacy gritted her teeth. Anubis approached her with outstretched arms. She let him lead her into the dance, hesitatingly, worried.

– Let's throw ourselves into it, he said lightly. – It's just as well. One can deny neither one's black nor white shadows.

The lake brushed against the shore, carefully, virtually undetected. Jill sat on her heels, studying the interaction zone with an intense curiosity, hidden behind distant eyes. Water seemed so harmless… so unimportant… almost. But during thousands of years, it could dig entire valleys. Everything depended on perspective. The life of a present-day human was so damned superficial. As long as one merely needed to turn a knob it was very easy to forget that, no matter the source of water, it was a Spring of Life.

She blinked, concentrated on what went on in her immediate surroundings. Gabi stood by her side, inside the circle of people. They juggled and performed cheap tricks for a while. Then they looked at each other and stopped. Gabi started shimmering. Then she started sparkling. Shadow enveloped everybody in the circle. Jill sensed their growing panic. She lit a fire in mid-air. No ceremonies, nothing obscuring what happened. To be certain they couldn't misunderstand what happened she held up her hands, enlarging the floating fire, bending it, forming it, making it obey her will.

It was night within the sphere, the sphere of shadow.

– This is… for real, isn't it? A boy almost stuttered, both fascinated and afraid.

– Yes, Jill replied. – This is no trick. This is the power within, the power of witches.

Both within and without the ring, the ones not yet initiated stared at the two female witches with wide-eyed, unveiled interest. They were captivated by the sight of the Storm incarnated. They had sought this, hungered for this, and had come here for precisely that reason… but they had never imagined they would find… what they had found. They had seen it inside the castle and saw it now, outside, undeniable. Whatever they had imagined within, previously in their life, now turned Real. Every thought, every emotion, every act.

Everything was just ghosts and shadows.

The sphere dissolved and daylight rushed back. All the people on the island hurried there. In acts without words, without thought a new, bigger circle was formed. In its center the 20+ witches sat. Surrounding them were the 80- initiates. Questions were asked, often stupid ones, answered patiently, encouragingly. Jill realized that this was something completely new. The Gods hadn't sat down and replied to the stupid questions of mortals much before. At least not in a very long time. Not as long as there had been Gods and mortals.

Jill replied to a question from Brian. He looked older than he had been just a few short weeks ago.

– You think my talents, these powers are what make me thick, don't you?

– Well, yes…

She turned slightly away, looking over the rise.

– I'll always be grateful for having them, as they're giving me a change for a deeper, richer life, but ultimately, they don't matter. It has become a cliché, but it is what's inside a person that counts.

She hit her chest and knocked on her head.

At first… at first all this had felt… unreal, as a sort of detachment. And she had expected it to continue like that, that she would turn into a sort of aloof being, as some of the old gods had been described. But it wasn't like that, wasn't like that at all. She didn't grow detached, but felt deeper, stronger than she had ever done. And she had forgotten how many times she had thought that thought since coming here.

There were demonstrations, show and tell. And it gave them all a good feeling. As they familiarized the others with their talents, they familiarized themselves… with themselves.

Gabi rose. Delphi rose.

– I'm gonna tell you a story, now, she told them, in the straight approach that the teachers and most adults found so frustrating, so infuriating.

Few of those gathered here thought in such limited ways anymore.

– Tell you a legend that in our days, people, the few remaining nomadic tribes in North Africa are most familiar with. Storyteller has told it to Storyteller through hundreds of generations… the story about the People of Legend. Many believe this is the Gypsy, but they're wrong. The people in question are far older than the gypsies.

Jill felt stirrings, the stirrings of Memory.

– The People of Legend are, or at least they were, held in high regard in North Africa. In a society where a nomadic lifestyle was seen as an absolute necessity for survival, for Life they were seen as the absolute Nomads. The stories are many and often contradict themselves, as old stories often do, but the core remains, a core far more solid than in more well-known stories…

– Nobody knows where they came from, originally. Who knows? Perhaps they quite simply appeared one day, from nowhere? But we know this: In a city, in a land history has forgotten they were seen as a threat to the ruling elite.

Flash: Riot control in the streets. Old streets, new streets, one and the same. People bleeding, people dying for speaking up, speaking and acting their mind, for being Human. Lillith concentrated about sharing this with them all, making sure they shared every fucking, bloody detail, every injustice, every heart of the Freedom Fighters.

– «It's better to die on your feet than to live on your knees», Gabi continued. – Emiliano Zapata said that, as many have said it before or after. As long as there has been the city, as long as there has been *civilization,* there has been injustice. Civilization destroys everything making Life worth Living. It has only existed for five hundred generations, but it has thoroughly fucked us up.

She stood there, with her hand like a fist, burning with Rage and they all shared it with her.

– This ancient line of Nomads was, by their very existence a threat to the emerging hierarchy. Every single Nomad was, is, but they especially, because they were gods refusing to buy the imposed idea of the hierarchy. They never stayed long in one place and were in all ways uncontrollable. They were driven off or forced to run. And even if they wanted to hide, they couldn't. Because they were unlike every other people on Earth, both of nature and look. Their eyes were like the beasts of the Earth and their fire was like that of thousands. Because of this they can never hide anywhere. The face isn't so special that they can't hide in a crowd, but the moment others see their eyes they know who… and what they are. This has been true throughout written history. There have been a few places where they have been able to enjoy a certain liberty, but only as a burning fuse, until the forces of intolerance rolled over another place where Freedom reigned. It has ever been thus. They have always been hunted. Admired and respected by the few, but mostly hated and feared. An entire tribe of witches and warriors, surviving to this day, only a handful left…

– The Janus Clan, one exclaimed astonished. – You're talking about the Janus Clan.

– So nice to have a participating and intelligent audience here tonight, Jill joked.

There was a bit of laughter, as everybody, both teller and listener attempted to catch their breath.

– Yes, Gabi stated, – I am talking about the Janus Clan, and it wasn't really difficult to realize either, was it, for the conscious being? They're one of the world's few groups of mutants living pretty much in the open, even if not many know what they're truly capable of. As you know they're active in

Phoenix Green Earth and that makes the ruling elite very, very worried. But not thrice as worried as they would have been if they had dared to admit for themselves the truth we all know. If they had *known*...

– Known what? It was the same boy, the one with a chip on his shoulder, staring sullenly at the others sitting there nodding.

– My mother says they're descendants of Satan, a girl giggled. – Just wait until she hears I'm here. She'll suffer a heart attack for sure.

– It sounds like you admire them? The boy said sharply. – What the hell for?

– Yes, why admire a bunch of thieves and insurgents and no-gooders and rebels, Bertram, Jill said, the very image of scorn, every word cutting him like knives. – Yes, why don't you buy hook, line and sinker what the establishment propaganda says about us all?

– It's really quite simple, Gabi said quietly. – They're what we all once were.

And everybody's Wild Heart thundered in their chest.

Perhaps even in Bertram, even if he left, even as he fled from the place of harmony and power.

– I feel sorry for him, Jill said. – He couldn't stand being confronted with his own prejudice... something we all must be from time to time.

– Me, too, Stacy broke in dryly, – but I'm even more reluctant to let him go. We're gonna meet him again, somewhere, somehow, sometime, and it won't be pretty.

– He's the Enemy, Jason said. – Faces may vary, but the realities of it are the same. He's the huge, mindless crowd, the eager servant of the caretakers of the Pyramid.

– Poor guy, Jill snickered. – He will miss the next story, the one that is mine to tell.

Her voice changed in mid-sentence, to her strange, singing speech.

After ten, twenty seconds she was elsewhere, they all were. Along a trail, a path of desperation, but also, eventually new Life.

– Many thousands of years ago a group of people, a tribe wandered across an enormous plain, a handful survivors from the sunken land, Atlantis... As its inhabitants they had lived closer to nature than present day people do, but they still had to relearn everything truly important, how to survive, to Live in the wilderness. They were few and the threat of starvation was never far away. True starvation, far worse than the pain they constantly felt in their stomach. Game was scarce and they were ill suited to hunt. What they needed more than anything was time, time to relearn how to kill, to kill to survive.

– One of their number, one that through the countless following generations has been given many names had a gift. Only one. But one very important. He had the ability to communicate with nature's smallest creatures. And he had two growths protruding from his forehead reminding one of buffalo horns... No matter, what he did was to keep flies and even smaller creatures away from the meat, causing far less of it to be spoiled. The hunt didn't get any better or simpler, but the small group managed better through times of scarce game. What he gave them was time, time to become what they were meant to be. They called him Ligthbringer. The Legend grew in the generations to come, as legends do. Among his names surviving to this day are the Horned God, Morningstar, Grandfather Death, Lucifer...

She let it sink in.

– I've heard several other stories about Lucifer, a boy said thoughtfully, jokingly. – Somebody has truly strived to destroy his reputation, right?

Laughter. Jill smiled.

– What happened to him? He asked, with an unruly curiosity.

– He lived many lives, as we all do... I can't tell you, don't remember, exactly what happened.

And she wanted to, wanted it desperately.

– But because his very essence was to lift veils, to reveal what is hidden and encourage independence, it was inevitable that he would clash with another powerful force in recent human history...

Warm sand found its way between her toes, burning her, making cold ice clutch her heart.

She stood alone on the beach a while later. Stacy sneaked up on her.

– Such a sjeahh, she pondered. – Wise, I mean. He was truly wise. He left before they grew too dependent on him.

– He had to, Jill said, pondering too, the word the other had used. An old word, a language from a faraway time. – If he hadn't, he would've destroyed them and himself as certain as he earlier had been their salvation.

– Not like a certain other we're quite familiar with, huh? Stacy mumbled moody.

– We never did forget the lesson of Atlantis, did we? Not even *he* made us forget that, did he?

– Not anymore, no. He made us believe we had forgotten, that asshole.

Jill studied the pack of kids running in and out of the forest, into and out of the water, splashing and laughing. Virtually all of them could swim. Even the youngest had learned it here, in an amazingly short period of time. They had learned in creative, inspiring surroundings.

We're doing something right here.

– We've become so sensible, Jill said suddenly. Stacy looked at her with humor in her eyes. – I know it's a strange thing to say. But I just can't believe how much we've grown. We are just eighteen, after all, you know.

Stacy waited while she kept looking.

– We've also become ruthlessly sensible, Jill said, a stroke of pain in her voice.

The pain was sort of comforting. Laurie had never, as they knew her, harbored *any* reservations about using her power to get what she wanted. And it had destroyed her, long before her actual death.

– I can see us not coming here, she said dreamily, – scattered in the wind, being picked up one by one by... other parties. Laurie made us come. And she did teach us something. Mostly how it shouldn't be done, but still.

Not all of Laurie's teaching had been bad, though most of it was tainted by power hunger, her prevalent desire to be on top.

She had said all the time, what Jason had said, she had just been a lot slicker about it.

– She did instill a sort of confidence in us, though probably in spite of, not because of.

Laurie had given them confidence, all right, but only confidence as part of the group. Her «teaching» had indeed «left out» the stimulation of their ability and will to stand on their own. But she hadn't, couldn't really dominate the wild ride of the Spirit Quest, could only do her best to steer it. And she had failed miserably.

While waking up that Sunday the results had been, at first, as Laurie had wished it to be, a confirmation of the group, conformity instead of individuality. But one of the first actions Jill, and also some of the others had taken was to establish themselves independently of, if not actually outside, the group.

– She tried to qualm the unrest in us. Unrest isn't bad, but great. We are natural nomads. Suppress that and we're hardly more than ants on the ground, sheep in a field.

And now the visions, the confusion, the clarity came from within, not being imposed from some outside source.

– Laurie lacked resolve and means. Stacy finally spoke as she grabbed Jill's arm. Jill looked at her. – She didn't have the power necessary to successfully prevail with her agenda... *We* do! We have Power to do whatever we want.

– Yes, Jill replied. – Yes.

And she grabbed Stacy's arm.

Then her eyes sparkled roguishly.

– Come, she said invitingly. – Let's go for a swim.

– Swim? Stacy squinted her eyes.

But before she could decide one way or another, Jill had pulled her with her out in the lake.

Bubbles. Like air in hot blood, pumping from a wild heart. The emotions inside of me are like a drowning body that must reach the surface. How long have I been under? How many seconds, minutes, lifetimes?

Stacy was breathing the life-giving air and she laughed aloud, unconditionally.

There hadn't been too much laughter in her life.

Laughter flowed above the waters, drifted among the trees, bubbled and boiled in and out of the lake of fire and the enchanted house… as the sun fell and fell. Many of the people present had arrived only a few days ago. They had sought so long, bird and fish, deep and far. Finally… they had found the Place. A conviction not at all fading with their further experience that day, that Night.

Twilight emerged, without, within. All their Shadows turned longer, mixing with the one growing around them. And when Stacy Larkin far from shore simply rose straight up from the water and started walking on it and Jill Stafford joined her, very much of everything seemed to fall in place for everybody. The two dark-skinned girls hardly got their feet wet, after they had ascended from the water. The water splashed a bit, like dust would do on a road, that's all. They walked towards shore with a smile on their lips. The low murmur rose to a silent choir as eventually everybody present had their eyes on them.

The old world was no longer a half-forgotten memory.

Smoke drifted above the water. The moon hung heavily in the air above the group of people. The humans couldn't be sure it was real, but they imagined they saw its mirror image in the strangely calm surface. An enthusiastic, expectant inner voice told them that whatever they had seen so far was nothing compared to what was to come.

A beast howled between the dark trees. Everybody heard it and experienced joyfully the cold trickle of fear and excitement down the spine. Those sitting in the forest glen moved a bit, just a bit closer together. And those who sat on the island, too… since they suddenly had to convince themselves that the howl hadn't come from inside the house, deep below the ground, from the deepest abyss. Jill and Stacy performed as dragons, blowing fire from their mouth, devouring it, spitting it back out. They stood on the shore, one on the island, one by the forest, dragons blowing fire high in the air. The flames turned into balls of fire falling into the water and a cone of steam and smoke rose high above them. Twin balls. Twin cones, turning once more into Fire, a huge bird of fire and Life, slowly fading in the mirror image in the strangely calm water surface.

– We're children of light and darkness, incorporating both, owing loyalty to none. Jill and Stacy spoke simultaneously, as one. – We walk, through fire, through Shadow, from the night we are born. We retain the newborn's hunger for life.

She/They paused. Pleased, Lillith registered that the children had made good their promise, their bragging. They approached carrying newly made pottery jars, in one odd shape after another. Large and small, painted in beautiful and ugly decorations.

– From ancient times the word *persona* means mask. We're all carrying masks. And each person is potentially many. Everything we have been and everything we may become is deciding who we are.

Both girls stopped suddenly, hesitatingly, wondering.

– We went deep… Jill said, while Stacy didn't move her lips.

– There's something… Stacy said, while Jill didn't move her lips.

There was a spasm then, below… but so much stronger than it used to be.

The blood, *she could smell the blood.*

She looked down and the thick, red fluid was flowing down her thighs and onto the ground, the sand.

There were screams of horror, on both beaches.

They held up hands, once more speaking and acting in unison.

– It's okay, I'm okay… I think…

They all stood frozen, undetermined.

– It's her fucking period, a girl exclaimed exasperated.

Everybody looked thunderstruck at the two girls, bathing in their own blood.

– Yes, I do believe that's it. Jill shook her head. Stacy smiled preoccupied.

And then everybody kept staring. The sand under their feet, by their feet. The yellow dusty sand… turned green. The first few seconds there was only grass, but then a wide variety of growths started sprouting from the former «dead» ground, Life's potential realized in moments, surrounding the Witch, the ground, the growth shimmering in red, yellow and green.

The two of them, after an undetermined timespan stretching on like years, finally emerged from the small forest they inadvertently had created with a dazed expression in their eyes. They stumbled in their dizziness and people rushed forward to help.

– NO! They cried, stopping everybody in their tracks.

They touched their forehead, sweating, with slowly receding swelling around their eyes.

– Not yet. Not yet…

You'll die, they thought, exactly like moths to the flame.

Jill remembered. How a strange growing fungus nobody had been able to explain, had forced her to change the fucking tampon in her crotch four and even five times a day. And there had been more blood than usual the previous month.

Of course, she didn't really lose more blood than others. It just expanded and made it appear that way. Everything also happened faster, more violent.

Her blood was saturated in energy, in Life.

She/They straightened, smiling.

– Life is letting go, she cried hoarsely. – Preparing, gaining power for the next cycle. We're ready now, prepared for another initiation, our ascension into the depths. Rejoice, my friends…

– In Death, there's Life

The blood… it was still a part of her. She was a part of the new forest as it stretched and grew, as she regained her strength, as she regained what she had given, as the sensation of not being there, of being there slowly faded, but not completely. Never more!

Steady beat of low-pitched drums resonated on the Hill. The celebration reinvented itself once again.

What had been interrupted began anew, fresh and wild.

Gabi accepted one and one jar from the children, as Loeh did on her side, and they started painting Jill, painting Stacy. Hands, fingers and hair were used as brushes and swabs. Jill giggled a bit. Gabi stopped, uncertain.

– It's okay, Jill shook her head. – I'm just… ticklish…

She was here, there, everywhere. So strange this, like she was painting herself. She saw herself through the painter's eyes and it… the background turned indistinct. Did she see the forest behind her… or the house?

She/They stood before everybody. White eyes in stripes and forms in gray, white and black, shimmering in fire. The children started painting everybody. All present either standing or sitting, started swaying. The rhythm and the close/distant music vibrated in them, in the ground, the very Earth below them. The fires hissed. Everybody laughed loud and unafraid.

– The paint has dried, Jill shouted. – It won't go away for days. Time to thread the water, to burn the fire, cast the Shadow.

And the excess began. It started with a volcanic eruption and worked itself up from there. They lost themselves and found themselves there on the spot.

Jill stood on the island shore, not really aware of how she had gotten there. She didn't care.

– Let's DO IT!

The highchairs were thrown at the fire. Jill burned with joy, as she and others, using the strength of their arms and hands carried one to the biggest pyre in front of the castle. It was an act filled with both symbolic and actual power.

And the Dance to Life began. All remaining fabric was torn off sweaty bodies like spider's web on a dark trek. No matter how tight, no matter how protective they had felt. Everett could actually sense the tightness of clothes, of skin, of his own, and others. At first, he didn't realize what was happening. His skin felt unbelievably tight… and then the Change started.

Then the Werewolf, a creature from the Earth's mythic past stood right there, in their midst. There was fear, inevitably, but not exceedingly so. They had thought they had seen it all during the day, during the first shimmers of night, but they realized now they had seen nothing yet. They stared, at the face, but another part of the body stole virtually all the attention.

Its huge cock stood erect and dripping. He attempted to speak, but he managed merely a low growl. There was no rage this time, only passion, and lust, indescribable lust. Males and females stared in disbelief, as their own mindless lust was raised even a few more notches.

– My cute beast. Jill purred.

She stood frozen in her tracks, immersed in hot magma, like every other female close by. The two-legged beast wagged to Jill and Tam and carried them off into the forest, into the deep sea between the trees.

Kieron loosened his shirt and kicked it away.

And the Dance to Life turned Wild.

Wild, as an unstoppable hurricane traveling the endless sea.

Jill swam in a sea of hot embraces. As she floated away from one body, another took its place. Shy, horny girls had come and relieved her in the two-legged animal's embrace. She had been riding it, him. He had taken her hard, making her scream in her Hunger. Tam had fallen asleep a few bodies away, completely spent. Jill sat with closed eyes, swaying on a male's body. She didn't know who it was and didn't care.

The Passion, the Hunger of Human Beings…

It's like turning a full cup upside down. Blood will run like water, but... No matter how long you're holding it thus, it will remain forever full.

Bodies crawled and floated everywhere around her. She knew hands and lips on the body, belonging to both men and women. It felt so good, so infinitely good. She sucked up energy from the very air, like a swamp after a prolonged drought. And she returned it. This was how it was supposed to be. No veiled thoughts, hardly any thoughts at all, rudimentary flashes of need and instinct. Jill had held back, allowed it to build and now she reaped the reward.

The highchairs had burned, leaving only smoldering ashes. Forest and lake breathed around them, as they were themselves. The light was both decreased and enhanced, and so were the shadows. Light and Shadow flickered and wandered, on the ground, in the trees, in the very air. A group of witches started to sing and run in the woods. From the city below they saw the wood nymph dance. Wild, unafraid males and females celebrating the fact that they were alive. Witchdance, as the city's oldest had been told it from their oldest during childhood erupted everywhere on the Hill. Stories from the mists of time, now about to evaporate in the shadow heat. A spirit dance touching ancient memories. The American natives had danced like this at Wounded Knee; making the appointed «official for Indian affairs» go apeshit in his panic. Like the outlaws had celebrated Life in the Sherwood Forest and caused rumors to fly about resident spirits, ghosts, apparitions, demons…

Vicky danced, encircling the man-wolf, in a mix of daze and mindless desire.

The red flower petals whirled in the air, with a few black and white mixed in. Someone, somewhere played the first part of «spring» from Antonio Vivaldi's Four Seasons. Harps, flutes and violins changing into something unknown, sliding into drums. Spellcast drums in the enchanted forest. Those who watched (with binoculars) from below, saw a cluster of sweaty bodies, and they saw Victoria, daughter of one of the city's most prominent men *ride* the giant dressed in a wolf costume. Fire and plants stretched and twisted. Even the forest itself seemed to be Alive, to move visibly before their eyes. Two police officers, a man and a woman were present among the onlookers. They didn't know if they should call for backup or leave this evil place and forget everything they had seen. They remained, unmoving.

A mist started drifting down from the forest. Jill emerged from the forest and began the descent from the hill. Instantly Stacy walked by her side. The mist surrounded them.

Parlor tricks, they thought despairingly, grinning.

The mist rose from the ground now, all the way to the city limits, surrounding all people present. Completely nude they stopped before the gathered crowd. Wild, with misty eyes and sweaty skin. Two males appeared a few steps behind them (out of the mist, people thought despairingly). Half erect, dripping cocks were clearly visible in the shadows.

– Why are you here? Stephen Bachman asked in a very aggressive, aggravated manner.

– You called out to us, Stephen, Jill replied softly.

He froze and with eyes filled with pain, he looked down at the shrunken covered shape he held in his arms.

– We'll take care of her, Stephen, Stacy commanded. – Put her down.

He obeyed. The girl lay on the ground, constantly twisting and moaning in pain.

– Can you hear us, Sylvia? The two asked her, speaking in tandem.

– Yes… The girl looked wide-eyed at them, as they knelt by her side, as they touched her skin, a skin so rough that it seemed to be covered by scales.

– How did you know her name… and mine? Bachman almost shouted.

– What has *happened* to her? Stacy pulled up her head. People gasped. Her eyes had turned white again. She hadn't been able to keep it from happening with the wrath swelling in her. – Why hasn't she been given medical care?

– We… tried, Bachman replied weakly, as if apologizing. – We had health insurance and everything, but nothing helped… much.

– It's the factory, Jill stated tightly, lividly. – As long as she lives close to it, she will never completely recover. No one will, as long as there are factories.

– What do you want me to do? Bachman shouted.

He stared at them with something very much resembling hatred.

– You must choose a side, Stephen, Stacy told him harshly. – We must all do that. Decide whether or not we're Users or Preservers. And those who wash their hands in the struggle aren't neutral, but on the tyrants' side of the fence.

Jill studied her a moment, until they both concentrated all their attention on Sylvia.

– You'll feel strong heat and strong pain, sweet one. It isn't dangerous and will be over soon.

They surrounded the poisoned girl in their powerful healing embrace. The gathered people gasped aloud, as two pair of hands started glowing, started glowing so hard that nobody could look straight at it without being blinded. Sylvia moaned… and then she screamed. Several onlookers swore afterwards on the fact that they had seen smoke and smelled chlorine. The glow faded, like a low flame on an almost burned-out fire. The scale-like skin turned smooth once more. Almost retroactively Jill sensed a camera being used and overexposed the digital image with white heat.

– Rise and walk, she told the girl, couldn't help herself…

Sylvia immersed her naked body in the blanket and straightened on legs that were nothing but unsteady. She began to jump up and down in a sudden state of euphoria. The blanket would easily have slipped from her fingers, if not for her strong, healthy grip. The father grabbed her. She stared at Jill and Stacy with something going far beyond awe.

– Thanks, Bachman said hoarsely, dragging his daughter away from the witches.

– What about Tremayne? Stacy cried after him.

Tremayne was his son.

– He's just coughing a bit, the man shook his head. – He'll be all right. A boy can take a little coughing.

– He will soon be as ill as Sylvia was, Jill said. – Or worse. If he catches the Betrayal, we may not be able to save him.

The man walked away with bowed head.

The two dark-haired females didn't feel tired even if they had used more energy than they would have wanted. Unnatural compounds were always more difficult to remove from a body and the diseases human-created poisons caused harder to cure than what existed naturally in the surroundings. And at the «heart» of it all was the general weakening of the spirit, of will modern human beings were subjected to. They didn't feel tired. Not even Stephen's lack of spine, what he shared with most of his present-day brethren destroyed the moment for them.

They turned to return to the forest, the hill, but stopped when the two police officers blocked their path.

– You will come with us, the male officer attempted to sound authoritative. – You're under arrest for indecent exposure.

Several of the onlookers smiled and laughed openly. The uniform alone would usually have given the man and woman complete control of the situation. Now they just looked ridiculous.

– We're not doing anything wrong, Percy. The words smothered him, like Jill's sweaty, seemingly oiled body. – You are, in your attempt to keep us from doing what we do. We're celebrating this day and night, honoring Life. What better way to do it than to with abandon surrender to the «reproductive act», the most fundamental possible, the strongest desire in our life?

He attempted to give voice to a reply, but couldn't do it. The weight of her breasts pushing at his chest, the erect nipples stabbing like knives in his heart stopped him from doing so. Her completely overpowering love made him groan in desire. Then… she pushed a hand at his rock-hard erection and smiled hungrily to him. He was pulled helplessly down the deep of her sea. She pushed her lips at his. He was a large man, broad-shouldered and slightly taller than her. She sensed the desperate resistance in him against giving in to emotions, needs, to his own most deeply felt passions, but it melted to nothing confronted with her heat.

– Don't think that will *work*. The woman spoke enraged. – It won't work on me.
– You really think so, Hazel? Stacy sneaked close to her from behind. – I don't believe you do. You don't sound very convincing, you know…
The witch grabbed her around the jaw. Hazel wanted to tear the hand away, but didn't even have the strength to move.
– Look at our men. Don't you long for their touch, long to feel their hard and large cocks inside? I know you do…
Do we take them, awaken them? Jill asked pondering.
Why not? Stacy returned. *They're not among the worst. There's hope for them and they've got potential, don't you agree? And they want to…*
– Come with us… Jill waved and called out to them, called to her everybody present. – And be Transformed.
– Everybody is welcome, Stacy said softly, – but know that you'll never be as you were.
A few remained. Some ran like rabbits. Most of those who had to this moment been only spectators to the celebration of life joined in. A crack in the air and the entire crowd disappeared in the burst of smoke. It was all so strange. They moved forward, but not by moving their feet. They heard the sounds of the city, music from one of the clubs and simultaneously also the sounds, the music of the forest. There was a moment without sight, without sound, and when sight, when sound once more *was*, Fire Lake's beauty appeared before them. Jill caught something in her throat. She felt exceedingly happy because no one had thought about putting water pipes up here.
The water surface mirrored nature and the deepest thoughts. Flames from many fires stretched to meet high in the air, eruptions of deep red dancing in the night. Jill and Stacy's eyes turned completely white. (For some reason) everybody looked at the lake. Suddenly the water started burning. Small flames making circles, a door opening up in the very air, a door of golden flames.
Jump through the Gates of Fire.
A broad passage they could all walk through simultaneously. They couldn't tell if anybody had actually talked, didn't dare to look at one another. How had they really come… where they were? They didn't know, weren't even sure they were here.
Stacy Larkin and Jill Stafford waited for them on the other side, as they also had seen them leave.
White, deep shadow eyes looked at them.
– You're naked now, Jill said, – like when you come into the world.
They were nude and it affected them strangely enough hardly at all. They had come so far from the world they had known, and they sensed the ties to that world slipping and fading.
– You're in the bewitched forest now. Stacy smiled to them. – All illusions fall. This is the world as it really and truly is, sensuous, unrestrained.
– Jesus Christ, the male police officer shouted in despair. – I have to get away from here, I'm cracking up.
– Is that your true desire, Percy? Stacy touched his cheek. – Isn't it true that you've looked for a place such as this your entire life, but given up because you feared it didn't exist?
– I…
In one single, rushed moment he had embraced her, pulled her hard to him.
He kissed her hard on the lips, with a longing, a desire he had always kept restrained, kept bottled up inside. And now he released everything. She shouted in joy and responded with a fervor he had a hard time accepting as real. As they fell to the ground, locked in a wild embrace.
Then thoughts of reality collapsed, and they no longer mattered.
– Where's my gun? Hazel stamped her feet at the ground. – I want my gun.
Jill gave it to her. Hazel grabbed it and instantly started checking it with a distrustful look, bordering on hatred. It was perfectly all right. The mechanism, the bullets, everything seemed to be all right.
Jill stood before her with a huge knife in her hand. What was her… intentions? Wide eyed and unable to move Hazel saw the witch cut herself, from the wrist to the elbow, deeply and destructively. Hazel had seen this before, seen such marks on people who had committed suicide. This was how it had to be done to be effective. To merely make incisions on the wrist wasn't in any way sufficient.
Blood flowed… but such a tiny amount. And in the course of seconds, as Hazel watched

transfixed… the hellish wounds closed completely. Skin healed and turned smooth once more, as if there never had been any wounds at all.

Hazel dropped her weapon. She didn't hear it actually hitting the ground. And that failed to either surprise or engage her.

– You may suspect we have used our sorcery to affect you, but you would be wrong. We don't need to. You, all of you came to us because you wanted to. Nothing is holding you back anymore. You can do what you want. We have the power to pluck you like withered husks of domestic flowers, but we prefer the wild, fresh ones on the plains, in the forest. You can't be sure, of course, that you're acting of your own, free will. You must decide that for yourself, like you did when you sought this place… like you've presumably done your entire life.

One of the male witches placed himself behind Hazel. Somehow, she knew he was there, well in advance before he put his hands on her shoulders, her nude shoulders. He kissed her greedily on the neck and she wanted so much to lean back and offer him her kisses, her already swollen lips.

– Don't fear that he doesn't desire you, Stacy said lazily. – He loves your tight ass, the round, smooth thighs, your pouting mouth, the entirety of your damn hardbody. You can hardly imagine how strongly he wishes to devour you…

Hands started exploring and Hazel let them. She stopped struggling against herself and pushed herself against he whom she didn't know by name. Her lips finally caught his and they were like fire. But the real eruption came from below. Unable to stand she fell on her knees, and he did, too. Behind her. He wouldn't…

– Yes, she breathed. – *Yes.*

Jill and Stacy played with the former police officer. He lay on his back, gasping, as they slipped up and down, on and off him. When he came, when his loins erupted in wild thrusts, he couldn't tell which one of them he ejaculated in, and he didn't care. Stacy smiled. Jill smiled. They registered joyfully, through the haze of their own, wild desire that the others had taken the cue and had engaged each other, had joined the sea of wet bodies, hot embraces. The ground had once again become like one big bed where everybody did everything with everybody. Jill sensed, welcomed the approach of the wild darkness. Consciousness faded and the deeper consciousness flashed for just a second, before eyes closed, the body relaxed, and the dream-sleep started.

There had been flickering eyes, as the fatigue finally claimed her. She, too, needed rest. There was the falling, the fading into darkness. She recalled no dreams when awakening, but felt fresh and rested in mind and body.

Her rest hadn't lasted long. People slept in heaps, but the fires still burned tall. Some of the children had probably kept building it, but not anymore. They had also fallen asleep.

She sensed movement on her right, even if she didn't see anything.

– Raven. It was Gabi. She waited between two fires, had placed herself between light and shadow, hungry for both. A thin voice, with a hoarseness impossible not to interpret correctly. – I'm… horny, Raven. My water is flowing. I can't resist any longer.

– You desire a male, don't you? Raven spoke evenly, in a soft, practical tone. – Who do you want, then?

– I don't know… can't you decide for me? I'll be happy to go to the one you choose.

– Okay, I'll do this for you, Jill said. – Look at it as a reward because you and Morgana did good tonight…

The girl reddened subjected to the hot, pondering stare.

– I'm thinking of Daniel, the woman offered teasingly.

– Yes, Daniel is great. Gabi lit up like a Christmas tree.

– He's just the right man to claim the virginity of hot, tight girls… An inexperienced boy closer to your age will only make a clumsy mess of it all.

She's so insecure and reserved. Not unlike me six short weeks ago.

– Come here, dear heart. If you want to be a woman, you must behave as one and not like a mouse. The pain only lasts a moment. The Power… The Power is Eternal…

– … *eternal…* the girl intoned, while taking one and one step forward on shaky legs, hardly able to carry her.

Jill heard an insistent voice in her thoughts. Stacy, inpatient, demanding.

We're waiting. Stop dawdling.

You know very well where I am, what I'm about to do.

– You *are* horny. She used her fingers to comb the girl's hair, pinching and patting her. – So strong is your desire that anybody could have plucked you. Off with your dress, you're ready.

Eyes filled with mist as the girl grabbed hold of the dress and dragged it above her head, dropped it behind her back. Jill smiled.

– Ready to fall, like a ripe fruit. Come…

Jill took the smaller, weaker hand in hers and led the girl away, to one of the many heaps of bodies. She pushed Daniel with her toes. He lay almost by himself on the edge of the heap. None of the others awakened. Eyes opened slowly, but clear.

– There is one who needs you, she called with a forked tongue.

He looked wide-eyed, first at the amazing view of Jill and then behind her. He froze, clearly uncertain.

– The spirit is willing, but the flesh is worn, he admitted, somewhat ambiguous.

– If the spirit is indeed willing, then so is the flesh, Jill enlightened him, as if disclosing a major secret. Then turning towards Gabi: – Dance, little heart. Dance for your prince.

Slowly first, lingering, sensuous as the fluidity reached her mind and then her limbs, Delphi danced. Eyes were huge, glossy. Small nipples grew erect on tight breasts and muscles spilled around her buttocks. She was swaying and dancing in one, in gracious movements, with an expression telling nothing. His throat turned dry in an instant. All expression was transferred to the body and its countless nuances and moves.

– Perhaps if you…

– Don't even think about it. You don't need any help.

She whispered into his ear, even if she stood a step away.

– *Look* at her… We could have offered her for sale and the bids would have piled up. It might be a long time until you get such a chance to cease the day. C'mon, man, think with your dick, not with your mind.

He did, not taking his eyes away from her. Not while… *noticing* the first pull, contraction below and not when the stiff throbbing thing was filled with so much blood that it hurt, and he feared it would crack.

– You're nuts, you know that, don't you? He whistled between gritted teeth.

– Thank you, Jill sang pleased.

The speed of the dance increased, almost imperceptible, before once more slowing down, as the virgin doll closed in on her prince, as no one pulled her strings anymore, as a hazy light glowed in her eyes. Daniel grabbed her carefully and placed her at his side. She moaned impatiently. He held back while touching and kissing her. They pushed against each other. She was far more active than he had imagined virgins would be (she was not exactly your run of the mill virgin, not your run of the mill anything). He pushed her at the ground, unable to hold back anymore, moving hard inside her. Her body turned soft in his hands. Minutes rushed like seconds, the moon howled in his ears and as she was moaning wildly her body turned rigid… And then it happened.

The pain and joy washed over Jill in waves as she sat course for the beach. She started running and hardly noticed how sand gave way to water, as she danced across the lake, moved by desires she couldn't name, towards the three, Stacy, Everett and Jason, awaiting her by the Gate of Fire, the entrance to the castle.

They walked through the gate and into the deep of the castle, to the room they would have called the library, if there had been more books there, which they spoke of as the Room of Knowledge. Or rather the Room Where One's Seeking Knowledge. Their Crossroads. To the right were the stone stairs leading to the Many Rooms and the Hall of Mirrors. And to the left - the Spiral Staircase. Where they had never set foot… until now.

– The Left Hand Path, my dear fellow witches. Stacy led on down the tailspin, dizzying path.

Round and round and round. Down, down, down. They couldn't tell when the metal stairs ended, and another stone path took its place. A fireball floated in the air an immeasurable distance ahead.

Stacy controlled it easily enough. Sometimes there were steps, sometimes not. A few minutes turned to many, as they penetrated ever deeper into the rock. They reached several levels on their way down. Each level had its own system of dark corridors and tunnels. They ignored them, as they ignored any distraction, making their way to the… bottom.

– It's so huge, Everett exclaimed. – Are we even… here anymore?

The… distractions, silent screams and impressions of death weighed heavily on them. The place was stinking of it. Skin turned to gooseflesh and bile rose in their throat. Something horribly insane had transpired in this place, this tomb of rock. They passed another passage and Everett growled, even if he was in his human form.

– I *know* this place.

They were bombarded with impressions, on many levels, within and without.

– There's more here, Stacy mumbled. – Infinitely more. It's just the stench of suffering and death that is so overwhelming.

– Is here… *here?* Everett asked the air, but received no reply.

The flashes came to them constantly now, overlaying each other. They saw an ancient city, and its tower. And the tower was a mirror, going down, not up. As you were going up, you went down. As you went down, you went up. An assembly of ghosts walked the gray streets. They weren't really transparent. Their ghostlike appearance was more in their complexion, in their demeanor, or lack thereof. There was no free will, no true motion.

And then Stacy saw the lake, the lake above or rather what was left of it, covered in tubes, by concrete and stink. She gasped in pain. The future… She saw the future, and everything was concrete, glass, tarmac and plastic. Everything was pain. The Wastelands had come to Earth and vanquished it. The others shared her vision. She made them share it and they shook in fear. Good.

Good.

It faded like all visions do. But this lingered, adding to the Nightmare she had experienced since her twelfth birthday.

They reached the bottom. More tunnels, broad and narrow tempted them. They chose the broadest one. Fire-colored light brightened/shadowed the path as they made their way further into the place. The broad corridor expanded until they could no longer see or even sense walls and ceiling, only sense the enormous room around them. The fireball illuminated only the floor immediately ahead and nothing more.

Jill created her own fireball, sent it up, up, up… Far away somewhere above they imagined they could see the ceiling. Or at least one ceiling. The sorceresses concentrated as each of them created an extra ball and made all four as powerful as possible. It was sufficient.

An enormous room, a hall revealed itself to them. Smooth rock, polished walls. Everything here, every spot of rock was touched by humans. *Many hands, bloody hands.* Jill and Stacy stared at each other over an abyss of suffering and death. There were so much here, so many impressions that they couldn't possibly take it all in, in fear of going insane. *An empty shell they could fill.* If they didn't guard themselves, they would be lost. *Lost.* Slowly, gloriously they were once more able to notice details. Four pairs of eyes were pulled to one area of the hall: A large flat rock placed on an altar. A human fit well on that rock. The entire altar fit into what was the five-pointed star of a Pentacle. A figure engraved into the ground, covering a huge area.

They climbed to one of balconies, searching a bit before finding a right one, looking at everything from above. Further exploring the tunnels, they found cells, they had to be cells, woven into the walls. There were no doors, only bars of hardened rock, a metal-like consistence. They saw the skeletons. A witch had used her magick and imprisoned these poor suckers. It had happened a long time ago, but it still felt raw, fresh to the sensitive observing his or her handiwork.

They returned to the Crossroads. Everything was so clear. Jill was willing to swear she could read the titles of the books, in the twilight many steps away. The four of them stood still a long time, finding satisfaction in the simple act of breathing. Skin on the cheek had a fresh color. They stared at each other alternately in ecstasy and terror.

– The past means nothing anymore, Stacy said in a very precise, accentuated, intense speech. – It never has. Our future, our present is down here, in Styx' staggering depths.

And the words, formal, boasting though they were, meant something to them, like a roaring echo in Memory. They nodded.

– There's more, Jason pointed out. – Here, now.

That's right, too. There was more to be done, before the night ended.

Anubis sniffed in the air, smelling a scent not of this world. They all felt what he did, a tingling in the frontal lobe.

– The water, he mumbled.

– What? Jill concentrated so hard that sweat poured from her skin. – Of course.

A shadow smile illuminated them all.

Driven by those very forces without name, they moved outside, pulled as one down to the water, towards something tangible, something rare. The werewolf bent down, wetting a paw, tasting the clear, fresh fluid.

– It's pure, he declared.

– Yes, it has a fantastic flavor compared to everything else I've tasted. Stacy shook her head in wonder. – We've found some spring here.

– No, you don't understand, Everett insisted. – It's *pure.* So much so that I, with my enhanced olfactory smell can't detect any trace of pollution.

They looked down, in an attempt to penetrate its depths. The water started… boiling? They looked up, at each other. In a flash… understanding.

Understanding, realization, action was one. Stacy gave Jill her left hand. Jill took it with her right. The two men placed themselves at each their side. They felt so much, in both their white and black shadows. And they couldn't deny any of them. Everybody held around each other, and the group started glowing, weakly as fireflies during twilight.

The water boiled and steamed when they stepped into it. They got wet on their feet. Then they dived, below the surface, suddenly their powers had brought them deep below. One single glowing ball showed the way into the stygian depths.

The Fire Lake… so deep. Jill felt so much of what they sought, so much close by, as if she could touch it, just by reaching a bit further.

She couldn't say for sure if she had expected what happened. They had gone so far down that they started to feel the pressure, but there was still no bottom, no bottom in sight. Instead, they imagined the resistance actually dwindling. They floated there in the deep waters, glimpsing the rock wall, but no surface, no bottom. The air in their lungs almost gone they should have been worried. Even their added stamina had its limits.

They felt like running, running high in the mountains. They felt wonder. In full control over their own movements, on route towards the big Unknown, they could hardly contain their excitement.

All four broke the surface, breathing, gulping the fresh air. They paused just a few seconds, treading the water before swimming towards the center of the lake with slow, lazy strokes. So strange to use their limbs to keep afloat again.

They looked around, shaking their head, looking at the Fire Lake. Or rather one fire lake. This was one very different from the one they had left just minutes ago. Or rather the surroundings were different. It was the same and yet not the same. Huge trees had in minutes seemingly covered the islet. The house had vanished. On the mainland, everywhere they looked they saw a nature wild and obviously untouched by humans. They swam to shore, very conscious of the heart beating in their chest. Jason looked astonished at the gooseflesh on his arm, caused by both physical and non-physical circumstances.

– It's noticeably colder, Stacy remarked. – See how wet the grass is? And green?

The ground was more of a swamp then the solid forest bed they knew.

– The future? Jason queried. – The past?

– The stars are where they're supposed to be, Everett pondered. – This is present day Earth, but without machines, technology, pollution. This Earth is pure.

– «This Earth» is the right term, Stacy said in wonder. – We're on another Earth, one where the pollution hasn't changed the temperature. This is the natural October climate at this latitude.

– A parallel dimension, Jill exclaimed excitedly. – Somewhere in the water we passed a portal to another world, another universe, with an Earth where cities at worst are rare, where there are no unnatural fires.

She smiled her roguish smile. The others grinned.

During the next few hours, they started their first, modest exploration of the new land, and found no traces of human life. Life flourished everywhere. They found marks of bear claws on trees, wolf tracks on the forest bed, and countless others they were unable to identify. Their senses virtually overloaded with impressions they stopped, taking it all in. Life was so varied here, such an incredible variety of species.

But no humans.

They walked to the eastern edge of the Hill (of this hill), as the horizon started to brighten. The forest didn't end there, but continued down the slope and as far as their eyes could see. Where there had been a field, there was only forest. No burned-out school, no city. Only trees. They researched the matter methodically, uncharacteristically by walking around the entire edge of the hill (this hill), but no matter what direction they looked they saw nothing resembling buildings, houses or any sort of construction.

– A huge, unspoiled Earth, Stacy stated.

They played wildly in the infinite forest. Their senses expanded towards their full potential and the unqualified vitality this world had to offer. An unborn force they had the power to awaken.

Jill ran through the forest running from Anubis with a smile on her lips. She knew she didn't have a chance of hiding from him for long. No one had. It wasn't merely his physical senses making him the ultimate hunter. His mind power was also enormously focused on the tracking of game, human or otherwise. She waited, her back against a tree. He appeared from behind some bushes a bit ahead of her, from the direction she would have run if she hadn't known he was waiting for her. The beast's eyes were fixated on her and would have paralyzed her, if she had been an ordinary, defenseless female instead of a growling she-cat.

– I heard a story once, about the Fenris Wolf, she purred, stretching lazily. – I have no intention of telling you where I heard it, but it goes like this:

The reality of the forest shifted in flashes into cave walls, wet torches, echoes of a raging river.

– A long, long time ago a human in the form of a wolf, a wolf talking like a man was chained at the gates of Hell. He became a guard, like those who had stolen his freedom. But one day, the story says, when Ragnarok is coming, he would break free of all chains and boundaries, and ravage the world and its humans and the societies where safety was put before all else would tremble in their foundation.

– Some story. He had come close. – But a bit too fantastic to be true, don't you think?

In one swift move he had caught her with his paws and claws.

– One among a thousand «unlikely» true stories, she grinned, suddenly breathing so much faster.

He turned her around, pushing her at the tree. Amidst her heaving and gasps she caught glimpses of that which moved up and down in his loins. He lifted her up and he fucked her. She sensed her breasts harden against the tree and every uneven interruption of the bark as her feet moved without control, up and down the rough surface. It didn't matter. She knew they could have been trapped on a narrow mountain trail, with the ground a thousand lengths below and not noticed.

They met Stacy and Jason by the shore of the lake. In the other two's lazy contentment, they recognized their own. A hunger just barely sated.

The four of them stood there in the sand, savoring the taste of the world with all their enhanced senses.

– We've found an entire, other dimension, Everett said. – It's a staggering thought. Even if it's only a confirmation of what I've always believed, believing and knowing, as we all know is two different things.

– The existence of one more is more than suggesting the existence of many, of thousands, of millions, of an infinite number. Stacy stood there, shaking her head. – It's fantastic. And we're the only ones who know.

– Except the infinite number of «us» standing «here» covering the Multiverse, Jason pointed out smiling.

Now, that was a staggering thought.

Jill cocked her head, listening, probing.

Gabi, Jill sent.

Yes? Gabi sounded sleepy, but she and the other non-telepaths had learned to reply to a sending well enough. *Where are you, Raven? ThankyouRaventhankyou…*

We will be with you shortly, Delphi. Is everything all right, honey?

The only reply she got was a storm of emotions, something resembling a huge smile…

All four of them smiled. They exchanged looks, exchanged trembles, as they took one last look at the world they left, one they most certainly would return to, if possible. They stared intensively, as if memorizing every tree, every molecule, until they as a group returned to the cold, humid depth they had come from.

Everything went easier this second time around. They knew what would happen, they knew the road, had walked it before. There was a floor, a bed in the lake, to a certain depth and then it just disappeared. Was this portal between dimensions a natural occurrence or had someone… opened it? The depth was hardly as dark as it was expected to be, something that was logical enough. After all, sunlight illuminated it from both sides. As the water got warmer as they got closer to the surface only a slight uncertainty haunted them. Would they return to the same world they had left? After all… they had moved into a vast, new territory and every bit of certainty had left their lives.

They had still a lot of air left in their lungs and let themselves float slowly the last stretch to the surface. It felt great to just relax and let the ascension take care of itself.

Something… They noticed it almost the instant they broke the surface, yes, perhaps even seconds before. Something different. They had arrived at the right… place. What they saw while looking around, stretching their senses was their home. Familiar and no longer unfamiliar faces smiling sleepily to each other. The castle of witches, seemingly in shadow, even bathing in sunlight, hardly visible during the night. Jill stretched her mind beyond the forest, below the hill and sensed easily the collective energy from Northfield's population. The four of them swam to shore at a pleasant pace. Even though they had held their breath for a considerable time, none of them was breathing much harder than normal. The heat surrounded them from the moment they left the water. Even Stacy started to sweat instantly. They had spent hours in a fairly colder climate, but that didn't explain it to their satisfaction. The temperature had increased one or two more notches compared to the morning the day before. And that day had been *hot.* The Sun had yet to rise quite a bit and the day was already as warm as midday yesterday. The four of them noticed it in every living thing around them. Animal and plant curled and suffered under the ruthless reign of the Sun. This wasn't even ordinary desert temperature, but akin to what Jill had felt when she as a spirit had floated above… above Death Valley. A baker's oven, roasting the skin, as if it was hot enough for lead to turn liquid.

Something lingered in the air. A silent accord that… yes… cracked deafening like thunder.

Morgana walked to them. She looked as worried, as shitty as they had ever seen her.

– I can feel it, she said aggressively.

– What is it? Jill asked.

She had her eyes on Everett. He was in his human form, but stood there crouching and sniffing as the animal he was, as they all were.

– The animals, he mumbled, – they're shitty as hell. They're… they're running in *panic* from what's coming… a pressure wave stronger than anything in collective memory. I hold up my hand,

(and he did)

– and it's as if I can actually *feel* it, as if a… switch in my brain is turned.

– What's coming? What?

She knew. She had the switch, too. They all did. We all do. She didn't have his enhanced rapport with animals, but all her instincts, her deeper parts screamed at her… to flee flee flee

Instinct and rationality combined, and convinced them all.

They didn't hear the wind chimes anymore. As one they turned their eyes to the portal and there wasn't the slightest movement. Emotions in a dozen nuances washed over them.

It was absolutely, completely calm wherever they turned.

The wind didn't blow anymore.

CHAPTER SEVENTEEN: The Storm

The hurricane Anton started its ravaging of the North American mainland a few minutes past five in the afternoon Eastern Standard Time. The state of Florida was among the first areas hit, and the entire state was virtually washed away to sea. A few hours earlier minor islands further south in the Gulf of Mexico had vanished. They were Gone. Nobody studying the footage of the violent waves, the raging sea thought the islands would ever reappear, even if the sea calmed down. If the sea ever calmed down. It had turned out to be impossible to reestablish contact with Jamaica. From Cuba and Haiti were heard only insane pleas for help. Almost none of the Bahamas Islands were possible to spot on the CNN satellite images.

Previous years' hurricanes like Andrew and Hugo and also Katrina earlier this year were as tiny wisps of wind compared to this. And Andrew and Hugo had been among the strongest ever measured, had moved up to 260 kilometer per hour. But they had been only level four hurricanes. Anton was the long-feared level six (off the scale) hurricane. Its winds exceeded easily 300 kilometers per hour and its rampage didn't seem to end. The meteorologists, the modern weathermen had predicted a hurricane, had as usual even warned people to leave their homes in the southern states, but they had failed completely concerning its strength. They had dubbed it a strong tropical storm, and people, after being hit by hurricanes on assembly line the entire season had grown used to ignoring general warnings.

The National Hurricane Center in Miami had used up all their 21 hurricane names this year and was forced to start over, for the first time in history. They managed just to give the approaching Storm its very appropriate name… before they were washed away along with the rest of Florida.

After crushing Georgia and major parts of Alabama, Anton continued its «mad rampage» (as put by a news anchor woman) northbound. It struck along a broad front in Tennessee, Kentucky and the Carolinas. In what had been deemed ordinary circumstances hurricanes lost their punch quite fast while traveling over land, but this one was so powerful that it took it much longer to lose any sort of punch. It was so strong and broad that it continued up the entire coastline and the sea outside with something like undiminished power. On some stretches of sea, it even picked up more energy and increased in force. It attacked the Potomac River and hit Washington DC like a soft boxing glove with a rock-hard hand inside. Manhattan and major parts of New York City and state were flooded. Buildings continued to collapse… yes, like houses of cards. Like castles of sand. West of the Appalachian Mountains, Anton set course for Chicago and Detroit, and people truly started to wonder if the Storm was ever going to stop. Evacuation around the Great Lakes virtually came to a halt. In Montreal and Toronto, the preparation for evacuation and for whatever would happen started. The question they asked themselves, those who weren't too numb to think was a simple one: Was there a sanctuary, a safe haven… anywhere?

The roads westward were still open. Only few cars of the Eastern American total had reached this far, but they still filled the roads to a standstill. The meteorologist, *meteoroliars* (as they were called more than ever these days) claimed that Kansas City and Winnipeg among others were safe areas, but their old cock and bull confidence had left them.

The spring tide flooded Boston Harbor. The water washed the heights and even the snobs on Beacon Hill got their feet wet. A tiny, everlasting moment most of the Metropolitan Area stayed under water, until the ocean pulled back or sank below the ground. Another second in eternity and silence reigned anew.

Then came the rain, in such torrents that many people with breathing problems died for lack of air. To call it torrential rain seemed like a horrible understatement. And Anton, at this time having lost a lot of its punch and momentum tore the air from the lungs of those being exposed to its rage and strangled them. Buildings blew apart. Houses were reduced to rubble. Cars and heavy trucks it pushed off the road. Nature *closed* roads in a matter of seconds.

Blood mixed with water transformed into waterfalls. Jill saw it. She kept her eyes wide open, no matter how it hurt. *Millions of souls suffered and died.* And her ability to influence it all was as non-existent as that of everybody else. They were all powerless.

The storm lasted three days. The rain kept splashing long after that. Devastated survivors emerged from the ruins, hungry for news, any news. The machinery started up again, slowly, painfully. The Army was deployed in the *unruliest* areas and was harshly, ruthlessly reestablishing Law and Order. A major number of the storm's victims, desperate for something to eat and for some news, any news received only a hail of bullets. Blood filled with adrenalin floated everywhere. Questions creating forbidden thoughts remained unresolved.

It was never clear how many had lost their lives during the storm and in the subsequent turmoil. Some claimed a million. Others believed it had to be twice that number. The official number, estimate was between five and six hundred thousand, depending on federal or local sources. One third of the US was declared a disaster area and a number of aid undertakings was eventually implemented. It seemed hopelessly lame and inadequate all of it. The president, George W. Bush, having been reelected on a wave of popular support created by his «fight against terror» and his resistance to implement restrictions on car use and industrial ventures, lost his popularity… yes, overnight. It didn't even help that leading meteoroliars went public to claim that the enhanced Greenhouse-Effect, the manmade Climate Change in fact wasn't responsible for Anton's escapades. Daily TV-footage from the worst hit areas killed any such attempt in what would usually have been an effective, calming propaganda. The state of Georgia emerged as one big ruin. The capital Atlanta, «the capitalistic miracle», made new and shiny the previous decade for the Summer Olympics didn't look like a city anymore, but like something between a garbage heap and a junk heap. Footage from Florida, «the Sunshine State» made the state a class of its own. Florida hardly emerged… at all. People could study in detail catatonic survivors on small sand islets in and around what had been Miami, Fort Lauderdale, Tampa, Orlando, Jacksonville… Florida stopped working as a state there and then. Georgia followed later the same year and remaining areas was split between the Carolinas and Alabama. Everything seemed wildly unreal to most people, of course, but through countless repetitions and eyewitness accounts reality finally got hammered into a stunned population.

Even the witches in Northfield had, to some degree experienced difficulties in digesting what had happened, everything changing. They, too, had, after all, like all present day-people been brainwashed since the cradle.

Massachusetts had been fairly, comparably lucky. Anton hadn't been much more than an ordinary storm this far north. The coast had been ravaged, but the inland had been (again quoting the before mentioned anchorwoman) «spared the worst». Northfield had suffered major structural damage and a lot of water flooding on the rock-hard soil. Life continued without major, continued interruptions. But Boston was so bad that one would be hard pressed to imagine anything worse other places.

If one didn't see it on TV, hear witnesses speaking about it wherever one went.

They had believed themselves ready when the storm hit Northfield. Several of them discovered that they were able to actually see the pressure wave in the air as patterns of energy, one single dark sky, flashing and sparkling. They were all in place in concrete cellars, either at the farm, in Square or the tavern. Without really discussing it, by a silent agreement none of the four mentioned anything about the catacombs below the castle. They all felt very strongly that Death thrived there.

The world below the lake remained an option. They would feel a bit of regret for not bringing their tribe there.

The farm had also originally been seen as a weak spot, but Stacy, a few other grownups and all the children had been trapped out there. They believed they had taken every precaution, with back up plans and the works, but the storm had moved faster than even they had feared, and it had attacked them like a black beast in the deepest night.

The roof had been torn off almost immediately. Everyone had recognized the tearing sound. They had never heard it hit the ground. The door down to the basement had dissolved like it was hundreds of years old. The windows hadn't really broken, but vanished from one moment to the next.

– We must get away from here, Stacy screamed at the top of her lungs, concentration broken, unable to use her power. *Jill heard her still.* – We'll DIE if we remain.

She seemed calm on the surface, but there was an underlying tone in the voice that they had never heard from her before, had thought they would never hear.

The strongest winds hit them in heaves and gusts. In between they could imagine it was close to quiet. They ran across the field. Stacy kept all the children close to her, embracing them within a shield of mind power. Sweat already immersed itself in eyes, closed tight in intense concentration. She hardly noticed the entire, massive farm-building behind them being transformed into a heap of wood. The grass was short and tight around them, but yet it heaved like rush in the water. They heard trees break far away. The invisible hand broke them easily, as if the trees had stood there, rotting for years. They heard the sound of matches breaking move closer, closer, closer. Jill crouched on a bed in the cellar in Square, sweating hard. Everett dried her forehead. They had removed her robe and covered the damp body in blankets. She had tried to close her mind to Stacy's thoughts, in vain. She (and Stacy) felt everything happening in Northfield.

We were unprepared. Damn us!

There was a gust of wind, of *Storm* cutting the field, the vulnerable two-legged creatures fighting their way across it. A child was pulled into the air. Stacy reached out with an invisible hand, grabbed the tiny body and kept it in her grip. It wasn't sufficient. She sensed the grip loosening. Then she pulled her deepest anger to the outside. She screamed in her Rage. The child ended up in her arms and she embraced it for all it was worth, quickly turning it over to one of the other, older children. There was another cut, another hole in the air itself, in space, in time. A boy was torn from her mental grip. The adrenalin flowed and made her entire body spark, but she couldn't hold on to him. She forced herself to watch, as he disappeared into the Storm. They never saw him again.

– It's no use, Morgana cried. – We're not getting anywhere.

A flash of realization was lit in Stacy's insane eyes. She grabbed the other witch's arm and tightened her grip. Morgana understood. She attempted to concentrate, in spite of the cold fire and light penetrating her. Stacy made the plants and grass grow incredibly fast and in its shadow tentacles of soil and stone from deep below the ground. They combined their powers in one, single burst. Many colored ropes tied themselves around everybody. Strong fiber, roots and soil, fluid rock rose as support. One single mass surrounding them all. Completely unmoved by the thunderous roar vibrating the air. *The grownups are worried. But not the children. They trust Stacy implicitly, trust her to do her best.*

Everett and Jill found them at dawn the next day, while a child of Anton set course for Europe, gathering strength on its journey across the Atlantic Ocean.

In the midst of the field, a field still basically covered with yellow, withered grass, they spotted the green circle, a dome reaching its highest level close to half a human length above ground. Jill sent for help and the others arrived with axes, hoes and spades.

– I don't get anything from her, Jill said, desperately walking in circles, while Everett attempted to comfort her. – No thoughts, no emotions, nothing.

Tam was carefully hacking around an «air-vent», expanding it, without making it collapse. Jill nodded. She told herself there was no immediate danger. Jason helped her to lift off bits and pieces as the hard/soft material of strange topsoil was chopped away.

They lay in a ring, all easy to get out in the open. They had been pulled into the ground by a force that, for a few seconds had been stronger than the Storm. They were covered to the thighs by a hard, packed substance. But it went easy enough to brush it away with hands alone. The «rope» tied around ankles and wrists dissolved when Jill made the plants pull back. Eyes were closed. They seemed to be locked in a sort of trance. Except for Stacy. She was alive, as her heart beat hard and strong, but something was clearly wrong. Her eyes were wide open, hard like glass. As she lay there frozen, she evidently didn't notice anything of her surroundings. She was catatonic.

Everybody was put on the ground. Morgana was severely weakened, and she had probably been close to death more than once during the night. Pulse was weak and the heartbeat irregular. The others awakened with a bit of shaking. One of the men had sprained an ankle. That was all. Jill took care of Morgana first, bathing her in the healing cocoon. The recovery was unusually slow, but eventually Morgana opened weary eyes. The man was less of a problem. But when the turn came to Stacy, Jill knelt hesitatingly, worried.

– You're correct, Jason confirmed. – There's nothing there. The bird has fled the nest.

Stacy Larkin had cast herself out in the Void, never to return.

Jill received nothing, other than a dark, empty Nothing and when she touched the rain wet skin the nothing started spreading to her. Overwhelming, overtaking her, devouring her like cold fire from a fake dragon.

No

Stacy blinked. The Life, the wildfire returned to her. Slowly she fought forth her unique, crooked grin.

– What happened? Jill queried hoarsely.

– I overextended myself. Unbelievably enough, Stacy shrugged. She rose and straightened, seemingly back in fine form. – I knew you would fix it.

Jill stumbled through Boston's ravaged streets, feeling as if she had overextended herself a thousand times. Tam supported her and kept her on her feet. She saw other witches walk in and out of the large tents. They had finished off quickly in Northfield. The small town had sustained mainly superficial damage.

Not like here. Was it luck that had made the administrative officer accept their help? They had felt they had to do something, no matter how small and insignificant. They had to help here in their local area. That was all they were able to do.

Another tent in an endless row. An endless row of beds. Andrea received them, showing them around, leading them to those who needed a true Healer the most. Jill was glad she could no longer see their faces, sense their despair, how they were withering, dying on the wine. How they mirrored the fact that they had given up a long time ago. Long before Jill's arrival, long before the Storm.

– You must rest, Tam insisted. – Feed on me… please.

– No, can't… won't.

– Feed on me and then you must rest.

No, she was tired as death, but didn't want to sleep. She had insane dreams. They started the moment she closed her eyes. She forced herself to keep them open. Perhaps she was too tired to sleep. She didn't want to dream. What she sensed around her now was Real. This was Reality, this all-embracing suffering on the road to darkness.

In a crossroads between the tents where many paths crossed, she met Stacy, her mirror image, her reflection, at least as pale and downtrodden. The skin color couldn't be said to be fresh anymore, but grayish yellow. The eyes dominated the sunken face. But the haunted expression and the terrible resolve remained. Her inner fire burned just as strong, if not stronger.

– We've entered the Kingdom of Death, sister. Voice was hollow, but steady. – This is a transition. The time is near. This is who we are.

She could just about see it, squinting her eyes, just beyond her grasp. Painfully, hesitatingly she reached for it.

The day moved slowly, so very slowly. She dragged herself along it. The change happened so slowly that she hardly noticed it at first.

Suddenly Jill discovered she didn't need support anymore. She straightened and started running so fast that Travis, he who presently accompanied her, couldn't keep up. The sunken cheeks, the pale skin disappeared. She got stronger, not weaker for every step she took. Was it that simple; was everything in the mind… her mind?

Despair and Will, Fire and Ice fought for dominance in her, as it did everywhere. The struggle was ongoing, and eternal.

The wind was blowing. Choppers roared deafening every time they took off and landed. The rain didn't let up, but continued to pour, not soft, not hard, even, unstoppable, insane. It hurt somewhere deep inside. She ignored it, simultaneously as she accepted death and suffering as a part of life.

She walked between two rows of beds. They all looked alike, and they all looked the same, like those she had walked between earlier today. All the humans on them looked the same. The witches struggled with their inborn talents, their medicines and valves, but didn't really register any difference in the hourly number of deaths. What happened was quite simply too big for them. And if they did happen to save some people from death… what use was that, what purpose did it serve?

Did they really do anything positive here? Didn't they merely postpone the suffering that sooner or later would come? She had known for a while that there weren't any satisfying answers to this, that she asked questions without answers, but just now it released the anger in her.

It was like Jason said. The winds of change would/had to come as an irresistible force.

The river Styx had brought her to the edge of the Kingdom of Death, and she learned what she was.

A married couple down the row, a bit away from the rest greeted her with dull, incomprehensive eyes. Their injuries were superficial. Broken bones, lacerations, major and minor wounds caused by flying objects. Less injuries than many others had any trouble with. They should have recovered nicely and quickly. They just withered and waned.

– You're one of them, aren't you? The man said hoarsely. – One of the magicians, with power over life and death?

– Help us, the woman begged weakly. – We're willing to do anything…

The sorceress wanted to shake them, ask if they were willing to sell her their souls, become her slaves.

– It's difficult, she replied tightly. – You're so lifeless, so unwilling to live.

She healed the wounds, only the wounds. Healed the physical body, nothing more. It demanded hardly any effort. They stared at her, thunderstruck and deeply miserable.

– Yes, that's right. The day is long and hard. And if you don't do anything drastic to change that, it will last the remainder of your lives.

She stood in deep shadow in a ramshackle warehouse block. The heat and the lights from the enormous fires danced in her face. This was where the countless dead from the city and around ended up and so very few knew of it. So much secrecy, so much ordinary men and women couldn't take, didn't want to know. What uncertain a grip those at the top of the pyramid had on the power. Jill had to smile (and her shadow smiled, too). They didn't know much, those cloak and dagger people, about what really went on in the shadows.

They knew very well the chance they took, the paranormals from Northfield, by coming here. There were Special Forces here, too. Not in the numbers of cities harder hit, but their presence was felt. In addition to the hidden watchdogs ever present in present day society.

But the shadowwalkers felt brave. If not overconfident.

The rumors were abundant, though. They had no chance of stopping that from happening. Perhaps there was one or more highly placed official here with sufficient knowledge to know facts from fiction, from exaggerations and who had immediate resources at disposal. They, those who had the ability to read thoughts, examined everybody they came close to. But they could never be sure.

She passed a soldier. He was definitely Intelligence. To her his hidden side glowed like an inflamed wound. She considered… teaching him something, but let it go, for now. There would come other occasions. Many others.

No streetlights. Ironically most present fires in the city this night were natural. All kinds of people smashed store windows and took whatever was there, in anger, fear and frustration. No realistic number of soldiers could stop that from happening. Civilization was such a fragile thing. The smile broadened. The generator-driven lanterns seemed pale in spite of the extensive darkness everywhere. Perhaps there was hope for the world, after all.

Sounds, she heard them everywhere. A door opened and closed, opened and closed in an unending loop. This second, somewhere in town a human stabbed another in the heart. She imagined she stood inside somewhere, in a cellar dark as coal.

She finally reached the tent the people from Northfield had been given. She actually felt a kind of exhaustion then, in her legs. And otherwise. It was time for sleep, for dreams. She only had to close her eyes, for the sensations to appear. She didn't even have to do that. Her life contained constant extrasensory perceptions. Seldom strong or clear enough, but present.

– Eat. Andrea put a bowl of oranges in front of her. It was she who was responsible for her health tonight.

Jill gulped down the fruit in a few, greedy swallows. In the other bed Stacy did the same. The juice erupted everywhere at their hands and face. Jill took Andrea's hands. Stacy took Udo's. They took enough energy to become a bit more awake. Awake enough to get sleepy. Two heads covered in black raven hair hit the soft pillow.

Lillith walked through a city. She couldn't tell which at first. It was unknown to her, but also strangely familiar. Suddenly it dawned on her. It was Miami, a few days back in time, a place that no longer existed except as a revenant in Time. Awakening had come practically instantly this time, the moment she closed her eyes, no REM phase. She knew she was bathing herself in Alpha waves. Heart was hardly beating, the pulse hardly measurable and difficult to find without sensitive instruments. Another exceptional feat becoming trivia to her.

The girl stretched lazily sitting in the warm sand, enjoying feeling the sun and heat vaporize the water on the skin. The sun shining from a cloudless sky. She sensed the heat entering the body, turning to something else. It shocked her, but not as much as she would have once believed. She was sixteen. Months had passed since her virginity had broken and she had been with several boys since then. But she hadn't truly dared to let go. This was the first time it had happened completely on its own. After hurried, worried looks around she dared to touch her breasts just a bit. The nipples hardened fast and painfully. The heat below grew hotter than the sun could ever make it. She jumped on her feet, packing her gear and started ashamed on her way back home. Doing her best to ignore the looks and lewd cries her Latino beauty caused. Usually she ignored her popularity, but now she was so ashamed that she didn't dare look up. Mama's thorough catholic upbringing raised its ugly head again. It remained, persisted, no matter how hard she wanted to escape it.

Lillith felt joy and unrest inside the girl, inside herself over the ease in which she had accomplished the task of «riding», becoming a passenger within the girl's body. She was conscious every nuance of what happened within the girl, both mentally and physically, much more so than within herself. Lillith was a passive rider because she wanted it that way. She could have possessed this body completely, or materialized outside it. But at the moment she was content with keeping it all as it was. Curiosity riddled her. What had pulled her to this girl? Not that she was a witch (she wasn't). It could have been the ethnical origin, the fact that she was of mixed blood. But Lillith believed, knew it wasn't that. What she sensed was something far more profound. Raven Moonstar had sought out this… observational platform for purely technical reasons. This girl was like everybody in Miami this day on her way to a meeting with Destiny, but something separated her from the majority of the city's population. She had a fire inside she wasn't consciously aware of, and she had coincidence on her side… She would survive.

She walked home to dinner and the downtrodden parents, the many siblings, a cliché of a Latino family. The dark light sparkled around them all and only to a lesser degree around her when she looked at herself in the mirror. Lillith, in her eagerness had to be careful to not take control over the body and thereby alter the girl's destiny.

The girl left the apartment as quickly as possible. She never stayed long if she could avoid it. Back, she walked. Back to the beach and the heat, chasing off the gray, unexciting existence.

Virtually all those present had turned their eyes, their focus to the south. As one they looked at the enormous wall of whirling dark already covering half of what just a few hours ago had been a lying, dishonest completely blue sky, a traitorous, fucking promise of eternal salvation.

The lightning turned *visible* in the darkened mass, in what basically still was a sunny afternoon. The frequent cracks of thunder hurt the ears of everybody present, even though they were still far away. Clouds, black as a snow free winter night filled the sky. Like a blanket keeping air from the sleeper. Yes, from the sleeper… *But not the dreamer.*

People turned and ran in panic, faced with the incomprehensible. Wind started to pull them, pull them hard. Lillith stared fascinated without eyes, at the drama unfolding. «Saw» the wind with its enormous speed tearing a hole in, ripping apart the very air. She laughed, both in fascination and fear. Nobody noticed her. A gush of wind, gaining speed tore off the roof of an office building. Another, even stronger gush and it broke in two like… yes, like a dry twig. Lillith perceived the energy patterns in the Storm. This was Nature at its purest, a raw, untamed force sweeping with it everybody and everything in its wake. An erupting volcano and the later earthquake rolled into one. An atomic bomb devastating a city. Everything at once. Humanity had done its best to tame and destroy nature, destroy Life, and now it was payback time.

Heaven and sea turned into one. «Horizon» was just a word. Air and fire became the same side of a coin with no other side. Wild electricity roasted people in their own fat. Sand dunes rolled like waves into the city and got washed away with the concrete. People lifted their arms at the heavens and begged their god to save them, save *them.* A bored, indifferent lord just shrugged and kept watching his TV-screen. But Lillith knew he was gritting his teeth. This was so absolutely contrary to his interests, his meticulously made plan. And she laughed in joy. Voluntarily or not, humanity had started on the journey back to nature and its own spacious place in it.

She turned restlessly in her bed. A doctor had entered the tent. He wasn't supposed to be here.

– Look at them. I told them both, to take it easier, to not push themselves so hard.

– They're only resting. Andrea's voice. – Don't go near them.

It looked like he was accepting this and was about to leave when he visibly froze in his tracks. He had spotted the electrodes the two of them had attached to their forehead. His eyes became like glued to the monitors. He paled.

– T-these readings… I've seen it before… many times. We're transmitting them the moment we die.

– They're similar, Andrea said patiently, but tense. – These are the result of ASC, Altered State of Consciousness. Go now, you don't belong here.

– Superstitious nonsense, the doctor spat and charged in between the two beds.

Andrea moved very fast, but stopped hesitatingly, not daring to get closer.

– Do they look like they're dying? She asked desperately, fearfully. She turned to Everett and Jason. – Do something.

Jason just smiled and studied it all with an interested expression. Everett and Tam stood frozen, about to charge forward.

The doc looked down at one of the girls, she who seemed the frailest, Jill Stafford. He had been helplessly attracted to her since he had first met her a few hours ago.

Two pair of eyes opened, wide, deep as the Universe. They didn't blink, just slid open, spooky, spookily, and it frightened him out of his wits, and he couldn't move a muscle. His words about superstition a few, short seconds ago seemed hollow, the silliest form of bravery.

He was grabbed around the arm, both his arms and kept in stasis. Jill held him with one hand in his left arm and the other girl, *Stacy,* in the other. The girls' lips moved in perfect synchronization.

– *You were warned,* the creature hissed. – *You do belong here, but you were warned*WARNED

Everett and Tam threw themselves at the three, grabbing Jill's right hand and Stacy's left. Jill and Stacy dug sharply into all three, dug deeply.

– Hear me, Everett cried, as pain cut into him. – Demon Mother, take the most from me. This is Charon, the ferryman, Anubis, the guardian speaking, he whom you have sought so long through the mists of Time. I… grant you *access.*

Three flashes turning into one single white. Three bodies like ragged dolls hitting the ground in a strange silence. Stacy and Jill falling back in the bed, corpse-like and still. All monitors flatlined.

Jason carefully and alert checked the three on the floor. Their breathing was labored, but even. Everett… Anubis, Jason corrected himself… sat up already. Jason reached out a hand. Anubis denied it, not unfriendly. There had always been some sort of rivalry between them, something they didn't yet understand. Andrea shook uncontrollably. Delphi stood by the entrance, unmoving. Everybody else who had slept in the tent awakened. Anubis straightened to his full height. He kept his human form, but was yet different.

– It has begun, he said.

Yes, the hour is coming. She dissolved the modifications of the mind, and her infinite power was unleashed.

She saw herself become one with the raging Storm, the Earth's primal force, Life's infinite power so long neglected, suffering in chains. She hung in the air, an enormous entity levitating under her own power, in front of the wind, wind followed by destruction incarnate. She hardly recognized what she would become. A giant shadow, whose eyes burned in the flames of the Abyss, the incarnation of force. She saw, exalted and terrified civilization die under her ruthless, irresistible Onslaught. A power with no equal released in her cauldron of a womb.

But was it truly… necessary? The planet was certainly well on its way to saving itself?

A moment's hesitation and Styx' whirlwind brought her far away on her Journey. Time, the mists of time was hers to reveal. A tree, bark at her back. She pushed herself at the tree, sweating and suffering, immersed in the Life of the forest. The birth water had come, the head of the baby, the boy was already visible between her thighs. Minutes later. The pool of blood on the ground flowed and glowed and burned. She held the boy, held him up, his head on the same level as hers. And as she watched his eyes opened… and they were glowing like fire. She recognized those eyes, she did. Mother, she was the mother of demons.

She walked through a hallway. It was raining white fluffy pieces, but not snow, raining cotton. A dark hallway. Somewhere she heard the sound and saw the flashes of a television set. The feet of a little girl revealed itself before her.

Her Journey brought her through time, so fast she could hardly comprehend anything but flashes. She saw, felt the tribe, her tribe fight and suffer and die. She saw countless variations of the future, but it boiled down to just a few possibilities.

Each breath was *pain,* air so thick with particles that no one could move outside and hardly even inside, without a mask. Breathing apparatus was the most common aid. Not everybody could afford gas masks. They were quickly worn out and only the very few had sufficient funds to procure oxygen bottles. Just like clean water and somewhat poison free food was a privilege reserved for the rich and powerful. And for those with proper connections further up in the Pyramid.

The night retreated from charging dust. All relief of darkness, of shadow ended. The sun, high in the sky was just about visible among the tall buildings. The day proceeded half gray, and the disk up there was just that, a disk, pale and gray, filtered through the completely rotten atmosphere. Beyond the city, one could, from the suburbs, on less bad days glimpse the mountains in the west. They were dirty brown, barren, not in any way tempting, not even as a refuge. The land between the cities was called the Wastelands and no one traveled through it without access to mechanical transport. Most people were born and died within the confines of the same city. This was the Supercity Kansas, a typical place on Earth around the middle of the twenty-first century (christian, western time). A planet of one voice, one will. This was *his* kingdom, and its day had come. He was Lord over all he surveyed. Everything that existed had come from his being. Such was it in the end and such must it have been in the beginning.

Humid and hot was the day. Humid and hot was the night. A heat making everything shrivel and die, without as within, as above so below. Nothing ever changed in the Shining City. Lillith, she called herself that all the time now, in her mind, as a way of pointing the finger, one last, rebellious thought, as she collected garbage on the edge of the city, close to the Wastelands, with the other unfortunates, for some reason or another having fallen through the cracks of the system.

The huge cracks.

Her reason for being here was simple: She didn't dare register anywhere. If she went through a DNA scan her mutant gene would stand out as a sore thumb. So, she hid among the garbage collectors, hiding her true self, hiding everything. She had hidden far worse places during the last fifty years. Many in her situation chose suicide before this denigrating, shameful existence, but they didn't know what she had firsthand knowledge of. He Who Was God and Wandered the Earth as a Man had gained control to such a degree that he had power over human souls, too. It was certainly known that His Domain included the soul, but very few realized what it *entailed.* And those who didn't believe turned believers after death. He caught them all in his net and threw them back into his sea, tailor-made to his specifications. Lillith knew it to be so. She still had a peripheral contact with the Shadowland. He had power over all living things, over life and death. It was said he could be many places simultaneously and the thought alone made Lillith gasp in fear. Where she walked and sweated, and strived to hold out the searing heat, she didn't seem much different from the others around her. But under the shit and smeared fat and the ragged clothes, she didn't have one single minor wound. Or burn. Or swelling. Her skin was as smooth as it had ever been. Under the tight bound headscarf all her hair remained. Her talents burned, if possible, stronger than ever, continued to increase as time passed. Her power kept the surveillance cameras from detecting her as anything else than another lowlife. Physically nothing was wrong. It was her spirit, her soul that was dwindling with every step she stumbled forward. And her reason. The certainty that she wouldn't be able to keep it going much longer. She would make a mistake. Or she would, one way or another, be discovered. She felt so tired. She had thought she had known the meaning of that word fifty years ago, but hadn't even come close. She stumbled on, one single individual in an endless row of condemned. The journey of the condemned back to the city central, the promised land.

The land of machine oil and rusty pipes. A bitter smile crossed her dirty face. Irony didn't work as well for her as it once had done.

The community standard of living was seen as better the closer one got to the center point. Out here the dead remained a considerable amount of time before they were removed, thrown into the patrolling combustion tanks, but in the inner city quite a lot of actually breathing people were incinerated. They were breathing, but they looked dead. Jill had often asked herself the question of how long she would stay young, youthful and strong. No answer was forthcoming. Perhaps it didn't matter. Perhaps she was doomed to wander back and forth in this hell forever.

Where she kept struggling forward, step by step, she saw him crush her, squeeze all the juice out of her, until nothing but a hollow, lifeless shell remained. He crushed the Earth itself. And he enjoyed it.

Flashes of pain, of sweet surrender. Flames erupted everywhere in the faint darkness. Fresh-looking plastic trees made out an alley on the sides of one of the main roads leading into the inner world of Metropolis Kansas, the last mile to the transparent white dome, the dome covering the sky-high pyramid. Its point was hardly visible as anything but a fever vision in the gray fog.

Five floaters, flying patrol cars slid through the air, towards the dome, just above the «trees», well above the crowd gathering like roaches along the route. It was funny, in a way. The floating cars still used the road. The sunlight, broken many times cast its shade over this insane a procession. One of the floaters, surrounded in a square by the four others, had no roof, no walls. Lillith was highly visible on the block they had placed her, heavily chained. Enraged and excited shouts rose from the crowd and the mob. It scarcely happened anymore these days that a spawn of Satan was captured. The crowd impatiently awaited this one's Burning. Lillith stood there, straight and proud. Suddenly her scarf was seemingly pulled off her head. The crowd went berserk. The long, black hair fell, well past her shoulders. Shouts of hatred and envy made white noise of any other sound. They realized that the chains didn't keep her from utilizing her demonic abilities. They shouted in joy as she got punished. The guards sent electric rays through her body. She fell to her knees. But the joy quieted as they realized that the cry was just as much in rage as in pain and despair.

She saw everything through a red haze and wanted to burn them all. They didn't throw anything at her. That act would have made laser beams incinerate the ones doing it. These people had long since learned their lesson. Instead, their fundamental hatred and fear washed over her like acid. She was responsible for everything wrong with the world, a heathen, spawn of godless and demons.

The transport passed through the air sludge, and she received a brief respite. Inside the dome it instantly picked up again, if possible, even worse than before. The air smelled better here, but tasted just as bad. Existence wasn't that different compared to fifty years ago. Now as then the subjects of the ruling class were told that everything would turn out fine and they wanted to believe it. And they did.

She glimpsed the entrance to the Pyramid far, far ahead, the building being so big that one couldn't take in everything in one glance, the entire silhouette created by sunlight from the west. Nothing obvious separated the pyramid from the rest of the dome, but to Lillith the force field was quite evident. An aura of disease, the center of rot and sick decay. The road there seemed both short and very long.

The floater landed. The soldiers (there were no faces, only helmets) dragged her down from it and brought her into an enormous white, clean hall, a place where there couldn't be much dust present. The flesh coated in uniform took her to a smaller room and chained her to the floor. Then they left. No ceremonies, only efficiency and obedience. A pull and the elevator started rising. She touched the floor. How clean and polished everything was.

How sterile.

They came and fetched her, the instant the elevator stopped, dolls in human shape. There were hardly thoughts in their heads, except for those necessary for them to perform their duties. They removed her chains and her headband. They put her in an enormous bathtub. They bathed and rinsed her, softly, efficiently. Water… Lillith had to close her eyes. How many years had passed since she had been bathing? How seductive wasn't it to feel the males and the females' hands on her skin, slaves at her disposal? They were nothing but drones that could be reprogrammed by a minor readjustment. Gooseflesh broke out all over her body.

She was dried, dolled up and perfumed. After cascades of water, they packed her body in towels and rubbed her with them until her skin had turned sensitive to the slightest touch. They dressed her up in elegant clothing, not exactly covering major parts of her body. They styled the long hair, but used the scissors sparingly. She saw herself in the mirror. Eyes were shining, like in a cold, hungry child brought into a warm, comfortable palace of riches.

A long hall, a red carpet. Tradition. Everything about this man was tradition. He was one of those who never changed. At least not during the fifty thousand years she had known him. She hadn't known him to the bone, though, hadn't realized how far he was willing to go and how far his guile could lead. And he had fooled her, as he had fooled the others, split them, split her. Then he had seduced her and made her his. He had grown so big and she so small. And she knew that just by making her think that way, he had won.

He sat on a throne at the top of a long staircase. People stood on both sides of the carpet, dressed like her, except for her uniform missing some important distinctions. There was no doubt that she was at the bottom of the heap. She was pushed down on her knees, and she knelt there, by the foot of the pyramid he sat on. The Supreme Being and his court looked down on her. A slight wave with his hand and she once more stood straight. He called her to him, and she ascended the stairs. She stood before him with lowered eyes.

– No lice. The pleasant tone made her skin crawl. – No truly foreign bacteria whatsoever. No bugs can come near you and live. A perfect body and a free spirit. You're a treasure and one with many talents. You must be, remaining undetected for so long. A long time has passed since I've encountered one such as you. How long have you been able to do what you do, my child?

The assembly snickered. The Almighty loved to play with the fresh meat.

– As long as I can r-recall, Master, she replied fearfully.

– You fear you'll burn, he said. – Don't. You're far too lovely to waste like that.

– Then thou find pleasure by the sight of thy humble servant, Sire?

– You interest me. Keep doing so and you've got nothing to fear.

He laughed and the court laughed with him, like a perfect echo. She followed his eyes to the carpet on the wall, a woven image of a cross and a pyramid. The carpet was pulled aside. There was nothing behind it, not even darkness. Flames erupted. A lot of flames, a lot of smoke. Nothing drifted into the room. He rose from his throne and reached out his hand.

– Walk with me through Purgatory, he bade her, – and be reborn.

So tiny, so huge. She walked by God's side. Ahead… awaited not as much flames, but ashes and smoke, what slowly but just as surely strangled anyone subjected to it. She kept walking. Nothing had changed. She knew this smoke well. It was the same she had been breathing all her life.

Lillith, the Lillith traveling through time and space, crouched like in a womb, drifting in the Void, shaking in disgust. She didn't have the strength to hold on any longer.

Further… drifting through the mists of time. No, not drifting. She flew. Over open sea. Something's rising from the molten sea. I. I AM

The Journey was nearly ended. In a flash she saw a possible future where the Dollmaster was just a distant memory.

And she was the one sitting on the throne. This was the woman who had ordered flagellated a servant for not kneeling properly, the Queen Goddess of Egypt.

She saw herself as a girl, saw her chubby legs as she strived to put one foot ahead of the other.

Sometimes the mirror girl, the big one, was there, sometimes not. And she saw them both, as adults, in another place, another time. Once the mirror girl stood behind her, offering her to the assembly gathered before them.

And she was alone with two adults.

– You took me away, she cried, the little girl cried.

– No, Jill, there was a fire...

There was smoke and her throat felt raw and constricted. She had been crying.

– You took me away, she cried.

– No, Jill, there was a fire...

– My name is NOT Jill! She cried out.

She passed through the final gate. She had reached the Kingdom, the Kingdom of Death.

A blinding black light and she opened her eyes.

CHAPTER EIGHTEEN: Mystic

The ground was already dry. It had stopped raining and the clouds had dispersed, had vanished. The sun made all humidity disappear. Shortly afterwards the ground and air were as dry as ever, the heat turned up a few more notches. The day before drowning had been people's main concern. Now many died because of the heat. The buildings of concrete and glass reflected the sunlight. There was no place to hide from the killing heat. People sought out the parks, but the few trees hardly gave sufficient respite.

Roads, sidewalks and open spaces were crowded with cars, smashed glass and dusty concrete, sand and dust arrived from far away. Jill walked in a daze quite similar to that of most people by her side, heading towards Boston Common.

– Shaken, my dear? Stacy patted her cheek lightly. Jill nodded, bowing her head. – Don't be.

The witches, walking along a growing crowd all made their way towards Boston Common and what awaited them there. Stacy whistled cheerfully and Jill caught herself doing the same.

– What irony. Stacy shook her head. – We sought a kind of mythical, remote Kingdom of Death, but it's here, right in front of us, merely a few steps ahead.

She illustrated her words by a wave of her hand.

– This is the Kingdom of Death. This is the Nightmare glimpsed by seers through millennia.

– Yes, Jill said intensively. – This world, not just this rubble.

Confusion and pain raged within her, she couldn't escape it.

Not because of this. She reveled in this.

The sky-high tombs in Boston and all other remaining cities on Earth still stretched towards the sky, over land and sea, and artificial fire burned the world. The Storm hadn't worsened this condition, but to the contrary improved upon it. The world needed more of it, much more.

Humanity had sailed down the river Styx and returned to shore on the wrong side.

Words, both in pain and exaltation echoed within Jill.

I'm NOT Jill

The little girl shouted.

I rose from the four dimensions' sea and learned what I am.

I AM

The grown girl shouted.

– Look at all this bullshit around us. Jill spoke part cowed, part aggressive. – So perishable.

– Rebirth is a natural part of the Cycle, Everett said smiling, casting long, worried looks at her. – All bodies, all fortresses raised to safety's praise are destined to become rubble. But not the Lifeforce itself. A new Storm will always come where it's necessary.

It was all so clear to Jill occasionally. What happened was a purification. Fire, water, earth and air were, in the final analysis Nature's way of cleansing itself, so that after the Storm had quieted, everything could start anew.

They started dancing, and many joined them well before they reached the stage in Boston Garden. There had long since existed plans for the rock group Mystic to play here, today, October 24. Merely during the last few days this planned event had changed to become something more, far more. Many guest artists had announced their arrival and participation, and even more would show up unannounced. An excited mood prevailed, and conversation had an excited sting attached to it. Rebellious shouts erupted from the crowd, emerging from the increasingly rebellious mood. Already at this early stage, at two o'clock, five hours before the concert was supposed to begin, the place was well over half-filled.

Wonderful, Jill thought, as she could virtually sense the energetic music already.

Excitement rose as Mystic entered the stage as early as 2.30. They didn't say anything. Without sermon they just started playing. They played cover tracks, other bands' compositions from the sixties and early seventies. It ended so fast, the two-hour set. Breathlessly people hardly got to ponder the sensational experience they had just lived through. Everything continued flowing and they didn't even think about catching their breath.

Other bands and single artists performed until 6.30. Then everything turned quiet among the audience, the participants to a buzz of anticipation. The last half hour wait was hardly any wait at all. Darkness descended and Boston Garden was filled to the brim.

Linsey Kendall re-entered the stage precisely at seven. The plain clothes he had worn earlier had been exchanged by his ever-changing shadow costume. As the crowd welcomed him, the stage turned dark, completely dark. Even the buzz eventually died. He started speaking. They heard nothing but his characteristic voice, dark, hollow, the edge of a sword.

– *It's dark. Let the ShadowWalk begin.* Listen to *Witchsong.*

A light was lit, one just about strong enough for people to glimpse details on the stage. It sparkled in the shoulder length red hair. The Mystical Rock, Mystic's own invention, started up from the electrical guitar he held in his hands, rough, soft and rough heathen moods slipping close to them all, crying proud, wild joy. Pulse quickened, sweat poured from already humid skin.

We walk
Through fire, through shadow
From the night we are born
An owl howls between
The dark trees
The Hunger of Life
from the newborn

Lights blinked off and on, subdued, hardly the sharp-edged blinding flares of an ordinary rock concert. This was a *Rock Concert*, in the classical sixties style, before things grew out of hand and grew too big. Even though this was big. And more. It was Mystic. Linsey and the other band members looked like phantoms and spirits and in flashes it seemed like they were levitating above the stage. Their play, their performance mimicked the music, a whisper rising to a scream. And the audience, the participants screamed and whispered back. Jill let the black hat slide below her neck, screaming as the mood assaulted her from all sides. Both the physical and cerebral hunger was fed and so easily, without her needing to take anything from anybody. She fed from the charged air. The words he sang, the way he sang them, so insightful and convincing. He *knew.*

– We are *Mystic,* he cried in the silence after the song's final beat, before the applause erupted. – Listen to our song of light and darkness. We are witches and witches have always been the Storytellers of the Night.

It's growing, Jill thought in fear and anticipation. He's one of the most high-profiled of us, but the attention is growing day by day.

Four songs followed, without much being said, but then - Jill felt it as if she knew him already - Linsey raised a hand. The stage once more remained in darkness. One could glimpse Linsey, his hand, but nothing else. He didn't have to utter a word or a sound, to make silence reign. Jill noted joyfully that the soldiers posted all over the area froze. Especially Secret Service and Intelligence members.

– I guess you're wondering how we managed *this?* The cheers charged him like a roar. His eyes flashed and burned. – Well, some of us… have *talked.*

– And the result is guaranteed to cause a stir in the dark corridors. It will be a cause for deep conversation and concern, like the one celebrating the seventieth birthday of Nelson Mandela, the No Nukes and Woodstock, and other great rock celebrations. For Rock is rebellion and works at its best when it causes the morning coffee to be stuck in the might's throat and is engaging those who are mostly talking, stirring them to action, encouraging them to break out of their confines. Someone will surely talk after this…

Brave laughter and applause. Many of those present knew very well that the expression «people have talked» was much used in Intelligence and clandestine governmental circuits.

– Many will be able to voice their opinions without obstructions or threats tonight. That's good. That doesn't happen often in our oppressive society. But as you well know some of them will sail under a bogus flag, speak here under false pretenses, pretending to be something they're not. Some are fairly obvious. You know who. In my eyes people like the «Bishop of California» will never be anything other than a two-legged wolf in sheep's clothing. He, like several others will speak to serve their own selfish gain, serve the society they profess to oppose.

A buzz rose from the audience. He had spoken straight from the heart, as was his custom, as many present weren't used to. There were supporters of the Bishop of California in the audience tonight and they stared at each other in shock.

– One last item: This is no tax-deductible event, no charity performance. This is not one of those countless gatherings collecting money to one «good» cause or another. No relief fund or part time indulgence with a short-term relief, keeping anything significant from being done. What's left after all the expenses have been paid will go in its entirety to Phoenix Green Earth. No, the government and the industry share the blame for the destruction. Let them pay for it a little this time. We will use the money the way we wish and what we wish is to tear down this world's pyramids.

He made one single guitar riff. The synthesizers joined with deep, naked sounds. And ancient ages, humanity's Life before the emergence of cities entered Boston Garden.

People turned Wild and the soldiers clutched their weapons. It happened quite frequently that the police and various authorities caused trouble during Mystic's concerts and performances. But not this time around. The publicity would be too devastating. All the thugs and eager servants had received strict orders to show restraint.

The band enjoyed breaks occasionally and let others play, as they were also the band for other artists. And others performed for an audience encompassing the world through the giant video screen. Musicians, artists, a wide array of performing arts. And also publicly well-known people from various alternative movements… and not so alternative movements.

Something was about to happen, they all sensed it. Linsey returned to the stage. He spent several minutes to achieve complete silence. The video monitor was turned off, all lights faded. Darkness descended, tighter than ever. Nothing happened. Not in minutes. Just a few voices were heard, and other voices hushing on them from the tight darkness. It slowly dawned on them all what this was about, and cheers rose like fire at the sky (and nothing burned). This was the start of one of the rare rock theater performances Mystic held without any pre-announcement.

Heavy piano sound filled the night, a variation of John Carpenter's opening title from his film The Fog. A figure emerged from the black velvet of the darkness. A red cloak and a Janus head with two adjacent faces. The figure turned and turned again. One face was a demon mask and the other was Death.

– *«Is all that we see or seem but a dream within a dream»?*

From that moment all sense of time and space disappeared. Whatever happened didn't merely happen on stage. Jill sensed the body's electricity increase violently and continue rising. A woman and a man with fire-eyes danced on the stage and the echo from the participants in the Garden, the Wild Garden, turned the dance into a frenzy, raw, passionate, ecstatic and certainly a performance that christians called indecent, heathen, satanic. An outlook on life dividing humanity from nature, quite simply had to be such a narrow, neurotic view.

The surroundings… dissolved. Jill didn't imagine it. She was about to learn the difference between real and imagined. They were led back to a time before the first church was raised, the first mosque, the first house of God, the first vocation to human denial of Nature, of Life, of Self.

Later, she didn't know how much later, as the very concept had lost its meaning after she had found out who she was… she looked at the big screen, at the flashing of electrical impulses. Two of the external features interested her immensely. Both made her both hot and cold. A recognition more than a discovery. A man, Martin Keller stood straight, immersed in a swarm of insects. They circled in orbits around him, and they sat directly on his skin. None bit him, even if many of the various species had the ability. His voice sounded strangely distinct, blanking out all the buzz. The buzz from the insects seemed… synchronized, as if they were modified to the modulation in his voice.

– No matter where you live today, he cried out, – whether in New York City or on a remote island in the arctic ocean, anyone willing to put up the $2000 for testing, will find more than 250 synthetic industrial chemicals in their body. Daily Ozone testing is a reality. The holes in the ozone layer are permanent now. The food and fishery crisis is intensifying. These are just a few of the countless self-inflicted problems we're dealing with in the present-day world. We grow more ill day by day, both we and our surroundings, by the industrial chemicals we're ingesting, of all the unnatural chemicals, poisons we're surrounding ourselves with. This is not caused by any alien influence. We, the present-day humans are all responsible for allowing this insane situation to arise and continue unabated. Those in power are telling us that Nature is something strange and dangerous and we listen…

Jill mumbled something. She couldn't tell what herself… but Lillith could. Gabi looked at her, enquiringly, as she sensed the happy excitement.

– Insects don't have a brain or mind we can affect, Jill said, – but he can… the *Lord of the Flies.*

Gabi looked at her in absolute astonishment.

Lillith knew him under many names. Peter Hardy, Piet van der Haart, Kjell Gudmundson and countless before that, in the mists of time. She had met him in the Valley of Kings, Egypt in the nineteen-thirties and in Egypt thousands of years ago. She recognized the Ankh-amulet around his neck.

Something happened then. Jill didn't quite get what. Not instantly. Martin Keller talked about human unity with the planet, about the alienation leading us to where we were today, in a hell of our own making.

The screen darkened. A new image emerged, like many bars overlapping each other. Birds flew in from the sky. An idyllic image. Huge wings in silhouette against sunset. It was only when the birds were shown in close ups the nightmare revealed itself. Open beaks exposed pointed, bloody teeth. Humans were attacked and torn apart piece by piece. A computer animation, so life-like.

The scene shifted. Sunrise. A man in a suit stood before a tall, futuristic building. Jill felt how the stomach content returned as bile in her mouth. A violent feeling of nausea overwhelmed her and didn't let go.

The man with the pleasant, cultivated voice started talking.

– Have your surroundings become strange? Do scary things happen in your neighborhood? The people are perhaps not the way you remember them. They might exhibit strange behavior or make you ill. The weather might seem changed? You know me, know my flock, my work. I have been given the task of uniting all the disparate flocks of God's sheep. We have our work cut out for us, and it can't be postponed. The Almighty, no matter the name He goes by, has long since given us all the task of submerging the Earth, conquering it in his Glory. This is a task well under way. Technology, the Almighty's holy tool, is available to us and we've used it well. It will eventually allow us to solve all our problems… if we let it. You see, lately a band of discontents has risen, threatening His Holy Work. They claim that technology is destructive, while it's not. They claim we humans use it badly, which we're not. It's time to deny those false prophets for what they truly are, agents of Satan. It's our destiny to obey His command and become Masters of the Earth. Those who in deed and words signal that they don't want to partake in the Great Plan can't be permitted to sabotage it any longer. They call our great leaders environmental pigs and tyrants. They're encouraging disobedience and discord and promiscuity. They can't be allowed to stop the New Age…

Laughter. Scornful, furious, enraged. But as shown earlier he had followers among the audience, and they let their presence be heard.

– Stop the *blasphemy* all of you, a girl cried. – He's a great prophet.

Nausea stuck in Jill's throat, and she couldn't take her eyes off the image on the screen. He hadn't changed a lot, he had hardly changed at all, he… With all her command over her own body she couldn't puke. She remained on the spot, shaking and sweating, so weak, so pathetic.

– H-he, she stuttered. – Brian Garrett, the Bishop of California… It's *Him.*

– Who? Jason said curiously, not that interested.

– The *Dollmaster.*

Jason paled. The very sight of him, like that, made them all pay attention, as Jill's words, their meaning sank in.

– It is time for you all to know, Stacy said concededly, an ironic smile crossing her face, just a slight shaking in her cheek revealing her mood.

Jill looked at her intimately, intensively, met the half sarcastic, half challenging look and then she threw up, violently, uncontrollably.

– GOD! Andrea exclaimed and shrunk in her tracks.

– Precisely, Gabi nodded.
– That shit is a recording, Jason snarled. – He can be anywhere, he can be here, damn it.
Gabi opened her mouth, but refrained from speaking. She clung to Jason, sore afraid.
– I would have felt his presence, Jill mumbled darkly. – It stays in the air wherever he walks, smelling like a host of rotten fruit. That's what he does, making fruit rot on the vine.
They tensed; body and mind, they who came from Northfield, they who knew, willing to do whatever it took, to stop the sleazy, ingratiating voice. He had talked enough.
Then the screen turned black seemingly of its own accord. It sparkled and died, as it spat smoke and brimstone. The face faded, even if there was a moment when it seemed that it wouldn't, that it lingered. Spontaneous applause broke out almost everywhere.
– I don't think he is here. Jill spat bile. – The Almighty isn't one who goes to places where he doesn't hold all the cards.
She felt better. It was as if a damp hand had been pulled back from the place. A hand with fingers like claws, hurting and mutilating its victims.
Linsey returned to the stage. He stood there with a raised fist.
– As you just witnessed our good friend, the self-baptized Bishop of California forced himself on us. The powerful voice was thick in its heated wrath. – He contacted us in advance and expressed his decisive desire to participate, but we, without hiding our disgust, asked him to stay in hell. He stands for everything we fight against. Under cover of leading an alternative movement, he and his lackeys are defending injustice, alienation, intolerance and elite rule everywhere. What is fundamentally wrong in the world he's presenting as the only, absolute solution. He wants more of the same.
He struck a naked, ghostly chord, smiling slowly, teasingly. An impressive figure he was, there on the stage, the little man, filling the vision of those assembled.
– I'm sorry to report that the stage monitor will be out of order for the remainder of the evening… Well, people, it's a beautiful night. We can manage without an overgrown TV, right?
More cries, more applause, renewing itself somewhere in the crowd, spreading from there to all over the place, never to quite end.
Linsey Kendall started singing. The music embraced everybody listening.

The soul is the dream
The dreams are the soul
Our Shadow, following us
Through pitch darkness

Once again, he shouted a greeting after the last, ear-shattering drumbeat, a brave, shocking cry because of its significance.
– Dreams belong to the night!
And the shattering crack spread throughout the eternal void. Mystic played to well after midnight. And afterwards the performances and festivities… quite simply continued. Many left the area after the music stopped, but many remained… listening to the music, the music of the airwaves. It changed to a party, a celebration, unnoticeable, as with a shadow following you as you walk towards the light. Journalists chased Linsey all night long, but he handled it in the same slick way he had handled everything else that night. He and the two other members of the Janus Clan had the same aura of explosive confidence.
– They're Ring Bearers. She almost jumped out of her skin. Gabi had joined her at her side, unnoticeable. – They carry pieces of their dead ancestors' eyes in their rings.
Jill studied Elizabeth Warren and Ted Warren. Their eyes and the content in the rings were the same. But Linsey's eyes, though he was a Bearer… they were normal.
Well, perhaps the eyes, but nothing else about him was normal.
Ted and Elizabeth were just as famous, infamous as Linsey, but tonight they kept to the background, so good at sliding in and out of the shadows that even experienced journalists were led astray.
It did help a bit that Linsey actually was the news tonight.
– You want to meet them, don't you? Jason spoke unexpectedly.

Without thinking more about it, the assembly from Northfield nodded eagerly. They were hardly more than ordinary, excited teenagers this particular night.

– Come with me, then.

They followed him, exchanging glances, shaking their heads, discarding their doubts.

The party, consisting of four to five minor parties retreated to an old, more or less standing storage building by the harbor. A house party had already started. Two powerfully built males sort of guarded the entrance, while entertaining people spitting fire from their mouth. The sweaty bodies flickered in the shifting light. Jill could glimpse the huge floor space within. Different types of music made war. Which was winning depended on your position at the moment. The fire-spitting men weren't really guards. There was no such thing. They just welcomed whoever came their way.

Inside, in a cacophony of sound and fury Jill faced Elizabeth and Ted for the first time.

They were young, they were old. Ageless would be a better word. The dark skin, the burning eyes, the dark, feathered hair. She felt an instant and profound, and scary rapport and couldn't help pulling back a little.

– Hallo, Jason, Elizabeth said softly. – How are you?

All the young adults stared at Jason, attempting not to stare at him.

– I'm okay, he replied. – I'm fine.

– We have missed you, the male Warren said, more accentuated, and unbelievably enough with a touch of uncertainty in his voice. – We have all missed you.

– I believe you, Jason said tightly. – Why shouldn't I?

– And these are your friends, the female Warren said, (uncharacteristically?) attempting to smooth things. – Your classmates from *school,* I gather? What an adorable bunch of raffle…

She greeted them all with a handshake and a kiss, a teasing grin. Jill got nothing from her, no impressions, no emotions, nothing at all, and she tried. She tried hard.

– You've had dreams, Elizabeth told her. – Of the future and the past and Beyond?

Jill nodded, unable to speak.

– Come, Elizabeth, Liz Warren bade them all, suddenly with a childish eagerness. – Let's find a quiet, noisy spot.

They are children, Jill thought. They are ancient.

Everything happened too quickly. The certainty that the two of them were studying them didn't matter, that they were looking them up and down was unimportant, but nothing really happened. Not on the surface anyway.

They talked normally, without raising their voice. It was as if they didn't sit in a hall full of noise and mayhem.

A girl threw herself off the balcony. She landed on a group of five people, without anybody getting hurt. No one could tell if they had stood on that particular spot by coincidence or not.

– You *are* recruiting, aren't you? Gabi asked very direct.

– We sure are, Ted laughed out loud. – Especially such… interesting young people gathered here this evening.

All the rumors, all the wild accusations circulating about him, about her didn't do them justice. Jill giggled. It didn't even come close.

– It might be interesting, Gabi said clearly arrogantly. – I mean, I'm not certain I want to, but it might be interesting.

– You will, Ted Warren said.

And the chill Jill felt down the spine was deep and profound.

A lot was said during the few minutes they spent in the company of the two Warrens, but these were the only words (of importance) she remembered.

There was some commotion by one of the platforms, one of the stages. The two Warrens looked at each other. They didn't have to, but they did so anyway.

– Sorry, kids, he said. – It has been swell, but we gotta go. See ya around, okay.

– Okay, Stacy mumbled.

The two Warrens disappeared into the crowd, into the smoke and mirrors.

They all waited as long as they could, a few seconds or so, before as one turning towards Jason.

Jason's eyes, his eyes ordinarily as blue as the night on a full moon flashed briefly with the fiery fire of the Janus Clan.

And Jill understood, startled before he opened his mouth to speak.

– He's my father, okay!

Silence reigned for seconds, without anybody speaking.

– He's hard, Morgana stated. – Hard as steel.

They all looked at her, eyes full of recrimination.

– I'm sorry, she persisted, – but it's the truth.

– I know, Jason said angrily. – I know.

– Something happened to him once, Gabi stated softly. – Something horrible.

And silence reigned, as their pocket of the Universe slowly was digested by another, much bigger piece.

The commotion persisted. Jill suddenly realized that the journalists and photographers had come running, rushing towards the stage for some time now.

It wasn't really a stage, but more of a low platform. They saw flashes of red, of red and black hair blowing in the wind.

Linsey Kendall called an improvised press-conference quickly, easily and lightly. He moved to the middle of the platform, while all the hungry sharks (missing their teeth) gathered below.

Handsome devil, Jill thought unfounded.

Silence reigned everywhere.

– You're attached to, yes, actually one of the founders of Phoenix Green Earth? A journalist charged forward by standing still. – What's the purpose of this organization?

– First of all, Linsey began. – We don't look at ourselves as an organization, at least not in a traditional sense. Call us rather a *fusion.* And these aren't just words, but facts. We're many small groups working together towards a common goal. What that goal is, shouldn't be too hard to understand. We've set out to lead humanity back to nature, back home. This will take care of many of today's problems and allow us to start over. The overgrown tribes called nations and countries will go. Religion, one of the major causes for the false legitimacy of the hierarchy, will go. Everything destroying Life on Earth will fade into unimportance. The world's pyramids shall crumble to dust. We don't want humanity to live in the overgrown anthills called cities. We want to leave the Stone Age, today's existence with refined rock all over, refined everything behind. The Stone Age is today, not ten thousand years ago, when something went terribly wrong, by the start and expansion of agriculture, the coming of the first cities. Humanity, natural nomads stopped being nomads and got stuck. We're nomads. It's our natural way of Life. We must rediscover what we have lost, *misplaced.* When that happens, we won't live in a perfect world. There's no such thing. But we will live closer to the living Earth, close to our Self… and we will *Live.*

Kendall's performances were always like this, more like a séance. He spellbound everybody listening to him. Jill knew he didn't use his power. He didn't need to, with his natural confidence and enthusiasm, something that almost made him glow. Perhaps that was a power, to speak from the heart, without pretense or conceit.

– Have you any idea why you and your family, the Janus Clan, infamous as you are, are enjoying such extended popularity in the current young generation?

– I can answer that, Jill cried out. Everybody's eyes and attention were directed at her. – Our generation, at least some of us, is the first realizing that present day human «life» is completely, absolutely, totally, utterly anathema to our survival, to the true Life we Hunger for, as Human Beings. We used to be both human and animal. Now we're neither. The Janus Clan is what we all once were.

He bowed eloquently. Eyes met eyes. His face was slightly rounded, a bit plump, quite ordinary really. But the eyes, ordinary as they seemed, were not. She saw there everything she would never forget. Both nodded and time continued its flow.

The very ironic press conference continued, but it had really ended. Everything important had already been said.

– Who do you think killed President Kennedy? A sharp voice after minutes of indifferent questions asked, as if Linsey was more qualified to answer that than anybody else present.

Suddenly silence reigned. Everybody held their collective breath in anticipation of the answer… and they weren't disappointed.

– That one is easy, too, Kendall smiled sardonically. – Everybody knows that representatives of the military/industrial complex did it, with the help of everybody in the central government who wasn't on vacation or sent to the South Pole that day…

Silence reigned still, a silence lasting several heartbeats. Then… a bark well prepared and thought of:

– What about you, Linsey? Is it your intention to become the next president of the United States?

The flash in the eye didn't go away, but intensified.

– President, *moi?* Laughter filled the empty space of silence.

– There are rumors…

– You know… Linsey showed his teeth. – I have heard those rumors myself…

– So, in your opinion, where are the rumors originating?

Another heartbeat.

– When I know anything worthwhile myself, you'll be the first to know. Thank you very much for your time, people. I'll see ya.

Another ambiguous comment, another flashing smile. This time, however, his fangs were clearly showing.

And then, he, too, melted away into the shadows. The strange performance had ended. The journalists chased him, but found nothing but others of their kind.

– The other two, one spat to his cameraman. – Quickly.

But the two other Warrens had also faded away, into the charcoal night.

Jill fumed around the mouth. The newsmen didn't really care, about what he said, about what anybody said, about anything. It was just a job to them. Even the so-called «crusading journalists», the few remaining, didn't do much more than scratch the surface.

Dawn, colors in rust and blood, shadows in gray. Inside the wreckage of a building, it was yet possible to hide in the shade. Music died from the speakers, one by one. This short day and night they had, for a little while, in an orgy of emotion and passion, managed to keep the Kingdom of Death at bay. Now, it crawled back under their skin.

Jill stood in the door, the doorway, on her way to full awakening, exactly in between where the two «spitfires» had been standing. Cuts and bruises hurt inside, and she couldn't really tell why they hurt more, now, than they usually did. Perhaps it wasn't any particular reason. Cuts and bruises did hurt… occasionally. She wanted to scream, in hatred and defiance. Her hands were already rolled into fists. She tightened them more. They bled and spread life and fire around her. She kept them open, and the red mist spread both outside and inside, until she felt faint and slowly, painfully let go of the fists and the blood flowed from them no more.

The Winds of Change… running wild

The two creatures stalking the streets of Northfield looked right at home here, more so than any of its citizens running around in disarray. They followed the smell of the fire, the scent of excitement, bravery and fear.

– I can actually smell it, Liz marveled. – I can smell it all. Is this how the animals do it?

She paused a bit, before adding:

– I can smell her rage, excitement and fear, too.

– It isn't even hard anymore, he pondered. – It's like the stink of waste stuck in the nose. It's almost overpowering.

It was as if the smell was drawing a picture in their mind, one different from, but at least as detailed as that seen through the eyes.

– And the plant life everywhere. Not trimmed either, but wild growing… and wild looking. If we didn't know better, we would think that the city council had invested in a green environment…

There was a tree standing in the middle of the road, surrounded by a lot of smaller trees and a circle of green grass.

– Perhaps they've put the waste to good use? He said brightly.

– Or they've hired a witch? She didn't want to be any less funny…

They heard the added commotion long before they actually saw anything, shrieks and shouts closing in on them.

A somewhat unified group turned a corner ahead of them.

– STRANG-ERS, the pack leader yelled in a parody of a thug. – Get them.

And they were about to, when they the next second took a closer look at the strangers, saw the seeming giants spit fire and emit cold, saw their feet hover just above the ground. The mob counted at least hundred «individuals». A majority of them started running. Some ran in blind panic straight forward, at the monsters they were running from. A major minority attacked just because their hatred overwhelmed their overwhelming fear.

Ted and Liz merely swept them away like lice. They heard bones break and skulls burst and couldn't say they didn't enjoy it all. Death fertilized the already fertile soil of the city turned tombstone further, transformed even more of it into seething, sizzling life.

He took one woman and lifted her up high above the ground, shaking her like a rag doll.

– DID YOU BURN THE WITCH? He roared and every word was like a snarl.

– Yes, we burned her, we burned her. AND SHE DISSOLVED IN FLAMES. GOD IS GOOD, GOD IS GREAT, HALLELUJAH

Ted looked into her windows to the soul and there was nothing there. He let her go in disgust and the woman collapsed on the ground, as the cackling laughter turned to tears and utter despair.

– God is with us, she sobbed and laughed chillingly.

He straightened, turning his face slightly, as if sniffing the wind.

– I can sense her. At least one of her is alive.

– Everything is Alive here, Liz said brightly. – She more than anything.

They kept walking. People pulled away, shrinking from the burning look, terrified of doing something that would catch the demons' attention.

The surroundings changed visibly around them, changed many times. They realized they were on their way into the older parts of the city. Buildings turned older and smaller. And the pervasive plant life everywhere turned even more pervasive. The very air changed… quality, turning thick as water, light as a breeze. They did indeed close in on something.

A crack broke the monotonous silence of the noise. A gun had been fired, had been fired close by. The two stalkers had smelled the four hiding behind the wall twenty seconds ago. They had seemingly ignored their presence. The bullet would have missed. The gun had been fired in haste, by a person obviously under pressure. Ted caught the bullet in his hand. All momentum left it and when he let go of it, it fell harmlessly in the dust.

– We're the investigative unit, he said aloud.

The silence turned heavier. Nothing more happened then. Ted and Liz walked into the dark alley. The four soldiers stared intensively at them. One of the soldiers didn't have his gun anymore. One of the others was holding it. The man without his gun was sweating hard and his eyes were huge as windows. He had cracked. The three others did remain calm somewhat.

They were professionals, after all, and had experienced a lot during their illustrious careers.

But nothing like this.

– You two do indeed look like the right choice for an investigative team, the soldier in charge said humorless. – I have heard about you, you know.

– We have heard about you, too, Cole, Liz said darkly.

The four wouldn't be any problem. They were completely out of their element, their line of expertise here.

– It's out t-there, the worn-down soldier stuttered. – The Ghoul.

Liz looked at the leader, deliberately sardonic.

– Someone is using a sophisticated movie projector, he shrugged.

He didn't believe it himself, but he was one of those persons who needed a «rational» explanation to cling to.

– That was no movie-p-projector, the other one babbled. – It… *looked* at me.
– Shut up, Jensen, Cole Bruckner snapped.
– It's TRUE! It floated above the fire, and it LOOKED at me… like She does.
He pointed accusingly at Liz. She smiled sweetly to him.
Jensen suddenly attacked Bruckner, attempting to wrest the gun from his hand. The pack leader pushed him away and struck him on the head with the rifle.
– Hey, that's enough.
One of the others spoke up and grabbed Bruckner in the arm. Bruckner kicked him in the groin.
The fourth man fired a bullet at the lieutenant, but missed. Then both fired simultaneously. The fourth man died with a hit in the head. Bruckner got hit in the chest and was pushed back at the wall.
– We have gotten everything we can from here, right? Ted turned calmly to Liz.
– You're right, she nodded. – Time to go.
They turned and walked away. They didn't look back.
Bruckner straightened and setting his machinegun on fully automatic, he fired a round at their backs.
Nothing happened really, except that the bullets lost all their forward momentum just after leaving the barrel, falling harmlessly in the dust.
– HELLO THERE! He shouted. – WHERE THE FUCK ARE YOU GOING
He sat down there in the dust. His face betrayed no expression. He just sat there, staring at nothing.
Cole Bruckner snapped that very instant. He had been close to do so several times before in his life, but now he flew off the handle completely and permanently.
– Such interesting people in this town, don't you think? Ted grinned and shook his head, dismissing what they had left behind.
– We should never leave, she grinned back.
It pulled at them, what awaited ahead. And all their focus turned forward, to the pervasive presence in their mind.
For a few blocks there had been no people, none but the four soldiers. Now, it thickened once more. No one looked at the approaching Warrens. Everybody looked in the same direction. They stood still, stood there in a daze, staring blindly ahead, surrounded by St. Elmo's Fire.
Liz and Ted approached the clearing. With rapid beating hearts they ran the last stretch… and stopped.
At the center of the broad street a pentacle burned. It burned and what burned was nothing but the dust on the ground. Flames rose high, but nothing except the actual figure lines were on fire.
– I would say this is it, don't you think? Liz said weakly, grinning wildly.
– I would say that's probably more than a correct assumption, Ted replied. – It is at the very least an excellent first step.
And like for the first time they saw the Hill. They saw it glowing in something far more sinister than St. Elmo's Fire. And they discovered the glowing gossamer line in the air, showing the way. The two Warrens obeyed willingly the siren's clarion call.
They followed the strands of night and fire, disappearing into the darkness.

CHAPTER NINETEEN: Samhain

The Lord of the Dead. The End of Summer.

Ground, long thirsty, long parched cracked beneath the cruel sun.

The festival of Samhain picked up again after the interruption October 26, after the night of the dying moon. The preparations for Halloween, the time of sacrifice, from midnight-to-midnight October 31, and the night beyond. The All Souls Night. The night when Shaman or Samhain, the Lord of the Kingdom of Death called to him the souls of the condemned, the demons of the Earth. A night when gates to hidden worlds opened wide.

In Northfield this year, more than any other place, a tradition thousands of years old was celebrated. Yes, one could claim that it was «relaunched» this year, on this place. A ritual both a challenge to, and a celebration of Death. But most of all a way of celebrating the Unknown.

Northfield, Newtown and Oldtown, had been immersed in the afternoon haze stretching beyond the northern and eastern fields and further into the uneven landscape. Most of the water fallen during the storm hadn't penetrated the hardened topsoil or at most softened just a bit of it. Now the remains evaporated. Every molecule of humidity, of vapor. The cleaning up had started, but the various crews and people seemed confused, dulled. Compared to their effort, the energy the witches and those within their circle put into their work definitely seemed paranormal. And they were followed by envious eyes.

Jill relaxed in a deep chair in the cool shade outside the Green Rose. She had taken a breather, a break because Tam, Luke and the others had insisted upon it. She had never before felt stronger, more rested, more awake… Her power seemed to be perpetually growing. It led to an awareness she both enjoyed and could have done without.

They had to do something right. She studied the relaxed hectic activity, the life and the joy. She did more than hearing… she sensed the birds singing. By using her power her mind flew across the fields, picking up at least as much as if she had been there physically. A few green spots had appeared after the rain, but not many. Most of the grass had remained yellow, dried, lifeless. Weeks of rain were needed for even the upper level to be drenched in water and it would still be dry soil further down. This area used to have huge amounts of rain. All the plants, all the animals here were adapted to a wet climate. The consequences of the stone desert's expansion made all life suffer.

The Halloween tradition had come to America with the European intruders. While it had waned in Europe it had sort of hibernated in a diluted form here, and now, as it returned everywhere, it was also celebrated with strength, in Newtown, Northfield. Perhaps because of the fact that people needed all the distractions they could find. Perhaps because of the re-emergence of witches all over world. Or perhaps because of the inevitable Change creeping under the skin of every living being on Earth. Jill certainly felt it, an almost tangible pressure under the eyelids, an electricity caressing the skin. Here, at least people turned to the witches, to get to know how it should be done. And the division among the city's population grew, as they chose sides for or against the witches, as tempers flared and hatred grew.

The mood, exalted and threatening, was clearly visible all over the city. Jill and Gabi took a walk through it all, feeling it all. Malvin, the huge, black kitten, took a stroll with them. He ran back and forth in between their legs and howled insulted when he didn't receive the attention he felt was due him. He had been so tiny such a short time ago. She was once again amazed by his fast growth, realizing that in many ways it mirrored hers. He walked with them, not at all frightened by the unfamiliar surroundings. His presence didn't exactly serve to diminish the interest and ugly stares concerning the little entourage.

And it was quite an impossible task to those attempting to close their eyes to the winds of change… the… extra quality. It was visible everywhere. Skeletons hung from trees and poles every year, but not in such numbers. The drawings, decorating hard surfaces were just a tad more daring. Skulls, grotesque masks, horrible monsters. Pumpkins resembling works of art in the way they terrorized everyone looking at them. Sharp-eyed observers also noted another detail in the decorations: The witches. They were drawn more normal, though slightly scary, compared to the ugliness of recent tradition the last centuries.

Children sang while trying out their insanely creative, terrifying costumes. Some didn't fit, or as some of the parents said it: «wasn't suitable as clothes». They were later placed on figures and dolls placed in fields and crossroads and in gardens and seemed to fill out any empty space they were found.
Jill shivered as she listened to the children's song.

Dancing round and round
lonely in the dark forest
The lake is burning
Burning the lovely witch
Calling to Life
Calling it to her
Death is coming
For her

A few blocks further ahead a man tore down skeletons wholesale and put them in the back of his truck. Another man charged forward to stop him.
– Stop this nonsense. What are you doing?
The man disliking skeletons didn't mince words. Without further delay he hit the interloper in the face. First there was an expression of utter astonishment in that man's face. Then, with his face concocted in rage, he hit back.
Jill considered intervening, but decided against it. Perhaps blowing off some steam would do them a bit of good.
She doubted it, though. Everything and everyone were charged these days… ready to blow.
– Hi, Goddess, a boy cried, good humored to her. – Any good Samhain tips to us?
– We're re-learning, just as you all, she shouted cheerfully back. – Trust yourself.
They walked through the Pyramid, as a reminder. The buzz there was quite different. An underlying whisper of eternal commercials, of how to live one's life, that was quite sickening.
– The present day «celebration» of Halloween is a joke, Gabi snarled, voice thick with venom and sarcasm. – It's so commercialized that absolutely everything of the ancient world is gone or horribly disfigured. The present world is about de-evolving, not evolving. Everything is prefabricated, everything is plastic. It's important for people to make their own costumes, to recreate themselves as they see fit.
Hope entered her voice during the last sentence. And hope and despair continued to war within her.
The walk ended, as it maybe was fated to by the factory.
The Factory towered above most structures, even within the might of the gray fog. Thick, black smoke erupted from the pipes. Tall fences surrounded the property. There was barbed wire everywhere. The private «protection» army stood lined up, side by side with the police officers, all inside the barricades. In front of the main gate a group of people sat tight. During days and nights of protests they had been moved away every time a truck had arrived or left. They had returned every time in ever-greater numbers. The crowd discovered the two (or three) new arrivals and cheered. The buzz, from the crowd, from everywhere turned loud in her ears. A powerful sense of Déjà Vu rose within her.
All those jailed because of Scott Thompson, all those earning regular meals at his expense, all those starving without that «free» meal, were present there, finally.
There were rebels and enraged people from town, finally fed up.
And the last major group, those who had arrived here from elsewhere, hadn't come here to hide. They hadn't come here to stand back, in any way.
Ivan, Rae, Travis and Tam waved from the middle of the crowd and Jill and Gabi (Malvin snarled) waved back. Jill received a wave of warm, aggressive joy from them and the rest of the protesters.
Jill and her two companions, one smaller and one seemingly very much smaller stepped within the dispersed circle. The heat and rage surrounded them. Jill raised a hand. Silence descended upon the place. She started speaking.
– First step is the questions you ask when you no longer accept what you experience in your

neighborhood. She sucked in the rage, the interest from the listeners, enhancing her strength, enhancing the rage and the interest, enhancing the people. – When you don't find satisfying answers there, you reach out, beyond the confines put on you by others and you're slowly realizing that something is horribly wrong. Then comes action and then your problems start in earnest. By revealing your major disagreement with the governing bodies, you expose yourself and become vulnerable, open to their complete attention and retaliation.

– Me, I don't feel I'm making such a sacrifice, a boy at the front of the gate grinned. – It's at the very least just as dangerous to obey and stay silent.

– Most people forget this, Jill nodded pleased. – They don't realize that they're easier to stamp on as long as they remain ants on the ground.

– HELLO THERE, BITCH. A higher-ranking police officer shouted to her. – Nobody has given you permission to hold a speech.

– We have permission to stay here, then? Jill spat. – Do you think we need permission from anybody, to do anything? You believe your masters are powerful? You-don't-know-what-Power-is!

– You really think you can get away with anything? He raged. – There are those among us who haven't forgotten about the school.

A girl cried out in anger from the left:

– They didn't burn down the school. Your comrades did, to frame them. And they won't get away with it, either. Dear Anton, finally developing a conscience, made sure of that.

Laughter. He shifted uncomfortably, nervously rubbing his palms together.

– You didn't take part in that, Jill said to him. – But perhaps you wanted to? Perhaps you want to do your own thing, your own *burning?*

His sleeves caught *fire.* He screamed and ran mindlessly away. The flames already licking most of his arms.

The witch turned to the other guards and police officers, their fear a warm glow inside her.

– Any of you feeling a need to do anything, to be brave, to beat up a defenseless protester? I know you won't. None of you will do anything from now on, except go home.

The gate, its chains and fortification started rattling, rattling a few seconds… before *breaking.* Gasps of horror and astonishment rose from the groups on both sides of the fence.

– *Go!* The Raging Witch *commands* it.

And they walked and they ran.

The Raging Witch, the witch of old reacting spontaneously and instantly while facing injustice. Jill Stafford felt pride and self-perpetuating joy threatening to overwhelm her. As she walked through the gate, as almost every protester present followed her. As they entered the buildings, the production halls, the offices, machinery started failing, until everything stopped and crashed.

– GO HOME, all of you, she shouted. – We have taken control of these facilities, this horrible Machine. We'll see to it that it stays turned off.

A group of clerks, workers and executives stood there waiting for them, with clubs, fists and guns.

– Every time you hit us, you will hit yourself. Every bullet you fire at us will hit you.

She smiled to them, and fear penetrated their very beings.

– You believe me, she said sweetly as they pulled back, as they retreated and left the factory area, never to return. – That's so sweet of you, so very, very sweet.

There was so much more she and both Gabi and the others could do, but not yet. Jill pulled herself together, reined herself in, with an effort of will. With an effort of will, she stopped.

– Are you ready? She asked those present. – This isn't the end, but the beginning. The battle will be long and hard, and it won't stop anytime soon.

– Yes, Luke shouted. – I am!

I am! He thought. This is who we are.

And others echoed his cry, his pain, his tenacity.

Slowly, slowly the dust settled (temporarily) on the factory floor, on the dry ground outside. Ten minutes passed. The journalists went apeshit out there, inside here, as they called in the story, reported to their networks, waited for more to happen, but for the time being… nothing did.

No policemen arrived, no private army. The dust settled. Silence reigned.

Everybody looked at the Witch, standing fierce and tall among them.
– There's so much to do, she said hesitatingly, – both here and there.
– You go, Luke told her. – We'll take care of things here. You've done enough, for now.
The flow, the flow of the walk continued. The witches left, except Ivan. They chose him to remain, in case of an emergency. The world, the world was changing. They caused the change, they helped it along.
Breathless they moved on, breathing hard, breathing fresh air.
The excitement, the rush from the factory stayed with them, it kept boiling their blood, as they walked ever closer to the old city, as they turned from Main Road, into Cross Street.
– You should be ashamed of yourselves, a voice cried from the sidewalk.
Jill stopped and turned, speaking in a voice full of pain and rage.
– No, YOU should be ashamed of yourselves, she cried, using all the contempt she could muster. – Are you sheep or human?
She who had spoken, and her followers shrunk into the background, fading into the nothingness from where they had come.
But there was more here. Jill didn't need enhanced senses to see how shitty Gabi became. The stakes had suddenly, through one single decision been raised significantly.
They heard it from far away, long before they actually entered Cross Street. The song rose from the full church. The number of churchgoers had risen steadily lately and they couldn't take all the credit for that, at least. But they felt the familiar chill in their bones, as they heard Joseph Parnell.
The walk from the factory had been absolutely undramatic, and even if the excitement stayed in them, it couldn't account for the silent buzz inside.
– Raven, you're bleeding, Gabi said calmly.
Jill looked down at her hips. There was a slight stain on her robe.
– Yes, she shrugged. – I must have cut myself in Boston. I have had some problems healing it. It's somehow comforting to have limits, I guess.
She concentrated, pulling up the robe, putting her hands on the naked hip. The blood stopped trickling and the wound closed.
Joseph Parnell spoke to his unusually large congregation.
– In our great town, he shouted with spittle flowing out of his mouth, wetting his skirt, – raffle, hooligans, heathens, blasphemers and spawn of Satan have found each other in unholy matrimony.
– AMEN, the congregation replied.
– They're all lost, he said filled to the brim with hatred. – The Lord will strike them down and condemn them all to Hell.
– AMEN
– Let us pray, he said scornfully. Jill saw it before her inner eye, as he reached for his bible. – LET US PRAY, for the Lord to deliver us from evil and for it to happen SOON.
– A - MEN!
The tiny group of witches walked away.
– Soon, Jill told them. – Very soon, now…
The chant started again, ringing in their ears, as they made their way down Main Street. New dust devils replaced those who had been lost during the rain, whirling around their feet. Gabi looked back.
– I can see it, she mumbled.
– What did you say, honey? Tam asked her.
The girl walked sideways several steps until she stopped.
– Look at the church, the girl said, frost in her voice.
Lillith did, and something in her atavistic memory stirred and revolted.
– Squint your eyes, your viewpoint a little.
Jill did. She saw the indescribable. It was Sunday (any day was Sunday) and the congregation sang. The song… and a blackened, sickening fog rose from the building in an even, uninterrupted flow, something from out of a horror movie, except the reality was far, far worse.
– It's Him, Gabi whispered. – He's gaining power from their prayer, their worship.
Jill paled, and the queasiness almost overwhelmed her once again.

This wasn't just happening here, but all over the world.

She looked at the girl. The calm was just a shell. She saw that easily, without enhanced senses.

Time and Space shifted, and she saw nothing but the void, and all her senses were blind.

She sat outside the Green Rose, still seeing the sickly dark cloud rise from the church, still hearing the insane chant from the many submissive people locked inside, locked inside their own, shrinking minds. She was able to hear the ice clink in the glass Jason drank from by the bar. She used Luke to see what happened inside the factory far away. There was a heightened activity, but quiet and relatively peaceful. The silence at the police station was of a different category. People dressed in uniform just sat there, staring bitterly at each other. Earlier it had been difficult, bordering on impossible for her to use her telepathic talents in crowds. They were less now, the difficulties. She could keep the shield around her thoughts, protecting herself and still send and receive, probe and project, if she kept a selective focus. And she could shift that focus so fast, so devilishly fast. She hardly needed to do it consciously any longer. She held a hand before her face, closing it into a fist, opening it. It wasn't harder than that. That was all there was to it.

There was also more to it. Her attention had started slipping, in a good way, sort of. It was as if it had expanded to the point where she existed several places simultaneously. At least with no discernible time span between the registered moments. She found herself inside the house down the street, where a loud party had continued for hours and hours. Sweaty bodies danced tightly. Incense lingered in the air. Everything dissolved, faded out. Several of the witches were present and had joined the uncomplicated joyride… but she couldn't.

– Wine, my Goddess? Sharon asked respectfully. She didn't kneel, but her entire attitude bespoke that of obedience and submission.

– Thanks. Jill took the glass with a distant look in her eyes. She had no change of avoiding the pleasure she felt over how completely Sharon had been transformed from a free and independent person to such an excellent servant.

Jason had seduced her and Jill herself had crushed the remains of will and independence. She had done it and didn't know how to undo it. Or… didn't she dare try? Loeh wandered around in Stacy's clutches. Jill knew that, she wasn't stupid. Priscilla and Rupert carried collars invisible to most people. The two of them had been sent here as slavers, but like a boomerang their intentions had backfired.

The well-known pain cut Jill, the one she didn't know where came from and the indecision haunting her didn't let go. They had to defend themselves… by any means possible and their core had to be hard…

But not hardened.

– Where is Stacy? She said aloud.

– I don't know, Jason replied. – I haven't seen her all day.

They sat around her the four of them. Jason, Everett, Gabi and Morgana. She shared the sight of the black air above the church with those who hadn't seen it.

– Humanity is a swamp he is squeezing dry, she told them straight out, flatly, – sucking all juice from.

– He did go a bit overboard, this time, didn't he? Everett pointed out. – I mean, in Boston, with the television broadcast.

– His confidence must be staggering, Morgana said. – After all those years of progress, of perpetual victory and only a few occasional setbacks, he doesn't hold the rest of us in very high regard, I suppose.

– We know so little about him, Jason said. – We must gather all the information about him we possibly can, using all the power at our disposal, and then we must strike at his most vulnerable spot.

– We might wanna check him out through conventional means, too, Morgana suggested, – gather information through the 'net.

– I don't think we should do that. Jill shook his head. – I know enough about it to know that one check on his name could make a warning flash in his headquarters.

– But millions check him out and visit his webpages every day…

– You don't understand how modern surveillance works, Gabi explained impatiently. – A computer program somewhere, anywhere could be set to react to certain keywords, locations or whatever, and then its human servants may check the selected content. And Garret has millions of people working directly for him, millions. He's a witch himself, remember? The way I see it, Boston is already an area of special interest to him, and only living near it puts us at risk.

– Yes, of course. Morgana looked down.

– But, of course, we're at risk anyway, Jason said harshly. – He might find us at any time, no matter what we do… or don't do.

And there was no way they could argue with that. So, they didn't.

They rose from their chairs, all of them, as if on cue, and walked inside the tavern. The smell of glasses and sweat and juices assaulted them. They still hadn't gotten used to their enhanced senses. It still bothered them as much as it pleased them.

The walk to the non-existing room, behind the non-existing door in the corridor behind the bar, was, as ever, a strange one. It was as if they faded, or the surroundings faded. Did they just imagine they were walking, that they were touching the handle with their hand, opening the door?

They were there, they were here.

– He has a lot more experience than I have, Gabi said, – but this is my Place of Power. With the telepathic shroud you guys are putting up, we should be secure here.

– Existence is vast, Morgana said, – No one, not even he, can focus on more than a shred of it.

– Yessss. It started as a spontaneous act, turning into an act of will. Jill stretched out her arms, reaching for Gabi. Something not matter rose from her body, the shimmering other Self she had learned to be somewhat comfortable with. – All of you, come with me, come with ussss…

They had to concentrate, but they, too managed to manifest their Self consciously. She smiled as she saw Jason and Everett in their pure, uncloaked forms, shivering in delight and fear as she stared into the skulls in their eyes, at the animal characteristics in their faces. And Morgana seemed to be joining the surroundings, becoming one with it all.

Gabi struggled. They sensed her pain, the pain of birth.

– I can't do it, she said miserably. – Even here I can't do it.

– She's too young, Jason said. – She isn't ready yet.

– Then we make her ready.

Jill walked to her, flowed to her.

– Look at me, she/it said, and the girl did. – I want you to seek out the energy from the churches, I want you to absorb it.

A shocked, hurt look showed in the girl's eyes.

– But I can't… It's not mine, it's…

– One church, not the one here, but somewhere else. You are a Dreamweaver. You can most certainly interrupt its flow, at least temporarily. I want you to taste it. I want to see what it's like.

The girl closed her eyes.

– I can feel it, she mumbled. – There is a lot of people singing, a city far from here… New Orleans. They're so happy, so trusting. I can't take the energy of their worship directly from them, not without a lot of grooming and preparation. It's His. But I can interrupt its flow. I can steal his gold, his dirty treasure…

Then almost immediately her eyes flew open.

– It hurts, she cried.

– Break contact, Jill commanded.

Something embraced them all, as it burst into the girl for the first time, as it tore into her.

She cried out short and sharp.

The something growing out of her was without form at first, then solidifying, organizing itself out of nothing, and an adult, ethereal Delphi stood before them.

– *I'm me,* she/it said. – *I'm so much more. I'm vast. It wasn't much I stole from him, it isn't much he's stealing. The process, though increasing in force is slow. He's using it to sustain himself, to sustain his body. But I… it gave me the push I needed… opened a door, a door to everything. I don't think he understands it, not even after all this time. He doesn't want to… doesn't want to… to See…*

A flash, a shift in perspective, both instinctive and conscious.

Five young boys and girls sat around a campfire. They didn't look like who they were, but they were whom they were, in every way that mattered.

– Layer upon layer of reality, Jill stated. – We're also using some of the same methods of deceit the Enemy does.
– Is this how it feels like, being reincarnated, Raven? Delphi asked. – My previous life already seems distant. How is it, to know your past lives?
– It feels distant, Raven said, – as if it happened a long time ago… And it did. How much do we, and people in general remember from childhood? Just flashes and bits, right? Memory must be prodded and stimulated constantly to not fade. I've wondered a bit about why most people don't remember much from their previous lives, and I think I know why: They're ashamed of themselves and want to remove the sides of themselves they're not comfortable with. They don't embrace the entirety of their Being, and are thus limiting themselves. We do embrace everything. We don't close ourselves off from major parts of ourselves. We are, at least glimpsing what we truly are.
– I think the transition is so intense, so destructive, so full of Life, Jason said, – that we need to forget, to remember slowly.
He seemed to search in the dust, on the forest floor. After a while he held up two fingers pressed together.
– I'm holding the Earth in my hands, he said. – I'm holding a universe. Remember how LSD feels like? In the eternities we live through, during the high rush, we glimpse ourselves, we glimpse Everything.
– To take LSD is certainly a good preparation to any spiritual Journey, including both a spiritual and physical rebirth.
Everett shifted uncomfortably where he stood, where he sat, and his spirit form ruthlessly exposed his insecurity.
– Forget the prejudices they've beaten into you, Jill snapped, her spirit form shifting to red (it was ridiculous how they brought their ridiculous characteristics with them, even here). – Listen. Can't you hear it? Can't you see stars being born and die?
He didn't reply and she paused, as they all looked at each other.
– I can't see it myself, she confessed. – It's just my… interpretation, I guess.
– Some claim we're born with all the memories, Gabi suggested angrily, – and that we're conditioned to forget in a society denying reincarnation as a possibility. Or as another theory goes: That we need to grow up in groups stimulating our creativity, our ability to see beyond the mundane.
– That's why we don't remember, one of the five teenagers sitting around the campfire said. – We've stopped preparing. That would have been a routine matter in the Life of the Ancients. Now it's something dirty, forbidden, a taboo.
It was a sort of brainstorm all this. They were also speaking with their mouth, but also, as it happened increasingly in their daily life, on several other, more intimate levels. Perhaps, in some ways, they were still sitting in their chairs outside the tavern, as they were traveling without moving.
– And so much is unknown, the younger teenager around the campfire spoke in choir with herself. – Even the scientists are speaking about dense matter, dark matter... matter they can't detect except indirectly, comprising major parts of even the known, generally accepted universe.
The others were silent, as ever, while she spoke, astonished.
– You guys have heard about dense matter, right? She prodded them, a bit patronizing.
They nodded, grinning.
– How typical, why don't they just call it ***unknown*** matter. Raven shook her head. – Admitting their ignorance.
– They are as he is, focusing on what is seen as tangible, experienced through the known senses.
– Let's say for the sake of argument, that they're basically correct in this. That the... the Unknown Matter is dominating the universe, existence as a whole. Then isn't it safe to say that since we're not residing in this unknown matter, that we're the shadow?
– Not according to Voodoun faith, as Loeh tells it. In their language Shadow means Soul, and our souls are exactly such a «Superverse» - matter being we're hinting at here.
– And if we go far enough back in human history most people had the same notion. Science is, as usual wrong or inaccurate or *late.*
Everybody and no one spoke, and they couldn't say who had said what.

They felt it all as real, for the first time, that very minute.
Everything was Ghosts and Shadows...
– I… I… Everett stuttered.
As new, vast, tiny parts of existence opened up to them, they stumbled upon new ideas, old ideas, putting them into context.
– The Dollmaster, Anubis said, even as Anubis he didn't dare speak the name, – he has time on his side.
– But we sailed the River, Circe said. – We slowed our descent. What happens if we slow it to a halt?
There was silence. There was the buzz, the roar of the waterfall.
– Don't you see? We may be dealing with one of the fundamental forces of existence here. If we... stop Time, won't we then gain... control of it?
Another flash, a burst of shadow. Jill sat outside the Green Rose, alone again. There were a lot of people present in the street with her, but she was alone. They danced exuberant, hip to hip, groin to groin, chest to chest in an overt sexual way, unashamed and free. Why couldn't she?
Time slowed down a bit. People had sought the shadow (not merely the shade). The Hill had hidden the sun. Shadow embraced Oldtown in its heat. The millions of impressions from the Journey faded as they always did, but some of them lingered, as they always did, more and more every time.
Gabi stood on a chair doing her thing, just happy about the fact that she was now just one in a long line of performers.
She quoted from H. G. Wells' the Island of Doctor Moreau with her usual flair:
– «Montgomery told me that the Law... became oddly weakened about nightfall; that then the animal was at its strongest; a spirit of adventure sprang up in them at the dusk; they would dare things they never seemed to dream about by day».
That was all she said this time. There were no additional words, no explanations. She wanted it to sink in, wanted them all to think it through, to think for themselves. They applauded as she stepped down. She waved back, laughing, hiding well her darker, brooding mood, the cloud hanging over them all. If he was watching now and didn't know, would he then suspect or just see one more group of unsuspecting witches ready for the pyre?
A man took her place on the stage. He bowed to the audience, drawing laughter. Jill stiffened.
– You guys would be a lot more convincing if you were capable of telling us what you wanted anyway. You're terrorizing a city, stopping the production in a factory. Why? «Umm.. err... we, like, are against the tyranny. Yeah, we're like, opposing the tyranny, man». What do you want to put up instead of this «tyranny»? «Umm.. uh... we want to live in villages, man. Like, live of the land, man.» Then why don't you just move there? «Umm.. uh...»
He was playing a concerned loyal citizen, «discussing» with a stupid rebel, one without any idea of what he or she was doing.
The general view on protesters and outsiders, as presented by governmental propaganda.
Some saw through him, saw him for what he was, but most of those present laughed and had a good time, not realizing the meaning hidden behind his words, his pleasant exterior.
– That was very sneaky. Jill didn't rise from the chair. – Do you have more authority propaganda for us?
And then almost everybody understood.
– C'mon, he said. – I was merely joking…
She smiled, with gray eyes clear as stone.
– I can take a joke, she said. – We all can, I presume, Falco?
The first hint of worry appeared in his glass-hard eyes.
– You're mistaken. My name is not Falco.
– Your name is Thomas Falcon, «Falco» among friends. Your current address is 16 Caledonian Road in New Jersey and you're a professional standup comedian.
He looked at her, glassy eyed and paralyzed.
– They've hired you, she blinked astonished. – They've actually hired you to make trouble.
He stared at her.
– What are you? He whispered. – What the fuck are you?

And he blinked, too, as he slowly started to back off, as he ran away from there, never to return.
She knew about the man hiring him, too. Nothing special about him. He had just hired him to do a job. Nothing special or especially threatening about it.
It had been easy, hardly more difficult than swatting a buzzing fly.
Later, still in the afternoon. Most people had gone inside. Jill sensed fur on naked legs. Malvin purred and stroked his pelt against her. That was the last she remembered before falling asleep. She dozed off and fell asleep quickly, as she always did these days. She knew when she was tired, and was able to sleep in the strangest of places. She had stopped conforming to any recognized pattern of behavior for some time now. She was awake when it fit her, slept when she was tired. It had worked well for a long time. To fall asleep represented no problem.
But it gave her ever less rest. The dreams, growing in clarity and texture, haunted her.
The house, the big house, burning, burning her. She saw herself being pulled howling and crying out of it and she saw herself being locked inside one of the rooms while it burned. So confusing, so horrible. She awoke in the sunshine and remembered just about as much as she used to, which was next to nothing. Only the fire and the distraught child, the child with the quiet, burning eyes and the hurt in her face.
– The same, persistent dream? Everett stood above her with a glass of water in his hand, a huge British Guinness pint glass. She grabbed it and drank greedily.
She nodded. Throat was still dry as sand.
Time was still flying. She rose from her chair (again). She knew there were ways to do what she needed to do in a group. A warm fellowship washing away loss and grief. She knew she had to do it alone.
– What about a short and intense trip to the woods? He suggested cheerfully, flashing his fangs.
– No, I must go. She shut him out and hid the flash of disgust she felt for him.
Knew how unfair it was. She had seen his horrible within. He, too, struggled with his savagery and boiling insides. But how could she avoid feeling frustrated over his self-control when she couldn't even marginally keep her own.
Self-recrimination would get her nowhere, she knew that. It wasn't just useless, counterproductive, but also ridiculous. She struck the brick wall with her right hand, and it hurt terribly. No one had seen anything. She stared hard at the tight fist, while the wound closed, and the skin turned smooth again. The bloodstains spread across the wall as if it was alive (and the blood was). The blood died eventually, cut off from the life-giving organism. What was the limit? How damaged could she be, until she would no longer be capable of repairing herself? Could one single cell, in a protein-rich solution, reproduce the entire organism?
She walked along Trail, leading to the Hill, confident that something solid, something tangible would come out of this, something she could hold on to. Nothing would grow on Trail, nothing at all. No animals crossed the dark soil. There was no life on the steep, broad path. Jill felt ill merely by being close to it. She had repeatedly attempted, as she did right now, to make something grow there. She had failed then as she failed now. It was true. Nothing grew in the Shadow of Death.
Driven forward she turned to the right well before the Hill, turning west, in the area between the forest and the plain. Before she truly understood what she was doing, she started circling. She moved in ever-smaller circles towards her goal. The Sun, the Sun behind Frazer's Hill shone on the Witchcircle, the ring of large mushrooms growing close to the cool forest.
She crossed the circle from the west. From the opposite direction her mirror image entered the natural round bowl… entered the Hollow. Or… did she arrive from the other side and the mirror image from this one? Jill sat down with her back to the sun, with her legs crossed, just inside the outer ring. The Mirror Image of the Other was in shadow. Illusions fell and the two moved as one.
Jill lowered her eyes, looking down at her hands, her killing hands. She looked up again, as her body stiffened. The landscape, her perception changed slowly this time, as if unwilling. She pushed on, biting her lower lip, tasting the blood in her mouth, smelling it in the air, the putrid air. Fog, light and dark, the entire specter, spectrum of the rainbow, descended upon the landscape, embracing the two unmoving figures. Shouldn't she… hadn't she… This time buildings rose from the ground, towering above it, forced itself up from it, devouring the green. There had been no sense of leaving her body

this time. It had happened so fast, so easy, like slipping on a pair of too big new shoes.

The huge cathedral, convent, the girl Vyla, everything had happened so fast, the Journey… without effort.

The young girl in a nun's clothes crouched on a cold stone bench in a cell dark even in the middle of the day. Night arrived and all the world's demons danced in the air around her. She pulled the thin blanket even tighter around her skinny body, once more drying the tear-wet face.

She wasn't the first Vyla. She had taken the name of another young woman, who had lived - and died - in the distant city of Barcelona many years before.

Now the same fate awaited her.

She had been compliant, hiding, hiding herself, buried her true Self in these clothes, this cold house. It had been no good. Nothing was.

She was Vyla, by nature and destiny. If she had just realized this before.

Sounds outside. Echoes of steps in the eternal night's dungeon. *She* came, followed by her loyal servants. A key was stuck in the iron lock and the heavy cell door pushed open. The Abbess, the chief nun entered the cell, followed by her most enthusiastic servants. *Lillith recognized Andrea and, yes, Udo, in quite a pleasant looking shell. Lillith had to stop herself from giggling.*

The Abbess closed in on the young girl suffering on her harsh bed.

– Sister Magdalena…

– That's not my name. Disheartened the girl attempted to make a fist of her weak hands. – I'm Vyla, *Vyla.*

The older woman shook her head in mock disappointment, in crushing disapproval.

– What a tragedy. I had such high hopes on your behalf… She pulled up the ragged nun robe and exposed the novice' naked legs. – Look at you, born with the mark of shame and you dare to be disobedient.

Vyla broke in continuous sobs. Tears ran freely now. Merely the other's close proximity made her sick.

– What you did to the boy… How could you do it, DO such a t-thing? How could you *imagine* doing such a thing?

The Abbess smiled in cold anger. She grabbed the girl's cheek, clutching it in her steel grip and shook her hard. Vyla wanted to scream, to tear herself away from the merciless grip, but she was so weak, so weak.

– He was *disobedient.* He dared to resist my will, my vaunted authority. He didn't know his place and paid dearly for it. He, lower than the ants on the ground, dared to demand independence, whatever that is. Like you, dear Juana, unable to submit to a higher authority. I am in charge here. I decide what's right and wrong. *I.* You're not just willful and disobedient, but also incorrigibly so. You refuse to repent. You will suffer the same fate as all sinners, who, being offered mercy, choose not to accept it. You have lost your right to carry the uniform, like you have lost so much else. As we all know: «Thou shall not suffer a witch to live».

Vyla was paralyzed and mute. She wanted so to crawl for the regal woman and beg for mercy, but something, an inner voice, an unbreakable will stopped her. When she was dragged off and undressed, fabric-by-fabric, it felt like the worst punishment imaginable, but she knew it wasn't so. What awaited her was a slow, humiliating, degrading journey towards Death.

The witch stood bent in the hay-wagon, heavily chained on hands and feet. Hair seemed torn off her head, short and ragged as it was. Images flashed before her eyes where she stood, dressed in a simple gray and dirty tunic. A pair of tongs, glowing iron and *the water tract.* The executioner, her Lord and Master. The crowd, the mob, the same threw rocks and pieces of wood over the circle of soldiers. Smoke from oozing torches made her throat dry and raw. She coughed, couldn't stop coughing. She had refused to bend, and they had broken her, crushed her. What would turn her into dust on the ground would perhaps be a kindness, a final kiss before Death.

The fire waited for her, in the form of dry wood. She felt a sick need to express gratitude because of this. They occasionally used wet wood.

There was a warrior inside her, refusing to give up, no matter how many times she was broken and crushed and burned, struck to Earth.

They tied her to the pole - again. With their grins and their scorn. In such a good spirit, now, when they got confirmed for themselves that they had chosen the correct path in life. *Never more, I swear. They shall never more feel the slightest peace, any kind of safety.* Yes, Jill opened her eyes, saw the city of Northfield, the creatures of power and their loyal servants, slaves. The passive, washing their hands. There were no neutrals, no innocents. It ended now, the acceptance of injustice. I swear. A Power, an irresistible Power…

Vyla stood tied to the pole. They had lit the pyre. Smoke and flames welled up, into the air, into sore lungs. The crowd chuckled and enjoyed themselves, and cried insults at the victim up there. They needed amusement like this to hold out their sorry lives. The only thing that mattered to them was the fact that they were down here in the warmth of the crowd and not there.

Then… celebration stopped as if… yes, by Magic. The cheerful mood vanished and in its stead was mumbles and silence. Vyla's eyes started glowing, stronger than the fire devouring her. This infinitely sharp look directed itself at the Abbess, Regal, triumphant. She stiffened.

– You do this terrible act, against me, who have never done anything to you.

They heard the strange voice, impossibly through the smoke. The woman shouldn't be able to breathe, at least not without heavy coughing, far less speak.

– One day or one night… and this is my promise to you all - you'll pay. Everybody, but especially you, seductress. You shall feel my vengeance for the rest of your life…

And Beyond.

One last time Vyla looked into the eyes of them all, into all their eyes and looked straight through the woman shrinking in the High Chair.

Lillith blinked and blinked, but saw only the void, while the completely unruly rage burned within her. THE WOMAN, SHE RECOGNIZED HER

Jill gasped and paled because of her own thoughts. She sensed something almost independent come to life within. A creature without face, and body and soul and blood. A wrath without peer.

– I accept you, she mumbled, – you're a part of me.

Blades flashed. A knife flashed. Stones ran red with blood. The stone ran red with blood.

A figure, a robed figure, a shadow in bright day floated through the air from far away. A half-faded road in the desert. Desert mist floated with it. A hood covered its head and hid its face (it is coming). In the one, visible hand it held a wand, a walking wand, with a tiny, golden skull decorating its top. An irresistible, unmoving force. Fire danced and burst around it, on its way.

Jill gasped in fear, in helpless fascination.

Barriers broke down, boundaries faded. Truths were revealed.

A room where heavy smoke lingered. Huge, black wax-candles burned on the table. Lillith saw the eight sitting and the woman standing. She knew what was happening and there was no way she would allow it to proceed. No way!

Not one more time, not ever.

She heard the tearing sound, the silent scream as it rose from each of the eight defenseless victims. She sensed beyond all doubt what was happening, what *Laurie* did to them. Laurie, who knew their soul names and had bound them, chained them to herself. But even that didn't sate her. She wanted to crush their personality, their very Self, turn them into empty shells she could fill and form at whim and use as probes, as extensions of her own being. The energy filled her, and she smiled in expectation.

The smile vanished. Lillith, hardly more than… than rage incarnated, knew that the enemy had discovered her presence. She knew what was coming and knew she would enjoy every moment of it.

– You knew. A hoarse, hateful voice cried at Laurie from the deepest Abyss. – YOU KNEW!

– Who are you? She demanded. – Show yourself. Who…

– We came here because something was missing in our lives. You used that, exploited it as the worst tyrant. You'll not exploit our vulnerability anymore. I will not allow it.

Laurie sought and strived to find something, anything solid to attack, in vain. She sensed nothing. No substance, nothing she could possibly control, only the indifferent… presence. She cried out in desperate, aggrieved indignation:

– What are you *talking* about? Laurie Isherwood stated incredulously. – I brought you together, brought you here, to serve me. You're here to do my bidding. You'll not be told anything more than

what I deem necessary, what I decide you need to know.
Lillith snapped her fingers and everything Laurie had done turned insignificant.
– *You've outlived your purpose. You're hardly more than dead wood we leave behind.*
Lillith stretched her claws growing out of the night, reaching for her prey. Let her sweat, let her suffer, as Laurie herself had done with her students, whose trust she had broken. The wrath couldn't be contained anymore. Lillith saw nothing but red and Laurie was torn apart and left in pieces.

The Nightraven wandered through a landscape of hot mist and searing heat. For every step forward it got that much closer, even if it was still far off. A creature without face, and body and soul and blood.

She levitated above the ground by Fire Lake, Raven Moonstar, the Moon Goddess. She, with many names, who was one. She looked down at Jill and Everett with a penetrating stare, a wrath just as horrifyingly strong.
– Who are you? The girl asked, quiver in her voice.
– *I am you?*
And later, while the young, ignorant girl lay writhing on the ground.
– *She must learn. We live in a predatory world. She or he who fails to see this, will be devoured.*

Closer…

Wrath threw her further through Time.
The streets of Northfield the evening of the initiation. She followed Jill and Jason. They discovered her, but couldn't fathom her.
Earlier that evening. She followed Jill, assessing, studying, wondering. She had been so innocent, so naïve. She knew she was being felt, if not seen. Good. Rage should be groomed, not muted.
The barrier was breaking down.
Several years earlier, before Northfield. A skinny, smaller Stacy. Her hair was cut straight on her brow and make-up was scarce. Clothes were expensive, such clothes that Jill had never worn. Gray eyes flashed and streetlight broke on the skin of sunken cheeks. She seemed like a normal sullen young girl, but to those who looked, there was that something of a haunted look on the edge of her eyes.
She danced around a bush. The bushes, the grass and the air were wet and cold. Suddenly the entire plant caught fire. It burned to a cinder so quickly, with such intensity that the entire street turned noticeable brighter. Stacy kept dancing, while laughing euphorically. The strong heat singed her clothes, but not her. She had always been taken by fire, attracted to it, and now she finally understood why. She had believed it had been because of the dream (the dream she had had since she was twelve), but that was evidently just a part of the truth. Another bush flared and burned to nothing, and she was about to light a third… when she stopped startled.
The air, the air itself, seemed to come alive. Invisible sparks (that she could see) appeared all over. A figure formed exactly where young Stacy had her eyes and she felt her skin crawl. She who floated there… was her. But different. Older, far more powerful. A Goddess of Vengeance. One who didn't need to take shit from anybody.
Abruptly the girl felt a horrible nausea and weak knees gave way. With tear-filled eyes she fearfully and painfully looked up.
– *Yes, kneel in the mud, little witch. So proud of yourself, just another weak poor beggar with illusions of grandeur. Pull yourself together or PERISH.*
go-go-go
Jill sat there, shaking. She could see the Nightraven's face now, the creature's body and soul and blood. It materialized right there before her, at the center of the Witchcircle. Jill's eyes opened so wide that it hurt. It appeared in all its wonder and horror. Jill couldn't take her eyes off it, during the waves of fascination and disgust washing over her, through her entire… being. The fangs, long and pointed, eyes burning in cold passion, claws growing from the fingers, and much more than even wide-open eyes could fathom. She looked at herself. And she looked at Stacy.
Just then the radiant and terrifying creature seemed to… divide itself. It split into two identical parts,

smaller, not so radiant and terrifying. It smiled in tandem, before returning to the two waiting bodies.

Jill gasped startled, as droplets of sweat, of cold fire erupted from her skin. It didn't feel in any way like it had before, with fatigue and orientation problems. Fully awake she kept her eyes on the opposite side of the circle, at Stacy. Stacy spoke first. She smiled cheerfully, ecstatic.

– I told you: We're alike… But the resemblance goes further than even I dared dream. We will all be surprised, won't we, *sister?*

The veil covering Jill's eyes lifted. Stacy started changing, subtle, dramatically in face and appearance. She revealed, removed the green contact lenses and familiar gray eyes appeared. Face turned slightly broader, the hair completely black, becoming complete raven hair. Jill shook her head, once, twice, but not more than that. This time she had no doubts she was looking at herself.

– I've known all the time we're identical twins, of course. But I took certain minor steps to ensure that you wouldn't easily realize this. It was simple enough to cast a spell over your thoughts, since you denied the truth. You didn't dare remember on your own. Only with my aid you've managed to dig up some minor stuff.

Thoughts raced through Jill's fevered mind. She had glimpsed something searching through Berkowitz's thoughts. The genetic testing the hospital had done on them. The samples were identical. How Stacy had looked different (similar to a mirror image). And she had denied that, too.

– The others suspected the truth, of course. Stacy continued virtually unabated. – But we seemed just different enough to keep them from convincing themselves. Only Loeh knew. According to her childhood teaching, the Voodoun faith, all identical twins share the same soul. As you know we also have our individual astral bodies, that we can go «out of the body» with, but that isn't quite the same, don't you agree?

– We k-killed. Jill lifted her hands.

– Yes, we have already given praise to Samhain, Sanheim, Shaman… Isn't it great? Few deserved more than Laurie and the hospital thugs to be chosen.

Stacy rose, confident, devil may care hatefully, lovingly. She turned to leave.

– Wait, Jill cried woolen, cunningly. – You can't leave me like this. You're still holding back on me. You must tell me who I am.

– That's for me to know, and you to find out. Stacy turned her head, looking, glancing back. – I sought you for so long and even if you didn't realize it, you sought me, too. Just a little further, now, and you're ready.

Jill remained there, on the spot. She looked at her hands. It wasn't these hands that had killed. She had… with the entirety of her being. And everything Stacy was. They who were Lillith - the Mother of Demons. She attempted to embrace herself with her arms, as she fell over to the side and laid still. She laid still until the sun set, and darkness fell.

2

She wandered aimlessly through Northfield's streets. No more than flashes of impressions penetrated the fog descending relentlessly on her thoughts.

She observed Rupert and Priscilla behind a till. She had asked them where they came from, and they had told her. Told the truth. They had been lying. They didn't come from a circle in Boston, but one with its primary location far from here. The two didn't know where it was themselves and it remained unclear to her, too. She couldn't see it. Not now.

Now, when she was limited.

Grinning skulls floated and danced in the air. She sensed the buzzing whisper everywhere, the flattering, scary, irritating voices that she didn't fathom. The souls of the condemned gathered and closed in on them, on them all.

She and Stacy entered the gathering on Main Street from opposite directions. The murmur started instantly. Big-eyed and speechless siblings welcomed them. Stacy still wore her hair differently, but aside from that… the two were no more different than Meta and Melanie or any other identical twins.

All the words, smiles and worried glances grew interchangeable in Jill's vision. While Stacy thrived in the added attention created by the revelation… Jill could not. She pulled back after a while, removing herself inconspicuously from everybody's company, allowing herself to be pulled wherever her body pulled her.

Jason and Sharon evidently held a small party in her place above the Green Rose tavern, with their closest protégées, Cynthia, Erica, Matt… and Andrea. All windows had been opened wide. The curtains, white, thin, transparent flickered in the wind. Fire burned in the wind, offering enticing secrets and hidden knowledge, information. Who could resist such a temptation?

Not she.

She measured the distance to the veranda… just a tiny… immeasurable moment… before jumping. She floated over the cornice and landed graciously on the cold marble floor. A rain of sparkles created a halo in the air, in her tracks. She knew perfectly well how she appeared to the people inside, slightly crouched, a creature of smoke and fire. A pair of stone-gray eyes flashing lively, just about visible, under the hat brim.

– Goddess… Sharon said hoarsely. – Welcome.

The big woman rose in the bed. The loose dress revealed more than it hid. She curtseyed in gratitude, in subservience. Jill nodded preoccupied, while letting her eyes, her burning stare extend the room, extend them all.

Jason hadn't really done anything yet, with Cynthia and Erica… or Matt or Andrea, except charming them to death.

– Moonstar… Andrea greeted her. – Tell me what to do.

Moonstar was or had been Stacy's name, but the others had started using that and Raven on both of them. Jill shook slightly, unnoticeable. She stood still, didn't lift a hand. Lines of fire emerged on the floor around Andrea. From one flash to the next a perfectly formed pentacle burned. Andrea reacted as Jill had anticipated, quickly, instinctively. She seemed to dance away from the flames, but after she had easily avoided a series of hungry protuberances it was clear what extraordinary reflexes she had developed. Laurie had held her down, as she had done with everybody. Now everybody's potential expressed itself.

The fire pulled back. Andrea stood there, breathing and sweating heavily, but with eyes clear and sparkling.

– I thank you… And then, after a brief hesitation. – Goddess.

She knelt, lowering her eyes, looking at the floor. Jill experienced a breath of irritation. Andrea was a born servant, always looking for a new Master. With such an attitude, or lack thereof she would never live, only exist. Jill fought back the irritation and gave the girl a hand, pulling her up.

The moon could be seen as many things, but not oppression.

She wished she had realized this earlier, so much earlier.

Jill directed her attention at Matt, without doing so openly. He was one of the many they had liberated and brought with them from the Asylum. For the first time in a very long while these people had a change to live, and she wouldn't let anybody destroy it. No way!

Matt, Erica and Cynthia stared glossy-eyed at her - and Andrea, but fortunately not, as misty as they could have been. Humans were once more getting accustomed to the presence of the gods.

– Time to relieve the poor suckers behind the bar. Jason talked for the first time since Jill's special arrival, lazily, relaxed.

Cynthia and Erica exchanged looks, but they walked down the stairs, followed quickly by Matt and Andrea. Jill was alone with Jason and Sharon.

Sharon stretched lazily in bed, before leaving it and stopping before Jill, gazing at the floor, with a respectful, but self-conscious smile.

– I've already given thanks to Master Jason many times… Goddess, but I wish to thank you, too. You have both transformed me, changed me into the person I've always wanted to be. My existence is at your mercy Queen Goddess.

She knelt graciously and skillfully. It seemed like she had been practicing for years.

Do we create worshippers in our own image? Jill wondered, gazing at Jason.

– Do you know what? He remained in bed, unfazed. – Little Sharon here is both supremely skilled and blindly loyal. I can ask her to put an arm around a neck and break it, and she will do it without the slightest hesitation. I wonder where she's coming from, I really do.

Jill pressed five fingers at the face of the kneeling woman and kept her hand there.

– Three times, at least we have come this close at being enslaved. He held the thumb and index finger close. – We were *this* close to become permanently controlled by others. It's time to learn the game, to play to win. To merely train in the use of our powers isn't sufficient. In short: We must learn ruthlessness.

He smiled his usual, teasing smile, but he stared at her with ferrety eyes. She felt a paralyzing cold and imagined him standing close to her, digging and searching for weaknesses. He was no longer the after all innocent young boy she had met not that long ago. This was somebody callous, dangerous. Why was she cold? Perhaps because what he was really doing was holding up a mirror and what she saw was herself.

– Stacy is correct, she said slightly sarcastic. – You do see yourself as Magneto.

– «I'm a siren, leading you to raging seas», he grinned.

– You're correct in one respect, she said sharply. – We have been playing and that won't do anymore. The game is done. Our flirt with the Path to Power must end. It ends NOW!

She ventured into Sharon's inner self. It happened easily, seductively. Jason had awakened a long-suppressed longing within the woman, a passionate desire to command, to rule, combined with a dog-like obedience. And with Jill's aid he had completed the process. It wasn't like what Stacy had done to Loeh, not so complete… but far more difficult to undo. So intricate and slick.

Inwards. It was so dank in here, and so cold. There was so much twisted and insane, brewing long before Jason had shown up. So much of the insane the world had to offer. She couldn't do anything about that just now, but she had more than sufficient power to undo Jason's influence and she could offer enlightenment, knowledge. Why not, wasn't she the one who lit the darkness?

A flash, blinding, an eternity. Jill blinked. The face was impassive and didn't expose her shock as she removed her hand.

Sharon eyes opened wide. She touched her head, rubbing her right hand's fingertips against her temple. Her lower lip started shaking.

– What did you DO? Why… Why did you do it?

With completely insane eyes, being filled with hatred, locked on Jill, she crawled, pushed, pulled herself towards the exit. A fear beyond any reason dominated the entire powerful built body. Jill was in a kind of perverse way happy about that. Some of that was self-preservation. Paralysis had spread to such a degree, to all parts of her being that she feared she wouldn't be able to defend herself, no matter what Sharon might decide in her fever hot brain. Jill faced realization, abruptly, painfully. In Sharon's mind she saw what she saw in the majority of those she encountered: Denial of Self and a deep panic of unwillingness to see the world as it was. Sharon had found comfort in the role she was raised to, in her existence as an obedient slave. Her flirt with a radical mindset had been just that. She found comfort in the sewing circles, they who talked much, but didn't act. Their political view remained an intellectual hobby they could simply leave if their «safe», daily life was threatened. Sharon had been offered *understanding* and rejected it with all the weakness she could muster.

– You're *evil*, Sharon Haldoway spat, crouching in the doorway. – EVIL! Spawn of the Prince of Darkness, eternally condemned on the last day. *Thou shall not suffer a witch to live.*

Then she was gone. She left Northfield, never to return.

Jill stood still, shaking in absolute horror. She wanted nothing more than to remain there, on the spot. She wanted to burn Sharon to dust, burn Jason and everybody who *displeased* her.

Shoulders sagged. Eyes changed to open wounds.

– You knew, she said thinly, weakly.

– Of course, he admitted unfazed. – She's brainwashed to live like a puppet on a string and doesn't want it any differently. Sheep don't want to be anything but sheep, you know that.

– She thought I did it because I wanted to hurt her…

– No, he corrected her. – If she had believed that, she would have knelt in the dust, cowering from the Goddess' Wrath.

Despair turned even more pronounced. He was so damn astute.

He finally rose from the bed and walked close to her. She backed off until she could back off no longer. He grabbed her arms brutally, painfully hard, turning her around, pushing her against the wall.

A sharp pull and he had exposed her butt. A simple touch or two and she stopped resisting him. He took her, excited and ravaged her.

– You're pathetic, he growled hoarsely into her ear, a vicious, distorted delight. – You're appealing to my protective instinct. I want to chain you in a dark, safe cellar, take you as mine, a willing, obedient toy. It would have been so *simple.* You're exposed now, so weak that it wouldn't have been much of an effort…

She felt him move freely within her, in the body, in the mind, in the depth. She saw him lead her away in chains, collar her and drag her off. He made Morgana build her a stone cage and he placed her there whenever he wished. A horrible vision making her shiver in horror… and excitement. When push came to shove, she, like Sharon, was a product of the society of her birth.

– … but you're no use to me like that…

He had taken control over all of her, both her subconscious and conscious functions. She hadn't thought it possible. The control was so absolute that he could afford to have her aware during it all. Her soul-name, more an emotion, a larynx sound of the soul, than a real thought… he found it easily, her most private part, what made her what she was, her *Acacia*, her *Ti Bon Ange.* Where she was one with every living being.

By that thought she came, he came, they came, in violent moves, a white glowing heat. One of her hands knocked weakly at the wall. Knock, knock, knock. Hand fell down, powerless arm, powerless Jill. He pulled out with a last, paralyzing and terrifying message:

I know who you are.

– Fourth time for you, he said softly. – *Lillith.*

She stiffened even more, like rock. A haunted look in her eyes exposed her. She pulled the skirt down her thighs. He pulled it back up instantly. Dully, she let him.

– You're such a tasty bitch, he said. – Give me a kiss, tasty bitch.

She offered him her lips and he took them. It burned and singed, and she moaned.

He grabbed her amulet, the one around her neck, making a fist around it, pulling it so hard that the cord broke.

– I'll hold on to this. It will be up to you to decide upon its importance.

He had let go of her. She felt it in every cell.

– You're Death, the destroyer of worlds, she whispered low and subdued.

One moment she stared hateful at him. Then her eyes turned dull and indifferent.

– You're absolutely right, she pushed out of her. – It's logical, isn't it… that the strong rule the weak?

3

Naked, exposed.

The streets, the humans there, everything blurred to nothing around her. What value had her views when they could be shaken that easily? What value had anything?

Dark, moody music flowed from speakers, flowing in the night air, pushing her off in the wind. Just a leaf in the Storm. Nothing else, nothing more.

The sky is cracking open
Like a dead leaf
Falling from a tree
Belief is shaken
A lie never forgotten
The jester is dancing
Triumphantly
Before your sore eyes
The crowd is laughing at you
Not him

The world is screaming at your feet

As you may hide in a circle
A way to survive
Be a number, the Jester dances
Instead of being alive
Deny the fire inside
And you deny yourself
The Jester is binding the Nomad
Carrying him off to jail

Flames, Hell's fire stretching at her. Ashes SHE TURNED TO ASHES

She noticed the presence of her twin, as she always noticed her. A short burst of rage and she closed her off, closed her out.

Oh, whom did she try to fool? They had grown up in different places, different environments and taken different paths But were still connected in ways that could never be broken.

Twins, separated early on. So long ago, such a short time ago. No matter, inevitably, now when they were together again Jill turned more into Stacy and Stacy turned more into Jill.

(As time crawled)

A campfire, a big one, burned in the middle of Main Street. And no one attempted to put a stop to it all. Unbelievable. She smiled. Wild dance continued around it and its close proximity. She felt a certain pride.

– I know who you are, too… She spoke to the very air, to no one, and no one listened. – Simple deduction. I'm a clever witch, you know…

She saw herself whisper in his ear, saw him stiffen.

Further down the street Gabi spoke, doing her thing. Ivan, having been relieved from his post at the factory, standing close by, made her easy to hear. Everybody heard her.

– Today, we live far from our natural surroundings. We live out of sync with our own rhythms. Violence is abundant in today's society. Primitive humans hardly killed another human. Today it has become the norm. A lot of shit is abundant in present day's society. Typically, the eager beavers of this society are attacking the symptoms, all kinds of symptoms of the problems… in an attempt at diverting the attention from what's causing the problems… Not so strange perhaps… considering the disease is society itself.

– We humans are creatures of passion, of emotional storms. In their infallible wisdom those who are running the show and their supporters want to strangle, to lock inside the Raging Storm. They don't realize, or won't realize that this seeming conflict between body and mind we're experiencing in today's world is so damn unnecessary. If they did that many other truths would also be torn apart and exposed as deceit and lies, and they would lose their illusory power.

Music danced in the dust by people's feet. They could see it, feel the girl's passion.

– We must not deny the wild animal, not even the beast in us. We are what we are. By suppressing parts of us, we're quite simply suppressing ourselves. If we acknowledge our deeper instincts, instead of fighting them, we may find anew the vitality and joy of Life such a natural part of our lives in previous ages…

Jill agreed, of course. She had herself said much of the same earlier. But she couldn't express it now. How could she be feeling so disharmonic… divided?

She left this place, too.

The unnatural darkness' heart surrounded her, pierced her soul. She found herself in Newtown. She had drifted so very far from home and the ever-stronger raging stream sucked her into the vortex like everybody else. The cauldron, the Storm, everything from Kelvin to Ra's seething insides. Phoenix Green Earth. She looked up, lifted her head. Everything was Life and Fire in the Universe, and everything returned to it. The connection wasn't broken, just tragically shrouded.

She heard Peter Barryman's voice as if from far away. Not the Storm's voice, but it rose in her and pulled her towards confrontation. And perhaps there and then, she decided how she wanted to live her life.

The public meeting was held on the marketplace in Newtown, by the crossroads. She smiled ironically. Barryman squeaked and chirped like an old man in a way cutting deep into her. Scott Thompson was present, too. Hidden, but not to her. She welcomed the cold anger, enjoyed it in such a way that she almost started crying.

– What GOES on in OUR beautiful city is a… HORROR of indecency and SUBVERSION. He who was supposed to teach the younger generation wisdom shouted insanely his curses at anybody who dared to disagree with him. – Good citizens of Northfield, we have tolerated this Satan's work far too long.

He was often interrupted by ecstatic applause and salutations. This particular one started extra forceful and promised to keep going for quite a while… when it suddenly quieted, dying like a burned-out fire leaving only ashes and stinking garbage. Garbage making people look at one another to see if the stench came from them.

The lone woman made a broad alley as she moved forward, and they moved away from her. Many looked ashamed at one-another and sneaked off. She stopped in the midst of the swirling mass, the mindless crowd, straight before Barryman.

– Peter here is scared, she shouted. – As he should be. Since bygone ages the rule of him and his like has been accepted. It's over now. Privileges will no longer be accepted. Not in any form.

– WHORE OF BABYLON, Barryman shouted insanely. – The Lord will strike you down.

– Yes, why doesn't he do just that? She challenged sarcastically. – I'm a Heathen, temptress and blasphemer, a fucking spawn of Satan. There can't be many worse in the world. He must be extremely busy since he can't come and take care of little me.

– Make her SHUT UP, an older lady screamed ad falsetto.

A young, red-faced girl took a step forward. She was one of those carrying clubs. Perhaps their goal for the evening had been more than merely vocalizing their anger?

The club dissolved in an instant, in a limited space of molten air. She who had held it released it, in horror and fear, but only the ashes reached the ground.

– I'm Surtur, cleansing the world with fire. They didn't fathom the witch's words, but understood the realities behind them. They weren't completely lost.

And they stood their ground. They didn't step closer, but didn't pull back either. She sensed the compact hostility everywhere. In the anger and the ice-cold black darkness state of their mind, the witch knew she could do little or nothing. Not in such a massive crowd. She pulled back, slowly, painfully, constantly on guard, moving her eyes, eyes able to kill. She grinned, spontaneously and diabolically. *Demonic.* One moment it had looked as if some of them wouldn't budge, move away from her path. Suddenly they couldn't move fast enough, and a broad path formed, an honor guard, full of respect. She had considered sending a tongue of flame in front of her as a warning, but unnecessary as it showed itself to be, she held back.

And she couldn't free herself from the thought that this had been a mistake. Huge crowds always exposed the weaknesses of her powers. What had she attempted to prove? She was sweating now and fought to keep them from discovering it. The smell of fear would make them go crazy in their hunger. She wouldn't have any recourse but burning them then and she didn't want t-that. She was Prometheus warming the world with fire.

Dark streets, dark city. Silence. They had yet to repair all the power lines. In Oldtown it didn't really matter, but here… here, the somberness turned overwhelming. She sought away from Oldtown without truly knowing why. She was a wounded animal seeking solitude… and something else. And she was vulnerable, and she knew it. This reminded her of the dreams. She was *hunted* and the pyre waited at the top of the mound.

It did hurt somewhere inside her, same place, same pain. She hardly recalled who she was. Short of breath she slipped along a dark brick wall, in a narrow night-black street. Tears flowed freely. Huge droplets, full of life hit the ground, whirling dust dry and dead. She coughed and it flowed even more from sore eyes.

Flash. The visions hit her then. Not from some distant past of future or faraway place. Here, now. She blinked. The black guard, they who earlier were only whispered about, was patrolling, haunting the streets of Northfield. Jill couldn't see them. All that power and she still couldn't see them. She had to see them through other people's eyes, and even that was hard. They were like ghosts, walking on air, walking on ground. Scott Thompson's enforcers, his terror guard. He had thrown caution to the wind, thrown away all semblance of respectability. She giggled, wondering if he truly realized what he was doing.

The mob, easily visible groups of people chased through Northfield.

The world was changing, but into what no one could say.

Wandering again, blinking, striving to remember. Head felt close to bursting. She whimpered in pain. Where was she going? What was she doing? Water, she needed it badly, for her sore throat.

Flash. Several minutes seemed to just disappear for her. She swallowed, whimpered, a despair deep as a well. She stumbled up the stairs to the water fountain outside Scott Thompson's Pyramid. She couldn't allow this to happen, couldn't lose control over herself. It would make her even more vulnerable, but also more dangerous than ever.

She drank until she no longer felt thirsty, sating for a while, but not more than that, her violent thirst. Stood on her knees and used her hands to lead more water into her mouth. It did no good. The Hunger didn't abate.

A cacophony of squeaks and chirps made her look up, made her *look*. That was when she discovered how an entire crowd was about to attack her. She had let them sneak close. The first stones were thrown. Then it started raining stones. If she had been Andrea, she wouldn't have had much trouble avoiding them, but her reflexes were not much better than that of an ordinary human. And not at all sufficient to the task. Many stones were knocked back at the attackers, seemingly turning in midair, but at least one penetrated her defense-screen. She had never practiced much in creating TK-shields and paid for that now. The stone hit her behind the ear. Pain and dizziness cut through her, a pain deeper than the mere physical, and she dropped to her knees. She clearly saw the blood, the tiny red droplets on the flagstones. She just about managed to stop herself from completing the fall and she stood there on all fours. She heard a beastly snarl and realized it originated from her own throat, her own deep, recessive mind. They stormed towards her with lifted clubs. Some stopped abruptly, terrified. Others managed to continue the attack, driven by their own, aching glow. Everybody along a straight line, along two straight lines was struck and pushed backwards, brutally, destructive. She knew what she was now, a for-real Warrior Witch. The admission felt good. *They're too many.* She knew that, but fought on. She heard bones break and blood flow as new attackers joined the star line and exposed themselves to her wrath.

One stormed in on her blind spot, a giant of a man. She turned. *The huge club fell in a flash. A blinding, white light and everything turned quiet.*

CHAPTER TWENTY: Tabula Rasa

Joining. An explosive release of fire and life… a Big Bang.

Millions of sperm cells shot from the male reproductive organ into the female's vagina. Many are lost during the intense swimming to the womb. Perhaps just a few thousand reach the single egg. Only *one* breaks through life's barrier, the soft membrane around the egg, immediately afterwards turning impenetrable. Two, incomplete cells become one complete.

This cell splits and becomes two new, complete, identical cells. These two stay together, splitting again and again and again, until they're millions. Many and varied.

This is what's usually happening… But in very rare occasions the first two cells are dividing completely and continue to grow independently of each other, until they've become millions, many and varied.

On even rarer occasions the division isn't complete. Two individuals, originally completely alike, remain in contact…

2

She ran, didn't know anything except that she had to keep running.

Smoke, light in the air. You can look at the patterns forever. You may learn much, but you may also disappear into the infinite and eternal. Lights blink and from the ashes smoke is rising anew. Lights blink anew. No beginning, no end.

Round and round the major vortex span. Car tires, wreckage and twisted metal pieces had been unevenly diverted everywhere, everything visible from the air and in the light cast from the powerful spotlights, like an indistinct shimmering twilight where all sharp edges were hidden. A curtain in a bedroom where light and shadow constantly moved. Indistinct phantoms become something alive, something tangible.

Haze and smoke drifted in front of the bus driving on the highway. The tour bus carried a group of European passengers across the American continent. The driver rubbed her eyes thoroughly, carefully one more time. She had been driving the entire day and what had to be most of the night. In the searing hot night, she expected the morning to come soon, but it didn't.

She swept a hand over the windscreen, tried again with the wipers, but there wasn't even the slightest humidity for hands or wipers to remove. The road in front of the bus remained fuzzy, no matter how she used the lights. She blinked again. The thought had struck her, more than once tonight, that there was some… body out there. She had thought she had seen someone under a road sign, seen the same figure… more than once, on this foreign road. A figure perhaps, but not the same one? Certainly not. She had been driving this route for years, so why should it be different tonight?

A girl crouched in the middle of the road. The driver heard whining of breaks and while looking down, realized that she had already pushed the breaks through the floor, that it was her foot on the pedal. The bus halted with a little less than a human length clearance to the figure in the shimmering light. The girl had dropped to the ground now and crouched there without moving much. The driver had felt strangely calm most of the recent seconds. Now the last few ounces of anger vanished.

Several of the passengers accompanied her out of the bus, into the hot night.

– Christ, she's almost nude.

They relaxed. It was only a girl lying there.

She's at the very least more naked than half naked, the driver thought critically.

The fact that she wore no bra or panties was very much visible. The black skirt and the remains of the strange clothes could hardly be called rags. They weren't old, but quite simply torn apart. The girl lay still, with her eyes closed. She was initially breathing irregularly, but her respiration slowly normalized itself. The driver bent down by her side, shaking her carefully.

The girl opened her eyes and lifted her head slightly.

– Is everything okay?

– Yes. She looked up at them with empty eyes.

– What's your name, dear? A middle-aged woman asked.

They could virtually see how the girl struggled to express herself.

– I… don't know. She held a hand at her head, and it was then they discovered the coagulated blood just above her left temple.

– It seems like someone has assaulted you, a man said. – Do you remember what happened?

– No. She looked bewildered at them all. – I don't remember.

They helped her up and discovered how tall she was. A young girl, probably not more than seventeen or eighteen, very young and very innocent and very vulnerable.

– I don't remember a thing, she cried. – I'm sorry.

– Perhaps you shouldn't dwell on that right now, the middle-aged lady with the funny accent said. – We would like you to come with us, at least until you're rested and have been checked by a physician, or we can leave you at the nearest police station.

She let herself be led into the bus. The women brought her to the bathroom, fixing her up and giving her new clothes. Cleaning the head-wound wasn't any trouble. It wasn't so bad after the hardened blood had been removed. She didn't betray any sound while they did that or when they put on the bandage. The clothes were another matter. They didn't find anything big enough before they had tried on her clothes belonging to one of the tallest men. They didn't really fit, of course, but at least they weren't too small.

They noticed how changed she seemed, dressed in «ordinary» clothes. Her distinctiveness was hardly muted, but not emphasized anymore. One of the more astute ladies noted how easy she stood in the moving bus, though.

Mile after mile raged by, outside, inside the bus, light and shadow playing across the girl's face. She strived desperately to remember. It was unproblematic for her to answer questions about public figures, who was President and such stuff... She drew a total blank when it came to personal information. Her life before she had appeared was Gone. Between the moments she imagined she could glimpse images, memories. They always slipped away. So, she sucked in everything being said around her instead.

– We will arrive in New York well before the Halloween parade in Greenwich Village, a girl in her early twenties giggled. – After that we're leaving for Washington DC… as soon as we're able…

– We have every intention of cutting loose, the boy holding around her giggled.

It echoed within her this, in the girl with no past. Nothing more than that. She sighed and suffered, allowing herself to be led by those around her.

– I must be a terrible burden to you, she said quickly, rushed. – Appearing out of nowhere like that…

The moment she said it, she realized how uncharacteristically it was for her. And she learned something.

– NONSENSE, dear, one or the women burst out. – We just appreciate a break in the regular schedule.

– It hasn't exactly been the most exciting holiday yet, the boy holding an arm around the girl admitted.

– The driver has just informed me that there isn't any police station near the road for some time, a man said. – I'm afraid you have to hold out with our company for a while.

The girl without a past nodded. She realized he attempted to comfort her… at least that he attempted to give her that impression. She didn't say anything.

It turned quiet in the bus eventually. The others fell asleep or tried their best to do so. The girl stared out of the window, fully awake. She had felt tired before entering the bus, but the trip seemed to have revitalized her. Everybody was falling asleep around her, but she felt as if she was constantly waking up. With her face pushed against the window she stared at the night outside and the light bulbs in front of the bus. The only light in the darkness was gray.

After quite a while, miles and miles of gray the bus turned off the road, into a place where rows of trucks filled all the open spaces and the stench of diesel and oil, and gasoline mixed with that of food and tobacco and sweat. A cafeteria. Lights grew and faded constantly here. Fire burned in the wind in such places. Most people couldn't see it. As little as they realized that Darkness surrounded them on all sides.

Drivers and guests who had stayed the night had just about started to fill the dining room. Truckers dominated, of course. There were very few others up this early, while it was still pitch-black outside. With the tourists it was the opposite. They had decided to stay the night after a quick meal.

– We can rent a room for you, one of the women offered. – It's no problem.

– Thanks, but I must keep moving.

– Let us at least equip you a bit.

– I don't need money. She didn't understand her own smile while saying that.

They interpreted it as false modesty and gave her a few bills each. The females embraced her. The males kept their distance. She knew they desired far more from her than a hug.

– I spoke with the manager, the boy holding the girl said. – He would drive you to the nearest police station as soon as he could disengage himself from the customers.

– Thank you. She smiled gratefully to him.

When the entire group had disappeared, she finally felt she could once more breathe easily. The fake, hypocritical kindness destroyed a bit of the fairly good mood the relative clarity brought.

She sat down by a lone table and ate a solid breakfast. Men came by and offered her a ride, but she rejected them. They didn't represent a problem. A few were pushy, but she got rid of them, too. She sat still, unmoving for a moment, staring at nothing. The entrance door opened and closed, and a cold breath touched her.

Who was she? Where did she come from? She rose abruptly from her chair, stood there hesitating for a second or two, before setting course for the lavatory, the restroom. «The brushing and painting place» they had called it back home. She had always resented that description.

She stopped, halted, gazed before her.

Into the mirror. A huge one, reaching from wall to wall, huge squares covered by steam, by mist. She saw herself unbelievably clear among cloud-colored dots in the air and on the walls. She stared openmouthed, not really surprised, but endlessly fascinated. Not so strange they had shown such interest… and such fear. She hadn't truly had any impression of herself before now. In this short night since she had been born.

The scarf they had given her had been used as a broad and thick sweatband (she didn't sweat). It covered well the wound and the entire white bandage. Slowly, in steady, confident moves she loosened the scarf and unwrapped the bandage. The white fabric was slightly red-colored on the spot where it had covered the wound. But when she bent forward, rubbed fingers at the skin, of the wound itself there was nothing left. The skin was smooth and pink, and it didn't hurt the least anymore. The former swollen tissue didn't stand out from the rest.

She tightened the belt around her waist to keep the too big dungaree pants from slipping off her. The white blouse fit her better. It was actually a bit tight… some places. She discovered without having to search herself too deeply that this didn't just please her, but made her feel unadulterated joy. She tied the scarf around the neck and then the outfit looked like it was made for her.

Faces. The door to the toilets revolved behind her. Flashes like lightning behind clear bright eyes. Gray eyes, wide-open eyes. One had to look carefully to see them move. Dark, moody music seethed from the speakers, filling the entire room. The darkness and the mood surrounded them all and wouldn't let go. The others here didn't realize it, but she did, and she thrived. She realized she was a creature of the night. As she had come out of the night, she was a part of it. Forever.

She started to move. One moment there was slow walk. The other a dance so obvious *heathen* that it made the onlookers gasp for breath. Hungry eyes couldn't look away. She saw clearly it wasn't merely her body they hungered for. They desired something far more, something they had lost, *misplaced* and they wanted to possess it, desperately, despairingly. She swayed and rocked, and her feet touched the floor only lightly. She had refused the tourists' offer of shoes and socks and was glad. The toes… her toes *touched* the floor. The rhythm of the dance shifted constantly between polished elegance and raw savagery, a performance of extremes melting together to one many-colored style. Eyes were half closed, dreaming one moment, sparkling hot and challenging the next.

Eyes, half closed or half open sought the sea of eyes, behind the flow of faces, behind the façade.

Dance slowed down, stopped, seemingly by itself. In a sea of gray and violet her body ground to a halt, as her spirit soared along infinite treks.

Her feet moved of their own volition.
He sat alone by a table in the middle of the room. She had noticed him almost the instant he entered the room, could hardly avoid it. She felt a thrill, the thrill of fear.
– Where are you going? She started without introduction.
– Your angle is wrong, he said brusquely. – The question is where *you* are going?
– I don't know… A slight smile crossed her lips.
– That suits me fine, he said, nodding, taking pity on her. – I think I can find room for you.
She sat down, studying him with an interest she could neither hold back nor hide. The huge body towered above her, even sitting. He wasn't that much taller, she ventured, but he was so big and had such thick, hard muscles. The hard, indifferent look he gave her, made her feel small. She had believed she had had that look and what was behind those eyes figured out, but realized she had been wrong.
– The cafeteria owner is supposed to drive me to the nearest police station…
– I'm sure they have a lot to ask you about, he said sarcastically.
The look told her he knew all about her anxiety, her fear of the police, her fear of everything.
– It isn't important, she said hastily, visually shrinking in her seat.
– Come with me, he ordered.
He hadn't been in a hurry about completing his meal. He wasn't in a hurry as he rose from his chair and left without dignifying her with another look.
She followed him. First hesitatingly, but then fidgeting, running, to keep up with him. The roar of many engines hit her immediately outside. Several of the trucks, the trailers had started up and were about to leave the parking lot. The wind seemed to increase. Powerful headlights flared in the night. She didn't recall much of the walk, if it was short or long, hard or easy.
He entered the driver's seat almost his full height above the ground with practiced ease. She was amazed over the fact that it didn't amaze her that she was able to do it just as well. Her moves felt alien to her, but she knew she was fit. She saw that by comparing her moves with most others she had met this night. They moved awkward, as if they were injured or something.
– You have great moves, girl. What's your name?
– Al-line. She said the first name coming to her and was glad he didn't notice the slight uncertainty in her voice.
His bedroom behind the cab was well equipped, bordering on the luxurious. A huge bed. A lot of space everywhere.
– I guess you have to start driving, to reach your destination fairly early, I mean?
And she seemed precisely as young as she, this body was. What strange thoughts. So strange and so… rational. *Yes, that was the right word.*
She shrugged and wanted to retreat to the driver's cab, realizing she went through the various stages.
He grabbed her shoulder with one of his big slabs of hands, tightening his grip. She moaned and fell back in his arms. He pulled her tight to him, her unprotected body, her wide-open mind drowning in his grip. He *held* her with one hand and started to paw, manhandle her with the other. Roughly, indifferently. Her breasts started swelling immediately and the nipples showing against the fabric of her blouse. She panted and turned her head, attempting to find his lips with her own.
– You love this, I saw that the instant I saw you. A knowing grin. – I've said that to many hot cunts, but never has it fit so well.
One single easy pull and he had torn her blouse to pieces. Sore breasts jumped out, liberated from their confines. He kept touching her, part by part, pulled down her pants in a way showing considerable expertise. She wished to twist, push the ever-hotter body against his, becoming one with it, but he held her tight, didn't allow her the slightest freedom. He awakened her slowly and painfully. She released a wail in despair, to no avail. He touched her on the inside of the thighs, but not where she most of all wanted. He rubbed fingers confidently across wet skin. She moaned in desperate lust, didn't manage to bring forth a single word, only sounds and all she saw was the same, knowing grin, an expression completely devoid of mercy. He stroked her with the palm of his right hand from her neck, down between the breasts, across the abdomen, turning to her left thigh, making her, making her wail in disappointment. And then, as his hand stopped moving altogether, she started crying. He laughed heartlessly.

– You're just a little girl, after all, pretending to be a woman. I rather thought that to be the case.

And just then, as her sobs turned uncontrollable, he pushed the hand against her hole of pain. She gasped and gasped, unable to breathe. Fully awakened now, she wanted nothing except for him to keep doing what he was doing. But he removed the hand… far too early. She attempted to speak, to beg him. He stopped her by putting a finger on her lips.

– Women are not supposed to speak without being told to do so, he said sternly. – And you shall only obey, serve and please. That's all being required of you.

She turned limp in his arms. He lifted her as if she was nothing and threw her on her back on the bed. She rocked up and down a few times before lying still. She wanted so to bury her hands in her hole of pain, but didn't dare. He was so dominating and so strong. She could do nothing but beg him with her eyes. He undressed completely calm, until he stood naked before her, above her. He was so big and while she watched, he grew even bigger.

His shadow fell over her, he fell on her body with his full weight. He pushed into her, and she felt pain, as if it was the first time. He held her tight and pushed into her, pushed and pulled without caring the slightest about her needs, about her. She was able to move her arms, but they were stretched far behind her head in the bed and their minor twists and turns were only resonant to his pushes and pulls. He wasn't directly brutal, he was too clever for that, only rough and remorseless. And she loved this. She showed that, in every little sound she released, in every move she made. In her every thought, her every action there were prayers to him to continue and never stop.

He pushed himself up on his knees and lifted her hips. To continue even more intensely. She opened and closed her mouth several times without a single sound escaping. Not until she reached climax did she manage to let go of a moan reminiscing of a scream. The body stiffened, until finally, after an endless time, she went limp once more, sinking into the bed like a ragged doll. He pulled out and let go, lying down on his back, relaxed and confident. She crawled close to him, pushing her smaller body tight to his and he put a protecting arm around her.

Everything was quiet. The roar and thunder outside didn't reach them, didn't reach her. She wanted to say something, but couldn't. He had taken away her speech.

He started *touching* her and her heat rose unresistingly. Her eyes sought helplessly his crotch. She saw he was well on his way back to full power and swallowed. Then she felt his big hand encircling her hole of pain and all thoughts left her once more. He turned her over on the side. She lay with her back to the massive body and couldn't see anything of it. He lifted one of her legs and then he slid unresistingly inside her. She greeted him with a happy sigh. This time he let her move and she writhed and threw her upper body back and forth, in horny gasps.

– I thought about putting restraints on you, but it isn't necessary, is it now?

A big, flat hand hit her left buttocks. There was another horny shout. He had loosened the restraints, but kept control. Every time he was the least unsatisfied with her, he slapped her butt. It made her comply, but also to moan in pleasure. She couldn't help it.

He grabbed her hair so hard that it stung in the scalp, and he pulled her head up, held her so hard in the uncomfortable position that it hurt very much, degrading her and the worst pain wasn't physical. She sniffed. Perhaps it was supposed to be like this. What did she know, who didn't recall anything about her former life?

She fell asleep, satisfied, exhausted, spent. After another explosion of heat and unreason her head dropped to the sheets and the eyes closed. She heard his satisfied hum, as he pulled out and released her, his patronizing laughter while he dressed and sat down by the wheel. Nothing of the hum as the motor heated up. Not the roar when the huge vehicle started moving. *She felt the shaking. The Earth itself was shaking.*

Another forest, not the same as in her earlier dreams. Another another. Her nude feet hardly touched the forest bed. Hammering hooves made the ground shake. She was on the run - again. Around her ankles and wrists, she wore golden slave bracelets, and on the thigh just below the left buttock, she had burned into her skin the palace slave's unique mark. She ran with a hammering heart and heaving breath, with a strength born of desperation and wild panic… like a mouse far from her hiding place. The forest was so big that it had to go on forever. It had to be possible to hide here, find a hole the hunters couldn't find or reach. Gray dots of mist floated around her wherever she turned, suffocating, paralyzing. She got lost fairly soon and stumbled around without any sense of direction and purpose. And she was the easiest kind of game: One who saw herself as one. She feared she was on her way back, to the place she escaped from. Perhaps, perhaps not. No matter, eventually she was recaptured, inevitably, welcomed. The guards, the soldiers stood around her, grinning, pleased with themselves. She was forced down on her knees and once more clad in the light chains of the palace slave. And the entire short walk back became a long, unending torture with scornful cries and the city people throwing harmless, stinging pieces of dirt on her. No one dared to risk damaging the property of the palace master. Well within the tall walls she threw herself on her knees, at the mercy of the Master and begged him to forgive her. I am just a stupid slave, master, punish me so I will never do it again.

… just a stupid slave girl… so I will never do it again… again… again…

She stretched her body. How long had she slept? She pressed a towel at her face, sensed the layer of sweat, the scent of body juices. Did she always dream like this? So intense and… realistic? She frowned. What was it Stephen Biko had said again, about the blacks (browns) in South Africa? Something about not being deserving of Freedom if they didn't find their own worth, their own way of living, independently of those seeing themselves as the master race. This was where Laurie had failed, time and time again. She had played the enemy's game and those doing that were doomed.

Another frown. Who was Laurie? She remembered. A name and it meant something to her. Why couldn't she

remember

the rest?

Hands remained tight fists in the time it took for her to rise from bed. Then she opened them purposely. The face dissolved in a lingering smile, one she recognized without remembering. She moved steadily on the shaky floor until she stood naked and promiscuous in the opening in front. She placed herself with her hands above her head, slightly bent forward and she let him see.

– Good morning, she greeted him huskily.

– It's afternoon, he replied tightly.

– It's morning to me, she chirped lightly. – I'm a girl who needs to sleep late.

Now, where did she get that from?

– In the closet you'll find a green dress, he said if possible even more curtly. – You'll find a lot of your size, but choose that.

She smiled with exposed… teeth and the wrinkle on his forehead turned more than visible. She was fairly positive that no matter how he had visualized their next conversation, it wasn't like this.

She had removed the wasp's sting before it had stung.

Yes, that was more than a correct expression.

She found the green dress and hummed merrily while trying it on. She stood before the mirror, studying the result with critical eyes. Yes… Critically speaking it was probably a bit too small, but she didn't mind. In this case tight was good… Earlier in her life she wouldn't have felt comfortable with the thought of standing naked or practically undressed in his presence, but now this little implication of shyness was like blown away.

The truck covered miles and miles on the highway. She sat in the passenger seat and took in every minor impression, every scrap of information the brain could possibly digest, a newborn, just out of the womb. Miles and miles, meter by meter, as the well-oiled machine brought them further south on the American east coast. Everything seemed the same in this eternal gray, but that wasn't so, not even here. The planet contained a myriad of variety, even here on this broad line of not-life. Life surged below the surface and fought to break through the hard covering, the thin crust.

They crossed the outer limits to New York City during what Aline strongly felt was a twilight hour, crossed the many-laned bridge to Manhattan. The tiny stretch of road took forever to cross, a horrible second of forever. Traffic slowed to a crawl in both directions. Aline would imagine that it hadn't always been this bad, that at least one direction, one line of cars driving either in or out of the peninsula usually had been flowing pretty okay. All problems, enormous for a very long time had increased exceptionally the last few years. This included the traffic, but didn't exclude others. Women and men stood on the roof of their cars, in their rage and despair and howled against each other, howled against the world. Suddenly, just like that, one or more walked to the edge of the bridge and without any sort of ceremony… they jumped off it. No one reacted in any visible way. The driver of the truck shook his head one single time.

– It gets worse and worse, he mumbled.

– Structures of pain and destruction keep us from the magic in our hearts, she expressed impulsively.

– Don't try to be a smart ass with me, girl. Shaking in rage he lifted a hand from the wheel a second.

She practically ignored him after that, stared out of the window with frozen eyes. Not on one single occurrence, but on many. Many shells of humans merely sitting there (wherever they sat), with empty expressions broadcasting a single message; that they couldn't go on anymore. She suddenly remembered a scene from the second modern Superman - movie Christopher Reeve had played the title role in. During a battle the crowd below had been bombarded with remains of buildings and walls. They had begged for Superman to save them. Aline had experienced the scene as horribly false. But most people were like that, she ventured. In their distress, their need they prayed to some god, any god for salvation. But no savior came. The world, the Universe quite simply didn't work like that. There was no one who could shake a magic wand and make things better.

But instead of doing anything themselves people fell ever deeper in the mire and passivity of an ordinary life, and in turn howling even higher for heavenly intervention.

All natural lights had faded when they finally reached the truck's temporary destination. Manhattan's appearance wasn't any better than the other parts of New York they had driven through. It was humid and gray and dark there. Central Park was dirty yellow and… horrible. There was hardly any green anywhere. Complains, screams and wails seemed to come from everywhere. The number of homeless had increased heavily in the entire so-called western, industrialized world the last year, the last ten years. Environmental refugees came from all over the planet now, not merely the so-called third world. And they came from within each nation, country. They had become visible for all to see, even to those constantly looking away.

The neon lights had killed those of nature. Manhattan's entertainment area still sparkled. The truck stopped outside a dodgy bar Off-Broadway somewhere. The driver looked at her. She could sense it like pinpricks of pain on her skin.

– Look at me, he ordered her.

She obeyed. Her lower lip started twitching under his remorseless scrutiny.

– That's good, he said pleased. – Now I've gotten your attention. Soon I will have it fully and completely.

He walked outside and with a small wave he signed for her to come with him. She followed him as if in a daze to the back of the truck. He pushed a button on the wall. A panel, a keyboard of numbers appeared. He hit the code, not caring if she saw it or not. A door opened and an electronic staircase helpfully offered its services. He walked inside without looking back. She couldn't tell whether or not she hesitated, but she did follow him, as she knew he wanted, as he had ordered her to. If he had ever lost control over her, he had easily, frighteningly easy regained it.

It was dark inside, but she could see well enough. She had no problem seeing in the dark.

She stood there, unable to move a single muscle, unable to even twitch.

A group of people crouched in the deeper parts of the truck. There was a mixed crowd of about thirty people, of Asian, African, Mexican descent. They weren't chained or anything. It wasn't necessary.

– These are workers, the driver commented, – even though one or two of the girls, if they survive the first couple of years may be good for a different kind of service.

She couldn't move, she couldn't think. She recognized the creepy feeling when he once more turned his entire attention at her.

– You don't want this for yourself, do you?

– N-no. She shook her head. – I'll be good. I'll be good, I promise.

– Good. He touched her under the jaw, as if assessing her. – I will introduce you to an associate of mine in New Orleans. You will be good then, too, won't you?

– Yes, she whispered. – Very, very good.

– Good. He patted her on the cheek. – I will turn you over to him, eventually, of course, after we've had some fun on the way south and you've learned a lot of the required proper behavior. The way you love squirming on your back or being on your knees, you'll love it down there. Eventually, after an introductory period you'll hardly do anything else. Anyway, I'm sure you agree it beats working in a fruit garden or poisonous factory. Your beauty and fire would have faded fast then, I assure you. Now you'll be fed and taken well care of, and you'll have your brains fucked out all day and night long.

She didn't speak. He didn't want her to. She had become acutely sensitive to his needs and desires. He smiled, looking straight through her meager shell and she bowed her head submissively.

– One more item on the program before we start enjoying the evening, he said brusquely.

There was another room further in. She followed him there. He turned on the lights, revealing a video camera and a computer. He turned on both. The screen showed another room, clearly far from here, a luxurious office built in a southern style. Aline understood and bit her lip. It took a while before a man appeared behind the desk.

– What took you so long? The driver asked.

– I was otherwise engaged, the man behind the desk said.

He was covered in sweat and had a pleased grin painted on his lips.

– Well, then you should *dis*engage yourself and take a look at this little specimen, the driver very casually suggested.

The other man looked at the screen on his end.

– Hello there. He whistled.

– Aline, ordered the driver. – Say hello to Flaherty.

– Hello, Flaherty, she obeyed.

– Now, reveal yourself to him. Ass and tits will be sufficient. We want to leave something to his imagination.

She turned and pulled up the dress, pushing her butt slightly back, letting the man watch her through the video camera. She turned again, exposing her breasts, pulling down the straps from her shoulder.

The driver, the man running her, nodded.

– I expect everything to be ready by arrival this time, he said to the camera. – And all the thick wallets present.

– I don't know, Flaherty said with doubt in his voice. – She seems a bit too experienced to me.

– Don't be put off by her eagerness, the driver laughed. – She is just easy to teach, that's all.

She didn't get the other one's reply. The computer was turned off, the lights were turned off, and then the fog surrounded her.

In the dodgy Off-Broadway bar the heavy smoke drifted between light and shadow, the gray surroundings. Here were all types of humans thrown into a whirlwind of pain, depression and desperation. A woman sat in a heap of broken glass and with a completely indifferent expression in her face she cut her wrist in a determined, precise incision. No one sacrificed a second look on her. Not that it mattered, but she wasn't in any real danger. If she had cut herself vertically, instead of horizontally it could have led to something. As it presently was going, a lot of other things competed better for people's attention. A man hit another while he kept pushing him at the wall, hit and hit and hit. It had been a while since the loser had stopped resisting. The bets continued unabated. How long would he who was doing the hitting keep it going? How many hits would it eventually turn out to be? Would he keep using his right hand? Was the poor sucker of a meatball still alive? How long would he stay that way?

A very lively place. Something was lit in Aline's lifeless eyes.

Two couples danced the night away without any interference from anyone, on a parquet floor of considerable size. No one *interfered*, and the reason was not hard to see. All four had double-edged knives in their hands and cut loose at each other. One of the men sank gargling to the floor with a severed throat. The woman, now fighting alone, kept it going just a short while longer after that. The victorious couple cut ruthlessly in her. Many of the spectators claimed she was deceased before hitting the floor. Two of them started a serious *argument* concerning this question. No one bothered to even look in their direction. Something like that was simply too ordinary in this context.

The woman (who at this time had cut both her wrists) triumphantly pushed the hands into two full glasses of beer. Here was actually something original and the crowd's curiosity was seriously aroused, looks turned in her direction and didn't turn away for a while. Her table virtually drowned in beer and blood. New bets were made. Even high-profile bookmakers became involved.

Aline sat with her back to two drinking buddies. She listened to their conversation. It wasn't completely uninteresting.

Feeling like broken glass, fractured, scattered.

– … hear that Bangladesh is under the water or under the weather again.

– Permanently this time, I gather, the other grumbled.

– A body can always hope. They toasted to that.

No bet was made this time.

– Thank you for taking me here, she said gratefully. – I'm enjoying myself.

He looked sharp-eyed at her, as usually thrown completely off center by her unexpected behavior. He just couldn't figure her out and it angered him.

– I've never met a man like you, she said, kissing his hand. – You're completely ruthless and indifferent, so hard and cold.

– You're such a cute girl, he laughed, – so easy to teach and mold.

She crawled shyly, humbly onto his lap. He felt triumph swell within. Such a jewel and she belonged to him. She would belong to him more and more with every passing day. He was looking forward to teaching her, to break her completely and rebuild her the way he saw fit. One touch under the dress and she was aroused. Her eyes turned misty in gratitude.

– Dance with me, she pleaded as she jumped up and reached out her hand.

– I'll let you dance alone tonight. He strived to keep the voice even.

He felt weakened, out of whack, not his usual self at all. Had he come down with something? Something sneaky that had been there all day and didn't go away. Fuck, he had never allowed himself to be hampered by such shit as bacteria or viruses. Dancing wouldn't have been a hurdle, but he didn't feel like dancing the particular dance going on, on the floor right now. Later… But not just now.

She did. He saw it in her every move, in her eyes and attitude. Perhaps she was lacking in experience. Perhaps. There was no lack of will. He started to grow excited in spite of himself. Was it possible that he had stumbled over a real treasure this time? He was tempted to call Flaherty again and make him contact the big guns on this one.

The couple that had *cleared* the dance floor a few minutes earlier still dominated it. No one challenged their spot. Aline didn't either, but was far more forward than the others obviously dancing with caution. They didn't dance, not for real. Aline did, showing off for them, without reservations, unconditionally. Interest flared in the couple's eyes.

Who was she? Was this how the Human Being truly was, totally fearless face to face with complete and utter horror?

They moved close to her, until they covered her on both sides.

– We're about to ditch this hovel, the man said hoarsely. – We have an Omega desire for you to join us.

Strange tides flowed from them through her, and from her through them.

– I would like that, she said candidly. – But my man is very possessive. I would need his permission and I don't think he will give it, at least not tonight, in the very foul mood stalking him.

– Possessive, huh, the man grinned. – He runs you, huh?

– He runs me well, she nodded.

– I've got no problems with that, the man mumbled. – A man gotta protect his property these days.

The woman looked angry at him, before turning to Aline.

– Well, we might meet again one day, and perhaps by then, the status will have changed?

The woman smiled ambiguously.

Aline felt their contempt.

The heavy smoke drifted between light and shadow, between the girl's sparkling eyes. Here were all types of humans thrown into a whirlwind of pain, depression, savagery, joy and desperation. The driver, her runner stared at her, and she returned his stare fearlessly. If he hadn't realized it before, he realized it now, how truly different she was. Her smile both mystical and blinding, both bright and full of shadows.

The wind was blowing. It rushed between the stone buildings, sucking with it paper and dust in its wake. The city was both dry and humid simultaneously and both states were equally bad. Aline felt in every nerve ending how little she belonged here. She was sick and tired of cities. At an earlier stage in her life, she had accepted them with gritted teeth, but that ended here and now.

She was a tabula rasa, a clean slate, an empty vessel to be filled by anyone.

If it truly was like that, she wanted to do it herself.

Her eyes caught a sprouting green bud in the transition between the sidewalk and the road, grown from a thin layer of dusty soil. Life didn't need much encouragement. Not even here, in the lap of Death. It returned, Life, time and time again, inevitable. A sort of living death had dominated for so long, but now Life returned, as an angel of vengeance.

The driver had made a necessary trip to the restroom, a very long trip. He had a disturbed look in his face he fought to get rid of. He walked outside, both angry and apprehensive. The wind grabbed hold of him and blew him away. When reaching the driver's cab, she yet wasn't anywhere in sight. He fumbled with the lock and the door slipped open… before he got a chance to unlock it. Shaking his head, he climbed on board. The keys were supposed to be in his pocket. He would never have given them to her, would he? As he pulled aside the curtain to his small traveling apartment, as he gazed into the darkness, he realized that he never had been able to control her. It had just seemed that way. There were ways. He had his ways. Any woman knew the difference between a slap and a pat on the head. She was a bit of a challenge that was all. He sort-of welcomed one, after such a long time of having it easy. His anger grew, as he imagined the darkness itself coming for him, engulfing him. His hands were shaking, and he had to grab hold of the doorframe to stop it. He found, after prolonged fumbling the light switch, switching it, in relief, in panic. Nothing happened.

The lamp on the table was switched on. It blinded him. He saw the table, but little else. And long, pitch-black shadows dominated the remaining parts of the room.

The girl had placed herself on all fours on the bed, between the light and the shadow. She had swept a thin blanket around her, but the lines of her body were clearly and easily visible, framed as it was by the light behind. He swallowed and immediately got a hard and painful erection.

It was as if he drifted towards the bed. Clothes seemed to evaporate like humidity near fire.

– I don't mind showing what I've got, you know, she said huskily, posing for him. – Nudity isn't such a big issue to me.

He stumbled and fell on his knees on the bed. She met him sitting on her heels, serving him sultry kisses.

– It isn't easy with a willing woman, is it now? She spoke hoarsely, from deep in her throat. – Many can't handle it.

She swept the blanket around them, putting her arms around him, rubbing the hot body incitingly against his. He lost count of time, lost all count of time. He could vaguely recall grabbing her and pushing her down on her back. His second trust already felt like forever. He gasped in helpless pleasure as he pushed and pulled, pulled and pushed. She clung to him in the entire body's length. It didn't matter if she was under him, on the side or above him, instinctively, *she realized*, like putting one foot ahead of the other. Her eyes opened, shining like opaque glass, clear and deep as Space. He gasped. Behind, below the overwhelming joy he felt, he felt fear, overwhelming fear.

Oh, what a sweet boy you are. I can see everything you wanted to do with me. It tickles so sweet within me, all your affectionate punishment.

Did she speak? He couldn't tell. Beyond fear now, he screamed, howled, terrified of the darkness.

They had come together several times, many times, he couldn't tell how many. He lay exhausted on his back. She hovered over him like a vulture, like a predator. With a few, simple moves she made him ready once more. He was unable to lift his arms, but his sore and battered cock rose broad, long and hard. She licked her lips and started to move back and forth above him, while the broad hips ascended and descended his stiffness. Up, down, down up. He moaned in pain and pleasure. She rocked up and down on him as she willed now, did whatever she wanted with him, smiled and looked down on him with her predator eyes. It was this image that would haunt him in the many upcoming lonely nights.

– You certainly can't. She dismounted and sat down on the edge of the bed. He felt a light kiss on his cheek. He strived desperately to lift his arms, to move, in vain. Strong and radiant she spoke, but he hardly heard it as much more than a whisper, like the roar of the Storm. – You were wrong about me. I'm not like the others, not like the needy, squirming hens you have picked up.

Time faded, everything faded, and he thought she had left, left him alone, when he suddenly heard her voice from the darkness.

– You didn't measure up, after all, she told him scornfully.

She lifted his head and kissed him greedily on the lips. It hurt. God help him. It hurt.

– You wanted to sell me, she said smiling. – Making me surrender into servitude and slavery.

His eyes just closed. He fell asleep instantly and slept hard, the sleep of the dead. She put her claws into his thigh. No reaction. He would sleep a very long time.

She felt great. While searching in the closet her thoughts raced away in a calm and harmonic manner. She still didn't know who or what she was… but she knew what she wasn't. The same discovery he had made.

So many great clothes, so much to pick from. But she was in no way indecisive, didn't need to try anything on. She chose right the first time. A black, tight blouse revealing her midsection and dungarees in the same color.

She walked outside. Deeply entranced by the morning she drew her breath deeply and deeply sated. She sensed it in every cell in her body. The pollution didn't affect her.

After a short hesitation she walked to the hidden door. She pushed the button on the wall, hitting the numbers in correct sequence without the slightest hesitation. There was the walk up the stairs, inside, even if she couldn't quite fathom it. She fathomed it all, every single step on her way. Her senses had grown remarkably astute. She looked with burning eyes on the human waste before her.

– You came here looking for something better, to the land of plenty. I'm gonna tell you a badly hidden secret. America… the entire world was… is created by the suffering and death of slaves. You may leave here and continue your miserable existence, your mockery of a life… or you can choose to do something about it.

She said nothing more. She turned and left, and left the door open behind her.

Ten, fifteen steps beyond the nearest corner she discovered the parked white Dodge Van across the street, seemingly black in the silhouette of the morning. She had no difficulties seeing the man and the woman inside.

As she approached the window slid open in an electronic hum.

– We're headed towards Washington Dee Cee, he put to her, his wolfish grin very appealing.

The woman opened the door on the other side, stepping out, allowing Aline to step inside first. She sat between the two of them as the man started up the engine and they drove off, leaving New York City, heading further south. Manhattan Bridge was silent, ghostlike in the early morning light.

Out on the highway miles just seemed to slip away. Even in bright daylight the surroundings had a surreal, unreal quality to Aline. They drove south, with the sun on their left side. Aline could hardly look out of the window. Her eyes had become extremely sensitive to light. And her ears… One moment when she had to hold her hands pressed to her ears to lower the roar of the engine, she wondered if she was able to feel everything, sense everything in the entire world.

– Rough night, darling darkling? The woman who had presented herself as Stella offered.

Aline didn't know what to say and nodded.

– Don't worry, I have something redeeming anything.

Two fingers between the lips, a taste on her tongue. She was tempted to spit out what Stella had put in her mouth, but she did swallow it.

They waited for something, she could sense it. Their expectation, as the man pressed the pedal through the floor was quite tangible. She waited for something, didn't really know what. A sound rose from within. Stella's blond afro-hair suddenly seemed like flying desert sand, her blue eyes a sea with a forever unreachable shore. A smell ravaged her nose, a rain of embers. She discovered that her sex was sticky wet.

Eyes closed and the rain of embers exploded.

– You gave me Ecstasy, she mumbled. – Why did you do that? It wasn't necessary, not necessary at all.

– Relax, baby. Stella rubbed her cheek. – We just wanted you to enjoy yourself, we just want you to feel good.

Teeth gritting, she discovered a playing tongue in her ear, teeth biting the lobe, demanding hands wandering the body. Aline allowed it to happen.

– So hard and so soft…

Wasn't she supposed to be afraid of this woman? And the man, too? They killed and mutilated, and did whatever they desired without fear of consequences. What stopped them from doing something really bad to her?

She moaned, as Stella grew more direct in her approach. She realized then, that she would always be a bitch, a horny beast.

That was a very easy question to answer.

She did.

She grabbed Stella's hair and pulled her close, kissing the other girl on the lips, hungrily, demandingly, mercilessly.

– Didn't I tell you? The man, Carl, laughed hard. – She's a predator.

Stella pulled a knife from a hidden pocket. The blade appeared in its full beauty. Aline, in a kind of detached manner, saw it, not as others saw it, but as patterns of soul and fire. It had been cleaned, but if one looked at it without eyes, blood ran freely. Aline laughed aloud, laughed Stella in her face. Anger grew in the blue eyes. Aline offered her a palm. In its center… skin seemed to crack. A single drop of blood found its way from its abyss. Stella's anger was supplanted with wonder and then it was as if a film covered the blue eyes. Knife fell to the floor. Stella led the mouth to the offered palm and started licking, carefully at first, but then she swallowed greedily. Blood flowed from the corner of her mouth. Aline grabbed her hair once more, lifted up the head, kissing the blood red lips. Stella went completely limp, docile in her complete Joy. Aline put the head in her lap and started rubbing the other woman between her thighs.

– I'm a night beast, Aline breathed. – The Blood is the Life. Life is the Blood.

– Jesus, Carl breathed. – What did you do? You're a fucking witch.

– Thanks… She smiled brightly to him.

Stella erupted in orgasm. She writhed and moaned, before falling silent, laying still. She crouched on her back, staring up at the girl with worship in her eyes.

Aline put a hand around the man's neck and started to rub it gently, ever more insistent and dangerously. Sweat broke out all over his body, in such amount that she could easily smell it. She moved close to him, to his mouth. Her lips were close to his ear.

– Do you want a taste? She whispered. – I know you will…

He grew hard and pushed against the fabric of his trousers. She grabbed hold of his hair and bent his head back. It wasn't necessary, but she wanted it that way.

She pushed a palm at his mouth. A single drop, liberated from the skin dropped down on his tongue. The blood expanded violently, and he had to swallow and swallow away, almost choking on it all. He shouted wildly during the sudden, raw ejaculation and the hot sticky wetness filled his pants.

The car had skid to a halt. He hadn't seen anything, hadn't heard anything…

– You're such a good boy. She gave him a wet kiss on his cheek. – Be real good, now. We're about to have company.

Three figures, two men and a woman made their way to the car. The woman had stood alone on the road, until the car had stopped. Then the men had appeared.

All windows were open. It was hot and getting hotter.

– Hi! Aline waved to them.

– Hi… The woman looked uncertain at her buddies.

– Such great breaks you've got, one of the men, the largest of them greeted the three inside the car ironically.

– We stopped when we discovered you two shy boys. Aline smiled to them, exposing her teeth. – You three are such an aesthetically great group. You're sort of… complementing us.

– Well, yes… All the previously so confident hitchhikers now had major difficulties finding the right words.

– We're heading south, to Washington DC, Aline offered very, very courteously.

– Eh, that's great… We're on our way… there, too.

– You're more than welcome to join us, Stella said huskily. Hoarse voice, husky eyes, hungry mouth.

– No problemo, Carl nodded eagerly.
– We have enough room in the back, Aline told them sweetly. – More than enough room.
It was at that moment the three rough, experienced hitchhikers started running seriously scared.

3

Within the car's eternal dark endless night Aline, Stella and Carl had chosen a partner, pushing themselves against cold carcasses soon to be hot. Aline looked pleased down on Dan as she rode him roughly and ruthlessly. Pleased, but she yet saw hunger in the mirror image's eyes.
– Come, she called. – Come to me.
And they came to her. She knew their names, the thoughts and the immediate thoughts of them all, what motivated and frightened them. They were helpless before this siren leading them further out on the raging sea than they had ever wanted.
They all gathered, and they loved her and gathered close to her, all of them tightly and she was bathing in their energies, in bursts of waterfalls quickening her.
She remembered (how could she ever have forgotten). Memory and awakening came to her in minute-by-minute, second-by-second flashes of compressed information. Every human was unique, like a snowflake. Not a single one was identical to another. In the present-day world, most people had lost their identity. Everybody was like shards going through the meat grinder. Instead of encouraging variety, the ideal was the formless, gray masses…
But not she.
Fire and light. She was back in Newtown, outside the Pyramid. The club hit her head and she was falling backwards. The world faded, life faded. Then, when it seemed like she would fall and hit the ground hard, her body froze, levitating, hovering in the air. An empty look, eyes sparkling in dark fire froze all attention at the man with the club. From one moment to the next it happened: The huge man dissolved in a flaming inferno where the air itself burned in terrifying Rage. There was nothing left of him but ashes.
The Avenging Angel directed the attention at the unmoving mob. They who had believed they had corralled her.
– Lord Jesus Christ, there's a hole in her skull.
They were able to see the brain bubble and flow in there. And blood and something that could only be pus flow from the wound. The expression in which she looked at them, at all of them simultaneously wasn't an expression at all, but something cold and dead completely surpassing their comprehension.
They threw away everything in their hands and ran away from there. They would never stop.

4

A house on a larger property a bit upstream on Potomac River, just outside Washington DC.
She walked through the heavily decorated gate.
– Good evening, Miss Stacy, the guard, the sentry greeted her, opening the gate. – Welcome back.
– Thanks, Bernard, she said cheerfully. – Has anything of significance happened in this ruin in the time I've been away?
– Nothing… major, Miss Stacy, he coughed, attempting to hold on to the neutral tone.
She declined his offer of a car driving her to the main building and walked the entire way to Larkin Mansion. She passed the spring water before the main entrance, the heavily influenced and expensive Gothic front. Saw the light glimmer in the water drops.
An underling opened the door for her. She allowed that, as she cheerfully, bitterly imagined all the activity within her sudden appearance had created. A huge chandelier was part of the major decorative work in the main hall. She stopped for a moment and looked up at it. All the light bulbs and crystals rattled slightly.
The house was so large that it seemed empty, even though she positively knew that the servants were rushing back and forth everywhere. She saw that, just by slightly closing her eyes. So large… so

perishable. She turned her attention to the side, walking into a long, well-lit corridor/minor hall. No dark corners here. Everything was hidden inside dark and deep closets.

Aline Larkin entered the luxurious lengthy dining room where her parents dined. They actually sat opposing each other at each their end of the long table. It didn't just happen in the movies. Aline didn't hide the very evident sour expression.

– New hair again, darling? Mother said in her usual detached manner.

– Yes, I grew tired of the other look, the girl replied lightly.

– Well, you're in time for dinner, the man said. – For once.

– Hi, father, she greeted him in a mocking cheerfulness.

– … even if one can hardly say you're dressed for the occasion, he kept going indifferently. – One can hardly say you're dressed at all.

– Nice to see you, too, she mumbled.

She sat down, between them. Food was put before her. She started eating automatically. The entire scene with the servants rushing back and forth with filled plates, empty plates, stiff, empty masks… it all seemed totally insane to her.

– Do you want me well done, too? She asked suddenly, smiling lovely and teasingly. – Like the food?

And she rose and stretched her body, stretched her arms above her head, high above. She made herself as narrow as she could around the waist and the skirt slid a considerable distance down her hips. The scar was extremely well exposed.

– How can you behave like that, Stacy? Mrs. Larkin exclaimed visibly shaken. – What if the servants saw you? This is a new low, even for you.

The mother chatted away. The father sat there silently, broodingly. But the mutant sensed his worry behind the façade, the stoic mask. He had noticed, and was now debating with himself whether or not memory played tricks on him, whether or not the scar truly was on the wrong side.

She walked lightly up the marble staircase. How fabulously strange. She had never been here before in her life, but yet felt as if she had walked through it all many times. She didn't have to read anyone's mind to find the bedroom, Stacy's room. She stopped just inside the closed door, looking around. It could just as well been hers.

Mirror, mirror on the wall…

She placed herself before the smooth, shimmering surface and saw herself in full figure. In the mirror she saw flames behind her and she started sweating.

Mommy, daddy there's a fire

(Stacy, where's Stacy?)

Closing her eyes did no good, she knew that too well, now, when she remembered. She sought her inner self, and the visions and the voices stopped, and her beating heart didn't hammer that much.

Her eyes burned in cold calm. The face was a study in pre-deliberation, the face of an adult, one who had accepted life's cruelty. The eyes didn't expose her anymore.

The mirror, the image and its surface started shimmering like the air above the ground during the day in deserts. A desert a long time ago and far ahead. By closing her eyes, she saw everything even clearer. A city, a fortress in the long passed past, inside a deep forest. A man and a woman with a child, a boy. Not he who would become the Dollmaster, certainly not, rather the opposite. She sat there with her back to a tree coddling him in her arms. He suckled eagerly on a breast. Then he opened his eyes, and his eyes were fire. Fire would rise behind the eyes of this child, until he was nothing but fire. She drew breath hard, remembering, recalling ever more. Her mirror image changed. It didn't disappear this time, but her features started to distort into that of a demon. She-Demon, warrior witch…

She smiled.

The mirror image continued its change, becoming ever more terrifying and fascinating. She felt something, a ripple. She knew that Stacy was on her way then. A stirring inside, outside heralded her arrival. There was a ripple in the air. A hole formed, one making it hard to see the wall behind. It was like they had been presuming. Distance was no hurdle to Delphi. The very concept became meaningless. That, too.

There was no barrier anymore. Jill was capable of reading Stacy's most private thoughts.

And Stacy had always been capable of reading Jill's innermost thought.

– They have attempted to keep us apart our whole life, Jill said surprised, nonplussed. – But they have failed.

– Many have, Stacy confirmed nodding. She stood on the middle of the floor in a dying radiance. – Most of all the two who did the actual fertilization. They were so disgusted by the thought of being parents to Siamese twins that the process of splitting us at the hips wasn't enough for them. They feared to such a degree they would be socially shunned by their peers, that they planned the fire, the separation, everything. One girl with a beauty mark could be explained away, tolerated, not two freaks with ugly scars fitting like hands in gloves.

– They even attempted to obscure our birth records, moving our birthday from October thirty-first to April thirtieth, Jill blinked, blinked twice.

For some strange reason, this made it all worse.

– They did that, too, Stacy said subdued, – but succeeded only in giving us an advantage, making us legally independent from them six months earlier. It's all so funny, isn't it.

Jill smelled fire, willing to swear it was real. And it was. The fire in this house was as real now as it had been so many years ago. She crouched where she stood, imagining she was once again a little girl, helplessly left to others' mercy. A force of will and she straightened her back, standing straight and proud.

– I turned twelve in a dream and realized it all, Stacy continued subdued, horribly. – All the seemingly unrelated memories, nightmares.

– You knew everything, what we were, before we came here, to Northfield.

– As you learn from me, I learn from you. Stacy smiled dangerously, tinged with a certain despair. – But you're correct, of course. I did know what's important, what had to be done. I had planned it every day, every hour, every second for six years…

– Father, mother, they've destroyed you, Jill said painfully.

– In that case I welcome the destruction, Stacy boasted proudly. – And I feel I almost should thank them. Almost. What they did strengthened me, made me better suited to deal with a harsh reality. And in time I could share my wisdom with you.

Jill closed and opened her eyes a single time.

– But what's… the point?

– As you now know, cruelty is a point in itself, precious.

– But why all the *bother?*

Stacy took a few steps forward, bringing herself close to the sister. They stood there, like two mirror images.

– I wanted to give you a taste of what Life could be, give you a taste of hope and then show you how false all of it is. And I've succeeded, haven't I, *sister?*

– *Yes.* Their voices were the same. – Only hatred and power are real.

– There are compensations. A hand touching a cheek. – I realized that a long time ago. So will you.

– You feared I would run away again, Jill said hotly. – Never again.

Good.

Frantic knocking. The door opened before any of them had time to open their mouth. Mister and Missus Larkin entered the room, staring openmouthed at them.

– Mother, Father, Stacy said sweetly. – You've already met her, but allow me to present to you your daughter Aline, back from the dead, from the Kingdom of Death where you sent her.

– Hello, Jill said, just as sweetly.

– Hello, the Lady Larkin said weakly, automatically, keeping up appearances to the last.

– Did you truly believe you could keep us separated? Jill asked quietly, almost subdued. – How silly of you. No one could and no one will.

– The poor sod you sent to spy on me freaked out quite fast… Stacy laughed contemptuously. – He ran off soon enough.

– What are you going to d-do? Lady Larkin asked very tense.

– Well… Stacy grinned and dragged it out. – Proclaim the happy news, I gather. Isn't that the proper procedure in such cases?

– You can't do that. The Lady gasped. – Oswald, stop them.

– Bet on it, Wilma, they won't get out of this house without heavy escort.
He stared angrily at Stacy.
– What do you have to complain about, anyway? We have certainly seen to your needs well enough.
– You left me alone with you, Stacy spat. Naked wrath, building throughout adolescence emerged to the surface.
– We have access to a number of qualified houses we can place you, Lord Larkin said sternly. – Places where all rebellious sluts are taught good manners and correct behavior. An option we should have chosen from the start. FREDRICK
– No, thanks, Jill said. – We've already tried that and didn't find it to our liking.
Larkin grabbed his throat and fell coughing on the expensive carpet, spoiling it. The Lady stared almost triumphantly at her daughters, with a pale, sickly shine in the eyes.
– Behold the mutants, humanity's freaks, she cried. – Demon spawn, lost and condemned forever in God's Kingdom.
– You knew, Stacy said, gasping. – You knew!
Jill lifted an open hand, rolling it into a fist. Hard. Wilma screamed from a pain originating from all over the body. Jill didn't feel much. Even the omnipresent hatred wasn't all that prominent.
– Yes, mother, we're everything you feared and more.
There was no excuse. None. And no regret. Only the blackest hatred. They were two empty shells, the two creatures that stood and crouched before them. There was nothing left in them worth saving. No defense for what they had done, for what they would have done, if they had been given ample opportunity.
– What… are you? The complete stranger on the floor gasped.
– What you and others have made us, Stacy said.
– WHAT THE HELL
A huge figure appeared in the doorway, the Larkin «fixer». Stacy had always detested him.
– *Fredrick*, Jill called throatily.
He took a couple of uncertain steps forward before freezing in his tracks. She made him look at her, look at the sweet eighteen-year-old girl, giving him time so she could savor his fear. Suddenly his entire body caught fire simultaneously. Flames reached the roof and instantly the roof transformed into a sea of fire. The two sisters held hands, even though it wasn't strictly necessary anymore. The man, who during the years had done so many cleanups and dirty operations, turned to ashes.
The flames erupted in the kitchen, in the living room, everywhere in the building. The servants and others screamed and shouted in panic and ran to the nearest exit point. A few attempted to put out the fire, but its wrath increased with every drop of water, every grain of detergent, every blanket, every dose of foam used against it. The staircase, the marble itself started burning. The escape route was closed off. Wilma and Oswald Larkin were surrounded by hungry, devouring flames. Mirrors bent and cracked in the heat. The outer windows, too. Air was sucked in, nourishing the flames further.
We're about to lose control, Stacy stated soberly.
The inferno grew around them, such an amazing force. They had trouble breathing, but two pair of eyes still sparkled in fascination. The whisper grew louder, transfixing them with its power. They shook off the seductive siren whispers. The fire had grown beyond any control now and would shortly embrace the entire building in its kindness, a kindness speaking to the witches as well. But they wanted to live. They wanted more than ever to finally Live.
– Allow me to go outside, Jill insisted. – I still got tears to spare.
Stacy nodded. Their eyes met for a short moment, one part of a million, more than sufficient.
Jill jumped over the banister. A brief, temporary pain riddled her when a minor bone in her leg gave in the moment, she landed on the floor below. It dawned on her that she had always feared open fire. Stacy followed her with her eyes, in thought and deed, until she threw herself through a broken window and landed on the lawn outside. As she limped to the other shipwrecked people gathering a safe distance away from the raging inferno.
The portal appeared behind Stacy, and she once more walked through it, into the quiet darkness.
Jill fell on the lawn with cuts and bruises in face and skin and tears down her cheeks. In a flash the flames had surrounded her, and she had feared they would never more disappear. She saw that her

burns were worse and more extensive than on the people close to her, but hers would soon be gone. Her sharp hearing discerned the sound of the many emergency vehicles from when they were merely a shiver in the distance… until the sound was as big an inferno… as the one in everybody's immediate vision.

– It must be the gas, one mumbled. – A leak… yes, a leak is reasonable…

The mutant gave the heat one final push. One single flame erupted from the roof. The Larkin residence exploded in one single, enormous blow. The fire pillar grew sky-high, and it was as if the sun had descended upon them.

Even if they pretty much left her alone, it took time and infinite patience, she thought, until the initial investigation and formalities were over and done. She met with some of the stated friends of her parents and of Stacy, unknown people embracing her and mumbling «poor girl». She recognized all of them like an echo in her mind. The family lawyer discretely pushed a paper over the table for her to sign. She scanned him so hard that he virtually sat there shaking, without him realizing a thing. He was greedy, but basically honest. She signed on the dotted line. And then she went home. She took a taxi to the burned out, desolate Larkin estate, where there was hardly more than a ruin left of the once «proud» house. She placed herself by an old tree by the gate. One step more forward and she vanished into thin air.

In a rush of fire and colors she returned to Northfield. Gabi's room, the Green Rose itself had expanded into the street. They had waited for her, Gabi, Jason, Everett, Stacy… Many people had arrived at the evening market. Jill sensed the entire scale of emotion from them, sensed attraction and hatred, reluctance and benevolence, admiration and contempt…

She nodded to them all, grinning in pleasure and contempt.

So many had been pulled here, to this miniature world. Herself, mutants, witches, others. A few had come here to stop what happened here, but most sought and found it because they wanted Freedom. They had liberated themselves and no longer had any difficulty seeing and sensing what was right in front of them, right before their nose.

They had all come from faraway, actually or mentally, searching for something they would never find. What they had truly done was to make a Journey, making it without moving, without taking a physical step, a journey in the mind and thought, back to their Self, to the edge of the universe.

Dance little man. Dance the dance of life. Death is just something happening in the interim of each dance.

The eagles flew out of the gray shadow. They had all arrived at this place as agents of change and together they were a fire able to rock the forces of heaven and Earth.

They found themselves here, now, on the evening of October 30, 2005.

And their time had come.

CHAPTER TWENTY-ONE: Unmasking - All Soul's Night

Partytown, Partytown, Partytown, the many kids in the streets and the fields sang with and without voice.

The Pumpkin Man stuck his head up everywhere, smiling his wild and sinister smile. Smoke rose and fell in the air, as song and dance varied in intensity. Smoke and fire mixed in chaotic order, unabridged joy side by side with the ominous. Jill loved it. She froze down her spine in delight.

It was happening, all around her, visible and tangible.

Partytown, Partytown, Partytown…. Night slipped away almost imperceptibly. Day slipped away almost imperceptibly. The first masks appeared early in the morning. The city… ground to a halt. One could wonder if all the traditional activity… stopped. Twilight descended and fire was lit everywhere, also in large oil-barrels placed randomly around town. No cars drove up or down Main Road. Even the streets of Newtown were basically deserted. Doors and windows flapped back and forth in the wind. People had left their houses, not caring about closing or locking anything. Main Street was filled with people. So much was happening, as more and more individuals were throwing off their inhibitions. They entered Oldtown by the church and one of the first things they saw was a brown-skinned, sweaty creature jumping back and forth over a fire. She turned and turned in a whirl of smoke. Except for the long raven hair nothing was covering her anywhere.

A group of midget trolls approached her howling and shouting, dragging her away. Jill allowed it, laughingly as she listened to their song:

> Big Bad Wolf wandered on the forest trail
> Big Red Riding Hood after a while he met
> «How you have grown»
> He smiled with his big, shiny teeth
> She smiled back at him
> So sweetly and so innocently
> «So I can eat you faster», she sang
> Big Red Riding Hood devoured
> Big Bad Wolf whole and raw

The Witch laughed out loud, as she dismissed the children, as she continued her Walk. She met male eyes on her trek. Some looked away, but some didn't. Sensuality burned within her as a low, pleasant flame. Arousal pulsed and waned, and she enjoyed it to the max. There was no voice inside her telling her to cover herself. She felt no shame, and this time there was no doubt, this time she knew it was a good thing.

Stacy waited for her. Stacy and Loeh. She hurried to them. They were both dressed. Stacy gave Jill a robe. Jill was nice girl and robed. All three of them set course for Circle. They found a vacant room there. Earlier in their life the twins had wondered why tables awaited them, in a room filled with people. They did so no longer.

Loeh started shaking the moment she put her foot inside the familiar place. They pushed her gently inside. Door closed discreetly behind them. The twins didn't touch her. They didn't need to anymore. Their power had grown to such a degree that they no longer needed to touch people physically, even when it came to enhanced, expanded mental touch.

They liberated her from their web, cut all the threads they had used to bind her. In the inner landscape of the mind her *Ti Bon Ange,* her ID shone freely once more. She fell on her knees and in her mind her Self did the same. She hid her face in her palms.

– We have cut you to shreds, Jill threw challenging at her. – You must make yourself whole again. You must decide if you're a servant, an obedient tool, a blindly obedient slave. Did you enjoy it? To be a victim, being dependent on the slightest whim of a superior Being? In that case you can remain in the same position, shaking your tail, awaiting the next command.

– We will enjoy refitting your collar, Stacy said scornfully. – You were a sweet and attentive slave.

A resolute light appeared in the naked face. She didn't once remove her attention from the two while fighting her way up. They observed with satisfaction how she once more filled her own, inner space.

– I feel so small, Goddess, she said evenly. She addressed them as one person, the way she had always seen them. – You forced me to grow, without that being my expressed wish.

– As we will do with everybody, Jill stated. – We were practicing. You should be honored.

She was. And ashamed because of it.

– There isn't that much of a difference between you and what we're fighting.

– But the differences, few as they are, are crucial, Stacy pointed out. – You know that, now, now that you know who you are, priestess, Loa…

An image, familiar, painful appeared through her inner vision. A woman and a man swaying above a winding snake, under a rainbow. «The Serpent is the Earth. The Rainbow is the sky. Between those two extremes we must all live and die». Understanding flashed in her eyes. She shrunk a bit before straightening fully. The creature standing there before her, looking at her from all sides, in a thousand different ways, was both the old and the returned power. She both was and wasn't what she fought. A major part of what would push beyond both the Serpent and the Rainbow.

– I'm yours to command, Goddess, she said aloud. – I submit myself freely, eagerly and without reservations.

She had finally found the confidence she had sought so long, an inner strength big enough to confidently follow something bigger than herself.

2

– I don't know… Everett was a study in insecurities and restraint. – There must be another way than…

The four all looked at Gabi playing and laughing with the younger children. None of the four really spoke or said anything or even thought a thought. Perhaps it truly was possible to think too much.

Stacy spoke with authority and perfect calm. There was no room for doubt in her.

– I have Death in my right hand and Life in my left hand. What would you want me to do?

Jill and Jason didn't say anything. They didn't need to.

It took time, but finally Gabi looked at them and she stopped moving. She hesitated a bit before shushing the children off and approaching the quartet.

– I'm ready, she stated bravely.

The others still couldn't bring themselves to speak.

– As you have probably read Ted Warren spoke already in 1975 about Nature retaliating against misuse.

– Yes, he took part in a squatting project in London, didn't he? Jason was unusually eager. – In spite of the high number of buildings being squatted the establishment made that particular one its pet project.

– He and the Janus Clan are a part of this retaliation, this returned force, this twilight storm… Gabi proceeded. – As are we.

Music. From everywhere. Both what they heard through their ears and on a deeper level, expressing what could neither be expressed nor denied.

– Don't be sad, the girl said, a slight irritation discernible in her thin voice. – There's rain, there's sun, both are inevitable, and what's what no one can say… right?

Jill lifted her head. She sensed it already… a change in the Earth and the sky. Something… had been liberated, something long dormant. The sea had risen slowly and now the flood was here. It was happening. The transformation had begun. Magick returned from its long exile.

– It's time. We should make the final preparations.

Surprisingly enough, Everett said that. The others nodded.

Jill didn't get any feeling of surprise. Anubis' words, the entire scene made her experience a sense of Déjà vu, a «phantom memory», as it was called. She turned dizzy. And she knew. Lillith knew the memory to be true. Something still bothered her, had bothered her a considerable period of time. Most revelations, especially of this kind, revealed themselves late.

Late… The smile came easily. She still found it hard to think of herself as a spirit, a paranormal being more than this body, a psyche, a soul, thousands of years old. A wound, a string shaking in the quiet darkness told her that understanding should/had to come.

Soon.

She saw it all from above, as if from the sidelines. An ominous chord. Jill and Stacy had auras almost touching each other now, even while walking steps apart. An image strangely comforting. It was as it was supposed to be. The party had begun. Let the party begin.

– This… all this is hopeful, she said thoughtfully, scornfully. – But the Machine marches on. The Gray Fog will one day cover the entire Earth, if it isn't stopped.

– The gray fog? A boy, one of a group of youths walking with them wondered.

– The Gray Fog, Jill stated. – The concrete, glass, plastic and steel of technology, the spread of civilization devouring the land, the very air we breathe. The tailspin suicide run.

– We will stop it, Stacy assured them. – We will stop its mad rampage.

– How? The boy asked, both curious and afraid.

– By becoming an unstoppable force, Jill said, looking at Jason, taking his hand.

A lot of people usually did follow them around. Usually, they sat down and spoke with them, took their time, but now time was running short, short as the shrunken, yellow grass on the lawn they passed. They hurried on.

– Wait. The boy and a smaller group than minutes ago kept tailing them.

They stopped.

– It's… time? The boy looked at them. – Can we come with you?

– Everybody is welcome, Jason said. – Everybody not coming at us with poisonous words in their mouth and burning crosses in their hands.

– Are you sure? Jill said teasingly, darkly touching the boy under the shaking jaw. – It will certainly be interesting, but not necessarily altogether pleasant.

– We want to come, he said stubbornly. He was probably several years older than her and he felt like the child in her presence.

The bigger group moved on. It continued to grow as they closed in on the Hill, like strands tying itself around the rope, strands of night and fire burning ever fiercer in the darkening twilight.

He was still out of breath as he struggled to keep her pace.

– So, do you have any message to the world's leaders gathered on Mount Selmon this week?

– You're a journalist… She grinned at him.

He reddened.

– Don't mind her, Jason laughed. – She has made it her mission in life to make life miserable for all panting dogs chasing her…

– This suicide life will beat you down, Jeremy, she told him. – It does that to everybody, who doesn't leave it.

She paused, before walking on, looking at him with the eyes in the back of the head.

– As for your question: The «leaders» of the world have always closed themselves off from the people they're supposed to serve, but they, the modern version, haven't used barbed wire until recently, not protecting their «public meetings» with physical walls and an army of uniformed thugs. They will always find new ways to protect themselves from the wrath of their «subjects».

– Spineless politicians, out of touch with everyone. A girl spat somewhere from the back of the non-linear line.

– Yes, Jill said.

She saw it all from above, from a number of ever-changing positions, in flashes and turns.

– She knew your name, a girl whispered in Jeremy's ear. He walked a few steps, perhaps as much as ten steps behind the main group.

Yes, Pauline, I do.

Pauline shook. Suddenly Jill stood there before her. Pauline looked forward, and Jill was still there, too. She gasped. The shimmering figure levitated a few centimeters above the dusty ground.

– This is just to convince you we don't have our own intelligence service…

Jill laughed and the laughter seemed to come from everywhere.

I'm drunk with power.

She didn't share that thought with anyone (except the sister… sisters share everything).

The floating figure faded like a mirage. The group made their way with Gabi in their midst, surrounding her in a protective bubble. Eyes and more from the hundreds of gathered people followed them. The trickle running down Jill's spine turned thick as ice. She sensed the pressure in the air, long before she saw Daniel come running. He didn't exhibit any panic either without or within, but a guarded look was in place in his eyes.

I've sensed his coming for a long time.

She thought.

– Two new arrivals called from the bus station. I did my best to convince them, but they insisted on not entering the city, without being initiated by «Jill herself».

Several of the witches and others arrived running, out of breath. Jill frowned. Vicky, leading Adam, Kate, Udo and Andrea stopped before them, with worry in their eyes. Others stopped, a bit further away, doing their best to hide theirs.

Completely in vain, of course. Jill smiled.

– Mobs have gathered in several places in Newtown, Udo gasped, more worried than she had ever sensed him. Not so strange really. He knew very well what was happening.

Everything is happening simultaneously, like we reckoned it would.

– We knew this while rolling the ball, she said aloud. – The elite, the establishment won't just roll over and play dead. They won't give away their hard-won power voluntarily anywhere. Not here either.

– Everything must proceed as planned, Stacy stressed. – We can't postpone it any longer without jeopardizing the entire set-up.

– I'll go, Jill decided. – You'll manage without me for a while. But know *this:* I will find my way to Fire Lake, even if I must go through the fires of Hell.

Stacy nodded. Once. Once was enough.

– I'll go with you, Vicky stated.

Jill sensed that she couldn't be persuaded not to and allowed it.

– You, too. She called to her Adam, Andrea, Udo, Kate, Tam and Kieron.

Like a train leaving the station she removed herself from the majority of whom she belonged, where she most of all wanted to go. But the train she boarded now, that train she had been on her entire life.

Time to jump off…

Soon.

They sat course down Main Street. The clearly diminished group passed the church and its long, horrific shade fell on them. They wanted to walk in a big circle around it, but kept their calm.

– This is a monstrosity, Adam growled. – It's destroying humanity, destroying nature, all life.

An older woman, disappointed, bitter scowled at them.

– How dare you, she cast their hatred at them. – You're desecrating Our Lord's House. You should be ashamed of yourselves.

– We dare much, Jill replied furiously. – You can't imagine how much we dare, tired old shell. The shame is on you.

They pushed on, entering Newtown. Tall, modern buildings, a modern look, groomed as a part of the future Metropolis. A shade now, its matter ghostly, unreal. Jill felt the southern scent in the air, felt a southern smell deeper than any southern smell. What once had been was once again.

– Do you remember the parties you joined? She said, speaking to no one in particular. – Some of them were wild, but you weren't content. You wanted it to really break loose. The party, the people present, you wanted them to throw all caution to the wind. Well, my friends, this is it…

The sound of her voice was both cheerful and ominous, as they had learned to know her.

Eyes, frightened, envious, curious followed them as they crossed the unofficial demarcation line between the two parts of the city. People saw nothing special at first. But after a block or two… Wasn't the grass taller, greener and thicker? The poor, tiny, isolated collections of grass growing between the sidewalk and the road… started growing and multiplying. It had to be. No weeds had been removed recently. There had been no need. Suddenly there was a lot more of it. All plants and even the domestic growth seemed to… strut its stuff, almost threatening. Those who looked could virtually see Jill Stafford's footprints. The moment she lifted her foot there was a clear green print in its wake. The same with Kieron Dane, less distinct. *Life grows in the wake of the Witch.*

Felix West followed the tracks, some distance behind. He had ditched the video camera, all kinds of recording devices actually. He had two eyes, two ears and most of his faculties intact, thereby needing no extra, artificial tools.

He saw the same as everyone else. The clear green footprints appearing, seemingly by themselves a few seconds after the girl pressed her naked feet on the dusty ground. But he also saw more. He noticed the ravens. They had learned… discretion lately. Instead of flying close to the witch they occupied treetops and roofs some distance away, but they moved as she moved, flew as she flew. Sweat poured from his wide-open pores. His raving mad thoughts alone did that. The heat he experienced as second rate, incidental… He followed footprints, he followed the seamy ravens, like a bloodhound following… Yes, tracks of blood.

Using his inner eye, another eye he didn't want, he saw the scene be replayed time and time again. He recalled every little detail, even after all this time. His resolve increased to the point where it turned visible in his pale face. He had wanted to forget, put it all behind him, but now he finally realized that such occurrences should never be put behind anyone, should never be forgotten. How painful, how welcome it was, the pain making him keep moving forward.

Doomsday drums thundered the wastelands. Jill would have heard them, even if no one else could have. Today, though the shadow lightning struck so loud that everybody quite simply had to catch their beat. The act of pressing hands to the ears was no good. The drums thundered on a much deeper level than that.

Ugly faces glared at the small group from gatherings along their route. Creatures devoid of any mask threw rocks viciously, hatefully. Jill returned them easily, unscrupulously. The creatures attempted to protect themselves with their arms, in vain. They fled in panic. *That's right. Flee, like the sheep you are, like the hens you aspire to be.*

The city, yes, the entire area wasn't about to explode. It had already done so. Good. It was as it should be. Castles of sand collapsed from the pressure of a few, lazy waves. The looting had begun. Windows were broken and shops emptied. Police officers fired indiscriminately and hit many. But they were forced to halt the shooting contest fairly quickly or it would have been a massacre. But the berserker rage behind every strike with the ugly clubs hardly made that method any less… fatal. Somewhere inside the young girl felt sick, sick to the bone. She pushed on. This, bad as it was, was nothing compared to what was in store.

Torches. With her farsense, she saw insane creatures waving their torches in the air. Idiots! Didn't they know that fire was her friend?

The bus terminal had been built where the river was at its wildest. Now, with the river so reduced in stature, this was the only place for miles and miles where there was sufficient humidity in the air for it to give life to the dots of fog surrounding the modest brick building. Jill peeked inside (without being close to the building). It was as if her eyes flew through the night on wings of eagles. No dangers hid in there, none she recognized or was capable of recognizing.

The small group entered the twilight misty space. At least half of the light bulbs inside had been broken. It was late in the evening, at a time when more than two people were rare. Tonight, the place was filled to the brim. Some stood there, shaking in their tracks, set to take the first bus out of town, holding on to their luggage, their dearest belongings, as if it was everything they owned in this world, and suddenly it was. Some had just arrived, but didn't dare leave the building. To Jill the two newcomer witches stood clearly out from the crowd. They wore ordinary clothes. The hair was well done. They had attempted to look ordinary to the point of exaggeration. But the way they truly differed from most people wasn't in any obvious, outside appearance, but more in the way they moved, talked, walked and even stood still. Jill had learned to recognize those signs, the signs of a free human being, independent of whether or not they were born with additional talents. She didn't need to see their aura, but she did. It was almost blinding in its brilliance. These were two mighty witches. She knew they weren't attempting to hide anything from her. They allowed her access, as deep as she wanted, without resisting. Not that it would have done them any good. She was done tiptoeing around people, done caring about finer points of present-day morality. They were a veritable source of information these two. But it bothered her that they knew so much about her, and she had known so little about them.

– Greetings, the woman spoke with a minor, undetermined foreign accent. – We're co-leaders of a Coven in Boston and come here as representatives for our brothers and sisters. Your light shines like the sun in our minds. We're yours to command, *Goddess.*

They knelt graciously, submitting themselves to her mercy.

– Celeste, Elmore… I am Jill, called Raven… Nice to meet you. Welcome to us.

She reached out to them with her arms. They took one each and she pulled them up. They met her direct, penetrating look with a quiet calm. The initial awe lingered in both of them.

– Your power, Goddess, Celeste whispered. – I've never experienced its like. I've never heard about anything like it, except in the legends and myths. We're like ants in your presence.

– Are you? Lillith snarled. – Are you like sheep bowing your head to the mighty?

And her rage made them shrink, made them ashamed.

– No, Raven. Celeste stood straight. – We're our own beings.

Jill wanted to shake them, to test their mettle. What was happening outside prevented that. On the other side of the street the mob had gathered. She reached out with the arms of her mind and met a wall of distrust, hatred and intolerance - three aces making the present-day world turn. She considered contacting Delphi, making her «pick them up».

No. Her facial features hardened. Her own recent acid words to Celeste and Elmore echoed and burned within her. She - like everyone else - was free to go wherever she wanted. And no matter how many others who didn't want to use their birthright, she would never more let go of it.

The night sky was filled with stars. Smoke lingered in the air. There was hardly a single draft anywhere. Lights, from both natural and artificial fires were reflected in the many changing walls, a pattern never staying the same. Was that what was «wrong»? Couldn't these people stomach the fact that the world was and would always be different from their perception of it?

The mob had stopped throwing rocks, but they were still many and shouted curses at the tiny group. Citizens not outdoors this night had barricaded themselves indoors. They were perfectly aware of what was going on, what was going to happen. They remembered.

Jill made a useless attempt at blinking sweat from her eyes. There was something… something definitely threatening lurking in these shadows. The crowd could be a threat, naturally, but there was more. She felt directly threatened. Raven sent out her wings, to her side, back and front. She sought in vain what was hidden. She knew it was there, but was unable to localize it.

And there, and there, and there…

All the energetic, excited thoughts attacked her, and it was so hard to divide them. Feet moved in tandem with her feet. She recognized a thought pattern, virtually indistinguishable from her own. It wasn't her own, wasn't Stacy, but somebody imitating it. She felt she had almost identified it several times, until it slipped away anew. So similar, so opposite, muted, controlled, suppressed… A fleeting image, a glimpse of something, like an image of a spirit or a ghost passing her thoughts… a pyramid. All light was gone, all warmth. And she realized

realized

where all the flashes came from, all the flashes hitting her simultaneously.

Flashes, flashes of the mind. She stood on all fours in the midst of the violent dustbins. Her friends writhed on the ground, even more helpless than she was. Feet, *feet,* close. She screamed, a wail of pain and suffering (it hurt, it hurt). Paralyzed, body, mind, paralyzed, paralyzzzzzd. None of the voluntary or motorized functions… functioned. She gasped, a painful laughter filled with mud, with immeasurable pain. She registered her arms being pulled up. One so brutally that her shoulder was dislocated, being pulled off the joint. She was dragged on her feet that way. She sensed deadly cold on her skin, the metal's ice-cold touch. Chained. Chained like a beast. Here, too. Here, too. In public. No difference. Her eyes started focusing again. All the water filling them flowed, jumped outwards, so very painful that, too. It hurt somewhere, somewhere. Torches oozed everywhere, she thought. She was coughing. Her eyes cleared. So short a time had passed, so very short. She had been awake and on guard constantly. Still, she and her friends had been captured with ease. Heavy chains, coated in silver. Eyes, two narrow wounds, focused on Scott Thompson. He held a strange apparatus in his hands. It looked like a gun, but it sparked. The majority in the mob believed his statement about this being an efficient weapon against the witches. But he lied. The «weapon» was merely a decoy. Jill glimpsed Joan Davis in the crowd, glimpsed the pale shadow of what she had been. Nine more, with the aura of a witch, muted, distorted to a horrible degree, ten altogether, a gestalt, a union of thoughts and powers. And Thompson was its Master. The witches' will had been broken. Then they had been brainwashed, taught to obey Thompson in all things. They were nothing but marionettes masquerading as human beings. No flashes. An invisible beam of Thought, a psychokinetic trust burning and paralyzing the nervous system of its victims. A method so brutal, so vicious that Jill hadn't even considered using it.

– … our fault, Celeste cried in despair.

– I will never again hear such bullshit from you, Jill snarled. – This is, of course, the fault of those who have done this to us, *do you hear.*

Jill just managed to register Celeste's wide-eyed nod, before a man stepping forward rammed a long wand into her belly. As she helplessly bent forward, she received another hit on her mouth. She felt something break and blood flowed from within, flowed between her lips and onto the ground.

– The bastards don't even dare touch us, she spat

Her eyes focused on the man with the stick, and he started backing off.

The chain was pulled again. Hard. Harshly. The pain cut through her. Thompson stood there, intense, strong, ruthless.

– You demon spawn are disgusting to us, he said triumphantly, in superior confidence. – We won't touch you more than we have to, for what needs to be done.

They were pulled away by rope and chain, pushed by sticks and kicks.

Faces swam before Jill. Masks, grotesque, ordinary faces. Gloating hateful laughter. Echo - ho - ho ho-ooooo. Horrifying images of times past, times future. The shoulder hurt terribly. Her body hurt within and without. It healed quickly, but not as quickly as it would have if she could have helped. The pain, focus on the pain, the hatred.

The poison, that from the poisoned Earth and from eclipsed minds spread through her and she welcomed it. From the garbage-filled sea the ancient chant rose:

– Burn the witch, burn the witch. All witches must burn. They will burn in eternal damnation. We will look down at them from Our Father's Heaven. Thou shall not suffer a witch to live!

This wasn't anything new to her. She had been experiencing it (with variations) many times, so many times. The chapter she remembered best right now was from Madrid 1370 AD. Everything had been different then. She had been alone and close to powerless. Only one creature in the crowd had known what an evil this was. And now? When she was more alone than ever? Was that the price of power? An alienation bordering on insensitivity? No, that couldn't be right. She hated like everybody else, only far stronger. All humans lived as they died - alone.

She wondered about one detail in particular, wondered with a skewed grin confusing and angering them further. If they understood what was happening. Oh, they were fully aware of the fact that they were about to burn and murder a fellow human being and cared little about that, in their intolerance and ignorance… But they didn't realize its *significance.* They didn't hear, didn't see themselves, how their basic behavior, how everything was changing. Last time, during the Burning Times it had signaled a preliminary end of the Age of Magick. Now, another was born. After this night, no matter how long it lasted, how it ended everything would be changed.

Her face exposed her suffering. She couldn't help it. She pulled desperately in the chains, the physical and those clinging to her mind like a wet blanket. It led only to more pain. She didn't care, didn't didn't didn't. She was so weakened. It was easy for Thompson and his slaves to keep her mind, her will dulled. What she saw in the ten's mind made her sick, sick sick. Of hatred. He had bound them to him, the same way Anton Berkowitz had attempted with her. The gestalt whispered sweet words of seduction to her, but she resisted. They couldn't control her. Therefore, she had to burn. And Law and Order would be reinstated.

Faces writhed and twisted within her vision. She recognized names among the mob. Peter Barryman, Lieutenant Hugh O'Keefe, Joseph Parnell… Hester was here. And Stephen Bachman. She wanted them to come close, wanted it with such fervor that it hurt and alleviated the pain. But they, her keepers only came close when they had to, during short moments, and never in contact skin to skin.

They dragged her and her brothers and sisters to the pyre and she was helpless. She couldn't prevent it. They never gave her the slightest chance. They knew she was dangerous, had gathered enough information to know that.

They believed.

She felt him rise towards complete awakening, felt Samhain rise. Not so strange, really, as he gained strength from every little bugger dressing up. The end of summer, but also its beginning. He who every year this night in past times had called to him the condemned and offered them another change, a last straw. One who belonged in a kingdom of death quite different from where the Bishop of California ruled supreme. Jill sensed Samhain's increasingly powerful presence, but realized that neither he nor the others heard her and the other chained people's plea for help. She «heard» Thompson's scornful laughter. Her hatred, it had to be stronger than his. He tempted her with life, but if she gave in she would be *his* and it would result in a death far worse than what waited further ahead.

I'm going to bury you all, he raged. *Those among you I can't break I'll burn, disintegrate in Hell's Flames.*

And something valuable hardened further within her.

The humans around her… Nature's fire brightened their faces, exposing them ruthlessly… and she saw them for what they were. Sweat kept flowing into her eyes, but her vision stayed painfully clear. She saw their gloating, their intolerance and everything ugly inside express itself. And not even her hatred, making the blood burn like lava in her veins kept the disgust from dominating inside her.

They approached the local garbage disposal center, a pyre at the top of the small human-created metal hill. She could see it and so could the others, her siblings in spirit, suffering and dying by her side. So far no more than branches, pieces of wood and a pole. But everything awaited the finishing touch. The fire awaited liberty patiently. It had happened already, really, it merely waited for its time to come. Or perhaps it would never happen, as anything other than a fever hot nightmare. She was hot and cold alternatively. She had never been ill her entire life, she believed, so she couldn't really decide if she exhibited the actual symptoms, but she had heard (she believed) they were similar to her suffering right now.

The wind was blowing, she heard it, but in no way did she feel it against her body. And she heard the infernal song, penetrating her body and soul. An insanely flat sound, like black, deep jewels transformed to dust. They kept torches close to her face. She coughed and gasped for air and hurt eyes searched the crowd for one single friendly face, in vain.

The procession, the two lines ended up on each representative side of hatred's altar. Those who watched, those who were content with that, and those who needed a physical outlet for their fear and thundering distrust towards anything even remotely different. The king on his hill, Scott Thompson pushed his torch close to the girl's sooty face… and its fire died. They stared incredulously. Not the slightest flame remained, not the slightest smoke. Thompson was like paralyzed in the cunning eyes' lure. He couldn't look away.

– Don't look at me, he hissed. – Don't you dare look at me!

– You've seen something resembling this before, haven't you, Scott? She grinned, she grinned distorted, horribly. – Seen it look straight through you, exposing you mercilessly… And you're sore afraid, afraid that everybody will know you for what you are…

– Shut up. He slapped her, slapped her several times. – SHUT UP!

He stepped back, finally, after a long period of hits and kicks. The girl's head hung, as if she was dead.

Felix West stood in hiding, a stretch, a good stretch away. He saw what happened unbelievably clear, as he had a long time ago. He had thought it was behind him. The thoughts a few minutes earlier burned in his mind. He had been right then. Such atrocities never could or should be forgotten. Three names sounded repeatedly in his mind: *Bennett, Webster, Robertson.* He saw their equals in this mob. The chief of police, the mayor, the priest. The rifle started slipping in his sweaty hands. Never if he would allow it to happen one more time. Never, never, never ever.

Jill Stafford was separated from her brethren and led before a distant, regal, seething Scott Thompson. Her eyes focused on what he held in his left hand: A wand with a golden skull at the top. The sight did something to her. A many faced well of emotions coursed through her All. She started shaking. The black flash in the smooth surface blinded her.

– Kneel, she-demon, he intoned. There was no mercy in him, nothing she could hook onto, no hope of him, who threatened her, saving her.

The clot of spittle, blood and bile hit him precisely on the chin and spread like wildfire. He shouted in insane desperation. It rained hits from sticks and branches of young trees. She fell to her knees in infinite pain. In her thoughts danced lights and shadows, down the path of humiliation and degradation. Did fighting serve any purpose? Wasn't it here, while thinking about it she had been on her way her entire life? Here. If she had occasionally walked right, or left, or anywhere, what did it matter?

Sister! She cried in her despair. No reply. No indications of anyone hearing anything. The pain reaffirmed its attack, stronger than ever.

Tiny tears dripped on the ground before her. Tears of despair and relent. And witches in times past had had it far worse and suffered far worse torture than she had. She understood now why they had walked willingly to the stake and the pyre. They wanted it to be *over.*

– You brown-skinned bitch. She heard Olivia, screaming in her ear. – Now, you'll get what's coming to you.

The point of the wand, the skull was pushed under her jaw, forcing her to lift her head, to reveal her shame.

– She's ready now. Thompson sounded as if he did her a favor.

She saw herself in his mirror, the empty, staring eyes in the dirty and wet face of a young girl. She seemed like a worthy snack indeed. She heard the laughter of the males around her. They dragged her the last stretch to the place of execution, and they tied her to the pole in a hurry. They followed orders, though they may have wanted to be a bit closer, a bit longer, now, when brutal lust had supplanted the fear.

Torches were lifted dramatically and lowered at the dry material Jill had been placed on.

Vicky screamed.

– Take me instead, she begged, in the short moment of silence. – Please.

– We will take you, harlot, Peter Barryman shouted. She fell, after a brutal hit in her back. – Your father has more sons and daughters in which he can comfort himself, after suffering your heathen, unforgivable sins.

– You're insane, she gasped. – You're all completely…

He had lifted his stick when a thunderous crack was heard, a crack rolling between empty buildings. Felix West appeared out of the darkness, out of nothing. He held a rifle with a smoking barrel. The mob stared indecisive at him and each other.

– That's right, he said harshly. – Who do you think you are? How can you in any possible way even imagine the thought of doing this, that no matter what the youths have done, and they have done nothing, that it can be any worse than this?

– What are you doing, Felix? Hester asked incredulously. – Go home and sleep off the hangover or whatever is wrong with you, and allow us to proceed with our holy deed.

– That will never happen. He lifted his weapon and directed it at her. – I will shoot down the first who take a step towards me or the girl, I mean it…

A number of shots were fired, and he was hit from all sides. At least one of the bullets went through him and hit another. No one seemed to notice.

– Thus ends all traitors. Thompson raised a fist.

A flash for Jill's eyes. More than one. Every time her vision seemed to clear more. She saw the wand with the skull in the hand. She saw it become a sword, a sharp blade cutting through everything and everyone. Not in his hands.

In hers.

– Let it be, he cried in a dramatic gesture and lit the pyre.

Flash. The young, unpolished, always unpolished Jill Stafford stood inside a lit room, pressing her face against the window glass. She pressed harder, staring hard and long into the deepest darkness… and she saw the fire.

The fire grew, hungrily, greedily, so powerful that those in the front row instinctively attempted to pull back. A hopeless task. The entire compact mass stood there like a wall and blocked their retreat. Andrea howled, completely beside herself. Scornful laughter everywhere silenced her. Gasping she crouched on the ground, in a deep, black well where the sky seemed to fly away from her, faster than light.

– This is our fault, Celeste insisted heartbroken.

– Yes, Elmore said with bowed head. – If we hadn't come…

– No, Tam stated simply, pulling her chains with all her strength.

– THAT'S RIGHT. Jill's voice thundered across the street, heard by everybody. – DON'T YOU DARE BLAME YOURSELF. THE ACTION IS THEIRS, THE GUILT IS THEIRS AND THEIRS ALONE, THESE SLUGGISH CREATURES DARING TO CALL THEMSELVES HUMAN. AND THEY WILL PAY FOR EVERYTHING, ABSOLUTELY EVERYTHING, believe me. They have paid already, but that's nothing compared to what's to come.

NOTHING

Many screamed and ran away in panic, but distance gave no salvation and somewhere, deep down they knew that.

Laughter and scorn followed the runners on their way, but it had a touch of uncertainty in it, somewhere on its edge. Thompson lifted and lowered his wand. The chanting, monotone choir rose deafening from the mob, repeated like a mantra, without the slightest variation.

– THE WITCH IS BURNING THE WITCH IS BURNING THE WITCH IS BURNING WITCHES MUST BURN ALL WITCHES SHALL BURN

Thompson smiled triumphantly.

Jill could no longer feel the tight ropes on her body. She SCREAMED, a sound beyond description of pain and rage, as the flames surrounded her, one that no one present had ever thought they would hear. An experience they were convinced would never repeat itself. Something so beyond their experience that it felt completely and unconditionally unreal. Suffering, the concrete and real, now attacking and blowing their senses to pieces had always been something distant, irrelevant to them.

Felix West was still alive. He could hardly believe it, shot asunder as he was. And the pain, growing in jumps convinced him that he truly was alive. And unbelievably as it seemed, he could sense the other who had taken a bullet, that he was indeed much closer to death than he was himself. Felix lay there on his back and had such a marvelous view, such a beautiful line of sight to the stars. He had never seen them quite like that before. Never something even remotely close to this. He heard not an insignificant number of the crowd cry softly. They were harassed by everybody standing close to them, and had to feel very alone, but they kept their small act of defiance going. He fought to keep his eyes open, but they slipped close. It didn't matter. He saw better than ever before in his life. He sighed, couldn't decide whether or not he was still breathing. Life, life itself had been something remote to them. It was all changing now.

She felt it, in the last seconds of her life, Jill Stafford, like an empty house burning down. Her clothes falling off. Every single piece of skin burning. Her hair, eyes and ears charring. The inner Self of everybody here wanting to burn witches and it was UGLY. She thought, she reasoned, a place inside this heap of ashes? She lived anywhere? Her heart was still there. She heard it beat, incredibly hard and fast. The hatred of they who had done this to her. It flowed in the air around her, as something she was able to smell, taste and feel. It… strengthened her. She reached for it with her night claws and pulled it inside. She lit the fire and let it burn.

Freely, without boundaries.

Felix crouched there, moaning, unable to tell how long time had passed, if it was one second, one hour, one minute. He couldn't look at the poor chained witches, laying there awaiting their turn. He saw Tam struggle to free herself. The air, the very air was strange, shimmering in shadow. Every time he drew breath it was as if his blood turned to fire. A policewoman hit Tam with her rifle. But to do that it had been necessary to come close to her. Too close. The big girl grabbed her. Kieron charged her from behind, putting the chains around her neck in a strangling grip. A male officer came running. Tam grabbed him good and with a snarl… she tore him apart. The huge, powerful built man was quite simply torn apart. Many guns were fired. Tam stood her ground. Several others fell with desperate cries. Others just stood there frozen like marble statues. Felix managed to turn his head now. He saw without a shadow of a doubt Tamara Farley take several hits. Blood gushed from the holes. The first chain broke. The first one died, he who had taken the bullet penetrating Felix… and Felix… stared… did he see an energy, the psyche, the phantom image rise in the air… and then fade?

ding

At first, he was unable to identify the sound. He heard the sound of metal against metal, chains against chains unbelievably clear. But… instead of being sharp, as it was supposed to sound, the sound was soft… As if the metal wasn't as hard as it should be…

As if it had been softened by heat, in a forge hotter than anything that could possibly exist anywhere near this wretched place.

Ridiculous. He hummed to himself. He gasped hysterically.

The cry-out rising from the gathering crowd in that moment contained something beyond fear, beyond reason as they knew it.

The second man died. He had been dead the moment Tam tore him apart. But still he took his time dying. Most people were shocked by that. They couldn't imagine anybody living even for a second with «wounds» that severe.

And the thickness in the air intensified. They felt it. They did.

Round and round within the circle of hatred, it raged, the presence in their midst. The presence far beyond their pale wrath and hatred, the righteous anger they had felt so sweet just a few seconds earlier. In those few seconds containing an eternity, all their previous beliefs vanished as if someone was snapping their fingers.

And someone was.

She sensed the wind, she sensed it close, sensed every single nuance of its path. She saw them, saw them all, saw herself, through them, through herself. The pyre's flames rose sky high, hiding completely the tiny pole and the small, insignificant figure tied to it. Suddenly, there was a breath of air, or traction in the air, a hole, a vacuum that everything rushed to. The pyre was like vanquished. In its place hovered a human figure burning hotter than any pyre they had seen. While it, she, it rose in the air it was as if the fire was pulled into the inarguable female form growing and reforming, naked and frighteningly beautiful, piece by piece of skin, eye lashes, ears, distinctive features. Burned surface turned to festering sores and then, abruptly to smooth skin. What had been peeled off returned layer by layer. Through two, three instants where nobody dared blink the raven hair grew back, shoulder length and swaying in the wind.

Eyes inverted to reveal only the white, stared straight through them all. She kept herself levitating above them, without moving the slightest from her chosen position. Everybody on the ground was like frozen, stuck in their place. They wanted to run most of them did. They didn't dare and they couldn't even if they had dared. An irresistible force kept them in place. The Goddess' face was placid, unmovable like a mask. It betrayed no emotion, nothing of what went on behind the mask. She was more beautiful than ever and that made her even more terrifying. They fell on their knees, in the grip of fear and awe and a paralyzing fundamental terror beyond any comparison and comprehension. She wasn't like a force of nature. She was a force of nature, a fire, torrential rain or a storm. It was unimportant how she used her Power. It was so strong that it surpassed any judgment. It was unimportant how they saw her, if she was «good» or «evil». The only thing that mattered was that *she was.*

No one dreamed about defying her.

– So now is the question. Do I make thou reap thy reward, gentle souls? Let what you intended for me, happen to you?

Was she happy or sad? Did that question have any meaning anymore? She felt the Power seething, to the tip of the nails on her fingers or longest hair, a power greater than she had imagined was possible. Not greater than she had imagined. The Power flowed into her from the humans below. Their hatred, their fear and everything else filled her to the brim. And it felt indescribable and intoxicating. She smiled and seemed even more frightening and remorseless. Well, right now it pleased her to show mercy…

Suddenly there were several versions of her wandering among them. There was no need for her to give them any form to look at, but that was her will. The Goddess' will be done. She laughed. Tam felt the enormous heat and all her wounds vanished as if they had never been. Felix sat up, confused. Chains fell off. Not one of the wounded members of the mob was healed. They started sobbing when they realized that the Goddess had denied them, cast them out of her favor. The one Tam had torn apart remained dead. The big elf felt no regret. She looked at the Goddess with boundless worship in her eyes.

One of the spirit-forms picked up the wand Thompson had dropped on the ground. It smiled to him. He stared straight through the shimmering, ghostlike creature. She kept her eyes on him for a short moment in time, then turned indifferently away. The phantoms faded. The wand flew up in the air, into the witch's left hand. A simple thought broke his influence over the shadow guard. They all abruptly awakened from the waken nightmare. All the strings from his hand were cut. After this, he had nothing left to lose. So small he was, so pathetic.

The Goddess took a final look at the crowd, before losing interest in them, too. To these, to the majority of them, she would be the Goddess. They deserved no better.

She picked up a call, a wave she no longer had any difficulties recognizing. Everything had become so much clearer now, everything alive. In a glimpse, in a storm filling out the darkness she shared her knowledge with everyone below. It would strengthen a few and crush the many. By that act she turned her body and her attention westward, and set course for Frazer Hill, with an ever-increasing speed. Like one the crowd followed her with their eyes as she flew over the rooftops, vanished into the darkness in a halo of fading embers.

Silence reigned. Not one of the grave, but one alive shortly before a birth. They who cried now did so openly and they shook in fear. People began to leave, walk, crawl, run. Those who remained gathered close in a wild mix of worry, cheerfulness and joy.

– It has started, Tam stated. – Our journey Home.

– … so wonderful, Andrea whispered with abandon in her eyes.

Felix still fought to gather his thoughts. It didn't bother him that much, though. For the first time in his life, he was busy *feeling*.

– Everything seemed to go the mob's way, he exclaimed, shaking his head. – A well planned, well directed show meant to emphasize prejudice and the power of establishment. But we *felt* it, didn't we? Something wasn't right, but very right. And in the last act everything was turned upside down. Everything exploded in the face of those who so strongly believed they had control. Glorious…

– A boomerang striking back, Udo said. – It's like Ted Warren and others have said. Everything is now returned to those who have thrown it. A tidal wave destroying the sandcastles of destruction. All the castles of sand there are.

Mutants and «normals» embraced each other, embracing the tidal wave within themselves.

– Let's go, Tam cried and waved. – You're all free to join us.

And almost all did. Tam stopped briefly, as she saw Joan pull back, a study in contradicting emotions. Tam attempted to make eye contact with the obviously disturbed girl and believed she did, too, but Joan kept retreating. Tam shook her head, both in regret and to shake off the tingling of sadness.

They went on their way. In the front walked the woman with the pointed ears, bigger than ever.

And that was how they all felt.

3

Joseph Parnell kicked open the doors to the church. The heavy wood hit the wall with a loud crack. He went straight down to the sacristy and grabbed two heavy cans of gasoline. Calm and centered he carried the cans up the stairs. He splashed the fluid on the floor, the benches, the walls, the carpets and eventually the altar and himself. A flock of the lost had stood in silence outside and watched. Now they entered the building and sat down on the wet benches. Not a word was uttered. Parnell placed himself before the altar with a clenched fist.

– GOD! He cried in a poisonous voice. – I and your sheep intend to spend the night here in your house. You have until the first light tomorrow to prove you're real. If you by then haven't given us irrefutable proof of your existence, we will stop worshipping you.

4

Raging through the night, she did, She Who Filled the Darkness. She was levitating, hovering, floating high above the ground by her own power. It started to dawn on her what it meant, what it signified, what she had become. What she did demanded no effort, no effort at all. She knew she had absorbed destructive energy from the gathering around the pyre, that and everything else. It was just energy, to be used as she desired. She wouldn't have had any chance of mastering a power on this level, unless she had also found the strength within herself, strength, not only to hold out the pain, but also to draw advantage from it.

The ice-cold rage's fog cleared slowly. The intoxicating passion remained. She understood why some gods in times past were known for their berserker rages in their contact with mortals. That or for keeping an indifferent distance. A middle ground was… difficult.

That stops this night, one way or another.

Flames erupted from Fire Lake. She let herself slipping further down to the temple at the center of the lake. A place filled to the brim of untapped power. Power she would use as she saw fit.

A figure rose up from there to meet her, an individual just as vibrant and vital as she was.

Stacy… the other Raven Moonstar.

They met face to face above the timeless structure. Dark colors flared between them, above what was a portal between worlds. Stacy spoke. Voice was both rough and soft.

– Since I was the dominating one, I could govern the focus of your thoughts, enshroud what I wanted. We're equals now, and thanks to you, unbelievably powerful…

Dark hot anger boiled within Jill, directed at the sister and everything and everyone, but she didn't allow it to distract her from the goal she and Stacy had formulated.

– The fire, she uttered in her hollow voice. – It isn't just flames, anymore. It's like a part of me. I can feel it touch the very air, the very firmament of… of Forever.

– Yes, Stacy breathed, as the flames started bathing her, too, burning off her clothes, and she closed her eyes in ecstasy, as she opened them, and they were like her sister's mirror of fire.

The brief imbalance righted itself. They would always be equals.

– I can't even imagine the world like humans think it is, Jill said softly, roughly.

– What we imagine is so much more, Stacy bristled.

They descended, entering the house through each their window, descending further into the deep. They *sensed,* without truly knowing what awaited them. The Unknown did. They left the old world behind. Forever!

5

Scott Thompson didn't think, except for rudimentary necessities like putting one foot in front of the other. He didn't notice much of the hectic activity in his surroundings. The bus terminal was far from empty even though it was close to the midnight hour. Nobody talked much. He didn't say a word, but merely placed the money on the tile, everything he had in his pockets, and he received his ticket.

– You're traveling far, I see? You're lucky, it's one of the first departures.

The clerk didn't seem to recognize him. At least she didn't expose any recognition, far less respect. Once this would have angered him, but now he just felt numb, and he kept his silence.

He waited there on a bench. In the ten minutes before his bus was called, he didn't move an inch. Even when he rose and walked his fellow passengers suspected him of being a walking dead man. One who had died and had yet to acknowledge the fact.

He sat stuck in a seat. His tie was crooked. His shirt was lacking several buttons. A gift from the ruckus on the garbage disposal gathering. His jacket was torn in more than one place. The stench of garbage prevailed.

Busses rolled out of Northfield, seemingly on an assembly line. Scott Thompson was just one more lemming hitting the road after losing his foothold, still wondering about how and where he had made a bad turn. He couldn't imagine why. He had never before needed an imagination. Like so many before him losing control he had been convinced there was no such animal.

He would never return.

6

Drums hardly heard were felt, a pounding in the gut. The wind was blowing even stronger. Heavy bass echoed through walls, rooms, floors, mountain, ceiling. In the heated night bodies chanted their intoxicating song. Thoughts hummed and danced into the dark. Lillith heard them without ears, saw them without eyes, where she was led and led herself through the catacombs below Fire Lake. What she sensed in these old walls didn't frighten her anymore. It gave her merely a pleasant, ominous tingling down her spine. That was okay. She had made up her mind. From now on she would worry even when there wasn't anything to worry about. She didn't need the many oozing torches to show her the way. Neither of her did.

Rupert and Priscilla lifted up one velvet curtain each, revealing the ornament-covered entrance and Stacy and Jill stepped into the steamy surroundings. Loeh stood on the right, heating water and soft towels. To the left Kieron stood and made a smoking brew. Kieron represented Nature's ruthlessness, Loeh its generosity. At the room's center, Gabrielle, its innocence and ancient knowledge stretched on a flat rock covered by carpets.

She rested on her belly. Morgana and Daniel, Adam and Kate massaged and oiled the sun-tanned, denuded young girl. Eyes were misty and the mouth half open. She breathed so quietly that it was hardly audible. She looked very young there on the slab, but the heavy scent from her sex left no doubt about her condition. If she had been available, she would have been irresistible to anyone looking at her. And she was. Irresistible. As she was meant to be.

Jill stroked her head, a comforting gesture. The girl watched her with trust in her dazed eyes, without any implication of rebellion.

I picked her, chose her for this, Jill thought. The very first time I saw her.

Ivan played the flute somewhere. The sound seemed to come from everywhere, from all the passageways leading here. The result was a deep, mystical tone stirring the mind. Lillith was pleased with him. Even she was unable to easily get a fix on his position.

– Raven, you're bleeding, Gabi said weakly.

Jill, and Stacy, too looked down on their hips. Both were bleeding from the scar. They stared irritated and slightly exasperated at each other, as they calmed themselves, attempting to heal the wound. Nothing happened. In a flow of rapid movements Jill grabbed a knife from a table and jerked it into the main vein in the thigh. That wound healed instantly, without spilling more than a few drops of blood, and so, seemingly by default did the hip wound, both their hip wounds.

Loeh dried the blood with warm cloths. It left a pleasant feeling. Jill and Stacy both closed their eyes briefly, immersing themselves in the moment.

Someone was approaching. Jill instructed the temple guards to let them in, without delay. Elmore and Celeste entered, as expected filled with devotion. They fell on their knees before Stacy and Jill. They remained thus, silent, with their head bowed.

– Speak! Stacy bade them. Jill couldn't make herself say it.

– You are h-her, Elmore stuttered.

– You are truly Moonstar, Celeste said awestruck. – She-Who-Fills-the-Darkness.

– *You have my permission to call me Selene or Diana or whatever you want, I've had many names, I'll have many more.* Everybody there, everybody guarding the doorways shuddered. The two sisters had been choiring, and it was no longer possible to discern the slightest between them, the two figures. – *Rise, now, quickly, before I transform you into toads.*

– The moon is many things, but not oppression, Elmore recited as he and his mate fought their way back on their feet. Celeste spoke meekly in her shame. – Forgive us, Raven, we were stupid.

– You were stupid, Jill said softly. The look she sent them before turning her back to them wasn't unkind.

Kieron had completed the brew. He lifted the cup and offered it to Jill with both hands. Jill accepted it and turned her attention to Gabrielle. The girl had sat up and sat there with her legs outside the rock. Loeh put towels and blankets around her, keeping them hot. The shaking persisted.

– I'm frightened, Raven, she said weakly.

– Don't be frightened, Jill said. – There's nothing to be frightened of.

The small, delicate hands closed around the cup. She didn't take her eyes off she who stood over her. She who had been reborn this darkness and had become so much more what she was.

– Angel of Vengeance, she mumbled, and she drank.
She lowered the cup. Loeh took it away. It didn't take long before the cheeks turned a deeper color and the eyes turned misty, the eyelids heavy.
Daniel took a step forward. Quite sudden. All attention turned to him.
– This isn't right.
The implication of desperation and resolve was evident in his voice.
– It is right, Jill said.
– You shouldn't judge us, Dan, Stacy said softly. – And absolutely not with the twentieth century narrow morality.
– She is honored, Kieron stated. – She will become One with us all…
Jill stopped him with a wave of her hand.
– I know, I realize that. Daniel pushed on, gritting his teeth. – But I want to be closer to her than that.
– You're sure? Stacy cut in him. – You have thought about it?
– I have thought, he said in a rasping voice.
Loeh gave him the yet smoking brew. Gabrielle smiled radiantly to him. He led it to his lips and drank the remaining fluid. Gabrielle had drunk exactly half.
He got unsteady on his feet almost instantly. Kate and Adam helped him sit down. They undressed him and started to massage, to oil his body, his hard muscles, the increasingly fever-hot skin.
Jill looked cheerfully at Kieron. He bowed to her, in acknowledgement and respect.
– Morgana, walk with me, Lillith bade.
Jill and Stacy left the room, with Morgana in their wake.
All preparation is complete. The hour of the dead is close. We stand on the threshold. Our stationary journey will soon be done.
Crowds of people had gathered in the great hall. But it was so big it could have hosted many more. The walls were glimpsed, not seen. Torches had been placed on them and large fires lit close to them. Glimpsed in spots of light that could just as well, for what they knew, be reflections in smoke. They imagined the ceiling up there somewhere, but they couldn't see it. Smoke and mirrors surrounded them, but now they knew it all for what it was. They had all traveled here from faraway… and their time… their time had come.
– Tell me, dear Morgana, what does this place tell you, the mountain, the rock itself?
– This is the work of one whose power is similar to mine, Morgana replied excited and muted both. – But I could never have done anything like this during a human lifetime.
– Your power will also be many times increased tonight…
Time passed. Nobody could tell how much. The vortex of moments span faster, but did that make time pass faster or slower? The pieces of events tended to be compressed, as one sailed down the river Styx, as one dared the raging rapids. This close to the Kingdom of Death, on its very threshold, Time slowed to a halt.
There were flashes of light and shadow, fire and life. They swam to the shadowy beach, walked into the forest. There was a mountain there, but it didn't necessarily surround them. And there was a forest and a beach, and the river and the sea.
They heard a pulse, a sound reverberating through the mountain, unable to tell if it was a drum or the sound of a beating heart.
Lillith walked nude among her subjects, among her peers. The silvery bluish of the moon and the reddish yellow of the fire warred there on the rock floor. She watched their faces as she touched them, as they gave her of themselves. There was a variety of people and opinions and viewpoints she had only rarely encountered before, but many, across the spectrum had the shining faces she had indeed encountered too many times before. These events, this gathering had all the signs of ending up as a new religion, if she allowed it. And if she did, could the Dollmaster, who had been present at the start of countless religions, be far behind?
A majority of the shining faces would fall easily in line. And most of the rest would also submit. There would be exceptions, there always were, but she would deal with them.
The pentacle drawn on the floor did seem to glimmer, in the shattering of moon and fire. No one

stood inside the circle. No one had walked close to it. Talk died slowly, the sound of voices faded. The three crossed the line. The floating Dust flashed briefly the moment they did. Morgana placed herself on her knees, on all fours inside the pentacle. In the last few minutes before everything let go another altar, another flat rock rose from the floor, a perfect match to the other, far older. Morgana sensed the skin of the twins touch her, felt their power surrounding her, penetrating her and nothing they wanted her to do seemed too hard.

Feel Death's Power, young Circe, doesn't it feel good?

… such a pleasure, Raven, such a terrible pleasure. Thank you, oh, thank you.

She followed the two as they left the pentacle, as they ventured out into the world. She recalled what Stacy had said not long ago. Was it just a short hour?

There was movement, movement everywhere. Morgana sensed it through the rock. She sensed the rock, the mountain itself.

– I'm getting the shakes, she mumbled

– What was that? Jason said, suddenly there by her side.

Fear touched her a moment before turning to courage, face to face with the ultimate demon.

– It begins, she said.

– It does, doesn't it? He shook his head in wonder.

Lillith stood somewhere on the floor, on the same level as everybody else. Still, everybody could see her. Jeremy Zahn, the journalist saw her stand before him, even though another girl stood there, too. A lot of people stood there, but she stood there, too.

– You can just as well stop filming, she said huskily. – Nothing will show. You will never write any of this down, or show it in any current media anyway.

She spoke to him, she looked at him. But suddenly she was looking at everybody else, too.

Raven Moonstar spoke solemnly, ironically, jokingly, intensively, as casually as if she sat in a chair in a quiet living room, having a conversation with just one single person.

– Welcome, Strangers, she cried. – We welcome all Strangers, coming here from afar, strangers in the society of their birth and to each other… until tonight. We have people present from all the four corners of the Earth here tonight, and from all those corners we shall find our Magick.

– Tonight, we're gonna call down the moon, Jill cried.

– Samhain, Lord of the condemned, we call upon you, to join us, Stacy shouted.

– Set, the serpent god, reveal thyself, Jason called.

Everett stepped forth from the shadows, stepping into the shadows. There was a gasp, as they saw his eyes, his serpent eyes.

– Thalama is with us tonight, he spoke loudly. – Thalama, Goddess of Destiny.

And their words, their passion was like a whip, a turn of the wheel, turning faster and faster.

The majority of those assembled didn't understand the smirk in the four's faces. They thought it was a bit misplaced and that it was the lust for life shining through and in a way it was. So much strange was happening anyway. Too much to care about minor details.

Jill and Stacy walked to him, placing themselves on his back and front. He nodded, finally surrendering, finally conquering.

The Universe paused a bit, as the twins placed their hands on him, placed themselves on him. There was a flash, a burst of energy and nothing was held back. The use of her power didn't weaken Lillith any longer, but strengthened her.

And Anubis felt as if the universal floodgates opened up for him, for his benefit.

The room changed.

The voodoo priestess entered the floor. They who knew her did see that this was indeed Henriette Gallier, but they didn't recognize her. All pretense, all similarity of normality was gone from the naked body, its moves, its naked eyes.

The drum started beating, there on the floor. No one could see it, but they could sure as hell hear it. All eyes were on Loeh as she started dancing. She danced in a jungle, she danced in a tomb. All eyes were on Loeh and barely noticed two cages being carried in on the arena. Cages covered in fine-masked nets. Two doors were pulled aside, and the two snakes crawled out, crawled towards the writhing human snake. She bent down in a quick, fluid movement and picked them up. They started climbing her arms to her body, twitching around her entire upper body. Other dancers joined in, careful at first, keeping their distance, but she enticed them, teased them, and they danced closer.

– Come, Loeh whispered. – Receive the serpent's kiss upon thy brow.

Udo was the first. He was clearly frightened, but he had something to prove and rushed to the waiting priestess. The two snakes raised their heads and hissed at him (Loeh hissed at him). Venom ran freely from their (her) mouth. Two forked tongues touched his forehead. Venom flowed down his head, on both sides of his nose, mixing with the juice painted on his skin.

– Dance, Hungan, she hissed. – Dance thy soul. Release it from its confines.

He did and his movements looked very much like hers had… as he smeared his hands with the venom, as he licked his hands of it. Melanie and Meta were next. They licked each other's hands. Smoke flowed out of Udo's mouth. He screamed, he hissed as his body began convulsing, began changing.

– CHRIST! A boy cried out and fainted on the spot. Nobody heard him hit the floor.

Udo didn't turn into a snake, but he did metamorphose. He metamorphosed constantly, as he and the other dancers surrounded the Priestess. Slowly, slowly the dance ended. Jill flowed from the shadows, talking in an endless, repetitive mantra.

– I call down the moon, I call down my moon, I call down its power, I embrace the moon, I embrace the moon, I am *the* moon. *I'm Demon.*

She stopped before Loeh. The snakes hissed and bit her on both shoulders, emptying all their considerable remaining venom into her. She collapsed on the ground and in that instant Loeh's eyes turned completely white. The Loa had possessed her, had become her. Jill's body rose from the floor and the two bodies moved as one. The big snake slid across the floor towards them. No one knew such big snakes existed and they gasped in horror, fascination and attraction, and arousal struck them all, sudden, without mercy, and they couldn't move. Only the Raven moved, flapping her wings, her four wings, as she welcomed Set of Osiris, the Desert Serpent, the guardian of the tomb. Jill could feel reason leave her (reason flooded her), as she saw herself dance close to her. Then she had three bodies (three lovely flesh bodies), then four and five and six.

The snake, the serpent crawled to her, coiled around her legs (her shameful legs), her body (her body full of sin, lovely, lovely sin), and she accepted it, becoming it. Felt its Power, the Power of the Earth, the Infinity of the Rainbow. And the song she sang was the Litany of Sin, and the word and the shame returned to the meaningless casket from whence it had come, so long ago, with the growth, cancer growth of civilization. And civilization itself, the thin layer of nothingness, dissolved without, within…

And the Human Being was reborn.

Udo's body twisted to impossible forms. Jill felt it twist as her perception constantly changed. Udo was a shape changer all right and he was capable of changing into anything. Slowly, slowly the light of consciousness returned to Udo and the three other host bodies. They fell to Earth, as the serpent kept coiling Jill and Loeh. The Loa left her, returning in full to Jill, to Lillith, Lillith dancing and Lillith floating above the dancers, sucking up the power. The serpent paled and became like smoke, and in its place stood Baron Samedi, the ruler of the lower kingdoms, one of the many incarnations of the ruler of the old kingdoms of death. Everett looked markedly different. The most obvious difference was that the air seemed to constantly swirl and shift around him. His features were fully human, but he looked more inhuman than he ever had looked when he had been the wolf… or even the serpent. He and the black maiden danced, the Serpent and the Rainbow. And then the Loa's servant pulled back and left the floor to the wolf and the Two Who Were One. Jill rose in the air, effortlessly. She didn't even have to think about it anymore. It happened instinctively. Keeping the huge wolf body levitated hardly demanded any extra concentration.

I am a Goddess. It's a fact. All the old stories are true, all the myths and legends have a basis in fact. They weren't exaggerated at all.

In fact, knowing what she now knew, they were on the contrary quite pale compared to Reality.

Man/Woman danced, encircling each other, back-to-back. They communed and everybody heard.

I'm Anubis - the Mystery of Death

And her reply: Or perhaps his reply had come first? Who could say.

I am Mysteriam - the Secret of Life.

She lowered them back down on the floor and the dance turned wild, passionate… When it ended, she should have been exhausted, spent, but she wasn't.

Loeh came to her, wild like a beast in an ancient jungle, but yet rational. It was that way with all of them now. Passion and reason ruled side by side, the way it should be, the way it was.

– I'm so much more, Raven, she said, flooded in excitement. – Thank you. Thank you.

– We all are. Stacy and Jill spoke in unison. – Just a bit further now, and we will be what we have always been.

They turned and spoke, they turned and sang.

– We are the resurrected Power. The ceremony tonight is for us, not for any possible god. Just a little further now and we will gain access to the one power unheard of, even among the ancients. By Gabi and Daniel's sacrifice we will surpass the druids and the shamans of earlier ages. We will gain access to Time, *time,* my friends. An irresistible force came to those with access to Time's River and we'll go Beyond that. This is a unique opportunity. There have never been this many witches gathered under such circumstances. We will proceed. That hasn't changed. We will finish this… and then we will go out in the world and make it ours.

Seven entered the pentacle. Stacy, Jill, Everett, Loeh, Travis, Morgana… and Jason. It shimmered strangely as he crossed the outer line. Stacy and Jill stood side by side, in the point of the five-point star pointing at the crowd, the living crowd, both audience and participants. No one knew any longer who was who of the twins. They believed Jill was the one holding the wand with the skull and Stacy had the hood covering her forehead. But no one was certain.

Loeh stared at the six, proud and fierce. She had at least two of the gods she had worshipped since she was a child standing in front of her, as living, breathing humans. They were exactly as terrible and great as she had always expected. The Loa had taken possession of her, complete and utter possession, and then raised her up again to walk among them as equals.

She took her position at the center of the pentacle. The remaining four walked to the other four points. It had already started, everything. The initiation was done. They had suffered a far harder path than most initiates. They hadn't fasted, but they had suffered ordeals and raised themselves up by their hair time and time and time again. No further ceremony was necessary to begin this beguine.

There was a rush of wind. Jill suddenly saw herself from above, spinning round and round the seven (or was that six?), as if through a video camera (but of course with a far greater clarity than any artificial equipment was capable of). She saw herself rise in the air, saw Stacy rise with her. Flashes of naked bodies appeared to her inner and outer vision. She felt the Power. The two bodies worked as capacitors, as collectors of the ambient energy drifting at them as mist, as Dust from outside the pentacle, from the gathering.

– *Fuck,* Lillith bade them with a flash of a smile, a pointed stare. – *Fuck your brains out.*

There was laughter, incredulity and eagerness. Some had already started, started the sex-magick. As she was enticing them, the isolated pools of water turned to a raging sea. The energy within her grew and as it grew, she called for more and it kept growing. Everybody outside the circle made this sacrifice. She grinned. Dark laughter echoed through the ancient halls. As an ocean of naked bodies writhed and twisted on the cold hard stone floor, on a soft forest bed the Gemini reached for its two bodies. They stretched out arms. One left and one right covered each other. Light and fire exploded from that point. Both individual figures turned completely white. *They gave us this of their free will.* The Energy washed over the other five. Everyone within the pentacle was bathing in it, bathing in fire and life. The twins descended back to the floor as they leaked like a dam. No one could contain this amount of energy for long. It is happening, it's happening. It was like a mantra, repeating itself in their mind, spurring them on. Jill sensed the expectation in her sister, in herself. Time hummed the last few seconds to midnight, and everything was perfect.

The white light faded as their feet touched the ground. The very moment flames erupted from the circle and lines making the pentacle, erupted from and burned on *stone.* The old clock in Oldtown chimed twelve times. Another, bigger pentacle formed by fire appeared in Main Street. People pulled away from it and wondered what would have happened if they had been caught within. On the burned-out garbage heap in Newtown the ash shook and was thrown up in the air. Where Jill had stood bound a tree and many green bushes grew. It happened violently and quickly and after hardly any time at all the green covered a major part of the garbage. More white flashes in the twins' eyes and similar occurrences transpired all over the city. The children in their frightening costumes laughed and enjoyed themselves. They saw no bogeyman, only nature unfolding.

Every time something new happened… *like pushing buttons.* The power intoxicated Jill, she couldn't deny it and didn't care anymore. It didn't matter. She saw the Earth from a distance, merely a piece of dust in her hand, the sun itself a small ball of fire. Another bigger pentacle, dark, lightless lines encircled the entire city of Northfield, preparing for what's to come. The two turned to Jason. He stood there, between them. The two put their hands on him. Night and Fire did. Two pair of eyes met his eyes.

– Perhaps you shouldn't do this, he said darkly.

– I know who you are, she burned.

Two pair of eyes flared. The power flowed into Jason and his entire body shook. He raised his hands above the head, slowly, painfully. A rush of darkness and everybody was able to see what Lillith had glimpsed for quite some time. Freely hovering shadows danced in the transition between worlds. The last borders weakened and dissolved as they watched. The air was filled with souls. Jason gasped and gasped for breath. He started growing, expanding, fading, becoming one with his surroundings. Lillith felt his presence like something solid, stronger than ever. The cave changed once more. Something resembling angry bees swarmed around Everett. He waved them off. Reality bulged and changed and shifted around him, too. Veils were pulled aside this night, and everybody appeared to the world and themselves as they were. Jill had already seen the ugly faces behind the masks of the people in the town. Now she saw far more. The world was as it was, hard and ruthless. The time for presumptions and self-conceit had ended.

Stacy's stare, Jill's stare… was cast across the room, the endless room, through the catacombs… at the ceiling far above where she once again got a funny feeling, a sense of that… not being there. The stare penetrated the gathering, the sexual activity still going on subsided.

– Prepare thyself, she thundered. – Know that thou are inexperienced in Magick. Know that this is your Goddess' strength. Random Magick was a thing of the past… until tonight, until this eternal night. Thou will shortly feel a dread rise within. My wish is that thou will give heed to this dread, to let it go, to let everything go, open thyself completely.

The hypnotic voice, the eyes appearing in the air before each and every one present, made them all feel distant, as if they weren't here, as if an outside force had taken control over them…

And it had.

Lillith made signs in the air. Ancient symbols, meaningless, inconceivable…

But not tonight. Not Now.

She left their free will. She desired their free will, their wonderful undisciplined attitude. It would assure rampant and powerful Magick.

I'm Chaos, she thought.

I'm Order, she thought.

She shook her head. Both concepts were meaningless. The clenched fist, the open hand, just silly deeds for nearsighted beings. And whatever she was, she wasn't that anymore.

She could see beyond the edge of the Universe.

How silly scientists are, she thought, in a moment's reflection. They claim we never can walk on distant planets without bulky mechanical vehicles. They claim primitive Man was confined to the Earth, when in truth it is now, yesterday, during the age of scientific «enlightenment» we were confined.

She looked at the assembly, at her warriors, *his* warriors.

He is coming, she thought. The human cauldron personified is on its way here. Good, I'll need him.

Samhain permutated the hall, now, ascendant wherever she turned her attention. This night was his, or it had been, and might be so again.

Anubis' power was growing, too. It kept growing for each waking second. Circe slipped into the rock, becoming more a part of it as time passed, making it one with her. Apollon was energy now and hardly anything else. This was their moment.

– I remember, now, Morgana cried to her, to Lillith, – remember clearer than ever. I bound you in rock once, long ago, but now nobody can bind you anymore.

The crack from the big drum thundered in the hall and the echo sent shockwaves through the mountain, through flesh and Shadow. The drum skipped a few heartbeats. A sound not a sound made people look up. Thousands of petal wings seemed to fall at them from the ceiling. The heated air slowed their descent. Step by step they had all traveled closer to this place in time and space. This was an All Souls Night in a way it hadn't been celebrated in millennia. The Human Being was both a spiritual being and the physical body and on a night such as this they realized what potential the combination held, a combination greater than the sum of its parts.

Everything was in place, and she was overjoyed. She had prepared lives for this.

A trip to the dark side, a push towards the ultimate limit.

Nobody, nothing will stop me now.

There was so much here. This place had existed for ages and ages, not only here, but many places.

The fires stretched high. The drums, the flutes and all kinds of strings sounded in the night above a darkened Earth. Eternity's doors opened, not merely two, but an infinite number. Two chanting processions carrying torches appeared slowly from two cave openings. Gabrielle walked as the second in her line as Daniel did in his. Meta and Melanie accompanied the girl, and Matt and Adam the boy. The assembly released a sigh of expectation, a hunger to see this through. Jill stood there, illuminated by the pentacle fire, the many bonfires outside the circle. She saw the sacrificial altars and she saw the sacrificial lambs. They were dressed in heavy, thoroughly prepared clothes, beautifully woven pants and jackets open in front, exposing their chest. The oil visible on the chest and the naked legs and arms made the various shades of light dance on their skin. Both moved sluggishly and with distant looks in their eyes. It seemed like they were somewhere else entirely.

Petals of white flowers descended at the floor. Just below the high ceiling bow people stood on terraces and threw the petal snow. The girl's body shook in expectation. Eyes were shining when focusing on the boy who would be her mate in Eternity. He wouldn't look at her; ashamed because this was the only thing he could do for her. He strived to deny the lust spreading throughout his being, the strongest desire in any human. It was far easier to deny Death, awaiting them in the form of the sorceress ahead.

Stacy and Jill raised their arms in ceremonial greeting. They had placed themselves between the two sacrificial altars. Music faded. People fell silent and silence reigned. Lights shifted constantly, coming from all directions, but it was still dark. The enticing mood increased while the light and dark kept shifting. The procession halted before the two rear points of the pentacle. One of the two who was She-Who-Fills-the-Darkness spoke and everybody listened.

She talked about Death as a transition, not the end, merely another new beginning in an endless number of beginnings, of metamorphosis and transformations. She told them that what lay ahead of them this night was something that had to be done, that the Earth and Life on it had to be saved, that everything had a price. Magick had a price. Nothing was free in this world. The voice sounded strong and clear everywhere in the cave. Emotions raged within them. They shared her despair, second thoughts and resolve. Impressions of green plains and deep forests, and the mountain of torches. How it had been and how it could become again. They saw the present-day garbage heap of a world and the Dollmaster's kingdom looming in the near future. *No price is too high.* None. She spoke about fate. She, Thalama - creator of destiny, inevitability.

She called to Gabi and Dan. They swayed the last, few steps to the circle and within it, before being received by Morgana and Travis, before being laid to rest on the hard rock. Anubis patted the girl on the cheek, and she felt comforted.

Jill drew the ritual knife with the shining blade from her belt. It felt as heavy now, as when it had hung from her body, as when she had first touched it on the wall in the farmhouse living room. She held it in both hands, looking closely at it. It seemed impossible, but it was the same knife she had used thousands of years ago on the plains of pre-Roman Britain. Blood flowed from it already, potent and sweet. Was she rationalizing? Was this truly necessary as she claimed, or did she deceive herself and thereby everybody who had placed their trust in her? Perhaps the price was too high.

The others saw only the young, confident sorceress. Nobody saw her slight hesitation except Stacy

(naturally).
– I sense that you're still riled by doubt, sister, Stacy said softly. – I'm not. Allow me to lead us also the last stretch. Your rage is far stronger than mine, but I'm craftier… more Driven.
Driven. By what fuel mattered little.
– I appreciate it, sister, but I'll do it. Jill tightened both her left and right hand around the handle, hardened herself for the last stretch.
– We all stand to gain by it, she nodded, – and we have no choice.
Stacy nodded, too. Was Jill mistaken… or did she glimpse a flash of sadness in the sister's burning direct stare? She let it go. It didn't matter. Nothing mattered.
– It's all right, Raven, the maiden (strictly speaking not a maiden anymore) spoke sleepily. – It really is.
– No, Raven corrected her. – It will never be «all right».
– I was here, you know. The maiden's eyes focused just a bit. – I'm not here anymore, but I could see me briefly in the preparation room a while ago. Remember… when I… disappeared? I went on a Journey. I can't really remember much about it, but some of it is coming back now.
– You… knew, Jill said, just about managing to stop herself from turning emotional, from keeping something from catching in her throat. – You *knew!*
– It's all right, the girl mumbled hardly audible, falling, returning to her sluggish state. – It's all right.
Jill pulled herself together; reminding herself what was at stake.
She looked objectively down at the skinny figure, both the skinny figures on the altars. These were the last rebels, the last hurdle to power undreamt of. The girl had gone through just a few bleedings. A perfect sacrifice. And then there was the line under the dot, the fantastic power hiding in the bashful human body. The boy complemented her in an excellent way. His power wasn't to be taken lightly. Everything was perfect.
Stacy started singing. Atonal, throaty, incomprehensible to her, but Jill understood and fear, so rare lately, touched her once more.

We worship death
We worship rot
We adore the entropy of the Universe
We are its agents
Its agents of Change

And more. The words, the incantations seemed to go on forever. The choir of multitudes in the cave picked up on her cue, her arrogant sign with the hand. They had no idea what they did, but they were an excellent dot over Stacy's line. Perfect. Stacy stretched out her arms, reached for the two sacrificial lambs with her Night Claws. It sparkled in ebony flashes when ancient, fundamental energies clawed at flesh. Stacy tied the girl and boy to each other with unbreakable bonds. Selene pulled back then. The boy and girl started moaning there on their back, moaning in lust, writhing sensual and chained bodies. There were no visible chains, but they could hardly move. The air was thick with desire and power. They were unable to go to each other and their eyes, their twitching bodies showed their desperation. And the magickal power intensified. Diana stepped forward. She raised the knife, its blade pointing at the girl's hammering heart. It had been a long hunt. Now it was done.
She observed the frail, helpless figure on the rock. Flashes in the shining blade mingled with the rolling thunder, as the wind increased to a Storm, in the other world so close to this one. Torrential rain fell on the other Fire Lake, on many other fire lakes. This lake was calm. Nothing moved, the air hardly more than a breeze. She saw so far, so very far. The chant ended and as there was not a breath, it echoed between the walls. She realized she hadn't known what had to be done until the moment it happened, the very moment the chant (not fading) built to a climax. The petals turned black, turned red, turned white, red and black again. She pushed the knife into herself, stabbed herself, right under the ribs. In a frozen eternity she saw herself and her twin sister cry out as one.
Fall so high to fall, so far down. The back and the back of the head hit the ground. *Hurts,* she thought sluggishly.

Darkness descended. Ice-cold winds raged from all sides. All fire shrank and flickered. Cold moonlight hit them all. The twins, Janus, the twin god's two bodies twitched on the back gasping for air.

Straight in the Chakra, the energy center. Well aimed… Why did you do it?

I had to…

We're leaking. Blood, Power, Life, everything…

… couldn't go through with it. Couldn't.

A spooky, translucent substance leaked through the punctured skin and rose in the air. Stacy's wound was just as deep and wide, in spite of her not being physically stabbed. That there wasn't any blade stuck in her punctured skin made the wound bleed faster. Everything lingered. Timelessness spread. Everything happened so slowly, so fast, so unintelligible to those who experienced it. Magick, the inner force had never vanished from human life, merely slept. An undistinguishable ember now laid bare in the wind, rising sky high. Jill didn't feel sluggish at all. She rather felt her fire burning hotter than ever.

Death was close.

The world darkened through two pair of eyes. But she saw, as everybody saw, two identical spirit forms appear above the two fallen angels. Two forms blending into one. People gasped. Even if the shock over what had happened was still raw in their minds, they found themselves astonished once more. They stared, unable to tear their eyes away. Every possible mood and emotion raged within them. Jill and Stacy's breathing turned shallow. They saw Lillith look down at them with affectionate amusement in her eyes. From the air they looked down at themselves, at Gabi and Dan. The two of them still writhed in heat. Stacy and Jill saw that the two altar stones and the immediate area were unchanged by the emerging cold and everything else happening… And then they understood.

Stacy attempted to move her arm, reach for the knife in the sister's abdomen. She managed just a centimeter or two before the movement lost all its strength. Jill couldn't breathe anymore. There had been one last heave, and then nothing. Anubis was the first breaking the mental paralysis. He threw himself forward, strong and supple, grabbing the knife with something far stronger than any human hand. It cracked awfully loud and in an explosion of sparks, he was thrown backwards. He remained on his back while shaking his head, on the brink of unconsciousness, on the brink of death. Only the robust quality of the pelt-covered body saved him. None of the others would stand a chance. Jill fought to move her arm, but it didn't work. Nothing worked. She stared vehemently at her four friends, her siblings. They understood. Lillith looked at the silver threads connecting her to Stacy and Jill. They were still thick and strong and glowing, but they were withering, dying… Jill screamed enraged. She could do that. Another, even louder scream made the walls shake. She moved one hand first, then the other so high up that they eventually tipped over and fell on her belly. *Hurts.* She started to claw herself towards the knife, incredibly slow. And it was the rage that had always sustained her, a will beyond the soul, but perhaps not the body… or the complete Human Being that made her move. She pulled out the knife in one last inhuman effort and it fell on the rock, playing the metal and rock tune, a sound so sweet.

The wind was blowing once more. It was ice-cold while touching everybody outside the circle, but desert hot when reaching Lillith. Her bodies reacted the way they always did when being lethally injured… violently.

Life's energy rose from the boy and the girl on the flat rocks, something shimmering, indefinite, with a life of its own. Just enough remained to leave both alive. A short while the glowing mist hovered hesitatingly in the air… until rushing into the two bodies on the floor. The phantom image vanished. A violent heat spread through the two on the floor, one also taken from everybody staying outside the circle. They fell to the ground, moaning and screaming. They recovered shortly, in pain, but alive. A few seconds passed. They looked up, staring.

This time Lillith kept it all inside. Some of the rampant, wild energy had already touched the others and left remains there, sufficient for the task ahead. Jill and Stacy straightened ninety degrees and kept themselves hovering, their feet a few centimeters above the ground. They felt such Joy, suchwildjoy. The wound had already closed, the pain a dying echo, hardly noticeable anymore. The fire, the circle of fire, the bonfires erupted anew. And from the circle surrounding Northfield a dark, shimmering wall rose, transforming it to a dome, no, a ball, effectively sealing the city off from the outside world. Tick, tack, tock. Northfield had frozen in time. The world kept going. Everett, Loeh, Morgana and Travis embraced them and shared with them, skin to skin.

Something is wrong. It was Morgana. *The ceiling...*

The pressure in the air, especially close to the ceiling increased to the point of becoming noticeable to all. Something had been wrong since the beginning, a disharmonic echo of a sound seemingly harmonic. *Time.* Understanding rode Stacy and Jill like a mare. It hit them like rusty knives in the heart. Lillith got a vision. The knife was buried in Gabi's heart. She and her eternal mate expired simultaneously. Their total life energy left them, rising in the air. But it didn't disappear into the six eagerly awaiting it. It kept rising towards...

... the ceiling. Reality as they knew it, in spite of it all got thoroughly trashed. The powers and abilities she had borrowed sang with such force within Lillith that she faced major difficulties handling it all. She made sure everybody could see what she saw. The entire ceiling of the cave was torn off, an impossible sight, and yet it happened, and they recognized, in the glow of a kind of St. Elmo's Fire the face of Brian Garrett - the Bishop of California, a contorted, enormous face, darkened by irritation and anger.

– He is Chronos, the God of Time, Gabi cried unbelievably clear, as she sat up on the rock. – We have been so stupid, so unbelievably stupid.

To the onlookers it seemed like the six standing inside the circle simply turned translucent and faded away. To them it felt like being pulled in all directions at once and air was sucked from their lungs.

Blinding black, blinding white. In a world of raging storms Anubis reacted instinctively. Something inexplicable flowed from the claws he dug into Loeh. He bathed her in his own St. Elmo's fire. She faded from their view, on her way back. Her eyes widened.

– Keep the fire burning, he screamed to her.

– With my life, she returned, already «far» away.

The ebony Lady reappeared close to Gabi and Dan. The fire, about to go out flared anew.

The surroundings embraced them in a bluish gray glare, an embrace horrible and sickening. Five beings, one for each point in the pentacle seemed to be adrift in the void. They knew better. *He* sent them through here (a place not here) to test them, to gauge their abilities.

Travis screamed. A rift appeared on his skin just below the elbow. Jill shook him furiously. *Pull yourself together. This is a battle fought in the realm of the soul and not affected by physical realities.*

But she could feel his, the Dollmaster's destructive power tear and pull at her, tear into them all, a disruption creating far more serious wounds than the immediate visible on Travis' arm.

Jill Stafford and Stacy Larkin had virtually no experience in this sort of thing. Lillith had to draw upon far older knowledge and even she had scant information about this place.

This was the Void. Even worse, it was his little, private part of it. There were no colors, nothing they could sense, absolutely nothing a human being had a change to hold on to. What little there was of anything solid, the five translated into their own version of reality.

Something appeared in their way. A tiny irrational hope grew in them when they discovered they were out in space, among the stars, in the cold, black Space and they felt no discomfort. They approached a star, large and beautiful, full of fire. This full of promises and conceit was Ahura Mazdah - the Almighty. They crashed into the mirage, and it was a gaping, black hole.

They wondered if they would have had any chance of avoiding it if they had wanted to. They didn't and concentrated about whatever would come. They shook in fear, but felt strong, alive. A chance such as this, to challenge He-Who-Corrupted-the-Wind would perhaps never come again. Not until it was too late.

Falling.

Sleepy. *She knew what was happening.* He peeled off her memories, the outer shell. The Black Hole erased her thoughts, memories, her superficial self. She had experienced something similar recently and all it took for that to happen was a hit on the head. She always found herself. Always. *Sleepy.* All the pain, wrath, all the hatred didn't allow her to soften.

The Black Hole towered everywhere. No matter where they looked, there it was. They were falling, falling, and had no change of escaping it. It devoured them. They fell for an eternity. An Eternity.

Jill attempted to speak. There was no sound. She saw nothing. She heard no thoughts. Those she projected got no reply. Her friends had disappeared. Her sister had disappeared, as if she never was. She didn't even see herself. There was nothing to see. Everything was being sucked away. Nothing remained… *but the Black Hole…*

7

Lovely and hot under the eiderdown. She wanted to stay there forever.

Threatening and dark steps outside.

She writhed painfully in the bed, didn't understand what was bothering her. Everything was great. Nothing was wrong. Everything was well. Everything!

The door to the bedroom opened and the mother - Mrs. Stafford - walked in.

– Time to get up, girl, mother said, strict, but not unfriendly. – You're unusually lazy today.

– Mother, it's way too early, Jill protested.

– You'll need the extra time in the tub. You have to be good and clean the first time you use the new school uniform. Come and hop in. I'll wash your back.

– What are you talking about, mother? I never wear a school uniform.

– What nonsense, mother laughed. – You've always been a well-mannered girl. You're a bit lazy sometimes, but we'll sort you out, your father and I.

Scared. The mild voice is scaring me.

– Yes, mother. The meek and obedient daughter replied.

The steaming hot water had already filled the tub. She slipped out of the nightgown and stepped into the miniature pool.

She stood in front of the mirror and did her hair into two thick plaits. The young girl still felt the mother's hands rubbing her skin, the lovely sense of being coddled. She dried and dried the steam off the mirror in an attempt to see her own mirror image. The hand's moves turned frenetic, chasing a dry spot. Then she saw, in a foggy glimpse, a twisted, horrifying face and stopped moving. She took one step back and forgot all about it.

The school uniform was a perfect fit, naturally. It was spacious and yet tight around the big body.

Breakfast with her parents. She ate with a visible frown painted on her brow. Had she really walked down the stairs in the old, drafty English house? They weren't wealthy her parents, but they cared well for her, wishing her the best. Her plaits, they gave her such a… proper, well-mannered, responsible look. Had she always been like this… so harmless?

– I have a SISTER! She hit the table with a clenched fist and had no idea she would do it until the moment she did it. – A twin, a mirror image of me, as I am a mirror image of her.

– Now, now, don't you get excited, now, honey, the father warned.

The mother rose with her meek, disarming expression.

– Oh, stop this nonsense, the cute schoolgirl said irritated.

She raised a hand and all movements in the room froze, like a picture. The mother's image stood still with one foot on its way up from the floor, like a sculpture.

As it was. Everything here was just an empty frame.

The surroundings shifted, dissolved to a fog drifting apart, drifting close.

Take a piece of reality. Distort it. Rearrange it on a whim. Congratulation, you've won the 96000 dollars question.

She had hung on the cross forever. Half lowered, as she was in a boiling pond there was not a piece of skin left on her body. Her life was fading, but she knew it would never fade completely. Not there, not in this place. With eyes, without eyes, she saw endless rows of crosses. Wherever she turned, left, right, up, down she saw nothing but the blood red air. A chain gang walked to a boiling pond. The chains fell off just before they reached the pond, but they k-kept walking anyway, falling into the boiling, boiling water. There were screams, but muted. She had convinced herself she had heard them forever. Fading, but never stop fading. More meat to the infernal machine, more meat to the infernal machine. Sweat poured into her eyes. She couldn't close them. Pain was everywhere, but she had no eyelids. Her entire body was nothing but a receptor for pain. Would that she was a slave. She wasn't even a slave… here. She was nothing, nothing but dust blowing in the wind. The sun, the blood red sun cooked the blood, cooked the flesh itself. Soul and life flowed on the ground like a river. There were no screams. Everybody here, millions and millions had long since lost any ability to scream. Wailing sounds echoed back and forth on the open, infinite plain, but it didn't rise from any throat or originate from any larynx, but rather from the flesh itself, having been reprocessed a million times. There existed no hope, because there existed no longer any desire for hope. No instincts remained, except the ability to take one step forward and only because the alternative, standing still and melt, was worse.

Run, she thought. Run

Sweat poured down her face. She sat by a table in an old castle, alone in the incredibly large dining room. She had been placed in the one end, by the head of the table, like a queen. The only lights were three glowing candles in the air above the table's middle. Her eyes slipped along the long furniture, beyond the flames seemingly burning in the very air itself. Everything shifted as she turned her head back and forth, to the left, to the right. The background seemed to flow and slip away every time she attempted to focus on a single point. So she gambled on several points simultaneously. She imagined glimpsing horrible creatures in the shadows of the flames, bound in ashes and iron.

– Show yourself, she demanded.

The air shimmered and torches flared along the walls (the living walls). She spotted her mirror image where she sat in the chair at the opposite side of the long table, in the same elegant dress. The lord of the manor stood behind her. She felt his hands on the naked shoulders and shuddered. Long, beautiful horns protruded from his forehead.

– Don't you go there, she said, choiring her contempt. – You're not the Horned God. You're nothing like him.

He changed before her eyes. The man who appeared to her was dressed in a dark suit. Hair was dark and oiled, and so long that the ponytail reached down at the middle of his back. The clothing was new, but the ponytail was ancient. He had kept it through the millennia of conquest and oppression. This was his true self.

– So, what do you think of my modest home?

– Dirty, Stacy commented.

– That pyramid idea does have merit, he said thoughtfully. – Perhaps I'll implement it sometime.

– More so, than you have already been doing? Jill cried bitterly.

He grinned curtly. They noticed they were shaking. He wasn't evil incarnated. There was no such animal. But he destroyed, corrupted everything he touched, and he did so willingly and eagerly. More than anything he was the spiritual death, what slowly, painfully killed all hope.

Suddenly they lay in chains in a cold, wet cell. The hay they had as bed looked more like a pond after heavy rainfall. They had been lying here so very, very long. They didn't dare look at each other, in fear of how they looked.

– I can see the bewildered, frightened expression in your cute faces, the brutal voice whispered from the darkness. – I like that expression.

They were back in the dining room, heavy in body and mind, from the consumed wine and food, glass-eyed and dull.

– You're only making it worse for yourselves, he kept whispering enticingly. – You don't stand a change. The witch-power has been heavily diluted and weakened through the generations. Join me voluntarily and achieve a power beyond your wildest dreams…

– You have no idea what I have gone through, monster. You don't realize it, but you have already lost. The Earth itself is set against you.

– So obstinate, he shook his head. – So sad. Do you know that the original sin actually was Disobedience. People didn't pay attention to my word. They didn't know their own good. How long do you think you can resist? A hundred years? A hundred thousand?

– Anyway, he continued after a few seconds, – they learned. As you will learn. You will listen and you will learn.

The voice stole the vacant space between them and him, making them soft and malleable.

– Once upon a time there were two Little Red Riding Hoods. They met the wolf in the forest and they lived happily all their days…

They found themselves outdoors. The wind was blowing. The grain-ears were swaying and swaying. A group of young girls sang in joy while working the fields. The bell chimed from the village and the girls walked home, to the village looking like a perfect anthill from above. Jill and Stacy left the other girls and headed for the small cabin in the forest glen. The others giggled and waved and laughed at them. The two stopped and looked at each other, tight-lipped and grim.

– What do you think was Jeshua Ben Pantera's last temptation? Jill asked.

– That one is easy, Stacy replied haughty. – That he could live and die as an ordinary man.

– It doesn't tempt me the slightest, Jill declared.

– Me neither.

They held hands and held on.

Dark. Throw light in shadow. Throw shadow in light.

Stacy and Jill walked down a dark street. It seemed they had been walking forever and there was no end in sight.

An old man carried a sign, a poster on his back.

– Heed the word of God, he cried. – Fear the wrath of God. Fear the love of God.

And then he cackled and leered at them. They hurried away from there, hurried away from the utter insanity.

They walked side by side in a subway. They glimpsed other people there, humans with dark, shapeless faces. There were lots of pigeons, picking their crumbs of life. Only three other humans had features making them stand out from the crowd. They felt increasing joy as they recognized Everett, Morgana and Travis. And also… in the deepest shadows, almost impossible to discover, they also recognized another.

A gust, one so powerful that it almost pulled the air from their lungs signaled the beginning of a Storm. The pigeons rose and transformed into eagles. So big and strong that wings and claws tore huge holes in the ceiling - keeping them all down. The five, together again felt the joy rise, too, as they rose, as they fought themselves upwards. The city surrounded them, attempting to pull them back down. Up in the sky they saw him clearly, the giant studying the anthill.

– We're not ants, Jill cried loud and clear. – We will never become ants.

– *You don't own me.* And now all five spoke with one voice, supported by a strange echo making Jill show her teeth. – *You will never own me.*

Beyond the illusion, to the core. The image of Garrett turned distorted, garbled.

The fire flickered and shrank everywhere in the cave. Loeh stood straight with her arms outstretched and her hands bent like claws. Sweat ran all over her body. The long hair was so wet that it seemed glued to the skin.

North Africa a few years after Zarathustra's time. In those days the now prominent Sahara Desert was just a tiny spot in Sudan somewhere. The coastal areas by the Mediterranean were like a Garden of Eden. A Roman army chief stood a comfortable distance from the vast forest. Those who watched him from the forest easily saw the ponytail sticking out from the helmet. They saw an officer step forward and salute him.

He waited a while before speaking, without turning the slightest.

– Chop down the forest, he said with an indifferent, distant voice.

– S-sire?

Then he turned. Eyes were daggers and the voice icy.

– I don't make it a habit of repeating myself, Centurion. Be jubilant for the fact that I choose to do so this one time. Chop down the entire forest, every single tree. I'm holding you personally responsible for the work being completed within reasonable time. Is that *understood?*

He's scared, Jill realized startled. *Scared of the forest.*

The forest opened up to them. They traveled its deepest paths.

Back in Norwegian mountains, way before anyone turned the land into a fortress by giving it a name. A fertility-ceremony by a river, a passage to the unknown. He was, of course present here, too, to distort and destroy. He was Frey, too. He was many gods. He had taken a people's strength and vitality many times. He had done it with many people.

Jill and the others realized that the struggle, the battle to this point, had been fought in their thoughts. Now they were fought in his. He didn't control anything anymore.

Gabi rose from the rock and on unsteady legs fought her way to Dan. A few, unsteady steps. He lay on his back with an enormous erection pointing at her. Both pair of eyes were cloudy, as if they were really someplace else. She crawled on top of him, twitched a bit and he hit the spot. A blissful smile of lust and she started swinging on him.

– Are you sure this is helping them… and not the opposite? He asked worriedly.

– I can feel it, she said, during a moment's concentration. – And the fire is the only method able to lead them back here.

Two shadowy figures walked into the circle, accompanied by gasps from the gathering. Lighting and sparks accompanied their breaching of the pentacle.

– She's right, Ted Warren told the assembly. Now I want you all to fuck. Fuck your brains out.

Gabi looked into two pair of fire-eyes through a flood of tears. She saw Ted and Elizabeth grab each other's hands, as they faded and vanished into the air.

Then it didn't matter anymore. Desire and passion removed all thoughts. Fire nearly put out, rose anew.

8

How many seconds had passed? How many bits of seconds, now when the dam on the River of Time broke? In a drafty room with a fireplace Time lost all meaning. The Maelstrom of Time constantly bit its own tail. Illusions fell like curtains embraced by flames. The world cleared. He, *the Enemy* had placed himself at the opposite side of the room, in front of the fireplace. Tentacles, strains of smoke and ashes stretched from him and tightened around them like glowing rings. They twisted in cramps, on the floor that was no floor.

Pain. Tearing, paralyzing pain. The maelstrom, the walls not walls showing them enticing images. Distractions from Death, the stench and everything reality's hell had to offer. He attempted to cloud their senses, their perception, weakening them, in order to more easily *fix* them in any way he saw fit.

– Never… MORE! The twin cry resounded across the Shadow World, across the Earth.

Garrett lost the cold smile never straying from his lips. He shook, shook, shook… Realization hit the five on the floor (not a floor, but a sea of blood, heaps of bones). They knew how Gabi's power worked. The sucking of power was instantaneous. And if Garrett's talent was anything like hers, and they were convinced it was, he should have sucked them dry already. The Janus-Goddesses started smiling.

It happened slowly, almost imperceptible at first, but with a roar growing louder and stronger. This in spite of the fact that they just borrowed a Dreamweaver's power, and he had thousands of years of experience in his favor.

They were sucking power from him. Lillith sensed the warm flow of energy. Yes, time to turn the wheel of destiny around, to turn the game of the Great Illusionist back on himself.

The tentacles, previously perceived as smoke and ashes, changed, started glowing in a silvery light. The transformation rushed from her to him and back. She felt it. It rose like a force of a thousand suns the instant the silver threads transformed into one single white light. A tear from the well of light. She felt it so strongly that she didn't manage to take advantage of the added power filling her up.

– You took, she spat furiously. – You took…

She hadn't taken a part of him just now… but retaken a part of herself he had stolen from her … so long ago.

The two who were Raven Moonstar crouched there on the bones. The silver threads had vanished, dissolved into nothing. It wasn't easy to decide which scream was the loudest - and worse. The two fairer. Or the roar of pain-mixed rage from the man standing shaking in front of the fireplace. Not beastly, not human and nothing in-between. Travis, he among them who understood least, couldn't imagine cries from the Abyss sounding worse.

He started laughing then, he who called himself Brian Garrett. *He doesn't realize what's happening.* Lillith fought to keep her concentration through the red fog. *Yes, the tears were blood.*

Blood-drops rose from the floor, defying gravity. Bones seemed to jump from the floor, joining to form skeletons. The blood was pulled in between the bones. The human forms attacked the Enemy. He brushed them off in crushing, angry moves. *It's me*, Lillith thought. *I'm doing it.* And there was nothing conscious about it, not even on a level the subconscious could fathom. It was something far deeper. And just an outer manifestation of what was really happening. She saw everything crystal clear and also knew why. *Daniel's talent.* His ability, his potential to measure *odds* in fractions of a second.

Morgana attacked him. Thick poles shot at him from all directions. They dissolved before actually reaching him. She couldn't make anything grow from the floor. Everett moved his hands. An indefinite, non-substance substance embraced the Enemy. He shook it off, not without certain difficulties. The voice cracked.

– You'll burn for this, *Anubis*. You'll all burn.

– *Never more.* The voice of the Fenris Wolf cracked and echoed in the Abyss.

Travis directed his hands at the Enemy as weapons. Energy beams shot from his hands. Garrett backed off a little, but then stopped. He grinned his ugly grin, one they recognized through thousands of atavistic dreams.

It's strengthening him. Stop. Travis, strengthen me, us. Circe, take our hands.

The force of Lillith's projected thoughts made the two hesitate no longer. Circe squeezed the hands Jill and Stacy reached out with. Travis shot his beams at her/them, time and time again. Everett changed, imperceptible. He appeared more human and far more frightening. He was Anubis - the Jackal God. They who had been living dead, who Ahura Mazdah had completely owned for so long, skeletons once more dressed in flesh and blood, finally saw a glimmer of hope. They danced ancient dance, in the forest, away from dry, warm sand, a thousand small candles. Prayers to he who dwelled in the crypt of eternity. Dwelled, guarded and now left it, bringing it with him. He attacked Ahura Mazdah with every single shred of it.

Jill and Stacy grabbed each other's hands, and in that moment, there was pain. The wound… the wound on their hips was suddenly bleeding and blood was flowing freely. She felt detached from the hurt, from life itself, as she focused on the Dollmaster's sarcastic, triumphant smile, as he, with a gesture stopped those he had condemned, all the wretched bones, in their flight.

– See? You have been bad witches, treated others bad and willfully hurt them. And all witches know that everything is returned threefold.

– There's no such thing as a rule of three. It's all just more bullshit, even predating Christianity. But not predating your machinations, I gather.

She pushed out the words, through sweat, through tears flowing like sweat. Something happened, something completely crazy, completely removed from any mundane reference. The blood, flowing freely now, from two wounds, formed strains in the air, thin ropes tying itself into that of the other sister, connecting them physically. A pull and they were pulled tight. Stacy and Jill were pulled tight together at the hip.

Searing pain. White light of nausea. She remembered now, how it felt being born. The complete uncertainty experienced when a child left, was taken from the safety of the womb. It had been a caesarian, of course. Otherwise, there wouldn't have been any birth, but only death. The mother was scared, uncertain and the disharmony echoed in the child.

A vision came to her, about Ahura Mazdah - the Only God, the Supreme Being. She saw him at this moment, supremely confident after his long row of victories. Merely minor setbacks, no losses. She saw him stand there laughing, towering above everything, saw him overcome the escalating Greenhouse Effect, the process that could save humanity from civilization's clammy hands. She saw torrential rain of ashes and poison, and she saw him, so powerful that his slightest whisper was Law, his voice the only one. Everybody existing did so at his mercy.

They had cut one of his threads. It couldn't mean much to him, because he didn't seem to care about it.

But to her…

… it meant everything.

He isn't doing this.

The merger started. The silent scream, gaining strength for centuries, was liberated. Everybody heard it, where we're all in an incomprehensible comprehensible way in touch. As below, so above.

It was as if the skin… melted. The speed of waving hands, kicking feet slowed down. Four arms and four feet in one body, as the extra limbs, too, were slowly submerged. She felt it happen, saw it through the others' eyes. Her two bodies… merged

Into One.

She stood straight. The Lost, reined in so long by the Dollmaster took flight. And he was helpless to prevent it. She struggled against a lump in the throat. So this was how it was, when the body and the soul was united. This was how it was supposed to be.

– I… know you, he said, straining to speak between gritted teeth. – But you shouldn't be capable of doing what you just did.

– You know me only as she you met in the Norwegian mountains and Egypt's dynasties, she said proudly. – Neither now nor then did you recognize *Lillith.* You turned overly confident quite fast, old man.

Her… inner being… erupted out in the open. There was no other way to explain what she felt. She had made herself extremely vulnerable… and extremely powerful.

– Lillith! He spat it out in boundless anger and fear. She took several steps backwards. Her name, spoken by him, spoken with such venom.

It shocked her, but didn't injure her. She made herself ready to fight back, while he removed all the stops. He hit his enemies hard, ruthlessly. The Maelstrom dissolved and whipped them. The content of the walls itself whipped them and dissolved. Then there was Nothing. Lillith managed to collect them all in a protective bubble, but they were swept away like dry leaves in the fall. She strained to sense Garrett, to get a sense of his whereabouts, in vain. Nothing strange by that. Since «direction» had ceased to have meaning. The bubble was crushed in a rain of garbage and ash. It passed through them, and *injured* them. A wave of the hand and Lillith halted their movement, she knew what she was doing. But the Gray Fog rose to greet them. «Space» no longer had any meaning. Cause and effect scrambled to bits. He could try and fail until he got it right, if she didn't pull herself together. He had gathered his power, focused it through ten thousand years. They had to do it right, now. There would be no more second changes.

Raven raven

(she hardly heard the cry in Eternity)

In a glimpse she saw the city below, a place very similar to the hell she had experienced during her Journey to the Kansas City of the middle twenty-first century, his model for the future. She managed to slow their descent, to diminish the speed in which they hit the ground. In spite of this it felt like breath was sucked out of their lungs. *Stupid cow, it's possiblepossiblepossible this is a struggle of the mind, but the most important realities remain in place. You'll die here and you'll perish. No second chance.*

She lifted her head. This both was and wasn't Chronos' place in California, his kingdom within his dome. His Place of Power, his Domain. She had come close to it, too close, during her first conscious out-of-body experience.

All four, Lillith, Anubis, Circe and Apollon felt the corrupt air and the corruption of the decaying ground, and it hurt them.

They found themselves in a street where everything seemed normal. People, cars, noise.

– I can hear their steps, Morgana cried, pressing her hands over the ears.

The people… they appeared whole and healthy, but a closer look exposed them for what they were, automatons without any life of their own. The Enemy closed in on them. Every step he took echoed under the white dome. From all sides they attacked, his legion of servants, eager in their desire to obey and please. They looked like shadows, but had hardly any substance, any own life. The four used their powers. Anubis powers did work. His claws and mist made them fall, made them scared, but they closed in on him, overwhelmed him. The three others couldn't do any harm to the approaching shapes. Lillith's telekinesis, her death-touch, her telepathy and her fire were all useless. Apollon's light just past harmlessly through them, without affecting them at all. Circe could delay their progress, by raising walls, but she was unable to stop them. They were formless, with no solid center to attack. The four attempted to flee, but they knew it was no use. The Enemy was everywhere. He was everywhere. Lillith glimpsed his face in all the empty shapes.

– Stupid woman, he said contemptuously. – To expose your weakness for all to see.

She exposed her fangs and snarled at him, unable to hide her fear, the fear of a cornered animal. She remembered how he had caught her, trapped her alone and trained her to do his bidding, made her nothing or less than nothing.

The secret name of God raven now

An echo in Eternity

– An echo? He stopped. – What…

– You're a fool, she said aloud. – Where do you think I've *been* all these years, all the time you lost track of me? Singing your mindless praise? You've started to believe your own propaganda about female inferiority…

The empty shapes attacked from all sides. An arm passed through Lillith, making her gasp in pain. Every new touch drained her, drained them. NO. She snarled. Her anger affected them no more than any other method she had attempted, but the rush made her fight on. And then she made headway, by affecting the air itself. She used Gabi's power in combination with her own and stopped the advancement from one side. But only one side. Anubis lay on the ground, struggling in vain as shadow knives cut into him. Apollon and Circe screamed. She healed them as the wounds appeared, but it was so hard, so hard. She fought on.

– NEVERMORE! She shouted and the ground, the very heavens, the very depths shook. – Show yourself, coward.

The laughter was filled with the scorn she deserved for expecting him to fight fair.

Another laughter, two voices in the dark. Everything seemed to freeze, the Dollmaster's laughter stopped as if cut.

– What…

Two beasts in human shape appeared out of nowhere, two pair of fire-eyes flashed as Ted and Liz Warren attacked the empty shapes, slicing them to ribbons. Lillith sensed triumph swell within. She knew those two. She remembered.

– Concentrate on the old fucker, Liz shouted. – We'll join you shortly.

The shapes gathered into one single shape, to no avail. Liz and Ted cut through it as if it was nothing and it was, animated to serve the will of its master.

Lillith stood slightly crouched, searching, searching.

– Peek-a-boo, she whispered. – I can see you.

Suddenly, a shape, a form appeared in front of her.

Chronos stood there as himself now. He grabbed her hair and lifted her up. As he did so he closed the two of them off inside a smaller, white bubble. He tightened a grip around her jaw, making blood flow.

– You're such a prize, he marveled. – You know that I rather want you with me than against me, my spiteful little she-demon…

– I'm not yours, she spat, as the trickles of blood formed shapes around her.

He touched her, kissed her on the lips. She registered despairingly that she was unable to suck a single shred of power from him. He was so superior, so crushingly confident.

Anubis, Circe and Apollon attacked the globe. They didn't even scratch it. Was it even possible? It wasn't matter. Wouldn't it, even if they did manage to scratch it, just fix itself instantly?

– Oh, your brood, the two minor demons over there, was certainly a surprise, my dear Lillith. But I've dealt with surprises before, and as soon as I have you under my heel once more, it will be easy enough dealing with all of them. They have caused me a bit of trouble during the millennia. I admit it, I didn't know what they were, what their origin was. But now that I know, they, too, will be mine.

– I remember, she mumbled. – I remember…

He knows my rage and is confident he can use it safely, but he doesn't know me. Not anymore.

Liz and Ted attacked the globe and cut huge openings in it. The claws, the talons protruding from their fingers were visible in the air.

Garrett froze, his surprise and fear visible in his features, in his body language, as he stared in disbelief at the two people he had avoided any direct contact with their entire lives.

Now, Lillith thought. Now is the time.

– jahavalo, she cried, she SHOUTED.

JAHAVALO

She penetrated down to his core and saw it crack.

He let her go, staggering back. She instantly attacked him, with a wrath building through many lives of experiencing prejudice and hatred. She burned him with red-yellow fire and fire she formed as night-claws. With fingers of flesh and blood and claws of black, crackling energy she held on to him. For the first time in ten thousand years Jahavalo *screamed.* In the air above, in the ground below cracks opened, opened wide.

He fought her off, throwing her away. She didn't fall, but hovered in the air, an angel of vengeance.

– STOP, he cried (ordered). – You don't know what you're doing. Stop, Lillith.

His wrath washed over her as a mild spring wind she easily shook off.

Prejudice and hatred wherever she turned. She was sick and tired of it. Intolerance directed at everybody different, encouraged and imposed so long, now. Enough.

Enough!

A figure stepped out of a black hole simply appearing in the air. Lillith felt the wrath mingle with a rush of excitement. Samhain was changed, as were they all. His eyes had turned to fire, the Janus Clan's unmistakable sign. But Jahavalo recognized him also, now.

And in that moment of further distraction Liz and Ted attacked him, tearing at him. There was no blood, but a sound of air wheezing out of a balloon. A swing with an arm and they were brutally thrown back. Blood and skin spurted from their many wounds.

– You're not ready yet, he snarled. – You're not whole. You will never be rising from your own ashes.

Lillith stretched out her arms, stretched out her claws like wings. The entire place seemed to be shaken apart. A gush of fresh air flowed in through the appearing cracks and Jahavalo's shadow-less shadows, his legion of mindless, soulless creatures got colors and contours, and many faded away. Energy flowed from Jahavalo's wounds. He managed to slow its flow, but not stop it. Otherwise, he seemed uninjured, invulnerable where he stood and cast his evil eye at them all. Lillith felt the rage keep rising and she let it, let it go. Let everything go. A flash of clarity gave her the most powerful revelation she had ever experienced. The blade flashed as she lifted and lowered it. The moment she had stabbed the virgin with the sacrificial knife he had taken control of her, torn out a valuable part of Lillith and made it his… and then *split her in two.* He had done it in the conviction that he would be able to control her. He had been sorely mistaken. She had kept growing and in time changed so much that he had no longer recognized her. What was ten thousand years? A tiny slice of human existence, not more. During that time, she had become a dynamic force with opposing polarities and her Power grew.

And now… now she was complete.

As complete as she could be, here and now.

He attacked her, but the corrupt energy moved so slowly, so ridiculously slow. She made it turn away from her and it dissolved harmlessly somewhere.

– And you see yourself as the Lord of Time…

She heard Samhain's scorn as he spoke to Jahavalo:

– This is what you have been afraid of all the time, isn't it? It isn't true the impression you've attempted to create, that the Power has been weakened since ancient days. It is, on the contrary increasing and growing in strength generation by generation. No wonder you started growing desperate during the Burning Times.

Shadows crackling in colors flowed from the black hole behind Samhain and his body aura got a strange, different glare. The focal beam he sent forth washed over Jahavalo like lye in an acid river.

The remaining shadow-less legion attacked. It wasn't that these figures reminded them of skeletons with pulled-over sunken skin that made them so scary, but the lack of humanity. They had been human once. Now they were something lacking life, lacking… everything.

Those moving at Morgana fell and decayed long before they reached her. Anubis smashed them to pieces with his huge paws and rays of St. Elmo's fire from his eyes. Apollon was like the sun itself and his wrath disintegrated the attackers.

There. A force of will, a push of rage and Lillith clawed a hole at the very air itself. What Gabi had done so easy in Northfield was so hard here, in Jahavalo's kingdom where he had been all-powerful.

As the cracks widened to an abyss, she saw his inner circle of servants in a churchlike building, under the invisible dome in California. They knelt and prayed with folded hands. All dressed in white uniforms, impossible to discern from each other. A few were mutants. Most were ordinary humans. Some of them lifted their head. They cried out and pointed with stiff limbs. They peeked into the inferno their Lord and Master had created, and for the first time they saw it for what it was, the Illusion supplanted by brutal reality.

His hateful attack penetrated her defenses. He filled her with bliss, with indifference. She wanted so much to lie down and never do anything else other than lay there, warm and safe under the eiderdown. She fell on the ground, close to the huge crack. She realized she was truly staring into the Abyss.

It hurt, a hurricane of pain molesting her.

She ran across the field with Death's Legion in pursuit. The forest awaited her, tempting her ahead. She might reach it, perhaps… Slowly, consciously she stopped, turning around, facing the enemy on his turf. Time is up, it's Time. Time to pick up the fighting glove and never again throw it away.

It had started. Shaking hands found the knife handle in her belt, as she focused everything, everything she was on Jahavalo. He no longer could focus his power on two fronts simultaneously. A line of raw energy flowed between Samhain and Anubis, as they joined forces for the first time in millennia. A snarling Jahavalo turned his attention towards them.

The eyes, the senses, even their inner senses stemming from their *Ti Bon Ange* couldn't correctly discern what happened and far less properly represent it, translate it to images of the Mind. Samhain knew his kingdom, his realm and Jahavalo his, but now it was mixed into something no one could control. The black hole seemed to be expanding, but shrinking, too. Jahavalo screamed uncontrollably. The scream itself seemed to tear him apart. He faded, to appear further away. He screamed in protest. Jason, Ted, Liz, Everett, Morgana and Travis also screamed, but there was pain tinted with joy, an embrace of the new, unknown. While he only wanted to exploit, subdue it and that was impossible. The wild energy-storm was unlike anything before experienced on Earth. Lillith sensed the life and the power flow within, flow time and time again. Jahavalo no longer had any advantage in this place. It belonged to him no longer.

You thought we had forgotten completely, didn't you? That you could just collect us on your little doomsday? Frustrating, isn't it, to see everything you have worked for turn to ashes? This is how it goes, O'Mighty One when one builds one's house on a foundation of mud.

The Earth was shaking, on both sides of the crack in the air. Along the San Andreas Fault Line small rocks started rolling, then bigger rocks. Time flew. Jahavalo's faithful fled from the doomed building, from their home. They fled in terror and would never stop. The building collapsed, the entire property turned to rubble.

Time had hardly passed inside the shadow-world, but outside the sun had risen and was already about to set the next day in the San Francisco Bay.

Smoke, lights in the air. You can look at the patterns forever. You can learn much, but you may also disappear in the infinite and the eternal. Lights blink and from the ashes smoke rises anew. Lights blink anew. No beginning, no end.

The major crack expanded to a cleft, dramatically. The land on each side divided completely. Jahavalo stood on one side. Samhain, Anubis, Circe and Apollon crouched on the other. On one small island in the middle were Liz and Ted. A gust from the Abyss and Lillith was pulled into it. Circe got her with strains grown from the ground. She could do that easily now. Anubis grabbed Lillith with his fur-covered arms. Lillith crawled away from the cliff, but didn't relax until she noticed the pull had gone. She had stared into the Abyss and what had stared back had been herself.

She heard Jahavalo's scornful voice, forced herself to listen to it and to it only.

– You have hurt me, I admit that willingly. You have set me back considerably, but I have had setbacks before, as you know… In the long run it matters little. I'm eternal. You'll never be rid of me.

– We can't let him get away, Lillith mumbled. – We can't…

She met Anubis' eyes and he understood. But before he could react, she had torn herself loose from him and started running.

Towards the Abyss.

She released the wild animal, even *the Beast* inside. No reservations, no ties anymore. Nothing held her back. She jumped at Jahavalo across the ever-expanding abyss, hitting him low. She attacked with fangs and claws and her entire being. Her features changed, as she became the She-Demon she had appeared as in her dream visions. The force with which she hit the Enemy made him fall back with her over him. He had attempted to avoid her, stop her and now he attempted to throw her off. Everything in vain. The force of the wilderness he had been denigrating for so long now held him in its grip and wouldn't let go.

The two parcels of land, the two islands now drifted further apart, on the sea of the Abyss. The smaller island with the two fire-eyed people disappeared in the horizon. The portal to the physical world had vanished completely from burning visions.

– Not a chance. Jason shook his head, holding a hand lightly on Everett's shoulder.

I stare back at you. She hissed at him where they crouched, locked in each other's deadly embrace.

Seconds, eternities… Fantasy, reality. What did it matter in the scheme of things? They were merely words, a hook, a peg to hang viewpoints on, to claim one's viewpoint to be equal to reality. All that mattered was what happened between beings on a personal level.

He cut deep in her. It did him no good. The added pain only made her more determined, fueled the pain, the wrath and hatred to the highest possible level. One last distraction: A pyramid, a stone-stairs, a throne in gold and marble. She was one of the Shadow-Women in Old Egypt, one of the Chosen, with power over life and death, an exalted life, where nothing outside the pyramid had any value. Was *this* Lillith Raven Moonstar's last temptation? She almost laughed.

She buried herself in him, pulled and tore him apart.

There was a gasp and he lay still. She straightened. He died under her and lost his grip on his last remaining threads, those to the majority of the Earth's population.

– You thought you could crush the Earth's Wild Heart, she exclaimed triumphantly. – You were wrong. You're merely an illusionist, a *deceiver.*

And she lifted her hands above her head. Something sparked and flared, the sacrificial knife, changing (she made it hers) to something… a bigger form. A sword. She clenched her hands around its ornamented handle and pushed it down through Jahavalo, through his energy-center. He belched, one last sound in contempt, disgust for everything living. She stretched her body, fought her way up on two legs, legs shaking.

Such a violent storm of energy, one ever bigger in time and space, was released that the four at a distance had trouble seeing she who was bathing in it.

They feared she would drown in it and gasped in relief when she appeared from the raging inferno.

Everything shifted and they weren't wherever they had been anymore (they weren't moving). Indistinct images started flashing on and off around them. They couldn't possibly register it all, as it assaulted them in an onslaught, a torrential rain of… of everything.

The past. They floated as ghosts through ancient Atlantis. A land and a city build into the land itself. In spite of this it carried within itself the seeds of its own destruction.

They floated across the gulf of Space, so far into the future that time itself was about to end. The Earth had become cosmic dust ages ago. The Universe itself approached the end. One single star, a sun black and darkened hung above them. They felt, incredibly enough that they were capable of seeing the atoms' ever slower movements. A figure seemed to observe them. It was «quite a bit away» from them, but so enormous that they imagined it much closer. Transparent or just One with everything here, they couldn't tell. A hood, a pair of glowing eyes, a shapeless robe. They couldn't tell if it was male or female, human or other. A Creature without face, body, soul and blood. Lillith froze on her back, her entire back. She got nothing from it. No thoughts, emotions. Something… She couldn't tell if it was Jahavalo, herself, Samhain or anybody else. But no matter how Alien the creature was, there was something undetermined there she… a connection there… she recognized.

She looked down at Jahavalo. He would breathe in and out a few more times. Then it would be over. How ironic, he who had been the very symbol of Death and Destruction fought so hard to stay alive.

The soul had yet to leave the shattered body. She knew very well she could *disintegrate* him, put out his light for all time. The only way she could do that was to do what he had done, become like him, become him. That was what - the one thing - she never wanted to do.

She lifted her head. Hair blew back on her head. Slowly, while she stretched out her arms towards what awaited ahead, she started to smile.

– Time to go home, she cried to the four on the other rock.

Both rocks were falling into the black hole. Her friends started fading, but she didn't.
– Lillith, come with us, Travis cried desperately.
– Don't worry about me, she shouted back. – I wish to live, now, more than ever.
They got a last glimpse of her as she vanished into the black hole, the well, which bottom no sunlight reached.

9

Samhain first appeared through the hole in the air inside the pentacle under Fire Lake. Then Anubis, Circe and Apollon. It happened quickly, like an «easy» birth. Delphi and her Daniel had fallen asleep. They awoke in the roar rising from those outside the circle. Both opened their eyes from their rock bed. Everett stretched his huge body. The pulse of Life beat stronger in him, in them all.
– Can anybody pinch me, pinch me hard and check if I'm dreaming? He exclaimed with a huge… Well, he certainly exposed his amazing row of teeth.
Delphi and Circe did pinch him from each side. It didn't hurt, but he sensed it. He sensed it.
– It doesn't prove shit. Morgana rubbed herself sensually at his bloodstained fur. – We're simply your dream fairies eagerly awaiting your every command.
Loeh knelt, completely exhausted. It showed in her strained features. Jason crouched slightly and encouraged her.
– Just a little longer, now. I and Anubis will take turns in keeping the portal open, so you don't need to strain yourself anymore. You can do it.
– I must do it, she whispered. – It… went well?
– Better than we could have ever hoped for, he nodded.
He stretched out his arms. The roar in the air increased. The portal turned visible to them all.
Silence had once more descended upon the denizens in the cave. Anubis had taken over the task of keeping the portal open. The night was yet tight and dark, but dawn approached inevitably. The human wolf exchanged glances with Samhain. Jason shook his head, so imperceptible that he doubted anyone except Everett noticed. They kept awaiting her return.
She didn't come.

10

A cascade of colors. Blinding light. Lillith raced through a tunnel that was anything but dark, but the light in its end was so bright that the rest paled in comparison.
She hovered above the Sunset Land. Or one of them. She knew she shouldn't land and didn't care to, either. She had passed this place more times than she could recall and had put it behind her a long time ago.
Back on Earth, still non-corporal. Hovering along power lines. St. Louis the summer of 1993, when the city had become a part of the United States' new great lake. Straight lines, going straight ahead had for so long been a part of her life. *Night.* Distant lights. Hyde Park in London, the summer of 1988. Midnight, hot and humid. People were bathing naked in the Serpentine and writhed and stretched on land, as they fucked their brains out. It was a beautiful orgy and she turned quite hot where she hovered above them. More than one pointed at her. She was visible. She waved to them, couldn't help her playful mood and didn't want to. She visited a church in San Francisco two months after the incidents in California and Northfield. They attempted to celebrate Christmas there. It was even less of a success than it usually was. Something pulled her, attracted her. She didn't know what, but let herself be led carefully away. It didn't dawn on her until she was right there. A group of youths sat in a circle, around a circle-round table with three legs. Then she giggling realized what was going on. They were engaged in spiritism. A couple of them were latent witches or it would never have worked. She was quite relieved they didn't know what they were doing, or they could have trapped her, bound her to this place longer than she would have appreciated.
– This may seem a bit odd, just now, she grinned openly, *– but you shouldn't really trust higher forces. You should fight to govern your own life.*

Know that this goddess appreciates your curiosity.

Halloween, New York. The parade in Greenwich Village. She was almost home. People stopped and stared at the mirage above, surrounded by dancing lights and colors and shadow. A demon-mask covered her face. The creature vanished slowly, but they didn't feel like she was fading.

11

Darkness. Surrounded by smoke and lights and colors.

12

The pentacle was filled with light… and fire. Some looked at it from under the high ceiling. They saw better than those on the ground the form the energy-explosion took. Animal creatures, first a large bird, then a cat, a black panther. The images shifted constantly, both wonderful and terrifying.

Behind Lillith, in the hole appeared a massive assembly of small, intense pulsing orbs, pulsing in life and fire. They rose towards the ceiling, joining those already there.

The lights faded, the fire muted inside the circle, and it was filled with shadows. Lillith and the other Travelers also rose in the air, but stopped shortly above ground. They made a smaller circle. In the present-day glaring light, the circle was synonymous with something closed, finite. In the shadows of ancient fire, it symbolized infinity. The fire from the torches reached even higher.

In the darkness before dawn, I am at my strongest.

There's nowhere to hide from the hurricane.

Above the pentacle in Main Street the five appeared briefly. Almost no one had left the place. They had been doing everything and nothing and they had been waiting for something wonderful, for the end of the world.

– JESUS, a man exclaimed and fainted in his tracks.

A flock broke down the closed church-doors and raced in where the priest and his congregation sat unmoving like dolls. As sleepwalkers they joined the dolls.

On the edge between Main Street and Cross Avenue the ground around the pentacle started to… brighten. The effect spread quickly, to both streets and trail's broad beginnings, the extension of Main Street, towards Frazer Hill, and to the school's gate at the opposite side of the street. People moved to the side, up on the sidewalk, into the adjacent streets. Most remained. Curiosity conquered the fear.

Suddenly the entire Cross Avenue and Main Street exploded in an intense glow. A shape formed. Not a cross, but an Ankh - a symbol representing eternal life. It was as if everybody present was able to see it from the air. And in that instant grass and plants started growing, shooting up from the soil in the previously sterile Trail. In just a few moments the path towards the Hill was completely overgrown.

Thompson Chemicals dissolved around and before the astounded environmental protesters. The buildings quite simply fell apart. There weren't big chunks of material raining down, but more dust-like properties. The few police officers holding wake outside the closed gate ran off in a panic.

Inside the pyramid a dark figure, a creature showed itself to everybody simultaneously, no matter where in the building they were at the time.

– *Get out,* the voice that had to come from the grave, the tomb hissed.

Everything fell down. Without further warning. No one had been close to anything. By then the majority had already set course towards the exits. A scenario repeating itself in Gyrich Manor and all «finer homes» in the area. People stared at the Pyramid. Electricity had long since disappeared for miles and miles in all directions, but they saw it in a strange shimmering glow. It was surrounded by it. But it… the building that the day before had been polished and shining chrome, now seemed old and derelict. *It was.* Their eyes didn't lie. There was a loud crack, then another. The entire structure seemed to… crouch… and then collapse. Dust rose sky-high and when it settled, nothing but ruins remained.

Father and Son Gyrich stared embittered at the place they had lived, witnessed the symbol of their power and wealth be reduced to rubble. The nightmarish further implications were also clear to them. They weren't so stupid that they didn't realize that the world had changed. Their very source of power had been rocked. The father went bananas there and then. He would never leave the *clinic* where his son placed him.

Grass and plants erupted all over the city. Houses and high towers were being covered in green. People wandered around like sleepwalkers, or jumped up and down as if insane. Inside the church that had stood between what had been Newtown and Oldtown Joseph Parnell stared blindly at the grass growing from the exit and down the carpet to the altar. He took one last walk to the sacristy and returned carrying two more cans of gasoline. Without changing expression, he emptied the fluid over all the people present, everybody sitting unmoving on the benches. He pulled forth the matchbox.

Outside a group of curios bystanders observed the strange act. They didn't walk inside, they weren't stupid, but pulled back to a more than safe distance. The good reverend meticulously picked one match and led it toward the box.

– Don't do it, man, a longhaired, older hippie attempted.

One could easily hear that he didn't think it would be much use.

Sulfur and brimstone erupted. The burning match fell to the floor. One single flame turned to an ocean, to a mountain. Shortly thereafter the old wood-church was surrounded in flames. A few of the burning people screamed, at least once. The majority took merely a few steps and fell. A few didn't move at all.

As dawn's first rays of light appeared in the east all the churches in Northfield and vicinity caught fire. Every fire started in front of the altar and spread from there to it all. As empty paper houses they all burned. No one was home and no one attempted to put out the fire. People probably realized it would be a hopeless task and that was the reason for their inactivity in this matter. Probably. Anyway, it didn't take many minutes for it all to burn down. In some cases, the grass in the churchyard also caught fire, but it didn't spread outside the cemetery walls. The grass was just as dry there, but not a single blade of grass outside burned. Not one.

The power emanating from the five spread… yes, like ripples in the water, like a nuclear explosion. The force was fierce in a circle, a certain distance away from the explosion and was weakened the more the rings expanded. But… the «waste» would influence what happened far away, long after the dust settled. *What great irony. Lillith giggled.* Electricity failed all the way to Boston's suburbs. An occasional church started burning all over the American continent and it also happened other places in the world. *Thanks, Joe, for the idea. Have a great Journey.* Car engines and other engines coughed and died miles away. Fuel and easily combustible material exposed to air vanished in flames. Recently dead stood up and walked relaxed off. Cathedrals and buildings of worship crumbled all over the world. Christianity, Islam, Hinduism, Buddhism, the New Age religions, it was all the same, all religion. The world had changed, irrevocably. Stones kept falling in the water and the waves the rings created flooded distant shores. Night ended and a lot remained to do, but this was a start, the start.

A part of the eastern wall in the cave under Fire Lake shimmered. The rock dissolved to nothing, and a passageway formed, all the way out. Air rushed in. The fire flickered. Tongues of flames rose one last time, before fading and dying.

But the Fire… The Fire was eternal.

The five broke contact and descended to the floor. The glow that had charged the air in their proximity faded. A minor eternity total darkness ruled. When some of the fires and torches once more were lit, they burned with ordinary, low flames.

Lillith looked at the tunnel. It was tall and broad, but so long that the light outside didn't reach in here.

Good.

Loeh had collapsed on the ground. Lillith set down on her heels and bathed the totally exhausted girl in her healing energies.

– Thank you, Raven. Loeh lifted her head and kissed her hand.

– It's we… I who should give thanks.

The three times born witch took two steps to the left and reached out the hands to Gabi and Dan and they accepted them. She sensed the final, remaining part of the abilities, powers she had borrowed from them slip away, leaving her.

They knew, but still they looked uncertain at her. Or perhaps they looked at her with uncertainty precisely because they knew.

She picked up two things from the ground, the sword and the wand with the skull. The expectation and joy flowed at her in waves, but she also sensed the same uncertainty in many. They had only a general impression of what had happened, and they saw that one was missing from the circle.

– Which one are you? Adam asked with a clear, underlying aggression in his voice and stance. – Which of them?

– She is both, Loeh explained smiling. – Two bodies earlier sharing the same soul are now united.

– I am Lillith Raven Moonstar. She seemed to talk to any one and all of them. – Call me Stacy.

Everett looked at her so alike Jill with a lump in the throat. He knew that it had been the practical part of her who had decided upon the name, and he knew he had to accept her choice. People changed and each person was potential many.

– Let's go outside, she cried with her contagious excitement. – There's so much to do and so much to tell. The day is dawning.

As the swirling mass of them all started moving one of them cried out:

– Hail the Goddess!

She stopped. Everybody stopped. She almost smiled.

– I'm not a Goddess. There's no Goddess, no God, no supreme being, no divine plan.

She felt extremely relieved. The bullshit about gods was no longer of any consideration.

– S-so what are you, t-then? She turned towards him.

– I'm a Human Being, Felix, she replied softly. – I've always been.

There was a lot of laughter and good-humored snickering. It implied that they agreed with her statement. That pleased her. She had tried on the pedestal and not found it to her liking.

Light played and trembled in the long walk through the passage. Lillith wondered. Not much.

Lillith. Jill. Stacy. Tangled together like strands of night and fire. Where did one begin and another end?

It didn't matter.

They were One.

What had happened, what she had experienced, what had happened to her might seem incredible looked through the twenty-first century's narrow perspective, but she didn't feel any need to pinch her arm. She knew… with unqualified certainty that she wouldn't wake up one day discovering that it had all been a dream. She had felt herself awaken many times since her arrival in Northfield… But had she been truly Awake before this moment?

She knew, now, that she was indeed a fanatic. Raw, uncompromising. She was willing to threaten, damage, destroy to achieve what she desired. The truth felt so good. She was Prometheus - the Bringer of Fire, but she was also Surtur - the Fire Demon. She was awake and ready for whatever had to be done.

They appeared from the tunnel, a living, breathing entity, a Storm in motion, entering the land of the twilight storm. Their home. A safe haven of sorts, in the eye of the Storm. From here they would reach out into the world.

Bushes, trees and brushwood had grown between the Hill and the City. The tunnel was hidden, no matter where one looked at it from.

Good.

She stopped by a big rock where nothing grew. They who followed her looked attentively at her, studied the known and unknown woman. They noticed a few distinct physical changes. She was slightly taller, half a head or a bit less. The eyes had been gray. Now they were black. The hair was longer than it had been on both Jill and Stacy.

In ways they couldn't define… she was changed.

– There's a lot of talk about the price of Magick… she said aloud. – Well, I tell you it's a load of bullshit. It isn't when seeking Magick one must pay the highest price, if any at all, but when one is denying all Magick in oneself, making one a shell of a human being.

She called to her Morgana and Gabi. Without further communication the two of them put their hands on the rock. There was no visible change. Lillith lifted the sword and pushed it into the seemingly solid gray mass, pushed it in to the hilt. She took a step back, without commenting, letting them wonder. They recognized the crooked smile, but that, too, had gained another layer.

– Camelot is once more, finally ready to call its knights, she cried. – It's about time to stop the insanity, among ourselves, in the world at large.

The warm breeze played with the fabric in her robe, clothing different from what both Stacy and Jill had been wearing. She sensed the wind over every bit of skin on her body. All of her felt Life around her. She heard the beating of hearts, leaves whisper at the top of trees, birds' wings flap as they flew.

No one should be closed off from the opportunity to feel something like this.

No one!

She was hardly conscious of doing so, when calling forth Rupert and Priscilla and the two other temple guards Gabi had recruited from the Asylum's keepers. Communication with Gabi followed as no more than a passing glance, it was sufficient. The girl eagerly stepped forth and removed the invisible rings the four had been wearing around their neck. A slight touch and Lillith had removed any other mental chains they might have had.

– I know where you're coming from, she told them harshly. – You may all go back to your respective masters. Tell them how we are as enemies, that next time we meet we will show no mercy.

Priscilla mumbled something in fear and hatred. Then they faded into the general background. Lillith forgot about them the moment they faded, at least in the forefront of her attention. She walked among those who followed her, touched them, touched by them, as they touched her. Their, her wild heart beat in the dawn's light.

– We're born to challenge the Storm. She stretched out her arms in a fast and furry move. – And we shall. Isn't it wonderful to be alive?

It wasn't a question, but they made their reply anyway, with raised, clenched fists and loud cries.

To see the truth in the lie. That was what one had been reduced to. Well, that, too, was of the past, now.

– We're the nightmares that throughout recorded history have made feeble attempts to raise the general population from their slumber… It's time to get serious.

Black and fire-eyes met.

– My compliments, Jason said appraisingly. – A brilliant plan. Excellently executed.

Yes, it had gone well. Stacy had planned everything from the start… No, not Stacy, not Jill. She had done it. She - the Demon Mother.

– Praise from you means a lot, brother, she joked joyfully and gave him a smacker on his cheek.

She had turned halfway around when he spoke up.

– It's quite an unpleasant thought, isn't it, Jason said, – that some people prefer slavery?

– Well, then we'll force them to *unprefer* it, Lillith laughed.

– What about what you said about the logic in the strong ruling the weak, what about that? He put forth the thought in a curious tone.

– Why follow conventional logic? She replied pointedly.

That brought a smile to his face. He smiled cheerfully and evidently had a lot of fun.

So, the others saw, had she.

– They're okay, you know, she told him. – I can feel them not far from here. They're on their way. They're all on their way.

– I know, he said, slightly irritated. – I can, too.

They danced out of the forest, onto the green field that Main Street had become. Many of the people there joined them.

Jeremy, as curious, as miserable, as passionate as ever walked by her side a moment.

– I noticed the rituals were cut a bit… short here and there?

– We felt a bit awkward doing them. She shook her head cheerfully. – They were more concentration exercises than anything else…

She paused a bit before finishing:

– We were praying to ourselves.

The ruckus was simply phenomenal. Something was seemingly happening everywhere. The world was rushing back in. The world was rushing back out.

– Two weeks, Everett said startled. – The dome stayed up for two weeks, normal time.

It had, and the people on the outside had turned more and more frantic by each passing day. Lillith could feel all the commotion out there, the powerful, fundamental realization all over the planet that the world was no longer the same.

All their friends were present. More allies and enemies entered the city gates this moment. The third «investigative unit» of soldiers and Special Forces had done so quite some time ago, before the dome had dissolved and was already roaming the streets.

Nothing, everything had changed.

– So, is it war or peace? Loeh said aloud, even though she knew the answer.

A raven landed on her shoulder. She played preoccupied with its feathers.

There was silence for just a second then, as they listened.

– It's both and neither, Lillith said instantly, spontaneously. – Current society's idea of duality is stupid anyway. Look beyond the closed fist, the open hand. And something far more significant appears.

And as she watched them, watched herself, they all did it, moved beyond both the closed fist, the open hand.

– A friend of mine said something I like, she finally said. – He said that Time is always standing still, that we're moving through it…

– Whenever we dream, that's when we fly.

A lot of ravens landed on people's shoulders.

The crooked smile started the slowly emerging laughter.

The three times born witch stopped a bit and looked back. Above the Hill a virtually mythic mist hung, one, which only by the longest stretch of the imagination could be mistaken for morning fog. Small, glowing pellets rose from it, glowing like fireflies in a forest of shadows and spreading in all directions, before fading in open air.

The dead, they had, a minor assembly, followed her from the beyond, from the Sunset Land and joined the condemned called forth by Samhain, by Jason Gallagher. The majority would probably settle down here. But not all. This would certainly turn up the heat, making things lively around the world. That, too…

Raven Moonstar laughed out aloud, wildly. She crouched and hit her thighs and then laughed even louder, even wilder, tilting her head back. The raven birds, virtually sitting on the shoulder of every person in her close proximity squeaked and laughed very humanlike. The Dance to Life started anew. It was her fervent hope for herself that she would always keep it going like this, unpredictable and full of Life's Fire.

She had turned herself into a lethal weapon, a double-edged sword, a creature with many faces, of many masks and thus she would remain and grow. Forever!

There is no truth, she thought relaxed. Never, ever! The only truth is that there isn't any truth. Everything and everything we do is ultimately meaningless. It's when we realize this we realize the meaning of everything.

And it's good.

Human destiny, whatever it may turn out to be was once more its own.

Born again
Through fire, through shadow
The hunger of life prevails
We'll laugh at the devil
We'll make the devil laugh
We are human
And life is fire and pain and joy
We're showing the robots of civilization
Sitting in their coffins
On the highway
On the tombstone nightmare
Of the Gray Fog
That the human spirit
is still alive

Amos Keppler -**Witchnight** (2002)

POSTSCRIPT: another world

A cascade of colors. Blinding light. Lillith raced through a tunnel being anything but dark, but the light in its end was so bright that the rest paled in comparison.

She hovered above the Sunset Land. Or one of them. She knew she shouldn't land and didn't care to, either. She had passed this place more times than she could recall and had put it behind her a long time ago.

Back on Earth, still non-corporal. Hovering along power lines. St. Louis the summer of 1993, when the city had become a part of the United States' new great lake. Straight lines, going straight ahead, had for so long been a part of her life. The part over and done. *Night.* Long night. Distant lights. She had such power now that she could do just about anything. She had removed all the stops.

She traveled back in time to when there were no cities. Very much of the rape of the land was yet undone. Much of what she had known would be gone, but that was unimportant.

Wide and long stretches of plains. One single plain. A woman heavy with child was cooking when she abruptly stopped and left the kettle. She walked to and climbed one of the closest, highest buffs. It didn't take long. She was as if driven. A slight hesitation on the edge and then she jumped. She landed in the middle of a huge ravine. By the time anyone reached her both she and the baby were stone cold.

In another camp, several mountaintops away.

The girl with the funny mark on her leg had been having her first monthly bleeding the day before and during the night her eyes had turned dark as inside the deepest cave.

She stood by the river and washed clothes when a younger brother came and called her to the morning meal. She turned around. She sensed the wind rage by. She smiled and threw the bundle in her brother's fawn. He stumbled backwards. She laughed thrillingly. It was spring and everything was so very, very funny.

Time started anew.

AMOS KEPPLER 1989-06-01 – 1993-12-30 (Norwegian edition)
9. Night 12049, the fourth year in the time of Witchnight
(New Year's Eve is December 21st)
and 2001-08-12 (English, upgraded, expanded edition completed)
233. Night 12056, the first year in the time of the Twilight Storm.
Christmas is finally, definitely over.
(For the curious of mind... see http://midnight-fire.net/finally.html)
Printed version completed 2003-01-07
17. Night 12058, the third year in the time of the Twilight Storm
Hardcover version completed 2011-09-30
284. Night 12066, the eleventh year in the time of the Twilight Storm

APPENDIX

Related web pages/further study.

TUMOR (cancer cell): http://midnight-fire.net/civilization/tumor.html
The Paranormal - Power: http://midnight-fire.net/shadows/power.html
THE CAVES OF DOOM: http://midnight-fire.net/truecurrentevents/doom.html
1984: http://midnight-fire.net/civilization/1984.html
Chemical Cocktail: http://midnight-fire.net/truecurrentevents/cocktail.html
Raging Witch: http://midnight-fire.net/bookofshadows/ragingwitch.html

Phoenix Green Earth:
http://midnight-fire.net/phoenix
And all the countless other Midnight Fire Arena pages.

Author's word:

«ShadowWalk is a powerful tale of magick and empowerment which manages not to sound like a mind-body-spirit-self-obsessed-hippie book. This is full-on reality. Blood and sweat and shit - nothing's toned down or dulled. The intensity of life comes through strong and meaty. Real life bursting off the pages».

Review in Green Anarchist (the original and best) No. 68/69 Summer 2003.

Trim the story, tighten the plot, that was usually what I was told to do by potential editors, and only when their response to my writing was somewhat coherent and made sense at all.
I disagreed, of course, and told them so, and they drew a blank. It seemed like they hadn't even heard of vigorous storytelling, a sneaking suspicion that was indeed confirmed later. They just weren't used to people disagreeing with them. They wanted all young, hopeful authors to stand there with the hat in their hands and beg for favors. I am and was fortunately made of different material.

ShadowWalk began, at least in part as a sort of excess product of what was discarded from my writing on Dreams Belong to the Night. At first, I put everything that didn't fit in Dreams there, but eventually it grew, branched out from there to encompass many directions and dynamics. I wrote the books practically simultaneously. SW was a story I didn't choose, and that I initially didn't see as terribly important compared to what I saw as the main story, but one that gained its own importance as I wrote it. Roughly stated, Dreams is about politics, while SW is about religion, and the upcoming, still to be completed Phoenix Green Earth is about both.

The completed story in Norwegian, what I out of old habit sent around to established publishers in 1993 and 1994 was about 200 000 words, and that was what they told me to trim and tighten.

I had really decided to abandon any contact with established publishers after their treatment of Dreams in 1991, but as stated, out of habit I decided to give them one more change…

It was yet another bust, yet another bad experience, yet another show of their completely fucked up priorities.

One said I should keep the first chapter and start over. This as one example of the quality of their «advice».

A few years later, in 1997, when I started translating SW, I found that there was stuff there I wasn't pleased with, but my take on it was quite different from the editors employed by the established publishers…

I translated, rewrote and expanded what I now see as the first draft, and ended up with a slightly different story, carefully, cautiously polished here and there, but still the same. I expanded it from 200 000 words to 300 000… and all the new strange twists and turns made it an even better tale.

The editors wanted me to trim it with fifty percent. I ended up expanding it with fifty percent, a very pleasing result.

Another great irony here is that this is my most edited book.

Here is another reader's reaction that I can totally relate to:

> «SW may break all the rules of novel writing, but it works.
>
> And it makes sense if you aren't too brainwashed to understand and experience it. I never found it jumpy or disjointed. And I believe that it flows quite nicely and seems effortlessly elegant in the way it works.
>
> When a stream flows around rocks in a very not straight line, we still find it beautiful. It will be full of back eddies and undercurrents and twist and turns. But it is still flowing. It is making sense within its own environment.
>
> And just because it doesn't flow at one speed in one direction, you can't say that's wrong. What the stream does is right for the stream. What SW does is right for SW».

I didn't set out to break all rules of storytelling, but realized quickly that was what I was doing, and once I did, I set out to break them all the more. During the rewriting/translation/expansion I most certainly did. I followed one - 1- advice given me by the various editors and ignored/discarded the rest and removed myself and the story further from their vision (or lack of it), doing what felt natural and right.

It was really funny when I met one of them by chance several years later and told him about it. I could see that he wanted to murder me on the spot. No bull! These people, generally speaking are so set in their ways that they see any opposition to their sacred texts as an affront to their sanctity, and that is why authors should avoid them completely.

This is a story about witches written after I realized I was one myself, a fact making a considerable difference, of course. True witches are, inevitably Agents of Change, a threat to any establishment, any imposed reality. It's about special people, about the paranormal and its place in a society denying its very existence.

Like many of my stories the events described are practically autobiographical. Almost everything has really happened, one way or another.

One more thing to note about SW and Dreams is the high number of females and/or people with a darker skin hue. I got sick and tired of the one female, one Asian/African-American/European quota in films/novels and decided to go completely overboard in order to distance myself from it.

It felt perfectly natural.

Oh, yeah, this is my least violent book, I guess, at least in terms of showing physical violence. There aren't many guns, except in the hands of usually not very present military and semi-military personnel.

It's just as controversial as the rest, though. A reader wondered why I left out homosexuality when it was so filled with other controversial issues. I replied that it was partly a coincidence and partly that I didn't truly view homosexuality as a controversial issue, anyway, and then I asked him to read Dreams Belong to the Night when it was published in English. Well, man, it has been a fairly long wait, but now you can finally enjoy that one, too…

This is basically the same book that was first published as a paperback in 2003, with some corrections, changes and expansions.

It's a book about young adults, but isn't a Young Adult book…

Certainly not!

> «Before I read ShadowWalk I thought the advertising was overblown to say it was "one of the most controversial novels ever written". Then I read it and found that to just be fact».

The Janus Clan
(http://midnight-fire.net/sw)
ten chapters about the Wild Man in the modern world, a world on the edge (those written in fat fonts have been published:

The Defenseless
The Slaves
Birds Flying in the Dark
At the End of the Rainbow
Lewis of Modern York
The Werewolf of Locus Bradle
The Valley of Kings
Eye In the Sky
The Iron Cage
Phoenix Green Earth

www.ingramcontent.com/pod-product-compliance
Lightning Source LLC
Chambersburg PA
CBHW060604310726
48982CB00008B/1231/J

* 9 7 8 8 2 9 1 6 9 3 1 2 5 *